Pretty SAVAGE

T.A. KUNZ

Published by C.A. Kunz LLC.

This book is an original publication of C.A. Kunz LLC.

Published 2021.
ISBN: 978-1-954723-01-6

Visit the author's website: www.authortakunz.com

Cover design by Sarah Hansen at www.okaycreations.com
Cover art copyright © 2020 Sarah Hansen

Formatting by Champagne Book Design

For my family and friends. You have always believed in my writing, and have never stopped encouraging me to follow my dreams.

Donovan

THERE HE IS.

Mr. Filthy Chai Tea Latte.

I mean, that's obviously not his real name. It's his usual drink order. Chai tea, steamed milk, and two shots of espresso. A rebel's drink for sure. And since I haven't gotten up the guts to ask him his name yet, he remains Mr. Filthy Chai Tea Latte.

It's at times like this I wish we were like most coffee shops and requested a name for each order rather than just the to-gos. But the owner refuses to switch from the ever reliable—his words—order number system. Today, Mr. Filthy is number twenty-one.

My lucky number. Kismet?

At least once a week he meets here at The Pour Over with a group of similarly aged teens and they chat for hours. About what? Beats me. I've contemplated lingering by their table, performing menial tasks like restocking the oat milk at the drink prep area or wiping down nearby tables, in order to eavesdrop. But every time, I chicken out.

"A large filthy chai tea latte?" I ask before he has a chance to utter a word.

His eyebrow—pierced by the way—quirks up, and I realize I must've sounded like a major creeper for committing his order to memory.

A hint of a smile breaks the corner of his mouth. "Yeah. Thanks, Donovan."

I die.

I die.

I die.

My name rolls off his tongue like caramel sauce dripping down the side of a hot latte. I've clearly been working here too long if I'm making coffee metaphors already ... and it's only my second month.

Wait, he knows my name. How does he know my name? Has he asked about me?

I glance down at my apron and see my name tag resting there. The bright white letters radiate against the dark background. You could probably see it from space. Makes sense.

He pays with his phone and then, just like clockwork, drops a folded five-dollar bill into the tip jar. He's so intriguing, paying for his drink electronically but also having cash on hand. And when I'm at the register, he leaves five dollars. Every. Single. Time. He might do the same for everyone else, but I enjoy living in the fantasy that I'm his chosen recipient. I imagine them as little love notes he leaves behind for my eyes only.

Okay. Pull it together, man. Composure.

I take in the show as he strolls off to join his group at a table near the back of the café. His tall, dark, and mysterious routine never fails to work on me. I sigh internally, but I'm not convinced a little didn't seep out by accident.

"Smooth."

My co-worker Marcus stands there grinning like a fool. A ridiculously gorgeous fool, but a fool nonetheless. His slicked-back chestnut brown hair is perfectly shaped to accentuate his chiseled features. The solitary dimple on his left cheek adds an extra kick to the impish grin he sends my way.

I laugh. "Yeah, definitely not my best work."

"Nah, you did great. A real pro," he teases. "Hey, why don't you go talk to him? We're slow right now and someone does have to bring him his drink, you know."

He wriggles his brows at me. I roll my eyes.

Marcus is no stranger to affection. Unlike me, he probably hasn't been rejected by anyone. He exudes confidence, which comes in handy when he dons a dress and a wig to perform in drag on the weekends at the one and only gay bar in Haddon Falls, Mae's Lounge. Marcus becomes Miz Markie Marc. And yes, he does have a slight unhealthy obsession with Mark Wahlberg. Hence, the drag name. And he loves to refer to me as Donnie for the same reason.

"I don't even know if he likes guys in that way," I say. "Besides, he's sort of out of my league. I mean, will you just look at that jawline?"

"With the perfect amount of scruff too," adds Marcus.

"Exactly. And he has at least four or five inches on me in the height department."

"What a shame, Donnie."

"Huh?"

"Oh, nothing."

I know that's not all he wants to say. He has more. Marcus *loves* to give input ... and constructive criticism.

"It's just...."

And there it is.

"Uh-huh."

"It's just a shame you have such a low opinion of yourself, that's all. Sure, he might be a certified eight and a half or even a nine if he ran a proper comb through that disheveled mess he calls hair, but boy, look in a mirror once in a while. Not only do you have the lightest blue eyes I've ever seen, but you also have a beautiful full head of red hair." He leans forward slightly to examine the top of my head. "With no signs of balding in your future whatsoever, I might add." He relaxes back while swirling his hand in front of my face. "And with that complexion and bone structure? You pretty, my friend."

I'm overwhelmed by the compliments. I've never been great at accepting them. I pretend to blow them off as he moves to the end of the counter where Mr. Filthy Chai Tea Latte's drink is waiting. Marcus winks at me, scoops up the cup, and saunters over to the table near the back. He delivers the drink and then laughs while touching Mr. Filthy's shoulder. The whole table joins in, and just like that, Marcus has ensnared them all.

Nothing seems to ever faze Marcus. I wish I had his level of chill. Teach me your ways.

On his return, I try to look busy and not seem like I'd been observing the whole scene.

Marcus props himself up on the counter by his elbows and rests his chin daintily on his hands. "His name is Connor, he's most definitely into dudes, he's single, ready to mingle, and he's a Libra. You're welcome."

"How the hell did you find all of that out just by delivering his drink?"

"A drag queen never reveals her secrets. That's why our wigs are so massive. But also, the first two things were true. The others I may have made up in the moment. They just felt right."

"You're the worst, you know that?"

"If by worst you actually mean the best, then I accept the praise."

The door chime pulls our attention to the entrance of the café. My new bestie Lori rushes up to the counter seeming like she's ready to burst with news. Her wavy black hair bounces as she busts into an impromptu shoulder dance. Having friends like her and Marcus has made my transition to living in Haddon Falls considerably more tolerable.

"Guess what?" she asks. Marcus joins in by mimicking her head bops and shoulder shakes. "And this right here is why I love you, Miz Markie Marc."

Never a dull moment with these two.

Marcus pauses for a moment. "Girl, not in front of the breeders, okay?" he chastises before resuming to bop along with her.

"My bad, *Marcus*," she corrects with a giggle.

"Not that I don't appreciate whatever's happening here," I say, gesturing at the two of them, "but what's up?"

Lori comes to a dead stop and a grin curls her lips like the Cheshire Cat. "Trent invited me to Sophia Gomer's party tonight. *The* Trent."

Her excitement is infectious, and I can't help but match it. "Shut, up ... wait, which one is he again?"

"That's my cue to exit stage left," Marcus says. "High school? Been there, done that, hated every second of it, and wrote a memoir." With that, he heads over to bus one of the tables.

Ignoring him, Lori looks at me and groans. "Come on, you know Trent. I realize you're new to school, but you can't miss him in the halls. He's one of the top players on the varsity football team. And he's always with that hottie Harrison, the team's quarterback. Perfectly quaffed hair, nice abs, great calves and butt. *That* Trent."

"It's really cute that you think I pay any attention to sports in the slightest. Half of what you just said was completely lost on me."

"You and I are both fully aware that you don't have to know squat about sports to admire the men who play them," she argues.

"Touché," I say, stroking my chin and searching my memory banks. "Oh. Isn't Trent the one that a lot of people at school refer to as the 'Twat Waffle Casanova'?"

"Only in some circles," she fires back. "But he's not like that. He's nice. And, hello, more importantly he's interested in *moi*."

"So you're going then?"

"Obviously, and you're going to be my wingman." She aims a double finger point in my direction for emphasis.

"I don't know, Lori. I really should get a head start on my calculus homework tonight."

"Seriously?"

I shake my head with squinted eyes. "No."

She snickers. "Okay, so I'll pick you up at seven. When we get to Sophia's, we'll pregame in the car with some serious liquid courage and then Project Trent will be a go."

"It's a date."

One of the guys from Connor's table calls out to Lori, putting a pause on our conversation. She glances over her shoulder and sends him a quick wave before turning back to face me with an exaggerated eye roll.

"Who's that?"

My gaze lands on the guy in question. He sends over a wicked, knowing smile that gives me instant chills. Then his expression softens when he laughs at something said at the table.

"Don't worry your pretty little head about it," she replies. Her demeanor changes. She seems put off.

"Just curious is all. Do you know them?"

She raps her hot pink painted fingernails on the counter, looking back over her shoulder when she hears her name called again.

"Hey, I got to go," she tells me. "But I'll see you at seven, right?" Her smile seems forced, hollow even.

"Yeah, of course."

Why didn't she want to talk about that guy? I get that we're new friends, but this is the first time she's been cagey around me. Definitely going to pin that for later.

She moves toward the group in the back. Her overall confidence and presence has noticeably dimmed. I can't help but wonder how she knows them. I'm pretty sure they don't go to our school. And who is the guy whose lap she's currently sitting on? If I'd known her for longer than the month we've been in school together, I probably would've pressed her further on the subject.

"Would you call his skin tone olive?" Marcus inquires as he rejoins me behind the counter. "He looks Greek, right?"

"Who?" I ask absently, my attention on Lori.

"*Hello.*" He flashes me some dramatic side eye. "Connor. You know, the guy you've been standing there drooling over for the past few minutes. Don't think I haven't noticed. I see all."

That gets my full attention on him. "For your information, I was keeping an eye out for Lori over there."

"Uh-huh." He waves his hand in front of his face. "This right here is my convinced look. And if you believe that, then you're gullible as hell."

I laugh. "Hey, do you know how she fits in with that group?"

"Uh-uh. I ain't got time for your high school drama club. I'm four years sober from all of that grade school B.S. If you want any tips, tricks, advice, and the like, I shall direct you to my countless diaries on the subject."

"I'm serious, Marcus."

"Nope."

Three ... two ... one.

"Okay, okay, you've twisted my arm."

Marcus can never pass up an opportunity to gossip. Like a moth to a flame.

He purses his lips. "If I tell you, will you promise to get back to work?"

I nod. "Promise."

"I don't know much, but I've seen Lori in here a few times with them. It's been a while though. I think they're her old friends from middle school or something. At least that's what I've gathered from what she's told me."

"Doesn't she seem uneasy to you?"

He tosses a damp cloth at my chest. "Nope. Uh-uh. Back to work with you. I've played around in your high school games long enough, and there's a counter just waiting for you to scrub it down like the dirty thing that it is."

I give him a half-assed salute and begin wiping down the counter. My eyes find Lori again just in time to catch her laughing with the group and hugging all over the guy whose lap she's perched on. She's relaxed, more at ease.

I guess maybe it was all in my head.

TWO

Donovan

THE HONK FROM LORI'S CAR HAS ME SPRINTING down the stairs toward the front door. I grab my coat from the rack and house keys from the hook on the wall in the foyer. A throat clears behind me. It's my aunt. I figure it was the jingle of the keys that betrayed me and gave away my intentions.

"Where are you off to in such a hurry?"

I whirl around on my heel to meet her inquisitive stare. "I'm going to a party. Is that cool?"

She crosses her arms in front of her chest. The serious look on her face falters into a half smile. "I guess I should be happy you're making friends who invite you to parties, huh?"

I nod emphatically.

"Look," she says, "I know you've only been living with your aunt and I since the summer, and you're probably thinking because you're a senior and an *adult* now that you can just run around town all you want. We're going to give you your space, don't worry. And we trust you'll make the right decisions. But please, could you let us know when you have stuff like this going on? Helen is just as neurotic as your dad used to be and she'll worry about you, as will I."

"Sorry for not letting you know, Aunt Lucy. I just found out about it at work and it completely slipped my mind. I do appreciate everything both of you have done for me, really."

The car horn sounds again. I send my aunt an innocent smile while motioning to the door.

"All right, get going. But try to be home at a reasonable hour, okay?"

"You got it," I say before pulling open the door and rushing outside.

I'm pretty positive Lori's car has seen better days. It's not a clunker by any means, it just has its fair share of dents and scratches along its mostly shiny black exterior. At the very least, it makes me question her driving skills. The fact she's waving around a bottle of vodka and two purple sports drinks only adds to the evidence piling up in my head.

Maybe this isn't such a good idea.

I'm amused despite my observations. "Cool it with the drink waving," I tell Lori as I open the passenger door. "My aunt's probably watching us through the curtains."

"Oops, my bad," she replies with a mischievous grin as she stashes the drinks in a bag in the back seat.

After I settle into the passenger seat, she roughly pulls me toward her and declares, "Pre-party selfie!" She holds the phone out in front of us before snapping the pic. "We're so photogenic. I love it." Her thumbs fly across her phone's keyboard. "And … posted."

"I'm not photogenic. My face always looks like I'm holding in a fart or something."

"Holy crap, can you not? Are you kidding me? You have to know how you look, right?" She shows me the pic of us. "You're a certified little hottie, my friend."

"At least one of us thinks so," I murmur.

She giggles. "I literally can't with you."

She throws the car into drive and pulls away from the house.

The sun hangs low in the sky. It casts sinister shadows of bare gnarled branches, resembling long boney fingers creeping out for us on the road ahead. They conjure forth thoughts of the impending Halloween holiday. My favorite. The biting chill flowing through the open car windows adds the perfect flourish.

I've always loved fall, and here in Haddon Falls it's far from disappointing. Much better than the pseudo-fall I'm used to in the South where we'd get, like, two days of seventy-degree weather before it shot back up to a constant eighty until around December.

"Hey," Lori says, "I've got to make a quick stop before we head to Sophia's. We're kind of running early anyway."

"Sure. You're the one driving."

"And being fashionably late is key, darling." Her posh accent is perfection personified.

We pull into RJ's drugstore down the street from The Pour Over and she puts the car in park. "Be right back."

I grab one of the purple drinks from the back seat and twist off the cap. Without thinking, I take a huge gulp and instantly regret it. A burning sensation courses its way through my mouth and nose before swirling down my throat. I'm sent into a coughing fit as I struggle to get the cap back onto the bottle.

"Damn," I get out between coughs. "She's already mixed in the vodka."

My eyes land on the two deputy cruisers parked a few spots down. I tense up. There are no cars between us, giving them a clear visual of me. I not-so-discreetly try to lower the bottle out of view and shrink back against the seat, wanting to disappear. I'm sure the whole thing looked spastic to anyone on the outside.

Nailed it.

A familiar mix of people exit the store, catching my attention. Connor and a few members from his group are talking amongst themselves while sharing a large bag of chips. There's one girl and two guys with him.

I can't help but stare at the piece of human artwork as he passes by. He's exactly the kind of guy I'd go for. Actually, he checks most, if not all, of my aesthetic boxes.

Taller than me ... check.

Dark hair ... check.

Light colored eyes ... check.

Lean and cut ... check.

Killer smile ... check.

Well-kempt facial hair ... check.

Piercings and tattoos ... double check.

One obvious thing about Connor and his group is how different they all are from each other. They seem to belong to separate factions that each send a delegate to a meeting of the minds to discuss how to keep the peace between their crews.

If this were an eighties teen movie, they'd all fit the parts of the stock characters based on visuals alone. There's the jock, who, interestingly enough, usually orders the fruitiest teas we have on the menu. Then there's the queen bee who consistently gets the blonde roast with soy milk and one packet of Splenda. At least, that was the case until recently. Now it's been all pumpkin spice all the time.

Next is the geek, who only ever requests a double shot of espresso in a cup. The good girl prefers a light herbal green tea with a packet of raw sugar. At the opposite end of the spectrum, the outcast always orders his coffee strong, dark, and straight up with no additions.

I wonder how these people all became and stayed friends. It's fascinating, to say the least.

Connor—the rebel of the group—catches me staring. I avert my eyes. For some strange reason, I begin whistling awkwardly while acting like I'm searching for something in the car. I inch my eyes back over to where the group was, but they're gone now.

I'm a complete dork.

The lights surrounding the drugstore flicker to life as the sun sets. Lori's still not back. I begin an impromptu drum solo with my fingers on the dash as I grow fidgety.

She emerges from the store and hurries over to the car. "Sorry it took so long," she says, plopping down in the driver's seat. "They didn't have my prescription ready, so I had to wait. Damn depression." She shakes a sandwich-sized Ziploc bag containing a handful of pink pills before tossing it into the cup holder. "And they were out of bottles on top of that."

Is it legal to give out prescriptions without labels?

I shrug it off. This is a small town. I suppose even the pharmacist has to manage with what supplies are readily available.

I want to ask Lori about her depression since I've definitely been there before, but our friendship is still too new. I wouldn't want someone just coming out and asking about mine if the roles were reversed. It isn't my business anyway.

"No worries," I say. "I kept myself busy. But you could've warned me you prepped the drinks already."

She snorts. "You downed some, didn't you?"

"Sure did," I reply. I'm mildly amused by how entertained she is by the situation.

She bursts into a laughing fit. "Damn, man, sorry about that. I should've given you a heads up."

"It's all right. Honestly, I think it's exactly what I needed to start this night off right."

"Now that's what I like to hear," she says before throwing

the car into reverse and pulling out of the small lot and back onto the road.

When we reach Sophia Gomer's house, which in all reality should be called a mini mansion, there are vehicles everywhere. Cars are parked in the massive driveway, on the sprawling lawn, and in front of other houses along the street. Her party is most definitely matching the hype.

"There are houses like this in Haddon Falls?" I ask as Lori parallel parks on the street down a ways from the party.

"Not many. This is kind of the only neighborhood with houses like this. Everyone who lives in this area makes well over six figures. That's why Sophia always has parties, because the chick's family is seriously loaded. And her parents are rarely home because of some traveling business or whatever they're involved in."

"Must be nice," I say, peering out the window at the roof of the house which is still in view even from this distance.

Lori presents the bottles of purple liquid and I grab the one I drank from earlier. "Pre-game time, little Donnie." She taps her bottle against mine and proceeds to take a sizable gulp.

I follow suit, though admittedly she's handling the drinking a lot better than I am. I wouldn't consider myself a lightweight, but Lori puts away drinks like she's training for the liquor Olympics.

Looks like I may have to be DD tonight.

"Okay, one last selfie before we make our grand entrance," she says.

I stash my bottle off to the side as she readies her phone to take the pic. She pulls me in and yells, "Goofy face!"

I stick out my tongue and act like I've died from alcohol poisoning, which probably isn't far from the truth if I keep at this drink like I have been.

"Epic," she states as she goes to post the pic. "I can't wait for you to officially hang out with my bestie, Drea. You'll love her. We used to do things like this all the time." She flashes me a quick pic of the two of them at a concert.

"You don't anymore?"

"She's going through some stuff, but she'll be back. Then we'll be like the damn three musketeers. Senior year isn't ready for us."

I can tell something weighs heavy on her. Her mood suddenly shifts. After a moment, she shakes herself out of it and yells at the top of her lungs, "Project Trent, Commence!"

This should prove to be an interesting night.

THREE

Drea

IMAGE AFTER IMAGE, MY HEART SINKS FURTHER.

Swipe up.

Swipe up.

Swipe up.

If someone told me a month ago that I'd be standing in front of the house of arguably the most popular girl at Haddon Falls High scrolling through my supposed best friend's socials, alone and torturing myself instead of partying it up inside like every other teen in this town, I'd have called them crazy. Lori and I are inseparable, I would've said, and there's no way I'd be here without her.

Well, it turns out there's always room for change.

And now I've apparently become a glutton for punishment on the verge of being a masochist. She looks happy, but then again, that's Lori's M.O. Her "always on" photo smile, she calls it. Her mask, I like to tease. If I summed up her life with a solitary motto it'd be, "If you stay ready, you don't have to get ready."

I should be thrilled to see her posting these fun pictures, but given the current state of things, I'm not sure I can scrounge up

Swipe up.

Swipe up.

Swipe up.

The common thread throughout her most recent posts is Donovan Walsh, the new guy at school and Lori's shiny new best friend. My replacement. At least, that's the consensus among our mutual acquaintances.

I lower my phone and stow it away, ending the little stalker session. I can't say I'm terribly proud of my current love affair with jealousy and resentment. Especially because I'm about to enter the first major party of senior year and the last thing on my mind is having a good time.

But I have my reasons.

The front door to Sophia Gomer's house flies open and a group of people stumble out. The frontrunner of the pack is fellow cheerleader and Sophia's number two, Chloe Fern. A self-proclaimed high functioning hot mess. From the looks of it, she's definitely living up to her reputation. Out of the entire group, she seems to be the only one "talented" enough not to spill an ounce of her drink in the process.

"Drea, you so need to get on this level," she slurs, toasting me and sloshing some liquid from the cup.

There goes her no spilling streak.

She's right though. I am too sober to deal with this right now. I'm here with a purpose, and this is only serving as a distraction.

"Hey, Chloe, have you seen Lori?"

She shakes her cup as she gets closer. "Where do you think I got this? Lori's at the bar, like always." She pokes her index finger into my shoulder. "Hey, why haven't you been at practice?"

I go to answer her with the rehearsed little white lie I prepared for this exact kind of situation, but her attention shifts to three guys doing a keg stand in the front yard. "I call next," she announces, and stumbles away.

I nod and carry on the conversation at a low volume as if she were still there. "Thanks for asking about that, Chloe. I just went through a major trauma, no big deal. But I haven't fallen into a deep pit of despair yet, so fingers crossed." My words drip with sarcasm.

Awesome, now I'm talking to myself.

She glances back at me. "Did you say something?"

I shake my head and look away, hoping she loses interest and keeps moving along, kind of like a T-Rex with potential prey standing completely still.

When she returns her attention to the keg, I let out a relieved breath. I turn my own attention back to her response about Lori. I should've known. Lori tends to like being the main focus at these things, and at a high school party like this, where is most of the action? The makeshift bar, of course.

Don't get me wrong. I'm not hating on her need to be in the spotlight. Her extroverted nature is the thing that ripped me, clawing and screaming, from my introverted rut when I moved to Haddon Falls at the beginning of sophomore year. Lori was my first friend here. My best friend. There's no way I can ever repay her for what she's done for me. Period.

The sounds of the party meet me before I enter. In our little cheerleading world, there's an unwritten rule making attendance to these parties mandatory since our squad leader hosts them. Since I've been kind of MIA as of late, I felt maybe my presence here would suggest I haven't completely given up on the squad. At least, that's what I keep telling myself.

The moment I cross the door's threshold, I immediately regret my life choices.

This is too soon.

I'm not ready for this.

This is my first foray back into the Haddon Falls High social scene since my little hiatus. I know there will be triggers all around me, but I've got to push them aside. I have to find Lori.

I'm temporarily blinded by the rapid pulse of strobe lights assaulting my eyeballs. Flash silhouettes of bodies writhing on the "dance floor" to the deep throbbing base line register through my squinted eyes. A cacophonous mixture of shrieking laughter and multiple conversations crash into each other all at once. Sensory overload.

I don't know if I can do this.

I draw in a deep, calming breath and keep moving forward against the flow of the crowd. Several people feel the need to say they're happy to see me. I flash them a forced smile accompanied by a nod since it's all small talk anyway … nothing to make me stop and actually engage. I'm not surprised the usual suspects are in attendance. Every "it" person at our school is present and accounted for.

Sophia's burn-out of an older brother, Will, must be playing the part of DJ because the whole house feels like one giant EDM concert, complete with laser lights and fog machines. I try to blend in by "dancing" my way through the throng of people, but it's more like a shimmy with forward momentum. I want to at least give off the illusion I'm enjoying myself. High school is all about keeping up appearances, after all.

My entire body seizes up and skids to a halt. My eyes are pinned in disbelief to the sight in front of me. I clench my fists so hard my nails dig into my palms. My heartbeat quickens to a feverish rate and my vision tunnels.

The nerve.

The gall.

The audacity.

A picture-perfect pair stands there hovering dangerously close to one another. Their body language screams attraction as they exchange smiles. The only problem is the pair happens to be comprised of my supposed best friend, Lori, and the jerk face who shall remain nameless for a plethora of reasons.

Lori's hand trails up the aforementioned douche canoe's arm. He leans closer to her with a roguish grin complete with bedroom eyes. I try to bite back the words forming in my throat, but fail spectacularly.

"You've got to be kidding me!" The vigor in my voice surprises me. It didn't even sound like me to my own ears.

The forceful statement lands me on the receiving end of some serious stares from the surrounding crowd. I swear I hear a record scratch and the music die abruptly, but alas, it's all in my head.

Lori breaks away from the asshole's clutches with a playful shove and hurries over to me. "Bitch, you came! I'm so glad you're here." Her tone is hesitant but upbeat.

She envelopes me in a hug and squeezes tight. I reciprocate, but I'm still in a daze over what was just on display. The honeymoon phase fades away.

I tilt my head back and my eyes fix on hers. "Of all the guys in all of this town, why him?"

I glance over at the jerk in question in time to catch the snide smile smeared across his face. He throws me a pompous two finger wave while still holding onto his beer. I vomit a little in my mouth … metaphorically speaking, of course.

"Who? Trent? He's harmless," Lori says.

Harmless?

Harmless!?

Harmless!?!

My frustration mounts by the nanosecond. The hairs

on the back of my neck prickle and the sensation swirls down both of my arms. My body is wound so tight I should have a "Contents Under Pressure" warning sticker slapped on my forehead.

My jaw clenches. "Wow. So you're just going to stand there and pretend that *he* hasn't been the main source of my trauma for the past few weeks?" I say. "And then to top it all off, you call him harmless?"

She places her hands on my shoulders and applies the slightest pressure while holding my gaze. "Sweetie, you need to calm down. You're making a scene." A smile cracks through her serious demeanor. "This is a party where you're supposed to be having fun. Besides, I was just being friendly with Trent. Nothing more. Promise."

Lies.

A few weeks ago, that's how it all started between Trent and me too. *Friendly.* I'm not even sure why I was entertaining his company in the first place given his notorious man slut reputation. Call it a serious lapse in judgment. But after a shot of vodka here and a couple of beers there, it was suddenly morning and I was waking up in one of Sophia's guest rooms in nothing but my bra and panties. I had little recollection of the night before, but I know I didn't have enough alcohol that night to get black-out drunk.

"Regardless of you just being friendly with him," I say to Lori, "you know how I feel about Trent. He's a spoiled brat who takes advantage of girls and then hides behind his bros. He gets away with everything. I mean, come on, his dad's that sleazeball lawyer with his face on most of the benches downtown. Tell me that's not Shithead of the Year material right there."

"Now, Drea, even you said you can't remember what happened that night."

"Are you kidding me? It's not just something I imagined. My body felt wrong. Off. And he was the last person I remember being around that night," I seethe, keeping my voice low to avoid drawing more attention to us.

Too late.

"Okay, okay. Let's just drop this and try to have a good time. Loosen up, girl."

Her cavalier attitude hurts ... a lot. This isn't Lori. She's acting like a pod person. We've gone almost a month without talking or hanging out, and she's pretending like nothing happened. We're just picking up right where we left off, and I'm not sure how I feel about it. Where's my caring and loving best friend? What happened to that girl?

Donovan surprises Lori from behind and drapes his toned arms over her shoulders. A swift punch of jealousy slams into my gut at their playful interaction. That used to be me. It must be nice being the new guy yet blending in so quickly.

I wish I could be the new kid again.

He presents Lori a shot glass filled with clear liquid in one hand and a red Solo cup in the other.

"Choose your own adventure," he states while waving the two drinks back and forth in front of her face. She giggles before grabbing the shot and downing it. "Hey," Donovan says, looking up at me. "It's Drea right?"

I nod with a faint smile.

"Enjoying the party?"

"It's all right."

His brow furrows at my blunt reply. "I feel like I may have interrupted something."

"Actually—"

"Nope, not at all," Lori says, cutting me off. "We were *actually* about to go dance. Care to join?"

I flash her a withering stare, but only Donovan seems to catch it.

"Only if Drea wants to."

His reply shocks me. Lori speaks before I can.

"Don't be silly, Donnie. Of course she wants to. Isn't that right, Drea?"

I'd rather continue our conversation, but Lori's positive energy and illuminating presence wears me down and I surrender to it. I want to be furious with her. I *am* furious with her, but I've also missed us so much that I'm willing to push that feeling aside for the moment.

Call me weak. Call me desperate. But I'm already at my lowest point possible. Maybe I should start looking up.

"Sure. Why the hell not?"

"Yay! We should take a selfie to commemorate our little trio's first party together," shouts Lori.

She draws out her phone and immediately assumes the position. We file in behind her and I fake the fakest smile I've ever faked, and it shows. Donovan, on the other hand, seems to be a natural and instantly models it up. I guess when you look like you could grace the cover of *Teen Vogue*, modeling probably comes naturally.

Lucky me.

Four

Drea

ISTARE AT THE SIN-AGAINST-NATURE WINE AND alcoholic cider concoction Lori threw together as it swirls around in the red Solo cup I'm holding. I take a whiff of it followed by a sip, and am stunned it doesn't taste half bad. Like an oddly spiced sangria.

What am I still doing here?

Lori and Donovan are dancing it up and living their best lives in the living room while I'm parked here on the bench in the grand foyer. My mood darkens as I watch them. I can't fake my enjoyment with Lori any longer. Everything feels awkward and forced. I don't even think they've noticed I'm gone.

Trio, my ass.

"Well, well, well," I hear, and glance over to see Trent advancing. "Andrea Sullivan. It's great to see you again. I've been meaning to have a one-on-one conversation with you about some of the things you've said about me." He oozes douchebaggery.

I send him a dismissive hand wave. "I've got nothing to say to you, Trent, so keep on walking."

"On the contrary, I think we need to clear up a few details between us, so I'd appreciate it if you'd hear me out."

"Clear up what exactly? As far as I can tell, everything that has been said about you is true."

A slim laugh breaks his austere demeanor. He downs the can of beer in his hand before crushing it in his fist and tossing it off to the side. I cringe at the harsh sound.

I go to stand up and he moves in front of me, blocking my retreat. "I'm not afraid of you, Trent."

He raises his hands in submission. "Who said anything about you being afraid of me? I just want to chat with you. An innocent little chat."

That shit-eating grin is back on his face. All I want to do is smack it off.

"There you are, Drea," Lori calls out just in time. She and Donovan seem like they were just laughing about something between themselves.

"I was about to offer you this drink, but it appears you've still got one," Donovan says. His eyes move between me and Trent as though noting the palpable tension between us.

"We were just finishing up here," says Trent with a subtle nod in my direction. His eyes bore into mine.

I take advantage of the break in the conversation to make my exit. I'd rather be anywhere else other than right here at this moment. I can't stand breathing the same air as this bastard for one second more.

"And, Drea, if you ever want to get a drink and have a little talk about this whole misunderstanding, I'm game," Trent says loudly in my direction.

My shoulders stiffen and my gut churns at the mere thought. I pay his offer no mind and keep moving down the hall.

"Girl, hold up," Lori says, taking hold of my arm as I'm

about to push through the door into the kitchen. "What was that all about?"

I whip around to face her. "Oh, you mean that little episode of *To Catch a Predator* back there?"

"Look, I have no idea what's going on, but you, my friend, look like you need something to eat, stat," Donovan says, placing a hand on my shoulder. His light blue eyes are soft and kind with a hint of concern.

"Sure, I guess. I haven't really eaten much today."

That's an absolute lie since I'm one hell of an emotional eater.

"Pretzel chips and dip it is then. I'll be right back," he says, vanishing through the door into the next room.

"Donovan's great, isn't he?"

"Yeah, he's cool." I'm finding it hard to keep the jealousy from trickling out through my words.

Lori positions herself in front of me, making me look at her. "Wow, that's quite the compliment coming from you."

"Yeah, well…"

"You should come to the movies with us tomorrow."

Her cheerful tone grates on my nerves for some reason. "What?"

"Movie, tomorrow? There's that new one with the Hemsworth brothers, and they look delicious, as always."

She gives my arm a pat, but my only reaction is to send her a look of confusion coupled with frustration.

"You know I'm helping your mom out at her store tomorrow," I point out.

She shrugs. "All day?"

"Yeah, all day."

"Then we'll go after. Come on, it'll be good for you, especially considering the funk you've been in lately."

"Funk?" The way she puts it feels like a slap in the face.

"Yeah, I know you haven't been in the mood to party or even just hang out. But now that you've emerged from your hole, we can reconnect and have fun again."

I grab her by the shoulders and stare directly into her eyes. "Lori, Trent most likely drugged me. Do you understand what I'm telling you?" She nods, but something still seems to be lost in translation. "I don't even know what happened to me that night. But what I do know is there was something in that last drink I had. I feel it in my bones. And I know Trent didn't just tuck me in bed upstairs and watch me sleep. And, damn, I'm sorry if I've been in a *funk*, but can you honestly blame me?"

"Yeah, well, that's all I mean. You were going through some stuff."

She still looks unconvinced. I'm reaching my wits' end. I release her shoulders and slink back, putting some space between us. My facial features harden and I stare at her accusingly. "You don't believe that happened to me, do you?"

"Of course I do." Subtle shock mars her face. But only subtle.

"Yeah, I keep hearing you say that, but I don't see it."

She throws her arms up in the air and releases a full breath. "I just don't know what to do about it, okay? All I can think to do is be light and fun around you, which I thought I was doing, but it doesn't seem to be making a difference." She pauses and begins massaging her temples before continuing, "And I've been hanging out with Donovan lately—"

She stops suddenly. Her eyes meet mine. I can tell she's apprehensive to go there. "Which I don't mean in a weird way, like instead of you," she finishes.

There it is. The truth.

"No, that's fine. I get it," I say. "Actually, keep doing that. Yeah. You just keep hanging with your new best friend and staying light and fun, okay?"

I storm off, not knowing where my final destination will be, but it had to be better than sticking around Lori 2.0.

"Drea. Girl, come back," she yells after me, but I refuse to acknowledge the request.

I swipe away the tears forming in my eyes, attempting to keep the waterworks at bay. I weave through the party, hoping to find a discreet place to collect myself. I'm brought to a sudden stop when I collide with someone. I mutter an apology and try to step around them. Large hands take hold of the sides of my upper arms.

"Whoa, whoa ... Drea, are you okay?" the deep male voice asks.

Without looking up, I swat his arms away and take a step back.

Triggered.

I wipe away more tears and finally look up at the person I ran into. Harrison Daniels, the captain of the football team, stands there. His soft hazel eyes crash into mine.

Another apology bubbles up in my throat. "Sorry. Knee-jerk reaction. I shouldn't have done that."

"I get it. Personal space. That probably wasn't the best thing for me to do either."

His reply reminds me of his gentle nature. It also reminds me of the rumor that started circulating last year of him liking me.

"You've been crying," he says. "Do I need to kick someone's ass? Just point and say the word."

I shake my head. "Trust me, if there was an ass to kick, I would've already done it."

"True," he replies with a soft chuckle. "Hey, I haven't seen you around school lately, and you weren't cheering at the opening game last week."

Well, now I know he keeps tabs on me.

The faintest flutter of nerves rise within my stomach. "I've just got a busy senior year," I reply, and then mentally kick myself for lying to him. My year is anything but busy. "I've decided to embrace the hermit lifestyle for a bit."

Hermit lifestyle? Really? That's the best I could come up with?

"Got it," he says with a raised eyebrow. "Can I get you a drink or something to eat? Or find you a place to sit down?"

He's being so sweet, but I've seen him hanging around Trent more than ever lately. I don't understand why someone like him would associate with a jerk like Trent. I get that they're on the same team, but I'm a firm believer that you are who you hang out with.

"Actually, I was headed to the bathroom," I say, attempting to weasel out of the conversation. I don't want to be rude and just leave, but my current emotional state has me fearing the tears will return with a vengeance at a moment's notice. "Thanks for this though. It helped … in a strange way."

"That's actually my superpower. Helping in strange ways." His subtle grin is dangerous. Deadly, even. "Find me after maybe?"

"Honestly, I'm probably just gonna head home."

His expression falters. "Shame. Another time then."

"Yeah," I say, and then move past him, headed for the bathroom.

I push through the door, locking it behind me. My knees go weak and then buckle. I lean back against the door before sliding to sit on the cool tiles. The tears flow freely. I can't hold them back any longer.

My head collapses toward my lap. I lift my head and tap it back against the door as a sigh erupts from deep within me. Sadness fills the space anger had been camping out in, and I tap my head back once more.

My phone vibrates in my pocket. I retrieve it and see that Lori's calling. A picture of us during a much happier time accompanies the call, a time before she apparently decided my problems were too much for her to handle. A time when I thought we established how we truly felt about each other.

It continues to vibrate in my hand. I refuse to answer. The call ends and immediately starts up again, so I press the button on the side of the phone, ending the call.

I guess I was wrong. I hadn't reached my lowest point yet.

FIVE

THE JIGGLE OF THE BATHROOM DOOR'S HANDLE overhead snaps me out of my despondent stupor. The knock that follows has me dragging myself to my feet. I seriously can't believe I spent the last some-odd minutes crying in the bathroom at one of Sophia's parties.

Good grief, girl. Get a grip!

"One minute," I call out to the person on the other side of the door.

I do a quick makeup check in the mirror and grab a tissue from a box by the sink to dab away the mascara running down my cheeks. At this rate, it'd be the best idea ever for me to just go home and save myself any further embarrassment. I knew I shouldn't have come tonight, but I'm too stubborn for my own good sometimes.

I open the door and there's no one there. I guess it wasn't that much of an emergency. A couple of deep, relaxing breaths later has me ready enough to head out.

I have to leave ASAP.

In my current condition, the thought of navigating through

the sea of people between me and the front door seems daunting. The current song has the living room resembling a mosh pit full of flailing bodies. I take in one last lengthy breath and put one foot forward as desperation to get the hell out of here takes over.

"Hey, have you seen Lori anywhere?" Donovan asks as he rushes up to me through the crowd.

I shake my head, trying to hold myself together.

"When I came back from the kitchen, she wasn't there," he says. "And neither were you. I've looked everywhere, but no luck. Except for finding you now, of course."

"Have fun with that," I reply. "She's probably with Trent. Those two are made for each other."

The moment I utter those words, I feel a prick to my heart. I wouldn't wish Trent on anyone, no matter how they treated me. Then flashbacks of that party flood my brain. The way I felt before I apparently passed out next to him, and then the horrid feeling once I woke up. Dread builds in my gut.

"You don't think she'd actually leave with that creep, do you?" I ask. "Some silly flirting here and there is one thing, but she wouldn't actually be that stupid to go off alone with him, right?"

My rhetorical questions seem to be lost on Donovan, as he shrugs his shoulders and says, "I don't know, but he was the one who invited her to the party. I think he's sort of the only reason we came here tonight."

I barely hear Donovan's response as I survey the party for Lori. Then his words fully register.

"What? That doesn't sound like her," I say. "She isn't boy crazy. Trust me, I know."

At least, she never gave me that impression.

"All I'm saying is that she seemed to be really into him earlier," he says.

"Yeah, well, I didn't say she always has the best judgment, did I?" I snap back, and instantly feel guilty. "Sorry. I'm just a little frazzled."

"I understand," he says in a comforting tone. "You really care about her, don't you?"

His question catches me off-guard. His eyes reflect genuine worry, and I inexplicably feel like I could talk to him about anything.

Huh. He's annoyingly personable, isn't he?

"Lori and I have been through a lot together. So, yeah, I really care about her."

I pull out my phone and press on the last missed call from her to redial. It rings twice and then goes to voicemail. Donovan's phone rings. He takes it from his pocket and shows me that Lori's calling him.

"I guess that makes sense," I say under my breath.

"Lori, girl, where are you? I'm with Drea and we're looking all over for you."

His face falls into a look of confusion.

"What is it?"

"I'm not sure. It sounds like she's having a conversation with someone. I think she butt-dialed me."

I reach my hand out for the phone and he lets me take it. I only hear her end of the conversation. It seems the other person she's talking to isn't within range of the phone.

"Oh, please. You know you're hot."

(Inaudible voice)

"A little bit."

"Lori? Hello? Can you hear me?"

She doesn't respond. She just keeps chatting away. At least the conversation sounds pleasant.

I carve through the crowd, searching for any sign of her and this person she's talking to. I notice one of Will's college buddies, Max, a low-key drug dealer who sells Lori weed, posted up against the wall. He's clearly looking for potential customers.

"Have you seen Lori recently?" I ask.

Max shakes his head. "Nope. She hit me up earlier, but that was a while ago."

Lori's voice comes through the phone again, drawing me back into her conversation with this mystery person.

"Lori, it's Drea. Please answer me," I say, but she still doesn't seem to hear me.

I begin to systematically check the first floor, room by room.

"*Stop it. Someone might see us,*" I hear her say in a frisky tone.

It's frustrating that I can't hear the other person's response. I butt into a conversation between a few of our mutual friends and ask if they've seen her or Trent recently. None of them have, so I move on.

"Lori," I say again, more desperate now. The thought of Trent laying his greasy hands all over her sends me into a frenzy.

Donovan heads out to the backyard to expand our search as I hurry up the stairs to the second floor of the house. I fling open the first couple of doors I come across along the way only to find the rooms either empty or occupied by people who aren't Lori. I apologize to a couple making out in one of the rooms and continue down the hall.

No sign of Lori or Trent anywhere.

"*What the hell's wrong with you?*" I hear her ask. Her tone is no longer playful. "*Let go of me. This isn't cute anymore. Let go of me, I said. I'm not joking.*"

Panic burrows its way to my core and I begin throwing open more doors, not concerned if I interrupt anything happening in the rooms beyond them. The door to the second-floor bathroom is locked when I reach it. I knock forcefully.

"Occupied. Damn," I hear from the other side. It's clearly not them.

"Drea, what's happening?" Donovan's anxious face comes into view as he asks the question.

"I don't know. I can't find them, but she sounds upset," I reply, trying to keep my emotions in check.

"I'm going to keep looking. Are you going to be okay?" he asks, seeming in full distress mode.

I nod and he rushes back down the stairs.

"Lori, listen to my voice," I say loudly into the phone, hoping she finally hears me. "I'm here and I'm not leaving, okay? Please tell me where you are."

"*Let go of me!*"

(*Inaudible voice*)

"Lori! Please answer me! Tell me where you are!"

My mind leaps into worst case scenario territory. I don't know what to do. I hear her struggling on the other end of the call and feel positively helpless. There's a quick noise that sounds like a car horn, then nothing. When the call drops, my heart drops with it.

"Lori? *Lori?*"

I glance at my phone's screen. The call has ended. I immediately call her back, but it just rings.

No answer.

I hurry back to the first floor, dodging past a couple devouring each other's faces on the stairs along the way. They don't even budge when I almost crash into them. As I reach the bottom of the stairs, my eyes focus on my exit to the front yard where all the cars are parked.

Sophia Gomer's face pops into view right in front of me. "Wow, I did not expect to see you here tonight," she says with a faint smile.

"Yeah, I'm surprised too," I reply as my eyes pan back over to the front door. My anxiety kicks into high gear.

I need to get outside.

"I'm glad you came," she says, flipping her long, straight, honey brown hair over her shoulder. "Does this mean you're going to come back to us? We miss you on the cheerleading squad."

That's literally the last thing on my mind right now. Can't she see how upset I am?

"As much as I'd love to update you on all things cheerleading, I'm kind of in the middle of something," I reply. My eyes dart back toward the front door. "Have you seen Lori anywhere?"

"No. Is something wrong?" she asks, finally seeming to take note of my frantic state.

"I need to find her. I think she might be in trouble."

Her brow furrows. "Trouble? What kind of trouble?"

"I don't know. I just think something's wrong."

"Okay, okay. I'll go look for her too, if that helps," she replies. "We'll find her, don't worry."

"Thanks," I say, and then wade into the dancing crowd.

I leave the house behind and stop short on the front porch. A sea of cars fills my vision. I don't recognize Trent's amongst any of them. I try Lori's cell again and hear the faintest of ringtones echoing through the night, competing with the noise from the party behind me.

"Lori?" I shout as I move toward the melody.

I rule out all of the cars in the driveway and on the yard before the call times out. I try again. The ringtone grows louder the closer I get to the street.

"Lori?" I cry out again, more desperate this time.

The call again rolls to voicemail and I lose track of where the tune is coming from. I make one more attempt and hear the ringtone sound in the near vicinity. I see a small rectangular light source illuminated in the road a little ways from my position. Rushing over to it, I snatch up Lori's cell phone and see all of my missed calls.

"Hey, did you find something?" asks Donovan as he joins me.

I try to articulate and get out all I want to say, but the emotions surging through me make it almost impossible. "She's gone. That asshole has her."

"Hold up—slow down. Who has her? Trent?"

"They were all over each other when I got here and it sounded like they were continuing what they started before I interrupted them earlier. And then look," I say, presenting her phone for him to see. "She doesn't just leave her phone behind. She's always on this thing taking pictures and checking her damn socials."

"Okay, calm down. Do you want to call the cops? Because if you do, I'll call them this second."

I begin to hyperventilate. I can't catch my breath. The thought of anything happening to her, regardless of how she's treated me, causes me to spiral into hysterics.

"You need to calm down, Drea. Listen, I know what a panic attack looks like, all right? You are right in the middle of one. You need to breathe and focus on your surroundings, okay?"

I do as he instructs and take in a few long breaths. I focus on his face and breathe in synch with him to get my bearings.

"I'd call the cops, but I can't," I finally say.

"Why not?"

"I take it you've never dealt with cops in a situation like this before?"

"I try not to, but unfortunately I have dealt with them on occasion."

"That's not what I mean," I say at the peak of my frustration.

"If I call and tell them that I saw a drunk guy with my drunk friend at a party, they're going to either A, tell me that's just what kids in this town do, or B, break this whole party up." I pause to take a breather before continuing. "And if I tell them that I actually didn't see anything and I have no idea where the two of them went, they're going to start calling me *young lady* and asking if I've been drinking or taking drugs myself tonight."

Donovan's brow creases. "Sounds like you're speaking from personal experience. Has something like this happened to you before?"

"Yeah." My eyes move to Sophia's front porch. "In that house, actually, but I don't really remember it. That's part of the problem. You can't file a report if you don't know what you're filing it about. I just woke up here a few weeks ago after a party, and all I know is that nothing good happens when Trent's involved."

He nods. "Let's go do something about it then, okay? Come on." He reaches for my hand. "Let's find our friend."

I go to take his hand and then something dawns on me. "Harrison's still here at the party. If anyone would know where Trent is, it'd be him."

Looks like I'll be finding Harrison later after all.

Donovan

I TAKE DREA BY THE HAND AND WE HURRY BACK TOWARD
Sophia's house to find some guy named Harrison. It begins
to set in that I only started at this school a few weeks ago and
I'm already about to make waves with the Haddon Falls High elite.

There goes my plan for laying low senior year.

I sure hope Drea's right about all of this. But if she isn't, I only
have to deal with the fallout until graduation. I've dealt with much
worse for longer, that's for sure.

"Thank you, by the way," Drea says when we reach the edge
of the massive driveway.

"Of course. It's what friends do. Besides, it's about time we
start believing the victim, right?" I reply with a thin smile, and she
returns it.

We move into the house. Drea takes the lead toward the living
room where she last saw Harrison. It feels like even more people
are here now than before we went outside, and it's proving hard
to navigate through them all.

"Do you see him anywhere?" I ask near her ear, contending
with the surrounding noise.

"Not yet, no. There's beer pong set up in the kitchen. Let's go check there."

She jostles my hand when we enter the kitchen. Her eyes fixate on a tall, slender, but fit guy with dark brown hair. He looks nice enough. Not the stereotypical jock.

If that's Harrison, I wonder why he hangs out with a guy like Trent.

"Is that…?"

"Harrison," she shouts, cutting me off.

I guess I got my answer.

Harrison turns to us and his mouth forms into a smile. Drea releases my hand and hurries over to him. I follow close behind.

"I thought you were leaving," he says, his smile deepening.

He's quite the glorious sight from both close up and far away.

"I was, but I need to find Trent. Have you seen him?" Drea asks.

"Not in a while, no." His calm expression changes to match her agitated one. "Is everything okay?" His voice lowers to a whisper. "He wasn't the reason you were crying earlier, right? Because if he was—"

"No, but he might be with Lori, and I need to find them before something happens," she replies.

"Have you seen either of them?" I ask, trying to get any lead we can.

He switches his focus to me and shakes his head. "Last time I saw Lori, she was at the bar taking shots. I think you were with her."

"Yeah, that was when we first got here," I affirm. "That was hours ago though."

The worry seems to grow in Drea's eyes the longer we stand here. "Harrison, listen," she says, "can you call Trent maybe? I think he might do something to Lori if we don't find her."

Alarm springs into his hazel eyes. "Sure." He pulls out his phone and presses some buttons.

"Thank you." Drea bites her lower lip as we wait for the results of Harrison's call.

"Trent, where are you, man?" asks Harrison. Drea and I hang on to every word. "You're upstairs and kind of busy?"

Drea wastes no time and charges toward the stairs. I try to catch up with her, but moving through the party is like swimming against an ocean current.

"Drea, wait up," I call out.

She must not hear me over the pounding music because she doesn't stop. I finally reach a break in the crowd and sprint up the stairs to find her standing in front of a door near the end of the third floor hallway. She's banging on it and demanding Trent to open up.

She looks over at me when I close in. "It had to be this room, right? Out of all the rooms, he had to take her to this one," Drea spits out. "He's locked the door and won't open it, but I know he's in there."

"Is this where you woke up that day?" I ask. I don't want to trigger anything, but it's probably far too late for that worry given what's happened tonight.

She looks at me and I receive the answer to my question by her facial expression alone. I move in front of the door and pull out my wallet. I retrieve my "lucky" lock pick and kneel in front of the door handle. Thankfully, it's a simple privacy doorknob with a small hole in the middle for me to slide the slim piece of metal into and pop it open.

"Wait, you just carry that around with you?"

"Remember when I told you I've had run-ins with the cops? Well, this is why. I keep this around to remind me of my screw-ups. It's kind of ironic that I'm using it now to help someone," I say as I hear the lock disengage.

Drea rushes into the room, then comes to an abrupt stop.

"What the actual hell?" Trent yells. "Get out of here."

Trent and a random girl, not Lori, are wrapped up in each other. The girl grabs her blouse from beside her on the bed to cover up, but Trent just flaunts his shirtless form, clearly not bothered by it. The girl pulls on the blouse before scurrying out of the room.

"Where's Lori?" demands Drea. She's definitely more upset now.

"How the hell should I know?" he replies.

Drea balls her hands into fists by her side. She's holding them so tight, I'm afraid she might draw blood.

"Wrong answer. Where's Lori?" she asks in a louder voice.

"You're crazy hot when you get like this, you know that?"

I jump in between Drea and her making a big mistake. "Come on, man," I say. "Do you know where Lori is, or not? Several people here said you were hanging all over each other tonight, so you might as well 'fess up."

"Fine. You caught me. We were getting all hot and heavy in the garage, making out in Sophia's dad's sweet Bentley, and she accused me of going too far too fast and being too rough, so she split. Then I got another girl and brought her up here. End of story."

"You're such a disgusting pig, you know that?" Drea snaps.

"Oink, oink, baby."

Even I want to hit him for that one.

"What did you do with her?" insists Drea.

"I already told you, she bit off more than she could chew and she split, period."

"I heard the whole thing, Marcus," she says. "Lori butt-dialed Donovan while you two were together. You tried to force yourself on her."

Marcus rolls his eyes. "If you heard the whole thing then you know she was enjoying it at first and then left when I got a little too hands-on."

Drea hauls off and slaps him across the face. I'm not quick enough to intervene, not that I would have anyway because this guy's some kind of next level douchebag.

Trent pivots his face back to Drea while rubbing the offended area, a smirk firmly in place. "Have you forgotten who my dad is?"

"Like I give a damn," she says.

She rears back to send another blow his way, but this time I stop her.

No need to push our luck.

"You and Lori are both the same, you know that, Drea? You both talk a big game, but deep down you're just a pair of weak bitches," Trent says with a pompous laugh.

This guy is the worst.

I guide Drea off to the side and then go toe-to-toe with him.

He rises from the bed. "You gonna do something, princess?"

Princess?

Princess!?

Princess!?!

He looks so smug, just begging to be punched, so I accommodate him. He falls back against the bed, and for a moment, I feel victorious as he cups his hands over his nose. Then the adrenaline begins to subside and a surge of pain shoots through my entire hand.

"Ow! Crap that hurts." I shake my hand off to the side before drawing it to rest near my stomach. "I always thought hitting someone who deserved it would make you feel good, but, damn, this hurts a lot."

"I think you broke my nose, asshole," he whines, flat out on the bed resembling a turtle on its back.

"That's Mister Asshole to you, Trent," Drea grounds out as she kicks him in the shin, adding insult to injury.

"Come on. We still have to find Lori. He's not worth our time," I try to convince her.

"I still think he's lying. He knows where she is," she argues while I lead her back toward the doorway. She cranes her neck to look back over her shoulder into the room. "I'm calling the cops on your ass."

"Not if I call them first, sweetheart," he fires back, and I feel her body resonate with anger.

"Let's go. We don't need to end up in jail tonight, okay?" I try to calm her the best I can, but in the back of my mind there's a single question nagging away at me.

Where the hell are you, Lori?

SEVEN

Drea

A RANGE OF EMOTIONS ASSAULT ME ALL AT ONCE. I can't decide how I should feel in this moment. Slapping Trent felt therapeutic, but the way Donovan punched him felt more like retribution. He still deserves so much more, but what Donovan did back there was truly awesome. I can see why Lori likes him.

"How's your hand?" I ask. Guilt scratches at my heart since that whole exchange was mostly my fault.

"The feeling is coming back and I no longer hear ringing in my ears, so there's that. But that's not important. We still need to find Lori. Can you think of where she could be?"

I shake my head, trying to piece everything together and make sense of the situation. "I still don't get it. She'd never be this far away from her phone, ever."

"Does she know anyone who lives around here, maybe where she could've gone to lay low?" he asks.

"Not that I know of."

"Hey, are you two all right?" Harrison's voice sounds from down the hall.

"No," I curtly reply. "Your friend's face in there did this to my friend's hand."

"First of all, sorry about your hand. I'm sure Trent deserved it," he says to Donovan. "And second," he turns to address me, his hazel eyes firm, "Trent's not really my friend."

I almost get shivers from the seriousness of his tone. It's nice to hear him openly denounce Trent, but that still doesn't explain why he hangs out with him so much.

"Okay, then why are you always around each other?" I ask.

"We're on the same team, that's it. I swear. The coach has this thing about wanting all of us to be a tight-knit group this season. It's not by choice. He's kind of forcing it upon us. Believe me, I'm not a fan of Trent or his handiwork." His eyes plead with me to believe him.

"If that's true, why didn't you ever do anything to stop him? You and the rest of the football team have practically let him get away with murder, and you've all stood by doing absolutely nothing."

He goes silent, contemplative. His eyes have lost their usual sheen. I'm disappointed he doesn't have a rebuttal.

Say something, please. Prove me wrong.

"If we're done here, we should probably keep looking for Lori," Donovan says, interrupting the silence.

He moves to the stairs. I hang back for a moment. This is the worst staring contest I've ever participated in. When I avert my eyes, I hear Harrison release a sigh.

"Wait, Drea," he begins, and I delay my exit. "You still haven't found Lori?"

I shake my head. "Not yet, no." I turn and join Donovan by the stairs, leaving Harrison behind.

We proceed downstairs to the garage to fact check Trent's story. Hopefully there's some clue as to what happened or where Lori went. I'm getting antsy. Every minute that passes when we don't call the cops costs us precious time, possibly allowing for something else to go wrong.

"Trent said they were in the Bentley, right?" Donovan asks, approaching the car in question.

"Yeah. Maybe we should check inside."

I open the door to the back seat. Nothing looks out of the ordinary. The leather interior smells newish, but is mixed with a lingering scent of that strong cologne Trent wears. It reminds me of some kind of Axe body spray knock off. I feel around the seats and look down at the floor mats for any clues. Then I remember the sound I heard at the end of the call.

A car horn.

"Is there anything up there?" I ask Donovan, who is checking the front seats.

"Not really," he replies, poking his head up over the passenger's headrest to look at me.

"I could have sworn I heard a car horn at the end of my call with her."

"Huh, the driver's side door isn't closed all the way. Maybe she went out through there and hit the steering wheel by accident, which was the noise you heard," says Donovan.

"Maybe."

I continue my search. I pull down the center console between the two back seats and hear a rattle as it settles into positon. There's a pill of some sort in one of the cup holders, a small pink opaque capsule filled with a powdered substance.

"Hey, I think I just found some kind of drug."

"Like this one?" Donovan asks, meeting me at the center of the car holding up a similar-looking pill in his fingers. "Found this wedged into a crease in the driver's seat."

"I wonder if these belong to Trent," I say, staring at the pill. "Probably some date rape drug or something."

"They actually kind of look like the prescription Lori picked up before we came to the party," Donovan mentions while also examining the pink capsule.

"Wait, what prescription?" I ask, my confused gaze meeting his inquisitive one.

"For her depression," he replies. I can tell by his reaction to the look on my face he realizes something isn't right about what he just said.

"Lori is the furthest thing away from being depressed," I say. "Where did you say she got these?"

"We stopped by RJ's drugstore to pick it up before we came to the party tonight," he replies.

Drug dealer Max usually hangs out there.

I climb out of the car and notice Donovan's attention is fixed on the side door of the garage. It's propped open the slightest bit.

"Maybe she left through there," he suggests. "I think we would've seen Lori in the house earlier while you were on the phone with her if she went that way."

"Good point."

He opens the door the rest of the way and steps outside. He's illuminated by the sensor light above the door as he ventures further out. "The fence's gate is open. I'm going to check it out."

"Wait up, I'm coming with you," I reply, hurrying over to him.

The gate leading into the backyard is wide open, revealing a view of the side front yard lined by a tall, well-manicured hedgerow. "Why would she go back to her car when you were still here?" I ask. "She wouldn't have abandoned you like that."

"Yeah, it does seem odd. But then again, you found her phone near the street, right? And that's where her car's parked."

"I'm still confused by that. None of this makes any sense," I say in exasperation.

"We need to go check."

We pick up the pace through the front yard and onto the street. Donovan reaches Lori's car first, largely due to my poor choice of footwear. Heels and grass are not a good combo. From a distance, I watch him search the ground around the car for any clues with the assistance of the flashlight on his phone.

"Found another one of those pills. What the hell is going on?" he asks as I close in on the vehicle.

"I have no—"

The words get caught in my throat when a faint outline of something in the front seat of Lori's car is illuminated by a passing car's headlights.

"Donovan? Is someone in the front seat?" I ask. My voice quivers near the end of the question.

"In the driver's seat?" he echoes, pressing his face up against the window to get a better look inside. He shoots me a relieved look before opening the door. "Lori, we've been looking all over for..."

He pauses. Shock mars his expression.

"What? What is it? Is she in there?" I ask, rushing closer to the vehicle.

Donovan staggers away and turns to stop me before I reach the driver's side door. "Stop, Drea. You don't want to see this." His eyes are serious, his face growing paler by the second.

"Wait ... no. It can't be," I say, my heart breaking a little more with each passing syllable. I push past him, disregarding his warning.

I have to see for myself.

"Lori! No!"

My hand shoots up in front of my mouth, unsuccessfully

attempting to stifle the screams. Tears pool and then cascade down my face. My mind tries to comprehend what I'm seeing, but I refuse to believe my own eyes. I reach out to touch her, my hand trembling uncontrollably.

I'm desperate. I need her to wake up from this horrible nightmare. Her skin is cool and damp to the touch. My hand snaps back.

Her face has taken on a slight bluish hue and is cocked off to the side, facing me. In her hand is an empty Ziploc bag. A few more of the pink pills are on her lap, a stark contrast to the black jeans she's wearing.

I can hardly contain anything at this moment and fall to my knees in a fit of tears. My body succumbs to heavy sobs. The sting of the asphalt on my bare skin doesn't even register. I feel Donovan's arms wrap around me, but then I go numb.

I don't feel anything at all.

EIGHT

Donovan

I'VE NEVER SEEN A DEAD BODY BEFORE. SURE, I'VE SEEN my fair share of horror movies, but nothing prepares you for seeing death in real time. There's this crippling finality that sets in and paralyzes you, making you feel like a shell of your former self for an indeterminate amount of time as you look on in disbelief. Like an out-of-body experience. You feel like you'll never be the same afterward, like you've been tainted or marked. The sensation is worse if it's someone you know.

I can't even begin to imagine how Drea's feeling right now.

The only other person I've lost in my life was my dad when I was nine. I never did see his body though. It was a closed casket funeral. Drunk driver. But I didn't need to see his body to realize my life from that point on would never be the same. I was changed forever.

It only took about fifteen minutes for everyone to clear out of Sophia's house after the deputies showed up. It felt a hell of a lot longer than that. And since we're the ones who called them, we were asked to stick around and give our full statements about what transpired. Trent had to stay behind too due to the part he played in all of this. The officers naturally had questions for him.

I do my best to listen to the conversations happening around me. For the most part, the adults act like Drea and I aren't even there, making it easier to eavesdrop. From what I manage to overhear, the initial examination of Lori's body by the coroner suggests she died from a drug overdose. A possible suicide, they say, but it isn't conclusive.

When I share this with Drea during a lull in our interviews with the deputies, she isn't convinced. She thinks there's no way Lori took her own life. After finding out that Lori didn't, in fact, have depression like she told me, I'm inclined to believe Drea's gut feeling.

I can't believe she's gone. Just like that.

I'm still in a state of shock as I wait for Drea to finish talking with the deputies. My heart breaks while I watch her try to speak to them. She's a wreck, and I can't blame her one bit.

The bag of ice the paramedics gave me for my hand has all but melted and is now just a pouch of cold water. I find myself momentarily hypnotized by the condensation as it drips onto my red and white Converse sneakers.

Drip.

Drip.

Drip.

To say my aunts were worried when they learned the reason I wasn't home yet is an understatement. They offered to come pick me up, but I told them I wanted to wait for Drea to make sure she was okay. They were pacified when I told them one of the deputies offered to give me a ride home.

I'm definitely making an impression on everyone tonight, but not really in the good kind of way.

"Hey, new guy," I hear a familiar deep voice call out to me.

Harrison?

"It's Donovan, thanks," I reply.

"Sorry. Donovan, right," he says with a strained laugh.

I'm not sure why he's come to talk to me. It's strange he's hanging around while everyone has gone home. Even Trent has at this point. The only ones left other than the deputies are me, Drea, a couple of neighbor lookie-loos, and Sophia and her brother Will since they live here.

"This is crazy, huh?" he asks.

I'm not really feeling the small talk, but I respond anyway. "Yeah, definitely not how I thought my senior year would be starting out, that's for sure."

"Yeah, I don't think any of us did," he replies. I begin to say something, but then he pipes up again. "I think I'm gonna head out. I just wanted to make sure Drea was okay. Could you let her know that I'm really sorry for what happened?"

I nod. I can't tell if he's being nice or weird. Or both. Maybe he feels responsible in a way.

"You know," I say, "you can always tell her yourself."

He sends me a questioning look. "You and I both know that's probably not a good idea. I don't think she's too terribly happy with me at the moment."

He surprises a small smile out of me. "You've definitely got a point there. She doesn't seem to be on Team Harrison right now."

"So you'll tell her for me?" There's a hint of worry in his eyes.

"Sure."

"Thanks," he says, taking one last look over at Drea before proceeding toward his car.

I guess jocks can be complex.

I've already had my turn with the deputies and regurgitated

every detail my exhausted mind could remember. I'm sure I forgot something, but I'm also confident that between Drea's and my statements, they should get a pretty clear picture.

The young deputy who offered to give me a ride home places his hand on Drea's shoulder and says something before walking away. She looks shattered as she makes her way over to me. I'm feeling it too, and Lori wasn't even my best friend.

"My dad's here to pick me up. I'm getting my car tomorrow. I can't drive with my nerves like this." She pauses for a moment and sniffs, and I can tell she's on the verge of tears again. "Are you going to be okay getting home? Do you need a ride?"

"I'm good. I'm hitching a ride with one of the deputies. He offered when I explained I came with … well, when I said how I got here." I sense her becoming worse when I start to say Lori's name, so I refrain.

She draws me into an embrace, not saying a word. She weeps close to my ear and I hug her tighter. I want to say so much, but I feel like this isn't the time. Everything's too fresh, too raw.

As I release the hug, I say, "Please take care of yourself, okay?"

She just nods before moving away to join her dad by his car.

"Ready to head out?" the young deputy asks from beside his cruiser.

He'd told me his name earlier, but clearly it didn't take since I have to remind myself by not-so-subtly looking at the tag on chest.

Owens … right.

"Yeah."

I settle into the front seat of Deputy Owens's vehicle and instantly feel strange. I told him I'd be fine sitting in the back and that I didn't mind, but he insisted that was only for criminals, not innocent civilians.

I'm slightly ashamed I know what it feels like to be in the back of a cop car with cuffs on. The charge? Breaking and entering. The victim? My stepfather, but I just call him Carl. He calls me chief. Well, at least he did until my little incident involving the church where he's a pastor. Long story short, he's the main catalyst for me being here in Haddon Falls.

When we reach my new home, all of the lights are on and I see Aunt Helen pacing back and forth in front of the large living room window. Aunt Lucy, on the other hand, is sitting in her rocking chair on the front porch, partially illuminated by the porch light. Her rocking a little manic. As we slow down in front of the driveway, Aunt Lucy opens the front door and Aunt Helen rushes out, both speeding toward the deputy's car.

I'm out of the vehicle mere seconds before I'm encircled in both of their arms, sandwiched between them. They ask me if I'm okay at the same time, and I assure them that I will be.

"That must have been horrible to find Lori like that," Aunt Helen says, pulling back a little to see my face.

"Absolutely terrible," Aunt Lucy follows quickly after.

"I love that you're both concerned about me, but I think I need some time to process all of this. I just spent what seemed like forever explaining to complete strangers what happened tonight, and I think I'm all talked out."

They both let me go. "Of course. Completely understandable," Aunt Helen says as Aunt Lucy nods in agreement. They usher me into the house. "Can we get you anything?"

"No, that's okay. You both should get some sleep too. I'm just going to head up to my room and crash, if that's all right."

"Okay, well, let us know if you need anything at all," Aunt Lucy reiterates as I ascend the stairs.

"And again, we're so sorry about this. Please let us know if you want to talk about it," Aunt Helen implores. Her eagerness to talk about things makes her a great guidance counselor at the high school.

"Will do, thanks," I reply, and move through the door into my room.

The space feels just as empty as I do right now. I haven't made much of an effort to decorate since moving in. There are no posters on the bare, cream-colored walls, nor any character to speak of like I had in my last room. I left most of my stuff back in Mississippi. It was all a part of my old life. This is a new beginning for me, so I only brought along the essentials. Clean slate.

There's still a black trash bag full of clothes that I haven't unpacked propped up in the far corner of the room. Not knowing how long I'd be here, I'd lived out of three trash bags for weeks until I finally succumbed to putting some of my stuff away in order to feel a little more settled in. I'm fortunate my aunts took me in so quickly.

I flop back onto my bed and stare blankly up at the ceiling. The first thought to enter my mind is I wonder how Drea's doing. I realize I don't have her number to check up on her. It also occurs to me that I never told her what Harrison said. There didn't really seem to be a good time to bring it up.

I don't know how I'm going to fall asleep with the image of Lori's lifeless body burned into my brain. It makes me think about how fragile life is, but then again, I first learned that lesson back when I nine.

It never gets any easier.

NINE

Drea

SOMETHING TELLS ME LORI WOULD LOVE THE FACT HER locker now resembles a shrine. That little nugget of humor is the only positive thing to cross my mind as of late.

Today's the first of October. My favorite month. But now the thought of having a favorite time of the year seems pointless if I can't spend it with the one person I want to.

It's also Monday, which means the world has been without Lori in it for a total of two nights. People always complain about how much they hate Mondays, and how it's so hard to get going in the morning. Well, I can officially attest to that opinion. I don't think I've ever had a worse Monday in my whole life.

How does anyone return to a normal routine after seeing something like that? But that's what everyone wants me and the rest of the student body to try to do … return to normal. Or at least as normal as high school can be.

I knew Lori was popular, but standing in front of her locker now covered in pictures grabbed from her socials, printed out, and stuck to it with flowers and little tokens gathered below, I can't help but get choked up. It's at times like these I'm reminded that people might not suck as much as I'd like to think they do. Even if there are those who only pay their respects because they want to feel good about themselves by contributing to a current group grief session, it's still nice to see the overall end result.

I loosen the knot on the woven black and pink rope bracelet Lori made for me and slip it from around my wrist. It represented our two favorite colors, mine black and hers pink, intertwined in an endless loop. Like we were.

I rub it between my thumb and index finger and feel every frayed fiber. This is the first time I've removed it since she gave it to me a year ago. I'll never forget that night for as long as I live.

After some serious debating with myself, I loop the bracelet through the opening in the locker door's handle and re-secure the knot before stepping back. It's hard letting go of it like this, but it's only temporary. I want it to be a part of this tribute to her. I plan to collect the bracelet later to wear at the funeral. It just feels right to leave it here for now.

People pass around me like they're moving in slow motion as I continue to stare at the memorial display. Lori and I spent many mornings over the years standing at our lockers gossiping over everything and nothing at all, and I'm finding it hard to break that routine, though now all of the dialogue is in my head.

The animosity I've been holding in my soul over the past few weeks has all but faded away, replaced with uncertainty and regret. The idea of Lori committing suicide just doesn't make any sense. I'm even having a hard time believing she accidentally overdosed. And why did she lie to Donovan about having depression?

Something doesn't feel right. Trent has to be involved somehow.

"How you holding up?" A familiar voice wades through my thoughts.

I shake from my daze and see Donovan standing there. I haven't seen him since that night. He looks kind of like how I feel. His hands are stuffed in his pockets with his shoulders slumped forward. The slight bags under his eyes accentuate the dreary expression on his face.

"I'm not really sure how to answer that," I reply. "It all seems unreal. I keep thinking that soon I'm going to wake up."

"Yeah, I get what you mean." His voice quakes a little. "It's okay not to know. I don't either, to be honest."

"This is uncharted territory for me, you know? Probably for most of us," I say, returning my gaze to Lori's memorial.

Donovan's arm drapes over my shoulder and pulls me closer to him. I rest my head on his shoulder and there are no more words. We just stand there staring at Lori's locker, which resembles one of her many social media walls full of fun pictures. If I had any tears left to cry I would, but it seems as if I'm all tapped out.

A commotion rumbles through the hall. We both look and see students moving to the side, making way for the sheriff of Haddon Falls with a couple of deputies in tow.

"Those are the deputies from Saturday night," Donovan says. "I wonder what they're doing here."

"I don't know. Hopefully it's not more bad news."

My eyes drift back to Lori's locker. Out of my peripheral vision, I see someone in a black and red letterman's jacket approaching. Trent's voice smashes into me before I can turn and look at him. My entire body tenses.

"I know you hate me and I'm the very last person you want to see right now, but I wanted to say ... I'm sorry." His posture suggests he's being forced to stand there, like a sniper has his sights set on him, threating to shoot if he moves.

Flames of anger slide up my cheeks. Donovan's grip tightens

on my shoulder. "I think it'd be best if you just left, Trent," he says before I'm able to muster any kind of words to tell Trent off. I'm at a complete loss for what to say.

"I get it," he says, taking a step back.

I rip away from Donovan's arm and drop my stuff on the ground. The loud sound doesn't even faze me. "I don't think you do, Trent. I don't think you understand that my best friend is gone now because of you." I poke my finger into his chest. He just stares at me, not saying anything. I prod him harder a second time. It seems to trigger a reaction. His face reads a little more irritated. "You're to blame, you asshole! This." I point to Lori's locker. "Is your fault." My voice shakes, and I guess I'm not as tapped out as I thought because tears begin to stream down my face. "Just get the hell out of my face. I can't stand to look at you," I shout, and then turn back to face Donovan.

Someone takes hold of my wrist. I ball up my free hand into a fist, hauling off and swinging at the person behind me. It connects, hard, and my hands shoot up to stifle the horrified gasp that leaves my mouth when I realize who I just hit.

Harrison.

He stands there massaging his jaw, just staring at me. Trent stands off to his side, a look of surprise mixed with amusement on his face. The surrounding crowd seems just as stunned as I am at what just happened.

"All four of you, in the principal's office, now," one of the guidance counselors, Mrs. Walsh, booms from behind us. She comes to stand by our little foursome, a stern look locked on her face. With an insistent wave of her hand, she gestures us to follow.

It's feels like a shame march as everyone parts for us, all staring. Whispers roll throughout the hallway, making me feel worse.

Why did I have to be such a hot head back there?

I can feel Harrison's eyes on my back as we keep walking single file. Guilt doesn't even begin to describe how I'm feeling right now. There's no way he deserved all the rage I put behind that punch. It was reserved for the asshat beside him.

"Is all of this necessary, Aunt Helen?" Donovan asks from in front of me.

Huh, I didn't realize she was his aunt.

"We have a zero-tolerance policy for violence on campus, Donovan," she replies. "Considering the circumstances, this is all more than necessary."

Her response strikes me as odd.

"What do you mean by that?" Donovan takes the words from my mouth.

She moves ahead of us and opens the door to the front office. She steers us inside and doesn't answer his question. "Take a seat. One chair apart from each other, please," she instructs.

We all drop down into our respective spots like children in time out, complete with a disapproving huff from Trent at the end.

"I can't afford to get in trouble like this, Mrs. Walsh. I need to play in Thursday's game to impress a scout," Trent tosses his weak plea at her.

"Well you should've thought about that, huh?" she replies and then moves over to the desk of the principal's administrative assistant.

Trent grumbles and slumps back into his seat. "I can't believe this crap," he says, crossing his arms over his chest.

"Will you please shut up?" says Harrison.

"You know what, Harrison? It's your fault we're in here anyway. You're the one who made me go apologize to that psycho down there," he says, and I find myself consumed with the urge to smack him again.

Did Harrison really make him do that?

"Donovan, please come with me," Mrs. Walsh says.

Donovan flashes me an unsure look before following her down another hall toward the guidance offices. My leg bobs as I grow restless. I roll the hem of my shirt between my fingers as my mind floods with thoughts of Lori and the events that led me to this very moment. It seems like we've been sitting here for ages, and there's only so many things on the wall to look at to pass the time. At my height, I can barely see over the receptionist's counter while seated in this chair, so there's that.

The door to the principal's office swings open and the sheriff and two deputies file out. Their presence causes uncertainty to spring up within me. I wish I knew what they were doing here.

Does it have anything to do with Lori?

"Trent Blakemore, could you come in here, please?" Our principal, Mrs. Grayson, beckons.

He shoves himself away from his seat and trudges over to her office before disappearing behind the closed door.

Now's my chance. I have to say something to Harrison.

I tap on the chair between us, hoping to get his attention. He ignores me. I clear my throat to drive home the point and tap again.

"Quiet, please," Gloria, the principal's admin, calls out.

Not the person I wanted.

"Sorry, Gloria," I say.

Harrison laughs under his breath. I snap my head to face him. "It's not that funny, okay?"

He nods with a tickled expression. I huff and collapse back against the chair. There's a tap on the seat between us and I swivel my head to look at him. He isn't even looking at me. I think he just tapped on the chair for the hell of it.

Is he mocking me?

He faces me while showcasing a hesitant grin and taps again.

"Yes?" I whisper.

"Can I ask you a question?"

"Oh, so now you want to talk?"

He nods. "Can I ask you a question?"

"Sure, fine, ask away."

"Do you lift weights?"

"What?"

"I mean you'd have to, right? With a left hook like that? It was really impressive."

A small laugh escapes me. "That was your question?"

He shakes his head. "How's your hand?"

I'm the one who punched him and he's worried about my hand?

"Surprisingly well, considering what it hit," I reply.

He trails his fingertips across his jaw. "Yeah, this here cuts diamonds, so you must be pretty tough."

"Okay, that was extremely corny," I say, but I can't help but giggle again.

"Ah, but it did its job. You laughed," he says, his grin shrinking to a pleased smirk.

Gloria clears her throat. "Second warning, you two," she says.

We both toss our apologies her way before flattening back against our seats.

Screw a third warning. I need to apologize to him.

We both start to speak at a low volume at the same time. I'm surprised he's willing to risk getting in trouble just to talk to me. He has more to lose than I do since he's an integral part of the football team.

"Me first," he whispers.

"But I want to apologize," I argue, just as quiet.

"Okay, apology accepted. Now me," he says. "You were right. I've screwed up when it comes to Trent. I should've done or said something. I need to be better. So, all I need to know is will you forgive me?"

"Thank you for saying that." I take in a delicate breath and then release a contented sigh. "And yes, I forgive you."

"Good," he says. Then his expression becomes thoughtful. "And for what it's worth, I'm truly sorry about what happened to Lori."

"Yeah, I think that's the common consensus."

"Indeed," he agrees with a deep sigh.

A bout of silence falls between us as I lean my head back against the wall. I can't believe I went that long without thinking about Lori. And I'm conflicted, to say the least. Up until Harrison mentioned her, I'd been distracted for the first time since the waves of sadness began bombarding me that night. Huh, this is the second time he's done this for me. The first time was back at Sophia's party.

Maybe he's more than just a mere distraction from my problems.

TEN

Donovan

I'VE ALWAYS CONSIDERED MYSELF A GREAT KEEPER OF secrets. In fact, my small group of friends back home used to refer to me as their therapist. They all came to me with their problems, maybe because I'm also a pretty good listener or because I'm just quiet and unassuming.

No matter how big or small the secret, I've kept tight-lipped about them all, sometimes to a fault. There was even one time back in fourth grade when one of my good friends confided in me that he peed his pants during a field trip to the aquarium. I kept watch while he cleaned himself up and then helped get rid of the evidence so the rest of the class, including the teacher, were none the wiser. To this day, I have yet to utter a single word of it to anyone. I haven't even brought it up to him again.

Flash forward to now, and I'm struggling not to break all of my rules regarding secrets. I was just sworn to secrecy. If I were to divulge this sensitive information, I could get quite a few people in real trouble, including my aunt, though I've been assured the truth of this matter will be revealed once all the details have surfaced.

I'd asked my aunt how she learned what she shared with me

She said she overheard the start of the conversation when the sheriff first arrived. She had decided to step out of the principal's office after she heard more than she cared to know.

That's how I feel right now. Like I've heard more than I want to know. I leave my aunt's office and close the door absently behind me. My mind races. At first, I thought she was going to ream me for being involved in the altercation this morning, but it quickly turned into a secret meeting that couldn't be held around anyone else. Heavy is my heart, and heavier is my mind at the prospects of what this information means.

I wish I didn't know these details.

I wish I'd heard about this along with everyone else.

When I reach the main office, the bank of seats is empty. No Drea, Harrison, or Trent. Relief comes over me. Now I don't have to try and hide anything from them. I'm most concerned about keeping this from Drea.

If I don't see her, I don't have to lie to her.

"They've all been sent back to class," Gloria says, startling me from my thoughts. She rips off a piece of yellow paper with gibberish scribbled all over it and hands it to me. "Here's your hall pass."

I take it from her outstretched hand and say, "Thanks," before heading out.

The hall beyond the office is deserted with everyone in class. The stillness of the silence spikes the hair on the back of my neck, and I shudder as my mind reflects back on the conversation I just had with my aunt.

The shrill squeak of my sneakers echoes in the hall as I pick up the pace to my locker. I can't get there fast enough. The dial on my combo lock spins between my fingertips. I don't want to be caught in the hall by anyone, regardless of whether I have a pass or not. I somehow input the wrong combo and my locker fails to open on my first attempt.

Damn nerves.

I draw in a deep breath and focus. My input this time is more methodical and it pops open. As I reach for my books, a folded piece of paper lying on top of them catches my eye. I open it. There's only one line of text. A simple message.

Hi Donnie.

"What the hell is this?"

I flip it over to inspect the back to see if there's any indication of who put it in my locker or if there's more to the message, but there's nothing. A shiver travels down my spine and stalls at my lower back.

"Shouldn't you be in class?"

I peer around the locker door and watch as Deputy Owens approaches with another officer right behind him. My body freezes in place. I forget how to speak. My words become jumbled in my head and refuse to be relayed to my mouth so I can express them. I crumple up the strange piece of paper and toss it back into the locker before pulling out the hall pass just in case.

"Hello, Mr. Walsh. Didn't recognize you at first," Deputy Owens says.

I retrieve a couple of my books and shut the locker before facing him. "Guilty as charged," I respond, but then regret the poor choice of words.

They both chuckle. "How are you doing?" he probes.

"I guess okay, all things considered."

It's ridiculously hard to chat with them while knowing exactly why they're here, as they don't know that I know. I wish I could just stuff myself into my locker right now and slam the door.

"Glad to hear it," he says with a kind smile. "All right, get to class, mister."

It feels strange to be called mister by someone who looks only a few years older than me.

"You got it," I reply, moving past them and heading to my class.

All eyes dart over to me when I enter the classroom. That's the first thing I notice. The second thing I notice is Lori's empty desk next to mine. It's oddly unnerving having this many sets of eyes locked onto me while I move toward the teacher and hand him my hall pass. I almost want to take a few steps backward just to test if they'd all follow me.

Mr. Foster's somber eyes meet mine. "Please take your seat, Mr. Walsh," he says, motioning to my desk. "And please let me know if you need anything."

It was nice of him to offer, but all that did was give ammo to the rest of the class. Whispers flow through the room at a low hum, like a muffled swarm of locusts. I don't need to hear what they're saying, I already have a pretty good idea.

"Settle down, class, and resume working on the even problems on page fifty-nine in your textbook," orders Mr. Foster.

I slide into my seat and attempt to block out the continued murmurs around me. I open the book to the page he mentioned and turn my notebook to the next blank page. I'm poised with my mechanical pencil in hand and ready to write, but then my eyes wander over to the empty desk beside me. I imagine Lori sitting there making a goofy face because she's bored to tears over Mr. Foster's lecture. She'd always doodle in her notebook and write little messages to me. She'd swivel the notebook to face me, but not so apparent as to give away that we weren't paying attention.

In this moment, I find myself compelled to write my own message to her. My hand trembles with each passing letter I write, making my writing look unlike my own. I finish the message, and as my eyes read over it, a sigh escapes my lips. I keep reading it over and over again, but the words still seem surreal.

Who killed you, Lori?

ELEVEN

Drea

THERE WAS A TIME WHEN I COULDN'T WAIT FOR senior year so I could have a free period. I worked hard for it. Now I'm dreading it more than anything because that means I'll be alone with my thoughts. It's not that I'd prefer social interaction, it's just that my current state of mind has easily become my worst enemy.

It doesn't help matters at all that battling for a spot at the forefront of my mind is the ridiculous act of chivalry Harrison apparently displayed during his talk with the principal. I knew something was up when he left her office and flashed me the smirk to end all smirks accented with a suave head nod. The way he said, "You're up," also had my suspicions on high alert.

He'd done something. I was sure of it.

To my complete and utter surprise, he'd thrown himself on the sword for me. He demanded the detention reserved for me be doled out on him instead. He'd taken complete blame for what I did. My actions.

Why did he do that?

Ultimately, the principal dropped the whole thing entirely

because of the current atmosphere around campus. A part of me suspected the reason was she didn't want to deal with the fallout from giving our school's star quarterback detention before the big Homecoming game on Thursday. She did, however, give me one hell of a firm warning about violence at school right before she strongly encouraged me to take part in the grief counseling being offered. I guess it also helped that it was both mine and Harrison's first disciplinary visit to the principal's office.

I need to thank him.

After killing most of my free period in the library, I find myself standing at the intersection of two hallways. I'm torn. Down one hall is Harrison's locker and down the other is Donovan's. I have important things to discuss with both of them, but since I know where to find Harrison after school—football practice—I decide to head toward Donovan's.

A paper banner trimmed out in our school colors, black and red, is strung up overhead in the hall. **HOMECOMING** is painted in bold letters in the middle of it followed by details about the game on Thursday. Smaller poster-sized signs line the walls and are painted with bright neon colors advertising the Neon MasqueRave Ball on Friday. There's a reminder to pick up a blank mask for the dance from the ticket table. **WE WANT TO SEE YOUR CRAZY NEON DESIGNS** is in all caps at the bottom.

Being flanked by these posters serves as yet another painful reminder that Lori's gone. The MasqueRave Ball was her winning idea for a dance theme. It had been a close run for both her and Sophia's suggestion of "A Night Beneath the Hollywood Lights," but ultimately Lori's idea won out.

Life as a cheerleader meant that pep rallies, sporting events, and dances used to be high priorities of mine. Now they've all been knocked down several pegs on the list. And cheerleading is another thing I get to say goodbye to since I plan to tell Sophia after school that I'm officially dropping out.

My heart's just not in it anymore.

I lean against the locker next to Donovan's and feel the cool metal brush against my bare upper arm. My eyes wander to the clock on the wall and watch the hands tick down to the end of day. These last two minutes feel like they're lasting an eternity.

The bell chimes and the halls fill with students. I stand on my tippy toes and try to spot Donovan amongst the shifting crowd. I know he'll eventually come to his locker, but with every passing minute it gets closer to when I need to go chat with Sophia. I want to talk to her before practice starts so we can have a one-on-one, just her and me. I've avoided her inquiries regarding my status with the squad long enough. It isn't fair to her or the rest of the squad that she's holding my active spot against the rules. We're supposed to be allowed to miss three practices before we're benched until we prove we can change our behavior, but I've missed every single one since the start of the school year. That's way more than three practices, by the way.

The sound of lockers opening and closing resound throughout the hallway, but there's still no Donovan. I sigh, then rip a piece of paper from the notebook in my hands and jot down a quick message along with my cell number before slipping it through the horizontal slots in his locker.

My next stop is the gym.

The closer I get to the double doors leading into the gymnasium, the more I realize there isn't the usual warm-up music emanating from within. I actually don't hear any noise coming from inside at all. It's deathly quiet. No sneakers squeaking on the court, no cheering, no rustling of pompoms. Nothing. Just silence.

I peek inside. The lights are lower than usual, but still on, like they're on reserve or something. I've been in this building many times, but in this dim light it almost feels foreign ... creepy even. I open the door wider and take a step inside.

"Hello?" I ask into the vast emptiness of the space.

No response.

The sound my shoes decide to make as I cross the court is unpleasant. The bleachers are all still pulled out and the basketball goals aren't tucked up. A door opens and closes in the vicinity, but I still don't see anyone.

"Hello? Is someone there?" I ask again, and I'm met with the same response as before. Nothing.

An uneasy tingle grows under my skin while I scan the area, hoping to see someone pop out from anywhere just so I'm not alone. The feeling of being watched slithers in. Goosebumps sprout on my arms and legs before spreading across my entire body.

A noise resonates from the bleachers to my right. My neck twists to the side and focuses on them. One by one, each bay of bleachers begin retracting against the wall. I jump back.

"All right, this isn't funny at all. Who's there?"

My sudden surge of confidence diminishes when I again receive no answer. The severe sound the bleachers make as they crash against the back wall makes me flinch time and time again, all in rapid succession, booming throughout the entire gym.

BAM!

BAM!

BAM!

My heartbeat quickens. I try to move, but my feet are stuck in place. I'm almost entranced by the motion of the bleachers. My eyes can't help but follow each set as they collapse back.

The left side begins retracting and my focus switches to them. My fight or flight instinct kicks in, finally freeing my limbs to move. I take a step back and am brought to a sudden stop by what feels like a wall. A human wall. A scream is ripped from me as I twirl around.

"Hey, it's just me, Drea," Harrison says.

My hand clutches the area of my chest where my heart used to reside. It's firmly in my throat now. Then my eyes explore Harrison from head to toe. He's wearing a sleeveless black compression shirt that showcases his sculpted arms and accentuates his Adonis-like physique. The pair of black shorts he has on hits mid-thigh and leaves very little to the imagination. I snap back to reality when I realize I've been staring for too long.

"So all of that was you then?" I ask. It's a toss-up if my breathlessness is from my scare or Harrison himself.

"No. It's probably one of the janitors or something. I was just grabbing another football from the supply closet." He holds up the one in his hand. "Both of the ones we had at practice were flat."

"A janitor … right," I say, thinking that sounds like the most logical explanation.

"What are you doing in here? Cheerleading practice perhaps?" His tone is hopeful.

I nod. "Which seems to not be happening today."

"Yeah, I think at lunch Sophia mentioned something about moving it to tomorrow."

There goes my whole quitting today in person plan.

"Thanks for the update," I say.

"Sure. Anytime." He tosses the football from hand to hand as he holds my gaze. "Does this mean I'll be seeing you on the sidelines again soon?"

I stare at his mouth for a moment, distracted. "Perhaps," I blurt. The sting of my lie is exacerbated by the pleased expression on his face.

"I do believe that's the best news I've heard all day," he says.

Doubt over my plan to quit enters my mind. Is this a rash decision? Or is my heart just confused by the sweet sentiments from the guy in front of me?

"Well, I better get back to practice," he says, gesturing to the entrance. "Can't really play football without this." He chuckles with a wave of the ball.

Thank him already!

I return his laugh, but it sounds forced to my ears.

Do it now!

"Hey, Harrison? About the detention."

The corner of his mouth lifts in a half-smile. "You don't have to say anything."

"No, I know, but I want to," I reply, which adjusts the curve of his mouth into a full-blown smile. The look in his eyes makes it harder for me to find the words I want to say. "I just wanted to thank you. You didn't need to do what you did, and I appreciate that you did it."

I breathe a small sigh of relief over the fact I was able to get all of that out. I nibble on my lower lip when he doesn't reply right away. Instead, he just stares at me with that same debilitating smile.

"Well, that's all I wanted to say," I toss out.

"You're welcome. But I did it because it was the right thing to do. I'm trying to work on that whole thing. Besides, you didn't do too much damage to the chin, remember? So it's all good."

"I'm glad to hear that."

"See you tomorrow?" he asks as he starts toward the exit.

"Yeah, see you tomorrow."

He holds my gaze, and after a few steps backward, he decides to turn and fully commit to walking away. When he reaches the door, he tosses me one last flash of a grin before leaving.

My phone vibrates in my pocket. I pull it out to see a text light up the screen. It's from Sophia.

Hey Drea! I know you're still taking a break, but practice has been moved to tomorrow, just in case. Miss ya!

Guilt wreaks havoc on my stomach as I stare at the *"miss ya"* part of the text. I'm not surprised she sent this to me. She's made a habit of checking in before every practice. Not necessarily to see if I'm coming back, but just to do a mental health check, which I appreciate. She's also been in contact a few times since Saturday night. It's nice to know that someone like Sophia is looking out for me, though I hate she's having to bend the rules. And all of this doesn't help me feel any less guilty for wanting to quit on her.

I want to reply but I don't know what to say, and I most definitely don't want to have this conversation over text. I feel bad since I've been avoiding the whole squad today just so I didn't have to deal with this on top of everything else.

I can't keep avoiding everything though.

TWELVE

Donovan

I FEEL LIKE ABSOLUTE SHIT.

The stuff I wasn't able to put back in my locker at the end of the day—because I'm a terrible person—isn't fitting into my work cubby at the café. It's like the worst game of Tetris ever. It's also the karma I deserve for actively avoiding Drea all day due to my fear of not being able to keep this massive secret that claws at the back of my throat, wanting to be screamed from the hilltops. The worst part is I saw her waiting for me at my locker, but I couldn't pull myself to see her knowing what I know. Not until it's officially announced.

I don't think I could keep this from her face to face.

I snap my apron over my head and twist the strands behind my back, securing it in place. I go to pin my name tag onto the breast pocket and drive the pokey bit right into my thumb. It goes deep.

"Shit," I growl as I watch the blood flood the grooves of my fingerprint.

If that wasn't yet another obvious result of karma, I don't know what is.

I blot away the blood with a paper towel I snatch from the holder by the handwashing station in the back and apply a bandage. The blood soaks through the bandage and oozes a bit out the side, so I double it up.

"You all good back here?" Marcus asks, surprising me. "Sorry, I heard a small girl's scream and had to check it out."

I crack the first smile I think I have all day. "Just me, I'm afraid," I say as I struggle to adjust the apron to rest flatter in the front.

"Sorry, humor is my way of dealing with crappy situations. You can thank all those repressed emotions I have buried deep inside for that," he says, leaning against the frame of the door leading into the back area. "Enough about me. How are you doing? Really."

"Honestly, I've been better," I reply, finding it increasingly more difficult not to shout what really happened to Lori.

"Do you need a hug from a muscle queen?" he asks, extending his arms to me. "Because I could sure use one myself." When I take him up on his offer, he adds, "Aren't Miz Markie Marc hugs the best?"

"They're all right," I tease.

He pats my head. "I'm just going to pretend you agreed and said they're the best." He releases the hug and moves his hands to rest atop my shoulders. "You good?"

I nod.

"Great, now get to work," he orders.

Even though he grins when he says it, I send him a sarcastic glare before moving to the front of the café and taking my position behind the counter. It's surprisingly dead here today. More importantly, there isn't any sign of Connor or his group yet. I wonder how they're doing after finding out about Lori. Then the thought of them hearing about her potential death by suicide crosses my mind and I become overwhelmed again about knowing the truth. I know my aunt was just trying to give me a heads up on what was really going on, but I really wish she hadn't.

Through the large bank of windows near the front of the café, I recognize Drea and her straight, dark blonde hair moving toward the entrance. I immediately duck down below the counter and crawl on my hands and knees to the doorway leading to the back room. I come face to legs with Marcus's bare shins, which are shaved and smooth as hell, and I raise my gaze up to meet his.

"Uh, what are you doing?" he asks with a cocked eyebrow.

"Please take care of the girl coming in now," I say as the chime from the door opening rings throughout the entire café. My eyes grow wide. "And I'm not here, got it?"

He rolls his eyes and shrugs his shoulders before throwing me a thumbs up. I scramble in my crouched position to the back area and am finally able to breathe a sigh of relief. I fully acknowledge how ridiculous I'm being right now, but in my mind, this is all justifiable behavior given the situation.

I really am a terrible person.

Marcus sticks his head into the back room a few moments later. "She's gone. It's safe to come out. And what the hell was all of that about anyway?"

"Long story," I reply as I make my way to my feet. "Thanks, Marcus. I owe you one, seriously."

"Damn right you do," he says, planting his hands firmly on his hips. "Oh, and if you were curious about what she wanted, she told me that when I see you to tell you that hopefully you got the message she left for you in your locker and please text her when you can. Something about it being urgent." He uses air quotes around the last word.

So she was the one who left me that note? But I didn't see her number on there.

"Thanks again," I say.

"You're welcome, obviously."

Then his face shifts into an expression like an idea just occurred to him. He sends me a mischievous grin that would make the Grinch jealous. The overly self-assured expression makes its way up to his eyes.

"What?" I ask, not knowing if I really want to know.

"I just thought of how you're going to repay me for our little game of espionage."

"And how's that exactly?"

"We're putting on a special benefit gig tonight at Mae's, and you're going to help me with it," he says.

"Hold up, on a Monday? Who goes out on Mondays?"

He scoffs. "I just said it's a special gig, didn't I?" His expression eases into more serious, contemplative lines. "It's a fundraiser we've been organizing for weeks to bring awareness to self-harm. It was just National Suicide Prevention Awareness Month." He pauses to clear the emotion from his throat. "And given recent events, it seemed like a good time to finally do it. Not to mention our community struggles with this on the daily."

I come so close to yelling that Lori didn't die by suicide, but that's not all this event is about. My inquisitive eyes meet his.

"What, exactly, am I going to need to do?"

"I'm doing a little number to the song 'Firework' and I'm going to need you to strike some poses on stage. Nothing too complicated. Your only goal is to accentuate my beauty. Do you think you can handle that?"

My eyes narrow. "What am I wearing during this *little* number of yours?"

That mischievous grin slowly fills his face again. "Oh, you'll see," is all he replies.

"But what about my aunts? They're not going to let me be out that late on a school night."

I'm certain Aunt Helen will refuse to let me go for obvious

reasons. She wasn't even that keen on me going to work today after school.

Marcus places his hand on my shoulder and pats it. "Rest easy, young buck. We're out of here at eight. The show starts around nine and then we'll be closing the show at ten. I'll have you home by ten-thirty, eleven at the latest. Plus, you owe me, remember?"

"Yeah, well, good luck explaining that to my aunts," I retort.

"Oh, ye of little faith. You just leave that to me," he says as he lightly taps my cheek.

How is he going to pull this off?

THIRTEEN

Drea

THERE'S NO WAY AROUND IT. I HAVE TO PASS BY LORI'S street on the way home. I'd consciously avoided taking my usual route this morning, but I guess due to force of habit, I'm now approaching her street.

Is it too late to turn around and go the other way?

Her house is three streets down from mine in the same neighborhood. I remember the first time we realized we lived so close to each other. It was during our first conversation over a mutual frustration with a certain heroine from a popular teen book series. I was rereading the first book in the library while waiting for my dad to pick me up after school, and Lori was nearing the end of her first ever read-through. It was the beginning of sophomore year and I'd just moved from Northern California to Haddon Falls. The thought of starting a new school after just getting used to all things high school was both terrifying and exciting. But Lori quickly became my reason for wanting to stay in Haddon Falls. It was all history after that.

Contrary to how I was feeling moments ago, I'm compelled to flick my blinker and turn onto Lori's street. Not sure why, but something pulls at me to obey. While traveling down Winter Haven Avenue, my mind floods with memories of us driving through our neighborhood late at night … all the trouble we got into and the countless times we stayed out living our best lives while making the town of Haddon Falls our own personal playground.

Lori's house approaches on the right. I slow the car to stall in front of it. The lawn is covered in an array of colorful foliage shed by the surrounding trees, making them look sparser than the ones in their neighbor's yard. A gust of wind jostles them to and fro, tearing even more leaves from their twisted branches.

There are no cars in the driveway and no lights on in the house. All the windows are pitch black, and there's this sadness that looms over the property. My heart pains seeing her house looking empty and dark, just as she was the night we found her.

That's a morbid thought.

I put the car in park and just stare at the house. I feel like some kind of sentimental lurker.

Lori's bedroom is at the top left corner. Her curtains are closed. The *Panic! At the Disco* decal stuck to the inside of the window stands out against the bright pink fabric. That was the last concert we both went to over the summer. A picture from that night is the one that showed up whenever she called me. I had been convinced that night was an indication of how our senior year was going to go. But damn, was I wrong though.

Her curtain sways to the side and catches my attention.

Probably just the air conditioning kicking on.

Then the curtains part, revealing a slice of darkness between the pink panels of fabric just wide enough for someone to peer through before closing again.

Maybe someone's home.

Light fills the room and shines through the tiny gap left

between the closed curtains. I unbuckle my seatbelt and step out of the car, never letting the window leave my sight.

It's probably just her mom or brother.

Lori's dad usually works late, and her mom is a seamstress who sets her own hours at a boutique she owns with a couple other ladies around town. Lori's brother goes to the same middle school as my sister, so he's probably home by now too.

To settle my inquisitive mind, I look through the bank of tiny windows near the top of the garage door for a vehicle. I stand on the tips of my toes, but I'm still too short, so I jump. I get a brief glimpse of the space inside. No cars.

Then maybe her brother's home alone?

I take a few steps back and peer up at the window again. The light is still on. I move to the front door and knock twice. There's no answer. I knock a few more times with the same result. I walk out to the middle of the lawn and look again at Lori's window. The light's off now.

That's strange.

The front door cracks open, pulling my gaze as it creaks back. A girl my age is framed by the doorway. I don't recognize her. Her pleasant smile complements her light blonde pixie cut and pale pink fuzzy sweater.

But why is she here?

"Hello. Can I help you?" she asks.

"Not to be rude, but who are you?" I reply.

"Funny, I was thinking the same thing."

"What are doing here?"

"Again, I could ask you the same thing." Her smile now looks more shrewd than kind.

"Look, we're getting nowhere here. I'm Drea. I was Lori's friend," I say. "I live in the neighborhood."

"Oh." Her expression dulls. "I'm Nancy. I'm looking after her little brother. I was friends with Lori too. We went way back, but I go to another school. I can't believe what happened."

"Yeah, I can't either," I say, matching her melancholy tone.

She takes a step out onto the porch. "Is there something you need? Lori's parents aren't here. It's only me and little Nate."

"Not really, no. I was just driving by since I live around here. I saw Lori's bedroom light on and felt like checking in with her family to see how they're doing."

She sighs and motions back to the house. "Yeah, Nate was up there messing around. I was trying to get him to leave. That's why it took me so long to answer the door."

"Ah, I see. False alarm then," I say with a hollow laugh.

"Seems like it."

"Could you tell Lori's parents that I stopped by? I was supposed to help out at Mrs. Stine's store yesterday but ended up flaking on her for obvious reasons."

That jerk-face named guilt strikes again.

Her pleasant smile returns. "Of course."

"Thanks. It was nice to meet you," I say with a slight wave.

I begin to feel a bit foolish for how I handled our initial interaction. My suspicions about her weren't warranted. Jumping to conclusions is becoming a new trait of mine, I guess.

"Yeah, nice meeting you too. Drea, right?" she confirms.

"Yep."

"Take care," she says while moving back into the house.

"You too," I say to the closed door.

Huh, I wonder why Lori never told me about Nancy before.

Retreating back to the car, I pull away from Lori's house with my final destination being my own home.

I withhold a groan when I see my mom's van in the driveway already. The one thing I've had a reprieve from during my time of mourning is her not grilling me about why I've decided to take a break from cheerleading, but I can tell she's just itching to pick up where we left off.

It's only a matter of time.

"Is that you, honey?" my mom calls after I shut the front door. She sounds a mile away.

"Hi, Mom," I reply, searching around to find her. "Where are you?"

"I'm in the basement. The dang circuit breaker went out again while I was baking." The lights suddenly flicker on. "I swear, your father said he fixed that ages ago, but here we are." Her voice gets louder with every step up the basement stairs. "Hey, could you join me in the kitchen?"

When I enter the room, she's standing there looking like the picturesque version of a housewife. It's deceiving, as she's an absolute boss who just happens to really like to cook and bake for her family. My mom has always been a go-getter and highly driven in life, which is what she wants from me as well. And yes, she was also a cheerleader in high school.

Like mother, like daughter.

"What's up, Mom?"

Empty cans of pumpkin puree, boxes of cream cheese, and an open bag of sugar and flour clutter the countertop. It dawns on me what she's baking … her signature pumpkin pie cheesecake, which happens to be one of my all-time favorite comfort food desserts. She's really laying it on thick, but I'm not complaining.

"I'm making your favorite," she says as she clasps her hands in front of her chest.

"I see that. But there's no reason to go all out on my behalf," I reply, giving her a hug. I can tell she's waiting for one.

"I know, but I figured with everything that's been going on, it would be nice for something good, you know?" I sense she's apprehensive to actually mention the *thing* in question.

"I really appreciate this, Mom. Thank you." I place a kiss on her cheek before moving to leave the kitchen.

"So what brings you home so late?" she asks. The inflection in her voice sounds optimistic, and I deduce it has to do with me possibly being at cheerleading practice.

"No, Mom, I didn't rejoin the squad," I reply, turning around to meet her hopeful gaze. "I had a few things to do after school, that's all."

"But you love cheerleading and it makes you happy," she implores. "Maybe that's what you need right now."

"It used to, Mom, but not anymore. I've got plenty of more important things to concentrate on now instead."

"Okay, honey. I'm sorry I pushed. I just want to see you happy."

"Me too. Thanks again for the cheesecake," I say as I leave the kitchen and head for the stairs up to my room.

And the hits just keep on coming.

FOURTEEN

Donovan

I HAVE NO IDEA HOW MARCUS DID IT.

That silver-tongued Miz Markie Marc was able to convince my aunts to let me help with the charity gig tonight. When Aunt Helen called near the end of my work shift, she reminded me of our conversation at school—like I needed a reminder—and to be extra safe. She said she understands why I want to go support something like this. I mean, I do want to support the cause, just not exactly in the way Marcus told them I wanted to. Fact is, I'm more of an introvert. Sure, I've partied from time to time, but playing video games in the comfort of my own room and watching horror films are my true loves in life.

"Aww, we're going to pop your gay bar cherry tonight," Marcus says, giving me a light shoulder shove outside the back entrance of Mae's lounge. "This is a momentous occasion in a queer person's life you know."

It's the third time today he's referred to my gay bar cherry being popped, and I can tell he's quite tickled by it. It's true, I've never been to a gay bar or to any bar, at that. Most of them back home were eighteen and over, and this kind of deal has never been my scene. I consider myself more of a "suffer in silence on my own" type. Come to think of it, Marcus is my first openly gay friend.

Huh, that's a sobering thought.

I'm sure there were other queer people at my last high school, but they were most certainly not out and proud about it in the rural south. Neither was I, really. There wasn't a ton of room to be diverse. And if you happened to be, it just made life easier to pretend you weren't.

Sure, my closest friends had an inkling about me, but it wasn't something I advertised, especially with my new stepfather being a prominent pastor in town. That's not to say I didn't wonder what it would be like to have a friend who understood what I was going through day in and day out. I just never actively sought them out.

I'm glad Marcus didn't give me a choice.

His reaction was priceless when he initially told me he was a drag queen at Mae's and I told him I'd never been. He gasped dramatically and did what he called "clutching the pearls" to display his great shock over the news. He proceeded to spout off an entire dissertation on how gay bars help provide a safe space for our community, and are one of the rare places a queer person can feel and be their true selves without fear of being mocked, ridiculed, or judged. I appreciated his bravado.

The dressing room in Mae's Lounge is quaint but highly colorful. Each wall is painted a rich red color and the floor is comprised of black and white checked tiles. I can't quite put my finger on the exact aroma permeating the space, but it's like a hint of fresh flowers stuffed in a gym locker mixed with sweet perfume. At the back of the room are a few rolling racks with different outfits hung on them, positioned next to shelves filled with foam heads holding wigs of all colors and types. There's even an entire rolling rack dedicated to an obscene amount of multi-colored feather boas.

"Okay, so all you have to do is wear that black sequin suit," Marcus says, pointing to the outfit hanging on the rack nearest to us, "and hold those sparklers," he moves his finger to point at the box of them on the small table beside me, "while I do my routine. Feel free to ad lib any dance moves or steps, just as long as you stay in your area of the stage, understood?" Before I can reply, he speaks again. "Can you vogue by any chance?" I shake my head, but he doesn't look at me for an answer. "You know what? Never mind. Forget I asked."

Marcus's multi-tasking skills impress me. He was able to explain all of that without ever looking at me. He just continued to apply his makeup while staring into a vanity mirror lined with large, old-fashioned bulbs. He never missed a beat.

It's also fascinating to see how effortlessly he's able to go through his transformation. He calls it his "quick-ish drag," given our time crunch, and though he's only half done, he is most definitely selling the illusion.

"Got it. Like I said before, I'm good," I reply.

He turns to face me, one eye completely done with a full lash and the other one just started. "Uh-huh. We shall see, but I do appreciate the confidence," he says with a bit of sass.

I can't help but chuckle at his half-finished face. He gestures to my costume on the rack. "Get going, mister," he orders playfully. "The bathroom's there," he adds, returning his focus to the mirror.

I collect the garment and head off to change. The fit of the outfit is a tad snug, but overall I find it flattering as I scrutinize myself in the full body mirror attached to the back of the door. And, damn, is it shiny. Even in the low light, it shimmers like a million twinkling stars in a cloudless night sky. All I can think is how bad I feel for the audience's eyes when they're subjected to this.

"Come on, let's get a look at ya," Marcus says through the door. I jump out and strike a pose. He gives me a soft clap with a genuine smile on his face, which is, for the record, finished and beautiful. "You clean up nicely, sir." He gives me a thumbs up before carefully adjusting the pink and blue cotton candy swirl colored wig atop his head.

"Though I agree, I have to say this is hands-down the gayest thing I've ever done," I say with a laugh while staring down at a garment that somehow dances in the light without me moving at all. "And to think, I'm doing this before I've even had my first kiss."

He scoffs. "Oh, please, get out of here with that mess."

I shrug my shoulders. "What? It's the truth."

"Hold the phone. Are you telling me you've never been with a guy before? Wait. Donnie, are you a virgin?"

I feel the embarrassment crawl up my face and settle on my cheeks. I clear my throat and smooth down the front of the suit jacket, not really knowing how to answer the question. "I only came out to my family last year and I'm kind of a loner, so I didn't really have many opportunities to do so," I reply. I look back at Marcus, who's staring at me with wide eyes and mouth agape. "What?"

His facial features soften. "Oh, nothing, I just assumed … actually, you know what? I'm an asshole, and good for you," he says finally, and I perk up. "There's no need to rush anything, especially when you're just coming to terms with who you are."

"Well, that sure makes me sound like a complete loser," I say, feeling myself retracting again.

He snaps his fingers and spins on the stool away from the mirror to face me. "Uh-uh. You are the furthest thing from a loser, my friend. We all do things differently and there's no need to throw around labels. Just keep being you, Donnie, and I'm sure things will work out just fine. Trust and believe." He goes quiet for a moment. "Hey, I know I kind of forced you to do this—"

"Kind of?" I interrupt with a laugh.

"Oh, don't act like this won't be fun." He sounds offended, but I recognize his joking tone.

"Tons, I'm sure." I gesture up and down my outfit and receive Marcus's trademarked side-eye.

"Can you let me thank you, please?" When I nod, he says, "I just wanted to say I really appreciate you doing this with me. It means a lot, seriously. And I hope you get something out of it too. I only wish Lori could be here to see it all. Her and her little dances that she loved to do." Marcus's mood changes for a moment and he gets reflective while returning his attention back to the mirror. "I really miss that silly girl. She was good people."

"Yeah, she was," I choke out.

The dressing room door swings open and a male's voice calls into the room, "Two minutes to show time, Miz Markie Marc."

Marcus adjusts his wig once more, followed by the breast plate under his garment, and then does final checks on his makeup before standing to face me. "You ready?"

"As ready as I'll ever be."

He leads the way through the back halls of the bar until we reach a door leading to the stage. There are countless flyers and posters lining the walls for upcoming shows, and many for events that happened over the years. A lot of the older ones are torn, tea-stained, and have curled edges, making me wonder if they serve a dual purpose. Like to cover up the holes and cracks in the wall underneath.

"Just have fun out there, Donnie, okay?" Marcus whispers to me over his shoulder.

"And now, please give it up for Miz Markie Marc and her special guest, Donnie Wahlberg," the host announces, and roaring applause follows.

I turn to Marcus and mouth, "Donnie Wahlberg? Really?"

He mouths back, "Live with it."

We both ascend a short staircase that ends at a red velvety curtain. It parts, and a guy dressed in black wearing a headset has me present the sparklers to him before he carefully lights them. The song "Firework" blares from the speakers lining the stage. Marcus nudges me to move ahead of him.

"That's your cue," he says with a light chuckle.

Applause erupts again within the bar as I round the corner and enter onto the stage. I'm so focused on finding my spot that when I finally look out over the packed house, my chest tightens and the sparklers begin to slip within my sweaty palms. Even with all the lights in my face, I feel everyone staring at me since I'm the only up here. I draw in a deep breath and strike my first pose with the sparklers. It gets a fair amount of applause that grows exponentially louder once Marcus enters. I glance over my shoulder at him and he's perfectly lip synching to the song.

I face forward and adrenaline kicks in. I embrace the silliness of it all and do a few improvised maneuvers, which seem to be well-received if the applause is any indication that the audience loves it. Marcus is so in his element. He's a natural entertainer, and just like at the café, he has everyone captivated by his performance. The crowd eats it up.

I strike another pose and Marcus plays off it by taking one of the sparklers. He spins it around as he twirls gracefully across the stage before returning it to me. The man who lit the sparklers places a bucket of water at the front of the stage. He instructs me to dunk them in it as the song comes to a close. The crowd erupts with applause again as Marcus curtsies to the audience. He grabs my hand and we both do a bow before he points to me and the crowd cheers once more.

The stage lights dim, allowing me to clearly see the faces in the crowd. In the back of the bar, I see a lone figure dressed all in black posted up against the wall. The only detail I can really make out is the mask the figure is wearing. It's also black, but bears the basic outline of a fox's head in thin neon pink strips of light. The figure's hand slowly rises into the air and waves back and forth just as slowly, and ever so eerie.

Was that meant for me?

Marcus prompts me to do another bow. When I look back up, my eyes return to where I saw the masked figure.

They're gone.

"You turned it out tonight, Donnie," says Marcus as we return backstage.

"Thanks. You didn't do half bad yourself."

"Don't push it, mister. And because of that little exchange, I'm gonna need you to hit the bar and get me a glass of water," he orders, laughing and shooing me away with his hand. "Make sure they give you a large one, and don't let them cheat ya with those small-ass plastic Dixie cups."

I send him a lazy salute and retrace my steps back down the hall. There's a door next to the one leading to the stage with a sign above it that reads "To Front of House." I leave through that one. The whole way up to the bar, people keep yelling their praise at me over the music. I'm not sure what to do with all the attention. I just smile and nod as I keep moving forward.

The bartender heads over when I reach the counter. "Let me guess, Miz Markie Marc wants some water," he says with a chuckle.

I grin and nod. "Could I also have one, please? Oh, and both large."

He moves away to get the drinks and I turn around to take in the space while I wait. For some reason, I imagined Mae's Lounge would look seedier on the inside than it does considering the state of the building's exterior. But the bar has a comforting feel to it. Like a home.

My eyes stop where I saw that person with the mask earlier. There are now two guys there huddled close together, one with his arm around the other, and seeming content. He places a kiss on the cheek of the other and I wonder what all of that feels like. Marcus was right about this being a safe space. I'd probably never see that happening around town outside of this bar. Definitely not back home, that's for sure. Feeling like a voyeur, I avert my stare and face the bar counter again.

"You looked good up there, Donovan," a male's voice comes from beside me.

I look over and find myself lost in the greenest pair of eyes … eyes I've been lost in before. Even in these low lights, they seem to glow. It's Connor. He's standing there posted up against the bar, a stool down from where I am. He smiles at me before shifting his focus to the stage.

I instantly clam up. Everything clenches. The first thing that crosses my mind to say, I dismiss. A heat starts to creep up the back of my neck and my cheeks flush. My mouth feels like it's full of cotton wool when I finally respond.

"You really think so?"

"You don't?" he says.

A nervous laugh tickles my throat as I dodge his stare. It's piercing. I can still feel his eyes on me as I reach for one of the waters the bartender sets in front of me.

"I guess I looked all right," I say after taking a sizable gulp.

His lips turn up at the corners. "Yeah, okay, Mr. Modesty."

I drop my eyes again and take another drink. I cough a

little when the water decides to travel down the wrong tube. Regaining my composure at this point seems futile.

I keep my focus on the cup of water in front of me. It's the only thing I can do to maintain my cool. This is the longest we've spent in each other's company, and I'm a mess of nerves. Why is my heart beating so incredibly fast? Maybe it's just residual energy from the performance. Or it's simply just my body's irrepressible reaction to the guy next to me.

"So, what brings you out here?" I ask, then feel absolutely stupid over how formal I sounded.

"I'm the drummer for the band that opened the show. We came to support the cause." His intent gaze meets mine. "I assume that's why you're here too, right? Lori?"

Wow. He's in the band I heard earlier from the dressing room? They're really good.

"Yeah, one of the reasons," I reply, battling guilt over playing along with this façade.

"I wish I could say Lori's the only friend I've lost, but sadly she isn't."

His face goes pensive. My heart twinges for him.

"I'm sorry," is all I'm able to say before I need to take another swig of water.

"Yeah, well, the town will be a lot less bright without her, am I right?"

He raises his cup of water to me for a toast. I clink mine to his and notice my hand trembling.

"Agreed," I say.

A moment of quiet falls between us. "So, you're a drummer, huh?" I say, pushing through my nerves. I just want to hear him keep talking, regardless of what his voice is doing to me.

"Yeah. Just a small garage band, nothing serious really. It's just a few people coming together for the love of music," he replies.

"You all sounded really great. At least from what I heard backstage."

I take another swig of water to bring more relief to my overheating issue. Between the thick suit I'm wearing and standing this close to someone so incredibly good-looking, I have two reasons to be quite hot under the collar.

"Thanks," he replies with a grin. "We're all right."

"Now who's Mr. Modesty?"

His smile widens. "Well played."

"There you are, Donnie. I was beginning to worry one of these burly bears snatched you up for a late-night snack," Marcus jokes from behind me. I turn to face him with wide eyes and nod back in a subtle motion at Connor. "Oh, hi, Connor," he corrects, sending me a knowing glance. "You all sounded fantastic earlier. We were busy beautifying ourselves during your performance, but the feedback amongst the other queens backstage has been stellar, boy."

Connor lifts his hand in a casual wave of acknowledgement, still relaxed against the bar. "I appreciate that, Miz Markie Marc. And you were great too. Very entertaining."

"Hey, weren't you coming to get a cup of water, Miz Markie Marc?" I ask, trying to get him to move along.

Clueing in, Marcus says, "Oh, yeah. Thanks." He snatches up the cup next to mine and puckers his lips while throwing me playful daggers with his eyes. "You two don't do anything I wouldn't do, you hear?" he says before strolling off. "Or do. Whatever floats your boat."

My entire body seizes up with embarrassment when I hear Connor's low laugh behind me. A tense one escapes my lips, and I throw back the last bit of water in my cup. I'm dreading the moment I have to face him again.

Marcus spins back around. "Oh, and don't forget I have

to get you home by eleven. Which is quickly approaching, Cinderella. The very last thing I need are two angry lesbians on my ass," he says, not making the situation any less awkward.

Deciding to just grin and bear it, I spin around to face Connor. Thankfully, he's staring at his phone. He's in the middle of typing something and raises his eyes to meet mine when he finishes.

"Hey, are you working tomorrow?" he asks.

The butterflies assault my stomach in full force. I stutter out a yes, prompting him to smile.

"Good. I have to go help the band load up the equipment in my truck." Lifting his phone, he explains, "That was Carter, our lead singer. Not that you needed to know that." He issues a faint laugh, seeming fazed for the first time during our whole conversation. "I've got to head out, but I'll see you tomorrow, right?"

"Oh, are you all meeting up at the café tomorrow?" I ask, and then worry I sound like a stalker for keeping tabs on him and his group.

"No," he replies with another smile. His gorgeous eyes add the final touch. "See you tomorrow."

He places his hand on my upper arm before walking away. My hand trails up to rest on the spot he just touched.

I'm keeping this suit jacket forever, no matter what Marcus says.

I watch as Connor high fives a guy who's dressed like he's in the band. Maybe Carter? I recognize him as the guy who had Lori on his lap at the café. The Outcast. Dark coffee guy. I'm surprised to see him wearing such a colorful outfit given he's usually dressed in black or grey when he comes into The Pour Over. The pink and black tie he's wearing perfectly suits his punk ensemble.

On their way out, they pass the spot where I saw the person in the fox mask. The memory wipes the lingering smile from my face. The mysterious figure gave off such a creepy vibe ... the way they stood there and waved. I shudder just thinking about it.

Well, that officially killed the moment.

FIFTEEN

Drea

TUESDAY IS THE FIRST DAY IN A WHILE I WAKE without hitting snooze on my phone's alarm. I wish it was because I actually got a restful night's sleep, but quite the opposite is true. The grogginess consuming my entire being has me wondering if I slept at all.

The scent of my mom's breakfast blend coffee lingers in the air, serving as a much-needed kick in the ass to drag myself out of bed. Though I'm not a huge coffee drinker, the smell does inspire a craving for a cup of Earl Grey tea.

Showered and dressed, I make my way down to the kitchen. I steep a bag of tea in my favorite mug from the original Starbucks in Seattle. My dad went there on a business trip a couple of years ago and brought it back as an early birthday present.

Next to the toaster, there's a plate of toast my mom prepped before taking my sister to school. I grab a piece to nibble on while waiting for my tea timer to go off.

A rapid succession of knocks sounds at the door. I approach it with the toast held in my teeth. I remove it for a moment to glance out the peephole but see no one there. I return the bread to my mouth and unlock the door, pulling it open and peeking outside.

"Hello?" I ask around the piece of toast in my mouth.

There's no answer. On the porch sits a small rectangular-shaped object wrapped in crinkled brown paper. I finish off the bread and pick up the package. In my hands it feels about the same size as a thin, hardcover book. There's no writing on the outside or any indication of who it's for or who sent it. Before I can peel back the wrapping, the timer beckons me back to the kitchen. I place the package on the kitchen counter and go deal with the tea situation.

The smell of the Earl Grey tea is soothing as I hold the warm cup to my nose and draw in a lengthy whiff. As I take a sip my focus shifts to the shrouded book-shaped object on the counter. My mind mulls over what it could be. A burning sensation rolls over my tongue when I take too big of a slurp.

"Ow! Crap. Why didn't I blow on it first?"

Grabbing a paper towel, I wipe up the droplets that hit the floor. I grumble and snatch a piece of ice from the freezer, putting it in my mouth. The icy sensation swirls around and brings some much-needed relief.

My phone pings, signaling a text. It's from Sophia.

How are you doing? Will we see you at practice today?

I'm conflicted on how I should reply. Technically I'll be there, but only to quit for real. I decide to keep it simple and direct.

Plan on it.

A smiley face emoji followed by a GIF of cheerleaders in a pyramid formation appear in succession on my screen. The third message is actual text.

Yay! Practice will be out by the football field btw.

Well, that's just great.

Not only will I have to deal with Sophia and the rest of the squad's reaction to me quitting, I might also run into Harrison and Trent. I'd be lying if I said I'd mind seeing Harrison though.

This is not the time for thoughts like that.

I send off a winking face emoji and then stash my phone. Looking at the time, I realize I'm going to be late for school if I don't leave soon. I pour the tea into a to-go tumbler and my eyes land on the package again.

It's probably for Mom. She buys so much online.

I secure the lid on the tumbler and rush out the door to my car, putting the package out of my mind.

While strolling through the school's halls, one thing becomes clear to me. The dark grey emotional cloud that loomed over the student body seems to have dissipated some. People are settling back into their routines, but why shouldn't they? They have lives to live, futures to plan. It's human nature. I just wonder how long it will be before I'm once again considering such things.

Lori's locker memorial is still fully intact. It has even grown by quite a few additions. It's heartwarming to see how much of an impact she had on our collective lives. It serves as a reminder to me that I'm not the only one struggling with her absence. I'm still convinced I'll see her round a corner in one of the hallways between classes.

I miss her laugh. Her voice. Her touch.

When I open my locker, a folded piece of paper tumbles out onto the ground. I pick it up and see there's a simple message written on it.

Hi Drea.

Seems like Donovan got my note and decided to leave me one as well. I wonder why he didn't text me like I asked him too. Even after telling his co-worker at the café, he still hasn't messaged me yet. If I didn't know better, I'd think he was avoiding me. Maybe everything that happened yesterday coupled with Lori's death has him unsure how to be around me.

The warning bell dings. I grab the books for my first two classes and head out. I pause when I reach the hallway leading to Donovan's locker. He isn't there. I dip my chin to my chest and keep moving forward, preferring not to invite any small talk this morning.

The school day drags on at a snail's pace. Class after class, I find myself not able to focus on anything other than my current situation. It's still strange to sit in my AP Physics class and not see Lori in her seat. We'd always sit next to each other in any class we had together.

This summer changed all of that. After the incident, I needed space. I wanted to disappear. Now I find myself regretting quite a few decisions I made as a result of that night.

I'm possibly about to make yet another one later.

Ominous clouds hang heavy in the sky, obscuring the sun and adding a gloomy touch to my trek out to the football field after school. The smell of rain clings to the air. Storm clouds roll in the moment I move outside the confines of the school.

Maybe a sign of what's to come.

The squad's opening warmup cheer echoes in the distance. As I move through the gap between the two sections of metal bleachers, the football field comes into view. Red and black cheerleader uniforms performing tumbles and stretches fill my vision when I emerge. A tackle out on the field draws my attention when I hear football pads crashing into each other followed by a whistle.

"Drea, you made it." Sophia's voice drags my attention away from the field. The rest of the squad waves and yells out to me with energetic smiles galore. "Wait, where's your uniform?"

"Uh, about that," I begin.

Her face scrunches with disappointment. "You're quitting, aren't you?" Her tone mimics the look on her face.

I nod, averting my eyes to the ground.

"Look, I know you're going through a ridiculous amount of stuff right now," she says. "But I hope you know you're not alone. We all knew Lori, and we've decided to use cheer as our outlet. Are you sure you don't want to at least try?"

The hopeful look on her face stings like hell. "I wish I could," I say, wondering if I'm really making the right decision. "I'm being pulled in all of these different directions, and I don't want to continue bringing down the team more than I already have."

She releases a sigh and wraps me up in a hug. "I hate this so much, you know that? But I guess I understand. You take all the time you need, okay? There will always be a spot on this squad for you if you ever want to return, got it? I'll vouch the hell out for you, even if the coach doesn't want to allow it." She eases up on the embrace and steps back to look at me. "And please let me know if I, or any of the squad, can help in any way. We're all here for you."

"Thanks, Sophia. I really do appreciate it."

I'm always surprised by how genuinely kind Sophia is. Based on head cheerleader stereotypes, she should be a tyrannical, self-absorbed, narcissistic witch. Not to mention her family is one of the richest in our town. She's anything but all of those things though, and she's definitely one of the reasons I'll miss being a part of the squad. I just can't handle the rest of them treating me like I'm this fragile glass figurine while skirting around my feelings after everything that's happened.

I follow the narrow path that hugs the fence encircling the football field. It's been carved out by excessive foot traffic and splinters off toward the student parking lot. My eyes keep glancing out at the players on the field. Trent I could give two craps about, but I can't help but want to locate Harrison. Jersey number seventeen.

"Hey, Drea!"

I pause when I hear Harrison's deep voice come from the field. He jogs toward me in full football gear with his helmet in his hand. His dark brown hair tussles about in the wind as he makes his way over.

A part of me wants to stick around and see where this conversation goes, but the other part is nervous and reluctant and wants to limit further private interactions with him. I start to walk away, then hear him call out again.

"Drea, hey ... come on, wait up," he implores, and I feel obliged to stop.

"What's up?" I ask, not knowing how to feel or act right now. This whole situation is confusing, to say the least.

"I saw you with the squad and thought maybe you were practicing with them again," he says with a broad grin.

Why does he have to look at me like that? Why does he have to make me feel like this when I don't know how I should be feeling about anything?

"Actually, I just quit," I reply.

His sunny disposition wavers. "Oh, sorry to hear that." He places a hand on the chain-link fence, his fingers weaving amongst the holes. "I thought you were going to start up again. You always seemed to enjoy it. What changed your mind?"

I can't help but blush at his sincere interest, but guilt swiftly makes itself known. Like I'm somehow betraying myself and my lingering feelings for Lori.

I'm not ready to open myself up to someone else yet.

"Stalker much?" I reply, trying to keep things light.

He chuckles. "Maybe, but then again, you're impossible not to notice."

My blush deepens. "It's just, I thought it over and decided my schedule's too busy for cheerleading."

"Ah, that's right. The new hermit lifestyle you mentioned. How's that going?"

He remembered that?

I shrug. "All right, I guess. No regrets so far."

"Well, as long as you have no regrets, I say do what makes you happy."

"Is that why you play football? It makes you happy?" I ask, and realize I've never talked to him about it before.

"One of the reasons, yeah. Though getting to see you on the sidelines at the games had a lot to do with that," he replies.

I laugh that off, but there's a war raging on between my head and my heart. "I'm sure you'll manage just fine."

"Yeah, but just think how bad you'll feel if we lose because I can't stay focused without you cheering me on." Before I can give him a snark-fueled reply, he says, "I'm kidding."

My eyes narrow in a teasing manner. "You better be."

His expression sobers. "But you will be missed. I'd never kid about that."

"Oh, really?"

He leans in close to the fence. "Really."

A whistle blows in the distance, followed by the coach calling Harrison's name. He slips his helmet back on and pats it down. "Be safe going home, Drea." He taps on one of the fence posts before taking off to join the rest of his team on the field.

"Thanks," I say, but it's lost in a gust of wind.

A droplet of water hits my forehead. I blink and turn my eyes to the sky. The clouds have grown darker and more menacing. Another drop hits the back of my hand. The angered sky looks like it's about to open up any second, and I decide to make a dash for my car before I get soaked.

The rain intensifies once I reach the parking lot. Just enough to be annoying. I jump into my car and settle into the driver's seat just as large raindrops start pummeling the windshield in a full downpour.

I really hate driving in the rain.

Unfortunately, my neighborhood has a flooding problem and the roads leading to my house have become miniature lakes, causing me to drive extra careful so I don't hydroplane. There's a small break in the rain when I pull into the driveway, so I take advantage of it. I throw caution to the wind and sprint for the front door.

Everyone's home when I enter the house. My parents are glued to the TV in the living room and my sister's doing homework in the dining room. I shake off my coat and leave it on the rack by the front door.

"Hey, family," I announce.

"Honey, could you please come in here?" My mom's voice sounds off. Uneasy.

"What's going on?" I ask, still shivering from the cold rain.

My eyes hone in on the television. A news report flashes across the screen. When I see the headlines and accompanying photograph, the rest of the room hazes in my peripherals.

Lori's picture.

Toxicology report showed poison in her system.

Homicide.

The details process through my mind, confirming some of my suspicions. I knew Lori didn't do this to herself, either on purpose or by accident. Were the drugs poisoned without her knowing? Did someone actually mean to do this to her?

Regardless of the answers, it isn't any easier to accept the truth of what happened. My heart still throbs in pain as if Lori's died all over again. Each passing second still feels like a swift kick to the gut. My eyes dart between my mom and dad as they hurry to my side. Their arms close around me, helping to suppress some of the rage boiling up from within. All I can do is just stand here, motionless.

I'm ready to wake up now.

SIXTEEN

Donovan

THEY SAY ALL IT TAKES IS ONE THING TO LOOK forward to in order to help push through a rough patch. For me, that thing is the prospect of seeing Connor at the café. After a full day wracked with guilt over avoiding Drea yet again, I need something to raise my spirits. Truthfully, I'm beginning to feel I don't deserve this slice of happiness after the way I've treated her. I know we're not close friends, but it doesn't take a genius to realize she probably needs a friend of any kind now more than ever.

Every time I hear the door chime, my head cranes toward it with the hope of seeing Connor standing there. But it's never him. Maybe I'm delusional about the whole thing. Maybe I've read too much into it.

"Donnie, did you hear?" Marcus whispers from the back-room doorway.

I shake my head. "No. What?"

He releases a heavy sigh and his misty eyes glance up at the ceiling before returning to mine. He's having a hard time coming up with the words.

"What? What happened?" I press. Then a thought crosses my mind.

Did they reveal the truth about Lori?

"The news said Lori was murdered," he replies, confirming my suspicion. "Poisoned. It wasn't a suicide." Tears trail down his cheeks. "Who would do this to that sweet girl?"

I pull him into a hug, overcome with a mix of emotions. On one hand, it's a relief to know the truth is finally out there. But now it truly sinks in that this is real. It hits me like a sack of jagged rocks to the chest.

Someone. Killed. Lori.

Ever since I found out the truth, my mind's been flipping through the details of that night in an attempt to find any clues we may have missed. I've yet to come up with anything other than pointing to the obvious culprit. Did Trent really do this? I mean, I know he's a real piece of work, but is he capable of murder?

"I can't believe this," I say into Marcus's shoulder.

"And to think you found her and didn't know what really had happened. That's some crazy scary stuff, man," he says, leaning back to look at me.

An image of Lori in her car flashes across my mind. "Yeah, pretty damn scary."

"Do you need to leave work early? I'll completely understand if you do. I'll cover for you with the boss. I think this qualifies as a good reason."

I shake my head. "Work will help keep my mind occupied … give me something to focus on."

That statement rings true, but there's also a part of me that wants to stick around long enough to see Connor. He'll be a bright spot in this otherwise bleak scenario.

"I completely understand, Donnie. Let me know if anything changes. If you don't mind, I'm going to continue working on stuff in the back for a quick minute to help clear my head. Will you be good up here by yourself?" he asks.

I nod. A line three deep forms as Marcus leaves from behind the counter. None of them are Connor. I ring up each order and begin prepping the drinks and warming up the bakery items.

Drea pops into my mind. When I have a free minute, I start composing a text to her. I type a few words and then my fingers hesitate. What if she doesn't know yet? Do I want to be the first person to tell her? Right or wrong, I decide not to reach out now, deleting the text and returning the phone to my pocket.

Marcus emerges from the back as the little oven with the pastries in it beeps, signaling they're ready. He plates them and gathers the drinks on a tray. He sends a wan smile my way before calling out the orders.

The rest of the shift goes by with no Connor sightings. I guess I shouldn't be surprised. He probably heard the news about Lori and lost track of everything.

"Hey, Donnie, could you help me take the trash to the dumpster out back?" Marcus asks, poking his head out from the back room. "This is one of the last things we have to do before we close and then I get to head to Mae's. I'm bartending tonight and I'm already running late. Yippee."

"Of course," I reply.

I collect the trash bag from the can behind the counter and tie it up before heading to the back. A sudden crash followed by a high-pitched screech sounds near the rear door of the café.

"Damn it all to hell," whines Marcus. A pile of trash covers his shoes and there's a ripped open trash bag clutched in his fist.

"What happened? I thought I heard a little girl scream back here," I say, sending him a snarky grin.

"Ha, ha, very funny. You're hilarious. A real comedienne," he replies with one fist firmly planted against his hip.

"I know."

He rolls his eyes in dramatic fashion. "Anyway, it's me. That's what happened. A walking hazard, I swear." He throws the tattered trash bag to the floor, adding to the pile at his feet. "I was rushing to get this done so I could get out of here but ended up making more work for myself." He stares at the mess he made, looking defeated. "And now I'm definitely going to be late."

"Look, I got this. You go. I'll make sure to lock everything up."

He shoots me a squinty-eyed stare. "You sure you can handle closing the store by yourself? You've never done it before. And with me being the shift lead here, it'll be my ass on the line, Donnie."

"I know. I've closed with you several times already. I know the drill. You can count on me. Besides, do you want to be on time for your other job or not?"

He rushes over and goes to give me a hug, stopping short when he sees the look on my face. He sniffs and looks down at himself, remembering he's covered in trash.

"Air hug," he announces, and I mimic his motions. "You're a life saver, Donnie. I owe you big time. I'm gonna go wash up real quick. You seriously are the best."

When he runs off to the employee bathroom, I set down the full bag of trash in my hand and grab an empty one. A groan leaves my lips when my bare hand grazes something moist amongst the pile. Full body cringe. I grit my teeth and keep chipping away at the mound of mess on the floor.

"Okay," Marcus says when he returns. "I put the spare store keys in your cubby and I'm heading out now. I've already taken care of the money in the register and put it in the safe, so you don't have to worry about that. Just the trash and locking up is left. Thank you so much again."

"Don't mention it," I reply, continuing to shovel the loose trash into the bag.

I grab the nearby dustpan and broom to sweep up the remaining coffee grounds. The sound of the front door chime signals Marcus has officially left. It's followed by the sound of the lock engaging, and now I'm officially sealed inside. Alone.

Taking both of the garbage bags in hand, I bump open the door leading out into the alley with my hip and struggle to pull both bags through the opening. I flip up the plastic lid on the rusted mini red dumpster with the assistance of my elbow and toss each bag in one at a time. The sharp noise the lid makes as it falls closed resounds throughout the area, sounding a lot louder than I intended.

While standing there in the silence, I realize how alone I actually am. Usually Marcus and I bring stuff to the dumpster together. Now every single horror film I've ever seen bombards my mind with irrational fear.

A second crashing sound emanates from down the alleyway. My heart skips a beat as I suck in air. I try to focus on where the noise came from, but I can't see anything beyond the light of the lone lamppost's reach. That doesn't stop my body's response to feeling like I'm being watched. Every hair stands at attention. The sound of shoes dragging across gravel comes from the same direction, but there's still no visual confirmation.

Nope.

I rush inside and slam the door shut behind me. I can't engage the deadbolt lock quick enough. There's a competition between my breath and my heartbeat as to which can be louder in my ears. Just like how I felt outside, the café seems quieter now that I'm all alone and on high alert.

I don't think this plan was thought out very well.

Once I regain my composure, I return the broom and

dustpan to their proper spots in the corner of the room before collecting the keys from my cubby. After performing a quick check of the bathrooms, I give the front and back counter a wipe even though Marcus didn't say I had to. This is all a weak ploy to give my nerves some time to settle.

Plus, I'm safe in here with all the doors locked, right?

I soon find out that choosing to wipe down the counter in my current state is a mistake. My intermittent OCD sets in, and for the next ten minutes I work on getting a spot of a sticky, unknown substance off the surface by the register.

A knock at the entrance startles me from my laser focus. My head pops up to see a person standing there. Their face is shrouded while the rest of their body is highlighted by the limited lighting left on in the café.

The front door is locked, right?

My first instinct is to duck behind the counter to hide and wait for them to leave. For some reason, my mouth decides to betray me. "Sorry, we're closed," I say in an elevated voice.

"Hey, it's me … Connor. Can I come in?" His voice is muffled through the glass, but there's no denying it's him.

Marcus's voice pipes up in my head clear as day. "You better not let that boy in here after we've closed."

But it's Connor.

Marcus's voice returns with even more attitude. "I don't care if it's Mark Wahlberg himself, you can't let him in. You just bring him the goodies outside."

I move to the door and finally take in that wonderful face of Connor's. He looks weary and forlorn, which is understandable. He flashes me a faint half-smile and my stomach does a little flip-flop. Even at half strength, that smile is dangerous.

"Hey, Connor. I'm not supposed to let anyone in after we close," I say to him through the glass.

One of his eyebrows lift. "Do you always do what you're supposed to do?"

That look once again gets my heart pumping overtime. "I'm actually on my way out. I just have to grab my stuff real quick and I can meet you outside. Is that cool?"

He nods. "Sure. I'll be right here."

Like a human tornado, I tear through the café, headed for the back room. My fingers fumble with my name tag as I try to pin it to the cork board next to the employee cubbies. I yank off my apron, ball it up, and hurriedly shove it into my backpack to wash at home. I moan when the game of Tetris strikes again and I can't fit all of my stuff into the backpack along with the apron. I trade out the apron for everything else and sling it onto my left shoulder, followed by my backpack over the right one. I shut off the lights in succession along the way to the entrance before flipping the switch off on the final set.

I think that's a personal record.

"Thanks for waiting," I say, trying to catch my breath as I step out and lock the door behind me.

"Of course. I'm a very patient person," he replies with a soft laugh. He leans against the back end of his dark grey truck. "Sorry I didn't come earlier."

"No worries. I figured with the news about Lori that you were processing it or something."

He dodges my stare. "Yeah, that was pretty damn rough, not gonna lie. I was actually just with the group. We were in the middle of talking about having a little memorial for Lori when we found out what really happened."

"This whole situation is so messed up. I'm at a loss for what to do. It seems surreal, you know?"

His weary eyes meet mine again. "Yeah, I know what you mean."

I move over to the standing rack near the lamppost beside his truck and dial in the combo on the lock around my trusty transportation. My bike. "It's scary to think someone wanted to do that to her. I mean, who poisons someone?" I ask while wrestling the bike away from its confines. I rest the bike up against my hip and return my attention to Connor.

He seems momentarily charmed by the whole episode, but then his face grows serious. "A sick-in-the-head individual, that's who," he says. "Not to change the subject, but is that how you're getting home?" He points to my orange and black bicycle.

"Yep. This is my noble steed."

"Why don't you let me give you a lift instead?" he offers. "I'll feel terrible for leaving you to ride that home alone in the dark."

There are those damn butterflies again. But now they feel like they're breathing fire.

"That's really nice of you, but I'm good. Besides, I don't want you to go out of your way or anything. I'm used to this," I explain, strapping on my bike helmet.

How the hell was I able to reject that offer?

"Okay, that's adorable," he says, gesturing to the helmet with a grin. "I admire your commitment to bicycle safety."

Houston … he just called something I'm doing "adorable."

Silence takes my words captive for a moment before I eventually say, "Can never be too safe, I always say." My reply has me mentally rolling my eyes so hard.

I don't think I could've given a more Boy Scouts of America answer than that.

"Okay, so if you won't let me take you home, how about you come hang out with me and the gang tomorrow night. Are you working?" he inquires, pushing himself away from the truck and taking a step closer to me.

My heart thumps a little faster and the bike starts to feel

heavier against my hip. "It just so happens I'm off for the rest of the week since there's that whole Homecoming thing happening," I respond.

"Oh, yeah. That's right. Our schools are playing each other, huh?" he says, taking yet another step toward me.

I nod, and on the inside, I commence freaking out.

"So, what do you say? Tomorrow night?"

I'm wrapped up in the moment and am about to blurt out a resounding yes when I catch myself and get smacked back down to reality. "I'd like to say yes, but I'll have to get back to you."

His brow furrows, then eases into a look of understanding. "Was not expecting that answer, but I can roll with it. Overprotective parents?"

"You could say that," I say with a small laugh.

He outstretches his hand. "Here, let me give me you my number." I can't pull my phone out fast enough and immediately place it in his hand. "I need your cute face," he says with a smirk, handing it back to me.

"My what?" I murmur, hoping he'd actually said what I thought he did.

"For the phone."

An anxious snicker escapes me. "Oh, right."

I unlock the phone and pass it back to him. His thumbs glide across the keyboard. He holds the phone up and smolders like I've never seen anyone smolder before, like, ever. He snaps a pic of himself and then does something else with my cell before handing it back.

"Did you just give me your number and add a picture to it?" I ask with a nervous smile.

"Yeah. Is that a problem?" Unlike mine, his smile is full of confidence.

I shake my head. "Not at all."

"Good. Be sure to let me know about tomorrow, okay?" He rounds his truck and climbs into the driver's seat. The passenger side window rolls down. "Are you sure you don't need a private escort to your house? I could follow behind you the whole way. I swear, I don't mind."

"You're good, but I do really appreciate the offer." Inside, I'm kicking myself for not taking him up on it. Then another question comes to mind. "Hey, Connor?"

He pauses his attempt to start the truck. "Yeah?"

"Why do you always put a five-dollar bill in the tip jar? Twenty percent of a drink is, like, just over a buck."

I can't believe I just came out and asked that.

He laughs to himself. A suave-as-hell grin takes over his mouth. "You're worth way more than just twenty percent."

Wait, does this mean he only does it for me?

I go to reply, but instead, a noise issues forth sounding like I'm speaking in tongues. Absolute gibberish … most definitely not English. Instant humiliation.

"Night, Donovan," he says as he starts up his truck.

"Y-Yeah. Good night," I finally reply, but I'm not sure I even said it loud enough for him to hear.

The truck's taillights fill my vision as he drives away. I can't hold back the heavy sigh as it travels from the pit of my lungs and out of my mouth. I pinch myself just in case that was all a dream. It hurts and I wince in pain, proving beyond a shadow of a doubt that what just happened was indeed real.

Hold on, was I just asked out on my first date?

SEVENTEEN

Drea

I AM NUMB.

Emotionally numb.

My mind is tangled in a thick web of confusion. I stare at my ceiling in a daze. I've lost count of how many times I've traced the grooves above me with my eyes. I'm unable to move an inch. The position I'm lying in on my bed hasn't changed since I came up here hours ago. I'm not even sure how much time has passed. It feels like time has stopped and sped up all at once.

My mind has decided to stall at the anger stage of grieving. Heat lashes my body as rage froths up in my throat like bile. It's all focused toward the one individual who is most likely responsible. I slam one fist down by my side, leaving an impression in the sheet, followed by the other as I grit my teeth.

Trent.

A soft knock sounds at the door, ushering in my mom. "I saw your light still on. I wanted to make sure you hadn't fallen asleep without turning it off," she says from the doorway.

I roll over to face her. "I think it's safe to say I'm not going to get much sleep tonight."

"I see you didn't eat your dinner either," she says, picking up the plate sitting outside the door and setting it on my nightstand.

"I'm not hungry."

She tucks the stray strands of hair in front of my face behind my ear. "I know, sweetie. But you need to at least try."

"Can you blame me for not having an appetite?"

She sighs while shaking her head. "Of course not."

My eyes fix on the brown paper-wrapped package from this morning tucked under her arm. She notices it has caught my attention and presents it to me.

"By the way, do you know what this is? I found it on the kitchen counter and assumed it might be yours. Your dad has no idea, and neither do I."

I'm surprised to see it in the state I left it in earlier. I would've thought she'd have opened it already. My mom usually can't help but snoop into things.

"I was actually going to ask if it was yours," I say. "Especially considering your Amazon purchase history."

She scoffs friskily while tapping my arm. "Hey, I only buy the essentials through Amazon. Besides, there's no shipping label or anything on it, so there." We both giggle, but mine sounds forced to my ears. "Want me to open it?"

I shrug. "Sure. Whatever. Like I said, I don't know what it is."

She tears away the bit of brown paper encasing the object, revealing a small, hardcover book. The entire cover is black with a small neon pink geometric outline of a fox's head on the front, but nothing else. She flips the book around in her hands.

"Hmm. Maybe I bought this for you from Etsy," she says, handing it over to me.

I take it before abandoning it off to the side of the bed. "Gee. Thanks, Mom."

"But, of course … anything for my daughter," she says with a light laugh before placing a kiss on my forehead. Her face then becomes serious. "They're going to find who did this, you know."

"I hope you're right," I say as I escape her stare.

She trails the back of her hand across my cheek before collecting the dinner plate and alighting from the bed. "Please try and get some sleep, sweetie."

"Will do, Mom."

She closes the door behind her as she leaves. My eyes land on the diary. I slide it closer to me and flip it over, and then back to the front cover. It doesn't look new, and even seems worn around the edges, but maybe that's the look the seller was going for. I open it to the first page and see someone has already written in it.

"Mom better get her money back," I mutter.

This diary belongs to Carrie Phillips.

Carrie Phillips? Why does that name sound familiar?

I think Lori mentioned her once or twice before … something about them being friends, but I struggle to recall any specific details.

Why would someone leave this on my doorstep?

Page after page has entire sections scratched out with erratic pen strokes, like the work of a crazy person. It's seriously giving me some creep-tastic vibes. Some pages have even been ripped out completely, leaving only shreds behind in the fold. My hand hovers on a page with an intricate sketch of an old, weathered barn. It's so detailed I get the impression she'd been there many times, or at least was drawing it from a reference picture. There are more sketches on other pages that are just as detailed. One of a willow tree, one of the theater downtown, one of a boat dock, and one of an old-fashioned looking truck parked off to the side of the barn featured in the previous sketch. There's even a recreation of the fox head from the front cover. Under the image, the words **Fox Hunt** are dug into the paper with heavy pencil strokes.

I feel weird flipping through this. Peering into the personal thoughts of this Carrie girl just feels strange. Wrong. I'm still not sure why someone left this.

As far as I can tell from the legible entries, this Carrie girl is highly self-conscious and very sensitive about how others perceive her. She's also glad this group of people has accepted her as one of their own. She has a crush on a couple guys at her school, but their names are crossed out. At one point in the diary, she mentions a potential sleepover with some girls from the group that has her excited.

I wonder if Lori was one of those girls.

It's hard to get a grasp on who any of these people are because most details have been frustratingly removed. There's even a multiple-page entry retelling what I gather is a story about watching one of her crush's perform in a band inside someone's garage, but it jumps around so much due to missing pages and omitted details that it's hard to follow.

I thumb through the rest of the pages until I reach the final entry. It looks to be fully intact.

I can't take this anymore. I need to tell them all tonight. I need to tell my friends this secret I've been holding in for a while now. It's been eating away at me, as only you know, Diary. I have to come clean. I plan to bring it up during our game night tonight. Maybe the game will soften the blow, and that way I'll feel like I can actually say it. I know they'll support me and help me through this. They're partly to blame for me meeting him in the first place. I will be devastated if they treat me differently after this. If HE treats me differently because of this.

I just might die....

The last line is engraved into the paper with deep red ink near the bottom of the page. It doesn't resemble the handwriting from the rest of the diary and seems to have rage behind it.

Really disturbing.

I flip back a few pages and try to find any reference to the event she's talking about. If it was something she was keeping a secret, she had to write about it somewhere. I find an entry talking about going to an end-of-eighth-grade party with a bunch of people. Her first big party. Most of it is scratched out, but there are a few details that remain. It was apparently held at a popular girl's house, but just like with every other important detail, the name's been removed.

Maybe it was Sophia's house?

I shamefully admit that living vicariously through this girl has proven to be a welcome distraction. I still keep wondering about the significance of this diary. The fact it was left at my house has to mean something.

Does this have to do with Lori's death?

The hint of voyeurism I feel while flipping through the diary is still present, but I can't seem to pull myself away from it. I'd freak the hell out if I found out someone ever invaded my privacy like this.

I shut the diary and toss it onto my nightstand as remorse overpowers my curiosity. I flop back against the pillows gathered behind me and return my gaze to the grooves in the ceiling.

If only it were a sky full of stars.

Memories of Lori flood my mind. We used to take her car out to this clearing near Lake Wilson late at night, well after our curfew, and just stare up at the stars. We'd lie on her car's hood and look at the sky for hours, just talking. She couldn't wait for the day she'd be able to leave Haddon Falls behind. I wanted to leave with her too. But now that all feels like another life entirely.

I'm not sure I'll ever meet someone quite like Lori again.

My phone pings, signaling a message. It's from a number I don't have saved in my phone.

Hey, it's Donovan. How are you?

I'm one hundred percent positive he's texting me because, just like the rest of the town, he now knows the truth about Lori. It's so weird how death draws people together.

There are so many things I want to write back, but I'm finding it hard to convey all of those feelings through a text message. I want to both stay silent and scream at the top of my lungs. Like with most of my texts lately, I decide to be direct and straight to the point.

I can't believe someone poisoned her.

I stare at the screen, waiting for his response. My eyes keep rereading the words I sent over and over, but the more I read them, the less sense they make. I was already having a hard time accepting the fact Lori died by suicide. It didn't make sense at all. But her being killed by someone doesn't make a lot of sense either.

Who hated Lori that much?

My initial feelings about Trent being the main suspect begin to crumble under the weight of the facts assembling in my mind. My gut points to him, but even though he's the absolute worst, does that automatically make him a murderer?

My mind keeps drifting back to when Donovan punched him. He went down so easily. Is Trent just all talk and no bite? Maybe he killed Lori by accident?

Thoughts swirl wildly around in my head, and I realize it's easy to blame Trent. The scarier thought is what if it was someone else.

My cell beeps as Donovan's next text comes through.

I know. It's crazy. I can't sleep, and still don't think it's all sunken in yet. We really need to talk in person tomorrow. Meet in the morning by my locker first thing?

I impulsively type out **yeah, sounds good,** and then wonder what it is he needs to talk to me about that can't be said over the phone. I hit send and he replies back with, **see you then.**

I conclude there are three things on my must-do list for tomorrow. And every single one fills me with uncertainty over how they'll go.

1. *Talk to Donovan.*
2. *Ask Sophia about Carrie Phillips.*
3. *Confront Trent Blakemore.*

EIGHTEEN

Donovan

WHY AM I SO DAMN JITTERY?

Oh yeah, maybe it's because I have three cups of coffee coursing through me. All blonde roast. All back-to-back. At this point, I'm pretty sure I can see sound with this much caffeine in my system.

Long night and no sleep makes Donnie a shell of a person.

A lack of sleep isn't the only reason for my nerves. There's a hint of uncertainty and anxiety building underneath the jitteriness. The relief I'll feel once I talk with Drea in person will hopefully help ease some of it.

The halls are bustling with activity as I keep a look out for Drea. I was hoping to have enough time to cover everything before the bell rings, but at this rate, we'll have to resort to a quick hello with the promise of talking later. I'm even considering ditching first period and making her do the same thing to ensure we'll have enough time. I'm pretty sure a life or death situation calls for drastic measures, and the last time I checked, attending calculus wasn't that dire.

I glance down at my phone and exhale. There's still no reply to any of the three recent texts I've sent Drea. My anxiety surges again. I begin to type out a fourth message before stopping myself.

She'll answer when she can.

I delete the text and drop the cell to my side, resuming my lookout. Something I wasn't expecting to see this morning is the sheriff and Deputy Owens. The sheriff says something to the deputy before splintering off down the hall leading to the principal's office. Deputy Owens, on the other hand, continues moving toward me. I feel turned to stone watching him close in.

He flashes me a smile of greeting as he removes his broad-brimmed hat. Then his face turns serious. My mind immediately jumps to the worst possible scenario.

Did something happen to Drea?

"Morning, Mr. Walsh," he says, stopping in front of me.

I hitch my backpack further up on my shoulder when it starts to droop. "So formal, huh? I must have done something serious," I say, trying to bring some levity to the situation.

He fiddles with the brim of his hat. When his eyes meet mine again without a change of expression, I can't take it anymore. What is this all about?

His low laugh interrupts the silence between us. "Sorry, Donovan. I get so used to talking with older civilians in this town. It's a respect thing."

"No worries. I was just joking anyway." I close my locker. "So, did you need something?"

"Actually, yeah. But it's probably best coming from the sheriff himself," he says, prompting my stomach to sink to my toes. "Could you follow me to the principal's office, please?" He gestures forward, wanting me to move ahead of him.

My nerves are as follows:

Shot.

Fried.

Dead.

Something else must have happened. My mind is going crazy trying to figure it out.

"Are you sure you can't at least give me a hint?"

"Sorry, Donovan, wish I could. I was only ordered to bring you to the office."

I mean, I get it. He could possibly get in trouble for divulging anything too early to me, but any information would be appreciated. I'm finding it increasingly harder to deter my mind from leaping to insane conclusions.

The main office is like an ice box when we enter. I almost expect to see my breath. Either the air conditioning is stuck on tundra or my body is having a severe reaction to my current situation. The bell rings and I resign myself to the fact that I'll be late to first period yet again this week.

We're met by Gloria, who tells me to have a seat in one of the chairs lining the wall. The door to the principal's office creaks opens and Mrs. Grayson steps out. Her hardened facial features are pulled back tight, just like her high bun. She waves me over.

I swallow hard and rise from the chair. My feet feel like they're stuck in quicksand, and every step I take feels like I'm sinking deeper and deeper. My heartbeat pounds in my ears. It's so loud I don't even hear what the principal says to me as I round the corner and see the sheriff seated behind her desk.

He motions to the chair in front of him and I take a seat, but no words are exchanged. I feel like I'm either on trial for something I haven't done or I'm about to receive information that will make me wish I'd never gotten out of bed this morning.

"Thank you for coming in, Mr. Walsh," the sheriff says. "I know you've met Deputy Owens before, which is why I asked him to collect you."

"Yeah, we go way back." The nerves in my voice immediately make me wish I hadn't replied.

The sheriff clears his throat, jostling his thick, bushy mustache. It's painfully obvious that my attempt at humor is lost on him. His expression never changes as he disregards my comment and continues.

"I hope you've been able to get back to some semblance of normalcy these past couple of days. My apologies for having to interrupt that again. Hopefully this won't take up too much of your time. The fact is, Lori Stine was murdered, and you were one of the two people who found her body."

I breathe an internal sigh of relief that this isn't about anything happening to Drea.

He leans back in the oversized comfy desk chair resting clasped hands in his lap. "Now, we still have your statement on file. All we're looking for is any other possible leads you might be able to give us to help with this investigation." He leans forward, planting both elbows firmly on the desk, perching his chin on the back of his knuckles. "Do you have any other recollections from that night? Any detail you might have remembered since our first meeting?"

I comb through my memory trying to think of anything I can say that will help, but I got nothing. It's not like I haven't been doing this since that night anyway.

The intercom system chirps to life. "Could Andrea Sullivan and Trent Blakemore please report to the principal's office?" Gloria's voice comes through.

Uh-oh. Big mistake.

"I'm not trying to step on any toes here, but you might want to have someone out there separating those two when they arrive," I suggest.

The sheriff studies me for a moment then gestures for Deputy Owens to handle it. "Now, back to my question," he says.

"Actually, I have a quick question of my own."

His eyebrows rise. "Okay, shoot," he says, leaning back in the chair again.

"I'm not even sure you can answer this since it's an open investigation, but did Trent's story check out?"

He takes a moment, seeming to ponder if he should answer. "As far as I know, yes, it did," he says at last. "We've found a few people who can corroborate his statements. I can't go into much more detail than that, but that's one of the reasons I've asked all of you here. To try and get a better understanding of what happened that night. So any other information would be greatly appreciated."

I shrug my shoulders. "I don't really have anything else to say other than what I've said already."

He releases a sigh and nods as though this is what he expected. "Well, thank you for your time, Mister Walsh. We'll be in touch if we need anything further."

He motions to the door, dismissing me. The principal hands me a hall pass, and as I leave the room, I see Drea sitting at one end of the bank of chairs with Trent at the other. Deputy Owens is seated dead center between them. None of them look happy about it. Drea's tired eyes meet mine and she waves. I return it.

"Mr. Blakemore, could you please come into my office?" Mrs. Grayson says from her doorway.

I watch Trent lift from his seat. His expression is pitiful and lacks the usual cockiness. I move aside as Deputy Owens passes by, accompanying Trent inside the office.

I make a break for the seat next to Drea and we begin talking at the same time. "Wait, wait. Me first," I say, putting my hands up. She nods. "Where were you? Did you get any of my texts this morning?"

She groans. "I completely forgot to charge my phone last

night and it wouldn't turn on when I woke up late. It was a rough morning."

"I'm just glad to see you're okay," I say, prodding a faint smile from her. My voice lowers to a whisper. "Before you go in there, I have to tell you something I just found out. The sheriff said Trent's story checks out, so he might not be the killer."

"He's still guilty of being a crappy person," she grumbles.

"I agree. No doubt about it, but that still leaves a giant question mark about who did this."

"Mister Walsh, I believe you're wanted in class," Gloria says from over the counter. Her glasses are perched on the tip of her nose and she adjusts them to sit higher.

"Right." I turn back to Drea. "Meet me at lunch."

"Where?" she asks, her eyes panning over to Gloria, who is still leering at us.

"In that little courtyard off to the side of the main one."

"I'll be there," she says.

"Mister Walsh?" Gloria singles me out again with her pointed question, her voice raising an octave.

"Okay, okay, I'm going," I mutter, and head for the entrance.

I glance back over at Drea. She looks drained. Her head is leaned back against the wall and her eyes are barely being held open. The dark circles around them stand as proof of lack of sleep. I guess we're twins in that department.

We're not out of the woods yet, my friend.

NiNETEEN

Drea

THE VERY LAST PERSON I EXPECT TO FIND WAITING
for me as I leave the main office is Trent. Yet there he is,
leaning up against the bank of lockers across from me
as I exit. His eyes lock onto mine. His face bears a hint of unease
and his posture is slouched. This pleases me for some reason.

"Why?" is all I ask.

He lets out a low grumble and pushes himself off the lockers to stand on his own. He seems like he doesn't know what to
say. It's kind of nice to see him squirming there unsure of himself.
Like a predator caught in a trap.

"You know what? Never mind," I say. "I don't know why
I was even entertaining the idea of hearing you out in the first
place. Like every word out of your mouth won't be a lie anyway."

"Wait," he says, stopping my departure. His voice sounds
raspy and forced.

Is he on the verge of tears?

When I turn to face him, it's deliberate. He's now closer to
me and inching forward. I put my hands up.

"Six feet back please," I insist. "If you want me to hear you out, I'm gonna need my personal space." His hands lift as he takes a couple steps back. "And let me make one thing clear," I continue. "I'm only doing this because I currently lack the energy to be mean to you. You also kind of look like shit, so I guess this is me feeling the slightest shred of pity for you. But don't for a moment think I've forgotten what you've done to me, Lori, or the rest of the female population here at this school."

His light brown eyes dart away and then back to me. Their normal arrogant luster is gone. I've honestly never seen Trent like this.

"Look, I know you're probably not going to believe me, but I have to get this off my chest," he says, sounding even more pathetic than before.

Is this just an act, or does the master manipulator really sound sorry?

I cross my arms over my chest. "Well you better spit it out, because I need to get to class."

He clears his throat and takes a step forward, but then retracts. "I know I've done some crappy things."

"No arguments there."

He releases a heavy sigh over my cutting tone. "I've accepted that, and now have to deal with it. But I need you to believe me about these next two things because though I'm guilty of a lot that I've been let off the hook for, these two things I'm not."

It's shocking how much of his egotistical wall is crumbling at his feet. This is not Trent Blakemore standing in front of me. This is a broken boy. Gone are his polished looks and arrogant grins. Gone is his confidence. His ego is deflating right in front of me. I almost feel sorry for him, but it's a fleeting feeling.

"Go on," I say.

"The night you claim I did something to you, I promise you, I did nothing. The truth is, we were drinking and having a good time, but then you passed out on the couch. I left to take a leak, and when I came back, you were gone. And yeah, I started making out with another girl pretty much right after that, but I didn't do anything to you.

My gut reaction is to reply that he's lying, but there's this desperate energy he's giving off that leads me to believe he might actually be telling the truth.

"If you didn't do anything to me, then who did?"

He shrugs his shoulders. "I don't know. Like I said, I lost interest after I saw you gone." Before I can respond, he interjects, "I'm a pig, I know."

I nod in agreement. "And the second thing?"

"I didn't kill Lori. I swear."

It sounds like tears are bubbling up in his throat again. I don't want to believe him. I want to hate him. Despise him. Not trust a single syllable he's uttering.

But somewhere deep inside, I find myself thinking he's telling the truth. He's being unusually honest, even admitting to his past wrongdoings. He's either telling the truth or is desperate and is making a last ditch effort to convince someone he isn't guilty. I think back to what both Donovan and the sheriff said about his story checking out.

"Why are you telling me all of this?" I ask.

"I don't know. This whole situation has me all twisted up and thinking about shit. The thought that I could've been responsible, even on an emotional level, for someone's death has me shook ... made me wake the hell up." He exhales a heavy, uneven breath. "I know I don't deserve your forgiveness, or anyone's for that matter, but I am sorry ... for everything."

"For some strange, off-the-wall, ridiculous reason, I believe you. And I do forgive you, Trent. But not for you. I forgive you for me, so that I can release all of the anger and resentment I harbor toward you. I still want absolutely nothing to do with you, understood?"

He gives me a slow nod. "That's fair."

"I do have one question for you though."

"Okay. What is it?"

"Why were there pink pills in Sophia's dad's car?"

"Oh, that." His expression eases. "Lori had a few on her and said they were Molly. It didn't look like any Molly I'd ever seen, so I said I wasn't interested. She insisted, but I was too focused on hooking up. That's when she flipped out and tried to leave. I admit I may have gotten a little forceful with her, but I let her go because I didn't need her accusing me of anything."

I almost regret asking him the details.

"Thanks. You're still a piece of crap, but at least you had some useful information," I bluntly reply.

"You're right. I hope we can just move on from this."

"Oh, I can move on, but you have a lot of asshole soul-searching to do. Just because you attempted to make things right with me doesn't excuse the rest of your crappy behavior," I say.

He nods. "I know. I just mean that I hope this can be a new start for us."

"We'll see," I reply, and then turn to head down the hall toward my first class.

What the hell is with today? Opposite day much?

When lunch rolls around, I head straight for the little seating area branched off from the main courtyard. It's three stone benches nestled on a small patch of loose gravel surrounded by short trees and shrubbery. The perfect place to have a secret meeting. Donovan's already waiting for me when I get there.

"You will not believe the strange conversation I had with Trent this morning after talking with the sheriff," I say as I take a seat next to him on one of the benches.

"Wait, you talked with Trent? And he's still alive?"

"Surprising, right?" I say. "Actually he left me with a lot to consider. And I can't believe I'm saying this, but I think he's telling the truth. Which are words I never thought I'd ever say in reference to him."

He puts his hand up to my forehead. "Nope, you don't have a fever."

I appreciate his sense of humor during such weighty circumstances. "I know. I'm as shocked as you are," I say while lightly batting away his hand. "So, you mentioned in your text last night that you need to talk to me. What about?"

He goes quiet, seeming to mull something over. He has me worried when he chews on his lip, like he's afraid to say words.

"I just wanted to apologize in person for kind of low-key avoiding you these past couple of days," he eventually says. The faint smile he sends my way doesn't quite reach his eyes.

"Yeah, I sort of figured that's what you were doing. I understand though. Emotions are hard to deal with on this level."

Is there something else he's not telling me?

"Yeah … emotions," he says, and I can tell he's back in his head again. "I just felt like crap for doing that to you. It was a bad friend move on my part."

I pat his hand. "Don't worry about it, seriously."

"Thanks, Drea. So, how are you feeling today?" he asks, concern reflecting in his eyes.

"I'm hanging in there." My gaze locks onto Sophia making her way to her usual table in the main courtyard.

This is my chance to ask her about Carrie.

"Glad to hear that." Donovan's voice wades its way into my mind, but I'm still mainly focused on Sophia.

"Yeah. Hey, Donovan, give me a sec, okay? I'll be right back."

The entire trek over to Sophia, I rehearse what I'm going to say in my head. Thankfully she's alone for the moment. The rest of the squad is probably still in line getting food. She sees me approaching and waves. I return it and take a seat across from her. It almost feels like I'm about to interrogate her.

"I can't believe the news about Lori," she says in a dismal tone. She reaches over the table to grab my hand squeezing it lightly. "Drea, she was killed at my house. Someone at the party did this. I just can't believe it." Her voice shakes.

I go quiet for a moment while watching her roll through these very familiar emotions. "I know. I can't either. I still have no idea who would have done something like this," I reply, rubbing my thumb across the back of her hand. "If you don't mind, Sophia, I do actually have a question."

She withdraws her hand back to rest on the table. "Sure. Anything."

"Do you remember a girl named Carrie Phillips back in middle school?"

A flash of recognition crosses her face. "That name does sound familiar. Why?"

"I remember Lori mentioning her, but I don't have any details on her. Do you remember if she went to any of your parties, or if she was a part of any groups in school? Who her friends were?"

She leans closer as though I spurred a memory. "Wait. You said Carrie Phillips, right?" I nod. "I kind of remember her coming to one of my parties, now that you mention it. I think she died near the end of the summer before our freshman year. The reason never really came out. Accidental, I think. She wasn't really on my radar. I know that sounds harsh, but it's true."

"She died?" I ask, remembering that added line to the last entry in the diary.

This just took a totally morbid turn.

An icky sensation hits me right in the stomach. Like I just ate and then immediately went on the loopiest rollercoaster right after.

I read a dead girl's diary last night?

I think back to flipping through the pages and peering in on all the gory details. It feels gross. And the fact so much was scratched out now has me wondering what was there that someone didn't want anyone to see.

"Yeah, I'm pretty sure," Sophia says. "Why do you ask?"

I focus on regaining my composure. "No reason," I reply. "I was just curious. Like I said, I remember Lori talking about her and wanted to know if you knew who she was."

"Well, that's all I can remember. Sorry I can't be of more help."

A few members of the squad start filling the seats around us. They toss curious looks my way. I guess they're not over me quitting just yet. Neither am I, really. I get the feeling that I've been the subject of quite a few conversations at this table during lunch while I was absent. Not much I can do about it now, I muse as I brush off their stares and return my focus to Sophia.

"Can you remember anyone she hung out with?"

Sophia shakes her head as her attention shifts to the squad. After exchanging a few greetings, she turns back to me and lowers her voice so only I can hear her.

"Sorry," she says, "but I really need to get back to my lunch since we only have, like, twenty minutes. It's been nice chatting with you though."

I get the feeling Sophia knows more than she's letting on.

With everyone's eyes on me, I utter my quick, awkward goodbyes to the squad and leave. Things definitely feel different with them now. Strained. I guess I'm not surprised. It's not like I've been the easiest person to interact with lately. Social pariah number one.

On my way back to Donovan, so many questions whirl through my head, and all I crave are answers. I think it's about time I Google Carrie Phillips and see what shows up.

Who were you, Carrie?

TWENTY

Donovan

ABOUT HALFWAY UP THE STEEPEST HILL I'VE EVER BIKED, the guilt from the lie I told my aunts begins to set in. They think I'm working on a group project after school. In reality, I'm headed to meet Connor and his friends. His directions to the old barn were clear. I just wish I'd taken him up on his offer to pick me up from school since I find myself struggling with this incline.

There's a pattern emerging here.

Even in these cooler fall temperatures, the constant little streams of sweat cascading down my back consistently remind me of my current struggle. Normally I wouldn't be so adamant about this and I'd just walk my bike up the hill. Today it seems I'm trying to punish myself for not accepting the ride from Connor.

What the hell am I trying to prove here?

My feet are firmly planted on the pedals, pushing with all my might to beat this hill. My legs burn from excessive use, but I push through. Then my bike decides to forsake me. The right pedal gives way under my foot at literally the worst time, right as I'm about to reach the top. I stagger to the side before catching the bike between my legs as my feet hit the ground.

That could have been disastrous.

I stare down at the now limp pedal. Upon closer inspection, it seems fixable. I readjust it to lay flat and then jiggle it back into place as a temporary work-around. It takes a little force, but after three solid jabs with the palm of my hand, it pops back into what seems to be the right position. I wish I could say this was the first problem I've had with this bike.

Karma 3, Donovan 0.

Once I reach the apex of the hill, a full view of Lake Wilson fills my vision. It's breathtaking. The whole area is surrounded by trees with foliage that seems set ablaze. Way different than trees in the south this time of year. It's quite picturesque. Like an oil painting.

The road forks, and I veer right as detailed by Connor's text. I'm thankful for the cool air flowing through my clothes during the decline. Wind wafts through my hair, giving me the relief I need after sweating my ass off on that insane hill.

There's another quick dip in the road and I appreciate the continued leg rest. A large willow tree is nestled near the end of this particular decline, and a path big enough for a car to drive down comes into view beside it. I brake in front of the path and strain to see the end of it. The barn isn't visible from the road, and the trail grows darker and more winding the deeper into the woods it goes. My whole body shudders while staring down the new route in front of me.

Do I really have to go through there?

An old rickety wooden sign sits next to the path. It once hung there by two chains, but now one has broken free, causing the sign to sit crooked off to the side. The whole thing is strangled by layers of vines, obscuring some of the words. I can still decipher its message.

Wilson Farm
Absolutely No Trespassing

Connor's text mentioned the warning on the sign, but to ignore it since it's only to scare people off. One of the people in his group has family who owns the property. They apparently hang out there all the time.

My bike takes another beating maneuvering along the trail. Rocks and leaves crunch under the tires, and I keep hitting problematic spots of thick muck and dirt formed by the earlier rain. My shoes crust with mud after several course corrects through the sketchier parts. The bottoms of my pants aren't faring that well either. They're weighed down with moisture and clumps of dirt, making peddling even trickier.

The path splits again and I'm met with a tall wooden post and a shoddily made wooden plank sign attached to it. A crude yellow painted arrow points to the left with the words "Boat Dock" underneath. The arrow pointing right has "Wilson Family Farm" below it. I bear right, and before long the lane opens up, revealing my final destination.

An oversized wooden barn sits in the distance, nestled amid a thick fortification of trees looking like sentinels defending a stronghold. Its outward appearance mirrors the sign at the entrance to the trail. The wooden slats comprising the structure are worn and weathered, showing its age. Otherwise, it's a typical-looking barn on the outside ... big and boxy. I'm so preoccupied staring at it and trying to ward off a serious case of the wiggins that I have to suddenly swerve in order to avoid crashing into a sizable ditch. Barely missed it.

Cat-like reflexes.

I note Connor's truck right away, and then notice a few other cars parked nearby. One of the trucks parked amongst the rest has sizable dents and visible patches of rust, making it stand out compared to the rest of the vehicles, especially Connor's.

I pull out my phone and shoot a text to Connor announcing

my arrival. A few moments later, the large barn door swings open enough for him to step out. The smile lighting up his face almost has me forgetting I'm standing in the middle of the most stereotypical of horror settings. Almost.

Still as handsome as ever, I swear.

His mouth forms into a bold grin. He smooths his thick hair back like he's in one of those sexy shampoo ads. Heat sizzles up from my stomach, sending the butterfly dragons into a flurry that I'm sure he must notice.

"I can't believe you actually rode your bike all the way here," he says, breaking me from my daze.

My mouth is dry and I swear it is full of the dirt I just biked through to get here. "Yeah, you weren't lying about that hill. It's like biking up Mount Everest."

He laughs and shakes his head, glancing at my feet. "And your poor shoes," he adds.

"These old things," I say, but I'm honestly irked I got my favorite pair of Converse this muddy. "It's only some dirt. It'll wash off."

I hope.

He straddles the bike's front tire. "All right. Well, this time I insist you put your bike in the back of my truck. I'd much prefer to drive you home than make you bike all that way back. It's supposed to rain again, so that trail is gonna get nasty. And a little dangerous since it's all downhill on your way home." He places a hand on one of the handle bars. His green eyes gleam in the low-hanging sunlight.

"Thanks. I think I'll actually take you up on that offer this time."

"Good," he says with a warm smile as his other hand grips the second handlebar.

I dodge his dreamy gaze when I feel I've been staring into

his eyes for too long. He backs away toward his truck and lowers the back door leading to the bed. I roll the bike over and he assists hoisting it in before closing it back up.

When he drapes his arm around my shoulder, I lose all sense of anything else. "I don't know about you, but I'm ready to show you off," he says.

It sounds muted because of the clanging between my ears. All I can do is nervous laugh over this simple action of territorial possession. I've never had a guy show this kind of open affection toward me before. It's foreign. It feels fragile, like something I'm scared of breaking or that will flee at any moment. He's probably used to dishing out this kind of attention. It's probably as natural for him to include someone in his life this way like a friendly handshake or high five.

Not for me.

I've always had better relationships with girls than guys, mainly because I was safe for the girls to be around. Guys tended to think my then-unconfirmed affinity for the same sex was contagious or something. I mean, I had a handful of straight guy friends and acquaintances, but knowing that Connor wasn't straight had this kind of attention feeling different. Comfortable almost, but in the most unusual and exhilarating way.

He leads me toward the barn door and pulls it open wide enough for us to pass through together. The interior is pretty much what I'd expect the inside of a barn to look like with a few notable exceptions. The center of the space is set up like a makeshift living room, complete with two worn green couches and a coffee table nestled between them on top of a tattered gray area rug. There are also a few wooden chairs strewn about, along with an old looking recliner that's an interesting faded powder blue color. Most of the seats are occupied by members of Connor's group.

It seems a lot of the typical farming tools have been removed and all of the loose hay has been relocated to the back. There are still some bundled hay bales stashed along the sides, but this definitely has more of a lived-in feel than the abandoned barn's exterior gives off at first impression.

The talking ceases the minute we enter the barn. All eyes turn to us. I recognize every one of the other people from their visits to The Pour Over, so it'll be nice to put names with their faces.

"Donovan, this is everyone. Everyone this is Donovan," Connor says, motioning to the people sitting on the furniture in the center of the space.

They all wave at me and I do the same. As expected, the mood in the room is not cheerful. All of the smiles and welcoming gestures seem to be a result of trying to be hospitable, but are coming off as forced.

I can't blame them.

The "jock" speaks up first. "Hey, what's up, man? I'm Geoff." He has his fist firmly wrapped around a beer can and takes a drink promptly after addressing me. "So, you're the guy that has our Connor here gabbing nonstop, huh?"

His smile seems the most sincere so far. He flashes Connor a knowing glance and I immediately become flustered. My eyes want to peek over at Connor, but I'm too embarrassed.

"Okay, who wants a drink?" Connor abruptly asks, clearly attempting to change the subject. I see him give the "I'm watching you" two finger point to Geoff, which Geoff just laughs off. He seems content with himself for making Connor uncomfortable.

Carter, the guy I'd seen with Connor at Mae's, sends a slight nod my way. He's back to wearing his usual brooding black and grey. "Name's Carter, if Connor didn't mention me already, though he should have since we're in a band together." He sends Connor a withering stare before looking back at me. "You were pretty entertaining up on stage Monday night, by the way. Not a big fan of the music choice, but to each their own."

"Thanks, I guess," I reply with a hint of a laugh in my exhale.

"Is it true you actually rode your bike up Devil's Horn?" asks the girl with the short blonde hair sitting on the couch next to Carter.

Queen bee.

"Devil's Horn?" I repeat with inflection.

"That's what we call that big-ass twisty hill," Connor says. His voice sounds so close it gives me a quick jolt. His breath tickles the spot on my neck just below my earlobe.

"Yeah, and we call it that because it's actually claimed lives," says Geoff.

"Mainly cyclists," Carter adds with a devilish smirk. My eyes grow wide as I face Connor. He shakes his head, reassuring me that's not the case, which causes Carter to chuckle. "Sorry, I couldn't resist. I'm a jerk, I know," he continues. The blonde girl slaps his arm and then turns her attention to me.

"Don't mind him," she says. "Carter can't help himself. It's his go-to behavior under stress. A practical jokester, this one."

"And an amazing lead vocalist," he adds with a quick pat to his chest.

She ignores his comment. "I'm Nancy, by the way." Both she and the other girl in the group join me on either side, linking their arms with mine. "And this is Tawni," Nancy says, nodding to the willowy brunette.

"Something tells me we're going to get along just fine," Tawni says as they both guide me over to sit on the vacant couch.

Unlike with Connor, this is the kind of attention I'm used to. Girls always seem to act like this around me. I'm gay. I'm safe. I've always wondered if it's a girl's wish to have their very own GBF … gay best friend. I've even wondered if that's what initially drew Lori to be friends with me. Of course, with Nancy and Tawni, this could just be their way of making me feel welcome since I'm Connor's guest. Whatever the reason, it's refreshing to be amongst a group of people that all seem so accepting. I can see myself hanging out with these people. They remind me of the few friends I had back home.

As I scan the group, I realize there's one person missing from the normal crew. The "geek."

"You work at The Pour Over, right?" Tawni asks.

"Yep, that's me."

"I thought you looked familiar." She nods to the others with pride over the fact she remembered me. It's met with a couple eye rolls.

"Hey, Donovan, want anything to drink?" Connor asks, hovering over the portable cooler he has propped open.

"I'm good, thanks."

"Oh, come on. Have at least one," Geoff urges.

"He doesn't have to drink if he doesn't want to," Connor says, sending me a quick smile before he cracks open a beer for himself.

"But the games will be more fun that way," Geoff presses.

Connor didn't mention we'd be playing games tonight.

"Games? What games?" I ask, my eyes darting around the group.

I've never been a fan of games requiring group participation. I usually stress the hell out when it's my turn. Just the thought of having to stand up and do anything in front of these people—who I just officially met, by the way—makes me want to hurl. Now I'm questioning even accepting Connor's invitation in the first place.

"Nope. Can't say a thing until Shaun arrives," Carter says with a snicker.

Carter really likes messing with people, huh?

By process of elimination, I assume Shaun is the "geek."

"Oh, Carter. Would you stop it? You're making him nervous again". Patting my arm, she says, "Honestly, it's just a few little games we like to play every now and then. They're kind of nostalgic. No big deal."

Her tone is gentle as she looks around at the rest of the group for affirmation. They all nod in agreement. It eases my anxiety about the unexpected games a fraction.

Connor approaches me and extends his hand out for mine. "Okay, okay. I think you two have had your fair share of time with *my* guest," he says to the girls with a soft chuckle. "Take my hand if you want to survive."

"You're such a dork, Connor," Tawni says, and Nancy nods in agreement.

When I reach out to take Connor's hand, a sudden concern rushes through my mind. My palms are sweaty at the mere thought of touching his. I'd drop dead on the spot if it grossed him out. But the look on his face when our hands touch puts that fear to rest.

"Aww. How cute," Geoff says, landing himself on the receiving end of scoffs from the two ladies. "Hey, love is love. I appreciate all kinds." He toasts his beer up into the air.

"Ignore them," Connor says with a laugh.

He chucks one of the small pillows on the couch at Geoff, who's sitting in the recliner. Geoff catches it in mid-air and places it behind his head.

"Just what I needed. You're so thoughtful, Connor."

His laugh is infectious and has everyone cracking up. Connor rolls his eyes.

A side door I hadn't noticed before groans open, pulling everyone's attention. In steps who I assume is Shaun.

"Sorry, guys," he says. "Had to run an errand before heading over."

"Hey, Shaun," Connor greets him. "This is Donovan."

"Nice to meet you. Welcome to the Wilson family barn," he says. He lifts his retro, eighties-style hot pink glasses to sit on top of his shaggy dark hair before reaching out to shake my hand.

"Always so well spoken, Shaun," Carter slides in.

"That's what happens when you have an IQ higher than your shoe size," Shaun quips, making the group laugh.

Carter sends kisses to Shaun and says, "Love you too."

"Shaun's family owns this place," Connor explains.

"Yep," Shaun says. "For many years now. It's been abandoned for a while except for our little group's hangouts here. And I guess the little gang keeps getting smaller."

The mood in the room changes like the flip of a light switch. It had been feeling progressively warmer the longer I'd been there, but that all left with the uttering of that single sentence. It's clear the loss of Lori is taking a toll on them. It's taking a toll on me too, and I only knew her for a short while. I seriously can't imagine what they all must be going through, including Drea. I want to ask more about Lori, but worry it might sound too intrusive.

"Hey, Donovan, you found her right?" Carter asks.

So much for me asking about Lori being too intrusive.

"Seriously, dude?" Geoff remarks with an attempt to tap Carter. He misses and hits the couch instead.

"Yeah, not cool," adds Nancy.

Connor looks at me. "You don't have to talk about this. You know that, right?"

"Come on," Carter argues. "I'm only calling out the massive elephant in the room. Don't you guys all act like you aren't curious too. I don't mean any disrespect. It's just, first she killed herself and now they think she was murdered. Please, someone stop me if you don't want answers here."

It's like I'm standing underneath a giant heat lamp. All eyes are staring at me. What was once a fun gathering has now turned into what feels like a trial.

Did I make a mistake coming here?

"Carter, bro, we all want to know what happened to Lori," Geoff says. "And we all also know you had a thing for her."

"That has nothing to do with this, *bro*." He emphasizes bro in a mocking way. "Of course I really liked Lori, have since elementary school, but she was a friend to all of us, not just me. And the fact that we have no idea what happened to her is complete and utter bullshit."

I hear the hurt in his voice. For the first time since meeting him, his sarcastic demeanor has completely disappeared.

"I think we all need to just shut the hell up and change topics," says Shaun, putting an end to the tense conversation.

I, for one, am relieved. I was about to slink out the door and leave if it continued for much longer.

"I'm so sorry about this," Connor says, looking over at me. "If you want to leave, I'll completely understand. Maybe this was too soon. I just wanted you to meet my friends."

"No, he can't leave," argues Geoff. "We need an odd number of people to play tonight, dude."

"We can just play later when everyone's cooled off," replies Connor.

It suddenly dawns on me that I'm filling in for Lori with these games tonight. In some weird way, I feel obliged to participate in a kind of homage to her memory. It could prove cathartic.

I put my hand on Connor's arm and squeeze lightly. "It's okay. I want to stay."

A smile pulls at the corner of his mouth. "Are you sure?" he asks.

"Uh-huh. I'm sure."

"That's what I'm talking about," whoops Geoff with a victorious arm pump. "I'm getting the new guy a beer, even if he doesn't want one."

"Let's try and enjoy this for Lori, okay?" Tawni says as she looks around at everyone.

"Agreed," says Nancy.

A large gust of wind rattles the barn door, making me jump.

"You good?" Connor asks me.

I nod, holding his gaze. The sound of raindrops hitting the roof resonates throughout the space.

"There's that second wave I mentioned," Connor says as we both glance up. Then a roll of thunder in the distance adds to the ever-increasing ominous atmosphere.

Am I going to regret this?

TWENTY-ONE

Drea

PERFECT, JUST PERFECT.

It's raining. Scratch that, it's bucketing. It's as if someone slit open a raincloud right down the middle and its insides are gushing down in sheets. It's the perfect topper to this day.

Between what Trent said, me reaching a dead end on finding information about Carrie Phillips, and being no closer to figuring out who killed Lori, I find myself utterly collapsed. For the umpteenth day in a row, every single class today was a wash, my mind preoccupied with the many conspiracy theories racing through it. Everyone around me seems suspect of something. It's quite apparent I'm not the only one suspicious of others at school after Lori's murder announcement. Paranoia has woven its way through the rest of the student body. You can feel it in the air. See it in the way people stare at each other accusingly as they pass by in the halls.

Or maybe I'm just projecting my own feelings out there.

Despite knowing this storm was heading our way, I made the foolish decision to kill some time by helping Addie Monroe and the rest of the Homecoming committee after school to pre-pare the gym for the dance coming up this Friday. The cheerlead-ing squad helped out as well, which is how I got roped into it even though I'm no longer an active member. I guess the news of me quitting hasn't made the rounds yet. Besides, the Neon MasqueRave is a huge undertaking. Addie seemed desperate for help.

The whole ordeal was a couple hours of me awkwardly in-teracting in close quarters with people I'd been avoiding since the beginning of the year. I had hoped that working on Lori's idea for the dance would prove to be therapeutic, and I wanted to pump everyone there for information on Carrie. It didn't work out that way. I came away with no more info than I already had on Carrie, and working on the dance only made me miss Lori more.

Now I stand under the safety of the metal overhang, staring out at the student parking lot and waiting for this to all blow over. It figured I forgot my umbrella in my car today of all days. Not that it would help much since I'd still get drenched from the waist down with the direction the rain is falling.

Tension mounts between my temples, a dull ache that rap-idly transforms into a slow pound. This weather isn't helping matters at all.

"Afraid you'll melt?" a deep voice asks from behind me.

There's no mistaking that voice, and a small shiver of antici-pation tickles my spine. It's Harrison. I've heard it so much these past couple days that it's hard to forget now. Or is it that I don't want to forget it?

Get a grip.

He joins me at my side standing dangerously close. He smells nice … clean, like a brand-new bar of soap fresh out of the box. Then I am enveloped in a faint cloud of mint when he exhales.

"After you," I say, waving my hand out toward the parking lot.

He laughs and shakes his head. "So, are you going to be in the stands tomorrow at the game?"

I feel him look at me, but I keep staring forward, hoping he'll get the hint I'm not in the mood to talk. I suspect he knows and maybe just wants to push my buttons.

It's clear he's been flirting with me as of late. So have I with him, to an extent. It tears me up that I can't give him what he wants. I think deep down I want to, but I'm confused. There's a ton I have to sift through before I can get there. My life's too chaotic right now, some of which is my own doing.

It's not fair to him. I should be more direct. I should tell him I need space.

Instead, I remain silent because I'm at a loss for how to put it. Why can't I just tell him? Maybe I don't want to. Maybe I'm selfishly entertaining all of this because of how he makes me feel. The distraction of it all.

"I'm sort of nervous, to be honest," he continues. "There's going to be a college scout in the stands, so extra pressure."

"Oh, stop it. You'll do fine." The conviction in my voice surprises me when I speak. It's like I felt compelled to say it that way.

Why can't I feel compelled to say other things?

"Ah, you are still there. I was beginning to suspect I was talking to myself."

My head snaps to face him and slams into his hazel gaze. After a moment of me wavering on how to reply, I recoil and resume my staring contest with the parking lot.

Why am I like this right now?

He sighs, and it's like a knee to the gut. "You know you can always talk to me, right? About anything."

Thud.

Thud.

Thud.

There goes my damn heart again.

"I know," I reply. "I've just had a not so great day today."

"Understandable. Want to talk about it?" His voice is low and thoughtful.

"Not really," I reply with a light shake of my head.

Another sigh from him. Another hit to the gut.

"Fair enough," he says.

Though I can't admit it right now, I am grateful for his silence and his strong presence as he stands there next to me staring out at the rain. At the same time, I feel bad he's seeing me acting like this.

I glance up and spy a ghost of a smile on his lips.

What is he thinking about? Why is he putting himself through this?

"You don't have to stay here, you know," I say.

"I know."

Another bout of silence falls between us. It's nice. He's kind of like my calm in the midst of this storm. And he's quickly becoming my anchor.

Now there's a thought.

"Just so you … well, I think you should come tomorrow," he says after a couple minutes.

He presents his umbrella and props it open. I once again gaze up at his soft smile. This time, he's staring right at me.

"There's room for one more under here," he hints.

I shake my head delicately and avert my eyes. "Thank you, but I think I'm going to wait it out. Be alone with my thoughts, you know?"

I see him give a brief nod out of the corner of my eye before he takes a step off the curb and enters the rain. I lose sight of him the further he ventures out as the downpour obscures his image. I'd be lying if I said I wasn't a tad disappointed at myself for not going with him. It was sweet of him to offer like that, but I if had accepted, I'd be sending him signals I don't know if I'm ready to commit to yet.

"Okay, you can stop anytime you want to," I mutter at the rain.

A car pulls up in front of me under the metal awing. The passenger side window slides down and I duck to get a look at the driver. It's Harrison and his incredible smile again.

"Hop in. I'll take you to your car," he says.

"Seriously you don't have to. I can wait it out."

He taps the passenger seat. "I know, but humor me, please?"

I'm overcome by his thoughtfulness. I don't deserve his generosity. His attention.

It would be rude of me to decline.

He leans over and opens the door from the inside before retreating back. I grab the handle and pull it open the rest of the way. There's a bigger smile on his face as I relax into the seat.

"Where are you parked?"

"Near the back of the lot. By the fence next to the woods. I got here late today," I explain. I'm a jumbled mixture of nerves and contentment.

"Sounds good."

"Thank you," I say, glancing over at him, a small smile flickering on my lips.

"You're welcome."

My gaze drifts out the window. I focus on the erratic water trails zipping diagonally across the pane in an attempt to calm my ever-increasing heart rate.

"If you're cold, you can adjust the vents. I run warm, so my AC is always on full blast."

"I'm good, thanks."

I feel a little ridiculous sitting here freezing while trying to hold the shivers at bay in order to prove I wasn't lying. Then a question enters my mind. "Hey, Harrison?"

"Yeah?"

"Did you know a girl named Carrie Phillips?"

His shoulders droop as his face becomes reflective. "Wow, I haven't heard that name in a while. Yeah, I knew her. A really sad story."

"Sad story? You mean about how she died?"

"Exactly," he says as he pulls into an empty spot near my car.

"What did you know about her? Were you friends?"

"In a way, I guess. She died a week before our freshman year started. She moved here during eighth grade, and from what I remember she blended in pretty well at school. The guys were into her, that's for sure." He unbuckles his seatbelt and turns to face me. "What's with all the interest? And how is it you don't know about Carrie? She was, like, one of Lori's good friends. Didn't she ever talk about her?"

"She did, but not much." I go to open my door. "Never mind. Don't worry about it."

Walls back up.

"Wait a sec. I'll get that," says Harrison.

He leaves the car under the protection of his umbrella and approaches my door, pulling it open and shielding me from the rain as I take a step out. With one hand grasped around the umbrella, he holds open his letterman jacket with his other to help block the wind. We huddle close together as he escorts me to my car. I only hope he can't feel my heart racing from being this close to him.

He continues playing the part of human shield from the rain the best he can while I open my car door and get situated inside.

He holds the door open, maintaining a block from the rain with the umbrella.

"You're not alone in all of this, Drea," he says. "You have people you can rely on. Remember that, okay?"

I nod. "I'll try. Thank you."

"Of course. Take care, Drea," he says as he shuts the door.

I watch him hurry back to his vehicle and jump inside. He pulls out of the lot, leaving me a conflicted mess.

This would be easier if he was a jerk.

I sigh and pull out my cell to shoot a text to Donovan.

Call me tonight when you have time please.

I stow away the phone and stare out the window at the wind and rain lashing the wall of trees in front of me. I can relate to those trees. I hope, like them, my roots are strong enough to withstand everything heading my way.

Something tells me this is only the beginning.

TWENTY-TWO

Donovan

As the storm rages outside, I feel like I'm in this bubble of safety amongst Connor and his group. Gone is the tension from earlier, replaced with a fun atmosphere. We've played countless games already, charades being my least favorite thus far. I'm not a huge fan of being the center of attention, which is all charades is when it's your turn. It was exponentially more fun when the others were up.

I find myself relaxing more into this groove, like I'm carving out my own little niche with these people. It's refreshing, but I know the moment I leave this barn, reality will slam full-force into me. For now, this is what I need. What I've been craving. The feeling of belonging.

My phone vibrates in my pocket and I pull it out to see a text from Drea. A conflict between my heart and head ensues as I stare at the preview notification and see **Call me tonight**....

"Everything okay? Do you need to get going?" Connor leans over to ask.

I put my phone away. "No, I'm fine."

"Good," he says with a wide grin.

I could most definitely get used to this.

Guilt punches me in my gut when my mind floats back to Drea's text and I wonder if she needs me. Selfishly, I don't want this moment to end. I know if I text or call her back, this will all change. The bubble will burst.

And there goes the self-imposed guilt piling on thicker.

My hand suddenly feels wrapped in warmth. The warmth turns into a bonafide bonfire happening on my knee. Connor's hand rests on top of mine and I feel the heat spread from my hand up my arm before scattering across my whole body. I stare at our hands nestled together for probably longer than I should. My heart rate increases ten-fold as I shift my gaze up to him.

"Want another drink?" he asks.

My words get lost around my tongue for a second. "I'm okay. Thanks though," I finally get out.

Whatever comfort I was feeling goes right out the window after that whole exchange. I'm so tense I feel like a constipated meerkat or something.

He releases my hand and taps it softly. "Okay. Be right back."

"Donovan, are you ready for the final game of the evening?" Shaun asks as he cracks open a new can of beer.

"Sure, and I just want to say that I'm glad I came out tonight."

"I'd wait until after this next one to say that," says Carter.

His words cause a yellow caution flag to spring up in my head.

"Would you stop, Carter?" Tawni chastises him. "And you were doing so well up until then too."

"Oh, he knows I'm kidding. Don't you, Donnie?" he asks before taking a swig of his drink.

I'm surprised when he calls me Donnie. Lori and Marcus are the only two people who have used that nickname. I wonder if Lori talked about me with them or if he just came up with it on his own.

"Yeah, of course," I reply with an unsure laugh.

"Well, we're glad you came tonight too," Nancy adds with a smile.

"By the way, Donnie Boy, this next game is the reason why we needed an odd number," Geoff chimes in. "It's kind of a twist on Two Truths and One Lie."

"What's the twist?" I ask as Connor returns to the seat next me.

Shaun dips away for a moment and returns with a box ... a matte black cube, to be exact. He removes the lid and pulls out a mask, one that I immediately recognize from the night at Mae's Lounge when I performed with Marcus. This one has a cruder feel to it though, with the fox head lined out in thin strips of bright orange duct tape instead of neon pink glow bands.

"Hey, I saw something similar at the bar on Monday," I say.

Shaun shoots a look of confusion my way. "Really? This is the only one we have and it was homemade. Not sure what you saw, but it probably wasn't this."

"Have you played Two Truths and a Lie before, Donovan?" Nancy asks. She moves over to Shaun and snatches the mask away from him.

"Yeah, I think so. Maybe at a couple of middle school parties or something. Not recently though."

"We call our version Fox Hunt. Hence, the mask." Nancy puts it up to her face and then brings it back down to rest in her lap. "The rules of the game are simple. One person wears the mask and the rest of the group splits into two teams. We all write two truths and one lie on pieces of paper and then take turns reading them aloud. It's the job of the fox to sniff out the lies. If any person is able to fool the fox, then that team gets a point. The ones who get sniffed out, though, are *eaten* by the fox and have to sit out until one side is crowned the winner. Each round, the survivors have to get more personal with their truths and lies, and eliminated players on the opposite team will judge whether they went deep enough. The fox has to rely on their keen senses in order to tell who's lying or not. And yes, just in case you're wondering, the eye holes on the mask are covered for an added challenge," she concludes with a flourish.

Connor stands up and takes the mask from Nancy before returning to his seat. "Are you sure you want to play?"

I nod. "Sure, sounds interesting."

He hands me the mask. "Okay. Since you're the guest, you have the honor of being the fox for tonight's game."

"Where did you guys come up with the idea for this?" I ask, analyzing the mask. It's oddly eerie, yet simplistic.

"It was kind of the brain-child of Nancy, Shaun, and—" Geoff begins, then cuts himself off as he glances around the room at everyone in attendance. "Another friend not in the group anymore," he finishes.

Did the mood in the room just change again?

"Yeah, and the mask was actually made by them too," Tawni adds.

"But the reason we're playing this tonight is in honor of Lori," explains Nancy. "She had the record for most wins, so it seems fitting to end this night with a game she loved."

"So, you ready to play?" Carter asks, leaning forward, hands clasped.

"I think so," I reply.

"There's no think. Only do, Donnie boy," Geoff interjects.

For some reason them calling me Donnie hasn't been bothering me. Maybe it's because they sound genuine when they say it. Like a term of endearment. Like the way Lori meant it. I loathed every time my stepfather called me chief. It seemed demeaning somehow, like he refused to call me by my real name. Either that or he didn't care what my name was. Sometimes I wondered if he'd forgotten my name and started calling me chief to cover up that fact.

Shaun hands out a piece of paper and pen to each person. Connor directs me to sit in the powder blue recliner to isolate myself so I can't see what anyone is writing. When everyone finishes, they set their pens down on the coffee table and face me, all eyes focused in my direction.

"Okay, mask on," says Connor with that glorious smirk of his.

I slide on the mask. The whole room disappears. Claustrophobia immediately sets in. The nose holes are small, but thankfully still allow for enough air to pass through and prevent me from hyperventilating. My breathing bounces around within the cheap plastic, sounding loud in my ears. It's all I can focus on. I feel someone take my hand and I jump slightly at the touch.

"Holy crap! You can't do that," I squeak out with a laugh. Everyone else joins in.

"Sorry," I hear Connor say. "Just wanted to make sure you're okay. It's a little weird putting the mask on for the first time."

"I'm good. Just a little disorientated and claustrophobic, but I'm okay," I reply with an anxious laugh.

The sound of the rain pelting the barn's roof has intensified. I can now hear it over my breathing within the mask. A loud clap of thunder has me jumpy and unnerved. My body squirms from the sudden adrenaline rush.

"Ready?" Carter asks.

"Yep."

It takes me most of the first round to get my bearings with

the game and to become more at ease in the mask. Hearing everyone speak while I'm blindfolded makes their voices sound somehow foreign, though I do end up proving to myself that I've gotten a good feel for these people despite only spending a few hours with them.

The first out is Shaun. It's easy to determine his lie. He has a tell. His voice quivers slightly at the end of his third statement.

The second out is Geoff. His lie is another one that's easy to catch. He said he had his first drink of alcohol at the age of fifteen, but he mentioned earlier that his older brother gave him his first swig at thirteen.

The next out is Nancy. Hers is a little harder to figure out. I'm torn between two, but ultimately choose the right one, which is that she's never cheated on an exam in school. She seems like a smart girl, but her whole queen bee thing led me to think she's capable of cheating on at least one exam.

Stereotypes, I know.

Then it's on to round two with Connor, Carter, and Tawni. They all played really well the first round, which has me wondering about Connor. It seems like he's good at lying. Or is he just good at the game?

Not sure how I feel about that.

Carter ends up being the only one eliminated in the second round. Again, Connor is either a great liar or he's mastered this game. Connor and Tawni take a moment to write down their statements and then show the other eliminated players for approval. Tawni gets the okay, but I have yet to hear Connor cleared.

"Nope," I hear Geoff say. "Got to do better than that, man."

"Yeah, that's not going to cut it," Nancy seconds.

I assume Connor goes back to his paper and reworks his statements. Then he gets the all-clear.

"All right, Connor, read me yours," I say.

"I've hooked up with both girls and guys. I've been in trouble for arson. And I have a crush on someone in this room," he says.

There's no inflection in his voice whatsoever. He says each statement with a deadpan tone.

Is the crush one about me?

"I'm going to say that the lie is you have a crush on someone in this room."

"Nope," Connor replies.

An audible boo rings out.

"Hold on, I feel this was rigged," Tawni objects. "Why would Donovan pick that one unless he wanted Connor to win? It's an obvious truth, am I right?"

"Not so obvious to everyone, it seems," Nancy says.

Tawni issues a huff. "I still don't think it should've been included."

"Thems the rules," Shaun says. "We voted and it counts."

She groans in submission. "Fine."

I sit there quietly, realizing there's a very strong possibility that I'm the one Connor is crushing on. It suddenly feels like a million degrees under this mask.

Because who else could he be talking about?

"So, Connor's still in the game," Carter says. "Tawni, you're up."

"Ready, Donovan?" Tawni asks.

I nod.

"I'm still a virgin. I have a half-sister on my dad's side. I've kissed a girl, and I liked it."

I mull over her statements and come to the conclusion that the first and last one seem to be the most personal. She also had a slight change in tone while reading the middle one, making it stick out.

"I'm going to go with the one about having a half-sister," I say.

"Correct," Tawni replies with a playful whine.

"Connor's team wins," announces Geoff.

I pull off the mask and blink, allowing my eyes time to adjust to the light. Connor comes into focus. He's all smiles.

"Way to go, Donovan," he says, taking the mask from me.

"It was fun."

My stomach is doing a gymnastics routine because of the look in his eyes. His smile seals the deal.

We all jump when the barn door swings open and slams against the wall. A few of us audibly gasp. Rain drizzles in through the opening and the wind lashes about. The answer sheets from the game tumble off the coffee table and swirl around the rug. Loose hay on the ground is sent up into the air, creating a little dust cloud tornado.

Shaun collects the mask from Connor and stuffs it back into the box. "I think that's our sign to break for the night," he says with a laugh while returning the box to its resting place in a medium-sized industrial cabinet.

"I second that motion," Nancy agrees. "It was so nice hanging out you, Donovan." She gives me a light hug and then moves through the open barn door.

Geoff pats me on the shoulder. "Great playing tonight, Donnie boy." He shifts his focus to Connor as he backs away toward the exit. "You made a good choice, man."

I battle a flush of embarrassment when I feel Connor's gaze on me. Geoff chuckles and heads out.

"Congrats, Donnie. You made it through the gauntlet," Carter calls out to me as he leaves the barn. "Until next time."

Tawni is right behind him. She waves bye as another gust of wind blows through the space and whips her hair in front of her face.

Shaun leads Connor and me outside and closes up the barn behind us. "See you guys later," he shouts as we part ways and he disappears into his car.

Connor and I are the last two huddled under the barn's roofline. We're bathed in the light from the lantern attached above the door as we build up the courage to face the elements. It feels private, especially being all the way out in middle of nowhere Haddon Falls.

Eventually, Connor runs out first and I follow in step. He props open the passenger side door of his truck and waits for me to hop in with that trademark grin on his face.

"Your chariot awaits," he says.

Yeah, it's corny, but it's working for me.

"Why, thank you," I reply as I climb in.

He shuts the door behind me. The wind dies down to a hum inside the vehicle until he opens his door.

"Now aren't you glad I offered to drive you home tonight?" he asks with a soft laugh.

"Yeah. Thanks again. I really appreciate it."

"But of course."

He starts the truck and heads down the dirt path toward the main road. "Okay, so now that it's just us, you knew that the thing about me having a crush on someone in the barn was the truth, didn't you?"

"Don't get me wrong, I wanted it to be true, but on the offhand chance it wasn't, I took a shot. You were really good at that game, by the way."

"You weren't too bad yourself," he says. "And just so we're clear, it's you that I like."

My cheeks flush and my heart surges a mile a minute as I slowly turn to face him. He glances over at me and smiles when our eyes meet. My palms begin to sweat, so I wipe them on my jeans. My head is spinning in some kind of euphoria that I've never felt. I've never known someone who *like* likes me. Then my inner saboteur cuts in and takes over my mouth.

"But you hardly even know me," I say.

I instantly want to kick myself. Here's this seemingly amazing guy telling me he likes me, and all I can think to say is he doesn't really know me.

A light laugh parts his lips. "Then tell me about yourself so I can like you even more than I already do."

Well, there goes my brain, and heart, and pretty much everything that controls my functionality.

I don't even think I could answer him on my best day in my current condition. My mouth is suddenly parched as hell and the front cab of his truck feels like a freaking sauna. I move my hands to the air vents and turn them on full blast.

He chuckles. "That wasn't meant to stump you. I'd just like to get to know you better."

And he officially just made it more difficult.

"W-What do you want to know?" I stutter, not sure where to begin.

"Anything," he says. "Let's just start with where you're from. I know you're not from around here. You don't have that Haddon Falls tarnish."

That was simple enough. "Well, I was born in New Hampshire, but we left there when I was two. My family didn't stick around places very long since my dad was in the military."

"Military brat, huh?"

"Yeah. Haddon Falls marks the seventh place I've lived up 'til now. I moved here from Mississippi to live with my aunts. It's most definitely a better situation than I had back there."

"What happened, if you don't mind me asking?"

"It's a long story," I reply, feeling vulnerable all of a sudden.

"You don't have to tell me, but I've been told I'm a pretty good listener."

After a few moments, I cave. "My mom and Charles weren't exactly elated when I came out."

"Charles? Is that your dad?"

"No, stepdad. He's like this pinnacle of religion in their town … the most popular pastor in the area. That's why having his stepson come out wasn't the best look for him, and he's all about appearances. My mom was never a religious person until Charles came along. I constantly wonder how she would've reacted to me being gay before she met him. If she would have disapproved so much."

Connor glances over at me with a strained expression. "I'm really sorry. Sounds rough. There's definitely a mixed bag of homophobia here, but I think more tend to be open-minded even if they are religious."

"That's good to hear, I guess."

"So, your mom's okay with you living with your aunts?"

"It was my choice really. I only had two. This or be forced to become a missionary. My mom and my dad's sister don't talk much because of my aunt's lifestyle, but there's at least this mutual respect because of my dad. Being gay wasn't the only reason I had to leave though. I kind of got in trouble with the law. Angry teenager stuff."

"For what it's worth," Connor says, "I understand the whole angry teenager bit. My dad used to kick the crap out of my mom and me when I was younger. He'd even burn her with his cigarettes. So one day I lit his car on fire. Hence, the whole arson charge thing."

"Wait, you lit your dad's car on fire?"

He nods. "I'm not proud of it, but it was all I could think of at the time. His car was his most prized possession. Since he liked to burn someone I treasured, I did the same thing to him. He's in jail now, so there's that." He glances over at me as though gauging my reaction. His green eyes flicker from the headlights of a passing vehicle. "What about your dad?"

I avert my eyes to my hands clasped in my lap. "He died when I was nine."

"Damn, I'm sorry. And here I am going on about how terrible mine is."

"Oh, it's okay. You didn't have any way of knowing."

He shifts in his seat and twists his hand about the steering wheel. "Okay, lighter subject. Are you going to the Homecoming game tomorrow?"

"Yeah, I think so."

"Want to go together? I'll even sacrifice and sit on your school's side, no matter how much food is thrown at me," he says with a light chuckle.

"Yeah, that would be great. Hopefully you'll get to meet my friend, Drea."

"Drea ... that name sounds familiar," he says, appearing as though he's in deep thought as he keeps his eyes on the road.

"She was Lori's best friend. We found her that night together."

"That's where I've heard her name before. Wow, I can't even imagine being in your position with that. It was hard enough on our group to hear on the news, but to be the ones to actually find her, that's tough."

His demeanor changes. I can tell by the look on his face that he's withdrawing into his thoughts.

"Okay, lighter subject," I say this time. "What's your favorite color?"

A smile lifts his mouth and the sparkle returns to his eyes. "I'd say it's a tie between purple and orange," he says with a quick look over at me. "Yours?"

"Orange, definitely. A lot of people think it's a jarring or abrasive color, but I always feel better looking at most things that are orange. Pumpkins, for example. My favorite holiday also happens to be Halloween."

"Mine too," he says with another smile.

"Cool."

Wow, I sound like an absolute tool.

"Yeah, cool."

"You're going to want to make a right up here," I say.

The realization that we're almost to my house sets in. I don't want this to end. He follows my instruction and pulls up to the curb in front of my house, putting the truck in park. Fortunately, the rain has stopped.

"I had a really great time tonight," he says, adjusting in his seat in order to face me. "Even if things did get dicey at moments."

"Yeah, me too. Thanks for the invite," I reply, trying to sound composed. Inside, I'm a bundle of nerves over what might happen next.

I've never been in this position before, but I've seen this exact scene play out in countless movies and TV shows. All of those scenarios terrify the hell out of me and excite me at the same time.

"I guess this is good night then," I say.

"Unfortunately, yeah," he states, never losing my gaze.

I pull the door handle and pop it open. As I step out, I feel sudden physical resistance.

"Uh, Donovan," I hear Connor say. I turn back to face him and he's incredibly close. I hear a clicking sound and he releases a small laugh. "You're still buckled in."

Our faces hover so close to each other that what he just said barely registers at first. Then it sinks in. A nervous laugh tickles the back my throat.

"Oh, yeah ... that," I say. My heart is about to leap from my mouth at any moment. The heat from his body resonates and intermingles with mine.

"Don't worry. I'm not going to kiss you ... yet," he says close to my lips, teasing them.

"I-I wasn't worried."

"Do you need help getting your bike?" he asks, still close as hell.

"I think I can manage," I say as another tense laugh conjures forth.

"All right." He settles back against his seat, the grin never leaving his face. "Have a good night."

"Good night," I say, returning his grin with one of my own. "See you tomorrow?"

"Looking forward to it."

I leave the car, not sure what to make of what just happened. I'm disappointed but also relieved in some kind of odd way.

I just went on my first date!

I collect my bike from the back of the truck and proceed to watch Connor drive away until his taillights disappear around the corner. A content sigh parts my lips. I find myself wanting to hold onto this moment for a little longer.

After punching in the code on the keypad next to the garage door, it opens. I stash the bike off to the side, out of the way of my aunt's car, before heading into the house.

My phone vibrates and I pull it out to see it's reminding me of Drea's earlier text. I feel terrible about not being there for her and for not calling her like she'd asked me to. I type out a message.

Sorry it took me so long to get back to you. I know it's late. Can we talk tomorrow at school?

My phone vibrates shortly after I hit send. She must have

been sitting by her phone waiting for my reply, which makes me feel worse.

Ok. I'll make sure to get there early. I really need to talk to you about something.

I text back, **See you then**, before stashing my phone away. The lights are all still on inside the house. I can only assume my aunts stayed up to wait for me to return. They're both night owls anyway.

I'm sure they're going to want to know how my class project went tonight.

TWENTY-THREE

Drea

W HEN'S THE LAST TIME I WAS AT SCHOOL THIS *early?*

A deep yawn takes hold of my mouth before working its way through my whole body. I had yet another night where sleep apparently wasn't my body's top priority. It felt weird being up and ready with the rest of the household this morning. My parents felt the need to put me through a game of twenty questions as they tried to figure out why I wasn't still in bed.

I expected to see more people at the school already. Instead, the halls are unnervingly quiet, sans a few straggling overachievers putting last-minute touches on the Homecoming decorations and rare appearances from a janitor and a few teachers.

Actually, the halls are pretty loud, but not in terms of volume. It looks as if our mascot, Haddie the Bulldog, vomited school spirit everywhere overnight. If anyone was questioning whether or not today was the big Homecoming game, all they'd need to do is look around and see our colors plastered all over the place. Streamers, pompoms, banners, balloons … the works.

Nestled in the middle of everything is a single collapsible

table covered in a red and black tablecloth. Soon, a ballot box, a stack of ballots, and a tote of blank plastic masquerade masks will adorn the top of it. Then all votes for king and queen will be closely monitored by none other than the head of the Homecoming and Senior Prom committees, Addie Monroe. Lori was actually in the running for queen.

I haven't voted yet.

It's still weird seeing everyone trying to go on with their normal lives while there's an unsolved murder lingering over our small town. My hands-down suspect for the killer seems to have a clean alibi, and the only thing he's being considered for now is being crowned king at the dance on Friday.

Harrison is also on the ballot. The only reason I know is because I helped Addie print them last week. It was one of the few social things I've done since the summer.

I'm currently doing my best to avoid Harrison this morning while waiting for Donovan to arrive. I'm posted up right next to the school's entrance in order to keep a lookout for both him and Donovan. I decided last night the last thing my life needs right now is more complications.

Through the tall, thin rectangular window in the door, I watch Donovan speed up on his bike and park it in the rack. I hurry out to meet him. He tinkers with the lock on his bike before turning to look at me when I get closer.

"Thanks for getting here so early," I say.

"No problem. My aunts were curious why I was leaving before them, but I just said I was helping with Homecoming stuff," he replies. "So, what's up?"

"I have something you need to see." I take the diary out from my bag and hold it toward him. "This was left at my house. There was no indication who left it."

His eyes widen when he sees the cover. "This design of the

fox head … I've seen it twice now," he says, tracing the image with his fingertips. "Once at Mae's Lounge, I saw someone wearing it. Then last night, I played a game with this group who were all friends with Lori. They had a mask that looked like this, but it was orange instead of pink."

"Wait, hold up. You were with a group of people last night that knew Lori? And they had a mask that looked like this?"

He nods as he begins to flip through the diary. "Whoa, this is really disturbing. Why are there so many pages ripped out? And what's with all the crazy markings?"

"I don't know, but clearly someone wanted me to see this," I reply.

He turns to one of the sketches and stops. "I think this is the barn I went to last night. Actually, I'm sure of it. The willow tree too, and the sign." He flips the page again and stalls on the sketch of the fox head from the cover. "Here it is … the mask. And this is the game we played. Fox Hunt."

"So it sounds like the group you were with last night was friends with Carrie as well as Lori."

"Yeah, and this Carrie girl must be the friend they were tip-toeing around talking about last night. She helped create the game and made the mask I wore while playing," he explains.

"Apparently she went to middle school with a few people here," I say. "Everyone I've talked to said she died mysteriously. I looked her up last night and could only find an old news story about how she fell off a cliff into Lake Wilson while riding her bike. All of her social media pages have been wiped clean, like she's disappeared from the internet or something. I didn't think you could do that, but apparently there's a way."

He frowns. "Wait, she's dead? They were talking about her last night like she just left the group, not that she died." He exchanges a look with me that reflects the same eerie uncertainty I feel. "Do you think one of them left this at your house for some reason?"

"I don't know. Maybe," I reply. "How did you meet these people? Did Lori introduce you to them?"

"No. They come into the café to hang out. I actually saw Lori with them before the party that night. My co-worker was the one who pointed out they'd all been friends since middle school."

That has me rubbing a sudden chill from my arms. "Did they say what happened to Carrie?"

"No. They didn't even mention her by name. Like I said, they kind of dodged the whole thing and focused on Lori. I didn't think to ask more since she came up at the same time Lori did. I didn't want to pry."

My mind swirls with all this new information. "Funny that Lori never mentioned this group to me. The only one she ever said anything about was Carrie." I shake my head. "This is getting really weird. Do you think I could meet this group?"

"You're in luck," he says. "One of them, Connor, asked me to go to the Homecoming game tonight. I planned to introduce you to him anyway."

"Perfect. Maybe he can shed some light on this whole situation."

"Yeah."

Students begin passing by, filing into the school. I take the diary back from Donovan and tuck it in my bag. When I look up, I notice Donovan's eyes are fixed on something over my shoulder. I follow his line of sight and see Harrison headed our way.

There goes my plan to avoid him today.

"Want me to intervene?" asks Donovan.

"No, it's cool. He's been really nice lately. I'm trying not to like him, but he's making it very difficult."

"What's not to like?" he asks, elbowing me lightly in the side.

I flash him a "Really?" stare and he responds with a shoulder shrug.

"Good morning," Harrison speaks up behind me.

A twinge of nervousness nips at my gut.

"I've got to get to my locker before class," Donovan says as he begins to move away. Talk to you later, Drea. Later, Harrison."

I try to send him a signal to stick around, but he's already committed to his decision. My focus switches to Harrison, who's all smiles.

"Hey, I wanted to ask you something," he says.

"Sorry, no … I haven't voted for you yet for Homecoming king."

"That's not what I was going to ask. I don't really care about that. It does have to do with Homecoming though," he says, moving closer to me.

I tense. My hand clutches my bag tighter at the mere thought of what he might want to ask me.

"Oh," is all I manage to get out.

"Would you by any chance want to go with me to the dance tomorrow?"

His smile gives the question extra pizazz in the delivery department. My free hand brushes a few strands of loose hair behind my ear as my brain stalls on his question. The very last thing on my mind is the dance or any other normal high school activities. I seem to be one of the few who haven't just up and forgotten about what happened to Lori. Still, I'd be lying if I said I wasn't tempted by his offer.

"I don't know," I say and his face falls. "I appreciate you asking me. I do. But I'm just not sure I'm even going."

He combs his hand through his hair and it bounces right back into place. "I get it. No worries. But if you change your mind, the offer stands." He gives me a half smile. "You are coming to the game tonight though, right?"

I nod delicately. "Yeah."

A twinge of guilt pricks my heart because the main reason I'll be there is to talk with Donovan's date about Carrie. He doesn't need to know that though.

"Glad to hear it. I'll see you there then," he says.

I nod before he walks away.

He's getting a lot harder to deny.

When I enter the school, the voting table shines like a beacon in the night with Addie positioned behind it. She tries to wave me over, but I duck into the bathroom. I can't deal with her asking again if I've voted yet. I just can't bring myself to see Lori's name crossed out on the ballot. It's too soon.

Add that to the ever-growing list of things I'm trying to avoid.

The bathroom dampens the low roar of the student body crowding the hall outside. Luckily, I have all the books I need for my first couple classes due to homework last night, so there's no need to go to my locker before the first bell. Addie will have packed up by then and I can safely make my way to first period.

I head over to the bank of sinks lining the mirrored wall and brace myself on the one in the middle. My desperate desire to talk to Lori has hit a fever pitch. I want to confide in her about everything that's going on. One thing I could count on before our falling out was her ability to make me laugh. I miss that.

The large window in the bathroom blows open, slamming against the wall. I flatten my hand over my chest at the startling sound. Wind flows through the space, ruffling my clothes as I approach to close the window. I shut it and click the latch. Girls usually come in here and smoke by the window, which probably explains why it was left open.

A gaggle of girls enters the bathroom, clucking like a bunch of hens. I duck into the nearest stall and perch myself on top of the toilet seat, pretending I'm not there.

"And here I thought Harrison was going to ask you to the dance, Sophia," I overhear.

"Chloe, I don't blame him for wanting to ask Drea," Sophia replies, piquing my attention. "She's the charity case of the season. First, she removes herself from all of her extracurriculars, and then her best friend is murdered. Harrison has always had a big heart when it comes to stuff like that."

My cheeks are lashed with heat from the anger building inside me. Her words feel like multiple daggers in my back. I can't believe my ears. Here I thought Sophia was my friend, my teammate, but she's just a stereotypical mean girl in sheep's clothing. I want to burst out of the stall and see the look on her face, but stop short when someone else chimes in.

"I hear that's not the only big thing he has," another girl says, causing the gaggle to giggle.

"Drea may have him for Homecoming, but I'll have him for Senior Prom. Just wait and see, ladies," Sophia vows.

"You might have him for Homecoming too, girl," Chloe says. "Once he sees you crowned queen, he may just drop Little Miss Pity Party."

"That's definitely one positive thing to come from Lori's death," says Sophia with a smarmy titter. "She won't take my votes for queen."

That's it. I can't sit here and listen to this any longer.

I rip the latch on the stall door to the side and throw it open, sending it crashing against the neighboring stall. "Unbelievable! I seriously can't believe you, Sophia." It takes everything inside of me not to haul off and smack her across the face. "You're an incredibly selfish asshole, you know that?"

All four of the girls spin to look at me. Their faces reflect their dismay. Sophia starts to say something, but I cut her off.

"You're all just a bunch of catty little bitches."

With that, I rush out of the bathroom, not giving them a chance to respond. I slam right into a solid body and tumble to the hallway floor. My bag slides off my arm. I watch the contents spill out, scattering across the hall. My ass twinges in pain after the hard impact. My eyes drift up to see Trent standing there.

Great, just when I thought things couldn't get any worse.

"Damn, Drea, sorry," he says, extending his hand out for mine.

I take it begrudgingly and he helps me to my feet.

"Yeah, well, I guess I was the one who ran into you, so no harm, no foul," I say as I begin to collect my things and stuff them back into my bag. He bends down to help me. "Please don't," I tell him. "I may have let you help me up, but this isn't some way for you to work off community service hours with me."

"You know what, Drea? I'm really trying here," he says as he stands back up.

"Trent, please stop trying so hard. One apology isn't going to make up for everything you've done."

"Fine. Have it your way."

I notice the hall is focused on our interaction. Then Sophia and her squad exit the bathroom and join the crowd watching us. Their presence has my anger mounting.

"Just leave me alone, okay?"

"Maybe you should listen to her, Trent," I hear Harrison say nearby. He moves past me and stands nose to nose with Trent.

"Harrison, stop. I don't need you fighting my battles for me, okay? I got this," I say through clenched teeth.

Trent says something in a whisper that I can't hear. It drives Harrison over the edge. He grabs Trent by the shirt collar and shoves him up against the locker. The crunch of the metal echoes through the hall along with a chorus of collective gasps.

I grab Harrison by the shoulder. "Stop it! He isn't worth this."

He turns to me, his face flushed. The football coach shouts from down the hall and Harrison releases his grip on Trent. He storms off when he notices the coach approaching through the gathered crowd.

The first bell rings and the halls begin to empty. My eyes move over to Trent, who is busy adjusting his shirt's collar.

"I hope you're satisfied with yourself," he says, glaring at me.

All of the anger drains from me at once. "Not really," I murmur before taking off toward my first class.

I need to be better than this.

TWENTY-FOUR

Donovan

I WAS SUPPOSED TO BE OFF WORK TODAY. IT WAS SUPPOSED to be a day I could put most of my focus on Connor. Then Marcus sent me an SOS text requesting my help. The owner was scheduled to be here to assist him but had to bail at the last minute due to a family emergency. So, here I am.

For a Thursday, it's been pretty slow at The Pour Over. Thursdays are usually our busiest days, mostly full of students trying to get in some last-minute studying for tests on Friday. But today is the day of a special sporting event. I've never lived someplace where football is lauded this much as the one thing that brings the town together. Hell, even Marcus considered going, but only for a minute, and he loathes sports.

"We're closing up early tonight for the big game, remember?" he calls out to me from the back room. "I never get used to hearing myself say that."

His laugh has me reacting with one of my own.

"Yeah," I say. "I've already cleaned all the empty tables and taken out the trash from behind the counter and by the entrance."

He emerges from the back. "I realize this will sound very

un-Marcus like, but I think this game is exactly what this town needs right now. To come together and catch their breath after what's happened," he says somberly before ducking away again.

I guess it's a nice distraction, but I bet Lori's family and loved ones won't get the same from the game as the rest of the town. I, for one, am firmly in the camp of still a little paranoid about who did it.

I remove the pastry items from the display cabinet and begin making a box full of food donations for the local homeless shelter. It's one of the owner's big contributions to the community. He loves giving back.

The entrance door chimes, pulling my attention. It's Deputy Owens.

"Afternoon, deputy. How may I help you?" I ask with a smile.

He removes his hat and sunglasses. "Hey, Donovan. I didn't realize you worked here," he says, tucking his aviator glasses into the V-shaped opening at the top of his buttoned-up shirt.

"Yeah, been working here since the summer. Mainly on the weekends, but I pick up shifts here and there during the week after school too," I reply.

"Guess that makes sense why I've never seen you here. You're at school when I make my coffee runs for the department."

"Yeah. Hey, I know it's probably a long shot, me asking this, but have there been any developments with Lori's case?"

He shakes his head. "They're ruling things out little by little, but there's just not much evidence. I'd love to be able to give you more details, but I'm kind of out of the loop now myself."

"No, I get that. I appreciate whatever you can tell me," I reply, and then notice two more customers line up behind him. "So, can I get you anything?"

He takes a peek over his shoulder and realizes he's holding up the line. "Uh, is Marcus here?"

"Yeah, he's in the back. Want me to get him for you?"

"No, that's okay. If you could just tell him to call me after you close up," he replies.

I.

Am.

Gagged.

Why does Deputy Owens want Marcus to call him? Why does Marcus have his phone number?

The deputy places his hat back on his head and tips it toward me. "Have a good night at the game."

"Thanks. I'll have as good a night as I can while watching football," I reply with a chuckle.

He makes his exit and I tend to the next two customers. I poke my head into the back area and see Marcus returning from taking out the trash.

A grin sprouts on my face. "Uh, question, Marcus."

"Yeah. What's up?"

He's focused on replacing the trash bags in the empty bins and misses the look on my face. I lean up against the frame of the door and glance back to the entrance to make sure there are no customers waiting. There aren't. My eyes return to Marcus.

"Inquiring minds would love to know why Deputy Owens is looking for you."

He stiffens and then a smile tugs at his mouth. "Oh, is he here?" he asks, tossing a coy look my way.

"He was, but he left. He said for you to call him when you're done here."

He looks as though he's trying not to fully express his happiness. "Oh, okay. Thanks for letting me know."

He isn't fooling me with this "playing it cool" routine.

"So, are you two…?"

"Maybe," he replies with a dismissive wave. "We've got work to do, sir."

"How did this happen?" I ask, elated by the news. I think I'm receiving some of his glee through osmosis.

"Work first, then gossip," he says sternly, but his lips continue to struggle to keep the smile from creeping across them.

"Truth while we work," I counteroffer, placing my hands on my hips.

He rolls his eyes. "Fine," he says, prompting a pleased grin to light up my face. "He comes in here almost every day to get coffee. We've talked here and there, but it wasn't until we bumped into each other at Mae's that I knew he was bi. We just kind of hit it off, you know? It's no big deal, really."

I'm not convinced of that. His body language is telling a completely different story.

He likes him. I can't blame him. Deputy Owens is a catch for real.

"That's awesome, Marcus."

"Uh-uh. Don't do that."

"Do what?"

"Make more out of this than there is."

"You two are so cute together though," I say in a playful tone.

"Get out," he demands with a finger point. I open my mouth on another reply and he repeats, "Get out."

I grin at him. My eyes trail out to look at the café. It's a ghost town. It appears the last customer has left. The clock on the wall shows it's two minutes past closing, so I move over to the door and lock it before flipping the flimsy metal sign to closed. My phone buzzes in my pocket and I pull it out to see a text from Drea.

I can't find the diary anywhere. Did I give it to you? I could have sworn I had it with me at lunch.

I think back to lunch and try to remember if I saw her with the diary, but come away with nothing.

Nope, I don't have it. Could you have put it in your locker or left it somewhere?

The dots show up at the bottom of the message chain as she types her reply. Then it comes through.

I've checked everywhere. I still need to go home before the game. Let me know if you remember anything. And let me know when you get there with Connor. Even without the diary, I still have questions for him.

I type out, **Sounds good,** and then hit send before resuming packing up the box of food donations for the shelter. Connor's truck appears in my peripherals as it pulls up in front of the café and parks.

I thought we were meeting at my house.

He rounds his truck and makes his way to the entrance. I meet him there, click the lock, and crack the door open so we don't have to talk through the glass. The first thing I notice are his eyes. They're shifty and apprehensive. Standoffish, even. A direct contrast to the slight smile on his face. When he looks at me, I see the worry just below the surface of his poor attempt at forced happiness he's displaying on his lips.

"Hey, what's going on?" I ask.

His smile fades as his hands dive into his pockets and hang out there. His shoulders tilt forward and his gaze shifts down to the sign on the door. "I forgot you guys were closing early today. Is it too late for me to come in?"

"Sorry. Marcus will be counting the money from the till soon. No one's allowed in when that's happening. Is something wrong? I thought we were meeting at my house."

A heavy breath leaves his lips. "I went to your house first, but you weren't there. One of your aunts said you were at work. I know I could've just texted you, but I wanted to do this in person, especially after the last time when I practically stood you up."

My heart sinks. I'm not liking where this is going.

"Is something wrong?" I ask, desperately wanting him to spit it out.

His gaze drops to the ground. He rakes his fingers through his hair, pausing at the back of his neck. When his eyes meet mine again, my mind searches feverishly for an explanation as to why he's acting like this, almost as if I'm looking up symptoms on Web M.D. and come to find I have a life-threatening disease.

"No one has seen Shaun since last night," he says at last. "We have no idea where he is."

His voice cracks a little at the end. I immediately feel guilty for thinking this had something to do with us. I reach out to touch his arm.

"Really?" I ask. "No one has seen him? Not even his family?"

He shakes his head. "We've been calling his phone all day, but it just goes to voicemail. With what happened to Lori, we're all on edge and don't know what to do."

I open the door the rest of the way and step outside to wrap my arms around him. He squeezes me tight and I reciprocate.

"He'll show up, I'm sure of it."

"I hope so," he says near my ear. "This is just not like him."

"Do you want me to help? I'm almost done here. We could ditch the game and start looking for places you think he might be."

He pulls back to look at me. "It's really sweet of you to offer, but the group's meeting soon to form some kind of search party."

"Did you report this to the sheriff's office?"

"Yeah, we did earlier."

"I can still ditch the game and help you look," I offer with a hesitant smile.

"No, you should go." He looks exhausted. "I really appreciate you wanting to help though."

"Well, let me know if I can do anything, okay?" I say, taking hold of his hand. He gives it a quick squeeze.

"Thank you. I'll make this up to you, promise," he says, and that signature smile finally appears on his face.

"What about coming to the Homecoming dance with me tomorrow then?" I ask without thinking.

His smile wavers, and I mentally face palm at my inconsiderate question. Of course he's not going to want to go to the dance while his friend is missing.

What is wrong with me?

"Sorry, that was a stupid question, and horribly timed," I say. "Damn word vomit."

He leans close. "It's not a stupid question at all. I'll let you know tonight, okay?" He places a quick peck on my cheek before turning to leave.

I'm shook.

My hand trails up to my cheek and lands on the place where his lips just made contact. It's burning hot, and I stand there dumbfounded in bliss. He sends me a little wave before getting into his truck and driving off. I snap out of it when I hear tapping on the glass door behind me. It's Marcus.

"Boy, what are you doing? We got things to do," he says with a pointed stare.

I reach for the door handle and then it hits me.

Wait, Drea wanted to talk to Connor tonight.

TWENTY-FIVE

Drea

CHEERLEADING USED TO BRING ME SO MUCH JOY. It was one of the few things I looked forward to. It kept me striving for my goals and pushing myself to do things outside my comfort zone. It also introduced me to people I thought I'd never be friends with.

Lori used to tease me about cheerleading. She always said to watch my back, and if I didn't, she'd be right there if things ever went south with the squad. It's true that sometimes people can be too close to something to see the truth. Sitting in the stands at the Homecoming game and watching Sophia and her squad perform their little routine makes me regret spending so much time and energy on them.

The crowd, on the other hand, is living for them. They're cheering along with every chant and sending them roaring applause at every tumble and cartwheel they perform. I'm probably one of the few sitting here defiantly not participating. The things they said earlier are on repeat in my mind. I grip the metal bench tight, trying to work through my frustration over the entire situation.

The ultimate betrayal.

Donovan has yet to make an appearance. The game is about to begin and there hasn't even been one text exchanged. I take out my phone and type out a message.

Hey, where are you?

A few moments go by before he responds.

Change of plans. Had to take my bike. Be there soon.

A cold wind sweeps by, causing me to regret not having my coat. I foolishly left it in the car. This is becoming a bad habit of mine, forgetting things in car. I was so preoccupied with getting here on time to meet Donovan that grabbing it completely slipped my mind. Now that the sun is all but set, the wind is on cut-to-the-bone setting. I clutch my bag over my lap and pull it closer to my chest to help shield myself from the cruel breeze.

The band strikes up into the song "Go, Fight, Win," and the crowd erupts into a chant right along with it. Any other time, I'd be right there with them. Hell, I'd be leading the chant. But my mind is more than just a little distracted at the moment.

Two of the male cheerleaders flank our team's entrance to the field with the paper Homecoming banner that hung in the halls stretched between them. Two more cheerleaders join them with large confetti cannons as the band begins to play our school song. The cannons blast off and our team rushes the field. They tear through the banner, leaving it in tatters in their wake. Harrison leads the pack with rest of the players close behind. For a moment I wonder how he's doing after his little spat with Trent this morning.

Oh, to have been a fly on the wall in the locker room.

Then a thought occurs to me. As I trace back to the incident this morning—just before it, actually—

I remember crashing into Trent and my stuff going everywhere. Like a puzzle piece falling into place, I wonder if Trent took the diary for some reason. He was the only one helping me pick up my stuff.

Was I that distracted that I didn't notice? And why didn't this occur to me before now? My poor frazzled brain.

I see Donovan out of the corner of my eye making his way up the stands and I wave him over. He's alone. "Where's your date?"

"Yeah, he's not coming. That was the change in plans," he replies, and it seems something is weighing on him.

I make room for him as he moves down the long metal bleacher. "Is everything okay?" I probe as he takes a seat next to me.

"Not really, no. One of his friends may have gone missing," he explains in a somber tone.

"What? Missing? This is all too weird."

"Yeah, tell me about it."

"Are you going to be okay?" I ask as I pull him in for a side hug. Mostly to be sympathetic, but also partly because I'm freezing.

"Yeah. It's not me that I'm worried about though."

"Connor?"

"Exactly. I want to help, but I feel helpless, you know? And it's not like he wants me too either. It's making our whole situation confusing."

"I'm sorry, Donovan. Believe me, I understand more than you know," I reply. "Just give him space. I'm sure I don't have to remind you that we're all going through some serious stuff right now."

"I know. You're right."

I'm trying hard not to mention how I still want to talk to Connor and his group about all the questions I have. I realize it's probably not a good time to bring it up, but when will it be?

"Did you find the diary?" he asks, shifting out of the side hug.

I shake my head. "Nope, but speaking of," I say when my eyes spot Trent standing alone near the edge of the field doing stretches. "Could you hold our seats for a second? I need to go check on something."

"Sure."

Trent never leaves my sight as I make my descent. I weave through the line waiting for the concession stand and move to where he's stretching. I have to confront him about the diary. I have to get to the bottom of this. Things just don't disappear into thin air.

He sees me and sneers before turning his attention elsewhere.

"I have a question for you," I say.

"Not interested."

"Did you pick up a diary this morning when you tried to help me with my stuff?" I ask, even though his body language yells *go away*.

He doesn't answer.

"Well? Did you?" I ask again, but a little more forceful this time.

He turns to face me and huffs while taking a few steps forward. He grips the top of the fence separating us as his eyes meet mine. I catch a glimpse of Harrison watching this whole exchange from over Trent's shoulder.

"Why would I take your diary?" he replies tersely.

"It isn't mine. It belonged to Carrie Phillips."

His eyes narrow. His face gives him away. He seems surprised to hear her name.

"I don't have time for this," he says. He releases his grip on the fence and takes a couple of steps back. "Go Nancy Drew somewhere else, all right?"

"So you didn't take it?"

"Again, why would I?" he barks, sounding super defensive. "Now, if you don't mind, I have a scout to impress tonight, so get lost."

"You owe me, Trent."

He eats up the space between us, flames in his eyes. "I don't owe you crap, okay? I didn't do anything to you or Lori, so there's nothing to owe you," he seethes in a whisper before storming off toward the bench.

We'll see about that.

Sophia is at the end of the concession line when I head back to my seat. Our eyes find each other's instantly, and just as quickly, she looks away. I have this sudden urge to slap her upside the head, but instead take the high road and pass by without incident.

"Hey, Drea, wait up," I hear her call out from behind me.

This should be good.

I spin around and am met by her famous forced cheerleader smile. Actually, it's just her regular smile. I'm just pissed at her, and every little thing she does bothers me. I cross my arms over my chest and lean to the side, putting all of my weight on my hip, letting her know she better make this worthwhile. To be honest, I'm not even sure why I'm giving her any time after the things she said. I refuse to be the first one to talk.

"About this morning," she begins, "I know what we all said was terrible. Unforgivable, even. It's just how some of us are dealing with the things that are happening around us."

A scoff flies from my mouth at her audacity. "Wait. So let me get this straight. The way you deal with death is by being a horrible person?"

"Okay, I deserve that. You know what? I am horrible. But at least I own up to it. That's more than I can say for some people."

Is she for real right now?

My face stings from the heat spreading across my cheeks. My heart pounds as I try to bite back what I'm about to say. My teeth clench to halt the stream of choice words forthcoming. I draw in a deep breath and stare her square in the eyes.

"What exactly is that supposed to mean?"

A whistle sounds, announcing the start of the game. "I've got to get back out there," she says before heading off to the sidelines.

I'm left standing there with all this pent up aggression, watching her saunter off. I'm seriously at a loss of what to say or do. I rejoin Donovan in the stands with Sophia's words replaying in my head.

"What was that all about?"

Donovan's question cuts through my thoughts.

"Which thing?" I ask.

"Both."

I grumble. "Well, it occurred to me that maybe Trent took the diary this morning after the incident I told you about."

"Oh, yeah. The one where Harrison defended your honor."

"Yeah, but I didn't ask him to," I say, then shake my head. "Getting away from the point. Trent claims he didn't take it, but who knows who can be trusted right now?"

"Truer words have never been spoken," he agrees. "What about Sophia?"

"Oh, you know, just a continuation of *The Young and the Restless* Haddon Falls High edition," I say in jest, but in all reality, it's much more serious than that. I guess oddly placed humor is winning out today.

"Connor might be going to the Homecoming dance with me tomorrow night," Donovan says offhand. Something on the field has the crowd groaning in unison. When it settles, he continues, "So, maybe you can talk to him about Carrie if you go. Or you could tell me what you want to ask and I can ask him for you."

"I wasn't really planning on going to the dance, to be honest. Maybe though. I don't know. I don't see why you couldn't ask him questions yourself though," I say, just feeling all kinds of conflicted.

"Okay. Let's plan on that then," he says.

Our attention is drawn to the field again when the crowd erupts with cheers. Our team just intercepted a pass and is running it in for a touchdown. A collective moan rolls through the stands when there's a tackle before that happens. My response to the reactions of the crowd serves as a reminder of how very little I care about this game. I can sense Donovan's in the same boat since he keeps staring at his phone every three seconds.

"Have you heard from Connor yet?" I ask when he pulls his phone out again.

"No, I haven't. Is it weird that I'm this worried about someone I've only known for such a short time?" he asks, facing me and dropping his phone to his lap. His eyes fill with concern.

I shake my head. "No, especially with what's going on. It's natural to worry about someone you care about. Have you tried texting him?"

He nods. "A few times. I feel like an overprotective parent or something. I hope it's not annoying him."

"It isn't, promise."

"Hey, I think I'm going to get something from the snack bar. Want anything?" he asks, making his way to his feet. "I think I need to eat my feelings."

"I'm good. Thanks though," I reply and he takes off down the stairs.

My focus shifts back to the game. Trent snaps the ball to Harrison, who takes a few steps back, surveying the field for an open receiver. I find myself getting sucked into the game all of a sudden. Maybe it's serving as a good distraction, or it could have something to do with a certain quarterback.

Quit it, brain.

Harrison decides to try and run the ball in since they're close to a first down, but misses it shy of the line and is tackled to the ground. They set up for the next play and Trent goes to hike the ball to Harrison, but it fumbles from the hand-off. Trent stands up and puts his arms out, challenging Harrison. He pounds on his chest with his palm and the next thing I know, they're going at it, blow by blow. Then they're on the ground rolling around like one of those fights from a cartoon where it's just a dust cloud with limbs flailing around. Their teammates try to pull them off of one another, but to no avail. The stands erupt into jeers and boos. Whistle after whistle blares from the referees until they're able to separate them. One of the referees points at both of them and then off the field. Shock takes hold of the crowd as the jeers simmer.

Did they both just get ejected from the game?

I watch as they stomp off the field. The coach holds Harrison back, allowing some space between him and Trent as Trent continues past the stands and back toward the school. The coach tugs on the front grill of Harrison's helmet and proceeds to say something I presume is heated based solely on his facial expressions alone.

I hurry from the stands and bump into Donovan on his way back. "Holy crap, did you see what just happened?" he asks.

"Yeah, and I need to go catch Harrison before he leaves," I say, patting his arm and moving past him.

When I reach the bottom of the bleachers, I see Harrison in the distance moving toward the school. He looks to have a death grip on the windbreaker jacket in his left hand. His body exudes rage. I can almost see the steam pouring off of him.

"Harrison, hold up," I call out, but he keeps walking as if he didn't hear me. "Harrison, please."

He stops, but doesn't turn around. He snaps off his helmet and tucks it under his arm. "What?" he asks, low and breathy. He still refuses to face me.

"Can you look at me, please?" I ask. I can tell he's conflicted over it.

He slowly spins around. His eyes slam into mine before turning away. I expect him to say something, anything, but he doesn't. Radio silence.

"What happened out there?" I ask, taking a step forward.

He takes a step back. "Oh, you mean when Trent and I blew our damn chances with the scout in the stands? That?"

"Yeah, that."

He lets out a frustrated sigh. "That's between that jerk and myself, okay?"

"Okay, well, what was with this morning then?" I ask, needing him to answer at least one of my questions fully.

He goes silent. His hazel eyes shine in the stadium lights as they stare into mine. "Look, it's no secret that Trent gets around," he says at last. "He's always gone after the girls I like, has been doing it since middle school. It's been this little rivalry between us and one of the main reasons I can't stand him. He took Sam in sixth grade. Maddie in seventh grade. Carrie in eighth grade. Alex sophomore year," he explains, counting off each girl on his fingers. "I wasn't about to let him do that to you too."

I'm knocked speechless. Floored. Unable to form even the slightest of syllables.

"He decided to remind me this morning of when he tried to get with you at the party near the end of the summer. I was the one who found you passed out on the couch, and the mere thought of him taking advantage of you like that tore through me." He pauses for a moment, his eyes still locked on mine. "I know it's pretty obvious, but I like you, Drea. Have for a long time. And I wasn't about to let you fall prey to that asshole. That's why I did what I did this morning."

Did he just say what I think he did?

My heart melts into a puddle on the grass, and I just continue to stare into his intense expression. Then it moderates. No one has ever talked that openly with me before. But when the dust settles from his bold declaration, the rest of his confession sinks in.

"Wait, you took me upstairs? Not Trent?" I ask. He nods. "So, he was telling the truth about that then?" He nods again. My eyes narrow. "Wait. Why was I in my underwear?"

"You had an accident," he explains. "I think you can come to the conclusion yourself of what happened with the alcohol. Lori was the one who undressed you."

What the actual hell? Lori knew about this!?

"Wait, Lori helped you?"

"Yeah. She didn't tell you?" he replies with a look of confusion.

"No … she didn't." My heart aches over this revelation.

How could she let me go all that time thinking it was Trent who did this to me?

Betrayal wrecks my gut and shreds my heart. I feel like I'm going insane. Dizziness overruns me like I'm stuck spinning around on one of those sketchy carnival rides at the county fair. I get lost in my mind and feelings for a moment until Harrison's voice filters in again.

"I'm sorry. I thought you knew."

"Are you telling me the truth?"

"I wouldn't lie to you, Drea," he says. "That's the very last thing I'd do."

"None of this makes any sense," I argue. "Why wouldn't she tell me about this?"

He shrugs. "I don't know. But it's the truth, I promise."

"Okay," I reply in a daze.

I'm not even sure which way is up right now. My knees feel weak, like they're going to collapse at any moment. Tears mist my eyes. When I look up at Harrison, the last scraps of anger have left his face. His eyes take on a blue hue in this light.

A sigh escapes his lips. "Are you going to be okay?"

I swallow hard, trying to stop the tears from falling. "I don't know."

The next thing I know, my face is firmly planted against Harrison's chest. He just holds me. A warmth I haven't felt in a long time spreads across my entire body as we continue to stand here.

"You should probably hit the showers," I say, leaning back to look at him.

"Do I offend?" he asks with a smirk. "I've actually been told I have a pleasant natural smell of lemons."

"Please don't make me laugh right now," I say, releasing a hollow giggle through the tears.

"That's one thing I'll never stop doing," he confesses as he stares down at me. I hide my face in his chest again while swiping away the straggling tears.

We part, but there's still the same warmth present that I felt while in his arms draped around my shoulders. Harrison's jacket. He put it around me before taking a step back and moving away.

I drift into some sort of trance while watching him leave. All the facts whirl around in my mind like an emotion tornado. The farther he gets, the more my mood shifts to sadness, as if his presence provided some kind of calming positive energy through all the emotions coursing through me. A distraction. Then the remorse kicks in. I'm somewhat responsible for all of this. Every decision I've made. Every feeling I've felt. Every single one of the opinions I formed after that night at the party was wrong. Completely and spectacularly wrong. I'm the saboteur.

What have I done?

A pink glowing light catches my eye from under the bleachers when I turn around. A shrouded figure stands there watching me. They're wearing some sort of mask outlined with pink neon lights in the shape of a fox head. The person waves to me slow and methodical, almost robotic.

I shiver at the creepiness of the person's actions. They just stand there, moving their hand back and forth. Then it hits me. Donovan said he saw someone dressed like that at the bar, and the mask looks just like the outline on Carrie's diary like he mentioned. I dig into my bag for my cell to snap a pic of the person, but when I look back up with the phone ready, they're gone.

What the hell? Where did they go?

TWENTY-SIX

Donovan

FIVE TEXTS.

That's how many I've sent Connor that have gone unanswered. I'm trying to give him space, which is why I haven't called him yet, but I'd be lying if I said I wasn't itching to do that as well.

Maybe it's just how dark it is on my ride home, or the fact Drea said she may have seen the same masked figure I did at the game, but I'm kind of wigging out right now. It's deathly quiet, almost uncomfortably so. The only sounds I have to keep me company are my own humming and the strain of the bike chain as it clinks with every full rotation.

I keep thinking how wonderful it would be to be in a certain someone's truck, but that certain someone isn't even returning my texts.

Please let everything be okay.

This is yet another occasion where I wish I had a car instead of this bike that I love so much. There are no doors I can lock or windows to roll up tight. It's an old bike. I've had to fix it a few times. The pedals in particular, but it's been dependable … mostly.

The wind rips through my thin hoodie. It stings like an exposed nerve.

I should have layered up more.

Most of the houses along this street are dark. Lifeless. I take mental notes of the select few with their porch lights on and use them as checkpoints while trying to escape the ever-encroaching night. I can barely see past where the sporadic streetlights shine pockets of light onto the road. In the long stretches of darkness, I feel like I'm out in the middle of the ocean looking for the next lighthouse to guide me to shore, while at any moment I could be attacked by a great white shark.

My pocket vibrates, and I stall under one of the lampposts. I rest the bike between my legs with my feet firmly planted on the ground and dig in my pocket for my phone. I can't dig fast enough, cursing my pockets for being so tight. There's a text from Connor.

Sorry for my lack of contact. Been a crazy night. Still nothing from Shaun. Not sure what to do.

My heart goes out to him and his group. They just lost Lori, and now Shaun's MIA.

Then something hits me that I could never bring up to Connor. The kind of implication that could cause a major rift between us.

What if Shaun had something to do Lori's death and now he's run away?

I begin to type out a reply. I pause at the sound of light rustling in the near vicinity. In the still of the night, it resembles someone pulling a rake through leaves. My eyes dart around, looking for the source, but can't find it.

There's a house to my right that has gone perfectly overboard with their Halloween decorations. It's an elaborate cemetery setup with a full wrought iron gate façade. There are headstones of all shapes and sizes full of cracks and covered in grassy moss scattered about. A grouping of white sheet ghosts are gathered around the graves, but there's also the subtle outline of a lone black sheet ghost amongst them.

My eyes drop back to my phone since there are more important things to deal with than taking in the spooky display. I continue stamping out my text to Connor. Leaves crunch nearby again and my head snaps up quickly in hopes of catching the source of the sound. But I still don't see anything.

A feeling of being watched creeps in. It has me glancing all around, surveying my surroundings. Almost every house is dark except for the decorated one. My main source of light is the lamppost I'm currently positioned underneath.

A false cone of safety.

A heavy gust of wind sweeps by. It swirls through the trees and sends loose leaves tumbling along the sidewalk beside me. Then it falls silent again almost immediately. My eyes wander back over to the yard with the cemetery, and I take comfort in the fact nothing seems out of place.

Then I realize the black sheet ghost is gone. My eyes scan the yard feverishly, landing on two tall trees flanking the driveway. A figure resembling the ghost lingers there, just behind one of the trees.

What the hell?

My fight or flight response revs up the longer I watch the still, shrouded figure standing there. Its featureless face feels like it's staring directly through me. My phone vibrates again, scaring the ever-living crap out of me. It's a message from Drea.

Made it home safely. Hope you did too.

I return my attention to the tree. The figure is gone.

My heart leaps into my throat. I struggle to slip my phone back into my pocket. A sharp clang nearby sends me into high alert. Dread sours my stomach. The wrought iron gate rattles, but there wasn't a gust of wind to cause it. My eyes rise from my pocket to the gate.

The dark figure is standing there. But unlike it did from far away, this doesn't look like another decoration in the yard. It's a person. A flash of bright pink neon reveals their fox head mask as they take a step forward.

I place my feet back on the bike pedals to take off. My right foot slips and a sharp pain surges from my ankle up to my shin. The footsteps of the person grow louder the closer they get. I panic and push through the ache to correct my leg position. I press firmly on the pedal. It breaks clean off.

Fuck!

The figure is mere feet away. I see a glint of something gripped tightly in their right hand. I ditch the bike and shove it in their direction. I don't stick around to see if it connected, I just start running.

My lungs burn like a furnace as I maintain top speed. It's painfully obvious how out of shape I am even with my trim build. The pain on my shin from the bike pedal has become a fleeting memory as I just keep sprinting as fast as I can.

"Help!" I cry out, hoping to see any of the porch lights turn on. "Please, help!"

I peek over my shoulder and see the figure too close for comfort. The mask's neon lights are dark. There's just a shrouded form nipping on my heels. I pump my legs harder than I thought I could, counting on the massive amounts of adrenaline coursing through my system to keep me alive.

I take a sharp turn down a side street and cut through someone's yard. After clearing two knee-high hedgerows like they were hurdles on a racetrack, I transition out onto the main road. My head whips around to look behind me and no one's there. Just darkness. I struggle to catch my breath while surveying the area.

Where the hell did they go?

I draw out my phone and continue moving hastily down the street. I dial 911. Moments later, a person's voice comes through. My response is cut short by the screech of tires on asphalt. Headlights blind me. I'm stunned still. I was so focused on making the call that I didn't realize I'd stepped out into the middle of a four-way stop. I'm like a deer caught in headlights, staring at literal headlights. The dispatcher comes through the phone again, but I can't muster the words to reply. They hang up. Yellow and green lights flash from on top of the vehicle, snapping me out of my daze.

"Donovan? What are you doing?" Deputy Owens asks as he steps out of his vehicle.

I hurry over to him, relief washing over me. A stream of rambling pours from my mouth, and by the look on his face I can tell what I'm saying makes little sense.

"Hold up, calm down. Just tell me what happened," he says in a composed manner.

"Someone was chasing me. They looked like they had a knife or something," I say, still trying to catch my breath after rattling everything off.

"Well I don't see anyone here now, so maybe it was just some practical joker giving you a hard time," he says. "Things tend to get a little crazy around here during Homecoming. Also, why are you out here alone? Were you walking home from the game?"

I shake my head. "No, I had a bike, but I ditched it a few streets over when the person started chasing me."

"Here, get in the car. I'll take you back to your bike. Then we'll get you home. Sound good?"

"I can't," I reply. "The pedal's busted. I wouldn't be able to ride it home even if I wanted to."

The deputy smiles. "You're in luck. This vehicle just so happens to have a bike rack on the back. Come on, let's go collect it."

"Sure, I guess."

As we approach the scene of the incident, my bike it not where I left it. It's lying on the sidewalk.

"You stay here. I'll handle this," Deputy Owens states before heading outside.

I watch him roll the bike toward the rear of the vehicle. The car shifts slightly as he mounts and secures my bike to the rack. He returns to the driver's seat and settles in before handing me the broken pedal.

"I thought you might want this back," he says.

I nod. "Thanks."

"Oh, and I found this wedged in the spokes. It might explain your little run-in with the person from before." He hands me a flyer for the Neon MasqueRave Ball. "Not to downplay what the person did to you, but maybe it was some extreme publicity stunt."

"Yeah, I don't think so," I say, reliving the fear I felt as I stare out the window at the creepy Halloween yard display.

It most definitely felt like a real threat.

TWENTY-SEVEN

Drea

I MADE A PROMISE TO MYSELF THAT I'D AVOID SOCIAL MEDIA like the plague after Lori's death, but here I am breaking it a second time after snooping around for Carrie last night. I find myself searching through all of Lori's pictures for any trace or mention of Carrie. Or really any answers at all. After tonight's full disclosure moment with Harrison, I'm at a loss for how to feel about anything. To say my trust in people has leaned heavily into negative territory is putting it lightly. It's as if I've been sleepwalking through life for the past two years of high school, just accepting everything at face value. But life sure as hell has a way of waking you up.

I dive into her photos from eighth grade and begin sifting through picture by picture. Lori sure did take a lot.

One photo catches my attention, not because it has Lori and another girl dancing together, but it's the third girl in the picture next to Lori that piques my interest. The original tags were Lori, Carrie, and a girl named Nancy, but they're no longer clickable. She looks like the girl I met at Lori's house who was babysitting her little brother. Older now obviously, and a different haircut, but similar enough.

Should I message her? She seems to have known Carrie too.

For a moment, I contemplate sending her a message. Then I realize I have to be friends with her first.

Well crap.

I shoot her a friend request. Now all I can do is wait. But this is the least of my worries. I still have no idea why Lori never told me about what she and Harrison did the night of that party. Why did I pass out in the first place? Did someone actually put something in my drink? My head begins to throb with all the thoughts assaulting it.

The other element I'm at odds with is whether Harrison's actions were sweet or weird. In a way, I kind of feel like this strange prize he and Trent were fighting over, but then his recent behavior and his admission of liking me has me questioning that line of thinking.

Maybe Harrison is the real deal.

My eyes trail over to his black and red windbreaker lying on the end of my bed and a contemplative sigh parts my lips. My phone pings next to me on the desk. It's a text from Donovan. I've been waiting on a reply for a while now, and I'm relieved he finally sent me something.

Can I call you? I need to speak with you ASAP!

My first reaction is to reply back with **of course**, but then I just decide to call him myself. It rings once before he answers.

"Drea, I was attacked tonight," are the first words out of his mouth.

Worry clutches my gut at the desperate tone in his voice. He sounds serious.

"Are you okay? Who attacked you?" I reply.

"I'm okay as I can be, I guess. It was someone wearing that fox mask," he says.

A sudden chill spirals all over my body. My hairs stand on end and numerous goosebumps form over my arms and legs.

"Did you report this?" I ask.

He releases a sigh. "Yeah. Deputy Owens was the one who helped me get home. My bike's out of commission for the time being though. He's aware of the situation, but thinks maybe it was someone just messing around. He found a flyer for the Homecoming dance on my bike and thinks this may have been a stunt or something."

"You don't actually believe that, do you?" I ask, not completely convinced myself.

"With all the things going on, I have no idea what to believe. I even thought maybe this person left this on my bike to say that something big is going to happen tomorrow. Am I being too paranoid?"

I can tell by his voice he's anxious. "Who can we tell that will believe us?" I ask.

"I have no idea. There's no evidence that anything has happened other than what I witnessed. But what if Deputy Owens is right and this was just a sick prank? Like, let's prank the new guy or something."

"I honestly don't know," I say. A moment of silence falls between us. "Have you heard any updates from Connor?"

"Yeah, in that there are no updates. They still can't find their friend. And when I told him about what happened tonight, he freaked."

The power cuts out, plunging my entire room into darkness except for the streetlight pouring through the open curtains of the solitary window in my room. A small gasp escapes my throat.

"What was that?" he asks.

"The power just went out." I look out the window and it seems we're the only house that's been affected. "It's probably the damn breaker. We've been having issues with it lately."

"Are you home alone?"

The quaver in his voice sets my nerves on alert. "Yeah. My

parents are a couple houses down having drinks with our neighbors for their Thursday night couples' gathering, and my little sister is at her friend's house."

"And you're sure it's the breaker?"

"I hope so." The gravity of my situation finally settles in. "You don't think this could be for some other reason, do you?"

"Where's the breaker?"

"The basement. But my dad showed me how to restart it in case something like this ever happened."

"I'm staying on the phone with you."

His voice is still unsteady. I won't lie, he's making me more than just a little nervous. After everything that's happened recently, what if this isn't just a random power outage? Flashes of chase scenes from countless scary movies fill my mind.

"I'm putting you on speaker so I can use my phone's flashlight, okay?"

"Good idea."

"Here I go. Off to the basement," I say, but fail to move.

Dammit, I'm officially that girl.

The phone's cone of light shines on the closed bedroom door. A few coats clutter the hooks installed on the back of it, looking like a person standing there. I draw in a lengthy breath and, after a sharp exhale, move toward it. My hand hesitates on the door handle before twisting it open. The door creaks as if protesting being woken up from a nap.

Never noticed that sound before.

I immediately point the light down the hall. Everything seems normal. Nothing's out of place.

Donovan's soft breaths through the phone have me on edge. My heart thumps harder within my chest. With every step I take toward the stairs, my heart seems to pick up the pace. Donovan's breathing stops coming through.

"Hey, you still there?" I ask.

"Yeah," he responds immediately. The sudden loud response startles me as it echoes loudly through the hallway. "You okay?"

"Yep, just scaring the hell out of myself, that's all," I reply with a hollow laugh.

I'm trying to keep my cool, but knowing that Donovan was attacked tonight on his way home, I can't help but think this whole thing may not just be the breaker. Again with the horror movies. I regret ever watching a single one right now.

I reach the stairs and begin my descent to the first floor. I keep to the carpet runner going down the middle of the steps since I'm sure the bare wood is freezing cold. The stairs squeak under the pressure of each footstep.

"What was that?" Donovan asks, again making me jump.

I hit the volume button on the side of the phone to lower it to a less jarring level. "Donnie, I really appreciate you doing this, but I think I'm going to need you to be a silent observer here," I say breathlessly.

"Got it, sorry."

"Completely fine," I say and keep moving down the stairs.

Just as I thought, the wooden floor is freaking freezing. A shiver shoots up my leg when my bare foot touches it. I retract instantly and then step down fully like I'm testing the water in a swimming pool before jumping in. The silence of the house grows uncomfortable. All-encompassing. It amplifies every groan of the floorboards under my feet. With every creak, I jump like I've seen a pop-out scare from an actor in a haunted house attraction.

If someone's in here, they've got to know where I am.

My phone's light casts on the umbrella stand near the front door, revealing a potentially good weapon choice. My mom's ornamental wooden cane. It's affixed with metal pins of the flags from all the places she's traveled to, making it even more ideal to bash someone over the head with if the need arises. I retrieve it and keep moving toward the kitchen.

"Okay, I've made it to the door leading to the basement."

The door usually looks like a normal door, but for some reason it appears menacing in the dark with my phone's light pointed at it. The feeling of eyes on me sets in. I dart the phone around the kitchen and then down the hall toward the front door, but see nothing out of the ordinary.

"Have you gone in the basement yet?" he asks.

"Doing that now," I say, grabbing the door's handle.

The doorknob's mechanism clicks as it disengages. It rings out within the space, sounding loud in the quiet. The door slowly creaks open, but unlike my bedroom door, this one groans like it's in desperate need of some WD-40. It sounds ancient, like a door that's been sealed for hundreds of years.

"Okay, that's damn creepy sounding," he says.

"Donnie? What did I say?"

"Oh, yeah, right. Sorry."

Staring into the basement is how I imagine looking into a black hole would be. It's considerably darker than the rest of the house. As I shine the light down the stairs, it seems to be swallowed up, barely reaching the third step in front of me. But there are way more stairs than that between me and the breaker box.

This sucks so much ass right now.

My hand has a death-grip on the cane as I move down the old and noisy steps. The sound rings out like a symphony of moans.

The moment the rest of the basement comes into view, I bend down and move the light in sweeping motions across the space to make sure nothing is waiting in the shadows. My eyes seem to have adjusted more to the darkness. Thankfully, the basement looks like it always does except for the complete lack of light and the much creepier atmosphere because of that fact.

A sudden chill works its way through my chest. My arm wraps across my chest to cuddle up and ward it off. But I maintain my strangle-hold on the cane, ready to strike at any moment.

My phone's light shows the circuit breaker on the wall in front of me as I near the bottom of the stairs. I bound quickly down the last few steps and throw open the front panel, revealing the switches behind it. I start by turning each individual branch breaker switch to the off position. The snapping sound each one makes as I flip them off causes me to flinch a little. Then I flip the main breaker switch off and then back on. The power doesn't come back on. I whine in frustration since I don't know what I did wrong.

"Did it work?"

I appreciate that he spoke softly so as not to frighten me. "Working on it."

A noise has me panning the phone behind me, cutting through the darkness of the basement. Nothing's there. I return my focus back to the panel. Through my unnerved state, I realize I never switched the branch breakers back on, and immediately start flipping them to the on position. Light from the kitchen spills in through the open door at the top of the basement stairs, illuminating the top landing and first couple of steps. I breathe a huge sigh of relief while closing the breaker box panel.

"I take it you got the power back on?" he asks.

"Yep, just did. Thanks for staying on the phone with me during that whole ordeal," I say as I shut the basement door behind me.

"No worries. That's what friends are for, right?"

"True. Hey, are you going to be okay?" I ask when I still hear concern reflected in his voice.

He sighs. "I don't know. My nerves are still pretty shot. It just didn't feel like some kind of stunt, you know?"

"Are you still planning to go to the dance tomorrow?"

"I don't even know if I'm leaving my house tomorrow," he jokes, but it sounds strained. I can tell he's trying to find humor in the situation, but he's still on edge. "What about you?"

"I'm not sure where I stand with the one person who asked me to go, so if I do go it will probably be alone at this point," I reply with a heavy sigh.

"Harrison, huh?"

"Yeah. It's all just so confusing."

"What if we go together as friends?"

"What about going with Connor?"

"Like your situation, mine's also complicated," he says.

"You know what? Let's do it. Plus, if something does happen tomorrow night, at least we'll be together when it does," I say, hoping against hope that nothing actually does happen.

"Sounds like a plan." His tone is slightly more upbeat than before.

"Try to get some sleep, Donnie."

"You too, Drea. Good night."

"Yeah, good night."

After returning the cane to the umbrella stand, I round the bannister and begin up the stairs to my room. The power cuts again, and I'm left standing in near-pitch blackness. I stub my toe on one of the steps.

"Dammit."

In my attempt to rub the affected big toe, I stumble and crash knee and elbow first into the steps. The front door handle jostles violently, snapping me right out of my pain. My eyes sift through the darkness to hone in on the front door.

If it was my parents, they would have their keys to get back in.

I swallow back my question of "who's there" and decide to stay quiet. My instinct is to call Donovan back, but then the handle's movement ceases. I pick myself up from the sitting position on the stairs and slowly make my way forward to inspect the front door. I peer through the peephole but see nothing there. I suddenly feel significantly less safe inside my own house. Wasting no time, I again collect the cane from the stand and inch away from the door toward the hall leading to the kitchen. Something passes by the partitioned glass window on the door leading out to the backyard.

I can't pull out my phone fast enough. I pre-dial 911 and am ready to hit the call button. My phone's flashlight illuminates the back door. A shape darts in front of the door's window again. The handle begins to turn back and forth. The door swings open.

I scream at the top of my lungs with the cane in striking position. My phone's light catches the person's face. It's my dad. He rears back, startled.

"Dad, what are you doing? You scared the absolute crap out of me," I gasp.

He places his hand over his chest and lets out a sizable exhale. "Sorry, forgot both my keys and phone," he explains, short of breath. "I figured you'd be up in your room with your headphones on, so I didn't try to call out to let me in. I'm just glad I remembered that spare key to the back door. Though it wasn't in the flowerpot. It was under the door mat before." He chuckles to himself. "I probably put it there by mistake one day. What are you doing with your mom's cane?"

I glance at the cane, which I'm still holding aloft. "I thought someone was trying to break in and grabbed the first thing I thought would do the most damage," I say as I finally lower it.

"Understood, but you should probably put it back. If your mom knew you were trying to use it as a weapon, she'd flip."

"Well, I'd hope she'd understand the desperate need in this dire situation." A piece of paper in his hand catches my attention. "What's that?" I ask, pointing my light at it.

"Oh, this was on the front door. It looks like something from your school."

He hands it to me. My eyes grow wide when I scan the flyer for the MasqueRave Ball with the assistance of my phone's light.

Donovan said he got one of these too. What's going on?

My dad's groan draws my attention away from the flyer. "I see the circuit breaker is at it again."

"This is the second time since you've been gone tonight," I say while folding up the flyer and stuffing it into the pocket of my pajama bottoms.

He asks to borrow my phone to look for his on the kitchen counter. Once he finds it, he returns mine before proceeding into the basement to turn the lights back on. Moments later, we're bathed in light again.

He re-enters the kitchen. "I'm heading back over. We're right in the middle of a game of cards. You going to be okay here for another hour or so by yourself?"

"Actually, do you think I could tag along?"

He looks pleasantly surprised. "I don't see why not. It will be kind of boring over there for you though."

"No worries. I think I've met my fun quota tonight anyway. I'll just do homework or something," I say.

There's no way in hell I'm staying here alone any longer tonight.

TWENTY-EIGHT

Donovan

MY ROOM FILLS WITH BLUE LIGHT. I SHIFT MY EYES from staring at the ceiling to rest on the nightstand beside the bed. My phone's screen is lit up bright in the dark space. I reach over and retrieve it, hoping there's not more bad news waiting for me. It's a text from Connor.

Hey, you awake?

Did he just send me the equivalent of a "you up" text implying he wants a late night hook-up? I type back **yes**, and then see the little dots at the bottom of the screen move in a wave motion. His next message comes through.

I'm outside. I need to talk to you.

My heart doesn't know how to react to this. What does he want to talk to me about? My mind races with all the possibilities, hoping that something else hasn't happened. I hurry over to the window overlooking the front yard and see his truck parked on the road, but I don't see him anywhere.

I don't see you? Are you in your truck?

My eyes never leave the vehicle as I wait for any kind of signal that he's there. The front cab is dark and the headlights are off. It sits there quiet, just outside of the streetlight's reach. No trace of subtle rumblings from the engine. Then I glance down at my phone and see those dots dancing again. His text comes through.

Yeah. I didn't want to wait outside just in case your aunts or neighbors see me.

After sending my reply of, **okay, be right down**, I slip on my shoes, grab a shirt, and throw it on before sneaking out of the room. The whole house is silent, much like it usually is at one in the morning. My aunts are asleep, but I know they're light sleepers, so I need to be cautious. I make quick work of the stairs and then retrieve my coat from the hook by the door and slip out without alerting anyone. I close the door as quietly as possible before turning to face Connor's truck.

The wind picks up and flows through my coat before I have a chance to zip it up. Slashes of piercing cold batter my chest and whirl around my torso. I clench my arms around myself, securing the coat closed. The wind fights me the entire time. My teeth rattle as my pajama pants flap about.

As I close in on the truck, my eyes scrutinize the front cab. Movement inside the vehicle accompanies the passenger side door popping open. It swings to the side, revealing a glimpse of Connor's face before he settles back into the driver's seat.

There's a part of me that's glad to see him, but the look on his face makes me wonder even more about why he needs to talk to me. Hesitation takes hold of my legs, and I find it hard to keep moving forward. The next gust of frigid wind helps me push through it and climb into the passenger's seat. When I close the door, the sound of the wind outside reduces to a low drone. I sit there with more anticipation than I can handle, worrying about those first words that will come out of his mouth.

His silence is killing me.

"After what you told me earlier about the attack, I had to come see you," he says, but doesn't look over at me. His tone is reflective and somber. "I know we talked, but that wasn't enough," he continues before finally looking me straight in the eyes. He looks tired, fatigued.

"I appreciate it. Really, I do," I reply softly, overwhelmed with feelings. "I'm glad you're here, if that helps."

"It does," he says with a slight smile. "A little truth talk." He shifts in his seat to face me head on. "I didn't really have anything specific that I needed to talk to you about."

"Oh."

"Yeah, I just really needed to see you. Between what happened to Lori, not knowing where Shaun is, and what happened to you tonight, things have been so chaotic. I wanted to be around the one thing that's made me feel somewhat normal. Grounded. And that's you, Donovan."

"I'd hardly call me normal or grounded," I say, resorting to humor since I don't know what to do with all of this. New territory.

"All I know is that I feel at my most comfortable when you're around," he replies.

His green eyes shimmer even in the dark of the trunk's cab. I want to say so much, but I can't seem to find the words to express how I'm feeling. I'm speechless. I put my hand out and rest it palm up on the center console, waiting for him to make a move. I'm so nervous I can actually see my heartbeat pulsing in the vein in my wrist.

He notices my hand and flashes a slim smile before placing his on top of mine. Intense heat engulfs my palm and spirals up through my arm, followed by a tingling sensation when his fingers weave with mine.

"Mind if I stick around for a bit?" he asks. "I'm not really into the whole idea of being alone right now."

"I'd like that. It's not like I was going to get any sleep tonight anyway."

"I hear that," he says as his slim smile turns into a full-blown one.

He relaxes back in his seat and leans his head against the headrest. I scooch closer to him and lay my head on his shoulder. He gives my hand a light squeeze, and I can't hold back the smile forming on my face. He adjusts in his seat to lean his head against mine, and we just sit there, content for the moment. Pure, unadulterated comfort.

The more time we spend like this, the harder I think I'm falling for him. He just makes me feel a way I've never felt for anyone before. He's raw, genuine, caring, and quite a few other positive descriptors all wrapped up into one.

I never want this feeling to go away.

Tap.

Tap.

Tap.

I stir from the sound of knocking. I snap awake and my eyes focus on Connor fast asleep. My mind is in a haze as I try to gain my bearings. It's still dark out.

How long have I been asleep?

Tap.

Tap.

Tap.

My groggy eyes pan over to the passenger side window. The

vision of my aunt's face startles me wide awake. Her eyes narrow and the expression on her face is most certainly not a pleased one. My sudden reaction has Connor stirring next to me.

"Explanation, now," Aunt Helen demands.

I deduce by the fact she's still in her pajamas and has a coffee cup in her hand that it must be morning.

Oh crap!

"Out of the truck, please," she insists.

I open the door and she pulls it the rest of the way.

"Good morning, Aunt Helen," I say.

She just sends me one serious, disapproving parental stare. "Uh-huh," she says. "There I was, enjoying my morning cup of coffee on the porch, and then I look out to find a truck parked in front of our house—one that I've never seen before, mind you. Then lo and behold, when I investigate, I find you snuggled up with a boy I've only ever met once." Her stare shifts to Connor and then back at me. "And all of this after what happened to you last night."

"I'm so sorry," Connor says. "This is all on me. I was the one who asked Donovan to come talk. We lost track of time and I guess we fell asleep."

"We were only being a support for each other, Aunt Helen. I swear. We've both been going through a lot, and we needed this. I'm sorry I snuck out and fell asleep out here and worried you," I say in a plea for her understanding.

Her face softens a bit as her eyes dart back and forth from Connor to me. She releases a heavy sigh. "It's nice to see you again Connor," she says at last.

He nods. "You too, ma'am."

"Please don't call me ma'am. It makes me sound ancient," she says. "Call me Helen. And I think it's about time for the two of you to get ready for school, correct?" The disapproving parental stare returns in full force.

I lean over to give Connor a hug. It draws on longer than I initially anticipated. A throat clears behind me, and I release my grip on him. Our eyes meet for a moment and half of his mouth turns up into a smile.

"I'll see you later," he says as our faces hover close together.

"I look forward to it."

Another throat clearing rings out. Abandoning my desire to be near Connor, I leave the truck. The weary look on his face returns … the look that was present when I first saw him earlier. I'm left with a slight wave between us before he drives off.

My aunt wraps her arm around my shoulder. "Please don't do anything like that again, okay? You could've just asked us. I mean, we probably would've said no, but still, it would be nice to know where you are," she says as we walk back toward the house.

"I know. Like I said, I'm sorry. I just really needed to see him," I reply.

"I know, Donovan. I was young once too, you know. But with everything going on right now, you can't just do things like this. You shouldn't be so impulsive. Just let us know next time, okay?"

"I will, Aunt Helen. Promise."

I say the words to pacify her, but deep down, there's only one thing currently on my mind.

I miss him already.

TWENTY-NINE

Drea

THE SCHOOL IS ABUZZ WITH NEWS OF A GUY FROM our rival school, Taft High, being found dead in Lake Wilson. The story broke this morning during a local news broadcast. He'd been reported missing yesterday and then his car was found at the edge of the lake, followed by his body being recovered from the water shortly thereafter. They were calling it an accidental drowning since his car was littered with empty beer bottles. They're awaiting further details from the sheriff's office.

I open my locker and remove the few books I'll need, stuffing them in my bag next to Harrison's jacket. I plan to give it back to him sometime today.

"That was Connor's friend they found this morning," Donovan says in a hushed tone as he comes up beside me. "I've tried calling him, but he doesn't answer. All of my texts to him have gone unread."

"Damn, really?" I ask. He nods slightly. "That's terrible. I'm so sorry. Poor Connor."

"Yeah, we spent the night together last—"

"Wait, what?" I interrupt.

"Oh, no. Not like that," he rushes to reply. "We just stayed up talking in his truck. I feel awful for him. He seemed to be doing a little better and now this."

"I'm sure he'll respond soon. Like you said, he's going through a lot," I say.

I hope Connor's okay. Poor Donovan.

"Yeah, but that doesn't mean I don't want to still be there for him," he says.

"True, but that just means you're a good person and you care about him. Give him time. I promise he'll reach out when he's ready."

The warning bell resounds throughout the hallway as he says, "It's just really hard."

My heart goes out to him. At least whatever's left of it. "I know." I pull him in for a hug. "We should probably get to class. Let's continue this at lunch, okay?"

"Yeah, all right," he replies, pulling away.

As we go our separate ways, I'm reminded of a theory I've been kicking around for a while now. Are all of these incidents linked? This group all knew Carrie. Maybe Shaun did something to Lori and then did this to himself. I have no idea what kind of relationship Lori had with these people, so I'm going off of wild assumptions alone.

There are too many coincidences.

I consider mentioning this to Donovan later, but with his new relationship, I'm not sure how he'll take me implicating one of Connor's friends. My mind races with crazy theories.

The school day seems to stretch on and on in an endless succession of monotony. Standing now in front of Lori's locker during my free period, I become lost in thought while staring at the memorial. Some of the flowers have wilted, but fresh ones have been placed amongst them.

My bracelets still there.

It still hurts. Every day. But now those feelings are tainted by the new information about Lori and my incident over the summer. My feelings are now even more muddled with confusion than before, but I still find myself getting sentimental while scanning the photos plastered all over her locker.

Like the newly placed flowers, there are also a few new pictures posted on top of previous ones. The one constant of her memorial has been the photos. They cover every inch of the locker's face, leaving no room for more. These new additions stick out like a sore thumb.

They're from the night of Sophia's party. The night Lori died. There's one of Donovan, Lori, and me. There's one of just her and Donovan in what appears to be her car. And then there's one of just me and her.

My eyes narrow on that one. We never took a picture of just us that night. We're also wearing different clothes in the picture.

Then it hits me. It was from the party over the summer. I vaguely remember posing for it, but I don't think she ever posted this one to her socials.

It's not a selfie. Who took this photo?

The more I stare at it, the more I remember posing for it. As the memory resurfaces, I recall Trent taking this photo at Lori's request. Most of that night though is a complex web of misinformation and fragmented memories.

Did Trent put these here?

I need to ask him. I need to know if and why he did this. And why this photo in particular?

I make my way down the hall and then turn the corner, headed for Trent's last class of the day. Almost all of the football players are in the same math class together. Harrison is an exception though, since he's in AP Calculus.

Don't ask me how I know that.

I plan to wait outside until Trent emerges after the bell. He's one of the last people I want to see right now, but I need answers.

The bell sounds and people pour out of the classrooms lining the hall. My eyes focus on one door in particular, waiting for my moment to pounce, but that moment never comes. The last person seemingly leaves the room and I wait a minute before moving up to peer through the thin window on the door. Only the teacher remains at her desk.

"Really interested in Mrs. Fuller's calculus class, huh?" Harrison asks near me.

I pan my gaze up and see his face hovering overhead, staring through the same window. "Actually, I'm looking for Trent, if you can believe it," I reply, rearing back from the window.

"Oh … I haven't seen him. I heard he never showed up today. Probably at home moping over the scout. Hell knows I considered it," he says with a faint laugh.

"I'm sorry about that."

"It was partly my fault. I shouldn't have let Trent get to me like that. I've only got myself to blame really."

"So no one has heard from him since last night?" I ask.

"Not sure. It's not like I'm keeping tabs on him," he replies.

I move closer to him. "You really think he just skipped school because of that?"

He releases a scoff. "His ego took a huge blow last night. He'll be licking his wounds for a while, I'm sure." A frown forms between his eyebrows. "Why are you so concerned about him anyway?"

"I'm not. I just had a question about something dealing with Lori. I thought he might be able to give me some insight."

"I see." He dodges my gaze as he slings his backpack over his shoulder. "By the way, how are you holding up after last night?"

"As well as I can, I guess."

"I'm sorry again for how all of that came out."

"Yeah, but I'm glad you told me … everything."

A glimmer of a smile crosses his lips. There's this palpable awkward energy between us that I wish wasn't there. I can tell he wants to talk to me, and I want to talk to him, but here we are, just kind of tip-toeing around what we both want. Then I realize I never gave him an answer about the dance, and that's probably not helping matters given that it's tonight and all.

Would he even still want to go with me after all of this?

"Hey, I have to get going," he says. "I've got some stuff to do before tonight. If I somehow bump into Trent, I'll let him know you're looking for him."

We can't leave things like this.

He begins to walk away and I follow in step, moving against the flow of the crowded hallway. "Hey, wait up," I say while digging into my bag for his jacket. "I wanted to give this back to you." I present it to him. "And I also wanted to thank you. I realize I never did last night."

"No worries. You were cold and I didn't need it," he says with a slight wave of the jacket, and then starts to walk away again.

"I was hoping we could talk," I blurt.

He stops and turns around. "I'd really love to, but could we do this later? Like I said, I've got a lot to do before tonight," he replies, glancing down at his sporty-looking smartwatch. "I'm already running late. Raincheck?"

"Sure, raincheck," I reply, not really knowing how to take this whole exchange.

I should've just said yes to the dance.

I watch him move away until he's swallowed up by the throng of people. Guilt settles in my gut as I trudge back to my locker. Donovan's there waiting for me. A folded piece of paper is clutched in his hand and the look on his face doesn't bode well for our impending conversation. When his eyes meet mine from afar, the concerned look seems to worsen.

"What's wrong?" I ask when I reach my locker.

"This," he replies, handing over the folded piece of paper.

I open it. When I see what's on it, my eyes leap from the image back up to him.

"Isn't that a page from the diary you said you couldn't find?" he asks. "It's that tree by the trail leading to the barn I hung out at with Connor and his friends."

"Where did you get this?"

"It was in my locker. It wasn't in there this morning, so someone put it in there during the day." His eyes dart around with suspicion at the people in the hallway.

"Let's go check this out," I say. "Maybe there's a clue or something at this tree. Why else would this have been left in your locker?" Even as I ask the question, I wonder if this is a terrible idea.

He mulls it over for a moment. "I don't know, Drea. I mean, if there is someone out there doing all of this, should we really go poking around and blindly follow clues they could be leaving behind? Maybe we should just let the sheriff's office deal with it."

"No offense, but the officers in this town still haven't found Lori's murderer. I'd say they've had their chance," I reply, folding up the piece of paper and stuffing it in my bag. "I don't know about you, but I've already waited long enough for answers."

"Okay." After a moment's hesitation, he says, "Let's go then. It is still light out. What could possibly go wrong?"

Please let this be a real breadcrumb.

THIRTY

Donovan

WHILE SITTING IN DREA'S CAR, I CHECK MY CELL for the hundredth time hoping to miraculously see a response from Connor. Desperation begins to set in. I need to hear from him … to know he's okay. But all I can do is stare at my phone's screen and wait.

This is painful.

"Still nothing, huh?" asks Drea.

"Nope, nada." I put the phone down to rest it on my thigh.

"He'll get back to you."

I can tell she's trying to reassure me, but the tentative look on her face tells a different story.

"Yeah," I reply.

I hope so.

We're making quick work of Devil's Horn. It's noticeably easier than when I was on my bike, though that's not surprising.

"Did you know this road's apparently called Devil's Horn?" I ask, trying to distract myself from my thoughts.

"Yeah, it's kind of a Haddon Falls urban legend. Car accidents used to happen on this road all the time. They had to add those safety guardrails and signs," she explains, pointing them out as we pass by. "The town thinks it's haunted."

"I guess every town has their scary stories. There's this abandoned house in the neighborhood where I lived back in Mississippi that sat alone at the end of a cul-de-sac. People said it was haunted by a woman who died there. I feel like those myths are a dime a dozen though."

"Sounds about right," she replies as we reach the top of the hill.

"Take a right here. The tree will be a little ways on the left next the dirt path and sign."

We make our way through the peaks and valleys in the road before the tree comes into view. Drea slows the car and pulls up in front of the large willow. The area is blanketed in shade from the canopy of trees overhead filtering out most of the sunlight.

"That's it, all right," Drea says, glancing back and forth between the sketch and the tree. "Hey, there's a smudge in the middle here. It looks like something was written on the trunk in the drawing."

She hands me the paper. "Huh. You're right. Do you think this might be on the actual tree?"

"Only one way to find out."

We leave the safety of the car and approach the tree. I move to stand near the road and try to recreate the perspective of the sketch. There doesn't appear to be anything on the trunk from this angle.

"Find anything?" I ask, watching Drea inspect the opposite side.

"I think so." She waves me over. "Look at this."

There's a carving at about eye level. Four letters. Two on top of two others. Like initials. A capital C and P over a T and B, with a plus sign in the middle.

Drea hovers over my shoulder. "C, P, and T, B?" she says.

I turn and look at her. She seems to be pondering it over. Then her face lights up with an ah-ha moment.

"Carrie Phillips and Trent Blakemore." A finger snap emphasizes her words.

"Maybe Trent had a little fling with Carrie," I say. "But something tells me whoever did this thought it was more than that."

"Harrison did mention Trent went out with her, so that lines up with what we've found here."

"It sounds like we need to speak with Trent about Carrie, huh?" I ask, and she nods.

The low hum of an engine accompanied by the crunch of leaves and gravel under tires sounds from down the path. A lone car approaches. It's a deputy cruiser. On closer inspection, there's actually two of them, but one is further down the trail. Through the windshield of the first vehicle, I see the silhouette of a person in the back seat as it gets closer. It rolls past and Connor's image flashes into view when the sunlight shines in through the back windows.

"Connor!?" I cry.

He turns to look at me through the rear window. His face fills with both relief and worry.

I yank out my phone and call him. It rings twice and I hear an electronic tone spill out from the open window of the second cruiser as it comes to a crawl next to us. Deputy Owens holds up a plastic bag containing a cell phone. Not just any phone though. Connor's.

He tilts his tinted glasses down to reveal his eyes. "What are you two doing here? And Donovan, why are you calling this cell phone?" the deputy asks with a pointed stare.

"Why did you arrest Connor?" I demand, dropping the phone to my side.

"Both of you need to leave now. This area is technically a crime scene," he replies, completely ignoring my questions.

That only serves to infuriate me more. "What is going on?" I grind out.

He sighs. "I can't get into specifics, but we just discovered one hell of a scene at the boat dock, and your friend was right in the middle of it."

My stomach churns at the words from the deputy's lips. I'm a ball of emotions. My mind and body can't settle on just one. Confusion wracks my brain, paired with the doubt resting at the forefront of my mind.

Connor couldn't have been involved.

"What? What happened?" Drea asks.

"All I can say is that we're taking Mr. Easton in for questioning," he explains. His face becomes even more serious. "I'd advise you to head home right now. The sheriff will be following shortly behind me and he won't be as lenient with you, so get going."

"I need to see Connor," I fire back.

"Not gonna happen, I'm afraid. I'm not going to sugar coat this. He's in serious trouble, Donovan. I'm really trying to give you all I can, but I think the best thing you can do is just leave. Isn't there a dance tonight or something that you should be getting ready for anyway?"

"I don't give a damn about some dance," I snap. "That's the last thing on my mind right now."

Another sigh parts Deputy Owens's lips. The radio on his shoulder beeps before a familiar voice comes through. "The area is secure and I'm headed back to the station. I want to see your report on my desk ASAP. Am I understood, Deputy?"

"Ten-four, Sheriff. I'm on it. Over and out," he replies into the radio.

He glances over his shoulder at the path before turning his

gaze to us. "Leave, please. Neither you nor I need to deal with him right now. He's on quite the rampage with everything happening around here." His eyes plead with us to comply.

"Fine," I say.

"Hey, Deputy, could you keep us updated on anything you can?" Drea asks.

I'm clearly too angry to think straight or I would have asked the same thing.

The deputy grumbles and then retrieves his cell phone. "Sure, but I can't promise anything. What's the best number I can reach you at?"

Drea rattles off her cell number and then I do the same. He inputs them into his phone before stowing it away. "I know this whole situation is really difficult and confusing, but I'm not going to lie to you and say things look good. They don't. Just be prepared for that, okay?"

I nod, but all I want to do is cry out in frustration. I feel tears form in the corners of my eyes, but I fight them back. Helpless doesn't even begin to describe how I'm feeling in this moment. My heart is in pulpy shreds within my rib cage. I can't even imagine what's going to happen to Connor.

None of this makes a damn bit of sense.

Drea gives my arm a little tug. "Are you okay?"

"Not in the slightest. Not at all," I reply.

I watch the deputy drive away before my eyes move to the darkness of the trail leading deeper into the forest.

What the hell happened down there?

THIRTY-ONE

Drea

I GUESS I'M FLYING SOLO TONIGHT.

Leaving Donovan behind in his current state was rough, but I would've felt worse dragging him along to the dance while he's this distraught. I was surprised when he asked me to drop him off at school so he could pick up his bike. I was under the impression it was out of commission, but apparently his aunt let him borrow hers until they can get his fixed.

I decided to accompany him back to his house. I felt for him and his situation. I wanted to ensure he made it back safe, especially after the last time he rode his bike home alone. I also wanted to make sure he didn't do anything rash like go straight to the sheriff's office or something. I wouldn't have blamed him if he did though. I'm still worried he might try, but he promised me he wouldn't.

I want to believe Donovan when he says he trusts Connor is innocent. I understand his instant reflex to defend someone he cares about. But I don't know Connor like he does. It pains me to think this, but honestly, I don't know Donovan well enough even to know if he's thinking rationally or not.

A piece of me is relieved to know they've potentially caught someone who might be involved in all of this. It just kills the other piece of me that wants to see Connor absolved for no other reason than to give Donovan peace of mind.

This whole situation blows.

The entire drive to the school, my mind is preoccupied with thoughts about what I may be walking into. If the flyers we both received were an indication that something might happen at the dance, will I be able to deal with what lies ahead? A part of me is second guessing the idea of going at this alone, and wishes I'd forced Donovan to come along.

I approach the check-in table for the dance. "If a guy named Donovan Walsh shows up, this ticket is for him," I say, handing over his ticket stub. "He most likely won't come, but just in case."

My focus shifts to the gym's entrance. I'm surprised to see Deputy Owens standing there with two other officers. Our eyes meet and he nods in my direction. I feel safer with them here.

"What are you all doing here?" I ask, coming to stand near their gathered trio.

"Safety precautions," Deputy Owens answers as he surveys a handful of students filtering into the gym. "A lot has happened lately, and since all involved have been high school students, we thought it would be best to monitor the largest congregation of young adults we could think of."

"Oh, I see. Any updates … on anything?" I probe, desperate to receive any amount of positive news no matter how insignificant it might be.

He shakes his head as the other two officers break off and head inside the gym. "Where's Donovan? I figured he'd be here with you."

I release a small sigh. "Nope. He's at home. He's probably not coming. I bet you can guess why."

"Yeah. It's a tough situation," he replies, his demeanor subdued. "Sorry, I have to stay focused. Safety first. You should head in and try to enjoy yourself. Besides, talking to me is probably cramping your style."

"Hardly. I think I succeeded doing that way before this conversation."

A hint of a smile breaks through his stoic face. "I still think it'd be best for both of us if you head on inside."

I nod and begin to move away.

"Hey, Drea?" he calls me back.

I turn. "Yeah?"

"I know it's been hard for you too, with Lori's case. I want to personally say I'm sorry it hasn't been resolved it yet. I just want you to know it's been eating up the whole department, myself included."

"I appreciate that, Deputy."

He tilts his hat to me, and I take my leave inside the gym. For the past three days, the Homecoming committee and the cheerleading squad have been transforming our gym into a neon rave wonderland. They completely nailed the theme. I only wish Lori was here to see her idea come to fruition.

The basketball court is walled off from the bleachers with black drapery. The fabric is splattered with an array of neon colored paint which radiates brightly in the black lights positioned about the space. The whole room resonates like a hypnotic, surreal fantasy land. The dancefloor is just as vibrant with the glow of everyone's masks and dress attire. There are so many creative painted mask designs, and they add another layer to the overall visual spectacle.

My focus is drawn to the large stage erected at the far end of the gym. It's a full professional setup complete with a lighting rig above it and a massive sound system on either side. A DJ wearing a purple neon light-up cat head sits dead center on the stage controlling the songs blasting from the speakers.

The energy of the dance grows more infectious the further I venture inside. A laser light show swirls overhead, distorting the view up into the rafters, cementing the feeling of being in some kind of otherworldly place.

Beautiful chaos, indeed. Lori would have loved this.

I'm in a little black dress—with freaking pockets!—that I found in the back of my closet. The material allows quick movements, which is good since tonight I need to be ready for anything. A wide neon purple belt I borrowed from my mom is wrapped around my waist. It's made of cheap material that seems like it might tear if I simply look at it the wrong way. It matches the purple lightning bolt earrings I have on, so not a complete loss. Sensible black flats are on my feet. Never know when the need to run will arise. My mask is painted like a large neon yellow smiley face with its tongue sticking out. Basic. Effective.

It's becoming quite clear to me that finding Trent in this mess might be almost impossible with everyone wearing a mask. I decide to begin my search with the left side of the dancefloor. I'm hoping his mask has some kind of tell on it, if he's even here at all.

Giant inflatable neon balls are tossed out into the crowd by the DJ. Cheers ring out as people swat them around, back and forth, up and down. They flit through the air like brightly colored bubbles. One flies over at me. I react, bopping it back toward the middle of the dancefloor.

"Nice form," I hear.

I turn and am met by a tall figure wearing an all-black suit. Black tie, black button-up shirt, black gloves, and black shoes. The only touch of color is their mask, which is painted like an intricate green skull.

Harrison slides back his mask, revealing a hesitant grin underneath. "And your mask is also very fitting."

I slip mine back as well. "I kind of did it last minute," I admit, speaking at a high volume to compete with the current song's deep bass.

"Really? I couldn't tell." His playful tone is present and accounted for. "It still looks good though."

"Thank you." I suddenly want to pull the mask down to hide the blush that's forming.

"I've been working on mine since the day we got them," he says.

"It's beautiful. I had no idea you could paint like that."

A smirk curls the corner of his mouth. "Yeah, well, there's a lot you don't know about me."

Be direct with him.

The guilt over our last conversation creeps in. "Hey, Harrison, I should have told you yes the moment you asked me to the dance."

"Oh?" the smirk turns into a full-blown smile.

"I like you too, okay?"

His smile then grows into the largest grin I've ever seen on his face.

"There were just things … feelings … that I hadn't processed. I wasn't ready to open up again." He goes to speak, but I continue. "I'm bi. Those feelings were for another girl."

Well, damn. I just came out.

His face shows the faintest hint of surprise, and then it relaxes. "Thank you for telling me. I'm honestly flattered you feel comfortable enough with me to say something like that. I know it couldn't have been easy for you. I'm proud of you."

"Does this make you feel any different?"

"Are you asking if I still like you even though you're bi?"

I nod. It's surreal hearing him say I'm bi out loud. He's the first person other than me to say it.

My heart teeters on the edge of a cliff, waiting for his answer. Then his lips part with a contented sigh.

"Drea," he says, taking my hand, "I like you because I like *you*, regardless of anything else."

My heart stutters. No, it sings. "Really?"

"Of course. Why would that change anything?"

I beam. It's as if the many walls I'd been building up over the past month have crumbled away with that one statement.

"Would you like to dance?" he asks.

I want to say yes, scream it even. I want to throw my arms around him and not let go for the rest of the night. But then I remember one of the big reasons I'm here.

Reality is quite the boner killer.

"I'd love to, really. Please believe me. And I realize this is, like, the worst timing ever, but I'm kind of in the middle of—"

"Just one dance," he implores, interrupting me.

His beautiful eyes entrance me. He looks so gorgeous right now I'm finding it hard to focus. I can't believe I'm even considering denying him. Then I think about Donovan and wonder how he's doing, followed shortly by the situation that I'm dealing with outside of this secure dome of loveliness.

Distraction.

"I want to, I do. Seriously, more than you know," I say.

He gives my hand a light squeeze followed by a soft tug. "Then why not?"

I find myself drawn to acquiesce to his request. As if he were a giant magnet and I was made of metal filings, I gravitate toward him. We both keep exchanging foolish smiles as he leads me out to the dancefloor. We find our spot, and as he turns to face me, a purple light passes across his face, showcasing his striking features in one of my favorite colors. I snap a mental picture.

That's an image I'm going to hold onto for a long time.

There's a question that keeps nagging at my brain, fighting for my attention. I don't want to ruin the moment we're sharing, but deep down I know I have something important to take care of.

We continue dancing to the current song. I've decided to allow myself time to revel in this moment a little longer before its inevitable interruption. By me.

Then the next song begins. Slow and romantic.

"Thank you for that," he says. "I'm a man of my word, and a deal is a deal."

"Maybe just one more," I reply, stepping closer to him.

A smile fills his face. I find myself staring at his mouth, wondering what it would be like to kiss him. His full, magnificent lips.

He drapes his arms around my waist and his hands land at the small of my back. He pulls me closer with smooth precision. His arms are strong. Safe. I lean my head to rest on his shoulder as the blush creeps in. His muscles flex underneath his suit as we continue to sway to the song. He's an impressive dancer.

Yet another thing I didn't know about him.

"Where did you learn to dance?" I ask.

"Depends," he says with humor in his tone. "How am I doing?"

"Moderately well," I reply with a smile.

His chest vibrates from a low chuckle. "The coach had us all take ballet for a semester. And yes, before you ask, I'm surprisingly limber."

I can't hold back my laugh. "I wasn't going to ask that."

"Well, then just consider that a little nugget of special trivia about me."

The current song ends and another slow one begins. I decide

this is my moment. I've stalled long enough. I have to find Trent and I could use Harrison's help. Maybe I can get it without completely killing the mood.

"Harrison?"

"Yeah?"

"Do you think you'll win Homecoming king tonight?"

He lets out a short laugh. "Doesn't matter really."

"But it would be nice though, right?"

"It's just a popularity contest. Me winning won't define my future after high school."

"True, but wouldn't it be nice to beat Trent?"

A sharp exhale leaves his nose. "That ass texted me earlier saying he'd see me tonight." My ears perk up when he confirms Trent's attendance. "He joked about how I'd get the crown over his dead body. Typical A-hole Trent making everything a competition." He groans. "And speak of the smug bastard." He nods to the section of the dancefloor butting up against the seating area filled with tables and chairs.

"Wait, you see him? What's his mask look like?"

"He's the one with the large pink X's painted over the eyes and mouth. He showed it off in the locker room. It's clear he didn't put a lot of thought into the design," he says. "I guess you still need him to answer that question about Lori, huh?"

"Yeah, something like that."

I'm distracted by the vision of Trent's mask floating over Harrison's shoulder in the distance. He looks to be moving toward the exit on the opposite side of the gym. My pocket vibrates on my upper thigh. I dig into it and retrieve my phone.

"Everything okay?" Harrison asks.

I see a missed call from Donovan followed by a text.

I know I promised, but I'm heading to the station. Just wanted you to know.

"Hey, I have to make a call real quick," I say. "Be right back."

"Okay. I'll be here," he replies as I hurry off.

I press on the missed call from Donovan to redial. It goes straight to voicemail. I try again with the same result.

"Dammit," I say under my breath.

My eyes rise from the phone and zero in on Trent as he makes a beeline for the exit. I follow behind, pushing through the double doors and revealing the hallway beyond. No one's there. The majority of the fluorescent lights overhead are darkened, leaving the hallway shadowed. The red glow emanating from the exit sign over the door at one end of the hall acts as a beacon. A warning. I move my gaze to the other end and glimpse Trent about to turn down another hallway.

"Trent," I call out.

He doesn't stop. I pick up the pace in an attempt to catch him.

"Trent, wait up," I shout again.

I skid to a stop after taking the corner into the next hallway. Trent stands there, positioned partway down the hall, facing me. His hand rises into the air and it waves back and forth, slow and methodic.

"Trent, didn't you hear me calling you? I need to ask you something."

The more I talk, the more hesitation seizes my gut. Something doesn't feel right about this. There's a faint smell of gasoline hanging in the air.

I realize he's standing next to Lori's locker. The flowers on the ground are silhouetted in the dim light. I was so focused on him that I hadn't realized it until now.

He digs in his pocket and pulls something out. I can't see what it is from this far away. I take a few steps forward and hear a quick scratching noise as Trent fidgets with something in his hands. A flame flickers to life in front of his mask, casting an ee-rie glimmer.

Unease envelopes me. "Trent, what the hell are you doing?" I yell, taking a few more steps toward him.

He moves the match to hang over Lori's memorial and then presses it to the pictures on the locker, setting them ablaze. In a matter of seconds, the entire locker is engulfed in flames.

"No!" I scream, sprinting in his direction.

He drops the match to the ground. It ignites the rest of the memorial gathered at the base of the locker. The closer I get, the further he retreats, all the while waving at me. Tears fill my eyes as I attempt to stamp out the edge of the fire with my shoe, but I fail miserably. The flames intensify and I have nothing to help extinguish them. I'm forced to watch the whole thing burn, re-ducing a little piece of me to ash in the process.

It's beyond torturous. I stumble back and slump to my knees as the sobs completely take over my body. Sudden mois-ture showers down from above, soaking everything. I watch through waterlogged eyes as the fire is diminished to a puddle of black soot by the sprinkler system. The water mixes with the tears streaming down my cheeks as I continue to stare at the scorched remnants. The sound of the fire alarm filters in like some sort of messed up soundtrack to the scene.

"Drea?" Harrison calls out. His shoes slosh across the wet floor as he hurries over to me.

I'm at a loss for words as I just continue to stare at the mess left in Trent's wake. Harrison joins me on the floor and captures my shoulders with his arms.

"What happened?" he asks.

I shift my head to lay on his shoulder. My crying intensifies.

"Trent," is all I can muster.

"Trent?" he echoes.

I tilt back to look at him. "That asshole did this."

He tucks my head back onto his firm chest as the sprinklers die down to a dribble.

He's going to pay for this.

THIRTY-TWO

Donovan

THE RUSH OF CONFIDENCE I'D FELT IN MY DECISION to go to the station fades more and more the further away I get from home. Thoughts back to the night I was chased rear their ugly little heads and cause paranoia to sprout in my mind. I refuse to slow for anything. I'm not making the same mistake I did last time by stopping to look at my phone. It's buzzed a few times in my pocket, but I'm laser focused on getting to the station.

I need an explanation for all of this.

My bike makes quick work of the parking lot in front of the station and I park near the double glass doors at the entrance. My phone vibrates out of control and I sigh before retrieving it. There are a couple missed calls from Drea and even more texts.

Trent burned Lori's memorial.
The sprinkler system ruined the dance.
Everyone's leaving.
Please be safe and don't do anything dumb.

Anger and confusion fill my mind as I read through the

messages. I should've been there. Maybe I could've helped stop this from happening. My eyes rise to peer through the glass doors at the officer sitting behind the front desk before returning to the phone. My heart is leading me one way and my gut in dragging me in the opposite direction.

What am I going to do?

I release a sigh and tap on Drea's missed calls and redial. It just rings. No answer. I try again and decide to leave a voicemail after the prompt.

I engage the bike's kickstand and head for the entrance. As my hand's about to take hold of the door handle, my phone buzzes. I can't pull it out quick enough. The text isn't from Drea though, it's from Marcus.

S.O.S NEED HELP AT WORK!

And now my head is telling me to help Marcus.

Dammit, body, make a choice here.

It's almost nine o'clock. Closing time at the café. And I'm sure he needs assistance because he usually works at Mae's on Fridays. I type out a quick message to him, **be there as soon as I can**, before entering the station.

The bright lights overhead assault my eyes while they adjust from being outside. The officer behind the front desk raises her head and watches as I approach. She scans me head to toe. Her face is at first puzzled, but then turns more welcoming.

"May I help you?" she asks, sitting up straighter in her chair.

"Uh, yeah, my friend was brought here earlier. Just making sure he's okay. And I was wondering if there was any chance I could see him."

Her eyes squint at me and her mouth scrunches as she leans forward. She's just about to answer when our focus shifts to the sheriff emerging from the door behind her. He's surveying a packet of papers in his hands. His eyes move up from them and land on the officer before shifting over to me. They widen and then narrow, causing his brow to furrow.

"Mr. Walsh. What are you doing here?" he asks, lowering the papers to his side.

"I wanted to know if I could see Connor. You took him in earlier," I answer. My voice wavers at the thought of being denied.

He grumbles while moving his free hand up to smooth down the ends of his salt and pepper mustache with his thumb and index finger. "Sorry, no. Mr. Easton's in some serious trouble. He can't have visitors other than family."

"What did he even do?" I ask.

He crosses his arms over his chest. "I can't reveal those details. Just know it wasn't anything good." The serious look never leaves his face. "I suggest you head home, Mr. Walsh, or else you'll be wasting a lot of time out here for something that will never happen."

I sense him growing more exasperated the longer I stand there not obeying. It's as if I was in one of those Wild West stand-offs, but unfortunately for me, it seems my participation won't get me anywhere.

"Can you at least give him a message for me?" I ask, hoping he says yes.

He relaxes his stance and exhales deeply. "I can't promise anything, but if you write something down, I'll read it and decide if he'll get it or not."

He motions for the officer to present me with a notepad and a pen. Suddenly I'm struck with writer's block, and the pen in my hand just hovers over the page. There's so much I want to say, but my brain refuses to relay it through my hand. A grumble nearby has me glancing up from the page to see the sheriff staring at me, clearly losing his patience. I refocus on the paper and press the pen down to begin writing the first thing that comes to mind.

Connor, it's Donovan. I don't know what happened, but just know I'm here for you and I support you. Hopefully this was all a misunderstanding. We're going to get to the bottom of this, I promise. I miss you.

"Okay, I think that's enough," the sheriff says.

He moves up to take the pad and pen away. I take a step back as he looks it over. He tears the page from the pad and looks me directly in the eyes.

"I'm going to go give this to him, but in return, you have to leave."

I nod. "Thank you, sheriff," I say before taking a step toward the entrance.

All he does is nod, his facial expression unchanged. A message comes through on my phone when I get outside. It's from Marcus.

PLEASE HURRY!

His text has me mounting my bike and taking off toward The Pour Over. It's only a few blocks away from the station, so I should be there in no time. Weaving through the streets as fast as my legs will allow me, I arrive at the café in seemingly record time.

The interior is dark, lit only by the over-the-counter lights. When I pull on the door, it's locked. I press my face up against the glass and scan the inside but see no signs of movement. I take out my phone and shoot off a text to Marcus.

I'm here. Where are you?

A few seconds go by as I stare at the dots at the bottom of the screen before his response comes through.

Dealing with the trash situation. Come around back.

I abandon my bike and make my way to the alley behind the store. When I turn the corner, no one's there. The only sound I hear is the wind sweeping through and dragging the leaves across the gravel.

"Marcus?" I ask into the night.

No response.

I take a few steps forward and catch myself on the dumpster when my foot slips on a patch of loose gravel. Regaining my composure, I take my phone out and tap out another text to Marcus.

This isn't funny, Marcus. Where are you?

The dots never appear. I'm left staring at my screen with zero activity. My head pops up when a commotion comes from inside, just beyond the back door. I draw in a deep breath and move toward it, apprehension trying to seize my movements. My hand trembles as I reach for the door's handle.

What the hell am I doing?

With a swift yank, the door flies open, and I'm bathed in the lights from the back room. Framed in the doorway is a welcomed sight. I breathe a huge sigh of relief as I see Marcus standing there muttering to himself while restacking a few boxes of product that he clearly just knocked over. I take note of the earbuds in his ears and assume he did this while dancing to his music. It's happened several times before.

"Marcus," I call out to him, trying to be louder than his music. I take a few steps in and allow the door to close behind me. "Oh, Marcus. Marcus!"

His head whips around at me and he rolls back on his heels before plopping to the floor, flat on his ass. A startled laugh erupts from him as he removes the earbuds. I join in.

"Damn, you scared me," he declares with his hand placed firmly on his chest. "You can't just sneak up on someone wearing earbuds, boy."

"Sneak up? You knew I was here."

"What? No, I didn't," he replies, his face filling with confusion as he makes his way to his feet.

"Stop playing. You texted me to come help you out."

The more I speak, the more perplexed Marcus looks. It's honestly starting to bother me.

"Boy, please, bye," he says. "I haven't messaged you at all. Why would I? I knew you were at the dance, silly."

I pull out my phone and show him the texts. "Okay, stop joking around," I tell him. "I have the texts, Marcus."

He looks over the screen and then his eyes move up to mine as he hands the cell back to me. "Donnie, I swear I didn't send those."

"Uh-huh. Where's your phone then?" I ask, presenting my hand for him to give it to me.

He glances over his shoulder and motions to the front of the café. "It's on the front counter. I was taking advantage of this opportunity to work on my new squat routine by lifting the boxes of new product. Since the phone bulges too much in these tight pockets, I ditched it."

I move to the front counter and see nothing there. No phone anywhere. "Where did you say you left it?" I ask when he joins me.

"I swear I left it right here," he replies, tapping the space by the cash register. "Where the hell did it go?"

"Okay, this is officially not cool." A sudden chill rolls across my shoulders as an edgy prickle sprouts beneath my skin. "I'm calling it," I say, pressing on a previous missed call from him.

"It's ringing in my earbuds. Hold on."

Marcus struggles to find the power button with them around his neck. The ringtone sounds from the back of the café. I take the lead, leaving Marcus by the counter to go in search of the phone. The closer I get to the source of the sound, the more I realize it's coming from the same table Connor and his group usually occupy. More specifically, the phone is on the chair Connor usually sits in.

"Did you find it?" Marcus asks.

I turn to see him standing in front of the open doorway leading to the back area. "Yeah, found it." As I head toward him, I see the back room is now dark when moments before the light was on. "Marcus, did you shut the lights off back there?"

He turns to look behind him and then back at me before shaking his head. "Not that I remember, no."

My eyes grow wide. A sudden flash of a neon pink light appears over Marcus's shoulder. I swallow hard. The words get caught in my throat when I try to yell, but then they burst through.

"Marcus, behind you!"

As I shout those words, the mask's light vanishes. Marcus pivots to face the back room and I hurry over to him. My legs can't pump fast enough. Terror clutches my entire being.

"The door, Marcus! Close the door."

He grabs the door's handle and begins swinging it closed. I assist by gripping the elongated old-fashioned brass handle next to his hand and pull it along faster. The tip of a boot slips into the gap, halting our progress. A guttural scream leaves our collective lips as we both fight to get the door shut. A gloved hand grips the door's edge, revealed by the lights above the front counter. I dig down harder and help Marcus pull with all my might. Marcus stomps on the boot with his heel, but it seems to have little effect.

The gloved hand releases the door and thrusts through the opening. It swings wildly for Marcus. He dips, bobs, and weaves away from the person's grasp. A quick glimpse of the neon pink mask appears in the gap as the person strains to reach him. Marcus swats the hand away and kicks the front of the boot lodged between the door and the frame. It slips back, allowing us to close the door on the person's arm. A growl rings out from the other side, but the person still refuses to give up.

Thwack.

Thwack.

Thwack.

The thud of metal on wood resounds throughout.

Thwack.

Thwack.

Thwack.

Our eyes focus on the tip of a knife as it breaks through the middle of the door. It's ripped out, splintering off tiny pieces of wood around the resulting hole before it plunges back through. It digs back and forth, twisting, and turning, trying to breech further.

A pair of scissors we use to cut open stubbornly wrapped pastries rests on the counter just out of my range. "Marcus, grab those scissors," I grind out while maintaining my hold on the door.

He turns to look and then stretches out for them. The door gives a little and opens partway. Marcus returns his grip to the handle and pulls the door back to the position it was in before.

"I'll pull harder, just get the scissors," I say through clenched teeth.

He reaches out again. His fingertips graze the scissors. He strains to reach further. He takes a step toward the counter and extends his hand, finally able to snatch them up. He rears back and drives them into the gloved hand.

A deep cry of pain erupts from the other side of the door. The person's arm disappears from view. We slam the door closed and continue to hold on tight.

"One of us needs to call 911," I say.

"So on it," Marcus says, just as breathless as I am.

He grabs his phone from my coat pocket and dials for help. My eyes move to the front windows of the café overlooking the street. I watch as a figure dressed in black closes in on my bike. They turn to look into the store and their fox mask briefly lights up in neon pink before going dark again. I release my grip on the door's handle and take a few steps toward the entrance. The figure raises their hand into the air and waves.

I rush to the door and try to pull it open, but it's locked. The figure jumps onto my aunt's bike while I'm trying to disengage the lock. The figure takes off down the street as I jerk the door open.

"What the hell are you doing? The deputies are on their way," Marcus calls out to me as I stare at the bike being ridden off into the distance by some unknown person.

"Dammit, they just took my aunt's bike," I say, turning back to face Marcus.

"A bike?" he echoes. "All of this was over a damn bike?"

"I don't think so," I reply as my gaze drifts back down the street.

Was all that just to send a message?

THIRTY-THREE

Drea

I SHIVER IN THE FRONT SEAT OF HARRISON'S CAR EVEN with the vents pointed at me blasting hot air. A towel he grabbed from the gym's supply closet is draped over my shoulders. Harrison is in the driver's seat, and I can feel every time he glances over to look at me. I sense he wants to talk, but he has yet to say a single word since we entered the car.

"Sorry I'm getting your car seat wet." My eyes are pinned to my lap. "Are you sure this won't ruin the material?"

"I'm sure," he replies gently. "Besides, that's not important right now. Is the heat helping?"

I nod. "Sort of."

"Good."

A knock at my window pulls my gaze. Deputy Owens is standing there, tapping the butt of his flashlight onto the glass. Harrison hits the button to roll the window down.

"Hanging in there, Drea?" the deputy asks.

"Did you catch him yet?" I reply, pivoting from the question. It's pretty clear how I'm doing.

He shakes his head. "No. We did find the box of matches

and small gas can we think he used, but that's about it. We'll get him though. Eventually a criminal always slips up and makes a mistake."

"I hope you're right," I say.

Another deputy calls out to him and draws his attention. "Well, it seems a deputy's work is never done," he says as he turns back to us. "You take care of yourselves tonight, okay? We'll be in touch."

Harrison rolls up the window as the deputy leaves. We're alone in the silence of his car again. The only thing I can think of is how the deputy hasn't left me with much confidence they're going to actually find Trent.

"Did you believe him when he said that they'd catch Trent?" I ask.

"I don't know. With everything going on lately, it's clear that the officers in this town weren't prepared for stuff like this to happen. I mean, before Carrie, I don't think anything really ever happened here."

I turn to face him. He's staring at me already. His damp hair is still tousled from when he dried it off with a towel. A smirk forms on his lips before he turns his attention elsewhere.

"I know I already said it, but I'm sorry this is all happening. I know it's not my fault, but I'm still sorry," he says while gazing out at the nearly empty school parking lot. He looks over at me again. "I can't help but feel terrible over how much this is affecting you."

My heart swells. "You like me that much, huh?" I ask as I dodge his stare and return my eyes to my lap.

He releases a faint laugh. "Yeah. Thought we already covered that."

"We did, I just like hearing you say it." I lift my head to take in that grin I knew would be there. Old Reliable. "Hey, I never did say thank you for what you did at the party over the summer," I say. When I sense him about to interject, I continue, "I know you're going to say that I don't need to, but what you did that night, saving me from Trent, was sweet. At first when you told me, I thought it was a little strange, like I was this prize you two were fighting over, but the more I thought about it, the more I realized that you were just doing the right thing. So ... thank you."

He releases a deep sigh. "You're welcome. And just so we're clear on this, I would've still done it even if it weren't Trent. You were clearly being affected by something, and it wasn't just the alcohol," he says. "Actually, I wasn't completely on board with the idea of leaving you in the room. It was Lori who pushed the idea. I did find it weird she didn't just take you home, but then she kept saying that your parents would kill you if they saw you like that. I countered with why she didn't just take you home with her, but she kept insisting that leaving you at Sophia's was the best option." He frowns. "She was acting really bizarre about the whole thing. Super defensive about everything, which is why I ducked out. I figured your close friend knew what was best for you. Not to mention the whole 'her needing to undress you' thing."

"I'm still so confused by why she lied to me and didn't say anything at all about it."

"Yeah, I don't know," he replies with a shrug, and then digs into his coat pocket. "Oh, and I rescued this from the memorial. I hope you don't mind that I removed it."

He presents the pink and black rope bracelet. I hold out my hand and he places it in my palm. I thought I'd lost it to the fire. There's a slight char on one side, but it's still intact.

My eyes begin to collect water again as a surprised gasp leaves me. "Thank you, Harrison. How did you know this was mine?" I can't slip it on my wrist fast enough.

"I saw you add it," he confesses. "I was going to say hi that day, but you looked like you were having a private moment."

"I honestly can't thank you enough. This means so much to me, seriously."

"It seemed like it."

I lean closer to him, and then in one swift motion, I press my lips firmly to his. Our mouths mingle with one another in a sweet embrace, and I'm surprised how soft and supple his lips are. He deepens the kiss as his hand moves to rest at the back of my neck and pulls me even closer. The eagerness of his kiss proves how long he's been wanting to do this. I attempt to match his fervor while following along with his every move. I pull back slightly, releasing the lip lock, and our eyes meet. Breaths release.

"That's exactly how I imagined it would feel," he says with a grin.

I answer his grin with one of my own. "Is that so?"

He nods. "And it was well worth the wait."

An even larger and more foolish smile spreads across my face as the blush settles on my cheeks. "Glad to hear it," I say, shifting back into my seat.

His phone chimes and he removes it from his pocket. Mine goes off as well. I find missed calls and a voicemail from Donovan as well as a group text from Sophia. There's a number I don't have saved in my phone included in the message.

"Hey, did you get this message from Sophia?" he asks.

"Yeah, just got it, oddly enough. Surprising too, considering our last interaction wasn't all that friendly," I reply. "I'm ignoring it though."

I'm about to click on the voicemail from Donovan when Harrison pulls my attention back to him. "She included Trent on it."

"What the hell?"

That must be the number I don't have.

"Yeah, she's apparently continuing the Homecoming dance at her house. It seems like everyone's invited," he says while reading over the text.

"She's ridiculous. I bet she invited him to mess with me," I seethe. "She's the absolute worst."

I return my eyes to my cell and hit the voicemail from Donovan. It's quick. A straight-to-the-point apology for not being there when I needed him is followed up by his promise to not do anything stupid at the station. As I clear out the messages and missed calls, three texts from Donovan show up. They're time-stamped thirty minutes ago.

Marcus and I were just attacked with a knife by that person in the fox mask.

We're fine now, but they stole my bike.

The deputies said they're on their way. I hope you're okay!

"Holy crap, Donovan was attacked," I say, my heart lodged in my throat.

"What?" Harrison takes his eyes away from his phone. "When?"

"A little while ago."

"Is he okay?"

I nod. "I think so. He was able to text me, so I'm assuming yeah."

He goes quiet for a moment. "Did he get a good look at them?"

"I don't know, he didn't say," I reply, dropping my phone to my lap as my head collapses back against the headrest.

"That's absolutely crazy."

Could Trent be the person in the fox mask? But then how could he have been under the bleachers and in the locker room at the same time last night?

"Where's Donovan right now? Do you need to go see him?" Harrison's voice filters through my thoughts.

"Yeah, I probably should," I sigh.

He begins to say something and then his phone chimes. His eyes scrutinize the screen. "That asshole Trent just messaged me and asked if I was going to Sophia's. He's got some damn nerve, that's for sure," he fumes.

"You're kidding me, right? Why the hell would he show his face somewhere he knows he'll get ratted out? Everyone knows he was the one behind what happened tonight."

"I'm telling him to piss off. We should be focusing on Donovan anyway."

"Actually, I think I'm going to go see him alone, if you don't mind."

"What?" His head snaps to face me. "I'm not sure it's such a great idea for you to just be driving around town alone after all that's happened."

"I appreciate the whole chivalrous white knight routine, Harrison, but I think it'd be best if I went to meet Donovan on my own. You should go to Sophia's just in case Trent does actually show up."

He lets out a groan of frustration. "Are you sure I can't change your mind? I honestly don't feel like this is the best plan."

"I'm sure. When I get to the café, I'll let the deputies know that Trent might be at Sophia's. Then they can deal with it once they get there. You could stall Trent in the meantime."

"I guess I don't really have much of a choice, do I?" he asks with a quirked eyebrow. I shake my head. "Are you sure you don't want me to take you to see Donovan?"

I nod. "Yeah, go to the party. I'll let you know when I reach the café."

"All right, if that's really what you want to do."

"It is."

I lean over and plant another kiss on his lips. It's softer. More delicate.

The phone in my hand vibrates, interrupting our lip lock. I glance down and see Donovan's calling. I slump back against the seat.

"Hold that thought," I say before answering.

Donavan begins speaking before I have a chance to say hello. "Drea, you okay?"

"I was just about to ask you the same thing."

"The deputies just got here so I can't talk long, but I had to keep trying to get a hold of you," he says.

"I'm doing all right, I guess. Been better obviously, but how about you? How's Marcus?"

"Same," he replies quickly.

I can tell his attention is being pulled elsewhere. "I'm actually on my way over to see you," I say. "Harrison is going to some kind of after-party at Sophia's. Trent might be there and Harrison is going to scout it out."

"Wait, Trent's going to be there?" he asks, sounding like his full attention is back on our conversation.

"Maybe."

"Hey, don't worry about coming. We're good, especially since the officers are here. You should go see if Trent's at Sophia's and then give me a heads up so I can let the deputies know and we can get him. You could both distract him at the party."

"Are you sure?" I ask, my stomach in knots.

"Yeah, but please keep me updated on everything, okay?"

"Fine, but only if you're positive that this is the right thing to do."

"I am," he says. He pauses for a moment and I hear Deputy

Owens's voice in the background. "And if you could," Donovan adds, "give Trent a swift kick to the nuts for me."

"Most certainly."

"Hey, be careful," he says softly.

"You too."

As the call ends, my eyes pan over to Harrison. He seems to have heard the entire conversation, though he tries to play it off like he didn't.

"So, what did he say?"

"It seems we have a party to get to."

He smirks. "All right, then." His eyes linger on me for a moment before he looks away.

Let's just hope this isn't one giant mistake.

THIRTY-FOUR

Donovan

I WATCH AS DEPUTY OWENS HOLDS MARCUS IN A lengthy hug. Clearly he isn't bothered by his fellow deputy seeing this public display of affection. I'm struck with a shred of joy at the visual. It's nice to see something like this during such a dark time. It gives me hope.

Deputy Owens steps away from Marcus and strolls over to where I'm sitting at a table in the center of the café. He drags out one of the four chairs and spins it around before straddling it and sitting down. His worried eyes connect with mine.

"What happened here tonight?" His voice is full of concern.

"We were attacked by that same person I tried to tell you about last night."

He sighs and removes his hat, placing it off to the side on the table. "Did you see their face? Any identifying features?"

"Just the mask. They were dressed in all black. Same as yesterday."

"Huh. Maybe I should have put more weight into your story last night," he says, rubbing the back of his neck.

"And they stole my aunt's bike," I add.

"Look, we're going to get the bike back and catch who did this. I promise," he says, his eyes reflecting his confidence.

I decide to take a chance and reply, "Actually, to make it up to me, you could tell me what happened at the boat dock. I need to know."

A strained laugh parts his lips. "Well, this is quite the position to be in." He combs his hand through his light brown hair before leaning forward. "What you're asking me to do is completely against protocol. It's putting my job on the line, you realize that, right?"

I nod. "But you also realize that because of your inaction and not believing me, you almost got me and your boyfriend killed tonight," I snap back in a whisper.

He glances over at Marcus talking to the other deputy and then moves his eyes back to me. He takes a moment to think it over and eventually releases a groan before leaning in close again. "Okay, I'm going to tell you, but I hope you're prepared to understand that maybe Mr. Easton isn't as innocent as you think he is."

My heart cracks. I don't want to believe Connor is a bad person. Am I going to regret asking about this?

"We found him at the docks with two dead bodies in a pontoon boat tied off there," the deputy says, chilling my blood. "A male and female, both about your age, both with multiple stab wounds. There was blood all over the interior of the boat." His eyes lower to the table. "It was pretty horrific."

My words become caught in my throat. "Who were they?" I'm finally able to whisper.

He seems to search his memory banks. "I believe we identified them as Geoff Winchester and Nancy Loomis. Connor said he received a text from Geoff to meet him and Nancy there."

"Did you check his phone for that text? Or Geoff's?"

"Yeah, we verified both. There are still some timeline

discrepancies we're working through, but that's one of the many reasons we're holding Mr. Easton in custody."

"Was there anything else? Any clue, DNA, or anything tying Connor to their deaths?"

"I really shouldn't be discussing this with you," he says with a low grumble as he rears back from the table.

"Too late," I whisper. "You owe me."

He hesitates and then leans forward. "There was a gas can and matches near their bodies, which doesn't help Mr. Easton's case since he has a previous arson charge," Deputy Owens whispers even quieter.

My heart sinks with every word. I honestly don't know how to feel right now. In my gut, I know Connor couldn't have done this. I begin to feel even worse for him, knowing what he witnessed. And was now being charged for it? He must feel utterly lost and dejected.

"Wait," I say. "You said there was a gas can and matches, right?" He nods. "Well, didn't someone burn Lori's memorial tonight?" He nods again. "So that coupled with the possible timeline issues could mean there's a chance Connor isn't guilty of what happened at the docks. He was at the station during the dance, right?"

"We've taken that into account, but the sheriff is sticking to holding Mr. Easton for the maximum time he can until more evidence is gathered," he explains. "And how do you know what happened at the dance?" Just as I'm about to answer, he continues, "Never mind. Of course you know what happened."

"Yeah, high school gossip travels fast," I reply.

"Speaking of gossip, the sheriff told me you went to the station tonight to try and talk to your friend."

"He's more than a friend. But yeah, I did."

"You had to know you wouldn't be able to see him, right?"

"I had to try. I had to know why he was in there. To make sure he was okay. I was desperate."

He lets out another deep sigh. "I get it. And I sympathize with your situation, Donovan. I hope you realize that."

"And I hope you realize that I honestly believe Connor is innocent," I curtly reply.

"For your sake, I hope you're right."

He has to be innocent.

THIRTY-FIVE

Drea

"WHERE IS EVERYONE?"
My question causes a flash of confusion—
and maybe worry—to cross Harrison's face as
we pull into Sophia's massive driveway. The only other car there is
hers. A pristine, custom, rose-gold BMW.

"Please tell me we aren't the first ones here," I groan.

I'm not sure if I can deal with Sophia one-on-one.

"Well, the only way to find out is to head inside," he replies,
and shifts the car into park. He turns to me. "Are you sure you're
cool with this?"

His concern is nice, sweet even. "Yeah, I just have to rip off the
Band-Aid. Absorb the pain."

"All right," he says with a nod and a tentative smile.

Harrison's the first to exit the car. I watch him stroll away while
I sit there seemingly unable to move. I've apparently perfected my
ability to waver on decision-making these past few days to an annoying degree. He comes to an abrupt stop and looks back at me before
beginning his return to the driver's side door. One long, deep breath
later, I step outside the vehicle and notice a smirk appear on his face.

"You sure you're good?" His smirk wanes into a more serious expression.

"Yep … Band-Aid, remember?" I reply, and suck in yet another lengthy breath followed by a sharp exhale.

A rush of adrenaline hits my veins and I take the lead up to Sophia's front door. But it dissipates almost as rapidly as it developed the moment I go to ring the doorbell. I don't ring it, hesitating again when I'm struck by the fact there isn't any music coming from inside. Or talking. I see the lights are on through the windows and I test the doorknob. It's locked. With no competing noise, I knock instead. Three times.

There's some light scuffling on the other side of the door before the handle jiggles and the door is wrenched open. Sophia stands there, still wearing the frilly neon pink dress I assume she wore to the dance. Traces of streaked eyeliner are left on her cheeks, possibly a result of the fire sprinklers. Her hair is disheveled and looks like it was jostled around by a towel. The Homecoming Queen crown sits atop her head at an angle with the accompanying sash draped haphazardly across her chest.

Definitely not her best look.

Her eyes narrow. "Huh. I guess my invite to you wasn't as clear of a joke as I thought it'd be," she says while waving us inside. "The more the merrier, I guess."

I toss a look at Harrison and he just shrugs before gesturing for me to move in first. I draw in a quick breath and step forward.

"I mean, don't get me wrong," Sophia continues as we follow her into the living room. "Deep down, I wanted you to come, but I didn't actually think you'd show up."

"Well, here we are," I reply, blunt as can be.

"Yep, here you are," she echoes, spinning around to face us before plopping down onto the couch.

"Are more people coming?" asks Harrison when he notices I'm getting too annoyed to talk.

Sophia rolls her eyes. "Nope. I guess not even an official Sophia Gomer party seemed appealing to anyone after what happened tonight. I got a few replies saying people might head over after going home first to change, but I'm not holding my breath."

I find myself staring at the crown and sash the entire time she's talking. I can't help but get more irritated with each passing second. "How exactly did you get those? The dance was evacuated before the crowning ceremony happened."

She giggles to herself before snatching up a glass of pink colored wine from the side table next to her and taking a sip. Her face grows more pensive with each passing moment. "I stole them," she says. "From Lori." She takes another swig of her drink. "She won by, like, five votes. *Five votes.* All write-ins." Her eyes slim at my surprised expression. "Oh, come on. We both know she would've won regardless."

My tongue firmly travels across my teeth as I hold back the words I'd love to say.

"Did you have something to do with her death?" Harrison throws out there.

It's one of the many questions I've been biting back.

She scoffs. "What? Of course not. How could you even ask that?" Her attention shifts to me. "Speaking of Lori though, what did she have that I didn't?"

"What are you talking about?" I ask, equally confused and frustrated.

"You always liked her more than me. I tried so hard to be there for you, but you always kept me at arm's length. You always chose Lori. But I was your captain … your friend," she rambles, taking a sizable swig of the wine this time. "Why? What was it about her that made her so special?"

"It's complicated."

I drop my eyes to the floor to avoid her pointed stare. This is the first time anyone has asked point blank about my relationship—or whatever it was—with Lori. It felt like more than just a friendship, but we were both confused. Curious.

"Look, I'm not getting into this with you," I reply, placing my hands on my hips. "You've been drinking and don't know what you're saying."

She releases a sharp exhale before downing the rest of the wine. "She drugged you at my party, you know." The loud clink of the glass on the side table emphasizes her statement.

"*What?*"

"It was by complete accident, but you were the lucky winner that night. The drug was meant for Trent," she explains.

My blood begins to boil. "What in the actual hell are you talking about?" I ask, moving to stand in front of her. Heat slithers across my body. I'm closing in on the point of no return where I just lose it. The feeling of betrayal returns with a vengeance, and I'm even more conflicted about what I should believe.

She knocks her hand against the wineglass and tips it over, spilling out the last tiny dregs of liquid onto the cream-colored arm cushion. "Dammit, wine's all gone," she whines while standing the glass back up on the table. "Ah, crap. Mom's going to kill me."

"Sophia! Answers, please," I demand.

With a groan, she abandons her attempts to wipe away the dotted stain left behind from the spill and refocuses on me. "Do you remember when you asked me about Carrie?" she probes as she relaxes back against the couch. I nod. "Well, Mr. Twat Waffle Casanova himself, Trent, messed around with her. He forced her to do things she wasn't ready for and convinced her what they had was real. But then he broke her little heart." Her eyes meet mine and she seems to sober for a moment. "That's why she did what she did to herself."

"So, it wasn't an accident then?" I ask.

"That's where things get a little muddy," she replies.

"What happened?" I ask, losing my patience.

She takes a moment to herself and pivots her gaze to Harrison. "It all depends on who you believe. Isn't that right, Harrison?"

Her question slices through my chest and nicks my heart. My eyes dart over to Harrison and he goes from glaring at Sophia to flashing big doe eyes in my direction seconds later. His mouth gapes open to speak, but Sophia beats him to the punch.

"You haven't told her you were there that night, have you?" Sophia makes a disapproving sound with her mouth.

"What haven't you told me?" I ask, taking a step back when he takes one toward me with his hand extended.

He releases a short huff and recoils. "I was there when Carrie told everyone about her feelings for Trent. It came out during this silly game we were playing. Trent was his typical asshole self and denied her right then and there. She ran out of the barn and took off on her bike in the rain. A few of us chased after her on ours. I didn't actually see what happened to her though. I hung back to give Trent a piece of my mind first. But I remember seeing Lori and a few of our other friends all gathered at the drop-off looking down at Lake Wilson when I arrived."

"A car ran her off the road into the lake," Sophia butts in. "Her death was the catalyst for putting up the extra barricades and signs along Devil's Horn."

Harrison's gaze remains steady on mine. "I'm sorry I didn't tell you all of this earlier, Drea. I didn't think it was relevant to our conversation."

"We'll deal with that later," I say with a hand up before

casting a pointed glare at Sophia. "What in the hell does all of this have to do with Lori drugging me?"

"Lori came to me with this plan to get revenge on Trent since we were all tired of him doing whatever he wanted and getting away with it. Proper payback for what happened to Carrie. But we all know how that went, now don't we?"

"What were you going to do to him after he was drugged?" I ask, but I dread hearing the answer.

"I didn't know specifics, just that Lori mentioned someone wanted him knocked out and brought to the Wilson Family barn … where it all started," she replies.

"Did she try again at the party last weekend?" I fire off.

"Ding, ding, ding, we have a winner," she says with a slight giggle. Then her face grows more somber. "But apparently the drugs she had that night weren't the same as the ones you got, or we wouldn't be having this conversation right now."

"Who killed her, Sophia? You've got to have some idea," I insist.

"Uh, hello? Trent. I mean, he was the one who destroyed her memorial, right? And he was the last one with her that we know of."

"But his alibi was rock solid," I retort.

"Money talks, Drea. Believe me, I know," she says. "He could have easily paid someone else to do it."

"So, why did you invite him here tonight?" Harrison asks.

"Oh, that." Sophia rolls her eyes. "That was a joke too. Like he'd show up anyway. It was cruel of me to make that group text, Drea. I'm sorry. I guess I was just being my petty horrible self."

I draw in a deep, calming breath when I feel myself about to blow. I want to scream at the top of my lungs and expel all of these pent-up emotions. I'm like a nuclear reactor ready to go at any moment. A headache develops at my temples.

"Why do you expect me to believe you?"

"I don't," she replies. "All I can do is tell you the truth. It's up to you to believe it or not. I can't *expect* you to do anything."

Sophia's phone pings on the side table next to her wineglass. She fumbles around for it and knocks the glass onto the carpet. "Whoops," she mumbles before grabbing the phone. She pulls it in front of her. Her eyes broaden. Surprise overtakes her face.

"What is it?" I ask, unease creeping in from her expression.

Her eyes gradually pan up from the phone's screen. "It's Trent. He says he's waiting upstairs. He says you know where," she replies, showing me the text.

"What?" Harrison says, moving so he can see the message too.

I take the phone from her hand and scrutinize the text further, holding it so Harrison can see. The more I read it, the angrier I become. I hand Sophia back her cell and she returns it to rest on the side table.

"You don't actually think he's upstairs, do you?" she asks. "He's clearly messing with us."

"We'll see about that," I reply, storming toward the stairs.

"Where are you going?" asks Harrison. He reaches for my hand and brings me to a halt.

"The third floor," I say as calm as I can, but inside I'm fuming and am actually looking forward to unloading on Trent.

"You can't just go up there alone, okay?" The look in his eyes has a strange soothing effect on me.

"Well, if Trent's up there, I have some choice words for him too," Sophia pipes up. "He broke into my house, for one thing."

"All right, let's all go then," I suggest. "Three against one. I like those odds."

We ascend to the third floor and gather in front of the room in question. The door is shut. No light shines from underneath it, giving me pause. Harrison reaches for the knob, but I seize his hand, stopping him.

He shoots me a puzzled look. "Are we not going in?"

"Something feels off about this. The lights aren't on in the room. Why would he be waiting up here in the dark?" I say.

"Screw that. This is my house and he's getting the hell out of here," Sophia shouts, shoving her way between us in order to get to the door.

She pushes it open. A wide slice of light from the hallway spills into the space, cutting through the darkness of the room. She flips the switch moments later and I immediately focus on the bed. The top blanket has been removed and discarded off to the floor, leaving behind a solitary stark white sheet. A mass lies underneath it. The shape of a body. It's wrapped tight, showcasing the form, but the head area has an odd bulbous nature to it.

Sophia moves into the room first and then sidesteps to allow us to follow suit. We inch closer to the bed while exchanging uncertain glances. A single word is spray-painted on top of the sheet. The hot pink letters practically glow against the bright white fabric.

SLUT

"What the hell is that?" asks Sophia as she takes a substantial step back.

"Do you think someone's actually under there?" I ask Harrison, whose eyes have yet to leave the body-shaped object on the bed.

He snaps out of his apparent trance and glances over at me. "It's probably some sick joke that asshole set up ... has to be." He attempts to laugh it off before his face becomes grim again. His unsteady delivery doesn't instill much confidence.

"There's only one way to find out," I say, reaching out for the top of the sheet.

Harrison blocks my advance. "Actually, if you don't mind, let me do it."

His gaze is paralyzing. His eyes grave. My heart surges into overdrive for a multitude of reasons.

"Uh, okay," I stammer, withdrawing my hand.

Harrison takes hold of the loose flap near the top of the shape poking out from under the head area. He works the sheet from beneath it to get a better grip and then rips it away.

Sophia's shrill scream blares behind us. My hands shoot up to detain a sharp gasp that knocks the wind out of me. A queasy feeling invades *hard*. Harrison stands there, frozen, staring down at the person lying there. The tension resonating off his body is palpable.

It's Trent.

THIRTY-SIX

Drea

TRENT LIES THERE IN HIS FOOTBALL UNIFORM. IT'S unwashed and still grass-stained from the Homecoming game. A foul odor wafts into the air, a clash of rot and the strong cologne he wears. His skin is multiple shades of blue and gray, looking entirely drained of blood. The Homecoming King's crown is fit snug on top of his head. There's a piece of paper pinned to the jersey.

"I'm calling the sheriff," Sophia shouts as she flees the room.

"Sophia, we should stick together," I call out.

I rush toward the doorway after her, but she's already too far gone. In a restless panic, I rip my phone from my dress pocket and dial Donovan. He picks up almost instantly.

"Donovan, Trent's dead," I say. The words come out like I'm gasping for air.

"What? Where are you?" he asks in an anxious tone.

"At Sophia's. Someone used Trent's phone to text her that he was upstairs in her house, and when we came up here, we found his body."

"Wait. That means they might be still in the house," he says.

My blood runs cold, followed quickly by the rest of my body. "Please hurry! Bring Deputy Owens," I say into the phone.

"Be there as soon we can," he promises. "Please be careful, Drea."

I hang up and stow the phone back in my pocket. "What if who did this is still here?" I ask Harrison.

I watch as that thought rolls through stages in his mind before registering in his eyes. I'm shocked we both failed to reach this conclusion before. The rest of his face catches up with his eyes and fills with dread.

"Then we need to get Sophia and get out of here now," he replies.

"Agreed."

I hesitate before leaving the room. My eyes are glued to the piece of paper on Trent's jersey. I know I should leave everything as it is for the investigators, but I also know that paper is probably a significant clue that could point to Lori's killer … a killer the authorities have yet to identify.

Decision made, I keep my breathing shallow while retracing my steps back to Trent's body. The piece of paper isn't attached to his jersey like I originally suspected, but instead is nailed deep into his actual flesh. My fingernails capture the flat, rounded tip of the nail, and as I begin to pull, it snags on the porous mesh fabric.

FML

I switch to Plan B and carefully rip the paper free from the nail. It's another page from Carrie's diary. The sketch of the barn.

"What's that?" inquires Harrison.

I fold it up and put it in my other pocket. "A message."

A piercing scream echoes up from downstairs, interrupting Harrison's follow-up question. Our wide eyes crash into each other before we rush from the room. We reach the stairway in seconds and peek over the bannister to the lower floors. There's no activity.

"Sophia?" I call out, but receive no answer. "*Sophia?*"

Harrison shushes me. "We need to be quiet and get the hell out of here."

"What about Sophia? What if she needs our help?"

"What do you propose we do? Head down there and potentially stumble into a situation we can't get out of?" he asks in a low whisper. His questions cause my lower lip to become a battleground between my teeth while I think them over. "The deputies are on their way, right?" I nod. "Then let them handle this."

"What if that was you down there?" I fire back in a forceful whisper. "Wouldn't you want me to try and save you?"

"No. I'd want you to get to safety by any means necessary," he replies, direct as hell.

"Well, I guess for Sophia's sake it's a good thing I'm not you then," I say, shoving past him.

As I take my first step down, he grabs my shoulder and lightly pulls me back. He positions himself between me and the staircase. His hazel eyes are firm and focused.

"If we're going to do this, at least let me be in front, all right?"

I nod in agreement.

"And if anything happens, you run. Got it?"

"Yeah, got it," I reply.

His gaze drifts over my shoulder. "We should probably grab something to protect ourselves with." Moving past me, he snatches a large, decorative brass candlestick from a side table in the hallway. The candle topples off and falls to the floor with a thud. Though thankfully the sound was dulled by the area rug underneath the table. He swings the candlestick back and forth like he's attacking the air in front of him, but I assume he's checking its weight. "This should do." His other hand reaches for a metal vase. He dumps the fake flowers onto the floor and turns to me, presenting both items. "Any preference?"

I grab the thin metal vase. It's got some weight to it and feels sturdy in my hand. I spin it around in my grasp, my hand deciding on the best place to hold it. There's a perfect grip point near the base.

"Okay, ready?" Harrison asks.

I nod and crowd close against his backside as we begin our descent. By the time we reach the second-floor landing, terror has taken complete hold of me. Every footstep sounds louder than the last to my ears, and I begin to think maybe Harrison was right about just getting out of there.

A shimmer on the floor near the bannister catches my attention. "Is that a crown?" I ask over Harrison's shoulder.

"Looks like it, yeah. Stay close and stay alert." His voice quivers slightly, but his tone remains firm.

The entire trek across the second-floor landing, I stare at the crown resting on the floor. Like a crow attracted to shiny things, I bend down and allow Harrison to keep moving forward toward the next set of stairs.

He pauses and looks back. "What are you doing?" he whispers. "I said stay close. Leave it."

"All right," I reply as my fingertips trace the sparkling piece of intricately bent metal that was meant for Lori.

A faint noise sounds from somewhere nearby. I can't scramble to my feet fast enough.

"Now would be a good time to regroup," Harrison says, taking a few steps toward me, his hand outstretched for mine.

The noise happens again and seems to have come through an open door to our right. The room beyond is pitch black. I shudder as the feeling of being watched sets in, and can't fight the urge to study the space for any movement within.

"Seriously, Drea. We need to get out of here."

The moment he finishes that statement, a fox mask illuminates within the dark of the room. It rushes toward me. A throaty shriek escapes my lips. I lift the vase, but not in time. A cold, sharp pain glides across my arm after the attacker swipes wide with a knife. My free hand moves up to the wound and comes away covered in blood. That's when the pain really kicks in.

Harrison steps in to run interference. The figure dodges his swing with the candlestick. He's stabbed at as well, and knocked back against the wall for his efforts. I notice him favor his stomach as he tries to regain his footing. My heart cracks right in half.

"Harrison!"

The figure snaps its focus back to me like a shark smelling blood in the water. I raise the metal vase in front of me, pointing it at them and ready to strike. They cock their head to the side slowly, meticulously. At a dramatic angle. I stagger backward and press against the bannister in an effort to put distance between us. The figure's head whips back straight up and they charge at me. We collide. The vase flies from my hand. My vision of the surrounding area blurs and jumbles as we flip up and over the railing.

I manage to grab hold of the bannister, then almost immediately lose my grip when a severe ache throbs through my arm and it gives way. In a last-ditch effort, I struggle to secure my fingers around the spindles to catch myself. Sudden force strains my hold on the thin metal rods. An immense amount of pressure weighs me down. My hands burn as they slide along until I reach the point where the spindles meet the floor.

My eyes glance down and slam into the bright pink lights of the fox mask. The neon purple belt wrapped around the waist of my dress acts as the attacker's lifeline. Their grip on it is causing the buckle to dig into my gut. I can't hold back the shrill cry of pain as it's ripped from me.

"Let go!" I screech, thrashing about.

I try to shake them off, but it seems the more I move, the firmer their grip becomes, like a snake twisting around its prey.

"I got you," Harrison calls out as he appears above me.

I've never been happier to see that beautiful face. He leans over the railing to grab hold of my wrists. The groan of pain that follows as he struggles to hold on destroys me.

"Stop! You're hurting yourself," I shout at him.

"No pain, no gain," he says through another excruciating sounding groan.

I go into full leg-flail mode, trying to get the attacker to release me. The belt slips and adjusts off to one side due to the stress being inflicted on it. The material begins to tear as one by one the fibers rip apart. The buckle twists in an awkward angle, pressing deeper into my stomach before it gives way.

The person's grip weakens, and relief pours over my body as the extra weight sheds away. A heavy roar erupts from beneath me, followed by a sudden loud, sickening thud. My eyes travel down to look at the body dressed in all black unnaturally sprawled out. The lit mask flickers a couple times before shorting out completely. Just a dark hole where a face used to be.

Harrison pulls me up and over the railing until I can plant my feet firmly onto solid ground. I'm immediately enveloped in his arms. In safety.

"You saved my life," I say next to his ear.

He doesn't reply, he just squeezes me tighter as we stand there in the moment ... a quiet and comforting moment.

We peer over the railing and the person's still there. Still contorted into a painful looking position. An audible sigh of relief leaves us both at the same time. As we make our way down to the first floor, my eyes never leave the figure.

Now, standing over the body, my mind grows hazy. I'm still in shock, I think. Numbness overtakes me while I stare at them lying there motionless. I'm not sure if the reality of what just happened has truly set in yet. Tears well up in my eyes. My entire body feels like it's been hit by a semi-truck full of emotions that I've been holding inside.

This nightmare's finally over.

I kneel and lean in to reach for the mask. The urge for me to see who's been doing this overtakes every other one of my instincts. I need to know who's behind all of this.

"Careful, Drea," Harrison wheezes out. "They might still be alive."

"I don't think anyone could survive that fall," I reply, though in the back of my mind I'm imagining them springing to life at any moment.

My hand shakes as my fingertips stall at the base of the mask. I steady myself, warding off the trembles from the adrenaline, and fully commit to grabbing it. I pull it back and can hardly believe the sight in front of me.

What!? Sophia!?

A complex mix of emotions conjure forth as I stare at the person responsible for so much turmoil and chaos. And now I'll never know why. I want to scream, punch, and kick the air, but instead, I'm paralyzed in disbelief.

Her honey brunette hair cascades down around her shoulders as I flip the mask back further off her head. Blood is pooled in the corner of her mouth and has traveled down her chin, leaving droplets on her neck. Her face looks peaceful, not like that of a merciless killer.

"I don't get it. Why?" Harrison's confused tone echoes my own internal dialogue.

"We'll probably never know."

A faint moan draws my attention to him. He's supporting himself against the railing and his face has grown paler. "Are you okay?"

He pulls the left side of his suit jacket open to reveal a sizable slice to his midsection. "I guess it went a little deeper than I initially thought," he says as he stumbles down the last couple steps. He lands against the bannister and slides down to rest on the floor.

Concern consumes me. "Harrison!" I yell, moving to be by his side.

His hand hovers over the blood-soaked area on his shirt. My heart aches seeing him like this.

"I'm going to be okay. It's only a scratch." His attempt to laugh is ruined by a wince in pain.

A surprised giggle escapes my lips at his poor attempt at humor. I'm glad to see he's well enough to still joke around. "You're hurt. We need to get you to the hospital."

"It doesn't feel as bad as it looks. Promise. I think they somehow missed all my vital organs," he replies with a wan attempt at a reassuring smile, but I'm not fooled.

I loosen his tie and carefully remove it from around his neck. "Here, fold this up and hold it to your wound. Apply pressure, okay? We have to stall the bleeding."

He chuckles softly. "Look at you going all Doctor Sullivan on me."

"Yeah, well, there are plenty of sides to me you don't know about, Mr. Daniels."

"I'm looking forward to being introduced to all of them." His smile warms my heart and has me forgetting for a moment the waking nightmare we're currently in.

I reach for my phone to call Donovan, but I come away with nothing. Did it fall out of my pocket? My eyes search the area and land on a bright purple rectangle resting on the floor a little ways from me.

"Be right back," I say, patting Harrison's arm.

"Don't worry, not moving from this spot," he says with more humor.

I collect the phone and immediately notice the screen's shattered. I try to turn it on, but nothing happens. It's toast.

Dammit.

A loud bang resonates from the foyer. "Haddon Falls Sheriff's Department. Open up!" someone commands from the other side.

Deputy Owens!

I rush to the door and fling it open. A wave of relief crashes over me when I see the deputy standing there, gun in hand, as if he was pulled straight from one of the cop shows my parents watch.

"Drea, are you okay?" he asks. "What's the situation here?"

"Yeah, I'm okay. And I'll explain everything, but first we need an ambulance."

I hope they get here soon.

THIRTY-SEVEN

Donovan

I HAVE TO STOP MY HAND'S IMPULSE TO REACH FOR THE car door handle. It hesitates there before retreating to my lap. *No. Deputy Owens told me to stay put.*

It's taking every fiber of my being not to jump out of the deputy's cruiser right now, especially knowing people I care about are in danger. I'm at odds with every one of my decision-making organs over the conversation I had with the deputy about me staying in the vehicle before he left me in here alone. In the dark, I might add. I find myself checking each door yet again for, like, the millionth time to make sure they're still, in fact, locked.

I mean, who would be stupid enough to try and attack someone in a cop car, right? Right?

The yellow and green lights above the cruiser swirl around, causing the surrounding area to glow in a surreal manner. I asked why Deputy Owens turned them on in the first place, and he said they're tied to the camera on his dash. It begins to record audio and video when they're active. I'll be honest, I feel a touch safer knowing that fact. Just in case a certain fox decides to come out

I also appreciate that he left the car running. It's keeping the interior of the vehicle from becoming a freezer. But again, it's not just for my benefit. Apparently all the electronics in here would drain the battery if he didn't leave it running. He called it a "running idle state."

The more you know.

It's been almost seven minutes since he left—yes, I've been counting—and I'm beyond the point of becoming fidgety. I'm on super high alert and keep thinking I see shadows dart around outside the car in my peripherals.

"Screw this," I say at the peak of restlessness.

I jump out of the car and dash through the sprawling yard, stopping short at the front door. With a subtle twist of the knob, I crack it open in order to peek inside before pushing it the rest of the way. After taking a couple steps in, I spot Harrison over by the stairs posted up against the railing and clutching his side. Drea's next to him combing her hand through his hair. Something covered in a sheet is on the floor near them, but I can't make out what it is.

Trent?

"Drea," I whisper to avoid startling them, but they don't hear me. I move a few steps closer and go to call out again, but I'm halted by an alarming voice.

"Hold it right there!"

My hands immediately fly up in the air as I turn to face Deputy Owens. His gun is pointed in my general direction.

I think I just peed a little.

"It's me, it's me," I say.

He lowers the sidearm while releasing a sharp breath. "I thought I said to stay in the car." His tone is soaked in exasperation.

It only takes a few seconds before I'm wrapped up in Drea's

hug. "I'm so glad you're here," she exclaims as she squeezes me tight. It's a desperate hug. A relieved hug.

"Me too," I echo, fully embracing her. "Is Harrison okay?"

I wave to him. He returns it, but only barely. The slight smile that appears on his face is more reassuring.

"He was injured trying to save me," she replies. "He'll make it. We just need to get him to the hospital."

"I've already called for an ambulance and backup. They'll be here shortly," Deputy Owens chimes in.

"What happened here?" I ask. "Where's Sophia? I thought you said she was with you."

Drea pulls away, her expression grim. "Sophia did this, Donovan," she replies with tears forming in her eyes. "Her body's over there. She attacked us. She killed Trent, Lori … all of them."

"*What*? Why? How? This doesn't make any sense."

She shrugs and delicately shakes her head. "I don't know, but this means Connor didn't do anything. Deputy Owens told me he'd be freed after he gets back to the station. Right, Deputy?"

He nods. "Well, not exactly after I get back. There's still a chance he's involved with this whole thing, but it's looking a lot less likely now. And it seems there's enough evidence here to make a case for sure."

It's not exactly what I want to hear, but that statement causes me to beam nonetheless. I knew Connor couldn't have been involved with anything like this. I just knew it.

Then confusion wades its way through the fog of solace clouding my brain, grounding me.

"Hold on," I say. "How did Sophia attack Marcus and me at the diner and then have enough time to get back here before you arrived? And I know she was cheerleader fit, but the person who attacked us had enough strength to wrestle a door open while we were both pulling against them." I look between them and see the wheels spinning in both Drea's and Deputy Owen's heads. "Marcus stabbed the attacker in the left hand with some scissors." I hurry over to the sheet covering Sophia's body and lift it up enough to see her left hand. There's no hole or visible stab wound in her black glove. "See? It couldn't have been only her this whole time. There has to be another killer."

My own words send a severe shiver down my spine. It spreads and begins to overwhelm me.

"Dammit, you're right," says Drea. "Trent's body was upstairs on the third floor. There's no way Sophia got him up there all by herself. And she got a text from Trent's phone right in front of us. I can't believe I missed that!"

Deputy Owens seems to agree with everything we've said. "I've got to call this in," he says before stepping away.

Drea digs into her pocket and presents me with a piece of paper. "This was on Trent's body. It's from Carrie's diary. The barn sketch."

"What do you think it means? Is this where the other person wants us to go?"

She shrugs.

"That's for me to figure out," Deputy Owens says as he approaches us again.

The sound of sirens echoes outside the house, pausing our conversation. Red and blue flashing lights filter in through the slits of the blinds on the large windows lining the living room. The paramedics enter the house and Deputy Owens directs them to collect Harrison. Drea walks alongside him as he's loaded out on a stretcher before disappearing through the front door.

Deputy Owens faces me. "I want you to wait here for the other officers to arrive and get one of them to take you and Drea back to the station, understood?"

"Where are you going?"

"To the barn to see if there's any evidence there we can use."

"You're going alone?" I probe. "I should come with you."

"Hey, look, I appreciate your eagerness to help. I really do. But frankly, I've allowed you to be a part of this investigation more than I should have already." I begin to protest, but he continues talking over me. "Listen, I'm the one with the badge and the gun, okay? You're a civilian, so I'm asking—no, I'm telling you to go to the station and hang out there until I get back. Besides, the sheriff said he's going to meet me there with a couple other deputies."

"Okay, fine. By the book it is," I reply.

"Thank you."

Drea returns and Deputy Owens takes his leave. "Where's he going?" she asks, coming to stand in front of me. A gauze bandage is wrapped around her upper arm.

"He's going to the barn." My eyes zero in on the bandage again. "I'm sorry. I didn't even realize you got hurt."

She examines the injury. "No worries. It's barely anything," she says with a strained smile. "So, are we going to the barn or what?"

"I don't know. There's a part of me that wants to, but recently I've been trying to ignore that part."

She exhales sharply. "Yeah, maybe we should wait for the officers to show up first and then let them handle it."

I take a moment to think it over. My thoughts are interrupted by the chime of my cell phone. I retrieve it from my pocket and see a text from the very last person I'd expect one from.

Connor.

"What is it?" Drea asks while my eyes scan the text.

The barn holds all the answers you seek.

"Connor just sent me a text, but that's impossible. He's

locked up and doesn't have his phone," I say, confusion wracking my brain. "And there's no way they just let him go, right?"

She shakes her head. "Deputy Owens said there was a process. It wouldn't have happened this quickly."

"Wait, Deputy Owens. He was the last one with Connor's phone. Could he be involved?"

"No, I'm sure he would've turned it in as evidence," she says.

My mind becomes overloaded with facts and theories. Then something occurs to me. "He said the sheriff was meeting him at the barn. You don't think it could possibly be the sheriff, do you?"

"He most definitely would've had access to the phone," she confirms.

"Looks like we might have to just go anyway. Deputy Owens could be in serious trouble," I say. Then I'm struck by another realization. "Damn, we don't have any way of getting there."

Drea produces a set of keys. "I swiped these from Harrison's coat pocket just in case. I gave him a kiss to pacify him when he protested. It seemed like an even trade at the time."

I expel a drawn-out exhale. "Are we really about to do this?"

"We don't have to. We could just go to the station. Your call."

It takes only a second or two for me to decide what feels like the right thing to do. "No, we've got to go to the barn. You drive."

"We should probably leave a note on the front door for when the deputies get here. It wouldn't hurt to have some backup of our own," Drea points out.

"We can use the piece of diary paper."

She ducks away for a moment and then returns. "Here, I found a Sharpie and some tape in a drawer in the kitchen," she says. "I also grabbed this." She showcases a large butcher knife that would make any villain from a slasher film envious.

"Good ideas all around," I reply, taking the tape and marker from her.

I scrawl out a message with bold thick strokes. Clear and easy to read. Then I tape it to the outside of the front door in plain sight.

COME TO WILSON FAMILY BARN
DEPUTY IN TROUBLE!!!

"Ready to go?" asks Drea.

"I sure hope so."

Nerves, don't fail me now.

THIRTY-EIGHT

Donovan

WE'VE MADE A VERY SERIOUS MISTAKE.

I've seen this exact scenario play out in count-less horror films. A car pulls up to an isolated, weathered barn. The only light sources are the lone lantern above the oversized door and the vehicle's headlights. The surrounding forest resembles a dark, impenetrable barrier, walling in the unsuspecting victims. And it's just certain they'll be stumbling through that dense mess of trees to get away from the killer before the movie rolls credits.

Only this time, it's real life and not a piece of B-movie cinema.

On our approach, I notice two deputy cruisers idling off to the side near the broken-down truck. Both of their cab lights are on, but no one's inside. The visible exhaust leaving their tail pipes into the cool air gives off the impression they're still running. But there's no other activity aside from that. Nothing.

Drea rolls Harrison's car up in front of the barn's large door. The headlights are drowned out by the warm glow of the over-head lantern shining down from above.

"So, no element of surprise then? Got it," I say as the vehicle comes to a full stop. Sarcasm is present and accounted for.

"I figure we're safer in the car than we would be parking in the shadows somewhere and then going the rest of the way on foot. I don't know about you, but I can drive a lot faster than I can run," she replies.

"Fair point."

I glance over at the deputy vehicles again and notice the faint outline of a vehicle tucked back amongst the trees beside the white truck. I can't quite get a good look at it from here. No telling whose it is.

"What exactly are we thinking we can do here?" I ask into the quiet of the car. My voice sounds weirdly loud even though I thought I whispered.

"I was actually about to ask you the same thing," she says. We look at each other. "I guess I got caught up in the moment and didn't fully think this through. Oh—but we do have the knife. So there's that."

"We suck at this, don't we?" I say with a tense laugh as I crack open my door. The car's dome light turns on and I suddenly feel even more exposed.

"What are you doing? I'm not ready yet," Drea says, tugging on the sleeve of my coat. "We need to plan first."

My head whirls around to look at her. "Maybe that should have occurred to us before we came here."

BAM!

CRACK!

Our collective screams boom throughout the small car as it shakes from a sudden and violent impact. My heart has officially left my chest now. A body lays face down on the windshield. The glass is on the verge of being shattered, looking like crushed ice. I catch a glimpse of the person's face framed by dark hair. Her empty lifeless eyes peer back at me as a trickle of blood trails down the glass from the pool gathered near her gaped mouth.

Tawni? Dammit!

"Is she dead?" Drea asks in a panic. "Does she need our help?"

I slam my door closed. "She's dead! Go, go!"

"Where the hell did she come from?" shrieks Drea as she throws the car into reverse and slams on the gas.

We barrel backwards. The body shifts onto the hood, startling both of us. Our screaming continues. The car swerves hard to the left and Tawni's body is flung from the hood. A sudden bump near the back of the vehicle has the car tilting back, leaving us at an awkward angle.

"Crap, I think we're in a ditch," I say.

Drea puts the car into drive and tries to floor it, but we stay put. The tires rev and just seem to spin without gaining any traction. She reverses and encounters the same outcome.

"Dammit, we're stuck," she says while banging on the steering wheel in rapid succession. "What was that about us sucking at this?"

"What are we going to do now?" I ask. My voice squeaks a little at the end.

"I don't know, but we need to get the hell out of here, like, yesterday."

I whip out my phone. "I'm going to call the station."

I hit the button on the side of the cell to wake it up and go to press the phone icon. The screen flashes black and shows a low battery warning, then shuts off. I hit the button on the side again, but nothing happens.

"What's wrong?" she asks, her voice slightly higher than usual in her panic. "Are you going to call for help or what?"

I pan my uncertain gaze from the phone to her. "What's the worst thing I could say right now?"

"No. Did your freaking phone just die? Really? You've got to be kidding me."

I nod and stuff it back into my pocket. She slams her head back against the headrest and releases a lengthy moan.

"We're screwed," she says. "Absolutely, one hundred percent screwed."

"Hey, we need to stay positive, all right?"

I don't even believe myself right now.

She takes in a deep breath and lets out an even deeper exhale before looking at me. "Okay. What are our options?"

I wish I had an immediate answer, but unfortunately my mind is a big ball of mush trying to sift through this absolute worst-case scenario. My desperate eyes dart around before landing on the cruisers again.

"What do you think the odds are that there are keys in one of those vehicles?" I offer up.

At first it doesn't seem as though she likes the idea of leaving the safety of the car. But then again, neither do I.

"If how things have been going so far is any indication, I'd say the odds aren't great," she says.

"It's worth a check."

"Is it though?" Her voice goes up a couple more octaves with the question.

"Hey, we both decided to come out here," I say. "And now we've got to get ourselves out of this mess somehow."

She goes quiet for a moment and then sighs. "Fine. Let's not argue. We'll go check."

"Actually, you stay here and keep watch. If you see anything, flash the high beams. At least that might give me a fighting chance. There's no need for both of us to go."

Clearly my outer self has giant brass balls that my inner self lacks.

"Uh, problem," she says. "What if when you get over there the doors are locked? You could get trapped out there."

"Yeah, good point. But it's the only option I see at the moment."

She lets out another heavy sigh. "Please be careful. I can't lose you too, okay?"

Her words bring a slight smile to my face. "I will be, don't worry. And you be ready to flash the lights."

She nods. "Wait. If we're about to die—"

"We aren't."

"But if we are, I want you to know something before that happens," she says. Her timing is either terrible or perfect, depending on what leaves her mouth next.

"Okay," I reply with reluctance.

She gives me a brief nod. "Lori and I kissed over the summer. And I'm bi," she says, taking a deep, dramatic inhale between each statement.

"Wow. You really know how to wind a girl. I'm happy you've had this revelation. It's freeing, right? I'm happy for you," I say. She nods and I gather her in for a quick, enthusiastic hug. "Points to you for a great confession."

"Do you have anything to get off your chest before … you know?"

"I do, and I promise I'll tell you once we get out of this," I reply, causing a smile to form on her lips.

I reach for the door handle and pull it open.

"Wait. Take the knife with you," she says.

I look over and see her searching the back seat for it. She leans back with the knife in hand and holds it out for me to take.

"No, you keep it," I tell her. "I should be able to find something to use in the deputy's car."

"But what about the trip over there?"

"Then you'd be stuck in here without anything. I'd feel better if you kept it."

There are those big ole' brass balls again.

She sends me a look resembling both frustration and acceptance. We both nod, and with one last glance between us, I leave the protection of the car. I look back over my shoulder and say, "Lock the doors," before shutting the door behind me.

I hear the locks engage as I stare down the daunting task ahead of me … trekking the short distance between myself and the cruisers. From where I'm standing, it seems like they could be a distant mirage on the horizon promising false safety. It takes a moment to psyche myself up to put myself out in the open. To make myself vulnerable.

Taking the knife might've been the better choice.

I move out in front of the car and commence with my shaky approach. With the headlights to my back, they cast an elongated shadow out in front of me, looking like an impending omen. I realize I'm practically casting a beacon into the sky like freaking Batman, giving away my positon, and promptly jump out of the way of the lights. In the next minute, it's like I'm in a rave when the high beams start to flash. I spin around to face the car, eyes filled with terror, expecting the worst.

Drea pokes her head out of the now open passenger's side window. "Sorry, hand freaked out. False alarm," she whispers.

A steady exhale calms my nerves just enough to continue. The sound of static cuts through the multitude of forest noises filtering through the air. At first I'm convinced it's the wind, but then it happens again. The sound is coming from inside the closest vehicle.

The radio system.

I sprint for the door handle and tug. I'm surprised when it opens. I leap into the car and shut myself in right away. My hand reaches for the keys in the ignition, but they aren't there.

Great. Just great!

In the passenger's seat are a copy of the *Haddon Falls Daily*, a few light blue file folders, and other random paperwork strewn about. I dig around those to see if I can maybe find the keys, or at least something that could be useful to me.

Nothing. I lean over further to pop open the glove compartment and start feeling around inside. My hand bumps into a small flashlight. I click it on to see if it still works, and I'm relieved to find it does. I slip it into my pocket and relax back against the seat again.

If I were a spare set of keys, where would I be?

The static comes through the radio again. There are two walkie-talkies connected to the center console. A rigid plastic black one and a smooth plastic tan one with a polished finish.

Which one do I talk into?

"Deputy Owens, do you copy? What's your twenty?" The voice comes through the tan one.

I struggle to remove the hand radio from its holder. It's stuck. The moment it's free, I fumble with it in my fingers while trying to untangle the cord wrapped under the seat. I've never used one of these things before. There are a couple knobs and buttons all around it. I decide to press the large flat one on the side and get some feedback.

"Hello?" I say into it.

"Who is this?" the person on the other side asks.

"We're here at the Wilson Family Barn. We need help. There's a dead body, possibly more," I exclaim.

"Is this some kind of joke? How did you get on this channel?" the officer presses, annoyance present in her voice.

"I'm in Deputy Owens's car and he isn't here. I think he's in trouble, and so are we. We need help. Please come to the barn, now!" I say, my voice getting hoarse.

High beams flash through the window. My eyes dart over to Harrison's car. I cut into the person's response and say, "Please, hurry!"

My eyes return to look at the car. The headlights have stopped blinking.

Another false alarm?

I abandon the walkie and let the cord snap it down to the floor beneath the passenger's seat. It chirps to life again, startling me.

"Ten-four. We'll send assistance right away. Over and out," the officer replies, again drawing my attention away from Harrison's car.

A horn blares. My head whips to look back out the window. All I see is black. Unforgiving darkness. Then bright pink neon lights glow before my eyes. I'm so stunned I can't even muster a scream.

Well, shit.

I immediately hit the lock on the door. The figure's gloved hand rises into the air. It's clutched around the handle of a blade.

Tap.

Tap.

Tap.

The knife clinks against the glass three times, growing harder each time. I flinch more with every tap.

"Hey, asshole!"

Drea's voice booms from behind the figure. It's muffled through the window, but there's no doubt it's her. The figure turns to peer over their shoulder, their movements slow and deliberate. I catch a glimpse of Drea's silhouette standing in the distance, knife firmly gripped in her hand.

"Mine's a lot bigger than yours," she grinds out, showcasing the knife.

The figure taps the window one more time and then points the knife at me before turning their attention squarely on Drea. Alarm rocks through me. I bang on the glass.

"No … me. Come get me!" I say, but it seems to be in vain as the figure continues to stalk Drea. "Drea, run!"

She takes off toward the barn. The figure hurries after her.

I have to help her!

I throw open the car door and jump out. Drea enters the barn and manages to slam the door shut before the figure can interfere. They punch the door before slipping around the side of the barn, disappearing into the thick mass of surrounding foliage.

There are more entrances.

I rush to the front door of the barn and attempt to pull it open. I'm met with resistance. It won't budge. I bang on it.

"Drea, it's me," I say in a harsh whisper through the thin gap between two of the boards comprising the door. "Please, open up."

A high-pitched scream erupts from within the barn. My heart falls to the ground. I bang on the door harder this time.

"Drea, I'm coming!"

I curse my legs when they can't seem to carry me as fast as I want them to go as I sprint to the opposite side of the barn than the figure went to. With the help of the flashlight, I spot the side entrance Shaun used that night and waste no time bursting through it.

I find Drea standing there staring at a person sitting on the couch. A lamp resting on the side table next to the person casts an eerie glow on Drea's face. Her horrified look fills me with dismay.

Who's sitting there?

The person's back is to me, their silhouette static. Still, I close the door behind me and move in her direction, my eyes darting around in search of the masked figure. Drea pans her gaze to me and squeaks while pointing the knife in my direction.

"It's me, Drea," I say in a soothing manner.

"It's wasn't the sheriff," is all she says.

"What?"

She returns her attention to the person sitting there and I move the flashlight to follow her line of sight. The closer I get, the more the person's face comes into view until I can see them clearly. The body of the sheriff is propped up on the couch.

Blood. There's blood everywhere.

I have to avert my eyes from the gruesome sight he's been reduced to. My gag reflex activates, and I struggle to suppress the feeling.

"We should take his gun, right?" Drea stammers. Which means I have to look at the body again.

"Probably. It might be nice to have," I reply. "Maybe see if he has a flashlight you can grab too."

I try my hardest to keep the flashlight fixed on his utility belt so Drea can search more efficiently as I look and listen for the masked figure. My hand quakes, making the otherwise simple task difficult. She removes his flashlight from the left side of his belt and then goes for the gun. It's missing from the holster. It's empty. No dice.

"Okay, we're getting the hell out of here," I say.

I take her by the elbow and retrace my steps back to the door I came through. It's suddenly thrown open, slamming hard against the wall. A person slumps through the opening and stumbles toward us. They throw their hand up to shield their eyes from the shine of the flashlight.

Connor?

It's Connor!

My gut reaction is to run over and wrap him up in the

biggest hug I can muster, but I don't. I want to trust him, but his presence there leaves me with serious doubts. Doubts that I never thought I'd have about him. This hurts … so much.

"Connor!" I exclaim. "What are you doing here?"

"The sheriff brought me here. He said someone wanted to see me," he replies.

"Are you hurt?"

I want to go to him. To be there for him. But for some reason, I can't.

"Someone in a fox mask chased me around after—"

He's cut off by a loud sound that resonates behind us. Drea and I jump closer to each other as we twirl around to investigate it. We pan our flashlights over and reveal Carter standing there propped up with one arm against a stack of hay bales. A few farm tools are strewn about on the ground, presumably knocked over by him.

He pushes himself away from the hay bales to stand on his own, and hobbles toward us.

"Carter, were you hiding back there?" I ask.

"Yeah, from him." He points toward Connor. "You can't trust Connor, Donovan. He did that to the sheriff."

"I didn't, I swear," Connor shouts back. Drea's flashlight stays on Carter as I shift mine over to Connor. He takes a few steps forward. "Someone in a fox mask did that to him. You've got to believe me, Donovan." The distressed look in his eyes shatters my heart.

"Stop, both of you," yells Drea, brandishing the knife. "Don't either of you come any closer."

They both stop in their tracks. I drop the light to Connor's left hand. It's covered in a bandage. My heart sinks again. I look over at Carter and his is wrapped up as well, but in a piece of cloth.

"Connor, how did you hurt your hand?" I ask, hoping for the truth.

He stares at it and then back up at me. "I hurt it at the dock. I slipped on a pool of blood and cut it when I tried to break my fall."

"And you, Carter? How did you hurt your hand?"

Drea focuses the light on his face. He squints and holds up the hand in question to shield his eyes. She adjusts the light down and he looks me square in the eye. "I was attacked by that asshole in the fox mask," he replies, just as direct as Connor.

"You've got to believe me, Donovan. Why would I lie to you?" pleads Connor, pulling my attention back to him. "I think Carter's dangerous. I think he might be the fox."

Carter growls. "He's lying! How else do you think he got away from the sheriff unless he killed him, huh?"

"I escaped when the sheriff was attacked by the fox," Connor insists. "Then he chased after me. I barely got away with my life."

"Enough of this," Drea booms. "The sheriff's gun is gone. It's probably safe to say that whoever has it killed him and took it."

A moment of dead quiet falls on the space as we hold both potential suspects in our lights. Wind lashes the barn, causing some of the wood panels to rattle, breaking the silence. We're in a classic standoff.

What if neither one of them are the fox? What if the fox is watching all of us right now from the shadows?

"You both just couldn't play along," Carter says, his voice carrying throughout the barn.

He reaches behind his back and pulls out a gun, aiming it at us. A gasp escapes our collective lips as Drea huddles closer to me. I throw my arm out in front of her and try to position myself between Carter and our trio.

"Why did you do it, Carter?" I demand.

"Why? *Why?* How about we play a little game first, huh?" he asks with a cold, twisted smirk. "Here are three truths and one lie. Ready?" He pulls back the slider on the gun and lets it snap back, prepping the next bullet and adding a punch to his question. "One. Sophia poisoned Lori because she was jealous of what you and Lori had, Drea. Two. I killed that piece of shit Trent for what he did to Carrie. Three. I gutted the sheriff here because he covered up the real cause of Carrie's death to protect his drunk driving son who ran her off the road. Oh, and he made all us kids that witnessed it keep quiet," he says in a hushed tone with his hand up to his mouth like he's telling a secret. "And four. Someone used every single one of us to get their final revenge," he finishes with a flourish, nodding his head to look behind us with an even more sinister smirk than before.

I shine my light to Connor. "What's he talking about?"

"I don't know," he says. "It's true that the sheriff made all of us promise not to say anything about the accident, but I haven't done anything else. I swear!"

Carter lets out an exaggerated sigh. "Now, Connor, you know better than that. You broke the rules, man. No giving hints to the foxes. I may have let you cheat to win before, but I'm afraid tonight's the last time, bandmate."

Gunfire resounds behind us. My hands fly up to cover my ears, and the world slows down around me as I watch on in horror. Connor staggers back from the force of the bullet when it pierces his left shoulder. His painful groan rips through me. His hand moves up to the wound as he's rocked back off his feet and slams hard to the ground.

"Connor!" I yell, rushing to his side.

Blood floods around our hands as I place mine over his. Our teary eyes meet. "You're going to be all right." The words get caught in my throat at first, but I'm still able to get them out.

"I hate to be that guy, but I don't really see this working out in any of your favors," says Carter in an arrogant tone.

His voice grates on my nerves, but I can't seem to take my eyes from Connor's glossy green stare. He grips my wrist with his free hand as our stare deepens.

"I'm sorry you got involved with this," he says softly as a tear trickles down. "I only wanted to get to know you."

"Save your energy," I tell him. "You can apologize all you want when we get out of this, okay?"

He nods before wincing in pain.

"Hellooo?" Carter asks in a drawn-out manner. "In case you've forgotten, we're kind of in the middle of a game here. Not to mention I have a gun pointed at you."

A loud clunk reverberates through the barn. I look over in time to catch Deputy Owens standing over Carter's unconscious body with a large shovel gripped tightly in his hands.

"This damn punk shot at me," he huffs.

"Deputy Owens, you're okay!" announces Drea.

"For the most part, yeah," he says while snatching up the sheriff's gun from Carter's grip. "This isn't a toy, mister."

My attention returns to Connor. "See? We're going to be okay."

He nods delicately while squeezing my hand harder than before. A pale smile tries to come through but is marred by another pain-induced moan.

A guttural yell pierces the air. Drea's light glimmers off the knife in Carter's hand as he springs to life and lunges for the deputy.

"Deputy, behind you!" she cries.

Deputy Owens spins around, primed and ready to fire with the sheriff's gun still in hand.

BANG!

BANG!

BANG!

The barn lights up as each consecutive gunshot, like the snap flash of a strobe light. Carter's body flails with erratic motion as every bullet impacts his chest. His knees crash into the ground with a thump before he collapses forward, face first.

And then there were four.

THIRTY-NINE

Drea

"I F I NEVER SEE THE FLASHING LIGHTS OF AN ambulance for the rest of my life, it will still be too soon," I say to Donovan as we stand by watching the paramedics load Connor inside. He just nods. I wrap my arm around his shoulder and tug him close. "He's going to make it."

His water-logged eyes never leave the ambulance. "Yeah, I know."

"You can go with him if you want," I offer. "I'll just hitch a ride with Deputy Owens."

He sniffles. "I'd love that, but he told me not to. He feels responsible for what happened. He said he might need some time for things to settle … so it's not so awkward for him."

"He'll come around. It's obvious that he likes you, and you like him. So, maybe just give him some space?" I give his shoulder a quick jostle.

A hint of a hopeful smile sprouts on his lips, but then falters as the ambulance drives away. Deputy Owens finishes a conversation with two other deputies on the scene and breaks away, heading in our direction.

"Hey, you two," he says. "I believe I owe you both an apology."

"I think saving our lives is apology enough, Deputy," I reply.

"Yeah, you've more than made it up to us," Donovan adds with a shallow smirk. "But hearing you say that doesn't hurt either."

A half smile appears on the deputy's face. "Oh, and they found a bike fitting your description, Donovan."

Donovan perks up a little. "They did? Where?"

"Uh, well, in pieces inside the barn," the deputy says.

Donovan shrinks back and blows out a sharp breath. "Of course they did. Why would it still be intact? That'd be silly," he says, his tone full-on sarcastic.

"I'm sure there's some way we can get you a new one," the deputy replies.

"At this point, I'm just glad we didn't end up like the bike, to be honest," Donavan says. "I think it's time I invest in a car anyway. My luck with bikes lately seems like a sign."

"I second that," I add.

"Well, it seems the officers here have the situation under control," says Deputy Owens. "What do you say we all get out of here and head back to the station? We'll call your families when we get there."

"Sounds good," I reply and then look over at Donovan.

"Could you drop me off at the hospital where they're taking Connor?" he asks.

"Did you already change your mind about the whole 'space' thing?" I ask with a light elbow to his side.

He gives me a helpless shrug. "I have to see how he's doing."

"Hey, I get it," I say, briefly rubbing his shoulder in a show of support. "I was just kidding."

Deputy Owens smiles. "I think I can manage that."

Donovan takes shotgun while I climb into the back. It feels

weird sitting there walled off from the front cab by a layer of glass and a metal cage. The feeling could only be made worse if I were in handcuffs.

Glad I'm not claustrophobic.

Deputy Owens slips into the driver's seat. "Everybody good?" he asks, but it comes through a little muted. Donovan nods and the deputy glances back at me.

"Yep," I reply close to the divider.

He slides a square window of glass near the center of the divider to the side, allowing us to communicate clearer. "Sorry, about that. Don't usually have many backseat passengers."

"It's definitely cozy," I say, and he chuckles lightly.

Deputy Owens carefully maneuvers through the maze of vehicles parked out front of the barn. The ride along the trail leading to the main road is a bumpy one. The ground is uneven and rough on the tires.

Complete exhaustion begins to kick in. My eyelids are heavy, and I find myself wanting to nod off. They're trying to close up shop, but that's not happening any time soon while we're bouncing around like this. I'll wait until we're on the main road.

"You know, you two should be proud of yourselves for how you handled that situation back there," the deputy says.

"I wouldn't call what we did 'handling the situation,'" I confess with a hollow laugh.

"Yeah, not so much," Donovan concurs.

"Well, at any rate, at least it's all over now," he says.

A huff leaves my lips as I collapse back against the stiff, vinyl-covered seat. A cramp builds in my thigh, so I shift on the unforgiving material to get into a more comfortable position. My foot knocks into something on the floor. I drift my gaze downward, but can't make out what's there. It's too dark. I lean down and my eyes adjust the closer I get. A medium-sized black duffle bag sits there with the zipper partially unfastened. Something is sticking out from the small opening. It appears to be the corner of a book.

Donovan and the deputy are busy chatting, so I take the opportunity to investigate further. My curiosity gets the better of me. I discreetly reach down and slide the zipper all the way back. My eyes grow wide as the cover comes into full view when I pick it up. It's all black with the pink outline of a fox mask right smack in the center.

Why does he have Carrie's diary?

Then my eyes catch a second object that was right below it. A plastic evidence bag with a phone in it.

Connor's phone?

A small gasp slips out of me at the worst possible moment.

"Everything all right back there?" Deputy Owens asks.

The faint words leave me before I have a chance to think about them. "It's you."

"I beg your pardon?" he asks, his confused expression reflected in the rearview mirror.

"You're the one who used us all," I spew out like verbal diarrhea.

He scoffs. "What are you talking about?"

Donovan shoots me an equally puzzled look. "What's going on, Drea?"

"The person Carter was talking about," I say. "The one who used us all to get your revenge. It was you, Deputy. It was you the whole time." I showcase the diary and the phone for them to see. "I just found these in your bag."

Donovan's expression goes from confusion to shock almost instantly as his attention shifts from me to the deputy. "Deputy Owens, is this true?"

The deputy releases a frustrated sigh. "Carter was right about you two not being able to play along," he replies.

The car suddenly accelerates and makes a sharp turn onto the main road. I'm sent off balance and slam shoulder first into the car door. My head knocks against the window. Instant headache.

"What the hell are you doing?" Donovan asks as the car swerves erratically back and forth.

I'm tossed from one side to other by the car's dramatic movements. "Please stop!" I yell when I begin to feel sick to my stomach.

"Oh, like my half-sister probably pleaded with all her sup-posed friends—*your* friends—to stop following her that night," the deputy replies, jerking the wheel and causing the car to veer violently again.

Carrie was his half-sister?

"I'm sorry about what happened to Carrie, but what does this have to do with us?" I ask.

I'm sent crashing back against the unforgiving seat when he floors it again. My arms and legs burn from sliding along the harsh vinyl material. I reach for the seatbelt and fight with it to strap myself in.

"There are usually always civilian casualties, I'm afraid," he intones.

Through the windshield, I see we're approaching Devil's Horn. A left turn is coming up, but the deputy doesn't seem to be slowing or planning to turn.

Is he going to drive us off the cliff?

Donovan lunges for the wheel, stretching his seatbelt to the limit before it snaps him back. The deputy swings at him, but he dodges to the side and swats his hand away. He hurls him-self toward the steering wheel again and seizes it before spinning it sharply to the left. Donovan is knocked back against his seat with a quick shove. The car slams into the guardrail, sending sparks flying into the air as we glide along it. A harsh sound rings out and I cover my ears when it becomes too much to handle. We continue to skid along until the deputy course corrects back onto the road.

Chaos ensues in the front seat as a fight over the steering wheel rages on. I feel like a helpless spectator. Headlights shine through the front windshield. A collective scream fills the cab as the deputy regains control of the wheel in time to dodge the oncoming car. He turns the wheel hard. We spin out of control. The view through the windows blur in my peripherals. Like I'm on the worst kind of amusement park spinning ride in existence. My gut bubbles as I sink back against the seat harder to steady myself.

A sudden impact. A loud crunch.

Then nothing but darkness.

FORTY

Donovan

I BLINK MY EYES. BLURRY SLIVERS OF MY SURROUNDINGS come in lethargic waves. My right eye feels weighed down. Compromised. It's harder to open. A stinging sensation. I run the tips of my fingers across the closed eyelid. They come away damp. They're covered in blood. My blood. A dull ache rolls through my temple. A mess of confusion.

The range of movement for my chest and hips are limited by the taut seatbelt. I try to press forward, but there's no give. No slack. My legs feel constricted to the space near the center console. It takes a moment for me to gain my bearings. Attempting to do that while also competing with the massive headache trying to assault my brain is easier said than done.

I reach for the door handle, but it isn't where my hand instinctively lands. My palm grazes a sharp piece of something in the process. Upon further inspection, I see the door is actually bent inward. Almost split in half.

How am I still alive?

A mangled combination of metal and plastic pieces protrudes toward me from the door. My eyes peer out the shattered window and see the distorted outline of a thick pole with the assistance of a light from above. A lamppost. The door is securely wrapped around it.

I'm not getting out that way.

My gaze drifts out to the view through the front windshield. My brain registers the cliff's edge. Devil's Horn. But there's no guardrail here, meaning nothing is between us and the massive drop-off. The lake beyond appears like a huge blob of black matter outside of the light's reach. Infinite darkness.

My attention moves over to the limp body of Deputy Owens next to me before peering into the back seat at Drea. Both seem unconscious.

"Drea," I whisper, but get no answer.

I switch my focus back to the deputy. His head is leaned back against the seat and tilted away from me. There's a trickle of blood traveling down from his forehead, gathering on his cheek. I press the release for my seatbelt, first with the slightest pressure and then apply more at a slow pace. When it clicks free, I unbuckle and guide the strap to its resting position so it doesn't snap back. I lean toward him and wave my hand in front of his face to check his alertness. He doesn't react. His chest still rises and falls in rhythmic succession with a slight flaring of his nostrils. He's still alive.

My eyes locate the handle for the driver's side door. It seems like the only way I can get out of here.

I need to get to Drea.

I take in a shallow breath and carefully place my hand on the steering wheel to brace myself while I stretch over the deputy's body to reach the door's handle. It's just out of my grasp. I slide my hand further along the top of the steering wheel to get a better grip and reach out again.

Almost there.

My fingers grip the handle and I'm able to pull it. The door cracks open. My eyes dart over to Deputy Owens. No change. I push it the rest of the way and it continues to creak open. I cringe at the thought of the deputy waking up. I check again. He's still out cold.

Heart attack central.

My sweaty palms betray me in the worst way possible and slip off the wheel. My side rams right into the steering wheel. The horn blares. My hip crashes down onto the control panel containing all the center console's electronics. The flash of green and yellow lights shows through the open car door. I raise away from the steering wheel and steady myself. My eyes shoot over at the deputy. He's still unconscious.

Damn, that was close.

I slink back to my seat to shift myself into a seated position. I lift my leg up and over the deputy's lap, aiming to plant my foot on the edge of the open door's frame. My hand shoots up to grab the little handle above the door when I lose my balance. Now straddling the deputy's lap, I move my foot out further to touch down on the ground. I stare back at the last appendage I need to get to safety. Lifting it into the air, I bend at the knee and hold onto the door to steady myself as I retract my leg. Slow and deliberate movements.

Thread the needle.

Miraculously, I'm able to get my other leg out without incident. I lunge for the back door and yank it open. I unbuckle Drea and lightly tap her cheek to wake her. Her eyes flutter. She lifts her hand up to graze her head while letting out a low groan.

"Drea, I know it's hard, but we need to go now," I say, trying to pull her along.

She snaps to and assists herself out of the car. We begin to limp away. Then I stop to peer back at the cruiser.

"Wait here," I tell her.

"What are you doing?" she asks in a sluggish whisper.

"He still has a gun. If he catches us, he'll just shoot at us."

Her nervous whine behind me doesn't fill me with much confidence in the decision I've made. The short hike back to the driver's side door seems like I'm walking down an endless tunnel. I have to look down to make sure my feet are actually moving forward. My breathing is loud in my ears as I fight to quell my rampaging heartbeat. I spot the gun in its holster on the deputy's left hip.

The evil bastard's left-handed? He's giving them a terrible name.

I dip down and lean my hand in for the holster. At first my fingertips struggle to undo the button securing the flap in place. It's really locked in. I use my fingernail to dig under it and hear it click free. I grip the handle of the gun and tug it loose from its seated position.

My attention is fixed solely on the gun and its safe retrieval. The moment I get it free from the holster, my eyes glance up to see Deputy Owens staring right at me.

I roll back onto my heels, gun in hand, and land flat on my ass. He lurches forward and seizes control of the gun's barrel when I try to point it at him. I manage to get my finger over the trigger and pull. The shot misses and blows out the driver's side window. He moves on top of me and straddles my hips, pinning me to the ground. He works his left hand up to my throat while holding both of mine clutched around the gun at bay with his right.

"Get off of him, asshole," Drea blares. Her black shoe-clad foot enters my field of vision and connects with his head.

He groans and falls to the side, cradling his face in his hands. Drea helps me to my feet. I immediately point the gun at him again.

"Why did you do this?" I demand between desperate breaths.

He shakes his head while raising himself to sit up. His hand rubs his jaw as he contorts it back and forth. "I think you knocked out a tooth," he says, ignoring the question.

My anger mounts to the nth degree. "Answer me, dammit!"

He relaxes back against the side of the cruiser for support and stares directly at me. "Let me ask you a question, Donnie boy," he begins, and then hocks a ball of bloody spit off to the side. "If you were given a chance to get revenge on the person responsible for your father's death, would you?"

The question catches me off-guard. My hands quake as I try to maintain my aim at him.

His eyebrow quirks. "No opinion? Fine. How about you, Drea? Didn't you want to get revenge when your undercover girlfriend was murdered?"

"How the hell did you know about us?" Drea asks. Her voice trembles near the end of the question.

"Lori was the first one I coerced into helping me," he replies. "A picture of your little kiss on the hood of her car really set her off. The poor dear couldn't handle the thought of what that getting out would do to you. She was mine after that."

Initially, Drea stands there looking stunned, unable to give any kind of retaliation. Then she explodes and tries to rush him, but I hold her back.

"Go to hell, you bastard!" she shouts as tears begin to trail down her cheeks.

"Killing isn't the answer to anything," I finally say in response to his question. "No, I wouldn't want that."

"Oh, so you *can* talk?" he mocks me. "Come on, you can't deny that sometimes it's necessary."

"I couldn't live with myself if I did what you've done," I argue.

He begins to laugh, a low sound that croaks in the back of his throat. "Technically, I didn't do anything except save your lives back at the barn with the sheriff's gun, which I promptly returned to its rightful place. So, I guess he'll get the credit for that one." He pauses for a moment before continuing. "Your *friends* took care of the rest. They all picked each other off one by one because their secrets were too precious, too deadly, to be exposed."

"What are you talking about?" I demand.

He braces himself against the side of the vehicle in order to stand on his own. His hand sweeps across his forehead and he looks at the blood that comes away on his fingers. He laughs again under his breath.

"They were all the fox," he says. "They all have blood on their hands, whether figuratively or literally. I just made sure to set them up perfectly. With your help too, of course, my good little catalysts. But I never killed anyone until Carter, which, again, was to save your lives. So, in a roundabout way, you kind of owe me."

"We don't owe you anything," cries Drea.

"And this is the thanks I get," he sneers.

"You're sick, man, you know that?" I say.

"No!" he booms. "What's sick is a group of people chasing a young girl to her death. What's sick is a town's sheriff covering up said death by saying it was an accident, when in reality it was his drunk driving son who caused it." He draws in a deep, rough breath. "What's sick is that a group of people would kill the ones they supposedly love over things like jealousy, greed, lust, rage … or, in Carter's case, just because he enjoyed doing it. I really did luck out with that one. Now *that's* sick."

I go to reply, but he cuts me off. "Small town America likes to pretend things are just peachy. Safe in their quaint little bubbles.

But there's always chaos simmering just beneath the surface. Ready to boil over at any moment. So forgive me for wanting to exploit that for the sake of my sister!"

"You honestly think Carrie would have wanted you to do this?" I spit out.

"No, but then again, she never knew what was best for her in the first place. She was too innocent. Too naïve. Your classic, good girl type. All the boys wanted her attention. They all loved Carrie."

Drea scoffs. "Okay, we get it. Carrie was a perfect princess. Get on with it."

"How dare you reduce her to that?" he fires back. "Did you know that a week before she died, she called me at college to tell me what was going on here? Have you ever felt helpless, unable to be there for the ones you love? I was on the opposite side of the country and wanted to protect her, but couldn't. She told me about all the new friends she'd made here in Haddon Falls. About Trent. And after reading through her diary, I could see she was blind to how terrible these people really were. She was too close to it. She couldn't see how they were corrupting her."

"They tried to help your sister," Drea says. "Trent was the only one who hurt her."

"You're wrong. You didn't get to read what I did in that diary. They were manipulative," he replies forcefully. "They all had to pay."

"What about Harrison? Connor?" I ask, my patience wearing thin. "What about us? Your work isn't done if we're still alive, right? Civilian casualties and all that?"

"Well, both of you look like absolute shit, Harrison was stabbed, and Connor was shot. I'd say things worked out well enough." His smug reply has my cheeks flushed with anger. "Both of your deaths would have been a nice extra emotional toll on them, but I'll take what I can get."

"Take what you can get?" I repeat.

"Yeah. And let's not forget that at the end of the day, it'll be your word against mine ... a deputy who, mind you, hasn't done anything wrong. And if you kill me with my own gun, how will that look? You've got no evidence to back up your claims."

That statement resonates deep within me. Did we just lose this game? Is he right? His mouth coils into a sick grin at my blank expression.

"What are you proposing then?" I say. "We just give up and surrender?"

"We go our separate ways. Clean slate. I've got my revenge, and you have your lives to show for all of this," he replies. "And I'm sure you'll be seen as heroes in the eyes of this shithole town."

"Yeah, right," Drea says. "As if. You'll just come after us later."

"I guess you'll just have to take my word, now, won't cha?"

"I guess we don't really have a choice," I say, lowering the gun.

The deputy relaxes back against the cruiser. "Looks that way."

My eyes move to the flashing lights on top of the car. The memory of an earlier conversation with the deputy plays in my mind.

"Or do we?" I raise the gun at him as he stands back up. "You seem to have overlooked one thing in your otherwise flaw-less plan, Deputy."

"Oh? And what's that exactly?"

I close in on him before circling out toward the road, never letting him leave my sights. "Your dash cam has been recording this whole conversation. It picked up all the audio. Your confes-sion," I reply, just as self-assured as he sounded.

His eyes narrow. His jaw tenses. He glances over at the lights above the car and then down to the open door.

"Don't even think about it," I warn.

The deputy relaxes his stance. He puts his hands in the air next to his chest and a subtle laugh leaves his lips. "What are you going to do? Shoot me?"

"Haven't decided yet," I reply, taking an assertive step forward.

He inches along the side of the cruiser and slithers around the open car door until he's standing on his own, out in the open and away from the vehicle. Isolated. Each step I take forward he takes two back.

"You're not going to get away with this," he says when he nears the cliff's edge. "There's no way you're getting out of this without getting blood on your hands."

"Then it looks like we have something in common, huh?" I reply.

I surge forward, rushing him. His eyes widen as he takes a sizable step back. Gravel breaks away under his feet and slides down the cliff. His left leg buckles and slips back. His arms flail about before extending out for me.

"Help me!" he cries.

I'm not a killer.

I reach my hand out. He takes hold of it. He pulls me off my feet as he continues to fall. We crash to the ground. He continues to slide off the side of the cliff as I struggle to maintain my grip on his hand. My sweaty palms make the task even more difficult. I discard the gun off to the side in order to grab onto the deputy's other hand.

"Donovan," Drea shouts. She takes hold of my arms and attempts to help me pull the deputy to safety.

We're all struggling. My teeth clench tight, holding back a strained groan. For a split second, I notice Deputy Owens's eyes shift to the gun lying on the ground next to us. His eyes dart back over to me, suspicion present in his stare.

You've got to be kidding me. He wouldn't, would he?

He shakes his left hand free from my grasp and goes for the gun.

"Drea, the gun!" I yell.

She reacts quickly and knocks the weapon away from his reach. He struggles to get a hold of the rough terrain with his left hand, then tries to wrap it around mine still holding onto his right one. Our eyes slam into each other. I shake my head as I feel his hand slip through my clammy grasp.

Then suddenly, I'm holding onto nothing. He falls back, disappearing into the darkness below with a horrible scream. A loud, thunderous splash follows moments later.

Drea helps me to my feet, and I find myself in her arms, enveloped in a tight hug.

"That was incredibly stupid," she says, and squeezes me harder. "What were you thinking?"

"I know. I had a terrible lapse in judgment."

"You practically gave me a heart attack."

"I'm sorry," I say. "I hated how I felt when I saw him falling. I felt like I did that. That I was the one responsible. I wanted him to fall … and that scared me. I felt no better than him."

"I get that. I do, but you're nothing like him, Donovan." She pulls back to look at me. "What he did? There's no coming back from that, understand?"

I nod and proceed to bury my head into her shoulder. The tears I'd been holding back summon forth all at once, and I'm finally able to fully reciprocate the hug.

We separate after a moment. I move to stand at the edge to stare down through water-logged eyes.

"Karma one, Deputy Owens zero," I say under my breath.

"What?" asks Drea.

"Oh, nothing."

"Do you think he survived that fall?" she asks, joining by my side and peering down the cliff along with me.

"Nope."

"Good," she says, just as blunt.

I nudge the gun off the side of the cliff with the toe of my shoe and hear it hit the water.

"What are we going to tell the police?" Drea asks.

"The truth," I say. "I think there's been enough lies."

"Yeah. Besides, like you said, we've got all the evidence we need, right?"

I nod. Then I remember I still owe her a declaration for getting out of this.

"I've never truly been kissed," I admit. "But I plan to make Connor my first."

She looks over at me and smiles. "Your confession. You remembered."

I take hold of her hand and give it a light squeeze. "I promised, didn't I?"

"Yeah, that you did."

We continue staring out at the vast emptiness before us. For the first time in a long time, I feel free ... truly free to be who I am. After surviving this whole ordeal, I'm beginning to think the remainder of our senior year should be a walk in the park.

We've sure earned it.

A few weeks later ... Halloween

Donovan

It's my first holiday in Haddon Falls.

Unlike Halloween back where I'm from, the kids here apparently trick-or-treat around downtown before heading out into the neighborhoods. The Pour Over just so happens to be one of the prime stops.

"We need another jumbo bag of candy up here, Marcus," I call out to him from the front counter.

He hurries from the back room, a massive sack of candy in hand, and resupplies the large cauldron bowl near the register. Every time I see him in his costume, I do a double-take. He's decided to introduce Miz Markie Marc to the entire town. His rendition of the classic Marilyn Monroe in a ruffled white dress is a revelation. An almost spot-on recreation. And since it's for Halloween, no one seems bothered by it. Not to mention his female illusion is on-point, only compromised when he opens his mouth to speak.

"Are you sure you're only giving the little monsters two pieces each?" he asks with pursed lips, showcasing the signature Marilyn mole he's painted on his cheek.

"What answer could I give that won't land me on the end of one of your glares?" I ask.

He glares at me anyway. "Two. Your answer should always be two when it comes to this."

"Then yes, I've been giving out two to each kid."

He sees right through my lie. "You've been giving out more to costumes you like, haven't you?" His pointed stare cuts through me. "There's no way you've gone through this much candy if you haven't, Donnie."

I nod with a hesitant smirk. "But in my defense, some of them have been so stinking cute."

He rolls his eyes. "From this point on, two pieces each, got it? Or we're going to run out early. And then I'll sic those angry little rug rats on your flat behind."

"Hey, it's not flat," I say, glancing back at it. "I do squats."

"Do more," he says in a dead pan tone.

I send him a half-assed salute. "Yes, sir."

I'm glad to see him in better spirits after what happened with Deputy Owens. When the news broke about them finding the deputy's body in Lake Wilson, I hadn't had a chance to talk to Marcus. I was told I couldn't discuss the case since they were still looking through all the evidence, so he had no context of what really happened. It broke his heart.

Once it was all out there, it crushed Marcus even more. Mainly because he found out I'd been put through so much. He felt guilty for being so blind to the whole situation. Eventually, he chalked it up to him always attracting the crazies. We laughed about it in that moment, but I could tell he was still torn up over it, and so was I. Just like Marcus, I was tricked by the façade Deputy Owens put forth. I felt for Marcus for sure, but I think in some strange way this brought us closer.

I watch him return to the back room, thankful to still have him in my life.

"Trick or treat," a male's voice says behind me.

I turn around. Connor's standing there with a grin firmly planted on his face. His green eyes shimmer bright, like always. He's another person I'm glad is still in my life.

Oh, and we had our first kiss at the hospital. It wasn't exactly the most romantic of settings, but it didn't matter. The whole world melts away regardless when our lips meet.

Kissing him is my new favorite thing.

"Hey, you," I say. "I thought you were going to pick me up at home later to go over to Drea's."

He grumbles and extends his hand. "Trick or treat," he repeats, and somehow his grin grows wider.

Marcus pokes his head out from the back room. "Two. Pieces." His eyes slim at me before moving his focus to Connor. Then they relax. "Hey, Connor."

Connor shoots him a head nod. "Hey, Marcus. Or should I say, Miss Monroe?"

"Miz Markie Marc will do just fine, thank you," Marcus says with a little sass.

Connor chuckles while moving his attention back to me. Then they hone in on the candy cauldron. He clears his throat. I roll my eyes and withdraw two pieces to place on his outstretched palm.

I look over at Marcus and he mouths, "That's right," before he disappears again.

Connor's staring at me, all grins, when I turn back to face him. His lips are just begging to be kissed. I scan the area for any onlookers and the coast is clear.

"My turn," I say, and then lean in to plant a kiss on his lips.

A surprised expression shows on his face. "You always keep me on my toes, Donovan. And I think I like it," he says.

"You *think* you like it, huh?"

"I guess I'll need another sample, just to be absolutely sure," he says before planting a firmer kiss on my lips. "All right, I'm convinced. I like it."

His gentle laugh near my mouth causes my heart to flutter, and I lose track of everything around me. I become hot under the collar, and by the look in his eyes, he's feeling it too. I decide to put some space between us and slink back behind the counter even though that's literally the last thing I want right now.

The door chimes and more kids enter the café. "Trick or treat," their voices ring out from behind Connor. He chuckles to himself and side steps to allow them to approach the counter.

I drop two candies into each bag and have to fight myself not to put more into the bag of a kid dressed as an adorable lion. Marcus's voice enters my head in full force.

Two pieces of candy only, Donnie!

Once the group leaves, my eyes find Connor again. It isn't that difficult since he's hard not to see. The door chime annoyingly pulls my attention away from him again. My replacement for the rest of the candy shift enters.

"Hey, Marcus, I'm heading out. Blaire's here," I shout back to him.

He peeks around the corner. "All right, mister," he replies with a mischievous grin. "You two stay out of trouble now. Or you know what? Screw it. It's Halloween. Do whatever you want."

His laugh is contagious, and I find myself joining in. I hand off the orange and black striped apron to Blaire and make my way over to Connor. His eyes are welcoming at first, but then flash with a sense of seriousness. He extends his hand out for mine and pulls me closer when I grab hold. His intense stare causes a hint of worry to spring up within me.

"What's up?"

"There's something I want to take care of before we head over to Drea's. Is that okay?" he asks.

"Yeah, sure. I'll just head home and you can pick me up after," I reply, but am still left with concern over the look in his eyes.

He sighs. "Actually, I'd like you to be there, if you don't mind."

"Okay. If you want me there, of course I want to be there too."

A smile softens his face. "Great. Want to head out then?"

I nod and he leads me outside to his truck parked on the road. He props open the passenger side door and waits for me to get in. He rounds to the other side and settles into the driver's seat.

"Do I get any hints about what we're doing?" I inquire as my mind races with possibilities.

"Uh-uh. It's a surprise," he says with that signature grin of his.

Look, I'm not saying I don't like surprises, but after what we just went through, I'd rather not have too many more for the time being.

About halfway to our destination, I become very aware of our current route. We're headed toward Devil's Horn.

"Why are we going this way?" I ask. My voice tremors slightly.

"Okay, I guess there's no need for any more suspense. Check behind the seat under the towel."

I reach behind me and lift the towel to look underneath it. A familiar black cube sits there, the one from the barn that held the original fox mask.

"Uh, why is this in here?" I ask, apprehension feeling like a gut punch.

I trust Connor, but this is kind of strange, even for him.

"I'm getting rid of it … properly," he replies. "If the police took it, I'd never get the closure I need for all of this."

Relief pours over me. "How did you get it? The barn was on lockdown."

"It was. And yeah, this probably wasn't the smartest move on my part. But I snuck in a few nights ago and took it," he says. "I was surprised they hadn't found it yet, to be honest. But then again, it's our sheriff's department we're talking about here."

"You snuck in?"

"I know, I know. It was highly illegal of me to do that, but I couldn't go through life knowing something that has caused so much misery and heartache is still in existence."

I think about that and nod. "I understand. I'd probably do the same thing. And if you think this will help, I'm behind you one hundred and ten percent."

That grin I love to see so much returns. We reach the barricade running along the lake side of Devil's Horn and pull off onto the shoulder. Connor takes the box from the back seat and I follow him to the edge of the cliff, looking out onto Lake Wilson. Unlike the night a few weeks ago, the lake now appears serene. The water looks like it's made of glass, it's so still.

Connor removes the mask from the box and holds it out in front of him. The neon orange duct tape outline is showcased in the low-hanging sun. He produces a lighter from his pocket and positions it beneath the mask.

"New beginnings," he says before striking the lighter.

The flame flickers to life and ignites the bottom corner of the mask before spreading across the rest of it. Connor holds it until the fire grows dangerously close to his fingertips. Tears pool in his eyes before cascading down to his chin. I get a little choked up myself.

He releases the flaming remains of the mask to the ground and we watch together as the plastic crinkles up onto itself. It twists about and melts as the flames grow higher before engulfing it entirely. He grabs my hand as we continue watching the fiery display.

"It's officially over now," he whispers. He turns to me with misty eyes. "Thank you for doing this with me."

"Of course. New beginnings, right?" I say, leaning toward him.

"Yeah, new beginnings," he repeats, tilting toward me as well.

Our lips crash into each other in a sweet, all-encompassing embrace. His free hand cups my cheek as our mouths press harder together, deepening the kiss.

We pull apart and our foreheads touch. Our breath intermingles as our heads hang there. I sense the grin that forms on his mouth and can't help but muster one of my own.

This feeling. This feeling right here. It's what I've been wanting for what feels like forever. Now that I have it, I'm never letting go.

Not for anything.

Drea

My head rises and falls with each breath Harrison takes. Every time we cuddle, I have to take care to avoid his injury. After plenty of practice, I think I've found the perfect spot on his sculpted chest to rest my head. It's honestly magical.

The cool fall breeze flows through my bedroom's open window, causing me to snuggle up closer to him.

This is perfection.

The parents are out trick-or-treating with my little sister, and even though they've said countless times that I'm not to have boys up in my room when I'm home alone, they love Harrison. So in my head, he's got a free pass. Besides, the door's wide open. It's not like anything's going to happen. Strictly PG rating in here.

I tilt my head back and stare up at Harrison. His focus is solely on me. His mouth breaks into a smile when our eyes meet. Those soft hazel beauties always hit me right in the feels.

The doorbell rings, interrupting our moment. I faceplant into his chest. The scent of his subtle but intoxicating cologne wafts its way into my nostrils, fully snaring my senses.

"Dang candy duty," I mutter into his shirt.

"We could always turn off the porch light," he offers.

"Nope. Not an option, unfortunately." I raise my head again to look at him. "My mom doesn't want any candy left in the house. She's convinced my dad will cheat on his new diet. In her defense, he has no self-control when it comes to sweets," I continue with a soft laugh.

"I guess we should probably head downstairs anyway since I'm sure Donovan and Connor will show up soon, right?" he says at the peak of his full-body stretch.

"Oh, crap, what time is it?" I spring up from the bed and grab my phone from the nightstand. "That might be them at the door."

There's a text from Donovan that must have come in while we were napping. It says they'll be over in a little while. He mentions Connor needing to take care of something first. He ends with a note that he'll text when they get here. My eyes peer out the open window and see it's dark out.

"Any news from Donovan?"

"He said they'll be here in a bit. So that probably is, in fact, a trick-or-treater at the door."

Harrison takes my hand and halts my departure. "But cuddling," he whines in a playful manner. He rises to his knees on the bed and encircles his arms around my mid-section.

I giggle. "I'll be right back," I say, leaning in to plant a kiss on his lips.

The doorbell beckons me again, and I have to wrestle away from Harrison's arms which, admittedly, is a ridiculously difficult task to accomplish.

Once he releases me, I make quick work of the stairs to the first floor. "Coming," I announce while snatching up the Frankenstein head shaped bowl from the side table in the foyer. I open the door. "Thanks for wait—"

I pause when I find no one standing there. I poke my head outside and look from left to right, jumping a little when I glimpse the stuffed scarecrow sitting in the rocking chair on the porch. My sister insisted we put him out there. I finish giving the porch one last look over and crane my neck to peer beyond the yard at the children running along the sidewalk decked out in an assortment of costumes.

"Did I just get ding-dong ditched?"

I re-enter the house and shut the door behind me. I abandon the candy bowl back on the side table and watch as Harrison strolls down the stairs. He sweeps me up in his arms and holds me as we sway back and forth.

"Any kids in cool costumes?" he asks before giving me a peck on the mouth.

"Nope. I think one of the little assholes pranked us," I reply, returning his peck. "Or they just got justifiably impatient with me and left."

"Never," he states with a grin. The doorbell chimes. "Round two?"

I quickly collect the bowl again and rush the door, not giving them a chance to get away this time. There's a group of kids standing there when I open it. They all have their bags at the ready and collectively yell, "Trick or treat!"

"Aww, you all look so good," I say while dispensing out handfuls of candy.

The kids peel off one by one after they receive their treats, allowing the next one a chance. The last kid in line steps up and his costume causes my heart to skip a beat. He's dressed as a fox. Not a neon light masked fox, but a regular old fox.

"Like foxes, huh?" I ask him.

He extends his bag out while nodding, slow and methodical. A chill swims across my shoulders and down my arms. I toss a handful of candy into his bag and he turns abruptly before running off down the driveway. I shut the door and lean against it with a heavy sigh.

Am I going to feel like this every time I see a fox now?

Harrison's still standing there, his arms outstretched. I can't help but collapse into them. His strong hug releases all the tension I'm holding in.

The lights suddenly go out, leaving us standing in the dark. The tension instantly returns.

"You didn't have to go to this much trouble to get me alone in the dark, you know," he teases.

I groan. "That damn breaker. My dad swore he had someone fix it."

"You know, this could work out to our benefit. Kids will think we don't have any more candy," he says with a soft chuckle.

"Candy has to be all gone, remember?"

His face illuminates with the help of his phone's light. "Right," he says. "Lead the way."

He takes hold of my hand and our fingers lace together. I pull out my phone too and press on the flashlight button. I shine it down the hallway and move toward the basement with Harrison close behind. The door still sounds like it's in serious need of some lubrication as it creaks open, sounding loud in the quiet house.

"That's literally the creepiest thing I've ever heard," Harrison says.

"You're really not helping," I reply with a soft giggle.

We position our phones to shine down into the basement. Even with the help of both phones, the light still isn't strong enough to reach the bottom of the stairs.

"The breaker box is at the bottom," I say, but my feet fail to move forward.

"I got your back, Sullivan," he says close to my ear.

I love when he calls me by my last name. It's like we're on the same team.

I love having him on my team.

I take the first step slow and then the subsequent ones a lot quicker until I reach the breaker. After flipping all the switches, the lights come back on.

"Nerves of steel you got there, Sullivan," he says, and his phone's light reveals the grin on his face in the dark of the basement.

"Not too bad yourself, Daniels," I reply, making his grin grow.

When we reach the kitchen, Harrison's hands take hold of

my waist. He gently pulls me toward him. I crash against his firm chest as our hips mingle together. He sweeps my hair to one side, away from my neck, and places a soft kiss there. I allow myself to get swept up in this wonderful feeling, but then the reality of where we are slams into me.

"What if my parents walked in just now?" I say while playfully swatting him on the arm.

He acts offended. "First of all, I have it on good authority that your parents love me. And second, it's just so hard to not want to hold and kiss you whenever I see you. But if you want me to, I'll try to resist."

His smirk makes me want to smack and kiss him in equal measure.

"Thank you," I say with a quick kiss to his cheek. The doorbell rings yet again, and I can't hold back the moan that's incoming. "Something tells me this is going to be a long night."

I collect the bowl of candy and fling open the door. A smile fills my face at the sight of Donovan and Connor standing there.

"Trick or treat," they say together.

My smile falters and my eyes practically roll out of my skull. "Ha, ha, very funny. I thought you said you'd text when you got here." I step aside and they enter.

"Oh, yeah. Sorry about that. We were kind of distracted," replies Donovan. I flash him a playful look. "Not like that, you perv."

"Uh-huh," I say. Harrison exchanges hugs with them as I shut the door. "All right, since you two are such jokers, you can be on candy duty for the rest of the night." My delivery is frisky.

"Sounds good," replies Donovan, taking the bowl from my hands. He opens the door and sets it on the pumpkin shaped doormat outside before turning back to me. "Done and done." A cheeky grin lights up his entire face.

"Brilliant idea," says Harrison. "Why didn't we think of that?" He winks at me when I toss him a withering stare.

"Uh, I do believe that's called cheating," I say.

Donovan pulls me into a solid, warm hug. "It's good to see you, Drea," he says.

I squeeze him back. "You're lucky I like you, Donovan."

"Indeed I am."

"I hope you don't mind, but we were thinking we could watch *Hocus Pocus*," Connor pipes up, producing the movie case tucked inside his jacket. "It's one of Donovan's favorite Halloween movies."

"And it's cute scary, not scary scary," adds Donovan with a knowing glance.

"Sure," I say. "I think that's about all I could handle right now anyway."

The three boys move to the living room. I hang back to watch them take their seats on the couch. Harrison pats the empty space beside him.

"Coming?" he asks.

"Yeah."

I look down at the rope bracelet on my wrist. It hasn't left my arm since that night in Harrison's car. The bracelet will always remind me of Lori. That will never change. But now it also symbolizes something new. Both things born from a place of love.

"Drea, you're missing the beginning," Donovan says with a wave over to join them.

No, I'm not.

I know things will never be the same again. And that notion becomes more and more acceptable with each passing day. Of course I wish certain events hadn't played out the way they did, but when it's all said and done, you have to keep going.

Keep pushing forward. Keep on living … living for those you lost, and for those who would struggle without you in their lives.

As I look at these three people in front of me, I know I've found those individuals. We're bonded now through—let's face it—something that was pretty savage. And I've decided to live for the tiny moments in life that make it all worth it. Tiny moments like the one playing out in my living room right now. Because in the end, that's all we can really do.

This is the beginning I'm choosing to embrace.

THE END

acknowledgments

First and foremost I need to thank my family, with a very special shout out to my mom, for always being there when I needed to vent about anything book related. And for also never failing to encourage me to keep pursuing my dream no matter what. They're a huge reason why this book came about, and for that I'm eternally grateful.

Very special thanks to the wonderful author and editor, Raine Thomas (the Red Queen herself). I absolutely adore you and all you do to help clean up my writing! You've definitely made this book, and so many others, way more polished and refined. Not to mention, you're also one of the best people to bounce ideas off of!

Huge thanks should go to Sarah Hansen at Okay Creations for designing an absolutely stunning cover for this book. You've seriously given me something very striking to put on display, and I can't thank you enough! I am proud to have your cover represent this book.

Big thanks should go to Stacey Blake at Champagne Book Design for creating such a beautiful interior for this book. I'm absolutely head over heels with how this book looks, inside and out.

An extra special thanks goes to authors Gretchen McNeil, Susan Burdorf, Elisabeth Staab, Jennifer L. Armentrout, Abbi Glines, Colleen Hoover, and Cambria Hebert for being absolute all-stars who were all involved with beta reading and giving feedback in some capacity. You ladies are just too amazing for words, seriously!

I also want to thank EVERY SINGLE author, reader, blogger, and friend who's been so incredibly supportive of me and my love of writing (you know who you are). You all mean the world to me, and I can't even express in words how much I appreciate all of you!

Finally, thanks to *you*, the reader, for taking a chance on this book. By performing this simple act you are helping me make a lifelong dream come true, and you have no idea how much that means to me.

T.A. Kunz loves to connect with readers!
So, please don't hesitate to reach out to him here:

Website—www.authortakunz.com

Email—authort.a.kunz@gmail.com

Twitter—@Authortakunz1

Instagram—www.instagram.com/authorkunz

Facebook—www.facebook.com/authoradamkunz

CPSIA information can be obtained
at www.ICGtesting.com
Printed in the USA
LVHW091033150721
692780LV00011B/134/J

Chinese Views of Childhood

CHINESE VIEWS
OF CHILDHOOD

Edited by

Anne Behnke Kinney

UNIVERSITY OF HAWAI'I PRESS
Honolulu

95 96 97 98 99 00   5 4 3 2 1

Library of Congress Cataloging-in-Publication Data

Chinese views of childhood / edited by Anne Behnke Kinney.
p.   cm.
Includes index.
ISBN 0-8248-1681-1
1. Children—China—History.   2. Youth—China—History.
3. Children—China—Social conditions.   4. Youth—China—
Social conditions.   I. Kinney, Anne Behnke.
HQ792.C5C475   1995
305.23'0951—dc20
95-882
CIP

Designed by Paula Newcomb

Contents

Acknowledgments

I am first of all grateful to Dexter Whitehead, former director of the University of Virginia's Center for Advanced Studies, for helping to fund the conference at which these essays were first presented in 1990. I would also like to thank the Association of Asian Studies, the California Institute of Technology, and the Ellen Bayard Weedon Foundation for their contributions to the conference.

I am grateful to Viola Winner for her expertise in photographing some of the illustrations used in this book. Thanks also go to Ellen Laing and Keith Wilson for their advice on these selections. I am grateful to the National Palace Museum, Taipei, Taiwan, Republic of China, and to the Peabody Essex Institute in Salem, Massachusetts, for their permission to reproduce paintings and photographs from their collections in this book. Joseph Lipten provided valuable assistance in compiling the index.

Gail Moore and Judy Birckhead deserve thanks for the hours of technical assistance they provided. Final thanks go to Patricia Crosby for her patience, editorial expertise, and faith in this project.

Chinese Dynasties

Shang/Yin	1766–1122 B.C.
Zhou	1123–256 B.C.
Qin	221–207 B.C.
Han	206 B.C.–A.D. 220
Three Kingdoms	221–280
Jin	265–419
Six Dynasties	386–589
Sui	589–618
Tang	618–907
Five Dynasties	907–959
Song	960–1279
Yuan	1280–1368
Ming	1368–1644
Qing	1644–1911
Republic of China	1912
People's Republic of China	1949

Foreword

When setting out on a historical study of childhood, as these path-breaking scholars have done, one cannot be sure which of two approaches toward children will emerge from the resources. Some societies can only see childhood in terms of its potential—in relation, that is, to eventual adult roles. Others recognize childhood as a separate time with its own rights and tasks and its own fulfillment. This is not a moral distinction; some societies that indulge children in a world of their own do a poor job of preparing them for later life. But the difference is striking, nevertheless, and may best be seen in attitudes toward play: must play essentially be a training for later jobs, or is it viewed as the particular *business* of childhood?

Readers should consider these contributions in that light. Did Chinese culture and society, famous for its devotion to filial piety, offer children and youth the freedom to savor life's possibilities before getting down to the business of training for chosen or assigned roles? If not, how successful was it in inculcating the desire to maintain traditional ways?

The other distinction to be observed in a history of childhood relates to the sources used. Do they focus on the child's life directly, or mention the child only within the context of another, more central, topic? Are the sources the adult reports of the child's life, inevitably representing an adult perspective? Records of adult attitudes toward childhood might provide inferential evidence of the actual treatment of children, but they must be used with caution. More direct evidence could be used for a social history of children. But *literature* of all sorts only supports a cultural history of "childhood"— a construct comprised of adult expectations, hopes, and fears concerning the rising generation as opposed to a social history of the actual treatment of children.

This distinction should be kept in mind in postulating a field of the history of children. Such a field would cut across all historical specialities. Its distinctive concern would be the "status" (that is, the standing or position) of children with respect to:

1. The biological process (as a demographic entity): how welcome, how nurtured?
2. The social structure (family and larger authority structures, socialization, and discipline): how was traditional authority maintained?
3. The economy (the child as consumer, trainee, producer): what was the precise nature of the child's contribution to a given economy?
4. The culture (especially focusing on the educational program as an index of society's concerns): how was traditional culture transferred or undermined?
5. Ideology: how was the figure of the child used as an element in ethical, religious, or political thinking?
6. Literature and art: what did the figure of the child represent?
7. The psyche: what insecurities were induced and exploited (in the manner described in Erik Erikson's *Childhood and Society*), what impulses were indulged, what does adult affect indicate were the results of childhood experience?

All of these issues would need to be studied with an eye to differences according to gender, class, and birth order, as well as time and region.

There is some artificiality in such an attempt to treat the history of childhood as a separate field, and the contributors to the present collection had no such intention. It is more natural to consider childhood as an especially revealing aspect of the usual divisions within the discipline. But bringing together studies that represent such different approaches will alert others to the ways in which the treatment of the most vulnerable of humankind reveals the soul of a culture.

It seems possible that the importance of childhood experience in gender formation will dominate this field in the near future. And indeed, it could do so without distorting a history of childhood. All questions of gender identity involve childhood experience, just as almost all aspects of a history of childhood contain a gender element, as most of these studies show. We need only remember that considerations of gender do not exhaust the field.

These essays do not present a rounded history of childhood in China. They concentrate on the cultural and ideological aspects of such a history, which is the natural approach at this early stage. There is, after all, much more evidence of attitudes toward childhood than of actual treatment, especially for the remote past. Moreover, the adult meanings that inform this evidence present a challenge and even a provocation to the historian, who may be stimulated to reinterpret them in the light of wider views. The contributions on medicine and institutional care, however, do show the way toward a social history of children.

A concentration on this social dimension (the social structure and the economy) is naturally a second stage. Only after we know what adults thought they were doing with or for children can we assess their performance. This social history, in turn, will sharpen the questions that cultural historians will ask. One hopes that this pioneering collaboration may lead to just such a dialogue.

C. JOHN SOMMERVILLE

Introduction

ANNE BEHNKE KINNEY

This is a book about childhood in China. Given the great number
and diversity of works bearing on various aspects of Chinese civilization, it is curious that among all these studies the discussion of childhood is almost totally absent. In premodern Chinese culture, passage
into adulthood usually occurred anywhere between age fifteen and
twenty *sui* (fourteen and nineteen by Western reckoning). Thus the
sheer length of childhood in traditional China constitutes such a considerable proportion of a typical lifespan that we cannot afford to
neglect it. Furthermore, if one accepts the idea that it is during childhood that gender roles are learned and much of the identity is
formed, then understanding a culture's attitudes toward childhood
becomes crucial to understanding a people as a totality. The study of
childhood can also reveal much about how a culture perceives errors
of the past, how it attempts to shape the future, and how it maintains
traditional ways. Chinese views of childhood as they evolve from one
historical period to the next may thus reflect the judgments passed by
one generation on their predecessors and the ways in which the Chinese attempted, successfully or unsuccessfully, to avoid repeating
past mistakes. Therefore, in addition to heightening our sense of how
actual children figured in specific phases of China's cultural development, the study of Chinese notions of childhood can help to establish
the governing expectations and goals of particular eras in Chinese
history.

But as many of the essays in this collection demonstrate, rather
than reflecting any general sense of the pressures of the future or the
necessity of change, the treatment of children in premodern China
was fundamentally invested in the past. The desire to conform to the
past is evident in the consistency with which methods of childrearing
uphold traditional beliefs and aspirations—for example, the obliga-

tion to please and honor the ancestors, the imperative to maintain the patrilineage, the pressure to appraise a child's position in the family hierarchy in order to determine economic priorities (with infanticide one possible consequence), and the tendency to subordinate the child's interests to those of the enduring social unit. These distinctive traits are closely linked to ancestor worship, whose origins some scholars trace back as far as China's Neolithic period.

While traditional attitudes toward children may be rooted in the prehistoric past, in the opening essay of this volume I attempt to show how the widespread documentation of childhood in China begins in the Han dynasty (206 B.C.–A.D. 220). Many factors contribute to this phenomenon: the establishment of Confucianism as the state creed with its emphasis on educating youth; the flourishing of biographical writing, which took into account significant events of childhood; the Han obsession with discovering patterns in the birth, growth, and decline of dynasties, leading to an interest in similar patterns in the development and behavior of individuals; the establishment of a merit-based civil service, which expanded boys' opportunities for upward social mobility and encouraged their education; the increasing anxiety over the influence of women in political events and the resultant effort to educate girls about their proper roles in society; and finally, the frequency with which minors came to the throne in Han times to rule "all under heaven."

Many of the contributors to this volume have had to rely on a highly selective set of sources, which, through systematic bias and gross omissions, tell us a great deal about some facets of childhood but nothing about others. Han texts, for example, abound in idealized descriptions of youth, but these accounts mainly reflect adult expectations of the young and therefore provide only indirect evidence about the actual behavior of children. As might be expected, the farther we go back into Chinese history, the more limited our sources on childhood become. It is therefore inevitable that our understanding of childhood in early China will be less complete than that of later periods for which we have vast amounts of documentary evidence.

In Chapter 2, for example, Kenneth DeWoskin shows that the earliest examples of biographical writing in China occasionally include information on the youth of eminent figures; however, such accounts typically serve to foreshadow the nature of the adult personality rather than to illuminate an individual's childhood per se. Moreover, because historians in early China were concerned with the adult's accomplishments in public life, the desire to record acts of public service eclipsed interest in documenting the private events not only of childhood but of old age as well. Nevertheless, as DeWoskin points out, because biography (especially as found in the unofficial histories) engages questions crucial to our understanding of Chinese views of child development, it remains our single most valuable source of information concerning children in early China. These sources therefore provide us with a glimpse of what early intellectuals thought children derive from their ancestors; which characteristics are acquired through learning, which are a product of environment; and what constitutes the best way of shaping a child's moral and intellectual development.

In his essay DeWoskin observes: "The role of childhood in biographies relates to a set of historiographic questions bearing on the nature and function of the exemplary character, the emulation ideology of the society. . . and the rhetorical authority of the historical record." From one perspective, the representation of children in Han art reflects a similar set of concerns. In Chapter 3 Wu Hung discusses Han pictorial carvings of children who can be identified by name and concludes that there are no true portraits of children from the Han. The images of children that have been preserved (with one exception) serve instead to illustrate didactic tales that are largely concerned with the virtues of public duty and filial love. In many of the stories illustrated in the carvings, an adult is forced to choose between preserving another person's child for the sake of public good *(gongyi)* or his or her own child in an act of private, that is, selfish, love *(siai)*. In these accounts, public duty is usually portrayed as the duty of a younger brother toward the child of a deceased elder brother, that of a servant toward the child of a deceased master, or a wife's duty to her fatherless children or to her stepchildren. In all of these cases, duty is perceived as an obligation to the deceased parent as well as to the child. Private love—that is, love which does not involve the fulfillment of these social obligations—seems to have played a very small role in what was emphasized in these representations of the adult/child relationship.

Wu Hung links the prominence of the theme of public duty in Han pictorial carvings of children to the increasingly small size of the family in Qin (221–207 B.C.) and Han times. While smaller families may have intensified bonds between parents and children, the nuclear family system also gave rise to a heightened sense of anxiety concerning the security and survival of one's male children. In the event of the death of the father or both parents, a child's survival often depended upon the goodwill of caretakers outside the child's nuclear family or outside the patriline. But because these two groups of "outsiders" were likely to consider their own patrilineal interests (or the patriline of a second husband, in the case of a remarried widow) above the interests of their wards, they were deemed unreliable guardians. Han didactic stories and art therefore address these parental concerns by glorifying those who placed public duty toward orphans above private devotion to their own offspring or, in the case of widows, above devotion to the offspring of a second husband. In the context of Han carvings discussed by Wu Hung, the images of children thus serve primarily as symbols of public responsibility and not as likenesses of specific individuals. Indeed, Wu Hung shows that the representation of the child in Han pictorial carvings was so dominated by didactic themes that even the private "portrait" of a five-year-old boy who died in A.D. 170 was expressed, not in the highly personal and emotional manner of his eulogy, but in the stereotypical images of public art.

In Chapter 4, "Filial Paragons and Spoiled Brats," Richard Mather examines the emergence of a far more intimate treatment of childhood experience in texts from China's medieval period (third to sixth centuries A.D.). The new prominence of the private child at this time may owe much to contemporary intellectual trends, such as Neo-Taoism, which focused on the individual and the practice of self-cultivation in private life. Thus in these sources, far more frequently than in earlier texts, we find parents, often fathers, interacting with children against the backdrop of everyday life.

Portrayals of the intellectual at home with his children also reflect the new amenability to reclusion among educated men of this period. Those who embraced the eremitic ideal typically spurned government service along with the pretentious display of moral refinement that had come to be associated with the ambitious scholar-official of Han times. As Mather's essay demonstrates, the nonconformist attitudes that arose during this period also profoundly affected the ways in which children are portrayed in Six Dynasties texts. Although we still see children who, like their Han counterparts, are upheld as exemplars of courage, precocity, and virtue, we observe, perhaps for the first time in Chinese history, children noted approvingly for impertinence and disrespectful remarks to adults. But in spite of the superficially antiauthoritarian attitudes exemplified by a number of these children, it is likely that displays of disrespect toward superiors were tolerated only because they represented a fashionable intellectual pose adopted by parents and influential adults in elite Six Dynasties culture. It can be argued that childish irreverence and aimlessness in Six Dynasties texts therefore represent the social protest of adults more precisely than the actual rebelliousness of children.

While medieval texts afford us a more naturalistic glimpse of children, there are limitations to this view of childhood as well: the stories typically focus on the children of the gentry, and this small sampling of society is further reduced by its exclusion of all but a few girls. There is a general paucity of information on the lives of girls and young women in premodern Chinese texts, a significant point that engages many of the contributors to this volume. Nevertheless, there are various sources one can turn to to redress this imbalance. For example, Pei-yi Wu's contribution, Chapter 5, demonstrates that among available source materials concerning children in China between 800 and 1700, young daughters figure as prominently in mourning literature as sons. In fact, necrologies written for daughters may tell us more about children during this period than similar accounts of deceased sons because, as Pei-yi Wu points out, it was more acceptable for girls to behave like "children." Thus in contrast to the frequently stereotyped depictions of boys, which are largely concerned with foreshadowing adult behavior and accomplishments, portrayals of girls in this genre are often highly individualized.

As Wu Hung's essay demonstrates, examples of mourning literature written for children can be found as early as Han times. However, Pei-yi Wu shows that from about A.D. 800 onward, the corpus of writings commemorating a child's death began to grow steadily. Around 1520, the numbers of necrologies written for children sharply increased and became most prolific just before 1680. This surge, according to Pei-yi Wu, can be attributed, first of all, to the privileged status the Wang Yangming school of Neo-Confucianism extended to the child within its philosophical discourse. Proponents of this school equated the child's mind with spiritual perfection and in some cases regarded it as superior to the adult mind, which, they averred, was often confused and corrupted with too much learning. Followers of the Wang Yangming school also appear to have been particularly sensitive to the natural proclivities of children by forwarding an educational philosophy that, unlike more conventional attitudes toward instruction, allowed for a child's desire to play and move about without restraint. On this basis, the increase in literary works recounting the lives of deceased children may be plausibly linked to the school's reappraisal of childlike behavior as valuable in its own right.

As Pei-yi Wu points out, the growth of vernacular literature in China from the twelfth century onward also encouraged authors to write about people and topics of a more commonplace nature than those found in classical compositions, including the everyday activities of children. Vernacular literature furthermore employed a narrative style that promoted greater specificity. This specificity, coupled with the grieving parent's desire to preserve the memory of a deceased child in minute detail, provides us with some of the most vivid descriptions of children in premodern Chinese literature.

We can conjecture that Chinese (or any culture's) attitudes toward issues such as the burial and mourning of deceased infants and children are partially formulated in response to beliefs about when life begins and the point at which a child is regarded as fully human. In Chapter 6, Charlotte Furth's study of medical texts of the late imperial period leads us through notions about conception, gestation, birth, infancy, and sexual maturation, all viewed as steps in the gradual process of becoming human. Indeed, based on the cosmological foundations of medical wisdom in Ming and Qing times, birth was viewed as another step in an ongoing process rather than a final event. According to the works analyzed in Furth's study, the child became truly human with the development of intellectual and emotional rather than moral faculties. Furth notes that, like birth, adolescence was not regarded by medical experts as a significant stage in itself, and that in a certain sense, adulthood was not achieved until men and women had themselves married and contributed to the biological continuum of ancestors by producing descendants.

Nevertheless, many never survived long enough to fulfill this crucial filial obligation. Illness, famine, and misguided medical solutions posed a constant threat to a child's well-being. Many girls, however, did not survive childhood for very different reasons—namely, widely practiced female infanticide. In Chapter 7, Ann Waltner brings a new perspective to this important topic by examining female infanticide in Ming and Qing China and its relationship to dowry. As Waltner's essay demonstrates, in almost every period of recorded Chinese history there is evidence documenting the custom of killing unwanted female offspring at birth. Male children were clearly preferred for a number of reasons: only male descendants could perform sacrifices to the ancestors; moreover, sons were the only reliable source of support for parents in old age. Daughters, on the other hand, typically left their natal families after marriage and were expected to place the needs of in-laws above those of their own parents. Families therefore practiced female infanticide in an attempt to reserve limited resources for rearing male children who would eventually contribute labor and wealth to the family. Girls were thought to sap the family economy and offer nothing in return.

Waltner's essay, which examines data drawn largely from the highly commercialized Jiangnan region in the sixteenth and seventeenth centuries, shows how the increased size of a typical dowry lent even greater momentum to the practice of female infanticide. Thus families who had once regarded daughters as a strain on resources began to consider them an unaffordable luxury. Waltner links the spiraling costs of dowering a daughter to the tendency toward hypergamy (the custom whereby women prefer to marry men of higher social status) and the lure of upward social mobility: a daughter with a sizable dowry could attract a husband of a higher social status than a less generously dowered girl; her marriage to such a husband could furthermore forge socially or politically important alliances for her father or brothers. Families willing to make a large investment in particular daughters therefore stood to gain; others, unable to amass enough money to dower a daughter adequately, often drowned or killed girls at birth.

Waltner's chapter illustrates some of the extreme differences in the treatment of children based on gender in premodern China. The essay also illustrates how the birth of a child was at times regarded not so much as the birth of an individual with its own individual right to existence but as one link in a network or continuum of lives connecting ancestors with descendants. Extraneous or inappropriately placed links would weaken rather than strengthen the network. How welcome a child was often depended, therefore, upon how much it could contribute to the continuum, specifically the patriline.

With good reason, the concept of female infanticide is particularly repellant to the Western postmodern reader. Nonetheless, before we judge our premodern Chinese counterparts too severely, it is instructive to remember similar examples of such practices in Western culture. For example, John Boswell's study, *The Kindness of Strangers: The Abandonment of Children in Western Europe from Late Antiquity to the Renaissance,* provides a wide range of evidence documenting the custom of killing, abandoning, and selling unwanted children of both sexes. The account in Waltner's paper of how dowry affected female infanticide in Ming China is also paralleled in important ways by the Western legend of Saint Nicholas, the patron saint of children. Though now obscured by twentieth-century representations of Santa Claus, we should note that early versions of the legend describe how the saint provided dowries for and thus redeemed three girls whose father planned to sell them into prostitution.[1] Waltner's chapter demonstrates well how marriage practices in premodern China affected not only the adolescent but the infant as well.

In Qing times, although adolescence was not usually singled out as a significant developmental stage, it was the time when marriages were forged and careers were launched. This socially decisive stage in human development becomes a topic of lengthy scrutiny in Cao Xueqin's (d. 1763) fictional masterpiece *Dream of the Red Chamber.* In Chapter 8, Lucien Miller shows that by focusing on the psychological and sexual conflicts of a group of elite youths, it can be said that Cao Xueqin has "discovered" what we in the modern West think of as the adolescent: the teenager, who in body and mind has transcended the role of the child, but who is critical of the adult world and not yet a full participant in its institutions and responsibilities. Miller explores the discourse of adolescents who populate the *Dream of the Red Chamber,* which manifests itself in the novel as a kind of "illness narrative." He suggests that the vague and persistent malaise which afflicts these youths can be read as a somatic reaction (or a "neuraesthenic revolt" as Richard Mather suggests) to the major developmental task of adolescence: establishing an adult sense of identity. The role confusion and psychological disquiet that plague the *Dream's* adolescents are best illustrated by the behavior of the novel's protagonist, Jia Baoyu, who repeatedly retreats into the world of the child and at times into the domain and concerns of women to avoid pressures typically associated with Qing manhood— specifically, the inevitable demands to marry a wife of one's parents' choosing and to establish an official career. But Baoyu's tendency to avoid the responsibilities of adulthood by regressing into juvenile preoccupations continually frustrates the erotic, intellectual, and spiritual needs of his emerging adult self. Miller examines the tensions generated by the marginalization of youths such as Baoyu, capturing the ambiguities of adolescence and the bewildering prospect of adulthood in late imperial China.

Complementing Miller's study of elite youth, Angela Ki Che Leung examines the plight of abandoned and destitute children in Jiangnan during the last quarter of the nineteenth century. During this period

in Chinese history, local gentry organized "Societies for the Preservation of Infants" *(baoying hui)* to assist poor families who might
otherwise drown or abandon unwanted babies. Leung traces the
emergence of such charitable institutions to an earlier network of
philanthropic institutions for foundlings, which began to grow
steadily from the late eighteenth century onward. But because the
mortality of infants placed in these foundling hospitals was notori-
ously high, social activists such as Ouyang Zhaoxiong (fl. 1837)
argued that institutionalized babies cared for by wet nurses would
have a far better chance of survival if their mothers could be induced
by the payment of a monthly stipend to nurse the infants themselves.
In 1843, Yu Zhi, a member of the Wuxi gentry, wrote a pamphlet
proposing the establishment of "Societies for the Preservation of
Infants" designed to offer similar forms of extrainstitutional support
to indigent parents.

Relief institutions following Yu's model, as well as programs offering free vaccination, education, and vocational training, spread rapidly in post-Taiping Jiangnan. Leung attributes this growth to new
social conditions that arose in the aftermath of the rebellion: the
swelling numbers of homeless children who flocked to the cities to
beg for a living; the new sense that since many lives had been lost in
the uprising, many lives were now needed to reestablish order and
stability; and the arrival of foreign missionary foundling homes and
orphanages whose presence seemed to testify to the ineffectualness of
Chinese institutions. While we may view the formation and spread of
baoying hui and other relief programs for children as a pragmatic
response to pressing social problems, the appearance of these organizations also signals the emergence of a new concept of the child. As
Leung states, "the late-nineteenth-century society now perceived the
child as a complex social being with specific needs. To integrate these
beings into the larger society became as important to the philanthropists as safeguarding their fragile lives."

In addition to the new approaches to social problems that emerged
indigenously, as China approached the twentieth century, increased
contacts with foreign nations also elicited radical transformations in
government, education, marriage, and the rights of women. In the
sphere of literature, the depiction of children changed as well. In
Chapter 10, Catherine Pease explores the prevalence of the narrative
voice of the child in fiction of the May Fourth period (1919–1937).
She attributes this development to the acceptance of new ideas about
childhood and education by Chinese intellectuals who had gone to

Japan and the West as foreign students. Faced with the collapse of the imperial system, May Fourth writers were eager to embrace new ways of thinking that might offer solutions to the pressing social and political problems of their day. As Pease points out, the child-centered philosophy of thinkers such as John Dewey was particularly attractive to intellectuals of this era because it focused attention on those members of society most likely to effect the changes necessary for China's survival: youths like themselves and the future genera-tions of children who would continue their efforts. To May Fourth writers, the child's perspective provided fresh insights into social and political issues. It furthermore subverted the traditionally ingrained habit of equating age with wisdom and the tendency to search for answers to contemporary problems in ancient texts. Pease explores how May Fourth writers utilized child narrators to break through established social barriers and gain a clearer picture of the problems that plagued China in the early twentieth century.

A prominent factor in the reassessment of China's cultural heritage in the twentieth century was the growing antipathy toward the hier-archical nature of traditional culture and its reverence for old age. This tendency is epitomized, perhaps, by the early revolutionary thought of Mao Zedong (1893–1976) and his faith in youth move-ments as a potent force for political and social change. As a means to reinvigorate his revolution, Mao mobilized youth again in the Great Proletarian Cultural Revolution of the 1960s. In Chapter 11, Mark Lupher analyzes the social psychology of Red Guards during the opening phases of the Cultural Revolution and explores the relation-ship between youth and authority in this period of Chinese history. Rather than dismissing the political upheaval caused by these rebel youths as nothing more than a tragic "aberration," Lupher links this period in Chinese history to the youth-oriented May Fourth move-ment as well as to the student activism that took place in Tiananmen Square in 1989. He suggests that although Red Guards clearly engaged in acts of senseless violence, they also articulated issues of perennial importance in Chinese history—namely, the nature of power and authority. Like the Six Dynasties period, the Cultural Revolution provided Chinese youth with a rare opportunity to speak out against authority and challenge traditional notions of hierarchy.

The issue of authority in Chinese socialization has dominated recent discourse concerning childhood in both modern and pre-modern China, with works such as Richard Solomon's *Mao's Revo-lution and the Chinese Political Culture* (1971), Thomas Metzger's

Escape from Predicament (1977), and Jon Saari's *Legacies of Child-hood* (1990). Lupher argues that Mao's empowerment of youth sought to redefine the position of youth in society by delegitimizing authoritarian controls in both the state and the schools and by ridiculing traditional models of exemplary youthful behavior. From one perspective, Red Guard rebellion can be viewed as youth's obedient response to orders issued from on high. But Lupher suggests that far from sheepishly following the dictates of Chairman Mao, young Red Guards were more than willing to rebel against the established authority structure, which they had themselves regarded as oppressive, unfair, and corrupt. Nevertheless Lupher concludes that, true to authoritarian patterns in adult/child relationships throughout Chinese history, rebel youth (much like their Six Dynasties counterparts) openly challenged authority "only when given permission by the ultimate authority figure: Mao himself."

These essays converge on a number of key issues that have shaped Chinese views of childhood: the prominence of filial piety, which emphasizes what children owe parents rather than what parents owe children; the influence of ancestral cults, which stress the role of the male child as a living representative within a line of descent emerging from the past and extending into the future; and the domination of the patrilineage, with its estranging effect on female offspring, who are perceived as contributors to their husbands' lineage rather than that of their natal families. Equally important are the pressures exerted by traditional notions of hierarchy, which depress the status of girls as well as male children who succeed the firstborn son and contribute to the sense that sacrificing a child is acceptable if it works for the greater good of the family. The social order imposed by hierarchical ideals also determines the authoritarian nature of the parent/child relationship with, on the one hand, its constraints on individual autonomy and, on the other, its effectiveness in preparing children to adapt to the hierarchical structure of society as a whole. Also of crucial importance is the impact of yin/yang cosmology, which projects the cosmological processes of these two primordial forces (whose interactions bring all things into being) onto the human institutions of marriage and the family, with the result that social hierarchies (such as the superiority of the parent over the child) are understood as structures determined by nature and not as products of human agency.[2] Yin/yang cosmology also shapes medical, religious, and pedagogical views about the physical and moral development of children, including the age at which a child is said to become fully human. Thus we find not only the prevailing notion that childhood is a phase of human development which is not valued for its own merits but also, simultaneously, a deep reverence for the intellectual and moral potential of the child, which required development through education. (Confucius said: "Respect the young. How do you know that they will not one day be all that you are now?")[3] Our sources also suggest a general tendency to place a high premium on juvenile precocity, self-control, and studiousness and a correspondingly dim view of play and unrestrained activity, though such striving and immobility were generally frowned upon by the medical community. Finally we must take into account the circumscribed content of traditional Chinese education—which produced students trained in the Confucian classics for two millennia—and the relative insularity from foreign notions of education and child development until a late period in China's history.

While these issues may be said to characterize Chinese views of childhood, we must be cautious not to oversimplify. There are many possible inflections of these conventions and patterns depending upon the historical period, the geographical location, the gender, and the social status of the child or children in question. We must also take into account the fact that few of the notions concerning children and childrearing mentioned here went unchallenged even in premodern times, as many of the chapters in this volume demonstrate. Pei-yi Wu's study, for example, reveals that the general preference for sons was by no means universal and that gender bias in the family worked both ways. Other essays demonstrate the disparity between ritual prescription and actual practice in the treatment of children by revealing the frequency with which grieving parents ignored the dictates of canonical texts by arranging elaborate funerals for their deceased children. Chinese attitudes toward children clearly varied from family to family despite congruences in time, place, and social status. Thus, even as we attempt to generalize about Chinese views of children, we must also allow for the great complexity and variety intrinsic to these views at any given time.

Rather than providing comprehensive chronological coverage, this collection of essays examines Chinese views of childhood through the lenses of several different academic disciplines: literature, encompassing fiction, necrology, biography, and autobiography; institutional history, taking into account the role of the child in educational, welfare, and legal systems; the history of art; medicine; sociology; and Chinese cultural history. Because many of the attitudes toward childhood and childrearing that endured throughout the imperial period appear to have originated or were first recorded in Han times, this collection opens with three studies from the Han. The essays then progress from the Six Dynasties period and cover Chinese history through the opening phases of the Cultural Revolution. Important developments concerning pedagogy and elementary education in Tang and Song times have received much expert attention in *Neo-Confucian Education: The Formative Stage,* edited by William Theodore de Bary and John W. Chaffee, and, for late imperial times, in Benjamin Elman's and Alexander Woodside's *Education and Society in Late Imperial China, 1600–1900.* Dorothy Ko's pathbreaking work, *Teachers of the Inner Chambers: Women and Culture in China, 1573–1722,* explores education for girls in the Ming and Qing dynasties. Likewise, a number of excellent studies in English have been recently published on the category of writings termed "Family Instructions," in which there is also much useful information concerning childrearing.[4] And although these two fields have by no means been exhausted, the present volume has consciously focused on other less widely studied aspects of children's history in China. This collection is also enhanced by the foreword of C. John Sommerville, a noted historian of childhood in the Western tradition, which suggests guidelines for future studies of the history of children in premodern China.

A comprehensive survey of the role of the child in Chinese culture has yet to be written. But by identifying some of the attitudes and beliefs that have more or less consistently affected the treatment of children in China across the centuries, what is presented here should stimulate further research in this new area of sinological inquiry. And though the essays represent pioneering efforts, they offer many strong indications of how the study of childhood can illuminate significant features of China's past.

NOTES

1. Jacobus de Voragine, translated by William G. Ryan, *The Golden Legend: Readings on the Saints* 2 vols. (Princeton: Princeton University Press, 1993), vol. 1, pp. 21–22.

2. Two excellent English-language studies on this issue are Romeyn

Taylor, "Chinese Hierarchy in Comparative Perspective," *Journal of Asian Studies* 48(3) (August 1989):490–511; and William T. Rowe, "Women and the Family in Mid-Qing Social Thought: The Case of Chen Hongmou," *Late Imperial China* 13(2) (December 1992):1–41.

3. *Analects* 9:22; Arthur Waley, trans., *The Analects of Confucius* (New York: Vintage Books, 1938), p. 143.

4. See Teng Ssu-yu, *Family Instructions for the Yen Clan* (Leiden: Brill, 1965); Patricia Ebrey, *Confucianism and Family Ritual in Imperial China: A Social History of Writing About Rites* (Princeton: Princeton University Press, 1991); and John Dardess, "Childhood in Premodern China," in Joseph M. Hawes and N. Ray Hiner, eds., *Children in Historical and Comparative Perspective* (New York: Greenwood, 1991), pp. 71–94.

PART ONE

Early China

Overleaf: "Fuxi, Nüwa, and Child," from Feng Yunpeng and Feng Yun-yuan, "Shi suo," *juan* 3/7. 1821.

Dyed Silk: Han Notions of the Moral Development of Children

ANNE BEHNKE KINNEY

As early as the Shang dynasty (ca. 1700–1050 B.C.), kings made divinations about the births of their children and engravers recorded these prognostications in oracle-bone inscriptions.[1] Inscriptions on Western Zhou (ca. 1045–771 B.C.) bronze vessels also mention children in formulaic phrases that express wishes for "sons and grandsons," who would treasure the vessels and act as future guardians of the ancestral cult.[2] Children and childhood are also mentioned sporadically in the transmitted texts of the Eastern Zhou dynasty (771–256 B.C.), and though the infant becomes an important symbol of naturalness in the *Daode jing* (late fourth to early third centuries B.C.), in all of these early sources the image of the child is shadowy, indistinct, or, more frequently, absent.[3]

THE DISCOVERY OF CHILDHOOD

Textual evidence suggests that Chinese thinkers of the Han dynasty (206 B.C.–A.D. 220) were the first to focus on childhood in philosophical discussions, in history writing, and in educational theory. We may attribute this new interest in the child first of all to the consolidation of Confucian (or "Ruist") ascendancy in Han times. Eclectic in nature, Han Confucianism had absorbed modes of thought not originally associated with Ruist philosophy, most notably, cosmological speculation. In Warring States times (480–221 B.C.), theories about the origin and structure of the universe encouraged thinkers to conceptualize the human organism as a microcosm. Conception, fetal development, and the embryo's evolution into a fully human form were thus made to reflect contemporary notions about the generation of heaven and earth.[4] Han Confucian theories concerned

with correspondences between the heavenly, earthly, and human
spheres therefore began to include within their purview notions about
embryology and schematizations of the human maturation process.[5]

But the Han had an additional and perhaps more important incentive for attending closely to human development. Anxious not to
repeat the cataclysmic errors of China's first unified empire, the Qin
regime (221–207 B.C.), whose mighty state toppled after a brief fifteen years, the Han proved especially receptive to cosmological theories that sought to explain the cycles of human history. Late Warring
States assumptions about the cyclic domination of the Five Powers,
forces thought to order the universe in a regular sequence, gave rise
to theories claiming that rulers could predict and prepare for historical change. Han interpreters of these theories, such as Dong Zhongshu (ca. 174–104 B.C.), emphasized the importance of princely education in hope of producing wise and benevolent sovereigns who
were cognizant of these cosmic cycles and therefore capable of maintaining the heavenly mandate to rule.

While rulers were advised to ponder the forces that led to the rise
and fall of dynasties, we also find in Han times frequent reference to
contemplative and divinatory techniques that called for an examination of the origins of good and bad fortune in the lives of individuals.
The search for the point at which an individual begins to establish
habitually good or bad behavior naturally led thinkers further and
further back into childhood as the appropriate starting point for
moral education. Moral and well-educated princes, the early Han
emperors were told, would allow the house of Liu to preserve their
control of imperial power. It was moreover pointed out that the Qin's
recent downfall was partially due to the First Emperor's failure to
educate his son properly and surround him with wise teachers, for it
was when this ignorant and easily swayed youth ascended the throne
that the dynasty finally collapsed.[6]

Gradually the Han interest in childhood began to include all children, not just those of the imperial household. This broadened scope
was an outgrowth of the widespread acceptance of Xunzi's (fl. 298–
238 B.C.) theory that children come into the world with a host of
potentialities that require development through instruction. Idealistic
Confucians of the early Han moreover believed that once education
was made available to all, the population at large would be led into
an era of peace and high civilization. From a more practical perspective, the increased interest in furthering the public education of youth
(though still largely elite males) was a direct result of the establish-

ment of the civil service, which required an honest and educated staff to run the bureaucracy.[7] But as I will go on to show, the idealistic projects of the Former Han (206 B.C.– A.D. 8), which had been directed at extirpating the roots of wickedness and error in childhood, gradually led to a sense of failure and pessimism by Late Han times.

Princely Education

An important preliminary step in examining Han interest in the development of children is to consider more specifically the relation between the moral training of an emperor and the moral betterment of private individuals. The earliest reference to a program of princely education focusing on early childhood is found in the *Guoyu,* or *Conversations of the States* (ca. fourth century B.C.). The text relates a conversation between Duke Wen of Jin (r. 636–628 B.C.) and an advisor named Xu concerning the possibility of developing the ducal heir's virtue through the instruction of a tutor. The advisor cited the renowned virtue of King Wen (died ca. 1050 B.C.), which he claimed resulted not only from formal instruction but also from the spiritual purity and equanimity of the king's mother during her child's development in utero and her exemplary behavior throughout his early childhood.[8] This conversation reflects a philosophical concern that did not become fully developed until the last three centuries of the Zhou (fifth to third centuries B.C.)—specifically, the necessity of intellectual and moral qualities in addition to noble birth as requirements that entitled a man to rule.

Crucial to the formation of this ethic was the breakdown of the old aristocratic order at the end of the Spring and Autumn period (722–481 B.C.) and the rise of powerful leaders in Warring States times who in military, diplomatic, and administrative matters relied upon ministers of obscure origins but proven ability instead of their own noble kinsmen.[9] At the same time that ordinary men could entertain the possibility of rising to positions of prominence in the world, it became necessary for noblemen (who were not always educated) to acquire skills that would help them compete with and maintain their superiority over more accomplished commoners and ambitious rulers of enemy states. It is therefore no coincidence that discussion concerning the early education of aristocratic children first emerges in Warring States texts.

But it is not until Han times that we begin to see clear evidence of the widespread circulation and acceptance of theories concerning the moral instruction of small children, including the "instruction" of fetuses. Three of the most prominent thinkers of the early Han— Jia Yi (200–168 B.C.), Dong Zhongshu (ca. 174–104 B.C.), and Liu Xiang (ca. 80–7 B.C.)—all advocated the initiation of princely education as early as possible, and Dai De (late second to early first centuries B.C.), an imperially sponsored scholar of ritual texts, included the theme of fetal instruction in his *Da Dai liji*.[10] These educational theories gradually gained acceptance as the influence of Confucianism came to eclipse all contending schools of thought in the Han court.

Education Beyond the Sphere of Court Culture

The adoption of Confucianism as the state creed during the reign of Wudi (140–86 B.C.) ushered in a feeling of optimism about the ability of a Confucian emperor and a largely Confucian bureaucracy to establish a new order of high morals and advanced civilization.[11] The emperor was thought able to further the moral development of the general populace not only metaphysically, by the benevolent influence of his personal virtue, but also institutionally by the furtherance of formalized Confucian instruction. From the start, the twin projects of forming the emperor and morally informing the general populace were closely connected as elements of a program of social reform. The Han Ruist program was intent on correcting the Qin's errors in both educational spheres. The practical expression of this emphasis can be seen in the appointment of Confucian tutors for all heirs to the Han rulership from the time of Emperor Wu (r. 141–87 B.C.) onward and in the establishment of schools and academies throughout the empire dedicated to the education of boys and youths beyond the sphere of court culture.[12]

The Han is the first dynasty for which we have clear historical evidence about educational institutions established by the central government for the instruction of male children and youths throughout China.[13] The history of higher education in Han times is well documented.[14] We know, for example, that the Imperial Academy, which was established about 124 B.C., claimed by end of the Later Han (A.D. 25–220) more than thirty thousand students and that its curriculum consisted of study of the Confucian classics.[15] Boys between the ages of fifteen and eighteen *sui* attended the Imperial Academy.[16] Prior to this, at the provincial level, officially sponsored schools had also been set up in all kingdoms and commanderies sometime after 140 B.C.[17] No source, however, states the ages of students who attended these schools. Nonetheless, it is clear that the Han saw the rise of formal institutions sponsored by the state called *xiaoxue,* or "elementary schools," which, evidence strongly suggests, were devised for the education of young boys.

In A.D. 3, during the reign of Emperor Ping (1 B.C.–A.D. 6), the regent, Wang Mang, drew up a plan for the establishment of schools in all villages with as few as twenty-five families, though the extent to which this plan was ever realized remains unclear.[18] As Hans Bielenstein has noted, education during this period of Chinese history remained a luxury.[19] Each of these village schools was to be staffed by one expert in the *Classic of Filial Piety.* This text is generally thought to have been a "first reader" because it contains only 388 different characters, most of which appear frequently in Han and classical texts.[20] Han sources furthermore suggest that the *Classic of Filial Piety* was the standard beginning text for moral education.[21] It is therefore quite likely that these schools and perhaps some of the elementary schools established just after 140 B.C. offered instruction to young boys.

In A.D. 14, during Wang Mang's reign as usurper, he issued an edict which specifically mentions the *xiaoxue* and demanded that elementary students be taught a new system of numbering the days of the month, another subject that points to instruction directed at young children.[22] Other accounts of elementary education mentioned in Han sources, which describe instructional systems as found in high antiquity during the reigns of various sage-kings, are probably spurious.[23] Despite their questionable historical accuracy, these sources suggest that, generally speaking, male children at age eight *sui* (seven by Western reckoning) were thought ready to begin elementary education and concentrated on the acquisition of basic skills in reading, writing, and calculation.[24]

The Function of Public Education

Confucian schemes to transform the morals of the general populace relied on the charisma and good example of an emperor and local officials (including teachers) who were instructed in Confucian texts and who embodied and propagated their teachings. While emphasis on education derived in part from idealistic hopes of forging an era of "Great Peace" and the practical necessity of educating large numbers of youths to supply staff to an increasingly complex bureau-cracy, other concerns made promoting early education seem equally crucial.

The cataclysmic failure of Legalism in the preceding dynasty had rekindled the old Confucian distrust of law as the only means to pre-vent antisocial behavior. Although much of the apparatus of the Legalist state of Qin was preserved intact by Han officialdom, think-ers from the Confucian school believed that moral education would serve as a more effective deterrent to crime than the strict laws and punishments of the Qin regime. This view was based on the belief that by making children moral, Confucian education would prevent crime as well.

Toward the end of the Han, however, it became clear that Ruist educational techniques, even if implemented in early childhood, did not necessarily transform the darker side of human nature. A con-stant reminder of this fact was the failure of the Han state to control the power monopolies of its provincial elite and other privileged social groups. Growing disregard for the law also led a number of Ruist scholars in the Later Han to advocate the strict and at times harsh measures of Legalism. The movement from initial optimism into growing disappointment in the power of Confucianism to shape morals is reflected in Han views on methods for the prevention of deviant behavior both before birth and in early childhood.

THEORIES OF HUMAN NATURE

Questions concerning the genesis of evil in human conduct and ways to combat it were an integral part of the ongoing debate on human nature in early China. In the Han, there appears to have been little open support for the views of Mencius (ca. 371–289 B.C.), who, while stressing the need for moral cultivation, regarded human nature as essentially good and who furthermore approached a Taois-tic defense of simplicity in urging people to retain the morally pure heart of the infant.[25] With his contrasting emphasis on classical edu-cation and the notion that goodness is the result of the gradual accumulation of deeds and habits, the thought of Xunzi (fl. 298–238 B.C.) clearly dominated Han notions about how to make people moral and keep them from error.[26] Han critics, however, tended to disagree with a notion regularly imputed to Xunzi—namely, the doc-trine that human nature is essentially evil.[27] To the contrary, Han

intellectuals, in keeping with contemporary tendencies to perceive
reality in dualistic terms, believed that at birth a child could be
endowed with a nature that is either good or bad, or that both of
these qualities could be present, or that a child comes into the world
morally indeterminate and can be directed one way or another.[28]
Even in view of the various theories about the moral quality of this
endowment, most Han thinkers still concluded that good or bad, the
original nature of the child was, for the most part, malleable and in
some sense undeveloped or incomplete at birth and therefore in need
of the transforming power of instruction.

In this way, a belief in the power of "transformation" *(hua)* functioning in the personal, political, and cosmic spheres as a means to
develop or reverse inborn tendencies assumed central importance in
Han notions of human nature. Transformation was understood in its
most numinous sense as a supernatural force that could influence the
corporeal and spiritual constitution of human beings, enabling them
to realize the utopian ideal of *taiping,* the "Great Peace." At its most
mundane, transformation was regarded as the molding power of
education and virtuous example, which could transmute bad or
morally indeterminate characters into good. Used in conjunction
with diagnostic practices such as "examining minutiae" *(shenwei),*
and methods for instructing fetuses transformation was an essential
element in the neutralization of predetermined wickedness for those
who believed in the innate badness of human nature.

Before analyzing early Han ideas of this process, which for present
purposes are best represented by the thought of Liu Xiang (ca. 77–
6 B.C.), it is first necessary to discuss in more detail beliefs about
predetermined wickedness. As the preceding survey of Han notions
concerning human nature indicates, a number of thinkers believed
that wickedness was in some cases inborn. How was this determined,
and what were the implications of such a belief?

Predetermined Wickedness

Confucius once said: "By nature, people are nearly alike; by practice,
they get to be wide apart. There are only the wise of the highest class
and the stupid of the lowest class who cannot be changed."[29] Most
later interpreters of this statement emphasize the rarity of people
whose ignorance, that is, moral ignorance, "cannot be changed." Although Confucius' statement allows that some children are born with
inherently evil natures which cannot be altered, such a belief was

always eclipsed by the notion that most children can be transformed by various forms of instruction. Even so, the possibility remained that a newborn child could be inherently and incorrigibly bad.

Calendrics

Few records actually describe how to determine that an infant is evil by nature. The divination texts (ca. 217 B.C.) excavated at Shuihudi in 1975 make many pronouncements about infants based on which day they are born in the sixty-day cycle. But while certain birthdays portend goodness *(liang)*, the almanacs never explicitly state that a child born on a given day is inherently evil.[30] Nevertheless, other terminology is used which may indicate that children born on certain days were thought to be innately wicked. For example, some children are designated as "inauspicious" *(buji)* or "disadvantageous to their parents"; children born on other days in the sixty-day cycle were thought to be potentially "clever at robbery."[31] While these categories may refer to children who were considered to be endowed with inherently evil natures, we must turn to traditionally received texts for less ambiguous evidence.

According to transmitted texts, a belief prevalent from the Warring States to Han times posited that triplets and all children born in the first and fifth months were innately bad.[32] From the perspective of Han sources, the latter tradition was based on calendrics and yin/yang cosmology, which maintained that these births coincide with the intensely active and aggressive phase of the yearly yin/yang cycle, thereby imbuing the nature of such neonates with these dangerous traits. Han texts state that parents often refused to rear these offspring because popular belief maintained that a child born in the first or fifth month would grow up to murder one or both of its parents. Evidence drawn from the Han histories suggests that parents who believed these predictions typically abandoned or killed ill-omened children rather than attempting to "transform" them.[33]

Physiognomy

Classical accounts describe other signs indicating that an infant is predisposed to wickedness. The *Zuo zhuan* (compiled late fourth to early third centuries B.C.), for example, contains at least three separate anecdotes in which the "wolflike cries" of newborn boys were used as evidence of their inborn wickedness, and in one case as the justification to commit infanticide. These accounts strongly suggest that the parents in question did not believe it was possible to alter the child's nature.[34] Since the infants in question are also described as resembling tigers, bears, and wasps, the primary method used to determine the inborn nature appears to have been a crude form of physiognomy.

The ancient Chinese science of physiognomy was not, however, limited to analysis of physical appearance. Behavior and deportment were analyzed as well. For example, according to early sources much could be surmised about a child's character based on the manner in which it was born. A variety of texts suggest that children delivered in breech births were sometimes exposed.[35] In a Han-dynasty lexicon, the word for "breech" *(wu)* is equated with *(wu*)*, meaning "obstinate," "disobedient," or "unfilial."[36] Thus it is possible that the child's ability to physically torment its mother on its first day of life may have been interpreted as foreshadowing its future unfilial behavior or, in more extreme cases, as indicative of the child's murderous intent toward its parents.

Occasionally Han texts mention infants of such supernatural strength that they survive abandonment and exposure. Newborns possessed of such great vitality were thought to become profoundly virtuous or profoundly wicked adults, the former represented by figures such as Hou Ji, the legendary founder of agricultural sciences, and the latter by Zhao Feiyan, the unscrupulous concubine of Emperor Cheng (r. 33–7 B.C.). But since this trait alluded to both extreme goodness and badness, a powerful life force could not be interpreted without reference to less ambiguous indications of moral stature.

Some Han thinkers construed a child's rowdiness as a sign of an evil nature. The tyrannical nature of Zhou Xin (r. 1154–1122 B.C.), the last ruler of the Shang dynasty, was supposedly evident already in his childhood.[37] But Wang Chong (A.D. 27–97) argued that although goodness or badness is inborn, it is usually impossible to judge the nature of an infant based on its behavior because an infant is simply incapable of any great wickedness or virtue; a one-year-old baby will therefore not commit violent robbery, just as it will not exhibit the virtue of yielding. Not until the child is older will its nature become evident.[38]

In summary, then, a number of popular beliefs led to the labeling of some children, such as those born on the fifth day of the fifth month, as evil at birth. Mantic techniques such as calendrics and

physiognomy were closely associated with the divining of this information. Nonetheless, because Ruists like Wang Chong believed that
moral traits could not usually be detected at birth, that pure goodness and pure wickedness are extremely rare, and that most people
possess a potential for both good and evil, throughout the Han
parents were most often advised to control a child's moral constitution by developing its virtue while remaining vigilant for any signs of
emergent wickedness.[39]

LIU XIANG AND THE MORAL TRANSFORMATION OF CHILDREN

Liu Xiang was a seminal figure in the evolution of the Ruist school in
Former Han times. The Confucian reforms of Wudi (r. 141–87 B.C.)
in early Former Han times had been effected largely for pragmatic
purposes.[40] But by the time of the reign of Yuandi (r. 49–33 B.C.), a
form of Confucian idealism prevailed and Ruist projects such as educational reform were proposed with the quixotic goal of realizing the
era of *taiping*.[41] Liu Xiang's adult life spanned the reigns of Xuandi
(r. 74–49 B.C.), Yuandi, and Chengdi (33–7 B.C.). During this time,
Liu acted along with like-minded Confucians in the "reformist movement," whose political agenda advocated a codification of the "practices of the former sage-kings" and a formalization of Confucian
education as a means to social control. This philosophical stance was
directly opposed to the "modernist" fondness for the laws and conventions of the Legalist state of Qin.[42]

Liu Xiang's contribution to the concept of Confucian education is
unique in that the "Muyi zhuan" (Biographies of Maternal Paragons), a chapter in his *Lienü zhuan (Biographies of Exemplary
Women)*, is the earliest extant work to focus on methods for foster-
ing the moral development of children.[43] Liu's biographies thus
represent a radical departure from all previous expositions on Confucian education by setting forth in more than a few scattered comments methods for moral training in early childhood.

Mothers as Educators

It has already been demonstrated that theories concerning "fetal
instruction" can be dated back to the Warring States period (480–
221 B.C.). But in the educational theory of Xunzi, which was so
influential in Han times, nothing is said about the moral instruc-

tion of young children. For Xunzi, moral education begins with the memorization of the Five Classics (the *Odes, Annals, Music, Documents,* and *Rites*), an enterprise that in the Former Han normally began no earlier than age ten *sui* and as late as age fifteen *sui*.[44] Because Xunzi associated moral instruction with book learning, he furthermore denied that women, who were themselves denied education, were able to provide moral education for their children.[45] Liu Xiang's program of education as found in the *Lienü zhuan* therefore advances beyond Xunzi's theories in two crucial respects: it makes early childhood (including the prenatal stage) the starting point in a person's education, and it grants to women an important role in the moral development of their children and charges.[46]

Ideas concerning the transformation of the human personality found in the *Zhongyong* (attributed to Zisi, the grandson of Confucius), in Confucian interpolations in the *Book of Changes,* and in the work of Xunzi grant the power of transformation to the sage, the ruler, the gentleman *(junzi),* or the person who has developed sincerity *(cheng)* to the utmost. But in the *Lienü zhuan,* Liu stresses the transformative power of mothers over their children.[47] This process was to begin when the child is still in the womb.

Fetal Instruction

Liu Xiang advocated "fetal instruction" *(taijiao)* as a means to influence the moral development of the child at the earliest possible opportunity.[48] *Taijiao* demands that the pregnant mother take care in what she allows herself to see, eat, hear, and say and requires her to be ritually correct in her deportment. This prescription was based on the principle of "simulative transformation" *(xiaohua).* Liu believed that "people's resemblance to various things at birth is due to their mothers' being moved *(gan)* by these things."[49] He further claimed that if a woman is affected *(gan)* by good things, her child will be good; if she is affected by bad things, the child will be bad. Simulative transformation is a radical view of the environment's effect on both the spiritual and corporeal constitution of human beings. In this case, the environment is the womb, and the sensory stimuli that affect the mother simultaneously affect the fetus. Purely physical transformations were also thought to occur. For example, a birth defect, such as a harelip, was thought to be the result of the pregnant mother's eating hare.[50] We can surmise that *taijiao* was an accepted element of prenatal care among early Han aristocrats since a manual addressing this art was discovered in 1973 in the tomb of the son of the Marquis of Dai (d. 168 B.C.).[51]

Examining Minutiae

Like a number of earlier theories, Liu's own prenatal prescriptions were influenced by a concern for auspicious beginnings and ritual correctness. The notion that the manner in which a project is begun will affect all of its subsequent development has antecedents in the *Daode jing* and the *Book of Changes*.[52] The link between this view and ideas concerning child development is clearly illustrated by a broadly overlapping terminology. According to the "Xici" or "Great Appendix" to the *Yi jing*, the first action, event, or thought from which all good and evil in human experience arise is referred to as the *ji*, which we might gloss as "the embryonic," as the character for this term, according to one Han lexicon, derives from a picture of a fetus.[53] Another word that suggests the close connection between embryology and the gradual formation of good and bad fortune is *tai* ("fetal" or "gestatory"), a word used to describe the incipient stage of a given event or condition.[54] Similarly, Han texts stress the importance of examining *(shen)* the "minutiae" *(wei,* glossed in Han times as *ji* "embryonic") stage of a destructive tendency from its very inception, while it is still possible to control and contain it.[55] The increasing importance of *shenwei* and related practices such as fetal instruction among Han intellectuals owes much to their preoccupation with discovering the underlying reasons for the bestowal of the heavenly mandate and for the rise and fall of dynasties as a means to control such events.[56]

Prior to Liu Xiang, the *Da Dai liji* (ca. early first century B.C.) shows that one of the reasons why the Zhou dynasty was long-lived, in contrast to the brief tenure of the Qin, was because of the fetal and early childhood education of King Cheng (r. 1115–1078 B.C.).[57] The *Xinshu* of Jia Yi also cites the exemplary education of King Cheng and sums up by observing: "The gentleman is cautious about beginnings. . . . It is for this reason that the Way of Fetal Instruction was established."[58] Moreover, as we shall see, fetal instruction was soon utilized not just for the betterment of the dynasty but for the individual as well.[59]

After the child was born, its virtue could be maintained through a parent's scrupulous vigilance over the emergence of any bad tendency. In the *Lienü zhuan,* for example, Liu Xiang praises the exemplary behavior of a young noblewoman's duenna, who detected the first movement toward licentiousness in her charge and corrected her, thereby "preventing what was not yet an accomplished fact."[60] "Examining minutiae" was one measure advocated by Liu Xiang to keep good children on the correct path. But in cases where wickedness had actually become established in a child's nature, mothers were advised to transform *(hua)* this wickedness into virtue.

Gradual Transformation

In addition to the simple verb meaning "to transform," *hua* is combined with other words to form terms such as "to teach and transform" *(jiaohua)* and "to transform and instruct" *(huaxun).* These terms are fairly straightforward and need not detain us here. But another category of transformation mentioned in the *Lienü zhuan,* namely *jianhua* or "gradual transformation," requires detailed examination.[61]

The notion that virtue or wickedness is the result of a gradual accumulation of good or bad deeds has antecedents in the *Xunzi,* although the term *jian* first appears in connection with the word *hua* in the *Guanzi* (ca. 250 B.C.), where it is used to describe an aspect of transformation.[62] Liu Xiang, however, was the first to relate this idea explicitly to methods of childrearing. Liu's *Lienü zhuan* illustrates the concept of gradual transformation with an anecdote concerning the young Mencius.[63] Seeing the bad influence of various environments on her son, the mother of Mencius moved her residence three times and finally settled near a school where her son imitated the behavior of scholars. Liu Xiang praises this mother for her understanding of how children are gradually imbued with the values and behavior of those around them. Liu Xiang also shows gradual transformation utilized by the stepmother of a delinquent boy who is slowly brought back to the path of virtue through her persistent kindness and patience. Thus *jianhua* was thought to mold morally indeterminate characters into good and to correct personalities that had already been corrupted.

From a modern Western perspective there may seem to be nothing revolutionary in Liu's emphasis on gradual transformation as an element of childrearing. It is easier to see what is new here if we ask to what sort of parental engagement *jianhua* was opposed. A number of historical incidents recorded in the *Shiji* of Sima Qian (ca. 145–

90 B.C.) and elsewhere describe parents who belatedly and unhelpfully inflict extreme punishments on delinquent offspring whom they had habitually ignored or overindulged. Incidents such as these suggest a perceived lack of parental awareness concerning the necessity of providing gradual, consistent moral guidance for children and the disastrous effects of allowing a child to stray too far from the path of virtue without correction.[64] Furthermore, it appears that gradual transformation was perceived as a well-defined method, not merely a commonplace aspect of raising a child. Thus Ban Zhao (ca. A.D. 48–116) confesses that she "carelessly and stupidly" employed no particular method in the rearing of her children and that her daughters received no "gradual" *(jian)* training and instruction.[65]

Dyeing

Used alone or in other combinations, the term *hua* (transformation) has connotations that connect it to alchemy: it is also used to describe various chemical reactions.[66] But significantly, other metaphors used to describe the transformation or development of human nature are often drawn from the vocabulary of work traditionally associated with women: weaving and dyeing.[67] The word *jian*, which means "gradual," can also mean "to steep" or "to dye."[68] The slow process whereby textiles are steeped in dye and absorb color is an appropriate metaphor for the Han concept of how personalities are formed.

The source of this trope may be the *Book of Odes*.[69] But the earliest reliable reference is in the *Mozi* (late fifth to early fourth century B.C.), which employs the term *ran*, meaning "to dye." Here it is related that once, while watching silk being dyed, Mozi sighed and said: "Dyed in indigo, it becomes indigo; dyed in vermillion, it becomes vermillion. . . . Dyeing must therefore be done with extreme caution."[70] He then goes on to discuss how the state is "dyed" or imbued with the moral influence of its ministers. Xunzi also makes use of the metaphor of dyeing to suggest that education, though it stems from an imperfect source such as humankind, will transform an innately wicked nature as surely and inevitably as cloth can be dyed blue, though the pigment comes from the less vividly blue indigo plant.[71] Wang Chong elaborates on this metaphor, as well, but he is more specific than Mozi about the age at which the dye becomes set. Stressing that just as white silk dipped in indigo cannot be made white again, according to Wang Chong, at age fifteen *sui* the characteristics taken on by the personality become fixed and can no longer be changed.[72] No less a person than the eleven-year-old daughter of Wang Mang (r. A.D. 9–23), the future empress of Pingdi (r. 1 B.C.–A.D. 6), is described in the *Hanshu* as having been "dyed and steeped in virtue and thereby transformed." Dyeing white cloth and sending young children to school are also cosmologically linked as duties appropriate to the eighth month in Cui Shi's (ca. 110–170) *Four Peoples' Monthly Ordinances (Simin yueling)*, a guide that correlates human activities to the cycles of nature.[73]

The terms used to describe immersion in virtue vary somewhat from text to text. But all of these texts, including the *Lienü zhuan*, share the same extravagant premise: a morally pure environment. An idealistic prescription for total immersion in virtue to make children slowly and gradually good can be found, for example, in the *Da Dai liji*, which states: "If in looking to the left, to the right, behind, and in front, the child sees only upright persons, this child will also be upright, just as one who grows up in the state of Chu cannot help but speak Chu dialect."[74] In a more realistic vein, some texts emphasize the desirability of establishing a strong foundation of moral behavior in childhood because of the relative ease of inculcating virtuous conduct before the child becomes habituated to wickedness. The *Da Dai liji* stresses the importance of this immersion in childhood because "it is easier at this time to effect transformation."[75] In fact, Jia Yi, claiming to quote Confucius, states: "What is established in childhood becomes like the inborn nature; what is established as habit becomes natural."[76] This attitude stresses the crucial nature of early instruction in setting the tone for all of the child's subsequent development. But while the role of the mother and others with whom a young child might have regular contact was considered to be essential in establishing a solid foundation for moral development, the process was still not complete when the child left their sphere of influence.[77] For example, Liu's biography of Tai Si (the mother of King Wu) relates that when the young king reached adulthood, his father took on the responsibility of his son's education and thus "completed his virtue."[78] Nevertheless, in contrast to the role of the mother, the father's role in a child's moral development is still portrayed by Liu Xiang as relatively minor.

Liu Xiang's "Biographies of Maternal Paragons" outlines an entire program of moral education for the child from conception to adolescence, representing in the tradition of transmitted texts the first comprehensive and explicit discussion of the sort of moral training a child should receive before embarking on a course of study and self-

cultivation as recommended by thinkers such as Xunzi. Liu Xiang
was a realist: he recognized that moral development was a slow and
gradual process and that it was far easier to transform the malleable
nature of the child before bad habits and behavior had become
ingrained in the personality. But there is also a kind of sweeping
idealism in Liu's program, which envisions the good mother, such as
Tai Si, providing an environment for her sons so perfect that none of
them, "from infancy to adulthood, had ever observed anything perverse or vulgar."[79] In such prescriptions as "examining minutiae,"
Liu Xiang also displays an inordinate confidence in the reliability of
portents to signal imminent disaster. In this way, the lessons of the
Lienü zhuan imply that a truly vigilant parent is always able to antic-
ipate trouble and nip it in the bud. Moreover, Liu's system of education is presented as uniformly efficacious; there are no consoling
biographies devoted to good mothers who, in spite of their best
efforts, produce bad children. Clearly there are excellent rhetorical
reasons for presenting his case in this way, but Liu's idealistic representation of this program exemplifies the utopian visions of late
Former Han Confucian thinkers.

FILIAL PIETY

As we have seen, the educational theories of figures such as Liu
Xiang were more or less consistent with the childrearing methods
described in historical sources, so that theory and practice were
clearly related if not strictly linked. Nevertheless, quite surprisingly
in view of its practical importance, none of the philosophical texts
mentioned above devotes much attention to the place of filial piety in
the moral transformation of young children. We do, however, find
evidence suggesting that in the reign of Emperor Zhao (87–74 B.C.),
the *Classic of Filial Piety* was one of the first texts on morality mastered by boys in this period of Chinese history.[80] By the time of
the reign of Emperor Ping (1 B.C.–A.D. 6) we see the increasing
importance of this book, probably in the context of elementary education, through the establishment of teachers who specialized in the
Classic of Filial Piety in the schools of small villages throughout the
empire.[81]

I have already noted that the *Classic of Filial Piety* was a "first
reader" consisting of only 388 different characters. At first examina-

tion, the importance of this text in Han elementary education would seem to follow not just from the fact that the text is simple to read, but also from a natural association between children and filial piety. Yet the relationship between actual children and the virtue of filial piety is not as clear as it might seem. I would argue that throughout the Han the concept of *xiao*, or filial piety, is primarily associated with the duties and attitudes of *adult* offspring toward their parents. This is not to say that young children were not expected to obey and revere their parents. Children were clearly taught *about* filial piety, but they were normally not in a position to practice it. What is emphasized in the concept of *xiao* is that offspring cheerfully provide financial support to aged parents, produce offspring to carry on ancestral sacrifices, and preserve and bring honors (through public recognition) to the good name of the family—duties small children normally cannot perform.

The link between children and filial piety may be better understood when we examine a passage from the *Mencius* and a passage from the *Classic of Filial Piety*. Mencius said: "There are no young children who do not know loving their parents. . . . Loving one's parents is benevolence *(ren)*. . . . What is left to be done is simply the extension of [this feeling] to the whole empire."[82] According to this passage, a child's love for parents is the earliest manifestation of the virtue of benevolence. It is the extension of this feeling to other people that leads to the development of the cardinal virtues of Confucianism: filial piety, righteousness, propriety, wisdom, and fidelity. The *Classic of Filial Piety* states:

> Now the feeling of affection for parents grows up in early childhood. When the duty of nourishing those parents is exercised, the affection daily develops into a sense of awe. The sages proceed from the feeling of awe to teach the duties of respect, and from that affection to teach those of love. . . . What they proceeded from [i.e., affection for parents] was the root. The relation and duties between father and son thus belong to the heaven-conferred nature; they contain in them the principle of righteousness between ruler and subject.[83]

In this way, the *Classic of Filial Piety* utilizes a child's natural feelings of affection for its parents as a foundation for other virtues that become meaningful to children as they expand their social contacts from members of the immediate family to include individuals with whom they will live and work as adults. The *Classic of Filial Piety* is thus a text that prepares children for the gradual transition from a natural love of parents to a growing sense of reverence and obligation toward parents *(xiao)* as children become increasingly capable of providing care for their mothers and fathers.

Further information concerning the position of filial piety in the normal course of a child's moral development can be found in other Han texts. Thus far we have seen that the foundation of a child's moral development was thought to be established in utero, in infancy, and in early childhood. But according to Han schemes that plot the emergence or inculcation of specific virtues along chronological lines, the practice of filial piety was slated at a relatively late stage in a child's moral development. Thus the *Bohu tong*, for example, claims that at age seven the child begins to have understanding.[84] A treatise in the *Hanshu* also states that at age seven, boys enter elementary school where they begin to learn rules concerning home and family and precedents between young and old.[85] The *Liji* states that at age seven, a child begins to learn the virtue of yielding. At age nine, a boy devotes himself to the study of the correct deportment of a youth; that is, he learns how to serve his elders.[86] At age nineteen, he is capped and it is at this time that he begins the practice of filial piety.[87] This evidence suggests that a number of developmental milestones had to be reached before true filial piety was possible. Thus elementary instruction in the *Classic of Filial Piety* was a form of preparatory instruction for the filial duties children would later assume as adults. It is not until the Later Han that one sees young children praised as *xiao*, or filial, and even then the manifestation of this virtue was regarded as a form of precocious development.[88]

CHILD DEVELOPMENT

We have seen how Han Confucian thinkers charted a child's intellectual and moral progress along a gentle upward curve that began its ascent at conception. By the time of early adulthood, the moral and intellectual abilities were considered complete, but only in the sense that the child was now a fully functioning adult. From this state of readiness, the mature cultivation of virtue could begin and was supposed to continue throughout the course of a lifetime.[89] Like schematizations of the child's moral progress, Confucian attempts to chart the child's biological development also stress the incomplete nature of the infant and the body's gradual evolution into fully human form. This tendency stands in sharp contrast to the Taoist propensity to focus on the well-developed capacities and physical completeness of even the fetus. For example, in Liu Xiang's *Shuoyuan* we read:

> Now man at birth is incomplete in five respects: his eyes are without sight, he cannot eat, or walk, or speak, or reproduce. By three months he can focus his eyes, and then he can see; by eight months he grows teeth, and then he can eat; by one year his kneecap is formed, and then he can walk; by three years his skull has grown together, and then he can speak; by sixteen the semen passes and then he can reproduce.[90]

Yet the *Daode jing* suggests that a newborn boy "does not know the union of male and female yet its male member will stir; / This is because its virility is at its height."[91] The *Guanzi,* a text influenced by Taoist and Naturalist thought, also contains passages that marvel at the well-developed capacities observed in fetuses and newborns: "The mouth of a fetus three months old, though not yet complete, can already function. . . . In five months the fetus is complete, and in ten months it is born. After birth, the eyes see, the ears hear and the heart thinks."[92] The striking differences between these two views of fetal and child development suggest that Confucian references to the incompleteness of the infant and young child are not merely commonplace observations of biological development; they are, rather, generally representative of the Ruist emphasis on the deficiencies or undeveloped capacities of human life at birth and the perceived necessity of culture and education to make children fully human. Taoist thinkers, however, sought to denigrate the benefits of civilization and celebrated instead a natural simplicity and the spiritual superiority of the untutored child. The *Huainanzi* (ca. 139 B.C.), a syncretic compendium variously described as embodying Taoist or Huang-Lao thought, states:

> The substance of plain silk is white, but if you dye it in alum, it becomes black. . . . The nature of human beings is without wickedness, but if over a long period you immerse it in customs it changes. Thus changed, one forgets one's roots and merges with the natures of other [things]. Therefore, though the sun and moon wish to be brilliant, drifting clouds cover it . . . though human nature wishes to be calm, tastes and desires injure it.[93]

In summary, then, early Han Confucian descriptions of a child's intellectual, moral, and biological development are generally based on the notion that a virtuous adult is the culmination, and perhaps the triumph, of a long, gradual process which begins at conception. While ignoring childhood as a valuable stage of human development per se, the emphasis placed upon the undeveloped nature of the infant and the child also represents a bold challenge to the notion that privilege is a matter of birth alone. This theory originally served to warn young power holders about the dangers of complacency. But it was also this notion that allowed poor but determined boys to rise to positions of national importance. The young Ni Kuan (fl. 120 B.C.), for example, who hired himself out as a manual laborer to pay for his education and "carried a copy of the classics with him as he hoed," eventually rose to the status of imperial counselor.[94] Thus, according to early Han Confucian thought, a boy's future social worth depended not upon pedigree alone but on the gradual accumulation of virtue and learning as well. And though family wealth must have frequently determined a boy's access to education, the path to privilege, at least in theory, was open to all boys who could match Ni Kuan's perseverance.

LATER HAN THEORIES

In A.D. 9, the hope that a sage-king would assume the throne and bring the state into an era of *taiping* had culminated in the usurpation of Wang Mang, a self-proclaimed worthy who manipulated portents and omens of heavenly approval as a means to legitimize his rule. Wang Mang's seizure of the throne from the Liu ruling house and the swift collapse of his short-lived Xin dynasty or "interregnum" (A.D. 9–23) crushed the idealism and optimism of Former Han Confucianism, which had reached its most extravagant pitch at the time of Wang Mang's accession. In A.D. 25, the government was officially restored to the Liu ruling house. Nonetheless, a number of early Chinese scholars note signs of imperial decline already in the third and fourth reigns of the restored dynasty. Among other causes they attribute the spiraling weakness of the Later Han to the disruptive effects of a series of short-lived child emperors and the attendant corruption and extravagance of powerful cliques associated with imperial consort clans, regents, and eunuchs.[95] Under these conditions, the desire to transform the general populace through the benevolent influence of a properly educated emperor diminished in proportion to the growing sense of pessimism that such a goal could be realized.[96]

The Confucianization of the bureaucracy also failed to yield the expected results; Ruist officials too were prone to greed, ambition, and venality. Recommendation for office now depended more on a man's wealth and powerful connections than his personal merit. Hopes for spiritual and intellectual betterment, which had once been placed in the emperor and the state, were increasingly turned back on the individual.[97] Thus when thinkers such as Wang Chong (A.D. 27–97) discuss fetal instruction, they no longer refer to this practice as a means to strengthen the morals and thus the power of the ruling house to control and transform all under heaven. Instead, Wang Chong mentions *taijiao* as part of a larger argument concerning the self-cultivation of the individual.[98]

Nevertheless, by the beginning of the Later Han, in spite of the negativism that many philosophical texts of the day reflect, the Confucian literati had become an enormous and formidable social force, a vast network of scholars who were outspoken and influential in matters of national and local importance and who filled most of the state's bureaucratic positions.[99] In Later Han historical sources that recount the rise of such men, we also begin to see frequent reference to childhood as an important element of their biographies. One of the earliest and fairly thorough accounts of childhood can be found in Wang Chong's autobiography:

> In the third year of *jianwu*, Wang Chong was born. When playing with his companions, he disliked all frivolous games. His comrades would entrap birds, catch cicadas, play for money, and gambol on stilts. Wang Chong alone declined to take part in their games to the great amazement of his father. At the age of six, he received his first instruction and learned to behave with politeness, honesty, benevolence, obedience, propriety, and reverence. He was grave, earnest, and very quiet, and he had the will of a great man. His father never flogged him, his mother never gave him a harsh word, and the neighbors never scolded him. When he was eight years old, he went to school. There were over one hundred small boys in this school. As a punishment for faults they were made to bare the right shoulder or were whipped for bad writing. Wang Chong made daily progress and never committed any offense. When he could write sentences, his teacher explained to him the *Analects* and the *Shu jing*, of which he daily read a thousand characters. When he knew the classics and his virtue had thus been

developed, he left his teacher and devoted his private studies to writing and composing.[100]

The greater prominence of childhood in biography at this time may be linked to a more competitive climate in the search for bureaucratic employment. While the domination of important government posts by small cliques of prominent families made upward mobility more difficult, another impediment to advancement was the increasing numbers of educated youths and men who sought official appointment in an age that presented fewer opportunities for upward social mobility.[101] Under these conditions, the nature of one's upbringing may have helped to support claims of social superiority. On the one hand, families who had already attained social eminence and who desired to maintain their privileged status may have found it useful to stress a child's "breeding"—based on the assumption that cultural and moral influences unconsciously absorbed in early childhood are superior to the book learning and acquired tastes of the parvenu.[102] On the other hand, the biographical emphasis on childhood achievements may also be attributed to ambitious but less well-placed parents who were desirous of giving their sons an additional competitive edge and who encouraged precocious achievement as a means to launching their sons on the highroad of officialdom at the earliest opportunity.

For quite some time, Confucian educational theory had supported the idea of morally forming a child as early as possible. When this practice also helped to maintain or bring within reach elusive social and economic benefits, it is not surprising that young children are shown displaying Confucian virtues and erudition in increasing numbers. For example, in what is meant to be an extravagant boast of his own accomplishments, Dongfang Shuo, a contemporary of Emperor Wu (ca. 157–87 B.C.), states: "At the age of twelve I began to study writing, and after three winters I knew enough to handle ordinary texts and records. At fifteen I studied fencing; at sixteen, the *Odes* and *Documents*."[103] Dongfang Shuo would have received most of his education prior to the establishment of the Erudites *(boshi)* and their disciples at the Imperial Academy about 124 B.C., after which time the study of classical texts increasingly paved the way to official appointments and financial security.[104] But Dongfang Shuo's mastery of texts does not look very impressive in comparison to that of Emperor Yuan (r. 49–33 B.C.), who by age eleven was thoroughly versed in the *Analects* and the *Classic of Filial Piety*.[105] Even in the biographies of eminent figures who lived after Yuandi's reign, there are few comparable accounts of juvenile mastery of the classics. But by the time of the Later Han, the achievements of many boys far surpass those of Yuandi.

Thus in the *History of the Later Han* we see children age eight mastering the same texts that Emperor Yuan had not learned until age eleven.[106] By age eleven, Cui Yin (d. A.D. 92) was versed in the far more difficult *Odes, Spring and Autumn Annals,* and the *Book of Changes.*[107] As an eight-year-old, the historian Ban Gu (A.D. 32–92) is said to have been thoroughly versed in the *Odes* and skilled at composition and *fu* poetry.[108] As E. Bruce Brooks has pointed out, the increase in accounts of precocity is also linked to the growing precision with which culture was defined. The more Han intellectuals were able to define what constituted culture (in this case, an accepted canon of texts) and the more they defined textual memorization as cultural mastery, the more children were able to achieve precocious distinction.[109]

The early emergence of moral distinction in the behavior of historical figures is also first clearly noted in the *History of the Later Han,* perhaps for the first time in Chinese history. Thus Zhang Ba (fl. ca. A.D. 89–105) is described as understanding the virtues of yielding and filial piety at age two.[110] Not to be outdone, Zhou Xie (fl. ca. A.D. 124) displayed the virtues of yielding and incorruptibility three months after he was born.[111] These accomplishments must be considered in light of traditional conceptions of the moral development of children mentioned earlier, in which a child only began to learn the virtue of yielding at age seven.

The Later Han tendency to value precocious talent may be further linked to the honors occasionally offered to juvenile prodigies by the Later Han government. In A.D. 132, for example, two eleven-year-old boys noted for their mastery of classical texts were appointed by the director of the secretariat as "boy gentlemen." Afterwards, others seeking similar appointments were said to have flocked to the capital in "throngs thick as clouds."[112] Again in A.D. 146, an edict was issued seeking boys age ten and over who were known for remarkable talents and extraordinary behavior to be considered for recruitment.[113]

We can also understand the high premium placed on precocity when we take into account the fact that literate males served in the Han bureaucracy at a much earlier age than is generally recognized. During the Later Han, it was not uncommon for fifteen-year-old boys to fill official positions, and there is evidence of boys as young as age twelve who served in the bureaucracy.[114] In the case of a candidate under the age of fifteen, the selection process (when it was not influenced by nepotism) by necessity demanded scrutiny of the boy's childhood to assess his suitability for recommendation. Boys who assumed official posts at age thirteen, for example, would have been forced to exhibit at least a potential for government service at a fairly early age.

The increasing number of Later Han references to juvenile achievements, which are truly extraordinary in comparison to records from Former Han times, may therefore reflect, on the one hand, the elite's attempt to justify their social preeminence and, on the other, the increased competition for official posts, which required boys to prove themselves as early as possible.

But almost as soon as a high premium was placed on precocious ability, we see the emergence of a skeptical attitude toward the practice of basing official appointments and other honors on juvenile accomplishments and behavior. For example, the *Renwu zhi* or *Treatise on Human Ability* (ca. A.D. 240–250) of Liu Shao, a manual designed to aid in the process of selecting worthy men for office, argues that juvenile wisdom is not necessarily superior to wisdom that develops later in life.[115] Other statements on this issue reveal a cynical bitterness toward the reverential attitudes elicited by precocious ability. The *History of the Later Han* recounts how Zhu Bo, an erudite eleven-year-old, caused the poorly educated general Ma Yuan (d. A.D. 49) to feel ashamed of his newly acquired literacy. Ma Yuan's brother consoled the general by telling him: "Small vessels [those of limited capacity] are quickly completed; Zhu Bo's knowledge will go no farther than this."[116] The notion that precocious ability peaks early and comes to nothing soon became a standard rebuttal voiced by those who refused to be impressed by juvenile prodigies.

The possibility that some children are born wise also presented a number of ideological problems. The notion that a child prodigy could flourish without a teacher and without instruction posed a potential threat to the authority of the Confucian state. Nevertheless, orthodox Ruists could not deny the existence of Confucius' pronouncement that "those who are born wise surpass those who must study to become wise," which provided canonical evidence that some people are indeed above education.[117] As Homer Dubs once noted, people who did not need to be educated did not require the services of Confucian teachers and were beyond the authority of Ruist texts.

Mediating between the view that some are born wise and the notion that all people require education is a statement found in the *Comprehensive Discussions at the White Tiger Hall,* a text that purports to be the record of debates held in A.D. 79 concerning the establishment of orthodox interpretations of the classics:

> *Xue,* "to study," means *jue,* "to awake"; to awake to what one did not know. Therefore, a person studies in order to regulate his nature, concerned as he is to transform his emotions; for "an uncut jade will not form a vessel for use, and an uninstructed person will not know the Way." Zixia said: "The craftsmen dwell in their workshops to accomplish their art, a Noble Man studies to accomplish the Way." Thus, the "Quli" says: "At age ten one is said to be immature; he goes to school." Confucius said: "At fifteen I had my mind bent on learning; at thirty I stood firm." And: "Highest are those who are born wise; next are those who become wise by learning." For this reason a person, even if he has a natural aptitude for wisdom, must always have a teacher.[118]

The *Bohu tong* interprets the notion of inborn wisdom as merely a natural aptitude for learning and therefore stresses the importance of constant study under the guidance of a teacher. Moreover, because even the sage Confucius felt it necessary to "set his mind on learning" at age fifteen, to suggest that a person was above study was tantamount to ranking him as superior to Confucius, a comparison that few would be bold enough to make. Thus, despite the tendency in Later Han times to suggest that certain children had been born wise or incorruptible, a more moderate position actually prevailed, one stressing the necessity of Xunzi's dictum that "learning should never cease" and emphasizing the need for constant vigilance against the corrupting influences of the environment.[119]

Earlier we discussed Wang Chong's theory of the necessity of early moral education for children and the difficulty of changing an adolescent who had become habituated to wickedness. Living in a period of great social unrest, Wang Fu (ca. A.D. 90–163) also voiced his pessimism about reforming youth who had already gone far astray. In his essays he speaks of "worthless youths, who . . . burgle and rob, who murder . . . and exterminate entire families for the sake of wealth and sensual pleasure."[120] In Wang Fu's program of social reform, gone are the idealistic admonitions to "gradually transform" boys who have departed from the path of virtue. To remedy serious cases of delinquency, Wang Fu is of the opinion that "if the person is not executed, then the murdering will not cease."[121] He attributes some of the lawlessness of his era to the frequent amnesties granted to lawbreakers. Amnesties were thought to grant a new beginning to criminals.[122] But like Confucius, Wang Fu felt that "the substance of great evil can never be transformed."[123] If we believe what Wang Fu tells us about social conditions during his lifetime, incorrigible wickedness, a state once regarded by philosophers as rare, had in late Han times become commonplace. Although Wang Fu had no doubts about the power of transformation, his ideas about when transformation must take place distinguishes him from thinkers such as Liu Xiang. Taking the idea of examining minutiae to its logical conclusion, Wang Fu believed in transforming human wickedness even before conception.

Wang Fu's notion of transformation was not fundamentally the concern of mothers; nor was it the concern of the emperor, who according to Wang Fu should devote himself to the administrative aspects of statecraft. Wang Fu granted that the emperor could transform customs *(su)* and actions *(xing)* through his use of rewards and punishments.[124] And though this sort of transformation could produce an orderly, law-abiding society, it would never effect a fundamental change in the spiritual development of the general populace.[125]

What was truly essential to effect the moral transformation of the people was the transformation of their hearts, which was thought to encompass both their natures *(xing)* and their emotions *(qing)*, and this could only be done by a sage.[126] Wang Fu believed that by perfecting himself, the sage, through the all-pervasive influence of his virtue, could harmonize the cosmos before a child's birth. At the time of conception, the fetus would therefore take on the characteristics of cosmic harmony and at birth would be free of all perversity.[127] Under these conditions, it was also possible to realize the Age of Great Peace.[128] No one was more aware of the darkness and corruption of his own age than Wang Fu. It is therefore highly doubtful that Wang Fu believed that a sage would emerge and transform the world in his lifetime.

CONCLUSION

In summary, early Confucian thought was committed to the idea that a moral ruler is a good ruler. This notion led to the creation of various programs of study and self-cultivation for the betterment of the emperor. Early Chinese interests in historical cycles and the etiology of bad fortune led thinkers to scrutinize the developmental process of dynastic decline, which they linked to the errors of rulers. The search for the point at which the ruler first began to go astray naturally resulted in the analysis of a sovereign's childhood and infancy. The age at which the emperor required training was pushed back farther and farther until it was considered appropriate to begin training the fetus. This line of thought soon had implications that extended beyond the imperial house. With the Confucianization of China in the late Former Han came the increasing commitment to Ruist self-cultivation. Practices once recommended for sustaining the emperor, such as fetal instruction and total immersion in virtue, were therefore increasingly applied to those of much less exalted positions, resulting in a more acute awareness of the moral development of children among a larger sector of the population.

The traumatic failure of the Former Han Ruist educational program to bring about an age of *taiping* prompted a number of later thinkers to question why Confucian education does not always transform bad characters into good. Thinkers such as Wang Chong therefore stressed not just the advisability but the utter necessity of providing an environment that is conducive to a child's moral development in utero, since, as he claimed, a child may contain the seeds of wickedness from the time of conception.[129] Without fetal instruction, Wang Chong believed that the "extremely bad stuff of which [inherently evil] children are made would not absorb the blue or the red color [of moral instruction]."[130] In this way Wang Chong was able to reconcile a belief in the general efficacy of Confucian teaching with an awareness that it does not always achieve the desired results.

Political and social upheaval in the declining years of the Han proved to be an even greater challenge to the educational theories of Former Han Confucians. By suggesting that the only way to ensure the moral purity of a child is to harmonize cosmic forces before conception, Wang Fu takes a tradition of thinking about transformation to a logical but untenable extreme. Yet he appears to be leading us in a full circle with his suggestion that cosmic harmonization comes from the efforts of one and radiates outward, transforming everything in its path, in that this idea sounds like the older theory that the virtue of the emperor will extend to all his subjects and transform them. The crucial difference is that Wang Fu's transformation stems from the sage, who functions simultaneously but separately from the emperor. In fact, his sage is conceived of as superior to the emperor. Wang Fu's seeming idealism is furthermore tempered with the stark awareness that transformation on this scale is unlikely to occur anytime soon. In the interim, he urges strict observance of laws and punishments as necessary measures to restrain those he considers "incorrigible."[131]

POST-HAN

In December of the year 220, the last Han emperor abdicated in favor of Cao Pi, thus bringing the Han dynasty to an end. Earthquakes, rebellions, famines, and plagues had laid waste to the empire in its closing years. Out of this strife and uncertainty there arose a new commitment to naturalness *(ziran)* and a bitter scorn for humanity's blundering attempts to improve upon nature. Nowhere is the sense of disenchantment with Confucian educational schemes to improve morals more wrenching than in the following poem by Ruan Ji (210–263):

> Long ago, at fourteen or fifteen,
> high in purpose, I loved the Classics,
> hoping some day to be like Yan and Min.
> I threw open the window and let my hopeful eyes wander.
> Grave mounds cover the heights,
> ten thousand ages all brought to one!
> A thousand autumns, ten thousand years from now,
> what will be left of a "glorious name"?
> At last I understand Master Xian Men;
> I can laugh out loud at what I used to be![132]

For men such as Ruan Ji, the code of ethics endorsed by the Confucian state was no more than a glaring reminder of the moral failures of the age. A contemporary of Ruan Ji, Xi Kang (223–262), expressed a similar view: "My ambition has consisted in guarding the Uncarved Block, / In nourishing the Undyed Silk, and preserving Reality Whole."[133] Here too, after centuries in which educators advised parents to carve, polish, steep, and dye their children's virtue, is a renewed amenability to the Taoist ideal of the nature and heart of the untutored child.

NOTES

1. See, for example, David N. Keightley, *Sources of Shang History: The Oracle Bone Inscriptions of Bronze Age China* (Berkeley: University of California Press, 1978), pp. 34, 41, and fig. 12; Tsung-tung Chang, *Der Kult der Shang-dynastie im Spiegel der Orakelinschriften: Eine palaographische Studie zur Religion im archaischen China* (Wiesbaden: Otto Harrassowitz, 1970), pp. 101–102. I am grateful to E. Bruce Brooks, Richard Mather, Karen Turner, and three anonymous reviewers for their comments on this essay.

2. See, for example, Edward L. Shaughnessy, *Sources of Western Chou History: Inscribed Bronze Vessels* (Berkeley: University of California Press, 1991), pp. 83–87. For a brief reference to the education of young nobles, see p. 146, n. 48.

3. See, for example, *Daode jing,* chap. 55. In the *Daode jing,* the ideal of the infant is proffered as an antidote to contemporary greed for knowledge, power, and position; it therefore functions primarily as a symbol and tells us little about real children. For the role of the child in early Chinese ancestral rites see Michael Carr, "Personation of the Dead in Ancient China," *Computational Analyses of Asian and African Languages* 24 (March 1985):1–107.

4. See, for example, *Daode jing,* chap. 42. But the exchange of vocabulary worked both ways, and cosmogony is also discussed in terms of human regeneration. See, for example, *Daode jing,* chaps. 51–52, and *Guanzi, juan* 39 ("Shuidi").

5. See, for example, Dong Zhongshu, *Chunqiu fanlu,* in *Sibu congkan zhengbian* (Taipei: Taiwan shangwu yinshuguan, 1979), vol. 3, *juan* 3, pp. 1b–3b ("Ren fu tianshu"); *Huainanzi,* in *Sibu congkan zhengbian,* vol. 22, *juan* 7, pp. 1–2; *Hanshi waizhuan,* in *Sibu congkan zhengbian,* vol. 3, *juan* 1, pp. 9a–b.

6. See *Da Dai liji,* in *Sibu congkan zhengbian,* vol. 3, *juan* 3, pp. 1a–9b (chap. 48, "Baofu"). In his comments appended to the *Shiji* account of this event, Ban Gu goes so far as to call Huhai, the Second Emperor of Qin, *yu* ("stupid"); see *Shiji, juan* 6, p. 112; Takigawa Kametaru, *Shiki kaichū kōshō* (Taipei: Hongye shuju, 1977), p. 132. The Second Emperor of Qin probably ascended the throne at age nineteen or twenty (twenty-one *sui*); see *Shiji, juan* 6, p. 69. In the epilogue to this chapter, however, it is stated that Huhai was twelve *sui* when he became Second Emperor; see *Shiji, juan* 6, p. 110. Sima Qian outlines Huhai's upbringing in his biography of Li Si (d. 208 B.C.); *Shiji, juan* 87, pp. 15–46; translated by Derk Bodde in *China's First Unifier: A Study of Ch'in Dynasty Life as Seen in the Life of Li Ssu* (Hong Kong: Hong Kong University Press, 1967).

7. In the Later Han other cultural forces made furthering public education advisable. Citing the example of a Chinese administrator who set up

schools to sinicize the Yue people in A.D. 28, Hans Bielenstein has noted that "in South China, the influx of Chinese settlers, and the accelerated sinification of the region, undoubtedly encouraged the establishment of schools." See *Museum of Far Eastern Antiquities* 51 (1979):184; Fan Ye et al., *Hou Hanshu* (Beijing: Zhonghua shuju, 1965), *juan* 21, p. 758.

8. *Guoyu, Sibu congkan zhengbian,* vol. 14, *juan* 10, pp. 24a–b ("Jinyu," pt. 4, item 24); Shanghai Teacher's College, *Guoyu* (Shanghai: Shanghai guji chubanshe, 1978), vol. 2, pp. 386–387.

9. See Chou-yun Hsu, *Ancient China in Transition: An Analysis of Social Mobility, 722–222 B.C.* (Stanford: Stanford University Press, 1965), pp. 24–52.

10. *Da Dai liji, juan* 3, p. 7b (chap. 48, "Baofu"). See also *Liji* in Ruan Yuan, comp., *Shisanjing zhushu* (Beijing: Zhonghua shuju, 1980), vol. 1, *juan* 15, p. 134a ("Yueling"); Liu Xiang, *Lienü zhuan*, in *Sibu beiyao* (Taipei: Taiwan Zhonghua shuju, 1965), vol. 104, *juan* 1, p. 4b ("Muyi zhuan"); Jia Yi, *Xinshu*, p. 69, in *Sibu congkan zhengbian,* vol. 17, pt. 2, p. 69b (*juan* 10, "Taijiao zashi"); Dong Zhongshu in Ban Gu, *Hanshu* (Beijing: Zhonghua shuju, 1962), *juan* 56, p. 2510.

11. See, for example, Dong Zhongshu's "Shencha minghao" and "Shixing" in *Chunqiu fanlu, Sibu congkan zhengbian,* vol. 3, *juan* 10, pp. 1a–8b (chaps. 35–36): "Nature needs to be trained before becoming good. Since Heaven has produced the nature of man which has the basic substance for good but which is unable to be good [by itself], therefore it sets up the king to make it good. . . . It is the duty of the king to . . . complete the nature of the people." Translation by Wing-tsit Chan, *A Source Book in Chinese Philosophy* (Princeton: Princeton University Press, 1963), p. 276.

12. Nevertheless, Confucian tutors were employed prior to the reign of Wudi. Though known primarily as a Legalist, Chao Cuo (d. 154 B.C.), who served in the suite of the heir apparent (the future Emperor Jing), was also a specialist in one of the five Confucian classics, the *Book of Documents.* See *Shiji, juan* 101, pp. 16–17. After Jingdi came to the throne, he appointed Wang Zang, a Confucian authority on the *Odes,* as junior tutor to the heir apparent, the future Emperor Wu. See *Hanshu, juan* 88, p. 3608. Before the reign of Wudi, scholars of other philosophical schools are represented in the ranks of imperial tutors as well. The Huang-Lao school was particularly favored during this period. Its popularity, according to the histories, was due to the influential Empress Dowager Dou (d. 135 B.C.). Consort of Wendi and mother of Jingdi (r. 157–141 B.C.), she is said to have been devoted to writings of Huang-Lao and required her son (as well as her husband and other members of her family) to study the texts of this school. See *Shiji, juan* 49, p. 14. For studies of Huang-Lao thought see Karen Turner, "War, Punishment, and the Law of Nature in Early Chinese Concepts of the State," *Harvard Journal of Asiatic Studies* 53(2) (1993):285–324; R. P. Peerenboom, *Law and Morality in Ancient China: The Silk Manuscripts of Huang-Lao*

(Albany: State University of New York Press, 1993); and Harold D. Roth, "Psychology and Self-Cultivation in Early Taoistic Thought," *Harvard Journal of Asiatic Studies* 51(2) (1991):599–650.

13. Mencius speaks of schools as part of the model state in *Mencius* IIIA:2; *Mengzi zhushu* in *Shisanjing zhushu*, vol. 2, *juan* 5a, p. 38c. For a survey of sources concerning pre-Han educational institutions and practices see Yang Chengbin, *Qin Han Wei Jin Nanbeichao jiaoyu zhidu* (Taipei: Taiwan shangwu yinshuguan, 1977), pp. 1–48; and Cho-yun Hsu, *Ancient China in Transition*, pp. 99–106.

14. For a survey of these sources see Hans Bielenstein, "The Restoration of the Han Dynasty," *Bulletin of the Museum of Far Eastern Antiquities* 51 (1979):184–197.

15. *Hanshu, juan* 88, pp. 3593–3594; *Hou Hanshu, juan* 79a, p. 2547.

16. According to the idealized scheme of the "Shihuo zhi" (Treatise on Food and Money), boys at age fifteen *sui* should enter the Imperial Academy; *Hanshu, juan* 24a, p. 1122. Around 124 B.C. Gongsun Hong (chancellor from 124 to 118 B.C.) stipulated that boys eighteen *sui* and older could be admitted to the Imperial Academy; *Hanshu, juan* 88, p. 3594. Du Gen (fl. circa A.D. 107), a boy prodigy, is said to have entered the *taixue* at age thirteen *sui*; *Hou Hanshu, juan* 57, p. 1839.

17. *Hanshu, juan* 89, p. 3626.

18. *Hanshu, juan* 12, p. 355.

19. Bielenstein, "The Restoration of the Han Dynasty," pp. 184–185.

20. See Herrlee Creel, *Literary Chinese by the Inductive Method*, Vol. 1: *The Hsiao Ching* (Chicago: University of Chicago Press, 1943), p. 36. At least on one occasion, study of the *Xiao jing* was suggested as a means to civilize non-Chinese peoples of Liangzhou; see *Hou Hanshu, juan* 58, p. 1880. Certain magical properties were also attributed to this text; see *Hou Hanshu, juan* 81, p. 2694.

21. See, for example, Cui Shi, *Simin yueling*, in Yan Kejun, *Quan Shanggu Sandai Qin Han Sanguo Liuchao wen* (Beijing: Zhonghua shuju, 1958), *juan* 47, pp. 1a–7a. It is important to note, however, that primers teaching basic vocabulary also existed. See *Hanshu, juan* 30, pp. 1719–1721; *Hou Hanshu, juan* 10a, p. 418.

22. *Hanshu, juan* 99b, p. 4138.

23. See, for example, Ban Gu, *Bohu tongde lun, Sibu congkan zhengbian*, vol. 22, *juan* 4, p. 16b (chap. 15, "Biyong").

24. *Hanshu, juan* 24a, p. 1122.

25. *Mencius* IVB: 12; *Mengzi zhushu, juan* 8A, p. 62C. For a study of the subtleties and complexities connected with this theory see A. C. Graham, "The Background of the Mencian Theory of Human Nature," *Studies in Chinese Philosophy and Philosophical Literature* (Albany: State University of New York Press, 1990), pp. 7–66. Also see Roger Ames' argument concerning the elitist nature of the Mencian view of human goodness: "The

Mencian Concept of Renxing: Does It Mean Human Nature?" in Henry
Rosemont, Jr., ed., *Chinese Texts and Philosophical Contexts* (La Salle, Ill.:
Open Court, 1991), pp. 143–157.

26. For the influence of the school of Xunzi on Han Confucianism see
John Knoblock, *Xunzi: A Translation of the Complete Works* (Stanford:
Stanford University Press, 1988), vol. 1, pp. 36–49. Homer Dubs has suggested that the influence of Xunzi eclipsed that of Mencius because the
latter's philosophy was based on "moral intuitionalism," which "allows the
feelings of individuals to judge right and wrong." Dubs notes that "the leading Confucians were moreover teachers and advisors, sometimes of kings. If
one need merely to follow his feelings in order to do right, where is there any
need for teachers or advisors? Mencius was eliminating his own profession
and that of his followers, as well as rejecting the authority of the sages."
Dubs concludes that Confucianism is "ultimately dogmatic" and that Xunzi
"saw that the only safe foundation for authoritarianism is the belief that
human nature is fundamentally evil, for then man cannot trust his own reasoning." See "Mencius and Sun-dz on Human Nature," *Philosophy East
and West* 6(2) (1956):216. The authoritarian nature of Xunzi's Confucianism was also well suited to the rulers of the Han, who required a system of
control different from the Legalist methods of the Qin and the laissez-faire
policies of Huang-Laoists in the early Han court.

27. The idea that Xunzi regarded human nature as bad is an oversimpli-
fication of the thought of this philosopher, according to a number of modern
scholars. Nevertheless, thinkers of the Han such as Wang Chong and Xun
Yue characterized Xunzi's theory of inborn nature in this way. See Donald
Munro, *The Concept of Man in Early China* (Stanford: Stanford University
Press, 1969), pp. 77–81.

28. Dong Zhongshu believed that human nature is good (*yang*) but the
emotions are evil (*yin*). He further believed that instruction is necessary to
develop inborn goodness. See *Chunqiu fanlu, juan* 10, pp. 1a–8b (chaps.
35–36: "Shencha minghao" and "Shixing"). On the other hand, the *Hanshu*
biography of Dong Zhongshu claims that Dong thought nature could be
either good or bad; *Hanshu, juan* 56, p. 2501. The idea that human nature is
good and the emotions bad is echoed by Ban Gu (A.D. 32–92), *Bohu tong,
juan* 8, pp. 1a–4b ("Qingxing"), who in turn cites the *Gouming jue,* a
"weft" commentary on the *Xiao jing* for a similar statement. Xu Shen (fl.
A.D. 100) also subscribed to this belief. See Duan Yucai, annotator, *Shuowen
jiezi zhu* (Taipei: Yiwen yinshuguan, 1973), p. 506 (*juan* 10b, pp. 24a–b).
Liu Xiang (ca. 80–7 B.C.) countered the theory of Dong Zhongshu by posit-
ing that the original nature was yin and the emotions were yang; Huang
Hui, annotator, *Lunheng jiaoshi* (Taipei: Taiwan shangwu yinshuguan,
1964), vol. 1, pp. 134–135 ("Benxing"). Yang Xiong (53 B.C.–A.D.18)
thought of human nature as a mixture of good and evil and believed that by
developing the good or the bad a good or bad character would be formed;

Fayan, in *Sibu congkan zhengbian*, vol. 18, *juan* 3, p. 1a–4a ("Xiushen"). Huan Tan (43 B.C.–A.D. 28) maintained a view similar to that of Yang Xiong; see *Xinlun*, in *Quan Shanggu Sandai Qin Han Liuchao wen, juan* 13, pp. 6a–b (chap. 4, "Tiyan"). Wang Chong (A.D. 27–97) believed that the inborn nature can be good or bad or a mixture of the two; see *Lunheng*, "Benxing." Wang Fu (ca. 90–163) made no statement about original nature but regarded goodness and wickedness as the result of the accumulation of either good or bad deeds and agreed with Confucius' view (*Lunyu* 17:2–3) that only those of the highest intelligence and those of the most abysmal stupidity cannot be changed; see "Shenwei" and "Dehua" in Hu Chusheng, annotator, *Qianfu lun jishi* (Taipei: Dingwen shuju, 1979), pp. 230–238 and 596.

29. *Analects* 17:2–3; translation based on James Legge, *The Chinese Classics* (Hong Kong: University of Hong Kong Press, 1960), vol. 1, p. 318.

30. *Yunmeng Shuihudi Qinmu* (Beijing: Wenwu chubanshe, 1981), pl. 128, strip 875.

31. Ibid., pl. 164, strip 1142; pl. 128, strip 883.

32. Huang, *Lunheng*, vol. 1, pp. 260–261 ("Fuxu"), vol. 2, pp. 974–976 ("Sihui"); Ying Shao (fl. A.D. 165–204), Wang Liqi, annotator, *Fengsu tongyi jiaozhu* (Beijing: Zhonghua shuju, 1981), *Fengsu tongyi*, vol. 1, p. 128 ("Zhengshi"); *Shiji, juan* 75, pp. 4–5. Ying Shao describes this notion as a popular belief, although it must have extended to aristocratic circles as documented by the *Shiji* biography of Tian Wen, Lord Mengchang of Xue, cited above.

33. See Anne Behnke Kinney, "Infant Abandonment in Early China," *Early China* 18 (1993):107–138.

34. *Zuo zhuan*, Duke Zhao, year 28; Duke Wen, year 1; and Duke Xuan, year 4. Unlike the case of Tian Wen cited above, the *Zuo zhuan* prognostications are more or less accurate.

35. See Ying Shao, *Fengsu tongyi*, vol. 2, p. 561 ("Yiwen: 'Shiji' "). Although Ying Shao offers a different interpretation of the word *wu*, many commentators have convincingly argued that the term refers to breech births and not children born "wide awake" as Ying Shao suggests.

36. See Xu Shen, *Shuowen jiezi zhu*, chap. 7b, p. 25. Interpretations of the word *wu* can be found in connection with the account of Duke Zhuang of Zheng's birth as found in *Zuo zhuan*, Duke Yin, year 1. See Yang Bojun, *Chunqiu Zuo zhuan zhu* (Beijing: Zhonghua shuju, 1981), vol. 1, p. 10; Qian Zhongshu, *Guanzhui bian* (Hong Kong: Zhonghua shuju, 1980), vol. 1, pp. 167–168; Bernhard Karlgren, "Glosses on the *Tso chuan*," *Bulletin of the Museum of Far Eastern Antiquities* 41 (1969):1. Sima Qian's version of this story is found in *Shiji, juan* 42, p. 6.

37. Huang, *Lunheng*, vol. 1, pp. 125–126. Wang Chong derived this information from a version of the "Weizi" chapter of the *Shangshu* that differs from the standard transmitted text.

38. *Lunheng*, vol. 1, pp. 128–130 ("Benxing").

39. See Huang, *Lunheng*, vol. 1, p. 112 ("Guxiang") and Xunzi's chapter "Against Physiognomy," in *Sibu congkan zhengbian*, vol. 17, *juan* 3, pp. 1–12. Also see *Huainanzi*, *juan* 19, pp. 5–6 ("Xiuwu xun").

40. See Benjamin Wallacker, "Han Confucianism and Confucius in the Han," in *Ancient China: Studies in Early Civilization* (Hong Kong: Chinese University Press, 1978), pp. 223–228.

41. See Ch'en Ch'i-yun, *Hsun Yueh and the Mind of Late Han China* (Princeton: Princeton University Press, 1980), pp. 19–21; and Dong Zhong-shu's views on *taiping* in *Hanshu*, *juan* 56, p. 2506 ff.

42. For the terms "modernist" and "reformist" see Michael Loewe, *Crisis and Conflict in Han China* (London: Allen & Unwin, 1974), pp. 11–13.

43. Translated by Albert O'Hara in *The Position of Woman in Early China* (Taipei: Mei Ya Publications, 1971), pp. 13–48. It is possible that texts such as the *Lienü zhuan* existed prior to Liu's. Ban Jieyu, a contemporary of Liu Xiang, and the concubine of Emperor Cheng, mentions contemplating paintings of famous women as guides to correct deportment, as well as receiving instruction regarding the lives of exemplary mothers from a woman versed in the *Odes*; see Ban's untitled *fu* in *Hanshu*, *juan* 97b, p. 3985. Instruction of this sort sounds as if it might have been transmitted orally. The biography notes that in addition to the *Odes*, Ban could recite other works such as "The Modest Maiden," "Emblems of Virtue," and "The Instructress," all lost works that appear to be guides to correct feminine deportment. See *Hanshu*, *juan* 97b, p. 3984; titles tentatively translated by Burton Watson, *Courtier and Commoner in Ancient China* (New York: Columbia University Press, 1974), p. 262. These works may well have been precursors to the *Lienü zhuan* in a literary rather than subliterary genre.

44. *Xunzi*, *juan* 1, p. 11a (chap. 1, "Quanxue"). I base these age calculations on information found in sources such as those quoted earlier and in texts such as the *Liji*, "Neize," *juan* 28, pp. 243a–b.

45. *Xunzi*, *juan* 13, p. 23 ("Lilun").

46. See Charlotte Furth's essay in this volume (Chapter 6) for the disadvantages connected with this maternal responsibility.

47. *Zhongyong* 22–23; Legge, *The Chinese Classics*, vol. 1, pp. 415–417. *Zhongyong* 12 intimates that even ordinary women are capable of practicing the Way; Legge, *The Chinese Classics*, vol. 1, pp. 391–392. Women are therefore at least potentially capable of transforming others, though the author of the *Zhongyong* does not explicitly draw this conclusion.

48. See also *Da Dai liji*, *juan* 3, pp. 1a–9b ("Baofu"); *Lunheng*, vol. 1, p. 50 ("Mingyi"); *Lienü zhuan*, *juan* 1, p. 4; Han Ying's (fl. 150 B.C.) *Han-shi waizhuan*, *juan* 9, p. 1; Jia Yi's (201–169 B.C.) *Xinshu*, pt. 2, pp. 69a–74a ("Taijiao zashi").

49. *Lienü zhuan*, *juan* 1, p. 4.

50. *Lunheng,* vol. 1, p. 49 ("Mingyi"); see also *Liji,* "Yueling," *juan* 15, p. 134a.

51. The *Taichan shu,* or *Book of Pregnancy and Childbirth* (ca. 168 B.C.), found in 1973 in Tomb Three of Mawangdui also contains a passage concerning the practice of "fetal instruction," although this text does not employ the term *taijiao.* The emphasis in this text is placed on physical rather than moral transformations of the fetus. See *Mawangdui Hanmu boshu* (Beijing: Wenwu chubanshe, 1985), vol. 4, p. 136. Other sections of the *Taichan shu,* as well as another text found in the same tomb, the *Zaliao fang* (Prescriptions for Assorted Diseases), discuss how proper burial of the placenta will affect the welfare of the child. For a recent study of beliefs and practices surrounding the placenta in early China see Sabine Wilms, "Childbirth Customs in Early China," M.A. thesis, University of Arizona, 1992.

52. *Daode jing,* 64; *Yi jing,* "Xici," I:10, II:5, and II:8. This notion is also associated with the thought of Zou Yan; see *Shiji, juan* 74, p. 6.

53. See Joseph Needham's discussion of the word *ji* in *Science and Civilisation in China* (Cambridge: Cambridge University Press, 1956), vol. 2, pp. 78–80. The *Shuowen jiezi* defines the graph that Needham identifies as "embryoes" as "the image of a newborn child." If one construes *sheng* ("born") as "engendered," then Needham's interpretation is in keeping with the *Shuowen* definition. See Xu Shen, *Shuowen jiezi zhu,* chap. 4b, pp. 2b–3a. I am grateful to Richard Mather for pointing out that, contrary to Xu Shen's interpretation of this graph, *ji* is most often defined as a "spring" or "triggering mechanism."

54. See, for example, *Hanshu, juan* 51, p. 2360.

55. *Shuowen jiezi,* chap. 4b, pp. 2b–3a, defines *ji* ("the embryonic") as *wei* ("minutiae"). Other Han essays on "Examining Minutiae" include, for example, Jia Yi's (201–169 B.C.) "Shenwei," found in the *Xinshu,* Lu Jia's (fl. 202 B.C.) "Shenwei," found in the *Xinyu,* and Wang Fu's "Shenwei," found in the *Qianfu lun.*

56. See Wolfgang Bauer, *China and the Search for Happiness* (New York: Seabury Press, 1976), pp. 69–88.

57. See *Da Dai liji, juan* 3, pp. 1a–9b (chap. 48, "Baofu").

58. Jia Yi, *Xinshu,* pt. 2, p. 80 ("Taijiao"). It is clear that Jia stressed beginning moral education as early as possible primarily for political reasons. But given that Jia Yi was himself a child prodigy who was made a Senior Counselor of the Palace when he was barely twenty years old and that as a youth his progress was thwarted by conventional attitudes that rigidly equate age with ability, his personal experience might well have contributed to his interest in early education.

59. Ban Gu states that *Lienü zhuan* was written to warn the emperor about the political consequences of his relations with women; *Hanshu, juan* 36, pp. 1957–1958. And although the *Lienü zhuan* associates fetal instruction with the royal house of Zhou, the text, as a guide for women of both

common and aristocratic status on the subject of correct wifely and maternal deportment, addresses women more specifically than statesmen.

60. *Lienü zhuan, juan* 1, p. 6.

61. See, for example, *Lienü zhuan, juan* 1, pp. 10b, 12b–13a.

62. See *Xunzi*, "*Xing'e*," and "*Quanxue.*" See *Guanzi*, in *Sibu congkan zhengbian*, vol. 18, *juan* 2, p. 1b ("Qifa"). The dating and authorship of the *Guanzi* have been the subject of much controversy, although it is clear that the text was edited by Liu Xiang in the Han dynasty. Rickett discusses the nature of the "proto-*Guanzi*," which forms the core of present-day texts and dates from about 250 B.C. The passage under discussion, however, may be dated somewhat earlier, i.e., late fourth to early third century B.C. See W. Allyn Rickett, *Guanzi* (Princeton: Princeton University Press, 1985), vol. 1, p. 15.

63. *Lienü zhuan, juan* 1, p. 10b.

64. See, for example, the case of Liu Chang (d. circa 174 B.C.), King Li of Huainan, in *Shiji, juan* 118, pp. 1–10. After Liu Chang revolted and had been demoted and exiled, Emperor Wen's (r. 180–157 B.C.) advisor, Yuan Ang, stated: "The king of Huai-nan has always been willful by nature and yet Your Majesty failed to appoint strict tutors and chancellors for him. That is the reason things have come to this pass. Moreover, the king is a man of stubborn spirit. Now you have suddenly struck him down, and I fear that, exposed to the dew and damp of the road, he may eventually become ill and die." Translation by Burton Watson, *Records of the Grand Historian of China* (New York: Columbia University Press, 1961), vol. 2, pp. 364–365.

65. *Hou Hanshu, juan* 84, p. 2786.

66. Needham, *Science and Civilisation in China*, vol. 2, pp. 74–75. Here Needham notes that *hua* "tends to mean sudden and profound transmutation or alteration (as in a rapid chemical reaction)," but he admits that among the various words that mean "change" in classical Chinese, "there is no very strict frontier." Liu's use of the term *hua* to denote the slow changes of the personality suggests that rapidity is not necessarily implied in the word.

67. The mother of Mencius was famous for the practical recourse to such metaphors. She is said to have once cut the woof thread of her weaving to illustrate to her young son the dangers of interrupting his studies. See Han Ying (fl. 150 B.C.), *Hanshi waizhuan, juan* 9, p. 1a. For a slightly different version of this story see *Lienü zhuan, juan* 1, p. 10b.

68. "Steeping" is an important aspect of the thought of Dong Zhongshu (as represented by material cited in the *Hanshu*). Here Dong also mentions it as a method of transformation. But Dong uses the word "steeping" in reference to the transformative powers of the ruler on the people rather than parents' ability to transform children. Xunzi also uses this term to refer to the effects of the environment on moral development in his "Quanxue."

69. See *Hou Hanshu, juan* 48, pp. 1599–1600. Yang Zhong (fl. A.D. 76)

quotes the following lines from a lost ode: "White, white the raw silk, / What surrounds it dyes [*ran*] it." He goes on to state that only the wisest and the most ignorant cannot be changed and that most people need to be taught and transformed. He then mentions a traditional educational scheme whereby the son of a ruler is taught reading and arithmetic at eight *sui* and begins to study the classics at age fifteen.

70. Sun Yirang, annotator, *Mozi jiangu* (Taipei: Xinwenfeng chuban gongsi, 1978), *juan* 1, pp. 11–19 (chap. 3, "Suoran").

71. *Xunzi, juan* 1, p. 7 (chap. 1, "Quanxue").

72. Huang, *Lunheng*, vol. 1, pp. 64–65 ("Shuaixing"). There is much disagreement concerning the interpretation of this passage. It is important to note that elsewhere Wang Chong moderates this view by stating that even a person with a wicked nature can be made virtuous if taught by a sage or a superior man; Huang, *Lunheng*, vol. 1, pp. 64–65, 74 ("Shuaixing"). Though Wang Chong states that even under the tutelage of Yao and Shun there were those who remained wicked, Wang attributes this to the "extremely bad stuff they were made of [which] did not take the blue or the red color"; translated by Alfred Forke, *Lunheng* (New York: Paragon Book Gallery, 1962), vol. 1, p. 387; Huang, *Lunheng*, vol. 1, p. 129 ("Benxing"). Thus in the final analysis his view is most likely that while the transformation of bad characters into good is possible, even good characters can be made bad by bad environments; and once transformed in this way, it is very difficult and at times impossible to make them good again.

73. Cui Shi, *Simin yueling, juan* 47, p. 5a. Although the "Monthly Ordinances" ("Yueling") of the *Liji* (an earlier example of this sort of text) does not specifically link dyeing and early education, it associates the natural activity of young birds learning to fly with womens' work dyeing fabrics and both as occupations appropriate to the third month of summer; *juan* 16, p. 143a.

74. *Da Dai liji, juan* 3, p. 2a ("Baofu"). Although the term *jian* is not used in this passage, the process described is the same.

75. *Da Dai liji, juan* 3, p. 5a ("Baofu").

76. *Hanshu, juan* 48, p. 2248.

77. Whether or not young women normally received any additional moral training after marriage is not clear. But the *Lienü zhuan* account of the duenna *(fumu)* of the Lady of Qi and the writings of Ban Jieyu mention women (in Ban's case a "female historian" or *nüshi*) whose duty was to instruct or watch over these young women—often married around age fifteen *sui*—after they had gone to live in their husband's household.

78. *Lienü zhuan, juan* 1, p. 4.

79. Ibid.

80. *Hanshu, juan* 7, p. 223 (here Emperor Zhao is thirteen years old); *juan* 71, p. 3039 (Emperor Yuan is here eleven years old).

81. *Hanshu, juan* 12, p. 355.

82. *Mencius* 7A:15; translation based on D. C. Lau, *Mencius* (Harmondsworth: Penguin Books, 1970), p. 184.

83. *Xiao jing,* chap. 9; *Shisanjing zhushu,* vol. 2, *juan* 5, pp. 15c–16a; translation based on James Legge in The Texts of Confucianism, Part One: The *Shu King,* The Religious Portions of the *Shih King* and The *Hsiao King.* Max Müller, ed., *The Sacred Books of the East* (Oxford: Oxford University Press, 1899), vol. 3, pp. 478–479.

84. Ban Gu, *Bohu tong, juan* 4, p. 16b.

85. *Hanshu, juan* 24a, p. 1122.

86. *Liji,* "Neize," *juan* 28, p. 243a.

87. Ibid., p. 243b.

88. See, for example, *Hou Hanshu, juan* 36, p. 1241, for the biography of Zhang Ba; see also my essay, "The Theme of the Precocious Child in Early Chinese Literature," forthcoming in *T'oung Pao* 81 (1995).

89. See, for example, the injunction directed at boys during the capping or coming-of-age ceremony: "Cast away your childish ambitions, and cleave to the virtues of manhood. Then shall your years all be fair and your good fortune increase." See *Yi li,* in *Shisanjing zhushu,* vol. 1, *juan* 3, p. 13b; John Steele, trans., *The I-li or Book of Etiquette and Ceremonial* (London: Probsthain, 1917), p. 14.

90. Liu Xiang, *Shuoyuan,* in *Sibu congkan zhengbian,* vol. 17, *juan* 19, pp. 9b–10a. Parallel passages are found in *Hanshi waizhuan, juan* 1, pp. 9a–b; and *Da Dai liji, juan* 13, pp. 3a–b. The translation is based on James Hightower, *Han shih wai chuan: Han Ying's Illustrations of the Didactic Application of the "Classic of Songs"* (Cambridge, Mass.: Harvard University Press, 1952), pp. 27–28.

91. *Daode jing,* chap. 55; D. C. Lau, trans., *Lao Tzu: Tao te ching* (Harmondsworth: Penguin Books, 1967), p. 116.

92. From the "Shui ti" chapter of *Guanzi, juan* 14, p. 2a; translation based on Needham, *Science and Civilisation in China,* vol. 2, p. 43.

93. *Huainanzi, juan* 11, p. 4a. See also Roth, "Psychology in Taoistic Thought," pp. 606–607; for the history of this text see Harold Roth, *Textual History of the "Huai-nan Tzu"* (Ann Arbor: AAS Monograph Series, 1992).

94. *Hanshu, juan* 58, pp. 2628–2632. For a discussion of other poor boys who pursued education in the Han see Ch'ü T'ung-tsu, *Han Social Structure* (Seattle: University of Washington Press, 1972), pp. 101–107.

95. See, for example, Yang Liansheng, "Dong Han de haozu," *Qinghua xuebao* 11(4) (1936):1007–1063; and B. J. Mansvelt Beck, "The Fall of Han," in *The Cambridge History of China,* vol. 1, pp. 357–369.

96. See Ch'en Ch'i-yun, "Confucian, Legalist and Taoist Thought in Later Han," in *The Cambridge History of China,* vol. 1, pp. 781 and 783–786.

97. See Ch'en Ch'i-yun's discussion of the conflict between "inner" and "outer" worlds in Confucian thought in *Hsun Yueh and the Mind of Late Han China,* pp. 29–31.

98. Huang, *Lunheng,* vol. 1, pp. 49–51 (chap. 6, "Mingyi").

99. See Ch'en Ch'i-yun, "Han Dynasty China: Economy, Society and State Power," in *T'oung pao* 70(1–3) (1984):127–148; Hsu Cho-yun, "The Roles of the Literati and of Regionalism in the Fall of the Han Dynasty," in Norman Yoffee and George L. Cowgill, eds., *The Collapse of Ancient States and Civilization* (Tucson: University of Arizona Press, 1988), pp. 176–195; and Martin J. Powers, *Art and Political Expression in Early China* (New Haven: Yale University Press, 1991), pp. 92–96, 206–208.

100. Huang, *Lunheng,* vol. 2, pp. 1180; translation based on Forke, *Lun Heng,* vol. 1, pp. 64–65.

101. As Patricia Ebrey has pointed out, while opportunities for dramatic upward social mobility decreased during the Later Han, the number of men who were regarded as *shi,* or cultured gentlemen, continued to grow. It was from this pool of men that candidates for various bureaucratic posts were drawn. See Patricia Ebrey, "The Economic and Social History of the Later Han," in *The Cambridge History of China,* vol. 1, p. 631.

102. For similar views concerning social preeminence in France see Pierre Bourdieu, *Distinction: A Social Critique of the Judgement of Taste* (Cambridge, Mass.: Harvard University Press, 1984), pp. 2–3. I am grateful to an anonymous reader for bringing this point to my attention.

103. *Hanshu, juan* 65, p. 2841; Burton Watson, trans., *Courtier and Commoner in Ancient China: Selections from the "History of the Former Han" by Ban Gu* (New York: Columbia University Press, 1974), pp. 79–80.

104. *Hanshu, juan* 88, p. 3621.

105. *Hanshu, juan* 71, p. 3039.

106. *Hou Hanshu, juan* 36, p. 1226.

107. *Hou Hanshu, juan* 52, p. 1708.

108. *Hou Hanshu, juan* 40a, p. 1330.

109. Personal communication of May 21, 1994.

110. *Hou Hanshu, juan* 36, p. 1241.

111. *Hou Hanshu, juan* 53, p. 1742.

112. *Hou Hanshu, juan* 61, p. 2021; *juan* 6, p. 261.

113. *Hou Hanshu, juan* 7, p. 288.

114. *Hou Hanshu, juan* 48, p. 1597.

115. Liu Shao, *Renwu zhi,* chap. 10, "Qi Miu," in *Sibu congkan zhengbian,* vol. 22, pt. C, pp. 4b–5a. Translated by J. K. Shryock, *The Study of Human Abilities: The "Jen wu chih" of Liu Shao* (New York: Kraus Reprints, 1966), pp. 143–144.

116. *Hou Hanshu, juan* 24, p. 850.

117. *Analects* 16:9.

118. *Bohu tong, juan* 4, pp. 16–17; translation (with slight modifications) by Tjan Tjoe Som, *Po Hu T'ung: The Comprehensive Discussions in the White Tiger Hall* (Westport, Conn.: Hyperion Press, 1973), vol. 2, pp. 482–483.

119. *Xunzi, juan* 1, p. 7a.

120. Hu, *Qianfu lun*, p. 284 ("Shushe").

121. Ibid., p. 290.

122. See Brian E. McKnight, *The Quality of Mercy: Amnesties and Traditional Chinese Justice* (Honolulu: University of Hawai'i Press, 1981), pp. 1–36.

123. Hu, *Qianfu lun*, p. 291. In all fairness to the Master, one suspects that Confucius, unlike Wang Fu, regarded "great wickedness" as a fairly rare occurrence.

124. Hu, *Qianfu lun*, p. 587 ("Dehua").

125. Ibid., p. 584 ("Benxun").

126. Ibid., p. 593 ("Dehua").

127. Ibid., pp. 591–592 ("Dehua").

128. Ibid., p. 585 ("Benxun").

129. Huang, *Lunheng*, vol. 1, pp. 47–49 ("Mingyi").

130. Ibid., p. 129 ("Benxing"); translation based on Forke, *Lunheng*, vol. 1, p. 387.

131. Hu, *Qianfu lun*, p. 290 ("Shushe").

132. Ruan Ji, "Singing of Thoughts," no. 4; translated by Burton Watson, *The Columbia Book of Chinese Poetry: From Early Times to the Thirteenth Century* (New York: Columbia University Press, 1984), p. 150.

133. Xi Kang, "Youfen"; *Xi Kang ji*, in Lu Xun, *Lu Xun quanji* (Beijing: Zhonghua shuju, 1938), vol. 9, pp. 23–24; translated by Richard Mather, *Shih-shuo hsin-yü: A New Account of Tales of the World* (Minneapolis: University of Minnesota Press, 1976), p. xix.

GLOSSARY

buji	不吉	inauspicious
gan	感	to be moved
hua	化	transformation
huaxun	化訓	to transform and instruct
ji	幾	embryonic; trigger
jian	漸	gradual; to steep; to dye
jianhua	漸化	gradual transformation
liang	良	goodness
ran	染	to dye
shenwei	慎微	examining minutiae
taijiao	胎教	fetal instruction
taiping	太平	Great Peace
wu	寙	breech
*wu**	忤	obstinate; unfilial
xiaohua	肖化	simulative transformation

Famous Chinese Childhoods

KENNETH J. DEWOSKIN

The Chinese dynastic historian dealt with lives much more than with institutions or events. Emperors' lives *(benji)* were cotemporal with the eras; with each new emperor came a new reign title and a new year 1. Individual exemplary lives *(liezhuan)* were arrayed in chapter after chapter of the dynastic histories, for through the lives of exemplary individuals the significance of history for the whole of Chinese civilization was revealed. Absent the lives, the family chapters, and the genealogies, a dynastic history would consist of a dozen technical treatises and a few tables. Historians retold past dynasties by telling the lives of notable people, some well known through other means of preservation, some relatively obscure. Time past was demarcated by the rise, actions, and demise of men and women who rose above the mass of humanity. These biographies are economical, their subjects stereotypical, and their voices authoritative.

Looking for important Chinese childhoods in the histories, I will begin by stating some well-known features of Chinese dynastic histories. Several books and numerous articles explore the features of Chinese historiography, with special attention paid to biography writing and the construction and inventory of historical types.[1] To build on that work and turn attention to the treatment of childhood, I have picked a limited set of issues and will deal with them systematically. Within the general remarks and the topic I propose, these are the questions raised: In cogent records that emphasize public service and public acts, how and why are private dimensions of lives, such as childhood, included? What is exemplary? How are people selected for inclusion in the histories? What features of childhood are systematically of interest to the historians, and what is the relationship between the subjects' childhood features and their adulthood? What accounts for the way people are? What is inborn and what is acquired, and how are acts of acculturation constructed?

THE PRIVATE CHILD IN THE PUBLIC RECORD

At first glance, reporting on childhoods runs counter to the general features of dynastic history biographies. The histories are overwhelmingly committed to recording biographical moments of public importance rather than private interest. The moral, psychological, and emotional characteristics that demarcate notable people are, in the view of the Chinese historian, revealed entirely in public activities; their private lives seem beside the point. The top echelons of the imperial family are something of an exception, inasmuch as their lives in all respects define their times. Even so, the *benji* and the eras with which they coincide typically begin with the ascent of the emperor to power, not with his birth. There are a few exceptions to this pattern in early *benji,* but reckoning time by the life of an emperor relates to the establishment of reign titles *(nianhao)* in his administration.

Given the vast reserve of biographical materials found in the twenty-five histories, there is a trivial amount of information on personal lives, especially childhoods. But child fanciers can take some comfort in the fact that death fares no better. As anyone experienced in working with dynastic histories knows, simply establishing the year of births and deaths is under the best of circumstances a great deal of trouble; under the worst, impossible. Still, what little is in the dynastic history biographies about childhood, as well as what is not, is important to an understanding of the early Chinese view of childhood.

The general slighting of childhood records and the absence of birth and death information are related. Historiographic traditions and practices differ widely with respect to their use of dating for structure, scope and lifespan, and the degree of precision in all aspects of temporality. Such differences can be related to the perceived function of history writing in its own present and related to literary features in the larger narrative traditions to which it belongs. The dynastic historian's interest is focused on years of active participation in public life (or its active eschewal). It is not focused on the years of preparation or the years of demise. In the *Shiji,* many of the biographies commit a single sentence to youth, following the formula: "In his youth . . ." Others invoke the names of a few prominent ancestors but mention nothing of the youth of the subject. Still others begin their first lines with the subject already on the stage of public life, a mature and established adult. There seems to be little consistent obligation to position birth or other key moments in time or to relate public achievement with childhood development. It is worth asking the question: why did the early Chinese historian show little interest in a systematic presentation of key dates and childhood events?

Exemplary history writing was meant to instruct and admonish, or so all major historians tell us in their prefaces and postscripts. The words and deeds of exemplary figures have a timeless relevance. Their exact location in the long timespan of China's past is not crucial to their meanings for the present. Historical remove serves mainly to protect the likes of a minister at court who recounts the life of a loyal but undervalued official or the excesses of emperors in times gone by. It is never so important to know exactly when such people lived as to know for certain that they are not in the present and to know something about the circumstances of their lives and acts. The dynasties, large and approximate historically constructed periods, serve as adequately resolved temporal frames for most references to past figures.

The sequencing and scope of the lifetime covered relate to features of historical narrative familiar in other genres of Chinese narrative. We might describe Chinese narrative generally as showing a stronger interest in episodic, atomistic, facet-by-facet or frame-by-frame revelations of character, and the qualities of time at the moment, and a lesser interest in historical beginnings, continuity of events over time, causality, and what in the case of characters we would call "development." This is not to say that changes in characters are not of central importance, but they are revealed in the narrative by the exploration of critical moments, which may be revealed in adulthood as well as in childhood, not by the longitudinal narration of development with some commitment to an Aristotelian unity of presentation.

But there are exceptions, and the temporal frame of the biographies is not confined wholly to the period of public service or notoriety. That is, biographies do not strictly begin in the time when the subject comes to public attention, nor do they end when the subject dismounts the stage. What is of interest to historians and readers does extend beyond the period of public activity. This is most often minimal, a kind of necessary context; but in some notable instances, even in the dynastic histories, it is not minimal.

As one moves away from official historical sources to more informal ones—from official histories *(zhengshi)* to individual biographies *(biezhuan)*, unorthodox histories *(yeshi)*, and the like—one is more likely to find extensive records of childhood activity, more interest in the private to frame the public. This is partly comprehensible because the recordkeeping revealed in *biezhuan* was the result of private effort, often to correct perceived neglect of a character by the official historians. Our later discussion of Guan Lu, for example, a prognosticator whose childhood prowess is well documented as a presage of his adult capacities, comes entirely from a *biezhuan*. The official *Sanguozhi* biography makes no mention of his childhood whatever. The same is true in the extensive unofficial accounts of Han Emperor Wu, in whose fictionalized biographies rather exceptional tales of birth and early childhood are spun forth. The dynastic history accounts of Wu in the *Shiji* chapters twelve and twenty-eight make no mention of his childhood. His remarkable minister and confidant, Dongfang Shuo, is a similar case. Later I will provide specific examples of the fictionalized accounts of their birth and youth.

Among other informal historical records, anecdotal information on childhoods is found in biographies of women. Very few biographical accounts of women are found in the dynastic histories, excepting women of significance in the imperial household and those who are recorded in the collected biographies of exemplary women. Outside the dynastic histories, the *Lienü zhuan* name itself was as much a genre as a title, even though it often refers to the 125 biographies in the work attributed to Liu Xiang. Generation after generation of writers expanded Liu Xiang's work or compiled sequel collections. Local gazetteers as well appropriated its title. Women's biographies are useful sources for anecdotal information on childhood simply because women earned their place in history by virtue of their relationships with their husbands and sons.

REACHING THE HEAD OF THE CLASS

The issue of what is exemplary and who gets selected for inclusion in the histories is closely linked to the question of private and public lives. The lives selected were of importance to public issues and to the fundamental ethical and moral elements of the society. This encompassed a range of actors: emperors and empresses, leaders both civil and military, eminent artists and scientists, technicians and magicians, notable women, recluses, and scholars. All the lives included in the dynastic histories and their derivative genres are there because the subjects acted in ways that bore on public interest. Consistent with this reason for being selected in the first place is the discriminating emphasis given the public facets of individual lives.

The characters who populate Chinese historical writing are revealed living their public lives far more than their private. In certain subgenres, like the lives of exemplary women, private virtues within the family are typically discovered by officials and brought out for public acknowledgment and acclaim. As dynastic historiography matures, a favored technique is to let characters speak for themselves, through their memorials, their belletristic works, and their letters.

Exemplary characters are presented in the framework of a strong ideology that advocates modeling oneself on excellence and eschewing in oneself qualities that fall short of excellence. To paraphrase Confucius, in historical characters we see traits we would study and traits we would correct. Hence, exemplary does not mean only the good. Chinese biography has never confined itself to model characters who exemplify only the good in life. People are notable for more reasons than goodness and virtue. In the oldest records are the wicked rulers, the worthless sons, and the degenerate ministers that define the darker side of human nature. In the traditional interpretations of Confucius' role in the formation of Chinese historiography, blame was as significant as praise in his characterizations of exemplary Chunqiu figures. Sima Qian shows a fondness for exemplary characters whose very exemplification is problematic. In the collective biographies of harsh officials, for example, he states again and again that harsh officials are really a Qin-dynasty phenomenon and that good government is a matter of virtue, not punishments. Nonetheless, his ten subjects are all Han-dynasty officials, and in his concluding critique he subdivides the harsh officials into "good" and "bad" and separates those for whom he provided a biography from a list of those whom he would only name:

> Yet, among these ten men, those who were honest may serve as an example of conduct, and those who were corrupt may serve as a warning. These men, by their schemes and strategies, their teaching and leadership, worked to prevent evil and block the path of crime. . . . But when it comes to men like Feng Tang, the governor of Shu, who violently oppressed the people; Li Chen of Kuang-han who tore people limb for limb for his own pleasure; Mi P'u of Tung Province who sawed people's heads off; Lo Pi of T'ien-shui who bludgeoned people into making confessions; Ch'u Kuang of Ho-tung who executed people indiscriminately; Wu Chi of the capital and Yin Chou of Feng-i

who ruled like vipers or hawks; or Yen Feng of Shui-heng who beat
people to death unless they bribed him for their release—why bother
to describe all of them? Why bother to describe all of them?[2]

No one has contested the claim made for some twenty years by Western scholars of Chinese historiography that Chinese historical biography is committed to a set of stereotyped characters. Historians in
their work paint masks not unlike the Peking opera's; the taxonomy
of character types lends coherence to the whole enterprise of writing
lives. The practice of collecting characters in chapters like "The Lives
of Harsh Officials" attests to the imperative to classify biography
subjects explicitly.

Yet the complexity in individual lives is undeniably there, planted
securely in the tradition by Sima Qian. It is often ironic and problematic. Readers of the histories in traditional China were intellectually
deeply engaged in the particularities of the lives. They would hardly
mistake one for another, and their commentaries, notebooks *(biji)*,
essays, stories, and novels make clear to us that the interest in detail
and particularity in historical lives could approach obsession. Balanced with the forces of classification and stereotyping, then, were
the forces of finely differentiated details, the grist for those who
would ponder the very questions of classification and judgment
themselves. In other words, strong as the character stereotypes were,
the details of any individual life left rebuttable the correctness of any
classification and judgment. In diverse genres of literature and scholarship, Chinese men of letters explored the possibilities for interpreting the lives of past figures, most notably the morally marginal
knights, officials, mothers, and sons whose memorable acts left much
room for debate.

The function and effectiveness of a subject's writing included in
the biographical narrative are related to the principles of selection.
Written material quoted for a biographical subject is most often official writings with the customary formulaic formality. In fact, the
kinds of memorials that one often reads to exemplify the personal
qualities and character of a biography subject serve that purpose
rather poorly. The persona of the memorial writer is an utterly
impersonal one, a humble and ignorant minister, who dares not
assert his ego even to the extent of mentioning his own name. Voice
is suppressed. A quoted memorial stresses the political and literary
talent but not the temperament or soul of its author. The historiographic trend toward including official writing samples further con-

solidates the focus on public as opposed to private, the focus on adulthood and accomplishments as opposed to individual issues of childhood and potential.

The majority of biographies in the dynastic histories have one underlying plot: the mounting of the stage of public life and the dismounting. What I call "the stage of public life" is actually several stages, several arenas or venues of distinction, including those of court life, popular influence, artistic prominence, or the moral hall of fame (inhabited by such figures as Confucius, Bo Yi, Shu Qi, the recluse, and the retiring official). Obviously, the historiography is largely concerned with the development of a moral and literary story from the stuff that bears on public life. As the official historical processes are stabilized and bureaucratized, more and more publicly held materials (ranging from memorials written by the subject to eulogies presented by his mourners) find their way into the chapters.

THE ADULT IN CHILDHOOD

What role does childhood play in telling the life of an exemplary character? What contribution does telling something of the childhood make to the essential record of public life? At the most general level, the answers are not difficult. The childhoods of famous Chinese provide differentiating detail and engage the reader in two important questions. The first question is this: Is there a relationship, indeed a relationship of predictive potential, among ancestry, birth, childhood events, and adult life? It is easy to affirm its existence; every concept of human nature makes this assertion. But it is not so easy to say what kind of relationship it is. What do childhood events tell about adult life? How generalizable are they, and what is the technology of prediction? The second question is likewise one of "developmental" interest, but of a different sort: Where lies the boundary between the "inborn" and the "acquired"? What comes of our pattern-giving ancestors, conceptual and other prenatal interventions, and the particular genetic palette of our parents? What comes of our early nurture, tutoring, society, play, and tribulation? Most accounts of childhood in traditional Chinese history writing speak to these two questions.

There are three different kinds of materials that reveal something of subjects prior to their emergence as exemplary adult figures. First, we should note ancestral tracings, whether constructed as formal genealogical tables, as lists, or as miscellaneous observations of prominent ancestors. The second category comprises omens and other presages of distinction at conception, during gestation, or at birth. Finally, a biographical subject's notable behavior and capability in early childhood and adolescence, including precocity and charisma, often provide insights into character.

The interest in genealogy is divisible into two domains. First, there is a presumption that inborn nature and talent are patterned on one's ancestors, so a catalog of ancestors gives hints about the qualities of the individual being recorded. This is not a simple matter, and shortly we shall look at the relationship between inborn qualities and acquired or acculturated qualities. Second, a fundamental tenet of the Chinese understanding of ancestors is that they remain active forces in the present-day life of their descendants. The mechanisms by which this force is exerted are diverse, changing over time and place, and differing radically through varieties of elite and popular culture, but its existence is a fact. Hence genealogical notes in a biography attach names to one's predecessors who remain potent forces in the present.

Among the earliest *jinwen* (bronze script records), one frequently encounters the term *wenren*, which commentators generally interpret to mean "one of cultured virtue." *Wenren* refers in early *jinwen* to one's ancestors, perhaps pointing to the discernible similarities one shares with ancestors, a patterning. Beyond the current and active power of deceased ancestors over their living descendants, the perception of which motivates oracle-bone divination and ancestral sacrifice of every description, ancestors do set a pattern for their posterity, a feature acknowledged in the historian's keen interest in genealogy. Excellent examples are found throughout the *Shiji*. Among the biographies of the Five Sage Emperors, the biography of Shun, successor to Emperor Yao, begins:

> Yu Shun was named Chonghua. Chonghua's father was named Gusou. Gusou's father was named Qiaoniu. Qiaoniu's father was named Gouwang. Gouwang's father was named Jingkang. Jingkang's father was named Qiongchan. Qiongchan's father was named Emperor Zhuanxiang. Zhuanxiang's father was named Changyi. This goes back to the seventh generation before Shun. All the way from Qiongchan to Emperor Shun, they lived in obscurity as commoners.[3]

Biography subjects are often born with special favor. Notable parents bear notable children. Even for scholars we can find this notion of continuity stressed in their ancestry and upbringing. Good examples include Liu Xin, whose father Liu Xiang was also a scholar and bibliographer; Sima Qian, whose father Sima Tan was also a Taishigong diviner-historian; and Ge Hong, whose grandfather Ge Xuan was also an experimenter with elixirs of immortality and indeed was said to have achieved immortality. Not only are superior human qualities so transmitted but particular strengths and proclivities. Sons of historians become historians. Sons of technicians become technicians. This particular plot in the histories makes the point that official positions may be inherited by sons in some instances. In others, sons may have privileged access. In either case, the talents and learning needed to perform an official function flow smoothly down the patrilineal connection.

At the same time, historians recognize that the continuity from parent to child is not a simple and infallible process. In fact, although his genealogy is carefully recounted to reach back to a noble origin, Shun's immediate ancestry represents a family in deep decline, giving him anything but a prominent birthright:

> There is an unmarried man in a low position, called Shun of Yu. The emperor [Yao] said, "Yes, I have heard [of him]; what is he like?"
> [Si] Yue said, "He is the son of a blind man; his father was stupid, his mother was deceitful, [his brother] Xiang was arrogant. He has been able to be concordant and to be grandly filial; he has controlled himself and he has not come to wickedness."
> The emperor said, "I will try him: I will wive him and observe his behavior towards my two daughters."[4]

To amplify Shun's moral achievement as a harmonizer, the story puts him in this contentious immediate family situation. Shun's difficulty in dealing with his parents—who, in the words of Mencius, "were not in accord with him"—is spelled out in the "Wan Chang" chapters of the *Mengzi (Mencius)*. Here a series of childhood abuses are recounted. His parents ordered him to repair a grain storage tower, removed the ladder, and set fire to it. They ordered him to dig a well and attempted to bury him in it. His brother Xiang plotted to kill him—indeed was committed to it. Nonetheless, Shun elevated his brother to a princedom. In this remarkable early record of child abuse, Shun is canonized as a humble, forgiving, filial son whose extraordinary virtue was given extraordinary recognition.

Records of ancestral sacrifice dating as early as the Shang dynasty make it clear that ancestors were believed to be active in determining events that shaped the lives of their descendants. In addition to what we might understand as the transmission of characteristics to descendants, there was a potential for ancestors to play an active role in the birth, life, and death of descendants many generations down the chain. In conjunction with the potential role of ancestors, nature itself could act in signifying ways at important moments in human history. Both ancestral interventions and the responsive signing of nature appear to play a role in conceptual and prenatal signs. Coincidental omens, sweet dew, bright roving lights, dragons, mists and vapors, and bird and animal anomalies are found in many birth tales, most often with auspicious connotations. Early examples are found in the *Shiji,* in the "Yin benji," where the conception of the Shang founder Xie is described:

> Yin [founder] Xie's mother was named Jiandi, a daughter of the Yourong clan, and a second consort of the Emperor Ku. Three people went to bathe and saw a black bird drop an egg. Jiandi took it and swallowed it and consequently conceived Xie.[5]

Liu Xiang's *Lienü zhuan* expands on this account, describing how Jiandi was bathing with her sisters in the Xuanqiu waters when a many-colored egg was dropped to them. The sisters fought over the egg, and when Jiandi grabbed it, she put it in her mouth for protection and swallowed it by accident. As Xie matured, she taught him the moral principles, so that he was selected to be Minister of Education by Emperor Yao. In a consistent manner, the conception of the Zhou founder is described:

> Zhou [founder] Houji was named Qi. His mother, of the Youtai clan, was named Jiangyuan and was the primary consort of Emperor Ku. Jiangyuan was out in the wilds and spied a giant footprint. Her heart filled with joy, and she wanted to step into it. She did step into it, and she felt her body stir as if pregnant. After a time, she bore a child, but took this to be very inauspicious.[6]

The *Lienü zhuan* story of Qi's birth expands on the details. His name, which means "abandoned," was given him by his mother when she indeed abandoned him. Qi was miraculously protected from various hazards, and eventually when Jiangyuan saw the birds protecting the baby, she accepted it back. She taught him to plant mulberry and hemp, so that when he matured he was appointed Minister of Agriculture by Emperor Yao.

The grand ancestor of the lineage that founded the Qin dynasty, Dafei, was fathered by Daye, whose mother also had become pregnant by eating an egg dropped by a black bird.[7] Han founder Gaozu's mother was lying on the bank of a large pond and dreamt that she encountered a spirit. Thunder and lighting began and the sky darkened. Gaozu's father went out to search for her and saw a kraken dragon hovering on top of her. She became pregnant and gave birth to Gaozu.[8] Except for this remarkable conception, Gaozu's childhood as recounted in the *Shiji* is otherwise undistinguished; his youth, however, as we shall see, was ill spent.

The practice of recording remarkable conception and birth events grew with some vigor, so much so that extravagant stories of conceptual and prenatal interventions become commonplace in commentaries and informal histories. Recording extraordinary conceptions and births appears to be related to the development of biographies that sought to promote particular figures and lineages.[9] In a moment we shall encounter an example recounting the childhoods of Dongfang Shuo and his master Han Emperor Wu.

Childhood signs of precocity and distinction are usually, but not always, brief and obvious. Because subjects of official biographies are people who emerged into public life, even if they were not "officials" per se, there are often signs of such emergence recorded for their childhoods. By the Tang dynasty there was an *ertongke*—an examination that permitted prepubescent scholars to demonstrate their complete mastery of the classics, a demonstration that invariably brought them to the attention of local officials and secured their patronage. But well before we have the formalized examination to uncover precocity, the informal signs were of great interest to historians. The model for this in the *Shiji* is the first biography, that of the Yellow Emperor:

> The Yellow Emperor was the son of Shaodian, surnamed Gongsun. His name was Xuanyuan. At birth he was spiritually energized *(shenling)*, and as an infant he could talk. As a baby his knowledge was profound, and as he grew he was honest and agile. At maturity he was highly intelligent.[10]

Wang Chong undertook to explain that the Yellow Emperor could talk at birth because he had gestated for twenty months in his mother's womb and hence was nearly two years old at birth.[11] Of course, such notices of childhood prowess are not always so simple. Eventually they become more specific: either as augurs of the strengths the subject would show in adult life or as puzzling contrasts to adult characteristics.

Among the simpler examples is that of Guan Lu, a prognosticator recorded in the *Sanguozhi*:

> When Lu was only eight or nine years old he had already demonstrated a fondness for gazing up at the sky's traveling lights. Whenever he found someone who knew the skies, he would quiz him about the star's names, and at night Lu was seldom willing to go to sleep. His parents forbade his stargazing, but ultimately they could not stop him. Lu himself would say, "Though I am young, it is a feast for my eyes to look upon the sky's patterns." He often argued, "If creatures no nobler than barnyard chickens and wild geese can recognize the times, is it not obvious that humans could?"
>
> Whenever Lu was playing on a dirt field with his neighborhood friends, he would draw maps of the celestial star fields on the ground, and add the sun, moon, and planets. He was able to answer any and all questions asked of him and expound at length on astrological events. What he said was so extraordinary that even the experts of the village, some of whom had made long study of the skies, could not take issue with the young Lu. It was for these reasons that everyone recognized his highly unusual talent for such things.[12]

Earlier I mentioned that Guan Lu's official dynastic history biography makes no mention of his childhood; the quotation translated here is from a *biezhuan* that probably was maintained by a family or professional group interested in promoting the reputation and legacy of Guan Lu.

More puzzling are the childhood and youth of Han Gaozu. He had the marks of greatness: "a dragonlike face, with beautiful whiskers on his chin and cheeks; on his left thigh he had seventy-two black moles." His behavior was commendable in some ways: "He was kind and affectionate with others, liked to help people, and was very understanding." As a commoner, he struggled with minor posts, taking the examinations and getting only a minor district-level position. Less admirable, perhaps, he loved to drink, was fond of women, and lived on credit from the local wine shop owners. He avoided the industry typical for his family. But as Sima Qian tells us, "when he got drunk and lay down to sleep, the old women, to their great wonder, would always see something like a dragon over the place he was sleeping."[13] In the *Hanshu* biography of Gaozu, Ban Gu recalls his profound admiration for the Qin emperor. Since they are those of an emperor, Gaozu's personal moral qualities are of interest to the historian, although they were not promising. Still, the inborn greatness that brought Gaozu to found the Han dynasty was evident in special signs, but it was nowhere evident in his behavior or accomplishments or expressed interests.

Full rein is given the presentation of key prenatal and childhood events in more fictionalized biographical accounts. Here one finds all the story elements from the dynastic histories combined together in hyperbolic efforts to amplify the sense of biographical merit. In the *Record of Revelations of Secrets of Diverse States to Han Emperor Wu (Han Wudi bieguo dongming ji)*, compiled from materials that evolved during the centuries following the Han, Emperor Wu and his minister-jester Dongfang Shuo are provided quite an inventory of familiar birth and childhood elements:

Before Han Emperor Wu was born, Emperor Jing dreamt that a red pig plunged straight down from the clouds into the Pavilion of Revered Orchids. The emperor awakened and sat high up in the pavilion, where he saw a red dense mist approach and cloak the doors and windows. When he looked straight up, he saw cinnabar clouds soaring in a dense mass upwards. He changed the pavilion name from Pavilion of Revered Orchids to Hall of the Splendid Orchid.

Later, Lady Wang gave birth to Han Emperor Wu in this hall. At that point, green sparrows flocked around the Gate of the Ruling Fortress, so Emperor Jing changed its name to Gate of the Green Sparrows. . . .

Dongfang Shuo was styled Manqian. His father was Zhang Yi, styled Shaoping. Yi's wife was from the Tian clan. Yi was two hundred years old and had a face like a baby's.

Three days after Shuo's birth, his mother died. This was the third year of Emperor Jing's reign [154 B.C.].[14] A woman in the neighborhood took him in and reared him. By the time he was three, he knew all the world's esoteric omenologies, which he could recite aloud. He would often go about pointing at the skies and mumbling things to himself.

Once this woman lost track of Shuo, and he did not return for several months. So she beat him. He left again and did not return for a year. The woman was shocked to see him so suddenly, and she said, "You come back once a year from your wanderings. What kind of comforting attendance on me is this?"

Shuo replied, "I just went to the Sea of Purple Clay. Because the purple water stained my clothes, I went to the Gulf of Yu to wash up. I

left in the morning and returned by noon. What are you saying about
'a year'?"
    The woman asked, "Where did you go in all?" Shuo replied, "After
I washed my clothes, I rested at the Revered Terrace of the Dark Capital. His Lord King fed me there with Cinnabar Cloud Sauces. I ate
them and so stuffed myself I nearly died. Then, I drank half a dram of
Yellow Dew of the Dark Heavens. I immediately awoke and was on
my way home. Meeting a tiger resting alongside the road, I climbed on
it to ride back. But I spurred it on too much, so the tiger bit and
injured my foot.[15]

The biography continues with additional tales of Shuo's travels and
his early progress in the arts of the adept. Shuo is already capable of
"shrinking the world" and traveling to remote places as a child.
Biographers give no explanation for this. He did not attach himself
to a master and discovered no secret texts or elixirs. Yet we learn
from Shuo's own biography that the secrets are transmittable; he is
credited with writing a book to do just that.
    When Han Emperor Wu appears next in the *Record of Revela-
tions of Secrets of Diverse States to Han Emperor Wu,* he is already
an adult. In this highly developed fictional biography, the emperor is
provided the prenatal signs and the special conception, while his
minister Shuo is provided the precocious youthful adventures. In this
respect Han Emperor Wu is not unlike Gaozu. Specially conceived
and born amidst special signs, Emperor Wu still offers nothing in the
way of childhood accomplishments or distinction to commend him.
    We do learn something of Emperor Wu's childhood from other
texts. The *Taiping yulan* section on Emperor Wu credits a long
version of this story to the *Han Wu gushi,* an account that provides
additional prenatal signs presaging Wu's birth and some detail about
his childhood. Wu's mother dreamt the sun entered her bosom;
Emperor Jing dreamt Gaozu spoke to him and instructed him on
naming the infant. When still a child he is asked if he wishes to have
a wife and selects A Jiao from over a hundred young women. Ascending to the position of heir apparent by age seven, Wu shows his discernment in the following way:

> When Prime Minister Zhou Yafu was at his leisure, the heir apparent
> was on hand at the side. Yafu lost his composure and revealed a dis-
> turbing expression. The heir apparent just stared at him without
> pause. Yafu got up and left because of this, and the emperor asked Wu
> why he had stared at the man. Wu replied, "This man is frightening.
> He most certainly is capable of being a thief."[16]

Wu is subsequently called upon by the emperor to help adjudicate a difficult murder case in which a son kills his stepmother, claiming it to be vengeance for her murder of his father. Wu carefully weighs the facts and determines that the crime falls short of matricide. These displays of brilliance, all prior to Wu's fourteenth year, deeply impress Emperor Jing.

Ultimately the mapping of childhood behavior to adult life is complex, varied, and problematic. Childhood becomes an interest when the biographer sees literary interest in his subject and when the childhood behavior is useful for understanding or anticipating adult distinction. Overall, what is remarkable about the childhoods of Guan Lu, Han Emperor Wu, and Dongfang Shuo are those events in which they reveal the talents that make them exceptional public figures as adults. In the richer biographical accounts, the childhood signs are not always positive. Sometimes they are difficult to evaluate. An excellent example is the well-known life of Han Xin, marquis of Huai-yin.[17] Xin is described as poor and lacking any merit throughout his childhood—so poor, the historian tells us, he could not afford to bury his mother. In his encounter with the local butcher's son, Han Xin is called a coward. He submits to the name and is forced to crawl between his tormentor's legs. Han Xin's early years demonstrate cowardice and an obvious lack of capacity, if not lack of trust and filiality. After all, filial sons will sell themselves into slavery if necessary to bury a parent.

Whether Sima Qian had a credible source for this story or not, these early incidents serve the crucial literary function of creating a context for the remaining biography. More than any other dynastic historian, Qian constructed his characters to be complex and problematic, often ironic. As Han Xin moves or fails to move from contender to contender, as he blusters about, half winning, half losing, his highly ambiguous motives and capabilities constantly return the reader to reflect on his youthful failings cataloged at the outset. Again, what is told of his early years is utterly inadequate to construct a development of Han Xin from anything to anything, but there is just enough from Han Xin's youth to make puzzling any effort to understand his adulthood. Courage and cowardice, loyalty and treason, merit and misrepresentation—these are twin features of Han Xin's life, inseparable in his definitive moments. His childhood failings create a profound skepticism about Han Xin's virtues in his later successes, even as the successes accrue. His successes mount to a final and complete failure, validating the reader's skepticism about the basic virtues of the man. The critical decision that led Han Xin to

fail was the decision to remain loyal to Han. Was it an act of cowardice not to stand against Han on his own third of China? Was it an act
of loyalty to stand behind Gaozu in his final stand against Xiang Yu?

The temporal mode of this childhood-to-adulthood presentation is
more of simultaneity rather than seriality. There is constant presence
of the childhood behavior, because the adult counterparts are essentially the same. Within Han Xin's acts as an adult are the germinal
childhood acts. Definitive moments of his adult life may be read as a
return to childhood: his not standing up to the town bully and his
not standing up to Gaozu. The difference between the cowardly acts
of Han Xin in youth and those as an adult is one of visibility, not
substance. This same simultaneity of childhood and adult behavior
explains the choice of childhood events made by the official and
unofficial biographers of Guan Lu, Han Emperor Gaozu, and Dongfang Shuo. In childhood, they show fully developed intelligence and
knowledge, discernment and judgment. In contrast to a mode of narrative that stresses the simultaneity of childhood and adulthood, in
the West we have one in which serial development of character is
stressed. Our readings of biography, fictionalized or not, in the Western traditions are largely oriented toward the appreciation of what
we call "character development." Childhood is introduced so we can
understand the character's departure from it. In Western biography, a
character's return to childhood is pathological. This is not to say that
continuity is denied. But there is little sense that slices of childhood
life and slices of adult life can freely intermingle, perhaps even inter-
change. Continuity from childhood to adulthood is an aspect of consistency of behavior, but not identity of behavior.

STRAIGHTENING OUT THE WOOD

Biographers are interested in what children derive from ancestors,
their inborn endowments revealed in omens and presages, and their
early behavioral manifestations of distinction. But they also are interested in issues of acquired characteristics and acculturation, learning,
and conditioning. Some childhoods make the point that character is
contingent, determined by immediate causes, and that the development of significant moral qualities is wholly related to environmental
factors. There is a strong proclivity in Confucian thought, at least
through the Han, for this interpretation of human behavior. Xunzi
made the most detailed systematic statements of this principle in his

essays on human nature, including "Man's Nature Is Evil," "Encouraging Learning," and "Improving Yourself."[18]

> A piece of wood as straight as a plumb line may be bent in a circle as true as any drawn with a compass and, even after the wood has dried, it will not straighten out again. The bending process has made it that way. Thus, if wood is pressed against a straightening board, it can be made straight.[19]

The state had an obvious stake in controlling the educational agenda with a distinct set of values and model behavior, and over the centuries Chinese rulers have been consistently attentive to defining and enforcing a curriculum that sustained their authority. Selection through examinations and promotion based on accomplishments consistent with this agenda were realities of Chinese political life that encouraged study and submission to the range of training subsumed under the rubric of Confucianism.

Precedents for the kind of shaping described here abound in the Confucian canon. The *Analects* are ultimately a narrative of the process by which Confucius shaped the minds and bodies of students who came to him. His commitment to this process is stated in various ways. While the Master was in Chen he said: "I am going back! I am going back! The little children in my school are untamed and careless. While they are trained and in some ways complete, they do not know how to prune themselves."[20] The Han historians understood that acculturation was a necessary complement to genealogy in defining membership in the community of Han people. Thus when the ethnically central Han Chinese are contrasted to non-Han, early processes of training are identified as being importantly different. When the Xiongnu raise their children, writes Sima Qian, "little boys start out by learning to ride sheep and shoot birds and rats with a bow and arrow."[21] Model Han ministers, to take Sima Xiangru as an example, begin with a love of books.[22]

But the Confucian position on this issue was not without its twists. Even though the Master remarked that he found time spent contemplating questions to be useless compared to time spent in study, he also notes that there are those who are born already in possession of knowledge. Confucius said: "Those who know things at birth are the most superior. Those who know things through study come next. Next come those who learn through study under duress. The lowest of the people are those who, even under duress, do not learn."[23]

In his essay on real knowledge, Wang Chong argues that this comment must refer to Xiang Tuo, a precocious youth who was but seven years old when he served as a teacher to Confucius. Xiang Tuo as a model of precocity is widely reported in Han texts, including the *Huainanzi, Xinxu,* and *Lunheng.* Xiang Tuo is cited by another precocious youth, Gan Luo, who at age twelve served Qin minister Lü Buwei, when he successfully matched wits with the skillful advisor Zhang Tang.[24] Wang Chong raises the prevailing argument: at age seven Xiang Tuo could not yet have entered elementary school, so his knowledge had to be "by nature" *(xing zi zhi ye).*[25] But he objects to this claim of inborn knowledge: "When an infant is born, and its eyes first open, it has no knowledge, even though it possesses the nature of a Sage. Xiang Tuo was seven years old. At the age of three or four already he must have listened to other men's speeches."[26] Ultimately Wang Chong concludes that Xiang Tuo had a remarkable ability to learn through imitation and study (essentially the same thing) of admirable adults in his life.

Han accounts of the rearing of Mencius make a similar point: talented individuals are quick to learn from their environment. In the case of Mencius, he was not necessarily selective in his imitation of those around him. A roughly contemporaneous account, in the canon of good mother stories, describes Mencius as a blank slate and tells of his being moved from place to place as a child, each move a step in his mother's prudent efforts to control his environment:

> She was living near a graveyard when Mengzi was small, and he enjoyed going out to play as if he were working among the graves. He enthusiastically built up the graves and performed burials. His mother said, "This is not the place for me to keep my son." Then she departed and dwelt near a market place. Since he enjoyed playing as if his business were that of the merchant and bargainer, his mother again said, "This is not the place for me to live with my son." She once more moved her abode and dwelt beside a schoolhouse. He amused himself by setting up the instruments of worship and by bowing politely to those coming and going. Meng Mu said, "Truly my son can dwell here." Thereafter they dwelt there and as Mengzi grew up he learned the six liberal arts. In the end, he attained fame as a great scholar.[27]

Sima Qian tells us Mencius was an ineffectual scholar, one who retold the virtues of the sage-kings when other political advisors were building powerful armies and bustling economies.[28]

The historian's perception of shaping events in childhood and how they happen is influenced by the narrator's preference for atomistic and delineated critical moments. These are consistent with the general features of biography reviewed in the first part of this chapter. Shaping events do not unfold over time, nor do they necessarily fit into a sequence of influential events in a child's life. More likely, critical moments come in a series of discontinuous efforts or reversals of fortune. Shaping time, or at least its initial direction, is instantaneous, not a process over years of childhood growth. Hence the great general Xiang Yu, who contended with Han dynasty founder Liu Bang, was launched on his notable career as a formidable strategist in one pithy exchange with his uncle:

> When Xiang Yu was a boy he studied the art of writing. Failing to master this, he abandoned it and took up swordsmanship. When he failed at this also, his uncle, Xiang Liang, grew angry with him, but Xiang Yu declared, "Writing is good only for keeping records of people's names. Swordsmanship is useful only for attacking a single enemy and is likewise not worth studying. What I want to learn is the art of attacking ten thousand enemies!" With this, Xiang Liang began to teach his nephew the art of warfare, which pleased Yu greatly.[29]

CONCLUSION

I have posed several questions about the inclusion of childhood events in biographical narratives and have attempted to sample many genres. It is easily demonstrated that childhood plays a minor role in biographies, and its function when present is not primarily to inform a process of character development but to enrich our understanding of the adult. The role of childhood in biographies relates to a set of historiographic questions bearing on the nature and function of the exemplary character, the emulation ideology of the society (literate and not), and the rhetorical authority of the historical record. The mapping of traits from childhood to adulthood is complex but meaningful, and the cultivation of the individual and his inborn traits is likewise complex but suggestive.

The role of childhood in biographies relates to features of Chinese narratology—features that I would discuss under the rubric of the meaning and use of time in narrative, features that include the function of sequence and simultaneity, linearity and cyclicity, precedence and succession. Historians do not seem particularly concerned about constructing a continuous record, although the events in lives are generally told in chronological order. Rather, they are interested in a frame-by-frame illumination of the many facets of individual character and the many aspects of fate. Rather than attend to the evolution of character over time, they focus on the complexity and irreducibility of character at every point in time. A life is told, therefore, with a series of somewhat isolated observations, by no means confined temporally to the period of public service or notoriety, but always bearing on it morally. Such events may be found atomized in the subject's retirement or adolescence, dotage or infancy, even ancestry and posterity. Common biographies of Confucius begin with his ancestry of over one hundred generations; the roots of his greatness tap there. What I have called features of narratology commune with features of charactology. Frames of narrative are like snapshots. Confucius was conceived by a very aged father, Shuliang He. His mother, compliant and filial, volunteered to marry the aging He. In their telling, these events are not always in sequence; neither are they proximate in time or part of an etiological tracing. We are given something of a faceted crystal that we can turn and view in many lights from many sides; the subjects are complex actors in a world of complex factors.

In conclusion, to disambiguate the title of this essay, the childhoods of famous Chinese are not necessarily famous childhoods. That is to say, people who became notable in adult life were not necessarily notable as children; people who became notable in adult life did not necessarily experience events or influences that were notable as children. The balance of perceived significance between the inborn and the acquired is debated in the philosophical texts and explored in the biographies. While ultimately unresolved, the weight of early biographical materials suggests that true greatness—that which defines the Son of Heaven or the rarest adept—is an endowment from heaven and is displayed in signs of conception, birth, or exceptional childhood behavior. In these most exceptional cases, their childhoods are worthy of a glimpse. But for the vast majority of exemplary figures whose lives make up the bulk of Chinese history writing, they achieve what they do by pursuing a life of study and learning of the sanctioned corpus of knowledge and practice, building on a foundation of inborn talent. For these historical figures, what the historian needs to tell and the reader needs to know does not encompass the child.

NOTES

1. For a bibliography see Kenneth J. DeWoskin, "On Narrative Revolutions," *Chinese Literature: Essays, Articles, Reviews* 5(1–2) (July 1983): 29–45.

2. Sima Qian, *Shiji, juan* 122; Burton Watson, trans., *Records of the Grand Historian* (New York: Columbia University Press, 1961), vol. 2, p. 451.

3. *Shiji, juan* 1. Zhuanxiang was the grandson of the Yellow Emperor, third emperor to be recorded in the *Bamboo Annals*. The second of the basic annals in the *Shiji*, "Xia benji," traces the genealogy of Zhuanxiang back through Changyi to the Yellow Emperor in establishing the pedigree of Xia Emperor Yu.

4. Bernhard Karlgren, trans., *The Book of Documents (Shujing)* (Stockholm: Museum of Far Eastern Antiquities, 1950), p. 4.

5. *Shiji, juan* 3.

6. *Shiji, juan* 4.

7. *Shiji, juan* 5.

8. *Shiji, juan* 8; translated in Watson, *Records of the Grand Historian*, vol. 1, p. 77.

9. Within centuries of the codification of dynastic history biography writing, informal and unofficial biographies proliferated, written with specific audiences and interests in mind. For a discussion see Kenneth J. DeWoskin, *Doctors, Diviners, and Magicians of Ancient China: Biographies of Fang-shih* (New York: Columbia University Press, 1983), especially pp. 29–34.

10. *Shiji, juan* 1.

11. Wang Chong, *Lunheng*; translated by Alfred Forke, *Lunheng* (New York: Paragon Book Gallery, 1962), vol. 2, pp. 124–125.

12. Translated from the *Sanguozhi zhu*; see DeWoskin, *Doctors, Diviners and Magicians*, pp. 91–134.

13. *Shiji, juan* 8; translation from Watson, *Records of the Grand Historian*, vol. 1, pp. 77–78.

14. Two passages from the *Taiping yulan* (*Sibu congkan* ed.), *juan* 22, p. 7, and *juan* 360, p. 9a, describe Shuo's conception resulting from a visit by Venus to his mother.

15. I have relied on the textual collation and translation of Thomas Smith for this passage and for identification of the *Taiping yulan* materials. Smith's Ph.D. dissertation (University of Michigan, 1992) analyzes the major texts in the cycle of Han Emperor Wu material.

16. *Taiping yulan, juan* 88, p. 8. Zhou Yafu served both Emperor Wen and Emperor Jing. Eventually demoted by Emperor Jing, he ultimately fasted to death in protest. See *Shiji, juan* 57; *Hanshu, juan* 40.

17. *Shiji, juan* 92.

18. Burton Watson, trans., *Basic Writings of Hsun Tzu* (New York: Columbia University Press, 1963).

19. Ibid., p. 15.

20. *Analects* 5:21. The section is repeated by Sima Qian in *Shiji, juan* 121 ("The Biographies of Confucian Scholars"). The use of "prune" here reminds me of the marvelous analogy to human discipline in *Paradise Lost* (Book IX), when Adam describes his work in the garden: "The work under our labor grows, / luxurious by restraint; what we by day / Lop overgrown, or prune, or prop, or bind, / One night or two with wanton growth derides / Tending to wilde."

21. *Shiji, juan* 110; translated in Watson, *Records of the Grand Historian*, vol. 2, p. 155.

22. *Shiji, juan* 117; translated in Watson, *Records of the Grand Historian*, vol. 2, p. 297.

23. *Analects* 16:9.

24. *Shiji, juan* 71.

25. Forke, *Lunheng*, vol. 2, p. 120.

26. Ibid., p. 121.

27. Translated from the *Lienü zhuan* of Liu Xiang by Albert O'Hara, S.J., in *The Position of Woman in Early China* (Taipei: Meiya Publications, 1971), p. 39.

28. *Shiji, juan* 74. Mencius fails politically and retires to work on the *Book of Odes* and recollects Confucius in his writings.

29. *Shiji, juan* 7; translated in Watson, *Records of the Grand Historian*, vol. 1, p. 37.

GLOSSARY

benji	本紀	imperial annals
biezhuan	別傳	separate biography
biji	筆記	jottings
ertongke	兒童科	juvenile exam
jinwen	金文	bronze inscriptions
liezhuan	列傳	exemplary lives
nianhao	年號	reign titles
shenling	神靈	spiritually energized
wenren	文人	ancestors
xing zizhi ye	性自知也	(self-knowing) by nature
yeshi	野史	unorthodox histories
zhengshi	正史	official histories

3

Private Love and Public Duty:
Images of Children in Early Chinese Art

WU HUNG

A child who died in A.D. 170 is portrayed on a relief stone, originally part of an offering shrine but reused in a later tomb (Fig. 1).[1] The picture is divided into two registers. The child appears on the upper frieze, sitting on a dais in a dignified manner, and his name, Xu Aqu, is inscribed beside him. Three chubby boys are walking or running toward him; clad only in diapers, their tender age is also indicated by their *zongjiao* hairstyle: two round tufts protrude above their heads. They appear to be amusing their young master; one boy releases a bird, another pulls a goose, while the third boy drives it from behind.[2] The theme of entertainment is continued on the lower register on a grander scale: two musicians are playing a *qin* zither and a windpipe; their music accords with the performance of a male juggler and a female dancer. With her sleeves swirling, the dancer is jumping on top of large and small disk drums, beating out varying rhythms with her steps.[3] A eulogy in the Han poetic style called *zan* is inscribed beside the relief:

> *It is the Jianning era of the Han,*
> *The third year since our emperor [i.e., Emperor Ling] ascended the*
> * throne.*
> *In the third month of wuwu,*
> *On the fifteenth day of jiayin,*
> *We express our grief and sorrow*
> *For Xu Aqu our son.*

> *You were only five years old*
> *When you abandoned the glory of the living.*
> *You entered an endless night*
> *Never to see the sun and stars again.*

Fig. 1. Carving and inscription on Xu Aqu's shrine. A.D. 170 Excavated in 1973 at Nanyang vicinity, Henan province. Nanyang Museum. From *Nanyang Handai huaxiangshi* (Beijing: Wenwu chubanshe, 1985), pl. 204.

Your spirit wanders alone
In eternal darkness underground.
You have left your home forever;
How can we still hope to glimpse your dear face?

Longing for you with all our hearts,
We came to pay an audience to our ancestors;
Three times we increased offerings and incense
Mourning for our deceased kin.
You did not even recognize [your ancestors],
But ran east and west, crying and weeping.
Finally you vanished with them,
While still turning back from time to time.

Deeply moved, we, your father and mother... [inscription damaged]
To us all delicacies have become tasteless.
Wan and sallow,
We have exhausted our savings [to build your shrine and make
    offerings],
Hoping your spirit will last forever.
... [inscription damaged]

Visitors,
When you come here and see dust on this grave,
Please sweep it without delay.
Your kindness will make the deceased happy.

This carving occupies a special position in Han art. While most figurative images engraved on funerary monuments are part of illustrations of didactic stories from historical texts, this engraving is a *portrait* of a real, contemporary child.[4] The parents of Xu Aqu ordered the carving to be made as an expression of their grief over the death of a five-year-old boy, and in the eulogy they speak directly to their son. This eulogy, which assumes the parents' point of view, may be read together with another poem in a Han *yuefu* collection. In this poem an orphan appeals to his departed father and mother:

To be an orphan,
To be fated to be an orphan,
How bitter is this lot!

When my father and mother were alive
I used to ride in a carriage
With four fine horses.
But when they both died,
My brother and my sister-in-law
Sent me out to be a merchant.

I didn't get back till nightfall,
My hands were all sore
And I had no shoes.
I walked the cold earth
Treading on thorns and brambles.
As I stopped to pull out the thorns,
How bitter my heart was!
My tears fell and fell
And I went on sobbing and sobbing.
In winter I have no greatcoat;
Nor in summer thin clothes.
It is no pleasure to be alive.
I had rather quickly leave the earth
And go beneath the Yellow Springs.

I want to write a letter and send it
To my mother and father under the earth,
And tell them I can't go on any longer
Living with my brother and sister-in-law.[5]

In a broader sense, both poems—the Xu Aqu eulogy and the *yuefu* poem (which must have been written by an adult in imitation of a child's voice)—express a kind of intimate love and a consequent fear: a child, once he had lost his parents' protection, became extremely vulnerable. In the underground world he (or his soul) would be surrounded by dangerous ghosts and spirits; in the human world he would be subject to ill treatment, especially from those relatives who had no direct blood relationship with him but who were entrusted with his care; he would be helpless and lonely. Such anxiety about the security of one's children, specifically one's male children, seems to have heightened during Han times. Similar expressions are rarely found in pre-Han art and literature.

We may attribute this psychological crisis to China's transformation into a family-oriented society. Textual and archaeological evidence reveals that the basic social unit became increasingly small "nuclear families" comprised of a married couple and their unmarried children.[6] Encouraged by the Qin (221–207 B.C.) and Western Han (206 B.C.–A.D. 8) governments, this type of family soon became prevalent throughout the newly united country.[7] Although the official policy was somewhat modified in the Eastern Han (A.D. 25–220) and the "extended family" was promoted as an ideal model, the result was a more integrated residential pattern, not the elimination of the nuclear family as the essential social unit.[8] In fact, numerous instances of family struggles over property are reported in Eastern Han historical documents and are depicted in art and literature. Tension between families within a large household thus actually appear to have increased during this period.

From this social reality emerged the belief that only the bond between parent and child was reliable; all other kin and nonkin relationships were to be treated with suspicion. But the problem was that the parent/child tie was inevitably challenged and conditioned by death. When a child died young, his soul would enter eternal darkness. In trying to protect and nourish him, his parents would have to rely on religious means. Thus Xu Aqu's father and mother constructed an offering shrine for their son and entrusted him to the family's ancestors. But when parents were about to die, the problem would become far more serious and practical: who would take care of their orphaned child in this dangerous world? The answer was not easy. Parents had to entrust their children to certain "agents"—a stepmother, relative, friend, or servant. But the question remained, were these agents dependable and trustworthy? One solution to this problem was to cast the caretakers' responsibility toward the orphan as a serious "duty." Not coincidentally, such concerns became an important theme in the decoration of funerary monuments: numerous pictures focus on the fate of the orphan. But unlike the Xu Aqu carving, the emphasis of these pictures is "public duty," not "private love."

THE ORPHAN IN DIDACTIC ILLUSTRATIONS

The hardship faced by the orphan described in the *yuefu* poem quoted earlier is reiterated in the story of Min Sun (Fig. 2). The original tale is recorded in various versions of the *Biographies of Filial Sons (Xiaozi zhuan)*. It is said that after Sun's mother died his father remarried a woman who persecuted him:

> Sun's winter clothes were all filled with reed catkins, but his stepmother's own son wore clothes filled with thick cotton. Sun's father asked him to drive. The winter day was cold, and Sun dropped the horsewhip. When the stepmother's son drove, he managed everything well. The father was angry and interrogated him, but Sun kept silent. Then his father looked at the two sons' clothing and understood the reason.[9]

Once a child's father had also died, a stepmother might even threaten an orphan's life. Such a calamity is the subject of pictures illustrating the story of Jiang Zhangxun:

> Jiang Zhangxun had the style name Yuanqing. He lived with his stepmother . . . who was an immoral woman and hated him. Zhangxun was aware of this and went to his father's tomb yard, where he built a thatched shack and planted many pine trees. The trees grew luxuriantly, and local people often rested in their shade. Even travelers stopped there to relax. Because of this his stepmother hated him even more. She put poison into the wine Zhangxun drank, but he did not die. She then attempted to kill Zhangxun with a knife at night, but Zhangxun was roused suddenly from sleep and again did not die. His stepmother then sighed, saying: "He must be protected by heaven. It was a crime to intend to kill him."[10]

Fig. 2. Story of Min Sun. Wu Liang Shrine carving. A.D. 151 Jiaxiang, Shandong province. (*a*) Ink rubbing. From Rong Geng, *Han Wu Liang ci
huaxiang lu* (Beijing: Beiping kaogu xueshe, 1936), pp. 5b–6b. (*b*) Reconstruction. From Feng Yunpeng and Feng Yunyuan, "Shi suo" (Shanghai:
Shangwu yinshuguan), 3.20–21.

The underlying theme of both picture-stories can be summarized
by a quotation from Yan Zhitui's *Family Instructions for the Yan
Clan (Yanshi jiaxun):* "The second wife is certain to maltreat the son
of the previous wife."[11] Ironically, in both stories it was an orphan's
unconditional obedience and submission to cruelty that finally saved
him. Min Sun's obedience won back his father's love, and Jiang
Zhangxun's piety finally moved and reformed his immoral step-

mother. But the one-sided nature of these solutions highlights an important feature of Han didactic art: a human relationship, which by definition involves at least two parties, must be approached from at least two angles. Correspondingly, Han pictorial stories often provide a number of solutions to a problem by approaching it from various perspectives. For example, many narratives and their illustrations on Han monuments propagate the virtue of loyal ministers and assassins who carry out their masters' orders, while other stories and illustrations emphasize the virtue of magnanimous rulers who pay respect to their subjects.[12] As in the cases cited above, an orphan's difficulties might be avoided through the child's own and often extremely painful effort. A far better solution, however, was to induce the stepmother to act virtuously and fulfill her assigned duty. Thus another group of carvings suggests that instead of being a destructive force, the ideal stepmother was supposed to protect the orphan, even at the cost of sacrificing her own sons. In such a case she would be admired as an "exemplary woman," and her illustrated biography would be displayed on mortuary monuments to the public.

One such example is the Righteous Stepmother of Qi (Qi Yijimu) (Fig. 3). In the picture, a murdered man is lying on the ground; an official on horseback has come to arrest the criminal. The woman's two sons, one kneeling beside the corpse and the other standing behind it, are both confessing to the murder. According to the story recorded in the *Biographies of Exemplary Women (Lienü zhuan)*, the official could not decide which brother he should arrest. The mother, portrayed in the picture at far left, was finally required to make the decision and surrender one of her sons:

> The mother wept sadly and replied: "Kill the younger one!" The minister heard her reply and asked: "The youngest son is usually the most beloved, but now you want him killed. Why is that?" The mother replied: "The younger son is my own; the older son is the previous wife's son. When his father took ill and lay dying, he ordered me to raise him well and look after him, and I said, 'I promise.' Now, when you receive a trust from someone and you have accepted it with a promise, how can you forget such trust and be untrue to that promise? Moreover, to kill the older brother and let the younger brother live would be to cast aside a public duty for a private love; to make false one's words and to forget loyalty is to cheat the dead. If words are meaningless and promises are not distinguished [from nonpromises], how can I dwell on this earth? Although I love my son, how shall I speak of righteousness?" Her tears fell, bedewing her robe, and the minister related her words to the king.[13]

Fig. 3. Story of the Righteous Stepmother of Qi. Wu Liang Shrine carving.
(a) Ink rubbing (Rong Geng 1936:19a–20a). (b) Reconstruction (Feng Yunpeng and Feng Yunyuan, "Shi suo," 3.34–35).

Here we find the opposition between "private love" *(siai)* and
"public duty" *(gongyi)*: the stepmother was praised for her fulfillment of her "duty"—loyalty and righteousness—and she was given
the honorable title "Yi" (righteous). But in order to fulfill her duty
she had to give up her own private "love." In one sense a stepmother,
though called a "mother," was not so different from the more distant
relatives or even the servants of the orphan, whose responsibility, as
we find in carvings on Han funerary monuments, also fell into the

category of "public duty." Two pictures illustrate such righteous relatives: one is the Public-Spirited Aunt of Lu (Lu Yigujie); the other, the
Virtuous Aunt of Liang (Liang Jiegujie).[14]

It is said that the Public-Spirited Aunt met an enemy when she and
two boys were working in the fields. Pursued by cavalrymen, she
dropped one child while escaping with the other (Figs. 4a–b). When

Fig. 4. Story of the Public-Spirited Aunt of Lu. (a and b) Wu Liang Shrine
carving. Ink rubbing and reconstruction (Rong Geng 1936:36a–38a; Feng
Yunpeng and Feng Yunyuan, "Shi suo," 3.50–53). (c) Carving on the Front
Wu Family Shrine. From E. Chavannes, *Mission archéologique dans la Chine
septentrionale* (Paris: Imprimerie Nationale, 1913), vol. 2, pl. 49, no. 104.

she was finally caught, the commander discovered that the child she
had cast aside was actually her own, while the other was the son of
her brother. The commander inquired:

> "A mother always loves her son, and her love is deep in her heart.
> Today, you put him from you and carried the son of your brother.
> How is that?"
>   "To save my own son is a work of private love, but to save my
> brother's child is a public duty. Now, if I had turned my back on a
> public duty and pursued my private love, and if I had abandoned my
> brother's child to die to save my own child, even if by good fortune I
> should have escaped, still my sovereign would not tolerate me; the
> officials would not support me; and my compatriots would not live
> with me. If that were the case, then I should have no place to harbor
> my body and no ground for my tired feet to tread upon. . . ."[15]

A new theme is introduced: not only did the aunt have to place
"public duty" before her "private love," but her sacrifice was also
based on a practical concern about her own livelihood. The lesson of
the story thus appears to be a mixture of both enticements and
threats. Indeed, the unseen instructor of this lesson must have been
the brother (or the social group he represented), who successfully
transplanted his own fears into his sister's heart. We may condense
his instructions into a simple formula: those who fail to take care of
his (orphaned) son will be held in contempt by the whole world,
while those who fulfill this "public duty" will not only live in peace
but will be rewarded by the king. Thus while one version of the
picture-story highlights the theme of sacrifice (Figs. 4a–b), another
version represents its happy ending (Fig. 4c): two ministers come to
present gold and silk to the Public-Spirited Aunt, and the woman
kneels to thank them for the king's bounty. She is still holding her
nephew in her arms, and her own son is jumping happily behind his
glorious mother.

The woman's frightened voice in this story gives way to a cry of
horror in the tale of the Virtuous Aunt of Liang, another decorative
motif of Eastern Han funerary monuments (Fig. 5). It is said that
when the woman's house caught fire, her son and her brother's son
were both inside the house. She wanted to rescue her nephew, but in
her haste she picked up her own son. Upon discovering her error, she
ran back into the fire and committed suicide. The following words
are her final testament: "How can I tell every family in the state and
let everyone know the truth? . . . I would like to cast my son into the

Fig. 5. Story of the Virtuous Aunt of Liang. Wu Liang Shrine carving. (*a*) Ink rubbing (Rong Geng 1936:17b–18b). (*b*) Reconstruction (Feng Yunpeng and Feng Yunyuan, "Shi suo," 3.32–33).

fire, but this would violate a mother's love. In such a situation I cannot go on living." The official version of the story concludes with the remark of a certain "Noble Gentleman" *(junzi)*: "The Virtuous Aunt was pure and not debased. *The Book of Songs* says: 'That great gentleman would give his life rather than fail his lord.' This could be said of her."[16] By quoting this passage from one of the Confucian classics, the aunt's "public duty" toward her brother was compared to that of a minister to his lord.

These illustrations seem to support the argument that the didactic stories selected for mortuary monuments reflect people's intense concerns about posthumous family affairs. Among such concerns as the chastity of widows and the relationships between various family members, the safety of surviving children was overwhelmingly important. Nevertheless, we must not associate anxiety about one's progeny with purely personal or selfish concerns. The Confucian sage Mencius had announced several hundred years earlier that "Among the three sins of being unfilial, having no descendants is the greatest one."[17] Moreover, filial piety, as explained in the *Classic of Filial Piety*, was the most fundamental virtue of mankind. If a person had no descendants, his family line was broken and his ancestors could no longer enjoy offerings. What disaster could be greater than this in a family-centered society?

As mentioned earlier, within the context of Han funerary shrines, a common method to express posthumous concerns was to cite and illustrate the tale of a pertinent moral exemplar. The analogies that people drew did not necessarily coincide with reality; hagiographic tales only provided stereotypes, not real personages. Viewers of such pictures were expected to discern general parallels between themselves and a certain type. They would thus "identify" themselves with this type and follow the moral lesson it embodied. In addition to virtuous stepmothers and relatives, another such type was the loyal servant. A servant could play a considerable role in an orphan's life (and in fact servants in some households were poor, distant relatives of the families they served).[18] The epitome of the loyal servant during the Han was a man named Li Shan, a veteran servant in the family of a certain Li Yuan. Li Shan saved his young master from other "evil servants" and helped the boy recover stolen family property:

> During the Jianwu era [A.D. 25–55], an epidemic broke out, and people in Yuan's family died one after the other. Only an orphan, who was named Xu and had been born only a few weeks earlier, survived. The family had property worth a million cash. The maids and a man-servant plotted to murder Xu and then divide his property. Shan was deeply sympathetic about the [bad fortune] of the Li family, but he could not control the situation single-handedly. So he secretly carried Xu and fled, hiding in the territory of Xiaqiu in the Shanyang district. He nursed the child himself and fed him with raw cow's milk. He gave

a dry place to the child, while he himself stayed in a damp place. Although Xu was in his arms, he served the child as his elder master. Whenever something came up, he kneeled a long while before the child, reported on the matter, and then went to do it. The neighbors were inspired by his behavior, and all started to cultivate righteousness. When Xu reached the age of ten, Shan returned to the county to rebuild the household. He brought suit to the officials against the male and female servants, and all of them were arrested and put to death.[19]

This event must have created a sensation at the time: it was recorded in the chapter entitled "Distinctive Behavior" ("Duxing") in the Eastern Han official history, was transformed into several folk-tale versions, and was illustrated on funerary monuments. One of these illustrations is still extant. Its surviving portion shows an evil servant who is pulling the infant out of a basket (Fig. 6a). A nineteenth-century reproduction of the carving reconstructs the missing part: Li Shan kneels by the child and raises his arms in a gesture of reverence (Fig. 6b). This engraving graphically highlights the opposition between the evil and loyal servant; but the focus is still the orphan.

MOTHER AND CHILD

Although each of these stories concludes with a happy ending, the very act of depicting such stories on funerary monuments reveals a deep suspicion toward the intended viewers. The unspoken premise was that although "public duty" sounded glorious and might occasionally be carried out by relatives or servants, it was preferable to rely on direct kin, primarily parents themselves, whenever possible. This understanding was formulated in A.D. 79 in the Eastern Han official document known as the *Proceedings from White Tiger Hall* (*Baihu tong*). Here the relationship between natural parents and children was considered one of the Three Bonds, while "paternal uncles, brothers, clan members, maternal uncles, teachers, and friends" were called the "Six Strings" *(liuji)*. The text states: "The major relations are the Bonds, and the minor relations are the Strings."[20] Scholars have also proposed that during the Han various kin relationships were classified into two distinct systems: the first was a linear paternal line including the nine generations of a family from the great-great-grandfather down; the second included three

Fig. 6. Story of Li Shan.
Wu Liang Shrine carving.
(a) Ink rubbing (Rong
Geng 1936:43a–b). (b)
Reconstruction (Feng
Yunpeng and Feng Yun-
yuan, "Shi suo," 3.61).

indirect kin groups—paternal relatives, maternal relatives, and in-laws.[21] The last group was considered most distant and unreliable. The *Classic of Filial Piety* teaches that "the connecting link between serving one's father and serving one's mother is love."[22] Correspondingly, the care provided for one's children was also to be based on love, or in Mencius' words, "family feeling."[23]

The concept of "parents," however, is also a generalization: a father and mother were from different families and, logically and practically, must have had divergent and even conflicting concerns. The old question about a child's security thus surfaced again, but this time posed by the father to the mother. Specifically, was a mother's love toward her (husband's) sons forever trustworthy? Had not many mothers in old Chinese lore, from an empress to an ordinary housewife, betrayed their husbands' families by bringing their own brothers and nephews (i.e., their own paternal relatives) to power? Such anxiety is reflected in a letter by an Eastern Han gentleman named Feng Yan in which he bitterly accuses his wife of multiple crimes, including having "destroyed the Way of a good family." It is interesting, however, that according to Mr. Feng his personal nightmare proved a tragedy to which all members of his sex were vulnerable: "Since antiquity it has always been considered a great disaster to have one's household be dominated by a woman. Now this disaster has befallen me."[24]

Feng's statement also implies that if a man's wife outlived him, his household as well as his young children would inevitably be "dominated by a woman." Even worse, she might remarry and his children would then be brought to another household. This concern appears to have had a solid basis: according to numerous Han accounts, when a woman was widowed, her own parents often advised or even forced her to remarry.[25] In these cases, her own paternal family relationship resurfaced and overpowered her marital relationship, which, in a sense, had been broken by the husband's death. To keep the widow in the husband's household to take care of *his* children, the time-honored rhetoric of "public duty" was again employed. In other words, her "private love" toward her children had to be reinterpreted as a "duty" or "fidelity" *(xin)* to her deceased husband. Liang the Excellent, a widow who destroyed her face to avoid the danger of remarrying, best exemplifies this virtue. Remarking on her story, the Noble Gentleman says: "Liang was chaste, decorous, single-hearted, and pure. The *Book of Songs* says: 'You thought I had broken faith; I was true as the bright sun above.' This could be said of her."

> Gaoxing was a widow from the state of Liang. She was glorious in her beauty and praiseworthy in her conduct. Though her husband died, leaving her widowed early in life, she did not remarry. Many noblemen of Liang strove among themselves to marry her, but no one could win her. The King of Liang heard of this and sent his minister with betrothal gifts. Gaoxing said, "My husband unfortunately died early. I live in widowhood to raise his orphans, and I am afraid that I have not given them enough attention. Many honorable men have sought me, but I have fortunately succeeded in evading them. Today the king is seeking my hand. I have learned that the principle of a wife is that once having gone forth to marry, she will not change over, and that she

will keep all the rules of chastity and faithfulness. To forget the dead and to run to the living is not faithfulness; to be honored and forget the lowly is not chastity; and to abandon righteousness and follow gain is not worthy of a woman." Then she took up a mirror and knife, and cut off her nose, saying, "I have become a disfigured person. I did not commit suicide because I could not bear to see my children orphaned a second time. The king has sought me because of my beauty, but today, after having been disfigured, I may avoid the danger of remarrying." Thereupon, the minister made his report, and the king exalted her righteousness and praised her conduct. He restored her liberty and honored her with the title Gaoxing.[26]

Liang's testimony—that she must remain a widow to raise the orphans—is similar to the speech given by the Righteous Stepmother of Qi, in which she emphasizes the importance of keeping her "promise" to her deceased husband to raise his orphan. Indeed, once a wife had lost her husband, her conduct and morality were no longer judged on the grounds of being a good mother but with reference to her chastity and faithfulness. The difference between a widowed natural mother and a widowed stepmother had thus largely disappeared: they both bore the liability of keeping their "promises" to their dead husbands to bring up *his* sons. In fact, a widowed mother was approached not so differently from relatives and servants, since the virtue they shared was classified as "loyalty." We have read that the Virtuous Aunt of Liang was praised for her faithfulness to her brother, alluded to as her "lord," and that Li Shan served the infant orphan "as his elder master." The moral typically applied to a widow vis-à-vis her deceased husband was exactly same: "A loyal minister does not serve two lords, neither may a faithful widow marry a second husband."[27]

A widowed mother, however, differed from other guardian figures of the orphan in the demonstration of her fidelity: she was often forced to display some extreme proof, such as self-disfigurement, as testimony to her virtue. Liang's example is not necessarily fictional; plenty of similar instances can be found in historical accounts.[28] Women who disfigured themselves (by cutting off their hair, ears, fingers, or noses) were usually widowed mothers who were forced by parents or paternal relatives to remarry. Three such model widows named Peng Fei, Wang He, and Li Jin'e are presented in a single paragraph in the *Records of the Huayang Kingdom (Huayangguo zhi)*, which concludes with this observation: "They all brought up their sons and fulfilled their public duty."[29]

Widows' disfigurement must be understood as a kind of symbolic self-immolation. Incidents of widows' suicide were not uncommon during the Han, but as Liang testified, she did not commit suicide because she had to take care of her husband's children.[30] Her self-execution had to be performed symbolically, since in actuality she had to remain functional as a nursing mother. Women's self-disfigurement becomes even more alarming when we consider Feng Yan's letter. Here he blames his wife not only for her scandalous behavior but also for her slovenliness and lack of female refinement. But after her husband's death, a woman's beauty would have become useless and even dangerous. By removing such dangerous features she would become more "trustworthy" and secure in her widow-hood. Thus Liang the Excellent says: "After having been disfigured, I may avoid the danger of remarrying." It is not coincidental, there-fore, that the illustrator of her story on the Wu Liang Shrine chose the moment of her "symbolic suicide" as the subject of the illustra-tion (Fig. 7). In the picture, a chariot drawn by four horses halts on the left, and the king's messenger stands beside the chariot waiting for Liang's answer. A female servant acts as an intermediary to present the king's betrothal gifts to the widow. The famous beauty is holding a knife in the left hand about to cut off her own nose, while

A

Fig. 7. Story of Liang the Excellent. Wu Liang Shrine carving. (a) Ink rubbing (Rong Geng 1936:33a–35a). (b) Reconstruction (Feng Yunpeng and Feng Yunyuan, "Shi suo," 3.46–47).

B

the mirror she holds in her right hand brings the theme of disfigurement into sharp focus.

FATHERS AND SONS, ADULTS AND CHILDREN

By examining these pictures, we have gradually established the narrative vantage point from which the myth of "public duty" toward
children was created: it was determined by the "father." Significantly,
a father is never depicted on Han funerary monuments as taking care
of his son, nor is his responsibility to a motherless orphan referred to
as a kind of "public duty." The reason may be simple: he was the
invisible instructor behind all these moral lessons. He did not need
public exhortations to "public duty" because for men, in the institution of the patriline, private love coincided with public duty. For
women, private love and public duty were antithetical, and the
former had to be sacrificed to the latter (as demonstrated by all the
female exemplars discussed earlier).[31] The figures who are portrayed
as devoting their lives to orphans were virtuous widows, stepmothers, sisters-in-law, and loyal servants, because from the viewpoint of the husband/brother/master, these individuals were all un-
trustworthy: the widow naturally wishes to find a second home; "the
second wife is certain to maltreat the son of the previous wife";[32]
"sisters-in-law are the cause of many quarrels";[33] and servants commonly scheme against their masters. The hagiographic stories were
illustrated on funerary monuments to prevent these dangers, not to
reward good individuals.

A maxim in the Confucian classic, *Master Zuo's Commentaries on
the Spring and Autumn Annals (Chunqiu Zuoshi zhuan),* typifies this
anxious view: "If one be not of my kin, one is sure to have a different
heart."[34] Who could be closer kin to a son than his father? The relationship between a son and his father differed radically from all other
relationships including the mother/son relationship: the son bore his
father's surname and continued his father's family line. In other
words, the father identified himself with his son and considered the
son to be his incarnation. Moreover, in a patrilineal family the father/
son relationship was repeated generation after generation as indicated by the repetition of the family surname. A man was often
simultaneously both a father and a son, a situation that again differed fundamentally from one's relations with mother, wife, relatives,
friends, and servants who all belonged to or came from "other fami-

lies." Such a patrilineal chain demanded and produced a specific moral code to sustain it—namely, *xiao* or filial piety. Male heroes, when represented in a family context on funerary monuments, were therefore all filial paragons.

Generally speaking, filial piety is the virtue of a child toward his parents: "The essence of this primal virtue is none other than to honor and obey one's parents while they are alive, to sacrifice to them reverently after their death, and to adhere to their guidance throughout one's whole life."[35] By practicing filial piety one thus identifies oneself *as* a child. But to understand this point, the term "child" requires explication. We find that in early imperial China at least two different definitions of "child" coexisted. The first is based on age. Normally when a man reached the age of twenty he was considered an adult, and a special "capping ceremony" *(guanli)* was held to mark his coming of age. Before this age he was called a *tong* or *tongzi,* meaning simply "child." Some texts further separate *you* from *tong.* For example, the *Li ji (Record of Rites)* says: "The first

Fig. 8. The ages of man. Woodcut print. *Le Proprietaire des Choses* by Bartholomaens Anglicus, French, 1482. From A. Schorsch, *Images of Childhood* (New York: Mayflower Books, 1979), fig. 11.

父子莱　母子莱

惟莱子冠
□至□
兒之態令
有□君子嘉
此孝真大焉

A

父子莱　母子莱

老莱子楚人
也事親至孝
衣服斑連嬰
兒之態令親
有羅君子嘉
此孝真大焉

B

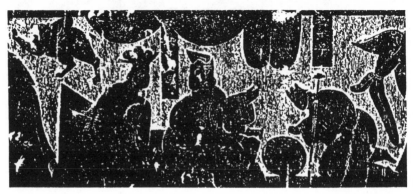

C

ten years in one's life are called *you*. After this age one begins to study."[36] A similar categorization existed in medieval Europe: a French woodcut print dated to 1482 (Fig. 8) includes four figures symbolizing four stages of childhood: the infant (tied in its cradle), the walking child (with an early walker), the playing child (with hobbyhorse), and the young student (wearing the long robe of a scholar).[37]

Another definition of "child" is based not on age but on family relationships; as a popular Chinese saying goes: "As long as his parents are alive a son is always a boy." This does not imply, as a modern person may imagine, that the son was treated by his parents as their "baby boy." Rather, it means that the son, though a grown-up man, should remain a boy—that is, he should behave like a child and cultivate the child's virtue of filial piety. The epitome of such "elderly boys" is Laizi, whose image was a favorite motif on Han funerary monuments (Fig. 9):

> Elder Laizi was a native of Chu. When he was seventy years old, his parents were still alive. With the ultimate filial piety, he often wore multicolored clothes to serve his parents food in the main hall. Once he hurt his feet. Afraid to sadden his parents, he made himself tumble stiffly to the ground and bawled like an infant. Confucius remarked: "One does not use the word 'old' when one's parents are getting old, because one fears this will make them grieve about their elderliness. A person like Elder Laizi can be called one who does not lose a child's heart."[38]

From Confucius' point of view, another famous "elderly boy" named Bo Yu, whose image also frequently appears on funerary monuments (Fig. 10), would be less filial than Elder Laizi because he, though a paragon, allowed his mother to become aware of her elderliness. At seventy, Bo Yu was still willing to be beaten by his mother whenever he made a mistake. But one day he wept and his mother asked him: "I did not see you weep when I punished you before. Why do you cry today?" To his mother's surprise he answered: "Before, when I offended you and you beat me with the stick, I often felt pain. But today your strength could not make me feel pain. That is why I

Fig. 9. Story of Laizi. Wu Liang Shrine carving. (a) Ink rubbing (Rong Geng 1936:7a–8a). (*b*) Reconstruction (Feng Yunpeng and Feng Yunyuan, "Shi suo," 3.22–23). (*c*) A scene on the seventh stone of the Front Chamber (Chavannes 1913: vol. 2, pl. 49, no. 104).

Fig. 10. Story of Bo Yu. Wu Liang Shrine carving. (*a*) Ink rubbing (Rong Geng 1936:39a–b). (*b*) Reconstruction (Feng Yunpeng and Feng Yunyuan, "Shi suo," 3.57). (*c*) A scene on the seventh stone of the Front Chamber (Chavannes 1913: vol. 2, pl. 49, no. 104).

am weeping."[39] If parents were not supposed to become "old" then the son had to be always "young," and this is exactly what the Laizi picture tells the viewer. This message is clearly manifested in the representation of the figures: Elder Laizi is portrayed as a boy with a small frame, a plump body, and wearing a three-pointed baby hat, while his aged parents (who in reality must have been close to one hundred years old) appear as a healthy young couple, the father wearing a gentleman's cap and the mother wearing an elaborate headdress. What the artist tried to express seems to have been the moral implication of the story, not a description of reality.

We can thus argue that the images of these men-children are not "portraiture" at all, an artistic genre defined by Richard Delbrücl as "the representation, intending to be like, of a definite individual."[40] In these carvings, the figures' physical likeness is vitiated to serve their moral content. To understand this method of representation we need only compare all nine filial sons "portrayed" on the famous Wu Liang Shrine. From textual sources we know that these men's ages range from five years old (see Zhao Xun, Fig. 12) to seventy years old (Laizi and Bo Yu), but in the pictures they are almost indistinguishable. Most of them kneel before their parents—a standard gesture of respect and submission. What these images depict is a particular species created by Han Confucian ideology that we may call the "ageless child." While a physically old filial son had to pretend to be young (and had to be represented as young), a filial son who really was young had to be mature enough to be insistently virtuous and morally unshakable. The former category is the "man-child" and the latter, the "child-man." The heroes' individuality is entirely omitted —like their "portraits," which have become simply tokens of ideas. What remains in these pictures is their morality, which, in the patrilineal society of Han China, was promoted as the foundation of the whole universe. The *Classic of Filial Piety* teaches: "Filiality is the first principle of heaven, the ultimate standard of earth, the norm of conduct for the people."[41] It is hardly possible to imagine anything more "public" than the duty of filial piety—or anything that is further removed from private family love.

On Han funerary monuments, real children and "ageless children" are depicted very differently. The former are mostly nameless creatures shown under the protection of virtuous mothers, stepmothers, relatives, and servants; the latter are famous paragons who are portrayed nourishing and protecting their parents. Furthermore, when a child was labeled "filial," even if he was only five years old, he had in a certain sense gained adulthood; he had become both a symbol of the most fundamental moral principle and an exemplar for the whole population. As this notion gained acceptance, a whole group of child-men emerged in both fiction and reality. For example, it is well known that from the time of Emperor Wu of the second century B.C., the Han government regularly selected officials through a recruitment system. People who had acquired reputations for being "filial and incorrupt" *(xiaolian)* were recommended by local officials to the throne on a regular basis. It is less well known, however, that the chosen ones included young boys who were not only morally distinguished but also well versed in the Confucian classics. They were honored with a special title: "Tongzi Lang," or "Boy Gentleman."[42]

Such Confucian prodigies, indeed the parents' dream-boys, were symbolized by fictional characters and represented in art. Xiang Tuo, a child of extraordinary wisdom and learning, was said to have been a teacher of Confucius himself. His image, often positioned between Confucius and Laozi, regularly appears on funerary monuments. In one representation of this theme (Fig. 11), while the small boy is shown holding a pull-toy, the two masters are gazing at him instead of evincing any interest in each other. As Audrey Spiro has remarked on this image, "the child is meant to be seen, not as an opponent, but as a Confucian prodigy, ready to discourse on the highest subjects."[43] Michel Soymié, moreover, has noted a tomb inscription found in Shandong dated to A.D. 179 that laments the premature death of a boy named Feng Sheng.[44] The inscription states that the child had memorized the whole *Classic of Poetry* and the ritual canon. Indeed, so great was his learning that he was called a second Xiang Tuo.

There were also children who instead of being known for their

A

B

Fig. 11. Xiang Tuo with Confucius and Laozi. Eastern Han, 2nd century A.D. Excavated in 1978 at Songshan, Jiaxiang, Shandong province. Ink rubbings. (*a*) W. 66 cm. (*b*) W. 68 cm. From Shandong Provincial Museum and Shandong Cultural Relics and Archaeology Institute, *Shandong Han huaxiangshi xuanji* (Ji'nan: Qilu shushe, 1982), pls. 186, 188.

mastery of the Confucian classics were distinguished by their moral conduct. Zhao Xun (Fig. 12) had consistently demonstrated his filial piety since he was five years old and thus "became well known, and his reputation spread far." He was finally promoted by the emperor himself to be a royal attendant.[45] The most interesting figure illustrated on Eastern Han funerary monuments, however, was the boy Yuan Gu (Fig. 13), whose filial piety transformed his vicious father into a filial son:

When Yuan Gu's grandfather was old, his parents detested the old man and wanted to abandon him. Gu, who was fifteen years old, entreated them piteously with tears, but his parents did not listen to him. They made a carriage and carried the grandfather away and abandoned him. Gu brought the carriage back. His father asked him, "What are you going to do with this inauspicious thing?" Gu replied: "I am afraid that when you get old, I will not be able to make a new carriage, and so I have brought it back." His father was ashamed and carried the grandfather back and cared for him. He overcame his selfishness and criticized himself. He finally became a "purely filial son" and Gu became a "purely filial grandson."[46]

Fig. 12. Story of Zhao Xun. Wu Liang Shrine carving. Ink rubbing (Rong Geng 1936:23b).

Fig. 13. Story of Yuan Gu. Wu Liang Shrine carving. Ink rubbing (Rong Geng 1936:24a–b).

The characters in this story belong to three generations. Yuan Gu's father violated filial piety in his treatment of his own father, while Yuan Gu demonstrated his extraordinary filial piety not only by rescuing his grandfather but, more importantly, by reforming his father. The moral lesson of the illustrated story is twofold: the father's behavior is criticized; but as a filial son, Yuan Gu cannot outspokenly criticize his father. Instead he employs a rhetorical method called *feng,* or remonstration, which conveys criticism indirectly through the use of metaphors and analogies. The key element in his rhetoric is the carriage, the rectangular shape near Yuan Gu's right hand, depicted purposefully in the center of the scene. By bringing back the carriage the boy hints at the parallel between his own relation with his father and his father's relation with the grandfather. The implication is clear: although the father is now in control, in time he may well become a victim of his own model. In fact, Yuan Gu makes no attempt to prove the universal nature of filial piety nor does he advise his father to follow this moral law. What he does is to appeal to his father's concerns about his own security and well-being. And he succeeds.

CONCLUSION

In this study I have tried to decipher the messages conveyed by children's images depicted on Han funerary monuments. What we have found is an essential paradox. Clearly the concept of "private love" was often associated with a child's relationship to its natural parents (especially the mother), while "public duty" was required from a child's stepmother, relatives, and servants. Upon closer investigation, however, it is equally clear that even one's relationship with one's own children or parents would eventually become a social responsibility bound by moral obligations assigned by society at large. Although "private love" was sometimes murmured, the most common themes of pictorial representation on funerary monuments are those associated with "public duty"—the loyalty of a stepmother, aunt, friend, or servant; the fidelity and chastity of a widowed mother; and the filial piety of a son. Executed on a memorial shrine or pillar gate, these pictures were displayed to the public, and their didactic function was again emphasized by inscriptions engraved alongside, such as the following: "We are stating clearly to people of virtue and kindheartedness within the four seas: Please regard these [pictures and] words and do not ignore them."[47]

The general social and moral implication of these carvings contradicts and dismisses any artistic representation of individuality, that is, an individual's distinctive features and personality. The images of children and figures on funerary monuments are thus symbols—"a particular [that] represents the more general"—which index people's mutual and conventional responsibilities in a community.[48] Even the Xu Aqu carving (Fig. 1)—the image of a "real" child—is not an exception: the "portrait" is based on a standard image of a male master receiving an audience and enjoying musical and dance performances. As the adult figures are replaced by children in this carving, Xu's "portrait" is again transformed into an idealized "public" image—as if the memory of the child could only survive in the stereotype of public art, and the parents' love for their son, so vividly expressed in the eulogy, could only be expressed in the generic language of funerary monuments.

NOTES

I want to express my thanks to Anne Behnke Kinney and Kenneth DeWoskin for their comments on this chapter. The issue of "public duty" in Han art is also a central topic of Martin Powers' important book, *Art and Political Expression in Early China* (New Haven: Yale University Press, 1991). Since Powers' book appeared after the completion of this essay, interested readers should consult his work.

1. Nanyang Museum, "Nanyang faxian Dong-Han Xu Aqu muzhi huaxiangshi," *Wenwu* 8 (1974):73–75. As the excavators have demonstrated, the tomb is not Xu Aqu's grave; the carving was reused as a building stone by fourth-century builders. For the practice of reusing early stone carvings in later tombs, see Wu Hung, *The Wu Liang Shrine: The Ideology of Early Chinese Pictorial Art* (Stanford: Stanford University Press, 1989).

2. In a letter to the author, Ellen Laing identified this second bird as a goose because "children playing with a goose" remained a popular motif in later Chinese art.

3. Such entertainment scenes are common in Eastern Han pictorial art and are discussed in Kenneth J. DeWoskin,"Music and Voices from the Han Tombs: Music, Dance and Entertainments During the Han," in Lucy Lim, ed., *Stories from China's Past* (San Francisco: Chinese Culture Center, 1987), pp. 64–71.

4. For a discussion of the definition of "portrait" in the Chinese context, see Audrey Spiro, *Contemplating the Ancients* (Berkeley: University of California Press, 1990), pp. 1–11. In this study I use the term in a stricter sense—not for fictional or mythological figures based on texts (which I call "illustration"), but only for images representing real personages.

5. Translation from Arthur Waley, *Chinese Poems* (London: Unwin, 1982), pp. 44–45.

6. For textual information, see Ch'u T'ung-tsu, *Han Social Structure* (Seattle: University of Washington Press, 1972), pp. 5, 8–9. Unlike pre-Qin cemeteries, which usually belonged to large clans or lineages, Western Han funerary sites were small and often included tombs for members of an individual family. A representative of this type of cemetery is the famous Mawangdui site whose three graves belonged to the first Marquis Dai named Li Cang, his wife, and one of their sons; the second Marquis Dai was not buried in this cemetery. Another product of the same social transformation was the "single-pit tomb" containing the corpses of a deceased couple, which became popular during the Western Han. See Institute of Archaeology, Chinese Academy of Social Sciences, *Xin Zhongguo de kaogu faxian he yanjiu* (Beijing: Wenwu chubanshe, 1984), pp. 413–415; Wang Zhongshu, *Han Civilization,* trans. K. C. Chang (New Haven: Yale University Press, 1982), pp. 175–177.

7. During the Qin–Western Han period a law required families with two or more adult sons living at home to pay double taxes. For textual sources and the impact of this law, see Ch'u, *Han Social Structure*, pp. 8–9.

8. Eastern Han authorities periodically established models of such "extended families" based on Confucian morality: in one place a scholar who lived with his paternal relatives and whose whole family held its property in common for three generations was highly praised. See Ch'u, *Han Social Structure*, p. 301; Wu Hung, *The Wu Liang Shrine*, pp. 32–37.

9. A version of the story is quoted in Ouyang Xun, *Yiwen leiju* (Shanghai: Zhonghua shuju, 1965), p. 369. The present translation is based on another version in Shi Jueshou's *Biographies of Filial Sons*. For a full discussion of the story see Wu Hung, *The Wu Liang Shrine*, pp. 278–280.

10. This story is recorded in a version of the *Biographies of Filial Sons* housed in Tokyo University. For a full English translation and discussion see Wu Hung, *The Wu Liang Shrine*, pp. 291–292.

11. Translation from Teng Ssu-yü, *Family Instructions of the Yen Clan* (Leiden: E. J. Brill, 1968), p. 13.

12. See Wu Hung, *The Wu Liang Shrine*, pp. 167–185.

13. Liu Xiang, *Lienü zhuan* (hereafter *LNZ*), in *Sibu congkan* (first series, reduced ed.) (Shanghai: Shangwu yinshuguan, 1937), vol. 60, p. 70; A. R. O'Hara, *The Position of Woman in Early China* (Washington, D.C.: Catholic University Press, 1945), p. 147. For a full discussion and translation of the story see Wu Hung, *The Wu Liang Shrine*, pp. 264–266.

14. The story of the Public-Spirited Aunt of Lu is illustrated on the Wu Liang Shrine and, according to textual information, also on Li Gang's shrine, which is no longer extant. The story of the Virtuous Aunt of Liang is depicted on the Wu Liang Shrine and on the Front Shrine in the Wu family cemetery. See Wu Hung, *The Wu Liang Shrine*, pp. 256–258, 262–264.

15. *LNZ*, p. 65; O'Hara, *The Position of Woman*, p. 138. For a full discussion and translation of the story see Wu Hung, *The Wu Liang Shrine*, pp. 256–258.

16. *LNZ*, p. 70; O'Hara, *The Position of Woman*, p. 147. For a full discussion and translation of the story see Wu Hung, *The Wu Liang Shrine*, pp. 262–264.

17. *Mengzi*, in Ruan Yuan, comp., *Shisanjing zhushu* (Beijing: Zhonghua shuju, 1980), p. 2723.

18. Besides the loyal servant Li Shan discussed later, a wet nurse is praised in the *Biographies of Exemplary Women* because she became a martyr rather than surrender the orphaned heir of the state of Wei. See *LNZ*, p. 69.

19. Fan Ye, comp., *Hou Hanshu* (Beijing: Zhonghua shuju, 1965), p. 2679; see Wu Hung, *The Wu Liang Shrine*, p. 295.

20. Ban Gu, *Baihu tong,* in *Congshu jicheng* (Shanghai: Shangwu yinshu-guan, 1935), nos. 238–239, *juan* 7, pp. 15a–b; see also Hsü Dau-lin, "The Myth of the 'Five Human Relations' of Confucius," *Monumenta Serica* 29 (1970–1971):30.

21. See Olga Lang, *Chinese Family and Society* (New Haven: Yale University Press, 1946), chaps. 2 and 14; Feng Han-yi, *The Chinese Kinship Systems* (Cambridge, Mass.: Harvard University Press, 1948).

22. Translation from M. L. Makra, *The Hsiao Ching* (New York: St. John's University Press, 1961), p. 11.

23. J. R. Ware, *The Sayings of Mencius* (New York: New American Library, 1960), p. 72.

24. Fan Ye, *Hou Hanshu,* pp. 1003–1004; translation from Patricia Ebrey, *Chinese Civilization and Society: A Source Book* (New York: Free Press, 1981), pp. 34–35.

25. See Yang Shuda, *Handai hunsang lishu kao* (Shanghai: Shangwu yin-shuguan, 1933), pp. 53–64.

26. *LNZ,* p. 58.

27. See T'ien Ju-kang, *Male Anxiety and Female Chastity: A Comparative Study of Chinese Ethical Values in Ming-Ch'ing Times* (Leiden: E. J. Bill, 1988), p. 17.

28. These examples are collected in Yang, *Handai hunsang lishu kao,* pp. 56–57.

29. *Huayangguo zhi* (Records of Huayang kingdom), in *Sibu congkan* (Shanghai: Shangwu yinshuguan, 1927), vol. 85, *juan* 10, p. 86; see Yang, *Handai hunsang lishu kao,* pp. 56–57.

30. Yang, *Handai hunsang lishu kao,* pp. 57–62.

31. I want to thank the anonymous reader who offered this penetrating view when commenting on a draft of this chapter.

32. Teng, *Family Instructions,* p. 13.

33. Ibid., p. 10.

34. James Legge, trans., *The Chinese Classics* (Oxford: Clarendon Press, 1871), vol. 5, p. 355.

35. T'ien, *Male Anxiety,* p. 149.

36. *Li ji,* in Ruan Yuan, *Shisanjing zhushu,* p. 1232.

37. See A. Schorsch, *Images of Childhood: An Illustrated Social History* (New York: Mayflower Books, 1979), pp. 23–26.

38. Li Fang, comp., *Taiping yulan* (Beijing: Zhonghua shuju, 1960), pp. 1907–1908. Another version of the story quoted in Xu Jian's *Chuxue ji* contains one more detail: "At age seventy he . . . played with a nesting chick beside his parents." See Huang Renheng, *Guxiao huizhuan* (Guangzhou: Juzhen yinwuju, 1925), p. 11b. This image is also found in Han pictorial carvings. For a full discussion of the Laizi story and pictorial illustrations see Wu Hung, *The Wu Liang Shrine,* pp. 280–281.

39. Shen Yue, *Song shu* (Beijing: Zhonghua shuju, 1974), p. 627.

For a full discussion of the story see Wu Hung, *The Wu Liang Shrine,* pp. 286–287.

40. J. D. Breckenridge, *Likeness: A Conceptual History of Ancient Portraiture* (Evanston: Northwestern University Press, 1968), p. 7. This definition is by no means final or universal. Spiro has demonstrated the necessity of redefining the art of portraiture in the context of ancient Chinese art; see Spiro, *Contemplating the Ancients,* pp. 1–11.

41. Makra, *The Hsiao Ching,* p. 15.

42. *Hou Hanshu,* pp. 2020–2021; see also Ma Duanlin, *Wenxian tongkao* (Taipei: Taiwan shangwu yinshuguan, 1983), *juan* 35, p. 8.

43. Spiro, *Contemplating the Ancients,* p. 31.

44. Michel Soymié, "L'Entrevue de Confucius et de Hiang To," *Journal Asiatique* 242 (1954):378.

45. Li Fang, *Taiping yulan,* p. 1909; see Huang Renheng, *Guxiao huizhuan,* p. 13b. For a full discussion of this story see Wu Hung, *The Wu Liang Shrine,* pp. 303–304.

46. Li Fang, *Taiping yulan,* p. 2360; see Huang Renheng, *Guxiao huizhuan,* pp. 28a–b. For a full discussion of the story see Wu Hung, *The Wu Liang Shrine,* pp. 304–305.

47. This passage is from the inscription on the An Guo Shrine, which also describes scenes on the memorial hall, including "personages of filial piety, excellent virtue, and benevolence." See Li Falin, *Shandong Han huaxiangshi yanjiu* (Ji'nan: Qilu shushe, 1982), p. 102.

48. Quoted in Rene Wellek, *A History of Modern Criticism* (New York: Yale University Press, 1955), vol. 1, p. 211.

GLOSSARY

duxing	獨行	distinctive behavior
feng	諷	remonstration
gongyi	公義	public duty
guanli	冠禮	capping ceremony
junzi	君子	noble gentleman
liuji	六紀	the Six Strings
sangang	三綱	the Three Bonds
siai	私愛	private love
tong	童	child
tongke	童科	boy's exam
tongzi lang	童子郎	boy gentlemen
xiao	孝	filial piety
xiaolian	孝廉	filial and incorrupt
xin	信	fidelity
xuanju	選舉	election

yi	義	righteous
you	幼	young child
yuefu	樂府	Music Bureau; ballad
zan	贊	eulogy
zongjiao	總角	child's tufted hairstyle

4

Filial Paragons and Spoiled Brats: A Glimpse of Medieval Chinese Children in the *Shishuo xinyu*

RICHARD B. MATHER

The Chinese-American anthropologist Francis L. K. Hsü used to complain facetiously that he had had "the worst of two worlds": he himself had been brought up in China, and he had had to bring up his own children in America. In China, even after forty years of anti-feudal indoctrination, filial piety *(xiao)* is still the expected mode of behavior toward one's parents, although, to be honest, it has been challenged in recent years. In America, especially after two hundred years of the Bill of Rights, the attitude of children toward their parents is far more ambivalent. However, I have no intention of getting involved in comparisons of Chinese and American familial ideals—a quicksand where far better informed souls have forborne to tread. Instead, I propose to look at a few individual cases involving children, selected from an anecdotal collection, *Shishuo xinyu* (A New Account of Tales of the World), compiled around the year 430 under the sponsorship of a prince of the Liu-Song dynasty in Jiankang (modern Nanjing).

The children who appear in these stories are all from gentry or aristocratic families, but for that level of society in that time, the stories tell us something about adult attitudes toward childrearing and about children's behavior in relation to their parents and other grown-ups. The time frame of the anecdotes is roughly the first four centuries of the common era, beginning essentially with the Later Han (A.D. 25–220), which saw the decline and fall of China's classical age, and ending with the Eastern Jin (317–420), a refugee dynasty based in Jiankang, south of the Yangzi River, whither a group of émigré families from the north had fled to escape barbarian domination after the fall of Luoyang (in Honan) in 311.

The period witnessed the erosion of many of China's classical values, as they had been codified by the Former Han (206 B.C.–A.D. 8), especially the authority of the Confucian classics and the traditional hierarchic social relationships between ruler and subject, parent and child, husband and wife, and so on. In their place there emerged a stronger awareness of individuals as persons in their own right, apart from their status in the social web. Such an awareness, of course, was not altogether new. In Taoist texts like the *Laozi* and *Zhuangzi,* a few eloquent voices had been raised even in classical times against what were felt to be the unnatural restrictions of social rituals.

But the new, post-Han outlook, often referred to as "Neo-Taoism," though it was fond of abstruse discussions of "being" *(you)* and "nonbeing" *(wu),* did bear some relation to social problems. What Neo-Taoists meant by "being" was the objective world of everyday experience, a crucial feature of which is language—the "names" developed by society to describe the relationships mentioned above. People who saw to it that these names matched their corresponding realities were referred to as adherents of the "Teaching of Names" *(mingjiao).* What Neo-Taoists meant by "nonbeing" was the absolute, undifferentiated source of being; it was another name for the Tao, the underlying principle of the universe. Rather than pattern their behavior on man-made "rites" *(li),* the Neo-Taoists preferred to follow the harmonious vibrations of the Tao in their own "feelings" *(qing)* and to do what was "natural" *(ziran).* Rather than bind themselves to "order" *(zhi)* artificially imposed by the state, some preferred to renounce the world and live untrammeled lives among hills and streams as recluses—a lifestyle that gained great popularity in this period, even if most persons who professed it were willing to mix their nonbeing with large doses of being. In actual practice, as we shall see, there were many variations and degrees of compliance with either extreme.

Let us begin by looking at the ideal of "filial piety" *(xiao)* itself, the traditionally prescribed attitude of children toward their parents. Confucius, with whose name this ideal has been consistently associated, offers a classic example of the paternal side of this two-way relationship. In the case of his own son, Li, as reported in the *Analects (Lunyu),* we are impressed by the extreme reserve with which Confucius treated him. The other disciples, curious to find out if Li got special instruction, once asked him what he had learned from his father. He reported:

[My father] was standing alone as I was hurrying past in the courtyard.
He asked me, "Have you been studying the *Book of Songs (Shi)?*"
I answered, "Not yet."
He said, "If you don't study the *Songs,* you will have no means of
conversing with others." So I went back and studied the *Songs.*[1]

The same process was repeated for the *Book of Rites (Li),* on which
occasion the Master added: "If you don't study the *Rites,* you will
have no means of establishing yourself." That was the sum of his
"special instruction." When Li died prematurely, his father did not
feel he could afford to buy him a double coffin.[2]

On another occasion the disciple Ziyou inquired about filial piety.
Confucius answered: "Nowadays a filial son is just a man who keeps
his parents in food. But even dogs and horses are given food. If there
is no feeling of *reverence (jing),* wherein lies the difference?"[3] And
again: "In serving his parents a son may gently remonstrate with
them. If he sees that they are not inclined to follow his suggestion, he
should resume his reverential attitude, but not abandon his purpose.
If he is belabored, he will not complain."[4]

Later, during the Former Han period, there appeared a work
called the *Book of Filial Piety (Xiaojing),* which purported to record
Confucius' conversations on this subject with his disciple, Zengzi,
and which has been extremely influential ever since. There the
Master declared: "Since body, hair, and skin have all been received
from one's parents, one dare not do them any injury—this is the basis
(ben) of filial piety. To establish oneself by acting morally, and to
make a name that resounds to later generations, thus bringing credit
to one's parents—this is the final aim, *(zhong)* of filial piety."[5] We
may safely assume, then, that filial piety is crucially important and
implies not only cheerful obedience to parents during childhood but
reverential support of them through their old age, and faithful worship of their spirits after their death. It also means care of one's own
health and safety and living in such a way that one's reputation will
reflect favorably upon the whole family.

To gain some idea of how this actually worked out in a particular
medieval family, let us listen to the words of Yan Zhitui (531–591)
in the preface to his *Family Instructions for the Yan Clan (Yanshi
jiaxun),* addressed to his own sons:

The habits and teaching of our family have always been regular and
strict. In my childhood I always had the advantage of good instruction

from my parents. With my two elder brothers I went to greet our parents each morning and evening to ask in winter whether they were warm and in summer whether they were cool. We walked steadily with regular steps, talked slowly with good manners, and moved about as dignified and reverent as though we were visiting the awe-inspiring rulers at court. They gave us good advice, asked about our particular interests, criticized our defects, and encouraged our good points— always zealous and sincere. When I was just nine years old, my father died. . . . I was brought up by loving brothers, who went through hardships and difficulties. They were kind, but not exacting; their guidance and advice were not strict. . . . I was greatly influenced by vulgar practices, uncontrolled in feelings, careless in speech, and slovenly in dress. . . . As these bad habits had become second nature, it was difficult to get rid of them entirely. . . . How pitiful that the lack of instruction brought me to this condition! Recalling past experience . . . I now leave these twenty chapters to warn and guard you boys.[6]

One of the first things to strike Americans in this passage from the Yan *Family Instructions* is the extreme formality alleged to prevail in parent/child relations. In gentry families of those times, at least, children normally were not brought up directly by their parents, even though they lived in the same household and saw each other every day. But, as I have observed, there were wide variations between families in this period. Take, for example, the respective families of Hua Xin (157–231) and Chen Ji (ca. 130–200). The *Shishuo* account relates:

Hua Xin in his treatment of his sons and younger brothers was extremely strict. Even at leisure within the bosom of the family he maintained a rigid formality as though attending a court ceremony. Chen Ji and his younger brother, Chen, on the other hand, were very free in their expression of tenderness and affection. Yet within the two households neither one on this account ever strayed from the path of harmony and peace.[7]

The successful outcome in both cases of such radically divergent approaches to childrearing—the one strict, the other seemingly permissive—was due, I suspect, more to the consistency of applying each method than to the method itself. But it is interesting to note at the same time the differences in temperament between the two fathers. Hua Xin is depicted in another *Shishuo* story as being so rigid in his posture of incorruptibility that he once threw away a piece of gold that had surfaced while he was hoeing his garden, fearing that keeping it would ruin his reputation.[8] Chen, on the other hand, in his own childhood apparently had been brought up rather informally. He served as groom whenever his father traveled by carriage,[9] and as cook when his father entertained guests.[10] One thing we miss in these accounts is the role that was played by the father as distinct from that played by the mother. Furthermore, since the vast majority of the children mentioned in the *Shishuo xinyu* are boys, what differences existed in their upbringing vis-à-vis the treatment of girls?

There is, however, an intriguing story about a certain Wang Cheng (269–312), the younger brother of Chancellor Wang Yan (256–311), whose mother had died when he was small. Wang Cheng had been brought up by his older brother's wife, Lady Guo, who was only thirteen years older than he was. By the time he was fourteen or fifteen, he was obviously beginning to feel his importance as a male member of the family and to resent her control over him. Lady Guo is depicted in the *Shishuo xinyu* as "avaricious and miserly." She had just ordered a slave to collect manure off the street to use for fuel in order to save the cost of firewood. Feeling very embarrassed for his sister-in-law's parsimony, Wang Cheng made the mistake of chiding her. Flying into a rage, Lady Guo cried, "When your mother was on her deathbed, she entrusted you, little boy, to my care, and not me, the new bride, to the little boy!" With that she seized him by the scruff of the neck and was about to administer a flogging. Cheng, who was physically very strong, struggled to free himself, and then leaping through a window, ran off as fast as his legs would take him.[11]

In the household of the statesman Xie An (320–385) and his wife, Madame Liu, it is apparent that Madame Liu expected her husband to share some of the responsibility for educating their sons. The *Shishuo xinyu* account reads:

> Xie An's wife, Madame Liu, was once instructing their sons [Xie Yao and Xie Yan], when she asked An, "Why is it that from the beginning until now I have never once seen you instructing your sons?"
> An replied, "Why, I'm *always* naturally instructing my sons!"[12]

Of course he meant he was setting them a good example, and nothing he might say could carry more weight than his actions. But I must admit his response sounds dangerously close to evasion. It should be pointed out in his defense, however, that he did, indeed, from time to time "teach and admonish" not only his own sons but all the younger members of his extended family. They were once gathered together, and Xie had been talking to them, evidently on some morally uplifting subject. Suddenly he stopped to ask:

> "Young people, after all, I'm not personally involved in your affairs, and yet here I am urging you to be fine people. Why?"
> No one could think of anything to say but An's nephew, Xie Xuan [343–388], who said, "It's like wanting to have fragrant orchids or jade trees growing by the steps or courtyard, that's all."[13]

The sixth-century commentator Liu Jun (462–521), in elucidating this incident, had nothing to say about Xuan's remark. Perhaps he thought it obvious that the younger generations should be an adornment to the family reputation, like fragrant plants in the courtyard. But this in itself was something of an innovation in light of the traditional concept that the male members of the family, at least, should bring honor to the family by serving as officials.

On another occasion, during a cold winter day, Xie An was again gathered with these same young people indoors, discussing the "meaning of literature" *(wenyi)*, when suddenly a flurry of snowflakes appeared in the courtyard. Clapping his hands with delight, An started a game of "chain verses" *(yuci)* with the line:

> "White snow flies and flurries—what does it resemble *(*zî)?*"
> His nephew, Xie Lang, matched it with:
> "Scattered salt in midair may perhaps be likened *(*ngjî).*"
> His niece, Xie Daoyun, chimed in with:
> "Even more, the willow-catkins on the wind uplifted *(*k'jî)!*"
> Xie An laughed aloud with sheer delight.[14]

Xie Daoyun was, by all accounts, a very gifted poet whose works (perhaps because she was "only a woman") have unhappily not been preserved. But it is significant that her uncle, at least, truly appreciated her. It is also told that after her marriage to Wang Ningzhi (d. 399), one of the less talented sons of the famous calligrapher Wang Xizhi (309–ca. 365), when she returned home for a visit, as was customary after the first year, she was deeply unhappy with her lot and sought comfort and advice from her favorite uncle. The only comfort Xie An could come up with was: "[Your husband] is, after all, the son of Wang Xizhi, and his ability as a person isn't all that bad."[15] Eventually, as it turned out, Wang Ningzhi, who was grand warden of a coastal town in what is now Zhejiang, was killed after refusing to take any defensive measures against the pillaging armies of the "Taoist" rebel Sun En (d. 402), preferring to rely on the protection of Taoist charms and exorcists instead.

There was one kind of education, however, that was not within the purview of fathers or uncles, at least not in the Yan family. According to Yan Zhitui, in matters relating to sex, "men of virtue do not personally teach their sons." Yan observes that these matters are alluded to elliptically, but never directly, in certain classical texts, especially the *Book of Songs* and the *Zuo Commentary*.[16] But one is still led to wonder: if not the parents, who then was expected to instruct the children in these matters?

In the troubled matter of discipline, Yan Zhitui's formula struck a happy medium. He wrote:

> Those of the highest intelligence will succeed without teaching: those of great stupidity, even if taught, will amount to nothing. Those of medium ability will remain ignorant *unless* taught. . . . As soon as a baby can recognize facial expressions and understand approval and disapproval, training should be begun in doing what he is told and stopping when he is so ordered. For several years punishment with the bamboo rod should be avoided. Parental strictness and dignity mingled with tenderness will usually lead boys and girls to a feeling of respect and carefulness and arouse filial piety.[17]

No examples are given in the *Shishuo xinyu* of severe punishment of small children. There is one story of a filial son who turned out well in spite of abuse from a jealous stepmother. This, too, is a standard scenario in the annals of filial children. Wang Xiang (185–269) had lost his own mother at an early age, and his father had remarried a Madame Zhu, who took an intense dislike to him. Nevertheless, he did everything he could to please her. One stormy night he protected her favorite plum tree with his own body against the wind and rain until dawn. On another occasion, in midwinter, he braved snow and ice to get her fresh fish for which she felt a sudden craving. But it was all to no avail. One night she tried to kill him in his bed as he slept, but he escaped harm, only because he had had to go to the toilet just before she entered the darkened room. It was then, according to the story, that "he realized his stepmother bore him an implacable resentment which could not be removed. Kneeling before her, he begged her to end his life. For the first time his stepmother came to her senses, and thereafter loved him as her own son."[18]

There are also cases in the *Shishuo xinyu* in which children manage to escape censure or punishment for behavior normally considered improper if they can justify what they have done. The same Chen Ji mentioned earlier, who as a parent treated his children with "tenderness and affection," when he was a boy of eight or nine was once cooking rice together with his younger brother, while his father, Chen Shi (104–187), was entertaining a guest. The two boys, listening with rapt attention to the adult conversation in the reception room, became so absorbed they neglected to place the rice in the bamboo steaming basket, but dumped it directly into the boiling water instead:

> [Their father], Chen Shi, called out, "That rice you're cooking—why isn't it steaming?"
>
> Ji and his brother, Chen, kneeling upright before their father, said, "Sir, you were talking with the guest and we were both listening on the sly and forgot to put it into the steaming basket and it's all turned to mush."
>
> Chen Shi asked, "Did you understand anything we said?"
>
> They replied, "We got a rough idea of it." Whereupon the two boys conversed with each other, each taking up the argument where the other left off, and in their version nothing was omitted or wrong.
>
> Chen Shi then said, "Well, in that case, plain mush is perfectly all right. Who needs to have rice?"[19]

In a similar story, Zhang Xuanzh (ca. 350–400) and his cousin, Gu Fu, both grandchildren of the celebrated conversationalist Gu He (288–351), and both around six years old, were playing in the same room where a very arcane "pure conversation" *(qingtan)* was being carried on between their grandfather and other distinguished guests. They became so spellbound by the grown-up conversation that

> their spirits and senses seemed no longer to belong to their bodies. At nightfall, seated beneath the lamp, the two boys rehearsed together the words of "guest" *(ke)* and "host" *(zhu)* [technical terms for the chief disputants in a *qingtan* debate], without any omissions or mistakes. Moving from his seat, and putting his mouth close to their ears, Gu whispered, "Never did I imagine that in our declining family there would ever again be born such treasures as these!"[20]

It was this kind of precocity—the ability to move from child's play to the sophisticated games of adults—that fascinated Prince Liu Yiqing (403–444) while gathering material for the *Shishuo xinyu* anthology. A whole chapter, "The Precociously Intelligent" *(Suhui),* is devoted to the exploits of these boy wonders. But it is well to remember that most of the episodes involved children who were only regurgitating verbatim what they had just heard and were not actually coming up with arguments of their own. There are also cases, however, where the children's answers were indeed original. In these cases, too, it is evident that the children's remarks owe a great deal to what they had absorbed from the prevailing "Neo-Taoist" preference for *Laozi* and *Zhuangzi* over Confucius himself, yet couched in language that made Confucius into a "sage" *(sheng)* in the truly Taoist sense, one who understood the meaning of "nonbeing" even better than the other two who had only talked about it from ignorance, while Confucius "embodied" *(ti)* it.

When the brothers Sun Qian (b. ca. 325) and Sun Fang were small, they paid a visit to Yu Liang (289–340), president of the Central Secretariat and brother-in-law of the Eastern Jin Emperor Ming (r. 323–325). Yu Liang asked their names *(ming)* and courtesy names *(zi)* and had each boy write them out for him. Fang's courtesy name was Qizhuang ("Equal with Zhuang").

> Yu asked Fang, "With which Zhuang do you wish to be equal?"
> Fang answered, "With Zhuang Zhou [i.e., Zhuangzi]."
> Yu asked, "Why don't you want to emulate Confucius?"
> Fang said, "The Sage [i.e., Confucius] was 'wise at birth' *(sheng er zhizhi):*[21] I'd have a hard time emulating him!"[22]

Yu Liang was delighted and thought the boy's answer surpassed even the famous remark attributed to the third-century prodigy Wang Bi (226–249), who, when asked to compare Confucius and the Taoist philosophers, replied: "Confucius *embodied* nonbeing *(tiwu).* Furthermore, since nonbeing may not become the subject of instruction, his words of necessity dealt with being *(you).* Laozi and Zhuangzi, themselves not yet being free of being, were continually offering instruction about something in which they felt themselves deficient."[23] There was, however, a rather significant age differential between the two: Wang Bi was twenty when he made his sage remark; Sun Qian was only seven or eight.

Sometimes there is only a fine line between "precocious intelligence" and mere impertinence. Some of these same quiz kids were also insufferable smart alecks. Zhang Xuanzhi—the one who dazzled his grandfather, Gu He, by repeating verbatim one side of the "pure conservation" he had just overheard—was on another occasion accosted by a stranger who observed that one of his front baby teeth was missing. (He was just seven at the time.) The stranger asked:

"Why have you opened up that doggie-gate in your mouth?"
Quick as an echo, Zhang shot back, "Just to let people like you go in and out."[24]

Sun Fang—the one who wanted to "be equal with Zhuangzi"—was once playing outside the front gate of his house when Yu Yuanzhi (ca. 325–360), the son of President Yu Liang's younger brother, Yu Yi (305–345), arrived at the house to pay a visit to Sun Fang's father, the historian Sun Sheng (302–373). Very properly using Sun's father's courtesy name, Yu Yuanzhi asked:

"Where is Sun Anguo?"
Sun Fang replied, "He's at the home of Yu Zhigong [Yu Yi's courtesy-name]."
Laughing aloud, Yu remarked, "The Suns are pretty *prosperous* [*sheng*, Sun Sheng's taboo name] to have a son like you!"
Fang immediately retorted, "Not as *luxuriantly luxuriant* [*yiyi*—Yu Yi's taboo name doubled] as the Yus!"
After Sun Fang came back in the house he proudly announced to everybody, "I definitely beat him; I got to repeat his old man's name twice!"[25]

It is hardly necessary to point out that for a young boy to refer to an elder—a distinguished elder at that—by his taboo name *(hui)*, something even adults are forbidden to do, was rather shocking, and, of course, it was intended to be. During the third and fourth centuries this irreverent sport had gained great popularity in some elite circles. The aim was to see which person could out-insult the other (a form of one-upmanship) without actually stating the insult directly. Puns using the same character as someone's taboo name were one way to do it, and numerous examples appear in the chapter of the *Shishuo* named "Taunting and Teasing" ("Paitiao"). It is not surprising that bright children might also play this game, but at the same time one cannot escape the feeling that such behavior would never have been tolerated in an earlier age.

Smart children understand well that when they are surrounded by an admiring audience they are somewhat insulated against heavy censure by their parents. There is the case of Xie Shang (308–357), for example, who, during a party hosted by his father, Xie Kun (280–322), one of the "Eight Free Spirits" (Bada), whose bibulous lifestyle was notorious, was holding everyone spellbound with his witty and literate remarks. One particularly effusive guest, who by then apparently was well in his cups, proclaimed: "The young lad is the Yan Hui of the entire company!" Yan Hui, of course, was Confucius' favorite disciple. Xie Shang quipped: "Since there's no Confucius in this crowd, how can you single out Yan Hui?"[26]

An even saucier bit of repartee is recorded of a twelfth-generation descendant of Confucius named Kong Rong (153–208). Every well-bred Chinese child has heard of Kong Rong; he was the little boy who took the smallest pear when they were being passed around, because he was the smallest one there. (*Kong Rong rangli:* "Kong Rong yielded [the larger] pears.")[27] This anecdote resonates with stories every well-bred American child has heard about George ("I Cannot Tell a Lie") Washington. A story less often heard about Kong Rong, however, concerns the time he accompanied his father to the Eastern Han capital in Luoyang. According to the *Shishuo* account:

> At that time Li Ying (110–169) was at the peak of his reputation as Commandant of the Capital Province. Those who came to his gate gained admittance only if they were men of exceptional talent and unblemished reputation, or if they were relatives on their father's or mother's side. Rong arrived [unaccompanied] at Li's gate and announced to the gatekeeper, "I am a relative of Commandant Li."
>
> After he had been let in and seated before his host, Li Ying asked him, "And what, exactly, is your relationship with me?"
>
> Rong answered, "Long ago, my ancestor, Kong Zhongni [i.e., Confucius], had the respectful relationship of student to teacher with your ancestor, Li Boyang [i.e., Laozi]. This means that your family and mine have carried on friendly relations for generations."

Li and the others present thought that was pretty clever for a nine-year-old. But another guest, the Great Officer of the Center, Chen Wei, came in later, and someone filled him in on what Kong Rong had just said. Wei snorted and said, "If a lad is clever when he's little, it doesn't necessarily mean he'll amount to anything when he grows up." Rong snapped back, "I imagine you must have been clever when you were little."[28]

It may be of some interest to know that the same Kong Rong, who at age nine astounded his elders with such devastating repartee, at age fifty-five was accused of making the following statement about the parent/child relationship, a remark that resulted in his execution on orders from the all-powerful general Cao Cao (155–220) in A.D. 208:

> As for the relation between a father and his son, what is particularly intimate about it? If one is discussing its fundamental meaning, [conception] comes about only as the result of sexual desire and nothing more. And as far as a son's relation to his mother is concerned, [his being in her womb] is like an object placed in a pottery jar. After it is taken out, it is separate, that's all.[29]

The charge has all the earmarks of malicious slander against Kong Rong by an enemy. Such blatant cynicism was probably never, even remotely, in Kong Rong's thoughts. But it is not insignificant that in the early third century someone of Kong's standing could actually be brought down by such a charge. There were people who were willing to challenge even the most sacred relationship of all. Kong Rong's two sons, who perished along with their mother and other close relatives with their father's downfall, also showed early signs of inheriting their father's wit. Another *Shishuo* story goes:

> Kong Rong had two sons. Once when the older one was five and the younger four, while their father was taking an afternoon nap, the younger one stole some wine from the head of the bed and drank it right down. The older one chided him, saying, "Why didn't you perform the usual rites [before drinking]?"
> He replied, "When it's stolen, who performs rites?"[30]

Not all the children who grace the pages of the *Shishuo xinyu* were "unusual" or even showed the redeeming qualities of the young wine thief we have just encountered. Wang Bin (ca. 275–333), a cousin of the Eastern Jin chancellor Wang Dao (276–339), had two sons—Pengzhi and Biaozhi. As babies they had revealed their rather elemental, animal-like natures, and had consequently picked up the "baby names" *(xiaozi)* of "Tiger Piglet" (Hutun) and "Tiger Calf" (Hudu). By the time they had reached their thirties and were still without notable distinction, the chancellor complained to another relative, the calligrapher Wang Xizhi: "Tiger Piglet and Tiger Calf have turned out to be just like their baby names."[31] Whether or not this judgment was fair, the younger one, Biaozhi, did actually become president of the Board of Civil Office before his death. His case reminds me somehow of the sardonic verse composed by the Song poet-painter Su Shi (1037–1101) on the birth of his son. I quote from the inimitable translation of Arthur Waley:

> Families, when a child is born,
> Want it to be intelligent.
> I, through intelligence,
> Having wrecked my whole life,
> Only hope the baby will prove
> Ignorant and stupid.
> Then he will crown a tranquil life
> By becoming a Cabinet Minister.[32]

There is only one case I am aware of in the *Shishuo* where a child's behavior is depicted as depraved—and this was only because in hindsight the compiler knew that he had grown up to become a usurper. Huan Xuan (369–404) was the youngest son by a concubine of the ambitious Eastern Jin general Huan Wen (312–373). Because of his unusual intelligence and other talents, his father declared him his heir. Then Huan Wen died in 373 when Xuan was only four. When the mourning period was over, at the end of the twenty-fifth month, Huan Wen's former staff officers, both civil and military, came to bid farewell to his heir. Xuan's uncle, Huan Chong (328–384), introduced them all to the boy with the words: "These are all your father's former officers and assistants." The instant he spoke, Xuan burst out crying, choking with uncontrollable sobs. All who were present were deeply moved.[33] On still another occasion, years later, in an unguarded moment, he ordered an attendant to take out a guest's wine cup, which had become cold, to "warm it up" *(wen)*. Immediately afterwards, realizing he had inadvertently uttered his deceased father's taboo name, he broke down, just as he had done as a child.[34] He was a curious contradiction—one moment almost overly sensitive, and the next cruelly calculating and cold-blooded. His father, Huan Wen, had gained prominent status through his spectacular military exploits and was prevented only by his premature death from overthrowing the Jin regime and founding his own dynasty. Huan

Xuan, filial son to the very end, briefly fulfilled his father's unrealized dream for three months during the year 404, when he ruled as "emperor" of the Chu dynasty, with its capital in Jiankang, before being killed by a new conqueror, Liu Yu, who eventually founded the Liu–Song dynasty (r. 420–422). With this background one can appreciate the following story in the *Shishuo:*

> When Huan Xuan was a little boy, he and his elder and younger cousins used to raise geese and have them fight. Every time Xuan's goose lost, it would make him very angry. One night [after such a defeat] he went to the goose pen and seized his cousins' geese, killing every one of them.
>
> Next morning, [beholding the devastation], members of the family became alarmed and fearful, thinking something supernatural and uncanny had happened. They reported it to Xuan's uncle, Huan Chong [who had raised him after his father's death]. Chong said, "There's no reason to think it uncanny. It's probably just one of Xuan's pranks and nothing more."
>
> Upon investigation, this turned out to be true.[35]

I have arranged these fragmentary and somewhat tantalizing glimpses of medieval Chinese children in a more-or-less descending scale, very much in the same order in which they appear in the *Shishuo* itself: from the sublimely filial and intelligent, through the merely cheeky and impertinent, to the stupidly dull, and finally, the cruel and malignant. The total impact of all these incidents tends to reinforce the impression gained from other sources for this period— that children from the third and fourth centuries, especially in the émigré regimes of the south, lived through a widespread if not universal questioning of the authoritarian, legalistic, and often repressive orthodoxy that had prevailed throughout most of the Former Han period. A new stirring of individual freedom with its concomitant relaxation of the classical social and familial relationships afforded some children, at least, a more nearly equal and intimate relation with their elders and greater opportunities to develop as individuals.

NOTES

I wish to express my indebtedness to the other participants at the Symposium on Children in Premodern China and to Anne Behnke Kinney in particular. Revisions also owe a good deal to Professor Ying-shih Yü's seminal article, "Individualism and the New-Taoist Movement in Wei-Chin China," in Donald Munro, ed., *Individualism and Holism: Studies in Confucian and Taoist Values* (Ann Arbor: Center for Chinese Studies, University of Michigan, 1985), pp. 121–155.

1. *Analects (Lunyu)* 16:13; James Legge, *The Chinese Classics* (Hong Kong: University of Hong Kong Press, 1960), vol. 1, pp. 315–316.

2. *Analects* 11:7; Legge, *Classics*, vol. 1, p. 239.

3. *Analects* 2:7; Legge, *Classics*, vol. 1, p. 148; see also W. T. DeBary, ed., *Sources of Chinese Tradition* (New York: Columbia University Press, 1960), p. 29.

4. *Analects* 4:18; Legge, *Classics*, vol. 1, p. 170; DeBary, *Sources*, p. 30.

5. *Xiaojing* (*Sibu congkan* ed.), *juan* 1, p. 1a.

6. Yan Zhitui, *Yanshi jiaxun* (*Zhuzi jicheng* ed.) *juan* 1, p. 1; translated by S. Y. Teng, *Family Instructions for the Yen Clan* (Leiden: E. J. Brill, 1968), pp. 1–2.

7. Liu Yiqing, *Shishuo xinyu*, chap. 1, item 10 (hereafter the first citation of *Shishuo xinyu* will refer to chapter and item number); Yu Jiaxi, ed., *Shishuo xinyu jiansu* (Beijing: Zhonghua shuju, 1983), p. 12; translated by R. B. Mather, *Shih-shuo hsin-yü: A New Account of Tales of the World* (Minneapolis: University of Minnesota Press, 1976), p. 7.

8. *Shishuo xinyu* I:11; Yu Jiaxi, p. 13; Mather, p. 7.

9. *Shishuo xinyu* I:6; Yu Jiaxi, p. 7; Mather, p. 5.

10. *Shishuo xinyu* XII:1; Yu Jiaxi, p. 587; Mather, p. 297.

11. *Shishuo xinyu* X:10; Yu Jiaxi, p. 559; Mather, p. 282.

12. *Shishuo xinyu* I:36; Yu Jiaxi, p. 38; Mather, p. 18.

13. *Shishuo xinyu* II:92; Yu Jiaxi, p. 145; Mather, p. 72.

14. *Shishuo xinyu* II:71; Yu Jiaxi, p. 131; Mather, p. 64.

15. *Shishuo xinyu* XIX:26; Yu Jiaxi, p. 697; Mather, p. 354.

16. *Yanshi jiaxun*, *juan* 2, p. 2; Teng, p. 5.

17. *Yanshi jiaxun*, *juan* 2, p. 1; Teng, p. 3.

18. *Shishuo xinyu* I:14; Yu Jiaxi, pp. 15–16; Mather, p. 8.

19. *Shishuo xinyu* XII:1; Yu Jiaxi, p. 587; Mather, p. 297.

20. *Shishuo xinyu* XII:4; Yu Jiaxi, p. 591; Mather, pp. 298–299.

21. *Analects* 16:9; Legge, *Classics*, vol. 1, p. 313. It should be noted to Confucius' credit, however, that he also said: "I am *not* one who was born wise. I love antiquity and am diligent in seeking [information about it]"; *Analects* 7:19; Legge, *Classics*, vol. 1, p. 201.

22. *Shishuo xinyu* II:50; Yu Jiaxi, p. 109; Mather, p. 54.

23. *Shishuo xinyu* IV:8; Yu Jiaxi, p. 199; Mather, p. 96.

24. *Shishuo xinyu* XXV:30; Yu Jiaxi, p. 803; Mather, p. 413.

25. *Shishuo xinyu* XXV:33; Yu Jiaxi, pp. 804–805; Mather, p. 414. The reduplicated binome, *yiyi,* appears frequently in the *Book of Songs* and elsewhere, meaning something like "luxuriant" (of vegetation).

26. *Shishuo xinyu* II:46; Yu Jiaxi, p. 107; Mather, p. 53.

27. See [*Kong*] *Rong biejuan;* cited in the commentary at *Shishuo xinyu* II: 3 (see note 28 below).

28. *Shishuo xinyu* II:3; Yu Jiaxi, p. 56; Mather, p. 26.

29. Fan Ye et al., comps. *Hou Hanshu* (Beijing: Zhonghua shuju, 1965), *juan* 70, p. 2278.

30. *Shishuo xinyu* II:4; Yu Jiaxi, p. 58; Mather, pp. 26–27.

31. *Shishuo xinyu* XXVI:8; Yu Jiaxi, p. 593; Mather, p. 432.

32. Arthur Waley, *Translations from the Chinese* (New York: Knopf, 1941), p. 324.

33. *Shishuo xinyu* XII:7; Yu Jiaxi, p. 593; Mather, pp. 299–300.

34. *Shishuo xinyu* XXIII:50; Yu Jiaxi, p. 762; Mather, p. 390.

35. *Shishuo xinyu* XXXI:8; Yu Jiaxi, pp. 889–890; Mather, p. 467.

GLOSSARY

Bada	八達	Eight Free Spirits
ben	本	basis
Hudu	虎犢	Tiger Calf
hui	諱	taboo name
Hutun	虎㹠	Tiger Piglet
jing	敬	reverence
ke	客	guest
*k'jí	起	uplifted
ming	名	name
*ngjí	擬	to be likened to
Paitiao	排調	Taunting and Teasing
qingtan	清談	pure conversation
sheng	聖	sage
sheng*	盛	prosperous
sheng er zhizhi	生而知之	born wise
Suhui	夙慧	Precociously Intelligent
tiwu	體無	to embody nonbeing
wen	溫	to warm
wenyi	文義	the meaning of literature
wu	無	nonbeing
xiao	孝	filial piety
xiaozi	小字	baby name
yiyi	翼翼	luxuriant
you	有	being
yuci	語次	chain verses
zhong	終	final aim
zhu	主	host
zi	字	courtesy name
*zí	似	to resemble

PART TWO

Mid- to Late
Imperial China

Overleaf: "Skeleton Puppet Master," by Li Song (fl. 1190–1230), in the Palace Museum, Beijing. From Zheng Zhenduo, Zheng Heng, and Xu Bangda, eds., *Songren huace* (Beijing: Zhongguo gudian yishu chubanshe, 1959), pl. 58.

5

Childhood Remembered: Parents and Children in China, 800 to 1700

PEI-YI WU

A major problem confronting historians of premodern Chinese child-hood is that of source material. In spite of the massive written records of the past, there was nothing in China that could even remotely compare to the diary of the court doctor Jean Héroard, who kept a day-to-day account of the infancy of the future King Louis XIII (1601–1643), beginning with the accouchement. Every-thing that a modern social historian likes to know can be found in it, often in minute detail: food, clothes, corporal punishment, toilet training, infantile sexuality, weaning, parental interactions, educa-tion. No wonder, then, that the history of childhood, for the last thirty years or so one of the most lively fields in Western history, began in France and still lags in China. Nonetheless, in the vast store of traditional Chinese writings there are several categories of mate-rials that can be made to yield useful information on various aspects of Chinese childhood. Accordingly, this essay explores several genres, primarily mourning literature, for descriptions of childhood and facts on related topics.

BIOGRAPHY

One may begin with biography, the most voluminous of all genres of Chinese prose writings, for the obvious reason that since childhood is an inevitable stage of life, any writing about a life is likely to touch on this matter. Biography, however, turns out to be of little use to us. What we would recognize as biography today went under a variety of names in traditional China. The subgenre that enjoyed the widest vogue and most resembled the modern form is the *zhuan*. In its verbal form the word means "to transmit," and it was used in its nominal form to denote a commentary or an exegesis of a canonical text. Hence even in its earliest days the didactic function of the *zhuan* had already been foreshadowed: it should contain what was worthy of transmission to posterity, and its contents should illustrate or demonstrate general principles. This fact contributed to the highly selective principle governing the type and quantity of incidents that could be included in a biography.[1] It is not surprising, then, that childhood is often completely neglected in traditional biographies, even in subgenres other than the *zhuan*. When childhood is touched at all, it is usually represented by a few standard topoi such as early signs of precocity or commendable acts of filial piety.[2]

Biographers writing about a subject's childhood tend to rely upon standard formulas even when, or especially because, the author knew the subject well. The brothers Cheng Hao (1032–1085) and Cheng Yi (1033–1107) were so close to each other philosophically that they were often mentioned in the same breath by their Neo-Confucian disciples and admirers. The only survivors among six boys, the two, born just a year apart, grew up together and remained almost inseparable as adults. After Cheng Hao died his younger brother wrote a biography for him that, running to some five thousand characters, is unusually long. The following is the childhood section in its entirety:

> The master, born with superb endowment, was different from ordinary children. One day he was carried by his great-aunt Lady Ren in her arms. As she was walking, her hairpin dropped without her knowledge. She did not look for it until several days later. The master was too young to talk, but he started to point with his finger. Lady Ren followed his directions and in the end found the hairpin. Everyone was amazed by the incident. When the master was not quite ten years old he could recite the *Book of Poetry* and the *Book of Documents*. His power of memory was unsurpassed. When he was ten years old he could compose poetry and rhymed prose. In his early teens he stayed in the school dormitory where he comported himself like a mature adult. None could see him without respect and admiration.[3]

AUTOBIOGRAPHY

Autobiography, often taking its cue from biography, is not much more helpful than biography in providing information on Chinese childhood. Occasionally we are given a brief outline of the autobiographer's schooling. The Tang historiographer Liu Zhiji (661–721)

seems to have had a less auspicious beginning than the Song master
Cheng Hao:

> As a child I received instructions from my father and had an early
> exposure to the classics. When I was a little older I was taught the
> *Book of Documents* in the ancient script version. As I was troubled
> by the text, which I found difficult and vexatious, I was unable
> to chant or memorize. I could not master it even though I was fre-
> quently beaten. In the meantime my father was explaining to my older
> brothers the *Zuo zhuan* version of the *Spring and Autumn Annals*.
> When I heard him I dropped the book I was supposed to study and lis-
> tened. Every time he finished his session I would take over and
> expound the lesson for my older brothers. I sighed and said to myself:
> "If all the books were like this, I would not be as slow as I have been."
> Impressed, my father began to teach me the *Zuo zhuan*, and in a year's
> time I finished reading and memorization. I was then just twelve years
> of age. Although my comprehension of my father's explanations was
> by no means profound, I understood the general idea of the book. My
> father and older brothers wanted me to read all the commentaries on
> the book so as to achieve a thorough mastery of this classic. I declined
> on the ground that this book did not cover the events that have
> occurred since the death of Confucius. Instead I begged that I might be
> allowed to read other books of history, thus broadening my knowl-
> edge of the field.[4]

Strange as it may seem, it is a rare father who is accorded an
important place in the son's autobiography. Tao Qian (365–427),
Deng Huoqu (1498–1570), and Chen Jiru (1558–1639) never mentioned their fathers; Mao Qiling (1623–1716), Hu Zhi (1517–1585),
Deqing (1546–1623), and Wang Jie (1603–1682?) did so only in
passing once or twice. In this respect, the contrast between autobiography and biography is conspicuous. Biography seldom begins without a genealogy, and the biographer almost always finds something
worthy of notice in the father of the subject. On this point even autobiographies that are otherwise virtually self-written biographies often
differ from their models. Some of the fathers of autobiographers
were quite prominent, pillars of the state or masters of learning, and
presumably exemplars for all, but they rarely earned an acknowledgment from the sons, as if emulation, the fundamental tenet of Confucian education, could be practiced only from afar. The most glaring
case is that of Han Chang (799–855), the son of Han Yu (768–824).
In his autonecrology, Han Chang describes his literary apprenticeship

under two mentors, but his father, the great defender of Confucianism, an innovative poet and the most celebrated essayist of the Tang, merits no more than a mention—and that only in the list of ancestors.[5] Although it is true that Han Yu, exiled by the emperor to the south, was an absent father during three years (803–806) of the autobiographer's early childhood, still the son must have benefited from the father's company from 807 on.[6]

The mother, however, is often remembered with affection and sometimes credited with the early education of the son. Mao Qiling begins his long autobiography with a dream that his mother had on the eve of his birth. She dreamt that a foreign monk came into the chamber and hung on the wall a monk's certificate, on the borders of which was a drawing of five dragons linked in a circle. After his birth she chose his name on the basis of a poetic allusion to the five mythic beasts. It was again the mother who acted as the first teacher:

> When I was five years of age I expressed a wish to begin reading books. As no tutor was available, my mother recited the *Great Learning* and I repeated after her. After I succeeded in committing the text to memory, I asked her what the corresponding characters were. My mother bought a popular edition of the book and told me to read the text by myself, using my memorized version as the guide. After two readings there was no character that I could not recognize.[7]

The father, a prominent man of letters in his own right, is mentioned only very briefly near the end of the long autobiography. It is extraordinary that neither he nor the grandfather had anything to do with the naming of the boy. His place in the life of the son, like that of so many fathers in biographies and autobiographies, is further diminished by the topos of the prophetic dream. On the eve of his birth, the child's future is typically prefigured: there may be a variety of signs and portents, for example, or he is shown to be a gift from a divinity or the reincarnation of another man. Under such circumstances, the father cannot have much to say about either the essential nature of the boy or how the course of the son's life will turn out.

This topos and the teleological principle of Chinese biography—that the adult traits are discernible in the child—tend to reinforce each other. Mao's life story is a case in point. As his narrative states, the significance of the certificate became clear to the mother twenty-two years later, when she learned that a monkish disguise saved her son from certain death. Later, during another crisis in Mao's life, a monk, who came from a border region, appeared in an outlandish habit. He saved Mao from his worst troubles, and the magic was wrought through the instruction of how to read the *Great Learning* in a new way. Although Mao does not specify what the dragon in his mother's dream prefigures, this symbol of elusiveness and swift transformations was quite appropriate for a decade of constant motion and frequent changes of disguise. The mythic creature also possesses other attributes that Mao shares: vigor, expansiveness, creative powers. No wonder that his early display of ease in memorizing texts and mastering the written language was repeated many times in adulthood.

The monk Deqing, also known as Hanshan, gives us the most detailed representation of premodern childhood in an autobiography—or for that matter in any kind of Chinese writing. As I have discussed him fully elsewhere, I shall not repeat his story, which combines all the themes—the mother's prophetic dream just before the birth of the child, her prominent role in the formation of the future adult, and the enigmatic absence of the father—mentioned in this section.[8]

WRITINGS ABOUT THE WET NURSE

Here we are exploring not a genre but a group of miscellaneous writings on a very important aspect of childhood. As there are references to the wet nurse in the *Shiji*, the first dynastic history, and in the canonical classics such as the *Liji* and the *Yili*, the practice of wet-nursing must have begun before the Han, probably even before the dawn of history. Although in recent years there has been much literature on her in the history of European childhood, nowhere else has she played so important a role as in China. From the Han dynasty to the Ming, there were numerous cases of emperors lavishing noble titles and other favors on their wet nurses and members of their families. Sometimes the bond between the charge and his nurse was so strong that she never left the palace. One does not have to be a Freudian to appreciate the closeness, both physical and psychological, children feel toward the women who suckle them. When such children grew up and ascended the imperial throne, their wet nurses often enjoyed a share of the absolute power. Some nurses are believed to have abused their positions of power by interceding with the emperor on the behalf of relatives and acquaintances and by interfering (usually through their allies) in the affairs of the state. The most notorious among them was Dame Ke (?–1628), whose faction dominated the court for three years. In a bitter struggle with Confucian ministers who led the opposition, hundreds were killed and more were exiled. The country never recovered from the resulting decimation of experienced and competent officials, and historians tend to hold the Ke faction at least partly responsible for the decline and fall of the Ming.

It is generally believed that among major dynasties the Ming had the worst emperors, and the childhood of the Ming sovereigns can be shown as an element in the formation of the deplorable traits they subsequently displayed as adults. The key may lie in their early separation from their mothers, their isolation from their siblings and from children of their age, their ritualistic and formal relationship with their tutors, the hostility or at best the indifference of their fathers, the claustrophobic palace environment rife with intrigues and suspicions, and, finally, the resultant dependence on their wet nurses and eunuchs. However important this topic may be, a detailed study of the childhood of Ming emperors must await a future occasion. Here we shall concern ourselves only with the Ming system of choosing imperial wet nurses. Little is known about the system in other dynasties, but we can obtain much information about its operation during the Ming from the memoir of a sixteenth-century magistrate of Wanping county, which had jurisdiction over much of Peking and its western suburbs.[9]

To qualify as a candidate for the position of wet nurse in the imperial household, a woman had to satisfy several stringent requirements. She had to be a presentable married woman, between fifteen and twenty years of age, with husband and children all alive. At the time of selection she was supposed to have given birth to a child about three months earlier. A physical examination of her was to be administered by an official midwife to ascertain the absence of hidden diseases and the adequacy of her lactation. Forty candidates were selected for each season, half of them having recently delivered boys and the other half girls. They along with their infants were then housed in the Bureau of Imperial Nurses, located just outside Dongan Gate. Another eighty qualified women were designated alternates. When a birth in the imperial household was imminent, a number of candidates would be called into the Forbidden City. The imperial infant would be suckled by several nurses for a month or so, and then one of them would be chosen. Thereupon the rest would be dismissed. Once a nurse was kept beyond the tryout period, she would stay in the palace to wait on her charge for the rest of her life. If the imperial infant was a boy, only nurses who had recently delivered girls were kept for the tryout period; for an infant princess, the reverse obtained.[10]

In more humble households the wet nurse was just as ubiquitous. Pediatric treatises often suggest standards by which wet nurses are to be chosen. She is also mentioned in other types of writings. Sometimes she played a role equivalent to that of the loyal masculine retainer, whose heroism and selflessness have long been sung in Chinese literature. The biography of Hou Yi in the *Songshi* discloses that when his son's whole family was massacred by rebels, only his infant grandson survived. The child owed his life to his wet nurse, who had replaced him with her own son—literally a case of killing one child to save another. Carrying the infant in her arms, the woman begged her way to the capital and returned her charge to his grandfather.[11]

The nurse's bond with her charge and her employers was so strong that often she would stay in the household to the end of her life. Two prominent men of letters wrote tombstone inscriptions for their wet nurses in which they expressed their gratitude. Han Yu, orphaned during his infancy, wrote:

> Nurse Xu . . . grew old among the Hans. She lived to see Yu, the child she once suckled, obtain the highest degree and rise through the ranks, marry, and have two sons and five daughters of his own. On every feast day Yu would lead his wife and children to offer felicitations to her, honoring her just as they would his mother.[12]

The wet nurse of Su Shi (1037–1101) filled several roles. For thirty-five years she waited on Su's mother as servant and seamstress. Earlier she had suckled Su's elder sister, and later she took care of Su Shi's three sons. The loyal retainer stayed in Su's employment as he moved from official post to post until she died at seventy-two in Huangzhou.[13]

However devoted the wet nurse and her charge may have been to each other, her own children could not but suffer the cruel consequences of her employment. This fact cannot long escape any keen observer, wherever he may be. Montaigne had the following to say:

> For a slight profit, we tear . . . their own infants from their mothers' arms, and make these mothers take charge of ours. We cause them to

abandon their children to some wretched nurse, to whom we do not wish to commit our own, or to some goat, forbidding them not only to be breastfed . . . but also to care for them in any way, so that they will be able to devote themselves completely to ours.[14]

In China there was no shortage of criticism of the practice on the same grounds. Hong Mai (1123–1202) and several authors of the popular genre termed "family instructions" advocated the abolition of wet-nursing.[15] Others suggested various reforms. Among the Neo-Confucian master Cheng Yi's many sayings recorded by his disciples, there is the following:

> In most cases employing a wet nurse is unavoidable. If the mother is unable to feed her child, someone must be employed. However, it is wrong to kill another mother's child as a result of feeding one's own child. If a wet nurse is absolutely necessary, employ two so that the milk for two babies can be used to feed three. If one of the wet nurses becomes sick or even dies, there will be no harm to one's own child and one will not be killing another person's child as a result of feeding one's own. The only thing is that it is expensive to employ two.[16]

Chen Longzheng (1585–1645) had a different solution:

> The rich like to spare themselves the trouble of suckling their young. The poor will substitute for them, in exchange for food, clothing, and cash which they will use to support their family. Such an arrangement is beneficial to both. However, in nursing other people's children the poor have to part with their own, entrusting them to childless families. Such families, usually poor, will soon find the undertaking a great inconvenience. Although they have agreed to it at the beginning, gradually they will come to resent the children. Resented, very few infants will survive. During my lifetime my family have hired more than ten wet nurses. When I was young I never thought about it. As I grew older I became very sorry for their hapless children. Our practice is no different from killing other people's children on behalf of our own children. Every time I thought about it, I broke out in sweat. Yet for a long time I could not find a way to save those children. The following is a tentative solution. Before anyone hires a wet nurse the employer should first find a family among her relatives where there is surplus milk and where her child is welcome. Beyond the contractual three-year wage paid to the woman there should be a subsidy of two and a half taels of silver to be paid to the foster family. The first payment will be in the amount of half a tael. After three months the child will be

brought to the employer's house to be inspected by the mother. If she is satisfied with the condition, one tael will be paid to the foster parents. The procedure will be repeated at the end of the first year.

Infancy is the most hazardous time for a child. The mother probably does not hire herself out until her child is several months old. After three months with the foster family the child will be more than six months old. After another year the child will be twenty months old. At the very beginning the foster parents may not feel much affection for the child. But tempted by the silver, they would put up with the trouble. From the age of one on, the child can laugh, stand, and walk. The foster family will cherish such a child even if they are not of the same flesh and blood. There is even more reason for them to take good care of their charge when the final tael is in sight.[17]

One might note that what Chen recommended as a solution for the care of the wet nurse's child was essentially the same practice that wealthy European families had for their own children. Another difference between the two systems is the longer period of nursing on the part of the Chinese.[18] Chen mentions a thirty-six-month contract with a wet nurse, while a sixteenth-century Chinese handbook on child care suggests that a child should be weaned at four or five *sui*.[19] In contrast, a 367 B.C. Greek document shows a twenty-four-month contract with a wet nurse. Lloyd deMause has prepared a table of "age in months at full weaning." Of the twenty-five cases he has collected, beginning with the Greek contract and ending with a German statistical study made in 1878–1882, only three indicate full weaning taking place beyond twenty-four months. In five cases the children were weaned at nine months or younger.[20]

PARENTS WRITING ABOUT CHILDREN

In recent years scholars have repeatedly asserted that childhood is a modern discovery. In Europe, "except for brief glimpses . . . children rarely appear in classical literature." Furthermore, they "seldom appear in medieval imaginative literature; when they do appear they tend to be precocious."[21] I shall not discuss the situation in early China as it is fully covered elsewhere in this volume. From the Tang to at least the fifteenth century, children were more written about in China than in Europe. We can find useful information about children in two types of writings. More and more poets from the Tang onward poured out their sorrows of parting from their children and mourning their deaths. The other type, closely linked to ritual, I shall call necrology for the lack of an established term. It includes the requiem (*jiwen*), grave notice (*kuangzhi*), tombstone inscription (*muzhih ming*), and other lesser-known genres. A necrology usually consists of two parts—a prose preface followed by a eulogy in verse—but sometimes one part by itself suffices. Its length varies from several lines to several thousand characters. Given the Chinese emphasis on death rites and the manner in which the past was remembered, necrology had a special place and constituted a sizable portion of traditional Chinese literature.[22]

There was an initial reluctance, both in classical Europe and ancient China, to accord children more than a minimum recognition in death rituals. But in China, as time went on, parents became increasingly ready to extend the same honor and care to dead children as to dead adults. There was not only a growing presence of children in necrology but also an increasingly sentimental representation of them. The trend was too consistent and too durable to be dismissed as simply a reflection of a shifting literary vogue. We shall proceed to explore these two types of Chinese writings in the hope of gaining a few insights into a most important topic: the parental attitude. As Lawrence Stone puts it, "the history of childhood is in fact the history of how parents treated children."[23]

The growing tendency to write about children with deep affection probably began with the ninth century. The case of Han Yu (768–824), mentioned earlier, was typical. Early in 819, Han Yu, then vice-minister of justice, remonstrated with the emperor against the plan of welcoming into the palace a relic bone of the Buddha. Offended by Han's bold language, the emperor demoted him to a minor post in the south. After his departure, his family was expelled from the capital as well. His fourth daughter Na, aged twelve, died en route and was hastily buried. The following year the emperor relented and appointed Han chancellor of the national university. On his way back to the capital, Han made a stop at his daughter's grave and wrote a moving poem of mourning. When he became mayor of the capital in 823, he had his daughter's remains removed to Heyang for reburial in the ancestral cemetery. For the removal he wrote a requiem (*jiwen*) and for the reburial he wrote a grave notice (*kuangzhi*). Han was not the first poet mourning the death of children, nor was his daughter the first child accorded a burial with two literary accessories. Before the Tang, however, it was a rare child whose death would occasion *both* kinds of commemoration. Another distinction is that in all three works Han displayed a more intense grief than had ever been expressed in previous literature. The requiem is especially moving:

> On such a day, such a month, and such a year, your dad and mom send your wet nurse to your grave with pure wine, seasonal fruit, and a variety of delicious food to be offered to the spirit of Nazi, their fourth daughter.
>
> Alas, you were gravely ill just when I was about to be exiled to the south. The parting came so suddenly that you were both startled and grieved. When I caught my last glimpse of you, I knew death would make our separation permanent. When you looked at me, you were too sad to cry. After I left for the south, the family was also driven out. You were helped into a sedan chair and traveled from early morning to night. Snow and ice injured your weakened flesh. Shaken and rocked, you did not have any rest. There was no time to eat and drink, so you suffered from frequent thirst and hunger. To die in the wild mountains was not the fate you deserved. It is usually the parents' guilt that brings calamities to their children. Was I not the cause of your coming to such a pass?
>
> You were buried hastily by the roadside in a coffin which could hardly be called a coffin. After you were interred the group had to leave. There was no one to care for your grave or watch over it. Your soul was solitary and your bones were cold. Although everyone must die, you died unjustly. When I traveled back from the south I made a stop at your grave. As I wept over you I could see your eyes and face. How could I ever forget your words and expressions?
>
> Now on an auspicious day I am having you moved to our ancestral cemetery. Do not be frightened or fearful: you will be safe along the way. There will be fragrant drink and sweet food for you, and you will arrive in your permanent resting place in a nice new coffin. Peace will be with you for ten thousand years![24]

Although the requiem (*jiwen*) is a literary genre represented even in the earliest Chinese anthologies, its origins go back to ancient death rites. It began as a performative text accompanying sacrifices and libations to the dead. Han Yu's piece was obviously written before the burial party set out, and it was the usual practice to leave the exact date of the service blank. Also remarkable about this requiem is that even four years after the death of the daughter her wet nurse's association with the family had not been severed. Apparently she acted as the parents' surrogate at the exhumation service. The grave notice (*kuangzhi*), however, indicates that at the reburial ceremony the wet nurse shared her functions with Han Yu's son or sons—the eldest was born in 799—and other family members of the younger generation.

Han Yu's innovations must be seen in the light of the hierarchical order of traditional Confucian society, which stipulated gradations in the elaborateness of the funeral and mourning ritual for each individual, depending on the age, station, gender, and generational ranking of the dead relative to the mourner or mourners. In the section on death rites the Confucian canonical classic, the *Yili*, compiled probably during the first century, divides *shang*, the mourning for those dying before adulthood, into three descending categories: *zhangshang*, for those aged sixteen to nineteen; *zhongshang*, for those aged twelve to fifteen; and *xiashang*, for children eight to eleven years old. Children who die before reaching the age of eight can be mourned by the parents, but not with outward ceremony. The length of the mourning period depends on the age of the child. For each month the child lived there will be a day of mourning: "An infant is given a name by the father when it is three months old. A father may weep at the death of a child with a name. He will not weep if the child is not yet named."[25] Coincidentally, Plutarch, who was more or less a contemporary of the compilers of the Confucian canonical classic just quoted, shared some of the same ideas. In his letter to his wife on the death of their young daughter Timoxena he states:

> It is not our way to pour out libations for children who die in infancy nor to perform the other ceremonies which the living do for the dead. This is because these infants are in no way involved with earth or earthly things; and so people do not stand around long at their funerals or keep watch at the tombs or at the laying out or at the side of the bodies.[26]

However much Plutarch may have cherished his young daughter, he did not challenge Roman conventions. On the other hand, the Confucian rules may not have been observed consistently. As Wu Hung's essay in this volume (Chapter 3) indicates, as early as A.D. 170 there was a fairly elaborate burial for a five-year-old boy. Nevertheless the tension between a parent's love and the force of convention seems to have persisted. Some parents would acknowledge the canonical stipulations; others would simply ignore them. An early example of this tension is seen in the case of the infant daughter of Cao Rui (205–239), Emperor Ming of the Wei. When the princess died before she completed her first year, the grieving father lavished all commemorative honors on the infant. He decided to accompany the cortege to the imperial burial mound, which was some distance outside the capital. A minister objected: since the emperor did not attend the burial of his father and mother, he argued, how could he now go out of the city "for a babe still in swaddling clothes"? The emperor prevailed.[27]

The same dilemma confronted the poet Li Shangyin (812–858?) when he mourned the death of his little niece and prepared a full-dress reburial for her: "I know I am doing more than what proprieties would allow for a child, but how can I do less than my deep feelings demand?" Again feelings triumphed over convention and Li wrote a long requiem for the five-year-old girl. In format the "Requiem for My Little Niece Jiji" does not differ much from Han Yu's piece, but I shall quote it in full because it contains descriptions of several children:

On the twenty-fifth day of the first month your uncle, with fruit and toys, brings back the body and soul of Jiji for burial in the family cemetery.

After you were born you were not taken to your hometown until four years later. After just a few months, alas, you were suddenly returned to nothingness. You had hardly lived beyond infancy, but the sadness you left behind is limitless. Why did you come, and what was the cause of your departure? Seeing you play as a little girl, who would have predicted the day of your death? At that time I moved the family to the capital, waiting for a transfer of office. Pressed constantly by events, I did not notice the fleeting of time. Five years had passed since your bones were temporarily interred here, amid pallid grass and withered roots next to an unused, weed-choked road. When you were hungry in the morning, who would hold you in his arms? At night who would find water to quench your thirst? It was my fault that your desolation was unrelieved. Now that I am planning to bury the remains of second elder sister in the family cemetery, I have the occasion of moving your coffin as well. With the help of geomancers I have chosen a plot for your grave and a tombstone with an inscription. I know I am doing more than what proprieties would allow for a child, but how can I do less than my deep feelings demand?

Since you died I have been blessed with several nephews and nieces. Clad in colorful swaddling clothes or short jackets, they often play with their hobbyhorses and jade hoops in the courtyard. Under the sun and in the breeze, they fondle flowers and crowd around me. Only you are missing and I wonder where your spirit has gone. I am even more fond of my nephews and nieces now that I have had no children with

my second wife. My heart burns with longing for the dead and love for
the living.

　　Your great grandfather and grandfather are not far from you. Just
look above the Rong River and next to the Tan Hill, you can see the
thick grove of pines surrounding their resting places. Your oldest and
second-oldest aunts are just next to you. Wandering about, you will
not be frightened of anything. Come and enjoy the pretty dresses,
sweets, and fragrant drink that I have brought for you. Your uncle is
making the offering to you and your father is weeping for you. Jiji, my
sad child, are you there?[28]

Tang poets often wrote about the death of their children. But their
classical allusions and ornate language seldom allow a modern
reader either a clear view of their feelings or a vivid description of the
children. Against this background Li Shangyin's requiem stands out.
While Li the poet yields to none in deliberate obscurity and allusive-
ness, as a grieving uncle he anticipates the expressiveness of a much
later age.

　　With Song poetry a change occurred. Simple words, direct observation, and plain narration give great immediacy to the representation of family life in an everyday setting. In 1084 poverty forced
Chen Shidao (1053–1102) to send his wife and their three children to
the care of her father, who had prospered as a judge in a distant
province. No parting scene—the father's sorrows, the daughter's
fears, the older son's fumbling attempt to be brave and dutiful—is
depicted with greater poignancy in Chinese poetry:

> *My daughter was just old enough to have her hair tied,*
> *Yet she already knew the sadness of parting.*
> *Using me as a pillow she refused to get up*
> *For fear that getting up she would have to let me go.*
> *The older son was just learning to talk.*
> *Unused to adult ceremonies, he had to struggle with his clothes*
> *When he took formal leave of me, saying: "Dad, I am going now."*
> *How can I ever bear to recall these words?*
> *The younger son was still in swaddling clothes.*
> *He was carried by his mother when they left.*
> *His cry is still ringing in my ears:*
> *Can anyone else understand how I feel?*[29]

The poet Lu You (1125–1209) must have been a loving father, too,
for even in his old age he dreamt he had another brood of children:

In my dream I had a little son and a little daughter,
For whom I felt boundless love.
I took them to doctors whenever there was anything wrong;
I bored every visitor with tales of their cleverness.
The morning rooster suddenly woke me up:
How can my love still be there?
Life is but a web of entanglements—
With a laugh I free myself of these fetters.[30]

His quick recovery from a sense of loss should not be seen as a sign of callousness. A few years earlier a daughter was born to him, but the girl lived no more than a year. The tombstone inscription he wrote for his daughter shows clearly that on that occasion Lu was not happy at all to have one entanglement dissolved:

I came to Xinding as county magistrate in the seventh month of the Bingwu year of the Chunxi reign [1186]. On the Dingyou day of the eighth month a daughter was born to me. She was first given the name of Runniang, then Dingniang. I loved her dearly because she was the youngest of my children. I called her "Nünü" rather than by her formal name. She was graceful and regal. Not given to tears or laughter, she was unlike other children. She grew two teeth in the seventh month of the following year. She fell ill and died on the Bingzi day of the eighth month. Her body was coffined in the Chengqi Monastery, northeast of the city. On the Renyin day of the ninth month she was buried on North Ridge. When she died I was much grieved. I shed tears inside the coffin and said: "They are my parting gifts to my daughter." Everyone who heard it wept bitterly. The mother of Nünü, Yangshi, is a native of Huayang of Szechwan.

The verse:

By a deserted hill and over a desolate ravine,
Amid frost and dew and surrounded by thorns and brush,
Lies my hapless daughter in a solitary grave.
No neighbor is seen in any direction.
When she was alive she never left the house.
In her death she is abandoned in a place like this.
How unkind I am![31]

That a girl from a commoner family and so young—Nünü was not quite a year old—was given a formal burial with all the trappings is a clear indication that by the twelfth century it was possible, at least among the educated, to depart from two conventions: minimum mourning for the very young and the favoring of sons over daughters. Whatever the practice of the populace, the mourning literature shows that daughters, at least in death, were just as cherished as the sons, if not more. There are even several cases of bias in favor of the daughter. Four sons and two daughters of the Song writer and statesman Ouyang Xiu (1007–1072) died in childhood, but only one, a daughter who perished at eight, was mourned in poetry. She was obviously his favorite child, for the relation between father and daughter seems to have been easy and close: "In the evening when I came home she would welcome me with a big smile. / In the morning when I was leaving she would pull me by my jacket. / The instant after she jumped into my arms she would dash away."[32] Ouyang was a prolific writer of necrologies, but he wrote none for his children. Perhaps the inhibition came from his knowledge of epigraphy—he was a passionate student and collector of stone and bronze inscriptions from previous dynasties. There were so few early precedents—none in his collection—for composing necrologies for the young.

In general, young daughters were depicted with more individuality than young sons. The reason for this bias may lie in differences in parental expectations. It was easier for little girls to be "children," while little boys were expected to behave in an exemplary manner, in a way that would prefigure the future men. The Song loyalist Wen Tianxiang (1236–1283) wrote during his last imprisonment by the Mongols a suite of six laments over the destruction of his family. His two sons are represented entirely by metaphors and allusions, but the daughters are given more specifics:

> Daughters I have two, both bright and sweet.
> The older one loved to practice calligraphy
> While the younger recited lessons sonorously.
> When a sudden blast of the north wind darkened the noonday sun
> The pair of white jades were abandoned by the roadside.
> The nest lost, the young swallows flitted in the autumn chill.
> Who will protect the girls, taken north with their mother?[33]

One could go on and on. I shall just cite one more case of an apparent partiality for a daughter. Ye Xianggao (1562–1627) had a distinguished official career, serving for several years as both minister of rites and grand secretary. Of his six sons, only one lived into adulthood. When his third daughter Jiang, born in 1590, died in 1602 he wrote a long grave notice in which he states: "As I am deficient in virtue, many of my children have died young. But I have never wept as bitterly as I do for this daughter."[34]

Another stereotype—the distant father who leaves child care to the women in the household—is contradicted in at least two cases. Huang Xingzeng (1490–1540) wrote a grave notice (*kuangzhi*) for his son who had lived less than a month.[35] This short necrology reveals an impoverished but loving father trying desperately to save a newborn child. The mother, herself weakened by undernourishment, struggled to care for the sick child. The father moved the infant to his bed, hoping to offer better care. Too poor to seek professional medical help, he delved into a Tang pediatric classic but to no avail. Huang, a Neo-Confucian scholar, followed the terminology laid down in the Confucian classic *Yili* and referred to the son as "dying under the age of *shang*," but he certainly ignored the canonical advice against a ceremonial burial for so young a child.

The other case had to do with Zhou Rudeng (1547–1629), another prominent Neo-Confucian. He lost his five-year-old youngest son on the day he was scheduled to set out for a new post in a distant city. In the grave notice for his son he describes his profound grief over the boy's death. After five days of indecision he was set to bury the son and begin the journey, but at the last minute could not bear the abrupt separation between father and son: "I had the coffin carried with me and after traveling for ten days we arrived at Jinghai. I dried my tears and said, 'This is where my son's bones will have a resting place.' " Zhou blames his career as an official for his son's illness:

> Ever since he was born I had personally attended to his feeding and clothing. Without reason I would never leave his side. He had not been sick for one day. After I became an official I was fully occupied with work. There were long periods when I saw very little of him.[36]

THE CULT OF THE CHILD

Both Huang Xingzeng and Zhou Rudeng were members of the Wang Yangming school of Neo-Confucianism. In fact Huang received instructions from the master himself. It was perhaps no accident that they were so solicitous of the welfare of their young children, for the child had a special place in the discourse of his school. Although no Confucian would have believed in the sinful state of the newborn, strict discipline and a didactic approach to elementary education had until this time been the staple of the Confucian attitude toward children.[37] With the Wang school the entire approach shifted. The innocence of children was strongly reaffirmed, and the preservation of this quality became more important than the mere acquisition of knowledge.

We shall begin with the founder of the school, Wang Shouren (1472–1529), better known as Wang Yangming. A corollary of Wang's theory of innate knowledge, the cornerstone of his teaching, is the elevation of the child in the Confucian hierarchy. "Everybody, from the infant in swaddling clothes to the old, is in full possession of this innate knowledge," Wang announced to his disciples.[38] When one disciple quoted an opinion that a child was incapable of the investigation of things, the starting point of the Confucian regimen as taught in the canonical classic the *Great Learning*, the master refuted him, saying: "When I speak of the investigation of things, it is the same endeavor from the child to the sages."[39] It is this affirmation of the child that led Wang to entertain a rather modern view of elementary education:

> It is in the nature of children to indulge in play and dislike restraint. It is like the budding of a plant. If it has plenty of freedom to expand, it will proliferate. If it meets with hindrance and obstruction, it will wither. When we teach children we must kindle their enthusiasm and make everything a joy. Then they will advance of their own accord without ceasing. It is just like plants nourished by timely rain and spring breezes. They will grow exuberantly. If they are visited upon with ice and frost, they will lose their vital force and weaken daily.[40]

Some followers of the Wang school, especially those in the Taizhou sect, to which Zhou Rudeng belonged, went even further, approaching what may be called a cult of the child—a similar trend appeared in Europe about two centuries later.[41] Lou Rufang (1515–1588) contrasted infants and adults by using a traditional opposition, the yin and the yang: "During infancy the yang forces are strong and the yin forces are weak. Although infants are not without thoughts, they depend on physical functions. Therefore they smile like the warm sun; they are open and cheerful like the dawn, vivacious like a fresh breeze."[42] Adults, however, having too much yin, tend to be stiff, anxious, and confused.

Li Zhi (1527–1602) wrote an article entitled "On the Heart of the Child" (*Tongxin shuo*) in which he exalted the child to an unprecedented level: "The heart of the child is absolutely not false but pure and true *(jue jia chun zhen)*. . . . If one loses the heart of the child then he loses his true heart."[43] Li advocated that everyone should try to preserve the heart of the child. To him the highly educated were at the greatest risk of losing their "heart of the child" because he believed that learning and experience tend to corrupt. Yuan Hongdao (1568–1610), too, equated the innocence of the child with perfection. In his literary criticism he selected the nebulous word *qu*, which means something like "taste" or "understanding," and assigned to it new and lofty aesthetic and metaphysical connotations. Here again the child is accorded a privileged status:

> *Qu* is more a matter of nature than of learning. When one is a child, one does not know that one has *qu*, but whatever a child does always has to do with *qu*. A child has no fixed expression in the face, no fixed gaze in the eyes. He babbles in trying to speak while his feet jump up and down without stopping. This is the time when the joy of life is unsurpassed. This is what is meant by Mencius when he speaks of "not losing [the heart of] the newborn infant" or by Laozi when he speaks of "the power of the babe." Theirs is the highest level of *qu*, the superior understanding, and the supreme enlightenment.[44]

Concurrent with the vogue of the Wang school was the proliferation of mourning literature commemorating the death of children. Not only did more and more parents write about their bereavements, but their unabashed avowal of affection and their unrestrained outpourings of grief contrast with the measured and succinct expressions in earlier centuries. If the romantic view of the purity of child in the West—beginning with Rousseau and going through Wordsworth and Dickens—led to the sentimental view of children in the nineteenth century, the Wang school, the most powerful intellectual and spiritual movement during the Ming, must have had a similar impact on the Chinese attitude as reflected in the mourning literature. This literature, scarce in early China but growing steadily after 800, took a sharp upturn around 1520 and reached its apex just before 1680. Infant mortality was probably high in all premodern societies, but now it was no longer accepted stoically and silently as a matter of course.[45] Lu Shen (1477–1544) lost eleven of his thirteen children. He poured out his sorrows for them all in his writings, and his collected works include necrologies for four daughters and two sons. Qu Dajun (1630–1696) repeatedly mourned the death of his young children and wrote more than twenty poems for his four-year-old daughter. The desperate cries of the distraught parents and the detailed accounts of the death scene sometimes border on maudlin sentimentalism. But if grief sometimes compels a total or near total recall, then we are the gainers because for the first time there was the possibility of a full portrayal of the child. We shall conclude our study with a discussion of a long necrology that makes the most of this possibility.

THE NECROLOGY OF SHEN AZHEN (1616–1619)

Exactly eight hundred years after Han Yu's daughter Hana died, another young girl perished. The child's seventeenth-century father, Shen Cheng (1588?–1624), an obscure man of letters, also expressed his grief and tried to calm the departed soul with a requiem. The two compositions could not be more unlike. The circumstances surrounding the two untimely deaths, the stations of the fathers, the ages of the two daughters—all differ. But the great contrast between the two requiems also reflects a number of cultural changes that occurred during the intervening eight centuries.

The increasingly affective attitude toward children—for which the Wang school of Neo-Confucianism may have been responsible—constitutes, I believe, one major difference between the articulateness of the two fathers. The other change is that of narrative style. Although Shen's is in four-character verse, his language is much closer to the vernacular than Han's. It is well known that the growth of vernacular literature from the twelfth century on changed both the perception and the representation of reality. Preferring a narrative style leaning toward mimesis (showing) rather than diegesis (telling), the readers of popular fiction and the audience of theater all demanded that everyday life be depicted with greater specificity. Moreover, as the society was becoming more and more egalitarian, so too were the topics and characters of literature. A ninth-century father of Shen's station would not even have thought of composing a requiem for so young a daughter, much less filling the composition with numerous quotidian details. It is those humble particularities that situate the young girl in the reality of an urban household, with all the accoutrements and activities attendant to her care and then to her death.

If Han Yu's necrology represents the beginning of a trend, Shen Cheng's composition is its culmination. Han Yu may have felt just as strongly about his daughter as Shen Cheng, but the ninth-century girl was a shadowy figure passively enduring her fate. While her father could still "see her eyes and face" when he stood over her temporary grave, the reader cannot share the vision. There is nothing in the text to suggest a real person. Even the standard topoi are absent. But the seventeenth-century girl, perishing after only three short years in this world, is nevertheless the most fully realized child in all traditional Chinese literature. Self-assured and perhaps a bit spoiled, she was playful, agile, and totally engaged with all the people, young or old, who came her way. Her individuality and complexity are lovingly recalled by her father: her innocent wiles and revelries, her little games and amusing mimicries, her quick though simple comprehension of the adult world, even her importunities. Why this became possible has been the heart of our story. The following is the complete text of the requiem:

> On the twenty-third day of the eleventh month of the *jiwei* year in the Wanli reign [1619], the eldest daughter Azhen of Shen Cheng died of complications from smallpox. She was temporarily interred in North Cemetery. Her mother, Madame Bo, chanted Buddhist scriptures daily in the hope of gaining merit for her. In addition, she urged me to write a plea for her, but I could not for some time bear to touch the pen. On the third seventh day of my daughter's death, having prepared food for offering to her, I wrote the following as a way of mourning for her. The text was to be burned on the playground where she used to romp.
>
> Alas, what a sad occasion! You were named Azhen because you were born in the year *binchen* [1616]. The character *zhen* was a combination of *bin* and *chen*. When you were born I was not pleased. A man over thirty wanted a son, not a daughter. But you won me over before you had completed your first year. Even then you would respond with giggles each time I made a face at you. You were then cared for by nurse Zhou. Whenever you became hungry, you were brought to your mother to be suckled. After you were fed, your nurse would carry you back to her room. As she had to get up many times during the night, she stayed in her day clothes all night. Because of you, she went through a great deal of hardship. Your mother would be angered if you were brought to her too often, but you would cry if your wish was not immediately gratified.

Last year, *wuwu* [1618], was a bad year for me. As I had to leave
for the examinations, I parted from you reluctantly several times.
Nurse Zhou died, and I failed my examinations. When I came home
you greeted me by holding onto my sleeves and demanding gifts of
toys. With you by my side my unhappiness was relieved. As you grew
more teeth, you became more intelligent. Addressing your parents,
you pronounced the words "dad" and "mom" perfectly. You often
knocked on the door and then quickly went inside and asked: "Who is
there?" When my nephew came you called him "brother." He teased
you by pretending to snatch your toys; you darted and dashed away.
When your mother's brother came, you seized him by his jacket while
gleefully shouting, "Mom! Mom!" When your uncle came you acted
the part of host. Holding up a wine cup, you invited your honored
guest to drink. Everybody burst out laughing. After you were born
your grandfather went to the country and then you went to Soochow.
As a result you had not seen each other for more than a year. When
you two met again you were asked if you knew who he was. Without
hesitation you responded: "By his white hat and white beard I know
he is my grand-dad." Your maternal grandfather you had never seen
before. As soon as you saw him for the first time you pronounced that
he came from Peking. Your maternal grandmother loved you as if you
had been her own child. Several times she took you back with her to
Soochow. There in the middle of the night you would ask her for toys,
and at dawn you would demand fruit. When your parents wanted to
keep you home you refused, saying to me: "Granny will miss me."

In the sixth month of this year you developed a skin rash. I went to
Soochow to bring you home. You kept rubbing the troubled spots and
looked sad. But you dared not cry, thinking that crying would dis-
please us.

Every time you reached for fruit or candy you always watched the
reaction of your parents. You would not put the food into your mouth
unless there was a sign of approval. During your play you would
sometimes injure one of your hands. Your little eyes would glower at
the wound, but you would hide your hand when you saw adults
approaching.

Your mother was too strict. From time to time she would discipline
you for fear that your habits would be carried into adulthood.
Although I agreed with her, I said to her when you were not around:
"A little child cannot be expected to know right and wrong. Let her be
until she is a little older."

When you were still in Soochow your parents were about to return
home in Loudong. You were asked whether you would go back with
them. You couldn't make up your mind. When you did come back I
was overwhelmed with joy. We played together—I taunted you and

surprised you, and you would play along by feinting dumb. You carried jujubes in a small basket and sipped porridge in a low chair. Sometimes you recited the *Great Learning* while bowing to Amit'ofo. Sometimes you would play a guessing game with me and the winner would chase the loser around the house. When you finally caught me you laughed jubilantly and clapped your hands. Who would have believed that not quite half a month later you would breathe your last? Was it decreed by heaven, or was it simply fate? Who could fathom the mystery?

When you were stricken I sent for the doctors. Some said you had measles while other believed it was the flu. It did not seem to be the flu, and it may have been measles. Looking back, I still cannot understand what happened. You had always been an articulate child but then you could not talk. Your voice was gone and you could hardly breathe. You could do nothing but open or shut your eyes. The family surrounded you and wept, and tears also flowed from your eyes. Alas, it is too painful to say any more!

It is the way of the world that one does not weep over the death of a daughter. But a man like me, who is still poor and friendless in his prime, should be content to have only daughters. He should have been happy to have a daughter as intelligent as you. Who would have expected the gods to treat me so cruelly! Ten days before you were stricken your sister A-hsün, younger than you by two years, came down with the same illness. Three days after she died, you too were gone.

Now that you no longer have playmates, you should at least have the company of your sister, whom you knew well. You can walk now but she is still unsteady on her feet. Hold her by the hand wherever you go. Be nice to her and compete not! If you meet your nurse again, ask her to guide you to your father's first wife, Madame Gu, and his mother, Madame Min. They will take you girls in. That was why I had you temporarily interred next to Gu. She will look after you, while you must take good care of your baby sister. In the future I shall choose a plot and make a permanent resting place for all of you.

I have been thinking of you all the time. If you know how much I miss you you will come back, again and again, in my dreams. If fate permits, be reborn as my next child. For such hopes I am sending you a copy of the Diamond Sutra as well as other books of spells and incantations. There are also offerings of meat and paper money for your use. When you see the King of the Underworld, kneel down with raised hands and plead for mercy. Say the following to him:

"Although I die young, I am truly guiltless. I was born into a poor family, and I never complained about the hardships. Fearing the God of Thunder, I never wasted even a grain of rice. I have always worn my

simple clothes with care. I am too young to bring suitable gifts for
Your Majesty. Please have pity on me and shield me from the exactions
of ghosts."

Just say the words to him and don't cry or be noisy. You must not
forget that the underworld is different from home.

I am writing this but you cannot read. I shall call your name and let
you know that your father is here. Azhen, Azhen, your sad father is
mourning you.[46]

NOTES

GJTSJC   Gujin tushu jicheng
LDW   Lidai zixuzhuan wenchao, ed. Guo Dengfeng (Taipei: Shangwu
            yinshuguan)
SBBY   Sibu beiyao
SBCK   Sibu congkan
SHGJCBS   Shanghai guji chubanshe

During an early stage of the research for this study I was supported by a
grant from the American Council of Learned Societies. The essay was
completed with a Pacific Cultural Foundation Subsidy and presented at
the Regional Seminar in Neo-Confucian Studies, New York, March 8,
1994.

1. On Chinese biography see Pei-yi Wu, *The Confucian's Progress: Autobiographical Writings in Traditional China* (Princeton: Princeton University
Press, 1990), pp. 4–5 and 20.

2. An interesting theme is the role of the mother in the education of the
son. *GJTSJC*, 324:28a–37b, records twenty-six cases of prominent figures
who were taught by their mothers, and even more cases of the mother as
role model or disciplinarian.

3. "Mingdao xiansheng xingzhuang," in *Er-Cheng wenji* (*Congshu
jicheng* ed.), p. 147. Throughout this chapter I follow the Chinese way of
reckoning age; e.g., here I translate *shisui* as "ten years old."

4. *Shitong tongshi* (*Universals in History* with collected annotations), ed.
Pu Qilong (Taipei: Shijie shuju, 1962), p. 138.

5. *LDW*, 2:339–341.

6. It is beyond the scope of this study to attempt a psychological portrait
of the Han family. As we shall see, Han Yu, orphaned at an early age, was
raised by his wet nurse. When it came to daughters, he seems to have been a
loving father.

7. Mao Qiling, *Mao Xihe xiansheng quanji* (1761), 11:1a.

8. Wu, *Confucian's Progress*, pp. 142–159.

9. Shen Bang, *Wanshu zaji* (Beijing: Xinhua shuju, 1961), pp. 74–76. The

Ming editions of the book are no longer extant in China. The modern book is based on a copy of the 1593 edition preserved in a Japanese library.

10. Whatever the scientific justifications for this sort of symmetrical arrangement, it probably had behind it the long-held Chinese belief in the yin/yang complementarity. Yet a contemporary French physician, Laurent Joubert, arrived at exactly the same idea a continent away, which he recommended to the public in his *Traité des erreurs populaires* (Lyon: 1608), p. 515. His student, Jean Héroard, attended the future Louis XIII and kept a detailed journal about the daily life of the dauphin from birth to adolescence. See Lloyd deMause, ed., *The History of Childhood* (New York: Harper & Row, 1974), pp. 264 and 284. An anonymous reader for the University of Hawai'i Press suggests that in both instances the symmetrical arrangement was designed to prevent the wet nurse from switching her own child for her employer's.

11. *GJTSJC*, 324:40b.

12. *Changli xiansheng ji* (*SBBY* ed.), 35:4b.

13. *GJTSJC*, 324:39b.

14. Quoted in David Hunt, *Parents and Children in History: The Psychology of Family life in Early Modern France* (New York: Basic Books, 1970), p. 104.

15. *GJTSJC*, 324:39a.

16. *Reflections on Things at Hand: The Neo-Confucian Anthology Compiled by Chu Hsi and Lü Tsu-ch'ien*, trans. Wing-tsit Chan (New York: Columbia University Press, 1967), p. 178.

17. *GJTSJC*, 324:39a. Chen Longzheng's compassion and earnestness represent the best of Song-Ming humanitarianism. It would take us too far afield to delve into the devices invented and efforts expended by the elite in improving the lot of abandoned or neglected children. Here I shall cite only one incident. When Ye Mengde (1077–1148) served as prefect in western Honan, a bad flood sent many refugees into his region. To feed the needy and starving he opened up all the "ever-level granaries" under his jurisdiction, and more than 100,000 lives were thus saved. "But I was unable to reach all the abandoned children. One day I asked my staff, 'Why is it that all those who are childless do not adopt the children?' They replied, 'People fear that sooner or later—no later than the first bumper crop—the parents will find their way to them and reclaim the children.' Examining the laws and precedents I discovered a stipulation to the effect that parents who abandoned their children during natural calamities could make no future claims to them. The man who made this law must have been a man of kindness. . . . I thereupon had the text of this stipulation printed on thousands of forms and distributed in all the districts and neighborhoods within and without the city. Whoever adopted a child would write down the circumstances on one of those forms, which in turn would be notarized in my office. Those who adopted a large number of children would receive awards

as well as surplus food from the ever-level granaries. The poor adoptive parents would receive appropriate subsidies. Altogether there were 3,800 forms notarized. This was the number of children who were rescued from a death in the ditches and placed in caring homes. Although this was only a trifle not worth talking about, I keep telling prefects and magistrates about it for fear that at the time of an emergency they may not be aware of this particular law or the way of making the most effective use of it." *Bishu luhua* (*Congshu jicheng* ed.), pp. 13–14.

18. Both circumstances tended to reinforce the Chinese dependency on the wet nurse. After the European child returned to the household of the parents, whatever bond there may have once been would gradually dissolve.

19. Liu Xi, *Huoyou bianlan* (Handbook for the preservation of children) (Xin'an, 1510), 1:6a.

20. DeMause, *The History of Childhood*, p. 36.

21. Leah S. Marcus, *Childhood and Cultural Despair: A Theme and Variations in Seventeenth-Century Literature* (Pittsburgh: University of Pittsburgh Press, 1978), pp. 9–10, 12.

22. The Europeans tended to be lithic; the Chinese, literary. See Pei-yi Wu, "Memories of K'ai-feng," *New Literary History* (Spring 1994): 47–60.

23. "The Massacre of the Innocents," *New York Review of Books*, November 14, 1974, p. 30.

24. *Changli xiansheng ji* (*SBBY* ed.), 35:3b–4a.

25. *Yili* (*SBBY* ed.), 11:14a.

26. Quoted in Robert Pattison, *The Child Figure in English Literature* (Athens: University of Georgia Press, 1978), p. 6.

27. *GJTSJC*, 712:41b. There were of course emperors who did not depart from conventions. For instance, the Chenghua Emperor (1447–1487) of the Ming lost his oldest son in 1466 and the next oldest in 1472. The funerals for the boys, who perished at a very early age, were very simple, conforming to the rules laid down in the *Yili*, the father's affection for the second son notwithstanding—the boy was made crown prince before he was even three years of age. The emperor heeded the advice of the minister of rites, who made an explicit reference to the stipulations in the canonical classic. See *Ming shilu leizuan*, eds., Li Guoxiang and Yang Chang (Wuhan: Wuhan chubanshe, 1992), pp. 195 and 197.

28. *Li Shangyin xuanji*, ed. Zhou Zhenfu (Shanghai: Guji chubanshe, 1986), pp. 350–351.

29. *Houshan jushi wenji* (Shanghai: SHGJCBS, 1984), 1:2b–3a.

30. *Jiannan shigao* (*SBBY* ed.), 60.3b.

31. *Weinan wenji* (*SBBY* ed.), 4b–5a.

32. *Ouyang Xiu quanji* (Beijing: Zhongguo shudian, 1986), p. 408.

33. *Wenshan xiansheng quanji* (*SBCK* ed.), 14:23b. Wen's "Six Laments" are modeled on Du Fu's "Seven Laments." The two compositions are similar in format and style down to the last detail, but Du (712–770)

said nothing in his laments about his suffering children—one of them, a young son, had died of hunger four years earlier. Wen devotes the third lament to his daughters and the fourth to his sons. Although Du in his voluminous writings often shows great affection for his children, there is no indication of any necrological attention to the dead boy.

34. *Cang xia cao* (National Library of Peiping microfilm), 10:5b–6a.

35. *Wuyue shanren ji* (NCL microfilm, EcF 6067), 38:13a–14b.

36. *Dong Yue zhengxue lu* (Taipei: Wenhai chubanshe, 1970), 2:1061–1062.

37. See Pei-yi Wu, "Education of Children During the Sung," in W. Theodore de Bary and John Chaffee, eds., *Neo-Confucian Education: The Formative Stage* (Berkeley: University of California Press, 1989), pp. 307–324.

38. *Wang Yangming quanshu* (Taipei: Zhengzhong shuju, 1955), 1:79. The term "innate knowledge" (*liangzhi*) comes originally from *Mencius* VIIA:15: "The ability possessed by men without having been acquired by learning is innate ability and the knowledge possessed by them without deliberation is innate knowledge." Translated by James Legge, *The Chinese Classics*, vol. 2, p. 456.

39. Ibid, p. 71.

40. Ibid.

41. For a sampling of sixteenth-century French attitudes toward children see Hunt, *Parents and Children in History*, p. 185: "Montaigne wrote bluntly that they had 'neither movement in the soul, nor recognizable form in the body, by which they could render themselves lovable.' Charron went so far as to claim that 'the faculties of the soul are opened' only after the child had reached the age of four or five. Bérulle summed up the opinions of a century when he characterized childhood as 'the meanest and most abject state of the human condition.' "

42. Huang Zongxi, *Mingru xuean* (Taipei: Shijie shuju, 1965), p. 350.

43. *Feng shu* (Beijing: Zhonghua shuju, 1961), p. 97.

44. *Yuan Hongdao ji qianjiao*, Qian Bocheng ed. (Shanghai: Shanghai guji chubanshe, 1981), pp. 463–464.

45. The increasingly affective parental attitude implied by the proliferation of mourning literature may suggest, paradoxically, a downward trend in infant mortality in late Ming China. Grieving parents were more inconsolable if they had been led to hope for more or if fewer neighbors and acquaintances suffered the same deprivations. See Lawrence Stone, *The Family, Sex and Marriage in England 1500–1800* (abridged ed.) (New York: Harper & Row, 1979), p. 57: "Even if mortality rates in England were lower than those of France, this will not alter the fact that to preserve their mental stability parents were obliged to limit the degree of their psychological involvement with their infant children. . . . It was very rash for parents to get too emotionally concerned about creatures whose expectation of life was so very

low." Chinese parents in late Ming times do not seem to have been deterred from emotional involvement with their young children.

46. "Ji Zhennü wen," in *Jindai sanwen chao*, ed. Shen Qiwu (Hong Kong: Tianhong chubanshe, 1957), pp. 262–264.

GLOSSARY

jiwen	祭文	requiem
jue jia chun zhen	絕假純真	absolutely not false but pure and true
kuangzhi	壙誌	grave notice
muzhi ming	墓誌銘	tombstone inscription
qu	趣	taste; understanding
shang	殤	mourning for those dying young
zhuan	傳	biography; to transmit

6

From Birth to Birth:
The Growing Body in Chinese Medicine

CHARLOTTE FURTH

How is a life located in time? Birth and growth from child to adult may be aspects of a universal human life cycle, but we are taught how to number our days. As a cultural reading of old age, the biblical three score years and ten, freighted with fleshly mortality, is profoundly unlike Confucius' summation of maturity at seventy: "I could follow my heart's desire and not transgress what is right." These examples show one commonplace repertory of markers for the passages of human time: numbers computed according to calendars or by some more organic pattern of the "ages of man."

In late imperial China a life might be numbered in a variety of ways: around natural phenomena—the sun, stars, moon, and planets; through the Heavenly Stems and Earthly Branches—ideographic symbols for sixty-year cycles of time; or according to the abstract binary sign system of the *Book of Changes*.[1] In marking human lives through numbers, this calendrical repertory had to deal with the complex relationship between "time's arrow" and "time's cycle." These are metaphors beautifully explicated by Stephen Jay Gould to evoke both "immanent pattern" and "contingent history" in the structure of geological "deep time." They are also understandable as flowing through human lives—seen now in terms of cycles of recurrence, and now by following the arrow of biography's irreversible events.[2]

Human time could also be patterned around ritual events. Chinese ceremonies prescribed in the classical *Book of Rites,* such as the third day and first month celebrations for an infant, the hairpinning and capping of teenaged girls and boys, and the rites of marriage, all punctuated growth and maturation from infancy to adolescence and adulthood. In marking lives through rituals, Confucian cosmology understood these ceremonies as culture's embellishment *(wen)* of a natural pattern *(wen)* inhering in heaven, earth, and humanity.

Medical authorities assumed, like almost everyone else, that both social arrangements and calendrical time intersected in the human person through a system of cosmologically ordained correspondences that ensured an overall harmony. They saw the life cycle of the human body—the domain of medicine—not so much as biology as a discourse on embodiment. It took as its subject not the physical body but patterns of change in human life. When medicine stressed process over event, function over anatomy, and environmental influences over inborn qualities, it was linking human growth and development with creative processes seen as part of the timeliness of heaven and earth's organic functioning. Because physicians emphasized no sharp nature/culture dualism, the ritual norms of society appeared to them just as much natural markers of human time as the cycles of the stars and seasons. The authority of medical thinking concerning the life cycle was based on its resonances with these worldviews; it did not derive from a privileged scientific metanarrative organizing the natural history of a physical body.

Nonetheless, even if culture taught doctors how to number human days, theirs was a mediating, not a passive, role: mediating between what they observed and what they assumed must be true about the cosmos at large, and between both of these and variable social practice. If the body was the natural vehicle for ritual performance, sometimes the evidence of the body was called on to judge what was ritually correct. Natural philosophy itself was not monolithic. Much in classical medicine was based on a Han dynasty cosmology that privileged time's cycles of yin and yang. Late imperial concepts of sexual development involved a more arrowlike view of primordial energies—*yuanqi*—as a finite resource bestowed by heaven at the beginning and nourished and husbanded for a natural complement of years (exceeded by only an exceptional few). Moreover, eclectic elements in medical thinking about birth drew upon pollution beliefs that fostered a view of human development more closely allied to certain early childhood rituals, where growth was viewed as progress away from the tainted beginnings associated with the body of the mother and infant disease. These variable elements gave medical voices diversity and enabled doctors to criticize as well as uphold dominant social conventions.

Although pharmacology and clinical practice changed substantially over imperial history, in thinking about the growing body, Ming–Qing medical thought was conservative. For understanding basic functions, one looked to the textual authority of a small corpus of medical classics, above all the Han dynasty *Yellow Emperor's Inner Canon*.[3] Since health issues of birth and growth involved women and children particularly, other important sources of authority were the relevant obstetrical and pediatric sections of the seventh- and eighth-century masters, Sun Simo (581–682),[4] Chao Yuanfang (fl. 605–616),[5] and Wang Tao (fl. 752).[6] In what follows I draw upon those words of these masters that were the common point of reference in the explanations of later generations, particularly the sixteenth through eighteenth centuries.

During this late imperial era, literate Chinese had access to a wide variety of contemporary medical works, ranging from texts on medical specialties to collections of case histories, as well as manuals for household use, reprints of classics, official encyclopedias, almanacs, and works of pharmacy. This voluminous literature was fostered by a thriving commercial publishing industry as well as by traditions of state and official patronage of medical knowledge in the interests of social welfare. The audience for the works discussed in this essay extended to a literate public far wider than medical experts who practiced healing as a livelihood. Thus we are dealing here with learning that was not cut off from upper-class daily life, where health was managed in the home and medical knowledge had cultural prestige as well as practical utility. What is less certain is how far such accepted wisdom of the high cultural mainstream resonated with the folklore of the myriad localities spread throughout China's vast hinterlands.

HUMAN ORIGINS: CREATION IN PROCESS

The cosmological roots of Chinese medicine are particularly clear when we consider the phenomenon of birth. In the Ming and Qing dynasties (1368–1911), a physician thinking about human origins would quite naturally turn first to the revered pages of the *Book of Changes*. Here he would find an account of universal creation modeled on sexual generation: "Heaven and earth intermingle *qi* [cosmic energy] and all things are transformed thereby; man and woman intermingle essences [the human aspect of cosmic energies] and all things are born thereby."[7] As yin and yang, the male and female principles pattern macrocosm and microcosm, including the role of each parent in the formation of new life.

In the *Book of Changes,* yang is associated with the first hexagram *"qian"* (first of the sixty-four foundational symbols), with *yuan* (origins), with *shi* (beginning), and with *qi* (as primary vitality of the body). Yin is associated with the second hexagram *"kun,"* with *cheng* (maturation or realization) and with *sheng* (growth) as well as *xue* (blood, also a primary vitality of the body). Altogether the eight basic trigrams constitute the universe, and each is given a role—father, mother, son, daughter, and so forth—so that the whole is interrelated on the pattern of members of a biological family.

Although the abstract and archaic nature of its language obscures this today, sexual imagery permeates the account of cosmogenesis in the *Book of Changes*. For cosmic and human creation in the process of coming into being, yang contributes that which occurs at the beginning, in a single moment, while yin contributes what develops over time through growth and differentiation. "*Qian* knows the great beginning; *kun* brings things to their maturation."[8] In this sexualization of the natural world, a gender hierarchy is implied in that yin qualities are dependent in any pairing. However, as has been said often, in the *Book of Changes* the dominant metaphor is one of complementary opposites. Yin and yang both have the power to influence and penetrate the other, leading to their mutual transformation. Yin may be second in rank, but its time of ascendency is no briefer, and in season it is able to match and overcome the forces of yang. Moreover, if this archaic dualism established sexual differentiation as a primordial aspect of generation or human embodiment, female/male was a relative, shifting aspect of the yin/yang relationship and not a fixed bipolar structure. The overall pattern of growth and development took place under the cosmogenic yin sign of *kun,* an openended process whereby time's arrow, once launched, maintained its life trajectory through the enabling reiteration of cycles from "yang within yin" to "yin within yang" propelling bodily growth and development.

In thinking about conception, then, cosmogenesis and sexual differentiation were separated by no more than a hair. Consider the following two typical accounts offered by leading sixteenth- and seventeeth-century medical writers. Li Shizhen (1518–1593), author of the famous summation of the Chinese materia medica, *Bencao gangmu,* put it this way:

> In the beginning "heaven and earth intermingle [influences]" as one *qi* to produce human beings; and so you have males and females. Human sexual fertilization occurs and so you have transformation and birth,

just as grass and trees propagate. There is one *qi* and afterwards ancestors and descendants, parents and children; what is planted continues
[to propagate].[9]

Wu Zhiwang, compiler of an authoritative and popular seventeenth-
century text on medicine for women, *The Salvation of Yin (Ji yin
gangmu)*, elaborated somewhat:

> What is it that congeals at the time of sexual union to make the fetus?
> Though it is none other than [male] Essence *(jing)* and [female] Blood
> *(xue)* made up of the material dregs that exist in the temporal world
> *(houtian)*, a tiny bit of preexistent perfected spirit *qi (xiantian zhen zhi
> lingqi)*, moved to germinate by the feelings of desire, miraculously is
> part of it.[10]

In these and other Chinese formulations, there are superficial resem-
blances to classical Western accounts of conception: the idea, for
example, that the fetus is created from a man's seminal fluid and a
woman's menstrual blood. It is also clear that Li and Wu thought
that the individual human life in some sense begins at conception.
But the parallels with Aristotelian or Christian views evaporate when
we look beneath the surface.

"Essence" *(jing)* in its material aspect is the fluid semen, while in
this period female "Essence" was identified primarily with menstrual
blood believed to be the woman's contribution at conception.[11] But
at a deeper level of medical understanding of the body, Essence is that
aspect of *qi* which is active at significant moments of change, when
phenomena move from one stage or form to another in transitions
like those from one of the five cosmic phases to the next. Thus generation—the mingling of blood and essence (semen)—is governed by
"Essence" in this more abstract sense as shaping the point of entry
into time (both as cycle and arrow). Conception becomes a moment
of fusion between cosmic creativity and embodied humanity. But the
moment of generation is also transitional, since what originates and
begins must develop and grow. *"Cheng,"* maturation, is necessarily
gradual; but it is also fundamental, as it is the yin phase of the total
process. In thinking of the substances involved, the priority of the
male contribution is not defined in terms of spirit and form versus
matter and food (or nurture) but is linked to timeliness. In thinking
of the process, what happens at the critical moment of transition into
existence is yang; yin is what performs its work over the long months
of gestation.

Into his account of conception quoted here, Wu Zhiwang introduced an additional dualism derived from popular Buddhism—the
dualism between the "spiritual" *(ling)* preexistent and the "material
form" *(xing*)*. But even these popular religious concepts do not
translate into an opposition between spirit and matter. In Buddhism
"material form" *(xing*)* embraces structure and pattern in the visible
world, while *"ling"* is possessed by all organic life as well as beings
awaiting reincarnation. Confucianists, on the other hand, adapted
the concept of *ling* to talk of the spirits of ancestors. Thus, from both
of these perspectives, the "spiritual" is associated with the cycles
linking lives across the boundary of death—that is, the principles
of the karmic transmission of souls or the ties linking ancestors
and descendants.[12] Wu Zhiwang's evocation of the "spiritual" was in
harmony with both Buddhist doctrines of reincarnation and Confucian beliefs in an ancestral "line" of descent transmitted across
generations.[13]

Another common way of characterizing what happens at the
moment of conception is revealed in commonplace medical discourse
concerning *"yuanqi,"* or, in the phrasing of Wu Zhiwang just cited,
"perfected *qi*" *(zhenqi)*. *Yuanqi* is a complex term with many different meanings in different historical contexts. However, by Ming–
Qing times it was commonly used by medical men to refer to "preexistent" *(xiantian)* aspects of *qi*—that is, those "outside time"
endowed by heaven at conception that make growth and development possible and underlie reproductive capabilities themselves.
Though "dependent on food and drink," *yuanqi* is not ultimately
renewable via metabolic processes. It was deemed especially vital to
reproduction and had an affinity for regions of the body associated
with generative functions: the Kidney system, ruled by Water (the
most yin of the Five Phases), and the Gate of Life *(ming men)*—at the
crossroads of all energy pathways below the navel. Grave illness
always threatened *yuanqi*. Its depletion was associated with aging:
when it is exhausted, the human being dies. In sum, the preexistent
heavenly endowment bestowed at conception precisely bridges transitions between lives in a biological continuum, translating the arrow
of biography into the cycle of generations in a lineage. In medical
texts, to conceive a child was literally "to plant descendants" *(zhong
zi)* or to "increase the descent lines" *(guang si)*. This language not
only privileged the male act of impregnation but focused upon *"si"*—
children as descendants, valuable from the embryonic stage for their
potential as posterity. The main weight of the medical tradition

suggests that we are dealing with primary vitalities connecting generations and making possible the mortality-transcending link of ancestors and descendants as embodied members of a single family line.

In cosmogony, yin and yang are the first differentiation. By analogy, the differentiation of the embryo into male or female is not a preexistent gift of heaven but was seen as the most fundamental of characteristics shaped by the forces of earth.[14] In late imperial times the medical consensus was that a woman's fertile period occurs as her menstrual flow ends and "new blood begins to grow." Beyond this there were conflicting accounts of the mechanisms involved in establishing the child's sex. Among competing theories inherited from the Han–Tang era, some stressed broad environmental and cosmological influences at the moment of conception (or, in some versions, during the first weeks of gestation). Others looked to yin/yang influences at work within the bodies of the parents themselves. The protean flexibility of the classical correspondence theory produced a welter of speculations concerning this most socially critical issue as medical specialists struggled to satisfy their clients' desire for sons.

Since yin and yang were forces permeating every aspect of the environment, very old speculations suggested that the sex of an unborn child would be determined by the total balance of cosmic and natural influences on events at the moment of sexual union. In his major work, *Prescriptions Worth a Thousand,* Sun Simo had taught that astrologically auspicious days, the particular time of day, the season of year, the weather and physical surroundings, were all potentially important, their totality creating a yin/yang force field, as it were, shaping the decisive moment. In keeping with this, there was a vast divinatory lore identifying favorable and unfavorable times, places, and directions of the compass for couples to consider when trying to conceive, with further refinements for the conception of a boy or a girl in particular.[15] In advising their clients about successful procreation, Tang and Song medical masters drew freely on Sun Simo's understanding of this tradition and on associated beliefs in star spirits, ghosts, and other supernatural influences.[16] In the late imperial era these traditions were kept alive in popular almanacs and in the lore of diviners.

Although most elite physicians of Ming–Qing times no longer stressed astrological and demonological influences on either fertility or ordinary illness, they had not abandoned entirely the logic embedded in such beliefs. Wu Zhiwang and others in the seventeenth century kept to the spirit of correspondence theory in recommending coitus at times permeated with ascending yang influences: the conjunction of hours of the day, times of the lunar month, and auspicious days of the calendar year (yang or yin days in the lunar calendar's stem/branch system of naming) allowed for a complex force field of favorable and unfavorable influences to shape the event.

But generally Ming–Qing medicine preferred explanations of embryonic sexual differentiation that located the forces at work within the human body rather than in the world at large. One popular old belief, identified in the seventeenth century with Taoism, taught that the sex of the child is determined by whether coitus takes place on days one, three, and five (yang numbers) or days two, four, and six (yin numbers) of the woman's new menstrual cycle.[17] Another favorite theory was based on the view of Master Chu Cheng, putative author of a sixth-century treatise that includes one of the few sustained discussions of reproductive processes in the older literature. Chu Cheng portrayed sexual differentiation as the result of a drama when "essence" met "blood" in the womb:

> If yin blood arrives first and yang essence then dashes against it, the blood opens to wrap around the essence; essence enters making bone and a male is formed. If yang *qi* enters first and yin blood later joins it, the essence opens to surround the blood; blood enters to make the foundation [*ben*] and a female is formed.[18]

This account was repeated as authoritative by Li Shizhen, Wu Zhiwang, and many others. It evokes the perennial Chinese topos of erotic encounters as combat—a literal war between the sexes. The sex of offspring is determined by a competition between the parents' own sexual powers, which in some accounts include the ability to provoke a partner's orgasm while witholding one's own. Beyond this, Chu Cheng attributed sickliness, infertility, and sexual anomaly in offspring to unions in which the parents' gendered vitalities were defective or out of balance with each other. This insight was compatible with a general medical insistence that successful procreation depended upon the conservation of primary vitalities through moderation and sexual restraint. Such explanations were based on the innermost, hidden workings of the body, unlike environmental theories that emphasized auspicious times and places—all of which common experience showed to be unreliable.[19]

But the internalist model of successful procreation also stressed the fundamental nature of sexual difference by linking gender differentiation to the primary cosmological polarity of yin and yang. When the sex of offspring (perceived as the outcome of the "union of yin and yang") depended on the relative powers of male and female parent, it translated biological chance into an event with a potential for social failure. In this way, medical reasoning became entangled in the socially charged imperatives of Confucian paternity. Occasionally a doctor would draw a bald conclusion: "If a woman has only girls, the father's "superintendant pulse" *(du mai)* is weak, and yang cannot overcome yin."[20]

However, this stress on male responsibility also prompted many doctors to criticize the common tendency to blame women for sterile or heirless unions. Faced with the inexact nature of medical knowledge about sexual differentiation, doctors balanced their claims to expertise with the popular appeal to fate as a larger cosmological or religious force governing human destiny. Such a mix of attitudes produced the following advice offered a male patient by an ordinary mid-Qing practitioner:

> Although whether one has descendants *(zi)* is fundamentally determined by fate, still the ancient saying was, "Those who have few desires will have many sons." Why is it that some who have few desires have girls? They don't know that yang influences have an affinity for the left side of the body and yin influences for the right.[21]

The husband was then advised to have intercourse on the favored days and to have his wife lie on her left side afterwards.

Sex, then, was the most fundamental characteristic that the potential human being acquired at conception. Here parents acted as embodied agents and channels of a natural pattern, not as the source of personal inherited characteristics. Again Chu Cheng was the physician whose ideas came to form the basis for late imperial medical discussion:

> In general children are filial to [i.e., resemble] their father and mother in form. Normally their bodily appearance does not depart from that of mother and father. If the father has a limp, the son's limbs are unfilial to his father [because they are whole]; if the mother has a squint, the son's eyes are unfilial to his mother [because they are normal].[22]

In glossing this passage both Li Shizhen and Wu Zhiwang explain that what is being discussed here is a child's "natural endowment" *(bin).* The Song philosopher Zhu Xi had said that "natural endowment is what is present at the beginning of life." Li Shizhen explained it this way: "In human beings the fundamental natural endowment comes from *qian* and *kun,* while material form *(xing*)* comes from a single [undifferentiated] *qi.*"[23] Li believed that "natural endowment" included qualities that all human beings share by virtue of what biologists today would call membership in the species—the human shape and human faculties. Other medical writers talked of natural endowment in terms of things like a tendency to be robust or sickly, fat or thin, long-lived or likely to die young. In a similar vein, those classified in popular literati writing as having "extraordinary endowments" *(yi bin)* included both the intellectually precocious and the monstrous or deformed, or even those with enormous sexual appetites.[24] The mention of reproductive capacities—fruitfulness in women and potency in men—showed further that such endowments included an individual's inborn excess or deficiency of some normal, hence normative, human quality.

Doctors were perfectly aware that children physically resemble individual parents and occasionally commented on it in a clinical context. But as a general principle, one received from parents at conception the inheritance of *"qian* and *kun"*—the human pattern in a more or less satisfactory replication of an ideal type. Unusual personal qualities—of intelligence, beauty, health, or vigor—were similarly imagined as either the innate gift of heaven (or karma or fate) or the product of potent environmental influences, including those active during gestation.[25] Such differentiating characteristics were those identified by Li Shizhen with "form" and, as he put it, were "shaped by the *qi* of wind and earth, and by customs which vary from place to place."[26] Among the various ways in which the customs of a locality fostered such imprinting, the possibility of human control was greatest over the uterine environment in gestation and was considered the particular responsibility of mothers.

Learned medicine, in understanding gestation as a process of differentiation whereby *qi* is transformed through the agency of yin/yang and the Five Phases *(wu xing),* was dealing with an aspect of the medical canon that had changed very little over a millennium.[27] From the earliest accounts, the periodization of gestation according to the passage of months established time's cycle as fundamental to the process. Thus the arrow of growth moved through a sequence of ten lunar months, each qualitatively equivalent to all the others. (See

Table 1.) Neither the written accounts nor the occasional crude drawings found in medical literature were concerned with observational accuracy concerning fetal form. What mattered was to identify each month faithfully by governing circulation tracts and associated organ systems, showing transitions propelled by the creative power of Essence. For the later months of gestation the transitions of Five Phase cosmology were invoked, governed by Essence as Water in the fourth month, as Fire in the fifth, and so on. In keeping with these transitions, the fetus developed from inner structures to outer ones and from softer to harder, moving from the formation of blood, to that of *qi*, flesh, bones, skin-as-hide, and finally to skin-as-hair. Here emphasis shifted from forms of energy at work to their actual materializaton.[28]

The effect of such theorizing was to emphasize the multiple qualitative transformations characteristic of fetal growth enabled by a "single *qi*" and moving from phase to phase and yin to yang in the context of gradual differentiation and development. As the editor of the *Salvation of Yin* stated it:

> The [embryo as] *pei* is *qi* materialized; the [embryo as] *gao* is *qi* coagulating; in a *tai* [fetus] the form of materialization becomes manifest. Preexistent [heaven] regulates creation and transformation, and so [Essences] of Water, Fire, Metal, Wood, Earth, and Stone order its transformations. Temporal *(houtian)* [earth] follows the suitable sequence [of phases] in maturation.[29]

There is no descent of soul, no emphasis on the mother's quickening, and no distinction between early and late miscarriage that might mark a decisive developmental leap in the character of fetal life as it matures. Such a view of human growth makes birth itself just another in a sequence of transitions whose overall impact is cumulative over gestation and infancy—a point of view reinforced by the custom of recording a human being's age in *"sui"*—that is, beginning the count during the gestational phase of life, starting with the month of conception.[30] Manifested in the transformations ordered by the endless alternation of yin and yang and the Five Phases, the developing fetus evolves within the overarching embrace of time's cycle.

Nonetheless, time's arrow pointed to the concrete specificities of beginnings and endings. The earliest months of pregnancy were uncertain times, when the facts of the case were ambiguous. Doctors offered a variety of methods for determining whether a woman was

Month	Name	Developmental Process
1	始胚 *shi pei* embryonic mud	union of yin and yang
2	始膏 *shi gao* embryonic fat	fetus begins to cohere; Essence (*jing*) maturing in the womb
3	始胎 *shi tai* fetus beginning	norms still undetermined; inner responds to outer; child's nature is influenced by material environment
4	形體成 *xing ti cheng* maturing form	*phase of Water*: Essence (*jing*) acts on blood
5	能動 *neng dong* able to move	*phase of Fire*: Essence acts on *qi*
6	筋骨立 *jin gu li* bones and sinews shaping	*phase of Metal*: Essence acts on sinews
7	毛髮生 *mao fa sheng* growing hair	*phase of Wood*: Essence acts on bone
8	臟腑真 *zang fu zhen* organ systems complete	*phase of Earth*: Essence acts on skin/flesh
9	穀氣入胃 *gu qi ru wei* can use the *qi* of food	*phase of Stone*: Essence acts on skin/hair
10	諸神備 *zhu shen bei* all faculties complete	all systems ready and interconnected; *qi* of heaven and earth descends into cinnabar field

Materialization	Governing Tract / Organ System
	足厥陰 / 肝 *zujueyin* / Liver
	足少陽 / 膽 *zushaoyang* / gall
sex is determined; mother can influence child by "fetal education"	手心 / 心 *shouxin* / Heart
maturing circulation tracts and functioning blood pulse carrying blood and *qi* to eyes and ears	手少陽 / 憔 *shoushaoyang* / triple burners
hair begins to grow; four limbs formed	足太陰 / 脾 *zutaiyin* / Spleen
sinews and bones maturing	足陽明 / 胃 *zuyangming* / stomach
bone maturing; skin/hair mature	手太陰 / 肺 *shoutaiyin* / Lung
skin/flesh maturing	手陽明 / 大腸 *shouyangming* / bowels
skin/hair mature; the six *fu* organs and joints are all ready	足少陰 / 腎 *zushaoyin* / Kidney
all powers of motion and powers of consciousness are ready	

in fact pregnant—a sure sign of ignorance—and often admitted that the canonical pulse method of diagnosis was only guesswork. Women took "menstrual regulating" *(tiao jing)* doses to bring on periods without acknowledging the possiblity that these might act as early abortifacients. While doctors themselves warned that early miscarriage often went unrecognized, their own experience as recorded in case histories was most often of miscarriage in the fifth or sixth month, rarely in the second or third. The inchoate nature of life during early gestation was acknowledged in the doctrine of "fetal education" *(tai jiao),* which taught that a mother's conduct in the first months had a particularly strong influence on the child's appearance, talent, or temperament.[31] Even the ten-month schema lacked a fixed nomenclature based on physical features for the first two months, while the name *tai,* appropriate from the third month forward, maintained some of the distinction conveyed in English between "fetus" and "embryo." Some said a *tai* could feed from its mother by mouth; significantly, it had a recognizable sex.

In the same way, approaching birth was marked by recognition that a phase of bodily separation was at hand. According to Sun Simo, in the tenth month the "*qi* of heaven and earth enters the cinnabar fields," implying that *yuanqi* was now concentrating at the Gate of Life *(ming men)* of reproductive vitalities and at the upper "cinnabar fields" of the chest and head, conceived of as the seats of consciousness. Also at this time, according to the seventeenth-century commentary on this text by Wu Zhiwang, "organ systems, flesh, bones, and human psyche *(ren shen)* are all ready."[32] Doctors moreover spoke of a child's "wish" to be born, and as labor approached they often dropped the term *tai* for *zi* (meaning "child," in the sense of descendant) or even *er* (baby).

The ambiguities of life in the fetal stage of development can be further elucidated by looking at the medical treatment of abortion. In Ming–Qing case histories, we find that doctors generally discouraged abortifacients in favor of prescriptions designed to strengthen mothers to withstand the rigors of childbearing. But it is clear that husbands could, without loss of face, try to procure abortifacients for wives thought to be sickly. This private matter was not so taboo as to be kept out of the pages of a public document like a printed case-book, and it was something a son might mention in writing of his mother's life and sufferings.[33] The medical disapproval of abortion was, as Francesca Bray has suggested, a matter of vocational ethics specific to the physicians' calling, supported by the belief that all miscarriage was dangerous to a woman's health. Doctors objected to female control of abortion (in the hands of "the six kinds of old women" including midwives), but they did not in principle give fetal life priority over a mother's well-being.[34] The same point of view was reinforced in forensic law, which punished those who, by injury such as a beating, caused a woman to abort, treating this act as a crime against the mother's person.[35] In cases of infanticide, the liminality of fetal life extended to the newborn. Again, doctors who commented on the practice were disapproving, but they saw it as an aspect of the suffering of mothers as well as inhumane vis-à-vis the child. In a popular eighteenth-century childbirth manual, *On Successful Childbirth (Da sheng pian)*, infanticide was seen as a gender issue, adding to the misery mothers faced for bearing girls.[36]

The pronatalist ethics of most Chinese doctors showed up not in protection of fetal life viewed independently of the mother but in medical concern about the gestational and neonatal environment that made the two so profoundly interdependent. Ming–Qing doctors did not often discuss the ancient ritual doctrines of "fetal education," and most no longer taught that a mother's conduct during the first months of pregnancy could influence the sex of her child. But pregnancy was surrounded from the beginning with strictures concerning diet, daily regimen, and moral behavior. These prescriptions for prenatal care reflected a belief in the interconnectedness of morality and health and in maternal responsibility for the uterine environment.

To be moved by emotions, especially passion or anger, to give way to lust, or to indulge in rich food or drink was to risk pathological fire within, endangering the child's health and well-being in utero and making it susceptible to disease in infancy. Although mothers themselves might be injured by these excesses and suffer from difficult delivery, medical advice on these matters focused on the child's welfare. On the positive side, gestation was also a time when wise mothers might benefit themselves and offspring through spiritual self-cultivation *(xiu shen)*, comparable to the moral discipline of a sage or worthy. On the negative side, the heat of passion and emotion, experienced as fire within the female body, was thought to be the primary source of "fetal poison" *(tai du)*—a medicalization of ancient ideas of birth pollution entrenched in popular Buddhism.[37] If the mother was immune to this poison, it was deemed toxic to the fetus. Moreover, fetal poisoning was considered inevitable, gave its name to a large group of neonatal illnesses, and was thought to be the principal cause of smallpox, an illness that struck universally in childhood during the Ming and Qing. Mothers seeking to bear and rear healthy children bore a grave responsibility for their welfare, which extended to responsibility for the child's chances of surviving this most feared of childhood diseases. Doctors taught that a child favored with good maternal care would be only lightly tainted by fetal poison, and thus its inevitable case of smallpox would be mild.[38]

In these ways the symbiosis between mother and child established during gestation was projected into the years of infancy—this time not as an aspect of microcosmic/macrocosmic rhythms of time's cycle, but rather as a material bond through a susceptibility to illness. Breastfeeding reinforced the materiality of this bond, for milk was imagined as "transformed" menstrual blood, which, after nourishing the fetus in utero, rises in the body after birth to become food for the infant. As in gestation, during lactation a nursing mother's conduct and emotions were thought to influence her milk and through it the child's development. Breastfeeding required a mother to maintain a mild diet and temperate passions while the child's grip on life remained precarious. In this form of medical discourse, the vision of life stages as patterned by numbers and cycles constituting human harmony with heaven and earth was disrupted. With birth entered death and disease, and with them some of the harsher contingencies of life stages as individual history. Despite medical commitments to a philosophy of the body based on an ideal of natural harmony, their evocation of the negative materiality of the maternal sphere marked early childhood as a conflict-ridden journey from nature to culture.

INFANCY: *YINGER*

Delivery separated the predominantly yang body of the new infant from its yin host, the mother, but few regarded the organ systems of the newborn as in any sense completely developed. As Sun Simo had said earlier: "A baby's *qi* and substance are subtle and weak. . . . Its bones and flesh are not yet consolidated."[39] Similarly, in the seventeenth century its frail life outside the womb was described as like that of "bubbles floating on the surface of the water or candles in the wind."[40] The weak, intermittent pulse discernible in infants under two years (three *sui*) was interpreted as evidence for the newborn's still-rudimentary systems of function, while consideration of its bodily openings mapped pathways of its new vulnerability to noxious influences *(xie)* from the outside world. These exposed openings included the skin, where the child's pores were conceived of as not yet fine and close, the fontanelle, and above all, the navel—the conduit of uterine life, which remained especially permeable in the first weeks. In fact, the immaturity and vulnerability of infancy had two sides: one was seen through its need to develop mature defenses from external contamination as it grew; the other was revealed in the infant's inherent propensity to disease, understood as a legacy from its polluted fetal state.

Side by side with this anxious picture of infancy was an account that stressed orderly cycles of growth manifested in cosmically resonant numbers. This normative process of infant development, described by late imperial physicians, was little changed from that outlined in the medical classics of Sun Simo and Wang Tao. As in the case of gestation, infant development was divided into alternations of symmetrical and equivalent yin/yang phases punctuated by critical leaps of growth.[41] In thinking about the underlying patterns at work here, medicine provided a theory of transitions that acknowledged the qualitatively unique characteristics of human growth in infancy. All infants, it was said, go through the process of "changing and steaming" *(bian zheng)*. This curious term draws on the medical concept of "steaming" as a kind of feverishness in the marrow and also on a metaphor of cooking—the qualitative transformation of foods by heat. Linked to *zheng* was *bian*, which means a cycle of change, also seen as involving qualitative transitions from one cosmic pole to another (i.e., the alternations of yin and yang). As a process of growth, the life of the infant was seen as dividing into cycles of thirty-two days (each a "change") and double cycles of sixty-four days (each a "steaming"). At the transition point in each cycle, about every thirty-two days on a small scale and about every sixty-four on a larger one, the child goes through a period of instability. This period, lasting about a week, is marked by fretfulness, feverishness, poor appetite, and possibly signs like a light rash, sweating, cold extremities, or night crying—things that seem like illnesses but in fact are minor crises of development. In the Ming–Qing versions of this theory, each cycle works on a particular organ system, according to the succession of the Five Phases *(wu xing)*. The "changing" works on physical aspects of organ systems, while the "steaming" affects consciousness. With each crisis phase, a qualitative leap in the child's development has occurred. At the end of eighteen cycles—that is, after 576 days—the process is finished. At a year-and-a-half the child is able to walk, understand speech, and can express the emotions of joy and sorrow. In light of these cognitive and emotional faculties, it has now "become human" *(cheng ren)*, matured, and is recognizable as a human person.[42]

"Steaming and changing," a very old idea articulated in the Tang and pre-Tang classics, was elaborated according to Five Phase correspondence theory. In the late imperial period, some doctors found its scholastic and mechanical numerology unconvincing. Debates over which alternative model of Five Phase theory applied ("mutual production" or "mutual conquest") cast further doubt on the theoretical foundations. It was also obvious that few infants experienced minor fretfulness and fever on such a predictable schedule. But for all its formalistic flavor, "steaming and changing" remained a staple topic in child care. A mid-Qing diarist wrote on his infant son's development, "Fathers should know about this," and noted telltale signs to look for on his child's ears, lips, and nose.[43] In sum, the developmental model of "steaming and changing" marked infancy, like gestation, as a time of rapid transitions of growth. On a practical level, it provided a way of understanding minor upsets and illnesses. More broadly, it suggested that the instability of infancy had a dual character. On the one hand, it was the mark of a frail grip on life; but on the other, changeability went with growth, leaping forward month by month in a dramatically transitory process that culminated in the maturation of the child's truly human nature.

As a theory of infant development, "steaming and changing" expressed confidence in a natural order regulating human growth according to the harmony of the numbers and rhythms of time's cycles. Much of the rest of pediatrics, however, emphasized the instability of infant life and the dangers surrounding it. Like parents, doctors frequently diagnosed a newborn's nature through portents— aspects of infant appearance or behavior seen as clues to its future destiny. Observation of abnormality here joined with the art of physiognomy and popular belief in spirit possession as explanations of infantile "queerness." A repertory of bodily signs indicated whether a child would be likely to live, be easy to rear, or be generally fortunate in its fate. Reliance on such portents suggests a period when the bond between parent and infant remained hesitant, as well as the degree to which human life in general was seen as something beyond human control.[44]

Medical accounts of infant vulnerability also encouraged mothers and nurses to uphold a protective pattern of care about which doctors were ultimately ambivalent. The medical image of a child's weak defenses encouraged caretakers to swaddle its body in thick wraps, rub medicinal paste on its fontanelle, and in summer cover its belly with a navel apron. A minority of experts who advocated "tempering" a child, along lines recommended by the seventh-century master Chao Yuanfang, found themselves arguing—probably in vain— against overfeeding, overdressing, and indoor seclusion, even as their own theories stressed the importance of a calm, protected, and emotionally temperate atmosphere in the nursery.[45]

If babies developed characteristic human faculties before they were two, the developing toddler still had to go through a further transition that dealt with the legacy of gestation and infancy: the heritage of "fetal poison." In the late imperial period, fetal poison was associated with neonatal disorders in the first month of life. It was also linked to later eruptive childhood diseases, especially the crisis of smallpox, foreshadowed from the time that the newborn went through ritual cleansing (the third day bath) and took cleansing tonics against fetal poison. "Light pox" *(xi dou)* medicines were routine in the first week and continued to be recommended for any child who had not undergone the disease. In the Ming and Qing eras, smallpox was almost universal in China and struck in early childhood. Chinese recognized its seasonal and endemic nature; it was severe, according to conventional wisdom, every third year. This observation did not invalidate the idea of fetal poison as an agent but, rather, led to the explanation that poisonous internal heat, absorbed from the mother's womb during gestation, needed to be stimulated by external climatic influences for illness to appear. The fact that those who recovered were thereafter immune reinforced the idea that something inborn was working itself out through the "heat" of an eruptive disease. Thus smallpox was seen as not merely fated, but as a necessary crisis of development that must be successfully negotiated before a child's future would be assured. Recovery from smallpox cleansed the child of the remnants of pollution inherited from the gestational state and allowed it to slough off the last bodily tie with the mother. Emerging finally from the polluted life-threatening disorders of infancy and early childhood, it passed from nature into culture and could be seen as now having a chance of living to grow up.[46]

The theory of fetal poison explained smallpox naturalistically, as inherent in the body. But smallpox also supported views of early childhood as a time beset with dangers difficult for human agency to control, subject to sickness and other accidents viewed as products of supernatural influences that required ritual mediation. As a visitation from "heaven," smallpox *(tian hua)* could also be seen as an illness bestowed by the "smallpox goddess" in the form of poisonous "heavenly flowers" blooming on the sufferer's skin. Similarly "fright wind" *(jing feng),* a pediatriac syndrome marked by crying, high fever, and convulsions, could be attributed to the temporary loss of a young child's unstable soul, calling for the services of a shaman. Many doctors criticized the use of ritual healers in such circumstances, but often their own ministrations in actual smallpox cases simply took the fatalistic form of prognostication: "After [sick children] have been feverish for a few days and a few spots appear, parents suspect smallpox and call in the doctors to forecast [by type of rash whether the outcome will be auspicious]."[47] In the eighteenth-century novel, *Dream of the Red Chamber,* when a young daughter of the aristocratic Jia family is afflicted, the doctor first announces that the outcome will be favorable, after which the parents set up an altar to the smallpox goddess and vow ritual abstention from sex for the duration of the illness.

Smallpox and other critical illnesses in early childhood evoked the metaphor of life as a journey leading through a succession of dangerous mountain "passes" *(guan)*—or in another sense of the term, "turning points"—moments of crisis where life and death hang in balance. In the world of popular religion, children were thought to face a gauntlet of "passes"—threats from accidents, wild animals, and baleful spirits as well as disease. Ming–Qing almanacs describe a standard repertory of such perils under the heading of "Passes of Baleful Influences" *(Sha guan)* and suggest astrological and ritual protections.[48] A Buddhist temple's processional way might be marked off by paper signs identifying the "passes" of various childhood diseases, where children could be taken and blessed.[49] In all these ways, medicine supported the ritual understanding of early childhood as a time of spiritual vulnerability complemented by physical weakness, marked by rites of passage as its inevitable dangers were negotiated.

From conception through infancy, then, becoming human is a gradual process not marked by sharply differentiated boundaries. Although "life" begins at conception, with entry into a ritual continuum linking ancestors and descendants, the process of "maturation" *(cheng)* extends past birth to the second year of life. Later, as the infant makes the transition from the perilous and tainted materiality of gestation and infancy, the significant markers of its emerging human nature have more to do with cognitive and emotional faculties rather than moral ones. There is no strong polarity between body and spirit here, and medical wisdom suggested that infancy was not to be associated with any morally privileged innocence such as philosophers claimed for the "childlike mind."[50] Even further, medical experts viewed the optimum patterns of a child's growth as distorted by the intense striving for moral and intellectual development that Confucian pedagogy encouraged.

Finally, much in a child's nature and destiny eluded human agency and was generally acknowledged to be a matter of fate. Often medical diagnosis concerning new life took the form of prediction concerning the sex of the fetus, the newborn's prospects for health, or the sick child's chances of recovery. Here medical experts were not simply relying on an empirical understanding of the course of disease; they were drawing upon a doctrine of signs based on the cosmologically rooted theories of correspondence—a method that linked their art to the frankly divinatory spheres of physiognomy and astrology.[51]

In sum, the foregoing readings of human beginnings accommodated both ritual commitments to family posterity and family contingencies based on the social experience of high infant mortality. They also illuminate some of the ways in which the Confucian belief that "children belong to parents" might have been culturally understood and filtered through the critical variable of gender. The enormous medical emphasis on the significance of sexual differentiation underscores the social importance of gender differences to Chinese families. The maternal power to influence events at conception by engendering daughters was read negatively as subversive of the agnatic line's need for posterity. The stress on environmental influences during gestation and lactation made mothers bear a heavy responsibility for their infants' health and vitality. Despite the shared body substances that blurred boundaries between mother and child down through weaning, the symbiosis between mother and babe was material in nature, not sentimentalized as a trope of family intimacy. This can also be seen in the wide social and medical toleration of wet nurses, whereby some elite women transferred the bodily task of lactation to menial surrogates. In keeping with this, it was the passage of time beyond infancy and the accumulation of social investment in a child that were critical to the full development of the parent/child relationship built around filiality in the patriarchial family. The

gradual, process-oriented view of early childhood growth marked
the infant/parent bond as no more than a preliminary phase of a
tie that was lifelong, culminating as adult sons and daughters-in-law
parented parents. Filial piety was not a childish virtue.

GROWING: SEXUAL MATURATION

Infancy *(yinger)* conjured up an image of a babe at the mother's
breast. Sun Simo defined it as the period under six *sui*, when a child's
"own circulation tracts do not support it fully, and so it hangs from
the mother's breast."[52] Other authorities sometimes placed the end of
the *yinger* stage at three *sui*. Although the transition would appear
clearly associated with weaning, elite medical accounts offered little
advice on this significant developmental issue and gave no consistent
picture of its actual timing.[53] Their discussion of infant growth was
shaped more by their own professional concerns with diagnosis and
prescription. The feeble pulse of children under three *sui* made this
preferred method of diagnosis difficult, while children under five or
six *sui* needed radically reduced quantities in prescriptions for ordinary illness. Textbooks suggest that pediatrics *(erke)* as a medical
specialty applied largely to children under five or six and that doctors
considered older children to be less medically special. Nonetheless,
practice could vary: the pediatric wasting disorders classified as
"malnutritions" *(gan)* were differentiated from similar syndromes in
those past puberty,[54] while in seventeenth-century casebooks one
finds instances where pediatric specialists treated adolescents.[55]

Further, though it associated the development of uniquely human
characteristics with cognitive and emotional capacities, medicine also
had little to say about early moral or intellectual development, which
figures so prominently in pedagogical writings. In fact, the chief
thrust of medical advice concerning these matters reflected a view of
bodily economy that was conservationist: vitality expended in precocious development or exertion would be lost in the long term:

> It is said that between the ages of three and ten *sui* a child's [future]
> length of life can be known by the elevation [high or low level of func-
> tion] of its nature *(xing)* and *qi*. In general those who are unusually
> clever when they are small do not live to old age; Xian Bo and Yan Hui
> were this sort. Children whose bodies are well knit and assured, who
> move slowly almost like simpletons, and whose spirits are like carved

jewels, are long-lived. Those who can guess others' minds and whose movements are quick and rapid also die young; Yang Xiu and Gong Ke were this sort. . . . The early blooming plum blossom does not last till the season is cold; the chrysanthemum is late to be ready and ends with the year. This tells us that the long-lived are those who are late to reach maturity *(wan chengzhe)*.[56]

Thus, in medical thinking, the issues of growth and longevity were linked, and both were tied to reproductive vitalities. The medically significant stage of growth that succeeded *yinger* began at seven or eight *sui* and was associated with sexual development. The *Inner Canon* provided the canonical point of reference, complete with the numerological patterning which signified that cosmological resonances were thought to be at work:

At seven *sui* a girl's Kidney *qi* is flourishing; her adult teeth come in and her hair grows long. At fourteen she comes into her reproductive capacities *(tiangui zhi);* her *ren* pulse moves and her *chong* pulse is abundant; her menses flow regularly and she can bear young. At twenty-one her Kidney *qi* is even and calm, and so her wisdom teeth come in and her growth has reached its apogee. . . . At eight *sui* a boy's Kidney *qi* is replete; his adult teeth come in and his hair grows long. At sixteen his Kidney *qi* is abundant, and he comes into his reproductive capacities *(tiangui zhi);* his seminal essence overflows and drains; he can unite yin and yang and so beget young. At twenty-four his Kidney *qi* is even and calm, and so his bones and sinews are strong, his wisdom teeth come in, and his growth has reached an apogee.[57]

As this passage shows, the visceral system identified specifically with sexual function was associated with the action of "Kidney" *(shen)*. Even though doctors did not think that preadolescent children have sexual feelings, the *Inner Canon* established seven or eight *sui* as the time when children could be regarded as sexualized beings by adults. Socially, seven or eight *sui* was when sex segregation began; formal learning—a discipline that medicine identified as risky to primary vitalities—also commenced around this time. For girls of all classes the separation of the sexes would be reinforced by the commencement of footbinding: although this was a procedure the male-dominated medical world ignored, its timing reinforced the understanding that this was a bodily change marking female sexual maturation.

Puberty in medical idiom, *"tiangui,"* stood for something far

broader than a transition into physical adolescence. As the eighteenth-century *Golden Mirror of Medicine* explained it: "*Tiangui* is a
heavenly endowment that originates in father and mother; essence
and blood are earthly creations produced by the nourishment of food
and drink."[58] Shared by males and females alike, *tiangui* is no less
than the capacity to reproduce in its totality, made possible by the
activation of the true *qi* of heaven bestowed at conception through
the function of the Kidney system working on female blood and male
essence. Only in late middle age would *tiangui* be exhausted, at forty-
nine in women (7 × 7) and at sixty-four in men (8 × 8), when fertility
has declined and doctors believed people normally ceased to feel
sexual desire.[59] Moreover, this decline goes with aging: "Kidney *qi*
weakens, hair falls out, and teeth wither." In the human body of
medical imagination, teeth and hair mark the developmental curve of
sexual life because they are manifestations of bone, itself governed by
the Kidney system. The lesson of the *Inner Canon* throughout is that
reproductive vitalities are the foundation of other forms of life
energy; they are responsible for longevity, so that the management of
these vitalities in youth is the key to vigor in great old age.

Such in fact was the interpretation of this passage offered by
Zhang Jingyue, one of the leading medical authorities of the seventeenth century. He linked *tiangui* (reproductive capability) and
yuanqi as follows:

> *Tiangui* is True Water generated by heaven; in the human body it is
> called original yin. It is original *qi (yuanqi)*. As the moment of genera-
> tion occurs, this preexistent *qi* is bestowed on parents, and in the
> course of generative development it is transformed in the body and
> called "temporal original *qi*" *(houtian yuanqi)*. In the beginning true
> yin *(zhen yin)* is infinitesimal, and as it increases blood and essence
> [reproductive fluids] thrive. True yin must be sufficient before blood
> and essence come into being; their relationship is one of before and
> after. Otherwise, after forty-nine and sixty-four [the end of reproduc-
> tive years] how can men and women still have some of this true yin cir-
> culating through their entire bodies along the paths of the *ying* and *wei*
> defensive systems, not yet completely dried up?[60]

The harmony of numbers here made the process of sexual maturation not only a manifestation of primary vitalities identified with life
itself, but also one that was homologous between the sexes. Just as in
infants the left side was designated "male" and the right side
"female," in maturing bodies the formal multiples of sevens and

eights (yin and yang numbers respectively) that ordered the timing of reproductive powers were understood as expressing the relations of cosmic complementary opposites. Medicine here noted puberty by calling attention to the homologous yin/yang dyad of blood and semen—functional reproductive vitalities—rather than secondary sex characteristics evocative of erotic dimorphisms of the flesh.

Reproductive vitalities mattered as a basic aspect of lifelong health, making those learned in medicine sensitive to functional manifestations in adolescence like nocturnal emission in boys and menstruation in girls. In late imperial China, however, adolescence, defined as the period between puberty and marriage, was not a ritually or socially distinct stage in the life cycle for most young people.[61] The coming-of-age rites recommended in the old ritual classics—hairpinning and capping—commonly were neglected or, in the case of girls, integrated into betrothal and marriage ceremonies. Medicine's mediation of the lag between physical growth and its social resolution in marriage took two main forms: the medicalization of certain sexual functions and the propagation of health advice supporting delayed marriage. First, since male continence was considered desirable to maximize fertility and longevity, spontaneous seminal emissions could be problematic, even in youths, if the boy was delicate or the emissions were frequent or accompanied by dreams. In girls erotic fantasies ("dreams of intercourse with ghosts") were always pathological signs, whether understood as spirit possession or as the manifestation of a disordered psyche *(shen)*. In these ways medical authority supported the prevention of erotic arousal in both sexes as best for young people's health, and Lucien Miller's construction of adolescence as a kind of illness in the hothouse fictional world of *Dream of the Red Chamber* (Chapter 8 in this volume) conforms to medical stereotypes.[62]

Second, in warning against early marriage, doctors admonished both sexes but gave more attention to its dangers in girls. They pointed to adolescent amenorrhea and menstrual irregularity as common signs that a girl was not yet ready for pregnancy. Reliable menstrual cycles, deemed fundamental to overall female health as well as fertility, were medically facilitated by a refined repertory of "menstrual regulating" prescription formulas. Case histories show that this was a major concern when doctors were consulted about the ailments of maidens. In counseling delay, Wu Zhiwang and others appealed to the classic *Book of Ritual* prescription of marriage ages: twenty for women and thirty for men. As Wu put it, the apogee of growth and reproductive vitality was reached some years after puberty, when a young couple's yin and yang were "replete" *(shi*)*. But only in the case of girls was this advice commonly accompanied by a warning that delaying a girl's marriage too long (more than ten years after puberty) was unwise.[63]

In sum, then, the notion of ripeness shaped thinking about age of marriage more strictly for females than for males. Ideally a stable menstrual cycle established her body's maturation, and social adulthood came to most women through marriage, followed as soon as possible by pregnancy. For males, differences in family circumstances could markedly affect marriage's timing—ranging from child marriages of preadolescent males, in families recruiting a daughter-in-law for her labor power, to prolonged bachelorhood among the poor. Girls married universally and did so relatively young (sixteen to twenty-two *sui*).[64] In their advice on marriage, medical authorities accommodated these social habits, thereby advocating gender differences that were at odds with the yin/yang homology of gender balance in natural philosophy.

More than marriage alone, successful reproduction marked true social maturity within the family. Newly married sons and daughters-in-law continued in roles of service shaped by filial duty, until such time as their own children established them as parents and ancestors-to-be, and the cycle connecting generations was complete. Male adulthood may have been a more socially contingent achievement than female, but there remained an important ritual sense in which the male body also was truly grown when he too had moved from birth to birth, taking his place in the ritual continuum linking generations.

METAPHORS OF BIRTH AND RENEWAL

Running through the classical medical writings on the growing body are sets of numbers that evoke time's cycles of recurrence. When late imperial medical men quoted these hoary passages on the ten months of gestation, the "steaming and changing" of infant growth, or the reproductive curve of the years of *"tiangui,"* they were well aware of the variability of their patients' personal life histories. Numbers were not meant to offer a statistical norm or a generalization applicable to a "population." Numbers marked off a rhythm of timeliness governed by the forces of yin and yang and the Five Phases. They evoked the ideal of normality, of health itself. Even more, they asserted that time's arrow took its flight within a spiraling field of creative renewal, overriding the closure of biography ending in old age and death. Similar metaphors of birth and renewal shaped myths of victory over death in Taoist religious traditions closely associated with medicine. Only the sage practitioner of "inner alchemy" *(nei dan)* combines the medically approved cultivation of long life *(yang sheng)* with the nurture of *yuanqi* within to gestate an "immortal embryo" —germinating in the Gate of Life below the navel and imagined as rising imperceptibly toward the head as the adept's spiritual powers increase. Bypassing the bodily continuum of human generation, the adept has by the moment of his own physical dissolution completed the creation of his reborn and perfected self. In other words, medical thought about the vitalities patterning the growing body also sustained the myth of Laozi's "old child"—whereby, in the microcosm of a single body, birth overpowers death, all energies are nourished and recycled, and nothing is ever finally lost.

NOTES

1. Richard J. Smith, *Fortunetellers and Philosophers: Divination in Traditional Chinese Society* (Boulder: Westview Press, 1991). For an account of these numerical systems applied to divination and astrology see chap. 5, "Knowing Fate."

2. Stephen Jay Gould, *Time's Arrow, Time's Cycle: Myth and Metaphor in the Discovery of Geological Deep Time* (Cambridge, Mass.: Harvard University Press, 1987).

3. *Huangdi neijing* (Yellow Emperor's Inner Canon). This is a composite work—the core dates back to the first century B.C.—and is found in three variant texts: *Su wen* (Basic questions), *Ling shu* (Divine pivot), and *Tai su* (Grand basis). In Ming-Qing China, as today, the works are known via these three texts dating from the eighth century A.D. The edition cited here is Nanjing Zhongyi xueyuan, eds., *Su wen* (Basic questions) (Shanghai: Shanghai kexue zhishu chubanshe, 1983).

4. Sun Simo, *Beiji qianjin yaofang* (Prescriptions worth a thousand for every emergency), in *Siku quanshu,* "Zibu," *juan* 40.

5. Chao Yuanfang, *Zhubing yuanhou lun* (Origins and symptoms of medical disorders), in *Siku quanshu,* "Zibu," *juan* 40.

6. Wang Tao, *Wai tai miyao* (Secret essentials of the imperial library), in *Siku quanshu,* "Zibu," *juan* 42–43.

7. *Yi jing* (Book of Changes), "Xici" (The Great Appendix), pt. 2, chap. 5, in *Shisanjing zhushu, juan* 8, p. 76c

8. See Fung Yu-lan, *History of Chinese Philosophy*, 2 vols. (Princeton: Princeton University Press, 1952), vol. 1, pp. 382–395, for an excellent summary of the passages in the *Book of Changes* that build the cosmos out of these primary oppositions.

9. Li Shizhen (1593, 1596), *Bencao gangmu* (Systematic materia medica), *juan* 52. I use a modern reprint of the 1596 edition in 4 vols. (Beijing: Renmin weisheng chubanshe, 1977, 1979). See vol. 4, p. 2970 (*juan* 52).

10. Wu Zhiwang (1620, 1665), *Ji yin gangmu* (Outline for the salvation of Yin), 1665 edition, ed. Wang Qi (Shanghai: Kezhi weisheng chubanshe, 1958), *juan* 6, p. 179. Identical phrasing is found in Tang Qianqing, *Da sheng yaozhi*, first published in 1762, p. 2a.

11. "Essence" was also identified with the woman's vaginal secretions during intercourse, but in the late imperial era these fluids were not emphasized as generative substances. However, as the quotation from Wu Zhiwang shows, some Chinese medical authorities did teach that orgasm in intercourse was a sign of successful conception.

12. The contrast between Buddhist and Catholic thinking was highlighted in the seventeenth century by debates between European Jesuit missionaries and Chinese scholars. Matteo Ricci's insistence that the immortal "rational soul" of the individual descends into the (male) fetus on the fortieth day after conception was criticized as one of many arbitrary and inflexible categories in Christian natural philosophy. See Jacques Gernet, "Christian and Chinese Visions of the World in the Seventeenth Century," *Chinese Science* 4 (September 1980):10–11.

13. As Arthur Wolf reminds us, the ancestral line points to the communion of spirits linking ancestors and descendants and is not reducible to biology.

14. Some Ming medical authorities, including Sun Yikui and Zhang Jiebin, claimed that the Kidney system, including the Gate of Life, was the first morphological element of the new human being preceding sexual differentiation and before growth depended on material nourishment. This was an effort to fit gestational development into the logic that mandated the formation of "preexistent" heavenly endowment first at conception and linked this endowment with the generative vitalities of *yuanqi*. Sun and others offered various theories about the anatomical relationship of the Kidney system and the Gate of Life. See Ren Yingqiu, *Zhongyi kejia xueshuo* (Discourses of schools of thought in Chinese medicine) (Shanghai: Kexue zhishu chubanshe, 1980), pp. 181–186.

15. Sun Simo, *Beiji qianjin yaofang*, *juan* 2; Wang Tao, *Wai tai miyao*, *juan* 33.

16. For Song variants see [Emperor] Hui Cong, *Sheng ji jing* (Classic of sagely salvation), ed. Liu Xiuqing (Beijing: Renmin weisheng chubanshe, 1990), *juan* 2; and Chen Ziming, *Furen daquan liangfang* (Complete good

prescriptions for women), ed. Yu Ying'ao et al. (Beijing: Renmin weisheng chubanshe, 1985), *juan* 9.

17. Wu Zhiwang and Li Shizhen reported the Taoist Canon *(Dao zang)* as their source. However, in rudimentary form this line of reasoning extends back to Western Han. The Mawangdui "Book of Pregnancy and Childbirth" *(Taichan shu)* states that on the first day after the end of menstrual flow a boy will be conceived, and on the second a girl. See *Mawangdui Han mu boshu* (Beijing: Wenwu chubanshe, 1985), p. 136.

18. Chu Cheng (479–501), *Chu Cheng yi shu* (Bequeathed writings of Chu Cheng). The first known printed edition dates from 1201 with a preface claiming to have been written in 936. This rare work was reprinted several times in the late Ming and widely quoted. Following the opinion of the eighteenth-century *Siku quanshu*, many think that the text was actually a Tang or Song forgery. I use the Ming version in *Shuo fu*, Tao Zongyi comp., reprinted in the *Sibu beiyao, juan* 74. In this quoted passage, instead of the term "foundation" *(ben)*, some texts say "womb" *(bao)*.

19. The Ming–Qing debate on earlier theories of sexual differentiation was in fact quite elaborate. An early summation by Yuan Huang (1533–1606) in *Qi si zhenquan* (Guide to praying for heirs; first published in 1591) was followed closely by Wu Zhiwang *(juan* 6) and Li Shizhen *(juan* 52). For Yuan Huang's text see *Congshu jicheng*, vol. 2986. For eighteenth-century views see the imperial medical encyclopedia, Wu Qian, comp. (1742), *Yi zong jin jian* (Golden mirror of medicine), *juan* 45, "Guang yu men" (On propagation). I use the reprint in 5 vol. (Beijing: Renmin weisheng chubanshe, 1973, 1981); see vol. 3, p. 46. For an ordinary doctor's comment see Cheng Congzhou (1632), *Cheng Maoxian yian* (Medical cases of Cheng Maoxian), *juan* 2, pp. 14b–15a.

20. Chen Xiuyuan, *Nüke yaozhi* (Essentials of medicine for women), "Zhongzi" (Begetting descendants) (Fuzhou: Fujian kexue zhishu chubanshe, 1983), p. 34. The dorsal "superintendant tract" *(du mai)* circulates *qi* from the Gate of Life below to the brain and back along the "conception tract" *(ren mai)*.

21. Fang Lüe, *Shangyoutang yian* (Medical cases from Honoring Friendship Hall), prefaces of 1846, 1847. The emphasis upon right and left sides did not just rely on yin/yang numerology but gained additional credibility from the well-known writings of the thirteenth-century medical master Zhu Danxi. Zhu had reported from his observation of a prolapsed uterus that the womb had two branches on its upper surface.

22. *Chu Cheng yishu* in *Shuo fu, juan* 74, p. 17a.

23. *Bencao gangmu, juan* 52; vol. 4, p. 2968.

24. Xu Ke, *Qing bai lei chao* (Shanghai: Commercial Press, 1917). See the section on "Yi bin" culled from a variety of Qing-era miscellanies.

25. What this line of reasoning shows, of course, is how far early modern

European notions of biological inheritance were shaped by metaphors reflecting an aristocratic preoccupation with family descent conceptualized as "blood." In ritual contexts Chinese sometimes spoke of "bone" to signify the fleshly tie between members of a patriline and claimed, as in the Sacred Edict of the Emperor Kangxi in the seventeenth century, that brothers are "bone and blood of one father." Ann Waltner argues convincingly that this is a ritual rather than a biological concept. See Waltner, *Getting an Heir: Adoption and the Construction of Kinship in Late Imperial China* (Honolulu: University of Hawai'i Press, 1990), chap. 1. Another religiously based belief about family inheritance may be found in popular Buddhism in the notion that a family's accumulated store of karmic merit is a treasury that individuals draw upon and add to by their own conduct. See Cynthia Brokaw, *The Ledgers of Merit and Demerit: Social Change and Moral Order in Late Imperial China* (Princeton: Princeton University Press, 1991).

26. *Bencao gangmu, juan* 52; vol. 4, p. 2968. This is the context for Li's famous discussion of environmental influences on human and animal characteristics: "Lice which inhabit human hair are black while pig lice are white; creatures which get their food from water smell rank; grass-eating creatures smell frowsy. Those who eat rich food and wear gauze and silk have big bellies and white skin like jadestone."

27. Earlier accounts of gestation are found in the *Huainanzi* and in the Mawangdui manuscripts—both dating from the Western Han. These are direct ancestors of later medical versions. For the *Huainanzi* see "Jing shen xun" (Instructions on essence and spirit), *juan* 7; see also *Mawangdui Han mu boshu*, p. 136.

28. See Sun Simo, *Beiji qianjin yaofang, juan* 2; Chao Yuanfang, *Zhubing yuanhou lun, juan* 41; and Wang Tao, *Wai tai miyao, juan* 33, for virtually identical versions of the ten months of gestation. For a seventeenth-century version see *Ji yin gangmu, juan* 6.

29. Comment by Wang Qi, editor of the *Ji yin gangmu*, in an eyebrow note in the 1665 edition; see also the 1958 reprint ed., *juan* 6, p. 187. Wang Qi continued to explain how the "mutual production" and "mutual conquest" sequences of the Five Phases both were operative in the process.

30. For a discussion see Kristofer Schipper, *Le corps Taoiste: corps physique—corps social* (Paris: Fayard, 1982), p. 161.

31. Sun Simo believed that sexual differentiation occurred as the fetus formed and argued that during the first three months of pregnancy "the inner responds to the outer and the child's nature will be influenced by the mother's circumstances." Such actions as riding horses, gazing on wild animals, and wearing a knife were part of a repertory for influencing events. In the Ming and Qing, such beliefs were no longer acceptable to most elite doctors, in keeping with a general shift to a more internalist analysis of body functioning. The minority who supported surviving folk versions of these beliefs explained that the child's sex was in fact "changed" by such ritual

manipulations. For earlier theories of fetal instruction see Anne Behnke Kinney's essay in this volume (Chapter 1).

32. *Ji yin gangmu, juan* 6, p. 187.

33. Hsiung Ping-chen has found several such references in literati biographies of their own mothers. See "Constructed Emotions: The Bond Between Mothers and Sons in Late Imperial China," *Late Imperial China* 15(1) (1994):91.

34. Francesca Bray, "Abortion in China 1600–1900: Ethics and Identity" (paper presented to the International Conference on the Construction of Gender and Sexuality in East and Southeast Asia, UCLA, December 9–11, 1990).

35. Sung Tz'u, *The Washing Away of Wrongs (Xi yuan ji lu)*, trans. Brian E. McKnight (Ann Arbor: University of Michigan Center for Chinese Studies, 1981), p. 84. The offense was considered a lesser one if the fetus was not yet formed, here defined as having visible head, mouth, eyes, ears, nose, hands, feet, and umbilical cord.

36. *Da sheng pian* (On successful childbirth). This text was first published in 1715. For an account of its publication history see Charlotte Furth, "Concepts of Pregnancy, Childbirth and Infancy in Ch'ing Dynasty China," *Journal of Asian Studies* 46(1) (February 1987):7–35.

37. For a detailed discussion of gestation and childbirth see Furth, "Concepts of Pregnancy, Childbirth and Infancy in Ch'ing Dynasty China."

38. "Fetal poison" as a gestational or pediatric category cannot be found in the early Tang-dynasty medical classics by Sun Simo, Chao Yuanfang, or Wang Tao. This suggests that the complex of beliefs surrounding fetal poison discussed in my 1987 article grew up later, as smallpox became endemic as a childhood disease. Earlier authorities simply noted that bathing a newborn with cleansing pig's gall would help prevent rashes and eczema in the future.

39. Sun Simo, *Beiji qianjin yaofang, juan* 8–9.

40. Author's preface in Chen Fuzheng, *You you jicheng* (Complete pediatrics), first published in 1750 (Shanghai: Shanghai kexue zhishi chubanshe, 1962, 1978).

41. Sun Simo, *Beiji qianjin yaofang, juan* 8; Wang Tao, *Wai tai miyao, juan* 35. For an eighteenth-century account see *Yi zong jin jian*, vol. 3, pp. 48–49 *(juan* 50).

42. The phrase is Cheng Fuzheng's. The *Yi zong jin jian* reads: "When changing and steaming have run their course, physique *(xing*)* and psyche *(shen)* are mature." See Wu Qian, *Yi zong jin jian*, vol. 3, pp. 48–49 *(juan* 50).

43. See *Xinglie riji* by "Jiaomengshi zhuren" (Master of Study of Creative Vitality), hand-copied diary in the library of the Research Institute of Traditional Chinese Medicine, Beijing, dated 1796, p. 4b.

44. For modern field research bearing on this issue, see Marjorie Topley, "Cosmic Antagonisms: A Mother-Child Syndrome," in Arthur P. Wolf, ed.,

Religion and Ritual in Chinese Society (Stanford: Stanford University Press, 1974), pp. 233–249.

45. Chao Yuanfang, *Zhubin yuanhou lun, juan* 45. Chao's advice was to have the child wear light clothing and to "let it see the sun and the moon," reminding his audience that grass grown in deep yin shade does not thrive.

46. For further discussion see Charlotte Furth, "Blood, Body and Gender: Medical Images of the Female Condition in China: 1600–1800," *Chinese Science* 7 (1986):43–66.

47. *Xinglie riji*, p. 7a.

48. See, for example, the various editions of the *Wanbao quanshu* (Almanac of ten thousand treasures), sections entitled "Xiaoer guan sha" (Gates of baleful influences on children) or "Xiaoer sha ge" (Songs to ward off baleful influences on children). In Taoist folklore "*sha*" are demon spirits. See also Smith, *Fortunetellers and Philosophers*, pp. 63–65.

49. For a twentieth-century description of one such temple in Qianfodong near Dunhuang, see Joseph Needham, *China and the Origins of Immunology* (Hong Kong: Center of Asian Studies, 1980), pp. 2–3.

50. See the essay by Pei-yi Wu in this volume (Chapter 5).

51. For a discussion of these arts see Smith, *Fortunetellers and Philosophers*, chap. 5.

52. Sun Simo, *Beiji qianjin yaofang, juan* 8.

53. One would expect more attention to the issue given its proven association with malnutrition. One intriguing possibility is that weaning was less of a health issue due to the widespread, medically recommended practice of giving infants prechewed solid food, often as early as the second month. A locus classicus for this advice is Sun Simo, *Beiji qianjin yaofang, juan* 9. The standard term for infant feeding was "*ru bu*"—referring to both liquid and solid nourishment.

54. According to the *Yi zong jin jian*, vol. 3, p. 63 (*juan* 52, "Yuke zabing: gan zheng men"): "Those under fifteen *sui* suffer from *gan;* those over fifteen *sui* suffer from *lao* (fatigue)." *Gan* are identified by moderns with anemias, deficiency disorders, and malnutrition in children.

55. See, for example, Zheng Chongguang, *Supu yian* (Medical cases from the plain garden), original preface 1707, cases 161–162; reprinted in *Zhen ben yi shu jicheng* (Collection of rare medical books) (Shanghai: Shanghai kexue zhishi chubanshe, 1986), vol. 13.

56. Sun Simo, *Beiji qianjin yaofang, juan* 9.

57. *Huangdi neijing: su wen*, "On Ancient Heavenly Truth" *(Shanggu tianzhen lun), juan* 1, Shanghai 1983 ed., pp. 4–5.

58. *Yi zong jin jian*, "Guang yu men" (On propagation), *juan* 45; vol. 3, p. 45.

59. Interpreting the numbers involved some ingenuity, since the *Book of Changes* correspondence theory identified odd numbers with *qian* and even with *kun*. However, since yin/yang cosmology also taught that every yin has

incipient yang within it, and vice versa, Wu Zhiwang explained as follows: "Males are yang and within every yang there must be a yin. Eight is the yin number within yang, so at eight a male's yang Essence ascends," etc. See *Ji yin gangmu*, p. 183.

60. Zhang Jingyue [Zhang Jiebin], *Zhi yi lu* (On doubtful matters), original ed. 1624, included in a rare Qing-era edition of Zhang's collected works: *Zhang Jingyue yishu shisan zhong* (Bequeathed works of Zhang Jingyue in thirteen sections) held by the Gest Library at Princeton. See sec. 11, vol. 3, pp. 36a/b.

61. There are undoubtedly many exceptions to this statement. One important exception was the many communities in southeast coastal China, both those identified as minority and those not, where boys' and girls' houses allowed adolescents to live away from the parental roof.

62. See the essay by Lucien Miller in this volume (Chapter 8).

63. In advising against delay, medical men were drawing upon the words of Chu Cheng.

64. This has been nicely demonstrated for the Song elite by Patricia Ebrey, using evidence from epitaphs. See her "Marriage Among the Song Elite" in Stevan Harrell, ed., *Chinese Microdemography* (Berkeley: University of California Press, forthcoming).

GLOSSARY

bao	胞	womb
ben	本	foundation
bian zheng	變烝	"changing and steaming"
bin	稟	natural endowment
cheng	成	maturation; realization
cheng ren	成人	to become human; to mature
chong	衝	"highway" (pulse)
du mai	督脉	"superintendent" (pulse)
er	兒	baby
erke	兒科	pediatrics
gan	疳	malnutrition
gao	膏	embryo; embryonic fat
guan	關	mountain pass; turning point
guang si	廣嗣	to increase descent lines
houtian	後天	the temporal world
houtian yuanqi	後天元氣	temporal original *qi*
jing	精	Essence; semen
jing feng	驚風	fright wind
kun	坤	second hexagram of the *Book of Changes*

ling	靈	spiritual; numinous
ming men	命門	the Gate of Life; vital gate
nei dan	內丹	inner alchemy
pei	胚	embryo; embryonic mud
qi	氣	cosmic energy; the primary vitality of the body
qian	乾	first hexagram in the *Book of Changes*
ren	任	"conception" pulse
ren mai	任脉	the "conception" tract
ren shen	人神	the human psyche
ru bu	乳哺	infant feeding
sha guan	煞關	passes of baleful influences
shen	神	Kidney system
sheng	生	growth; birth
shi	始	beginning
*shi**	實	replete
si	嗣	children (as descendants)
sui	歲	years
tai	胎	fetus
tai du	胎毒	fetal poison
tai jiao	胎教	fetal education
tian hua	天花	smallpox
tiangui	天癸	reproductive capability; puberty
tiangui zhi	天癸至	puberty arrives
tiao jing	調經	menstrual regulation
wan chengzhe	晚成者	those who are late to reach maturity
wei	衛	defensive *qi* sector
wen	文	patterns in nature; literary art
wu xing	五行	the Five Phases
xi dou	希痘	light pox
xiantian	先天	pre-existent
"*xiantian zhen zhi* ling qi"	先天真之靈氣	pre-existent perfected spirit *qi*
xie	邪	pathogen
xing	性	nature
*xing**	形	material form
xiu shen	修身	spiritual self-cultivation
xue	血	Blood
yang sheng	養生	to cultivate long life
yi bin	異稟	extraordinary endowment
ying	營	constructive *qi* sector
yinger	嬰兒	infancy

yuan	元	origins
yuanqi	元氣	primal *qi*
zhen qi	真氣	perfected *qi*
zhen yin	真陰	true yin
zhong zi	種子	to plant descendants; to beget young
zi	子	descendant

7

Infanticide and Dowry in Ming and Early Qing China

ANN WALTNER

In the past decade or so, historians of China have increasingly turned their attention to matters of private life, examining such subjects as family dynamics, sexuality, and childhood. In our attempts to reimagine the past, we are asking questions about the intimate details of personal lives. The sources available to us, however, are not always forthcoming about these matters. The questions we ask and the questions our sources address do not always converge. We are placed in the complex (and sometimes unenviable) position of pushing our sources to tell us what it is we want to know, rather than what it is they want to tell us. In this essay I address the question of infanticide in Ming (1368–1644) and early Qing (1644–1911) dynasty China. To do this, I have assembled information from a variety of sources. I will discuss the ways in which these sources address the logic of infanticide—not to determine whether or not the sources are accurate representations of social reality but to elucidate what kind of problem contemporaries saw infanticide to be.

The problems of studying infanticide are compounded by its resonance with other issues: the contemporary American debate on abortion, for example, and the continuing practice of female infanticide in China. Further, because infanticide (like footbinding) was an issue that was stressed by early observers as a marker of Chinese difference (and even barbarism), modern scholars who have tried to arrive at a more nuanced, if not more balanced, view of cultural difference have avoided it.[1] The difficulty of determining one's own position toward practices like infanticide and footbinding has also made them virtually untouched subjects for many years. Only now are we beginning to see serious scholarly work on these topics.[2] Demographers have begun to look at infanticide,[3] and feminist scholars interested in the cultural construction of the body have begun to investigate footbinding.[4]

We have long known that infanticide existed in traditional China. Anecdotal evidence abounds in both history and fiction. In "The Case of the Dead Infant," a story in the *San yan* collection edited by Feng Menglong (1574–1646), a widow renowned for her chastity kills the child conceived of an affair with a serving boy. From a historical record, we learn that when the official Zhu Wan (1494–1550) was born of a concubine, his father's principal wife and her three grown sons schemed to kill the infant, though he survived.[5] But these two examples, which illustrate infanticide as a means to conceal the fruit of an illicit affair on the one hand and as a strategy to seize domestic power on the other, do not explain the motivation behind all cases. I would like to suggest that infanticide, particularly female infanticide, was part of a population strategy in traditional China, that it formed a part of what Jack Goody would call a "hidden economy of kinship," and that it has a necessary connection with other aspects of the kinship system—specifically, with the status of women and the nature of dowry. It is on this latter point that I wish to concentrate.[6]

We are fortunately not limited to anecdote in our attempt to understand the practice of infanticide in traditional China. More information on attitudes may be found in a variety of normative texts, and population data may convey some sense of its frequency.

NORMATIVE TEXTS

Legal texts, magistrates' manuals, and moral texts are all useful sources of information about Ming attitudes toward infanticide. We can begin by noting that infanticide is not directly addressed by the Ming and Qing legal codes, though the killing of one's own child was. In the codes of both the Ming and the Qing dynasties, unreasonably killing one's own child was to be punished by sixty strokes and a year of penal servitude. The punishment seems light. Publishing and distributing prohibited books, for example, was punished more severely.[7] Killing a stranger (or a senior member of one's own family) might easily incur the death penalty. Principles of hierarchy pervade the Chinese legal system; parents might not have had the legal power of life and death over their offspring, but punishments for usurping that power were rather light. Nevertheless, the legal codes were not the only instruments with which the realm was ruled. While codes *(lü)* were conceptualized as unchanging for all time, certain issues were treated in administrative regulations *(li)*, which later might or might not be incorporated into the legal codes. Administrative regulations issued from the period 1500 to 1585 do proscribe infanticide specifically: the penalty is servitude at a military outpost one thousand *li** away from home.[8] The penalty is harsh, but not so harsh as that for murder.

Another important source of information on infanticide is the magistrate's manual. These works often mention infanticide as a practice that conscientious magistrates must attempt to curb. In late imperial China, the local magistrate was responsible for supervising a wide variety of tasks for which he generally had no specialized training. Experienced magistrates would therefore on occasion write manuals that outlined the tasks of governing and provided advice for other magistrates. They are a superb source for information on the problems of practical governance facing local magistrates in Ming and Qing China. In one such manual, Huang Liuhong (1630–ca. 1715) states that preventing infanticide was one of the tasks a lax magistrate was likely to shirk. Failure to cultivate fruit trees, to repair roads and pathways, or to prevent women from visiting temples all appear on the same list of potential failures. All of these seemingly disparate arenas for potential neglect are, Huang argued, "closely related to the maintenance of good social order" and hence of direct concern to a magistrate.[9] As we shall see, it is significant that the argument is cast in terms of preserving social order rather than in terms of preserving life. The chief means for combating infanticide at the magistrate's disposal, according to Huang, was the establishment of foundling homes. And indeed charters of foundling homes frequently mention that their purpose was to prevent, as one of them put it, "the cruelty of drowning babies."[10] In some cases, officials advised issuing emergency relief to stem the tide of this custom. Chen Longzheng, for example, describes an episode on the first day of the third lunar month of 1630, when the ghosts of boys and girls thrown in rivers by their parents in thousands of villages raised their voices in a collective outcry. Moved by the cries, Chen's wife persuaded him to distribute grain to relieve the famine that had precipitated the mass infanticide.[11]

The eradication of infanticide and abortion was also of interest to the compilers of morality books. These books, which appeared in the sixteenth and seventeenth centuries and rapidly attained popularity, are a distillation of Buddhist, Taoist, and Confucian ideas of morality. They prescribe good deeds and proscribe evil ones as a kind of moral checklist and as an aid to the attainment of nirvana or sagehood. Many texts ascribe a specific number of merits for the performance of a good deed and demerits for an evil one. In some cases, these texts treat abortion and infanticide as similar offenses; sometimes infanticide is treated as a more serious infraction. The *Gan ying pian* (Tract on Retribution and Response), for example, lists infanticide and abortion as paired misdeeds.[12] But the Yuan-dynasty (1280–1368) *Jingshi gongguoge* (Ledger of Merits and Demerits to Warn the World) distinguishes between the two. In that text, infanticide results in one thousand demerits, the most serious punishment, the same as that appropriate for the crime of offending one's parents, violating a chaste woman, selling a housemaid into prostitution, or causing a death. An abortion elicits three hundred demerits.[13] From the perspective of reward rather than punishment, Yuan Huang's (1533–1606) *Gongguoge* (Ledger of Merits and Demerits) allocates one hundred merits to the saving of a life, preserving a woman's chastity, preventing an abortion, and preventing someone from drowning an infant.[14] Preventing infanticide, it is interesting to note, is as meritorious as saving a life. But it is not the same deed: infanticide is analytically distinct from murder. The two infractions, given equal weight, receive separate mention. Medical texts present a picture of infancy that sheds light on the distinction between the two acts. As Charlotte Furth has explained, medical literature views birth as a matter of exposing an immature organ system to the outer world. Not until the phase of infancy *(yinger)* has passed does the child take on the attributes of full personhood.[15] Therefore, destroying an infant, however reprehensible the act may be, is not equivalent to murder because the infant still resides in a liminal state.

Infanticide seems to be an issue in all these genres, indicating both the prevalence of the custom and the persistence of opposition to it. The magistrate as well as the moralist had an interest in curbing infanticide. Nonetheless, the specific ways in which they articulated those interests, as we shall see, reveal much about their views on children, female infants in particular.

GENDER AND INFANTICIDE

The texts I have cited thus far speak of infanticide in traditional China as if it were not gender-specific. Yet from what we know, based on reports of anthropologists working in contemporary Chinese societies, on demographic analysis of population, and on the kind of textual evidence I outline below, baby girls were more likely

to be killed than baby boys.[16] Indeed some observers have gone so far
as to label daughters in some times and places as "luxuries."[17] A Chinese text written as early as the second century, the *Taiping jing,* rails
against infanticide directed at female babies in particular, while
noting the resultant scarcity of women and its cosmological implications:

> Now, ever since the world lost the *Tao,* there are many people who,
> not content with despising their daughters, kill them so that there are
> fewer women than men, which leads to the fact that *yin* is diminished
> and does not correspond any more to the norms of heaven and earth.[18]

That infanticide was likely to be gender-specific is also shown by a
provision in a Yuan-dynasty law stating that anyone who killed a
baby girl would have half their family property confiscated; there is
no mention of killing male infants. If the perpetrator were a bondservant, he would be punished to the same degree as a free *(liang)*
person. And if the officials in charge did not prosecute, they too
would be punished.[19] Moreover, although it is true that monetary
compensation was a more important form of punishment in the Yuan
than it was earlier or later (probably due to the influence of Mongol
customs), it is interesting, in light of the argument about dowry and
infanticide that I intend to make, that the penalty is the confiscation
of property rather than a more conventional punishment such as
beating or exile.[20] If dowry cost a family property, then so too would
female infanticide. But one Hunan magistrate of the late seventeenth
century suggested that rather than punishing those who killed their
daughters, those who permitted them to live should be rewarded.
Accordingly, any family who raised at least two daughters would be
awarded a wooden tablet extolling its virtue.[21]

As suggested earlier, population data also afford important clues
as to the prevalence of gender-specific infanticide. Sex ratios—ideally
age-specific sex ratios—should provide a good idea of the fate of girl
babies relative to that of boy babies. But the interpretation of
Chinese population data is difficult because females are seriously
underreported. The census, of which we have a preserved record in a
more or less regular fashion since the Han dynasty, was taken primarily for the purpose of assessing taxes. The basic unit of taxation
was the *ding,* the adult male. Nonadult females were of less interest
to the census taker than were adult males. Thus when one sees sex
ratios such as the one for Shanghai in 1572—460.4 males per 100

females—one is hard pressed to interpret them.[22] The figure is almost certainly not a real sex ratio: yet what does it represent?

Census records are not the only source for the study of the Chinese population. Lineage groups maintained their own genealogical records, many of which have been preserved. Here again, however, females, especially females who died young, are underreported. Moreover, the principles by which genealogies recorded members might vary. Because females, who marry out and produce heirs for other lineages, are not genealogically significant in the same sense that males are, they are generally not recorded with the same care. A lineage with a paucity of recorded daughters is not necessarily killing them: it may simply not be recording them.[23]

Nonetheless, despite the limitations of the sources, scholars have attempted to calculate Ming sex ratios. Let us look for a moment at some of these attempts. Detailed age-specific sex ratios are impossible to obtain because the census does not record ages, though in some areas a distinction is made between persons younger than sixteen and those older than sixteen. Ho Ping-ti finds that in Yongzhou (southwestern Hunan) in 1381–1382, the sex ratio for the population as a whole was 125.9 males per 100 females; for children it was 161.4 and for adults it was 109.2. The startling difference between the sex ratios of adults and children suggests that girl children might have been underreported. In Shanghai county, he finds the sex ratios among the population as a whole in 1391 to be 109.8; in 1412, 111.8; in 1520, 220.8; and in 1572, 460.4.[24] The latter figures (those of 1520 and 1572) are probably inaccurate. Most scholars agree that while the early Ming census is fairly sound, late Ming population data are suspect.[25] Michael Marmé finds the sex ratio in Ming Suzhou to be 108.7 males per 100 females.[26] John Dardess suggests that among members of the elite in Ming Taihe (Jiangxi province) there is what he calls a "theoretically real" sex ratio of 110 males to 100 females.[27] Other estimates of sex ratios in premodern China fall within a similar range: men outnumber women.[28]

SCARCITY OF WOMEN

Let us for a moment accept these sex ratios—though it should be stressed that much work remains to be done before we know all we need to know about sex ratios in traditional China. The sex ratios do indicate a scarcity of females. But it is important to note that traditional Chinese society not only had a net scarcity of females, it was polygamous. Although a man could marry only one principal wife, he was free to take as many concubines as he wished and could afford. Nonetheless, concubinage seems to have been restricted to the upper echelons of society. Estimates based on the number of concubines registered in genealogies suggest that between 1 and 4 percent of all consorts were concubines.[29] Moreover, unless one's principal wife had not borne a son, there was a slight aura of moral disfavor attached to the practice of collecting concubines. For example, the eighteenth-century ledger of merits and demerits, the *Meritorious Deeds at No Cost,* counsels men against keeping too many concubines.[30] If the principal wife had no son, then indeed a concubine was appropriate. The continuity of the line of descent was a moral priority of the first order. Yet even if a concubine were appropriate, supporting a second spouse could be expensive, and it could be difficult to find a suitable woman willing to join a household where she would be forever doomed to a position of subservience, not only to her husband, but also to his primary wife.

The shortage of women led to a shortage of wives. Eighteenth-century officials such as Chen Hongmou and Zhu Chun noted that in Jiangsu local bullies abducted young widows as brides.[31] That marriage was not universal (and that it was a universal ideal) is shown by *Meritorious Deeds at No Cost,* which counsels: "Help those who have been unable to marry to get married."[32] Family instructions also indicate that male marriage was not universal. Wang Shijin's family instructions reveal the presence of unmarried males and attribute a man's failure to find a wife to moral causes. He cites a proverb: "The sons of perverse families do not find wives; the sons of disorderly families do not find wives."[33] Marriage validated one's moral status, but it was not an option for all men. One modern demographer writing on Tongcheng (Anhui province) during the Ming–Qing period describes the situation as "an endemic 'marriage crunch' felt most keenly by lower class males."[34] The contemporary scholar T'ien Ju-k'ang describes a situation in Ming Fujian where in some areas half of the adult men were unmarried.[35] Although the evidence is sketchy, the implications are clear: women were scarce.

Why were women scarce? One might offer several hypotheses, but one inescapable suggestion is that women were scarce because female children were disadvantaged. Outright infanticide was probably compounded by relative neglect—male children were probably better nourished and in general had better access to family resources than did female children. Many aspects of the patrilineal society of Ming China favored male children. Only males could continue the family line by carrying out sacrifices to the ancestors, and male children provided a much better source of security in old age than did females. A woman's ties with and obligations to her family of birth were weakened by her marriage. She was expected to put the needs of her in-laws above those of her own parents, and she generally did. When families made decisions about the futures of their sons and daughters, the needs of the dead ancestors for sacrifices, the needs of the living parents for support in their old age, and the needs of unborn descendants for a continued patriline all favored male offspring.

The preference for male children could have deadly consequences for daughters. T'ien Ju-k'ang plausibly argues that the practice of female infanticide had become "rampant" in densely populated areas during the Ming. He cites a memorial by Zheng Jing, a subdirector of studies from Wenzhou, who reported to the throne in 1484 the seriousness of the problem there. When the Board of Censors forwarded the information, they added that the custom of female infanticide was also widespread in all of Zhejiang, Jiangxi, Fujian, and Nan Zhili.[36]

Matteo Ricci (1552–1610), the observant Italian Jesuit, also noted the practice of infanticide:

A far more serious evil here is the practice in some provinces of disposing of some infants by drowning them. The reason assigned for this is that their parents despair of being able to support them. At times this is done also by people who are not abjectly poor, for fear that the time might come when they would not be able to care for these children and they would be forced to sell them to unknown or cruel slave masters.[37]

Ricci does not describe infanticide as gender-linked but notes that it was practiced even among those who were not "abjectly poor." That infanticide was not limited to the destitute is corroborated by other sources. An essay by Ji Erbi contained in Li Yu's *Zizhi xinshu* (late seventeenth century) states that in Yanzhou (Zhejiang province), where he had served as an official, the custom of drowning girls prevailed among both the rich and the poor.[38] In many cases, however, the problem of female infanticide is clearly linked to poverty. Occasionally the economic pressure to dispose of female infants is reinforced by local custom. For example, the Ji'an gazetteer reports that in Anfu (southern Jiangxi) in the late Ming and early Qing, it was customary for a tenant who bore a girl baby to give the landlord a gift of silver before naming her. As a result, the gazetteer reports that many tenants drowned their daughters.[39] The account does not tell us why the landlords demanded silver at the birth of a daughter and not a son, but the presence of the custom indicates one of the ways in which class, local custom, and gender oppression could become intertwined.

THE FAMILY POLITICS OF FEMALE INFANTICIDE

Other sources provide us with some suggestions of the tortured domestic dynamics involved when a baby girl was killed. Wang Shijin tells us that women in mismanaged families are apt to drown their children, both boys and girls, and warns that infanticide implicates the entire family in trouble.[40] The gazetteer from Fuqing county in Fuzhou prefecture contains another account written in about 1625:

> The killing of newborn baby girls is the most horrible custom of this county. A survey by households reports that it is practiced by almost every family. After giving birth to a baby, the mothers are often in a semiconscious state and are afraid of touching cold water. The husbands are not allowed, nor willing, to enter the delivery room and the sisters-in-law are mainly nervous and scared. So the midwife is always the only person who has her wits about her and can do whatever she likes. Since she has no flesh-and-blood ties with the baby, she can lay her murderous hands on the newborn infant without a flinch. When a baby is born, the midwife holds it in her hands for examination. If it is a girl, she just throws her into a tub and asks the mother, "Keep it or not?" If the answer is "No," she calls for water and holds the baby upside down by the feet, dipping her head into the water. A healthy and strong infant will struggle and scream, so that the midwife will have to press the baby's head down firmly until her feeble cry dies away. All the while the mother is lying on the bed, helpless and heartbroken, bursting into tears. When the baby is motionless and dead, the midwife rises from her stool, tidies her dress, and asks for food and wine and her payment of money. Then she leaves the house in a triumphant mood, striding along with buoyant steps.[41]

Here the immediate villain is the midwife, who moves easily from drowning the child to asking for payment, feeling no remorse for her dreadful deed. Midwives in traditional China often had a somewhat unsavory reputation.[42] Family instructions warned against midwives as one of the categories of "six crones" whose visits brought disorder to the women's quarters.[43] Most births in traditional China were attended by a midwife: that such an essential person is labeled as dangerous in family instructions stems at least partially from the fact that at the birth she is "the only person who has her wits about her." Her authority at such a crucial moment in the life of a family is what marks her as dangerous. But the midwife does not decide on her own to kill the child: she asks the mother, who is later heartbroken at a decision that we must assume was not hers alone. Note that because the father is absent from the delivery room, he is absent from the entire drama. (The text tells us that he is not allowed there and, further, that he is unwilling to be there.) In this scene, female infanticide takes place in a world of women, and the murderous hands are those of the midwife, not those of a family member.

But the drama is constructed differently in another gazetteer. An entry in the Jiajing-era (1521–1567) gazetteer from Chun'an (Anhui) tells us that the reason people often did not raise their daughters was because of high dowries. The gazetteer goes on to tell us that in 1524 a magistrate named Yao Mingluan issued a proclamation that read:

> When people of Chun give birth to daughters, they often drown and kill them. Prohibitions do not stop it. I have reprinted an old song, exhorting people to raise their daughters, in order to startle them into awareness. The song says:
>
> > *Tigers and wolves: their nature is extremely evil,*
> > *But even they know the proper relation between father and child.*
> > *Among the myriad things only humans possess spirit* (ling),
> > *How is it that they alone are ignorant of this rule?*
> > *Giving birth to a boy or giving birth to a girl,*
> > *You should embrace them equally—that's all there is to it.*
> > *But those who have boys nourish them,*
> > *While those who have girls do not raise them.*
> > *I have heard that when a girl is killed,*
> > *Her being is miserable beyond compare.*
> > *Blood from the womb is still flowing out;*
> > *She has a mouth but she cannot speak.*
> > *She cries in the basin of water,*
> > *And after a long while, she dies.*
> > *Alas: the love between father and child*

Has declined to this point.
Therefore I instruct my people,
Not to kill their daughters.
Her hairpins and her clothes
Need not impoverish you.
Marry according to your station,
And man and woman will each get what is coming to them.
Let this song be distributed among the people,
And let my people remember it.[44]

Yao was the chief compiler of the gazetteer that features his reform efforts so prominently, and he was new to his posting in Chun'an when he promulgated this song in 1524. A native of Putian in Fujian, he received his *juren* degree in 1509 and his *jinshi* in 1520.[45] According-ing to a later edition of the Yanzhou local history, after his death the locals established a shrine to honor him.[46]

The practice of writing (or, in this case, distributing) morally uplifting songs in simple language was widespread in the Ming. Lü Kun (1536–1618), a late Ming magistrate and moralist, wrote and promulgated a number of ditties expounding moral reform.[47] Yang Dongming (1548–1642) went so far as to have short didactic songs performed for the edification of the indigent in the soup kitchens he sponsored.[48] These songs were one of the ways in which officials and literati bent on reform could reach illiterate people. As such, they are important sources of information on the ways in which political and moral propaganda was distributed. Reform of local customs to bring them in line with the value systems of the literati was a matter of high priority to officials. In the song promulgated by Yao Mingluan, infanticide is clearly marked as a class problem: the people who kill their baby girls are perhaps illiterate, and they kill their daughters because they fear the expense of raising and dowering them. Yet according to this ditty, raising daughters is expensive only if one has ambitions beyond one's station.

The poem begins by comparing the people of Chun'an to tigers and wolves, and it is not a comparison that redounds to the advantage of the locals. Human beings, who alone of the creatures of the universe possess spiritual efficacy *(ling)*, also are the only ones who kill their daughters. Nature is here used to criticize a human society that has become alienated from the emotional truths which even the most vicious of natural creatures, tigers and wolves, understand. Yao describes the bloody scene of the baby's murder with pathos and drama. And he concludes by telling people that if they marry according to their station, the need for the dreadful practice will stop.

Both the victim and the villain of the poem are gendered. It is clear that the child at risk in this poem is a girl: the gender of the child is specified in every instance but two. Moreover, in these two instances Yao invokes the moral imperative of familial relations—in the first case, invoking the proper relation between father and child that even the tigers and wolves follow; in the second, decrying that the love between father and child has decayed to the point where infanticide is possible. The father, not the mother, is presented as the authoritative figure, the parent in charge of the bloody deed. Infanticide in this story represents the dissolution of the father/child relationship.

In Chinese thought, the father/child relationship is of course one of the five primary relationships; it is seen as analogous to the bond between minister and ruler and therefore has important political resonances.[49] Since the relationship is hierarchical, the burden for its actualization falls on the status inferior. Nonetheless there is an ethical imperative on the status superior to behave in a moral and compassionate way. A man who could kill his daughter is thus morally damaged and, by analogy, might fail in the other relationships fundamental to social and cosmic order. Thus we can see here how the killing of girl babies is perceived as a pernicious custom that must be stopped. It is not merely a domestic issue; it has public and even political ramifications. An evil father is not a reliable subject.

I am not suggesting here that Yao is unsympathetic to the plight of girl babies; what I am suggesting is that he sees female infanticide as an issue which strikes at the very heart of the social order. It is an argument resonant with the *Taiping jing*'s concern with female infanticide destroying the cosmic balance of yin and yang. Yet according to the reports of Yao's famous successor, Hai Rui (1518–1587), who was magistrate in Chun'an from 1558 to 1562, children in Chun'an, Yao's efforts notwithstanding, remained in peril.[50]

THE CHANGING SIGNIFICANCE OF DOWRIES

The father may be the immediate agent of evil in Yao's poem, but the true villain in the piece is the dowry system. Because the dowry system is intimately connected with the lives of little girls, it is worth turning our attention to its mechanics.

Ming writers who deplored the practice of female infanticide frequently cite dowry as a primary cause. In the late fifteenth century, Zheng Jing reported to the Chenghua emperor that the widespread drowning of daughters he saw in Zhejiang was due to parents' concerns about marriage expenses. Zheng concluded his memorial by saying, "In terms of harming life and damaging customs *(shang sheng huai su)*, nothing is worse than this." The emperor's response acknowledged the gravity of the situation: "Human life *(renming)* is of utmost importance, and the bond between father and child is most intimate. Now we have people, who because of worries about marriage, damage benevolence and destroy righteousness." The emperor goes on to say that preventing infanticide is the responsibility of officials, and if people persist in providing lavish dowries, then neighbors should come forward to prevent them from doing so.[51] Zhang Mou (1437–1522) was another official concerned about the link between the prevalence of infanticide and the escalation of dowry.[52]

These concerns do not diminish with the passing of the dynasty. Lü Kun commented in the late sixteeenth century that in the Jiangnan region (the rich area of the Yangzi delta), female infanticide was high because of high dowries.[53] Another late Ming scholar, Liu Zongzhou, wrote that because marriage expenses were like a debt from a former life, poor people drowned baby girls.[54] Liu went on to observe that the attempts of another Jiangsu official at stopping the custom were to no avail until he finally hit upon the idea of limiting dowries.[55]

What are we to make of this putative connection between infanticide and dowry? I should begin by saying that we still do not know very much about dowries in the Ming. It is clear that they must have varied enormously with time, social class, and region. Until we get a firmer grip on the economics of marriage transactions in the Ming, our understanding of both gender relations and family formation and their implications for infanticide will remain hazy.[56] But let us speculate. Patricia Ebrey has argued that in the Song dynasty there was a change in the nature of marriage finance—that dowry contributed by the bride's family became, for the first time, more substantial than the brideprice contributed by the groom's family. She attributes this shift to a host of other changes that accompanied the Tang–Song transition. For example, increasing social mobility—indeed, changes in the way social structure was constituted—meant that affinal relatives (relatives through marriage) had potentially greater significance.[57] Ebrey cites Yuan Cai (1140–1190) on dowry: "Without going overboard, people should provide their daughters with dowries in line with their family's wealth. Rich families should not consider their daughters outsiders but give them a share of the property." Ebrey suggests that Yuan's ideas were widely held by members of the Song upper class and intimates that a daughter's right to a dowry was as absolute as a son's right to an inheritance.[58] Dowry seems to have persisted. Susan Mann has suggested that in the eighteenth century, dowry was the hallmark of a respectable marriage among even families of rather modest means.[59] It seems to be what distinguishes marriage as a wife from marriage as a concubine.[60] The one-way flow of wealth that marked the acquisition of a concubine demeaned her: it was as if she had been purchased.

Despite its continued importance, there were fundamental changes in the nature of dowry. A regulation of 1303 prohibited a widow or a divorcee from taking her dowry with her in the event that she should remarry. The dowry remained the property of the patriline of the husband.[61] Prior to this period, a widowed or divorced woman who left the family of her husband had been allowed to take her dowry with her. This change rendered dowry less firmly tied to the woman who received it (and to her father's patriline that granted it) and more clearly merged into the patrilineage of her husband. It has lost some of its power and much of its function as a bridge between kin groups. If the dowry remained with the family of the husband at the dissolution of the marriage, paying it would be much less attractive than if it remained with the wife or reverted to the family who granted it, whatever their economic position. Did Ming dowries seem more like expenses and less like investments than dowries of the Song?

THE COMPETITIVE MARRIAGE MARKET

We are now at the crux of a paradox. We have seen that marriageable women were scarce in relation to marriageable men due to infanticide and concubinage. But despite the relative scarcity of women, the pressures on families to dower their daughters well appear to have remained high. Marriage markets thus seem to have been competitive for both men and women.

But there are several ways in which high dowries can be explained in a situation of female scarcity. First of all, one does not want just any husband for one's daughter; one wants the right kind of husband. Marriage was an extremely important way of forging links among families in traditional China, and dowry was a statement about the relative status of the bride's family. And although a married daughter had left the family of her birth, a daughter who married well would increase the status of her natal family. A daughter who married a successful examination candidate would not, of course, enhance her father's status in the same way as a son who was a successful examination candidate himself, but it was the next best thing. In the felicitous phrase of Susan Mann, marriage was the ladder of success for women in traditional China.[62] Thus kin through marriage might significantly improve social standing or further a career, and an ample dowry was one way family might attract worthy kin.

The Ming complaints about dowry and their connection to infanticide that I have cited come from the highly commercialized Jiangnan region in the sixteenth and seventeenth centuries. Recent work has demonstrated the destabilizing impact of commercial wealth on Ming Jiangnan: social status could not be bought outright, but money could be very useful in facilitating status mobility.[63] The conflicted relationship between money and the sexual economy in late Ming Jiangnan has been explicated by Richard von Glahn in his study of the god Wutong, who was thought to seduce men's wives and daughters in exchange for granting wealth.[64] Contemporaries frequently railed against the extravagance of late Ming Jiangnan.[65] Indeed, in a social world where much money was present and opportunities for mobility were ample, dowries might well escalate.

Exacerbating the competitiveness of the marriage market was the fact that the ideal marriage was slightly hypergamous—that is to say, the bride came from a slightly lower social status than did the groom.[66] Chinese family instructions urge sons to take brides from families of slightly lower status, invoking domestic harmony rather than upward mobility. Liu Zongzhou suggests that a wife of lower status would be more respectful and serve her in-laws better than would a bride of equal status.[67] Wang Shijin advocates marrying a woman of lower status, too, citing as his authority the *Yanshi jiaxun,* dating from the Six Dynasties period.[68] The connection between hypergamy and dowry has been noted by a number of scholars, among them S. J. Tambiah. In India, he has written, the dowry givers are exchanging status for wealth.[69] But in premodern China, dowry was not the only determinant of a young woman's attractiveness on the marriage market. John Dardess has suggested that an ideal wife for a member of the Ming elite would be a "girl of quality": a modicum of musical or poetic training made for a more interesting wife, and some education would enable her to be a better mother for the next generation of scholar-bureaucrats. Nevertheless, Dardess also notes that the raising and educating of such a daughter represented a considerable expense and cites examples of families who had trouble finding suitable spouses for their elegant daughters.[70] Recent work by Dorothy Ko has shown just how profound an investment Jiangnan literati made in the education of their daughters.[71] The marriage market was probably not their only goal, but when one was strategizing about a daughter's future, the marriage market could never be absent from one's mind.

Clearly the accumulation of unmarried girls in the upper strata of society is a potential problem in any hypergamous system. How do members of the elite marry up? Tambiah reports two different North Indian solutions, and indeed the Rajput solution was female infanticide.[72] The analogy with India, though suggestive, is imperfect. Caste lines in India have no Chinese counterpart. The criteria defining an ideal husband in China were more broadly written than they were among the caste-bound Indian elite. Nonetheless, the notion that the number of females among the upper strata of society needed to be limited in order to retain the hypergamous nature of the marriage system is suggestive, though the situation is rife with grim irony.

Hypergamy is a system in which females occupy a structurally valued position. A daughter might reasonably be expected to attract a husband of superior social status, thereby enhancing her father's position. Hypergamy does not itself necessitate dowry, but an ample dowry doubtless made arranging an ambitious match easier for the woman's family. Furthermore, the scarcity of women in Ming China facilitated hypergamy, while hypergamy, in turn, encouraged ample dowries as well as cultivated daughters. The pressure created by this system may well have led families to kill girl babies rather than endure the sacrifices that raising them properly and dowering them adequately would entail.

THE CHINESE MARRIAGE SYSTEM AND THE GENDERED STATUS OF CHILDREN

What does this tell us about childhood in China—in particular, childhood for girls? Family strategizing often began in infancy, and while there would have been several ways in which to conceptualize a boy's future, marriage was the future career for virtually every girl. A boy could inherit his father's land and follow his occupation, or he could be educated for an official career or be trained for another profession. But because marriage was the career for girls, a female infant was, in this discourse, labeled as a dowry-needer. She was not granted the luxury of even a brief phase of ungendered childhood.[73]

Children were, moreover, viewed as being at the nexus of social reproduction. They were both the transmitters of social values from one generation to the next and the means by which families perpetuated themselves. The role of male children in this transmission is relatively straightforward: they are the carriers of the patrilineal name, the connection between dead ancestors and descendants yet unborn. But daughters are not heirs to the patriline, at least not in any ordinary sense. Their role in reproduction is crucial, but they do not reproduce their father's patriline; they serve as brides in someone else's lineage. This of course gives rise to another paradox, one that has often been noted by observers of the Chinese family. A bride is both essential and dangerous to the reproduction of a family. She is an outsider, whose influence on her husband's family is necessary but potentially disruptive.

But her disruptive influence does not function merely at the level of the individual family. We have seen a number of Ming literati writing about female infanticide in a way that demonstrates the connections between the domestic realm and public life. When baby girls are killed, order is threatened on all levels of society. A father who kills a baby girl, so Yao Mingluan implies, is not a reliable subject. The Chenghua emperor identifies infanticide as a practice that destroys the cardinal Confucian virtues of benevolence and righteousness. Huang Liuhong (who links infanticide with the failure to cultivate fruit trees and repair roads) views infanticide as a violation of public order. The ramifications of infanticide thus extend far beyond the domestic space where the crime was committed.

The conjunction of dowry and infanticide in the imagination of Ming men is especially instructive here. High dowries may in fact be to blame; but even if further research fails to confirm that high dowries were widespread, it is significant that Ming intellectuals singled out dowry as a leading cause of infanticide. Further, although several of our sources note that infanticide was practiced among the reasonably well off, the most protracted criticisms, all written by male literati, explicitly address female infanticide as a class issue. The long poem by Yao Mingluan assumes that the root of the problem is the ambition of the lower orders: if people knew their place, then dowries would be of appropriate size and little girls could thrive, modestly clad and coiffed in class-appropriate ways. As a solution to the problem, a number of magistrates sought to diminish infanticide by restricting dowry. Arguments against infanticide are arguments against a dowry system that permits families with daughters and money to foster politically and socially useful marriages. Thus the conjunction of dowry and hypergamy permits a certain amount of status mobility for men with daughters and money in a social setting where mobility should have been fostered by sons and education. Sixteenth- and seventeenth-century literati arguments against dowry are arguments for social stability and the status quo, made in a time when growing commercialization and mercantile wealth were threatening the rules of the old social order. A class of richly dowered brides represented a threat to the stability of the literati class as a whole.

Both those who dispose of baby girls and those who defend them have characterized girls as dangerous to the stability of the struggling family, on the one hand, and the stability of society as a whole on the other. An infant girl represents an economic problem to a family with limited resources. If she is killed, the repercussions of the act of violence can be felt in the public and cosmic spheres. If she survives and marries above her station, she carries the potential for another kind of disruption. In either case, the birth of an infant girl had the potential to precipitate a crisis that all too often ended in her death. It was her future as a bride that marked her as dangerous and placed her in mortal peril.

NOTES

1. See, for example, "The Prevalence of Infanticide in China," *Journal of the North China Branch of the Royal Asiatic Society* 20 (1885):25–50. For a cogent analysis of the traps that can ensnare Western feminist analysis see Chandra Mohanty, "Under Western Eyes: Feminist Scholarship and Colonial Discourses," *Feminist Review* 30 (1988):61–88.

2. See Anne Behnke Kinney, "Infant Abandonment in Early China," *Early China* (1983):107–138.

3. James Lee, Cameron Campbell, and Guofu Tan, "Infanticide and Family Planning in Late Imperial China: The Price and Population History of Rural Liaoning, 1774–1873," in Thomas M. Rawski and Lillian M. Li, eds., *Chinese History in Economic Perspective* (Berkeley and Los Angeles:

University of California Press, 1992), as well as other articles cited elsewhere in the notes to this chapter. See also Susan Greenhalgh and Jiali Li, "Engendering Reproductive Policy and Practice in Peasant China: For a Feminist Demography of Reproduction," *Signs* 20(3) (Spring 1995): 601–641.

4. See the passages on footbinding in Dorothy Ko, *Teachers of the Inner Chambers: Women and Culture in China, 1573–1722* (Stanford: Stanford University Press, 1994). See also C. Fred Blake, "Foot-Binding in Neo-Confucian China and the Appropriation of Female Labor," *Signs* 19(3) (Spring 1994):676–712. Ko organized a panel on footbinding at the 1994 meeting of the Association for Asian Studies, at which Angela Zito, Christina Turner, Blake, and Ko all presented papers. These studies are amplifying and challenging the views set forth in the recently reprinted work by Howard Levy, *The Lotus Lovers: The Complete History of the Curious Erotic Custom of Footbinding in China* (Buffalo: Prometheus Books, 1992).

5. Feng Menglong, "Kuang Taishou duan si haier," *Jingshi tongyan* (Hong Kong: Zhonghua shuju, 1978), p. 539. See the translation by C. T. Hsia and Susan Arnold Zonana, "The Case of the Dead Infant," in Y. W. Ma and Joseph S. M. Lau, eds., *Traditional Chinese Stories: Themes and Variations* (New York: Columbia University Press, 1982), pp. 122–134. For Zhu Wan, see his biography by Bodo Wiethoff in *Dictionary of Ming Biography* (New York: Columbia University Press, 1976), p. 372. The dynastic history does not mention his father's wife's attempts to starve him. See, however, his biography in the *Guochao xianzheng lu* (Taipei: Xuesheng shuju, 1965), 62/44a (vol. 4, p. 247).

6. On the notion of a "hidden economy of kinship" see Jack Goody, *The Development of Marriage and the Family in Europe* (Cambridge: Cambridge University Press, 1983).

7. *Da Qing lüli huitong xinzuan* (Taipei: Wenhai chubanshe, 1964), vol. 4, p. 2817; cited in Jonathan Ocko, *Bureaucratic Reform in Provincial China: Ting Jih-ch'ang in Restoration Kiangsu 1867–1870* (Cambridge, Mass.: Harvard University Press, 1983), p. 53. According to Ch'ü T'ung-tsu, during the Han dynasty infanticide was regarded as ordinary homicide and might lead to the death penalty. See his *Law and Society in Traditional China* (Paris: École pratique des hautes études, 1961), pp. 23–24, citing the *Hou Hanshu, juan* 67, pp. 34b–35a. But according to Ch'ü, during the Yuan, Ming, and Qing dynasties a parent's powers over children were much broader. In the latter period, a parent would not be punished for killing a child who had acted in an unfilial manner.

8. *Guochao xianzhang leibian, juan* 25; cited in T'ien Ju-k'ang, *Male Anxiety and Female Chastity: A Comparative Study of Chinese Ethical Values in Ming-Ch'ing Times* (Leiden: E. J. Brill, 1988), p. 29.

9. Huang Liuhong, "Fanli" (General rules) in *Fuhui quanshu;* translated by Djang Chu as *A Complete Book Concerning Happiness and Benevolence:*

A Manual for Local Magistrates in Seventeenth-Century China (Tucson: University of Arizona Press, 1984), p. 64.

10. Liu Zongzhou, *Renbu leiji* (Taipei: Guangwen shuju, 1971), *juan* 5, p. 38a (p. 119). On Liu, see T'ang Chun-i, "Liu Tsung-chou's Doctrine of Moral Mind and His Critique of Wang Yang-ming," in William Theodore de Bary, ed., *The Unfolding of Neo-Confucianism* (New York: Columbia University Press, 1975), pp. 305–329. See the essay by Angela Leung in this volume (Chapter 9) for a more detailed discussion of foundling homes.

11. Chen Longzheng, *Jiting waishu*, 2/21a.

12. James Webster, *The Kan Ying Pien: Book of Rewards and Punishments* (Shanghai: Presbyterian Mission Press, 1922), p. 26. The *Gan ying pian* is attributed to Ge Hong (284–363) but is probably of a much later date. A sixth-century text, *Yao xing lun*, in a passage preserved in the *Zhenglei bencao*, chap. 4, p. 107b, compiled by Tang Shenwen and others in 1249, describes mercury and mercuric sulfide as abortifacients; cited in Joseph Needham, *Science and Civilisation in China* (Cambridge: Cambridge University Press, 1974), vol. 5, pt. 2, p. 286. The *Yishuo*, a medical compendium compiled by Zheng Gao (fl. 1210), contains a section on medical ethics. An anecdote in that section about a woman named Bao Mudan makes it clear that abortifacients were known in thirteenth-century China. Bao earned quite a good living selling medications that induced abortions. But as a punishment for having caused many abortions, she developed severe headaches and running sores, and died. Cited in Paul Unschuld, *Medical Ethics in Imperial China: A Study in Historical Anthropology* (Berkeley and Los Angeles: University of California Press, 1979), pp. 48–49. The seriousness with which abortion was regarded during the Qing is evidenced by the fact that those who had performed abortions were not to be spared in general amnesties. See Brian McKnight, *The Quality of Mercy: Amnesties and Traditional Chinese Justice* (Honolulu: University of Hawai'i Press, 1981), p. 110.

13. Cited in Robert van Gulik, *Sexual Life in Ancient China* (Leiden: E. J. Brill, 1974), p. 249. The *Jingshi gongguoge* (Ledger of merits and demerits to warn the world) is a Yuan-dynasty text. It is perhaps worthy of note that an abortion incurred six hundred demerits if its purpose was to conceal an illicit affair.

14. *Gongguoge*, in *Xunzi yan; Congshu jicheng*, vol. 168, p. 13.

15. For a discussion of these views see Charlotte Furth, "Concepts of Pregnancy, Childbirth and Infancy in Ch'ing Dynasty China," *Journal of Asian Studies* 46(1) (February 1987):7–35. Furth stresses that at no time does the child's liminal state obscure its significance as posterity. See also Furth's essay in this volume (Chapter 6).

16. Ho Ping-ti, *Studies on the Population of China: 1366–1953* (Cambridge, Mass.: Harvard University Press, 1954), p. 57; James Lee and Robert Y. Eng, "Population and Family History in Eighteenth Century Manchuria:

Preliminary Results from Daoyi, 1774–1798," *Ch'ing-shih wen-t'i* 5(1) (1984):33.

17. Lee, Campbell, and Tan, "Infanticide and Family Planning," p. 175.

18. *Taiping jing* 35/34ff; cited and translated by Max Kaltenmark, "The Ideology of the T'ai-ping ching," in Holmes Welch and Anna Seidel, eds., *Facets of Taoism* (New Haven: Yale University Press, 1979), p. 20.

19. *Yuan shi* (Beijing: Zhonghua shuju, 1976), *juan* 103, p. 2640.

20. See Paul Heng-chao Ch'en, *Chinese Legal Tradition Under the Mongols: The Code of 1291 as Reconstructed* (Princeton: Princeton University Press, 1979), pp. 51–56.

21. Ho, *Population of China*, p. 60.

22. Ibid., p. 12.

23. This is in some ways analogous to the problem of the "missing girls" that confronts demographers and anthropologists trying to make sense of contemporary Chinese population ratios. See, for example, the discussion by Susan Greenhalgh in "Engendering Reproductive Policy and Practice in Peasant China."

24. See Ho, *Population of China*, p. 8 (Yongzhou); p. 12 (Shanghai). Sex ratios were calculated using Ho's figures.

25. Ho, *Population of China*, p. 4.

26. Michael Marmé, "Population and Possibility in Ming (1368–1644) Suzhou: A Quantified Model," *Ming Studies* 12 (1981):29–64.

27. John Dardess, "Ming Historical Demography: Notes from T'ai-ho County, Kiangsi," *Ming Studies* 17 (1983):72.

28. See the estimates by Barclay of 107 and Moise of 111.7, cited in Dardess, "Ming Historical Demography," p. 66.

29. Ted Telford finds about 1 percent of the consort population to be concubines. See his "Family and State in Qing China: Marriage in the Tongcheng Lineages, 1650–1880," in *Family Process and Political Process in Modern Chinese History* (Taipei: Academia Sinica, 1992), p. 929. Liu Tsui-jung finds 1 percent of the consort population in Hunan to be concubines, but finds 4 percent in South China; see "Formation and Function of Three Lineages in Hunan," in *Family Process*, pp. 337–338. One should of course keep in mind that not all concubines may be registered in genealogies.

30. Cited in Sakai Tadao, "Confucianism and Popular Educational Works," in William Theodore de Bary, ed., *Self and Society in Ming Thought* (New York: Columbia University Press, 1970), p. 354.

31. See Angela Ki Che Leung, "To Chasten Society: The Development of Widow Homes in the Qing, 1773–1911," *Late Imperial China* 14(2) (December 1993):6–7.

32. Cited in Sakai, "Confucianism and Popular Educational Works," p. 359.

33. Wang Shijin, "Guimen dang su," in "Wang Shijin zong gui," in Chen Hongmou, *Wuzhong yigui, Sibu beiyao*, 2/24b.

34. Telford, "Family and State in Qing China," p. 924.

35. T'ien Ju-k'ang, *Male Anxiety,* p. 31.

36. Ibid., p. 28. T'ien Ju-k'ang is citing *Guochao xianzhang leibian, juan* 25.

37. Louis J. Gallagher, trans., *China in the Sixteenth Century: The Journals of Matthew Ricci: 1583–1610* (New York: Random House, 1953), pp. 86–87.

38. "Jin ninü dianfu yi," Li Yu, *Zizhi xinshu,* in *Li Yu quanji* (Hangzhou: Zhejiang guji chubanshe, 1992), vol. 16, *juan* 7, p. 270. For a discussion of the *Zizhi xinshu* see Shelley Hsueh-lun Chang and Chun-shu Chang, *Crisis and Transformation in Seventeenth-Century China: Society, Culture and Modernity in Li Yü's World* (Ann Arbor: University of Michigan Press, 1992), p. 74. The first collection of *Zizhi xinshu,* from which this entry is taken, was published in 1663.

39. Fu Yiling, *Ming Qing nongcun shehui jingji* (Jiulong: Shiyong shuju, 1961), p. 83, citing a Ji'an gazetteer. Cited in Mark Elvin, *Pattern of the Chinese Past* (Stanford: Stanford University Press, 1974), pp. 256–257.

40. "Xunsu yigui," in *Wu zhong yigui,* 2/24b.

41. *Fujian tongzhi,* 1871 ed., *juan* 35; cited and translated in T'ien Ju-k'ang, *Male Anxiety,* p. 30.

42. In chapter two of the novel *Jin ping mei,* Dame Wang is a midwife, a go-between, a procuress, and one who does all manner of unsavory tasks.

43. For a brief discussion of the warnings against the "six kinds of old women" see Charlotte Furth, "The Patriarch's Legacy," in K. C. Liu, ed., *Orthodoxy in Late Imperial China* (Berkeley and Los Angeles: University of California Press, 1990), p. 197. See also the midwife's song in the novel *Jin ping mei,* chap. 30.

44. *Chun'an xianzhi,* Tianyi ke reprint ed. (Shanghai: Guji shudian, 1981), 1/5b–7a.

45. *Xinghua Putian xianzhi,* 13/26a, p. 344; *Ming Qing jinshi timing beilu suoyin* (Shanghai: Guji shudian, 1980), p. 1385. Two of his brothers also received the *jinshi* degree. The gazetteer for Putian reveals that there were two *yang ji yuan* (asylums) operational during Yao's lifetime, which cared for orphaned and abandoned children as well as elderly people who were sick or destitute; *Xinghua Putian xianzhi,* 13/26a, p. 344. Perhaps the better institutional arrangements for unwanted children in Putian made him respond particularly strongly to the conditions in Chun'an. T'ien Ju-k'ang (p. 30) writes that female infanticide was especially prevalent in Ming and Qing Fujian, even among the wealthy: perhaps that prevalence explains both the *yang ji yuan* and the ditty cajoling people to allow their daughters to live.

46. *Yanzhou fu zhi* (Taipei: Zhongguo fangzhi congshu, 1969), 12/38b (vol. 1, p. 261).

47. Joanna Handlin, *Action in Late Ming Thought: The Reorientation of*

Lü K'un and Other Scholar Officials (Berkeley and Los Angeles: University of California Press, 1983), pp. 144–147. For a discussion of such songs in morality books see Cynthia Brokaw, *The Ledgers of Merit and Demerit: Social Change and the Moral Order in Late Imperial China* (Princeton: Princeton University Press, 1991), pp. 218–219.

48. Handlin, *Action in Late Ming Thought*, p. 74.

49. The other three relationships are husband/wife, elder sibling/younger sibling, and friend/friend.

50. Hai Rui, *Hai Rui ji* (Beijing: Zhonghua shuju, 1962), p. 165. See also Michel Cartier, *Une réforme locale en Chine au XVIe siècle: Hai Jui à Chun'an* (Paris: Mouton, 1973), p. 88.

51. *Huang Ming ningzhang leibian*, preface dated 1578, microfilm held at Harvard University, 25/49a–b.

52. See the discussion in Chang and Chang, *Crisis and Transformation*, p. 135. The essay in which Zhang voices his concerns is in the *Lanxi xianzhi*. See the biography of Zhang (Chang Mou) by Ronald Dimberg and Julia Ching in *Dictionary of Ming Biography*, pp. 96–97.

53. Lü Kun is cited in Lee, "Infanticide and Family Planning in Late Imperial China," p. 166. For Lü Kun see Handlin, *Action in Late Ming Thought*. The 1575 edition of the Kuaiji gazetteer, also in Jiangnan, comments that female babies were often drowned at birth there because of high dowries; *Kuaiji xianzhi* (1575 ed.), 3/4a. The passage is repeated in the Kangxi edition of the gazetteer, 7/1a. The Hangzhou gazetteer of 1579 reports that in Lin'an xian it was common for people to drown female babies because of high dowries; *Hangzhou fuzhi* (1579 ed.), 20/24a.

54. Liu Zongzhou, *Renbu leiji, juan* 5, p. 32b (p. 108).

55. Ibid., p. 38a (p. 119).

56. What we need is a careful study of women and property in the Ming, such as those done for the Song by Bettine Birge and Patricia Ebrey. See Bettine Birge, "Women and Property in Sung Dynasty China" (Ph.D. dissertation, Columbia University, 1992), and Patricia Ebrey, *The Inner Quarters: Marriage and the Lives of Chinese Women in the Sung Period* (Berkeley and Los Angeles: University of California Press, 1993), especially pp. 99–113.

57. See particularly her discussion in "Shifts in Marriage Finance from the Sixth to Thirteenth Centuries," in Rubie S. Watson and Patricia Buckley Ebrey, *Marriage and Inequality in Chinese Society* (Berkeley and Los Angeles: University of California Press, 1991), pp. 97–132.

58. Patricia Ebrey, "Women in the Kinship System of the Southern Song Upper Class," in Richard W. Guisso and Stanley Johannesen, eds., *Women in China* (Youngstown, N.Y.: Philo Press, 1981), pp. 117–118.

59. Susan Mann, "Grooming a Daughter for Marriage," in Watson and Ebrey, *Marriage and Inequality*, pp. 204–205.

60. See the discussion in Sheieh Bau Hwa, "Concubines in Chinese

Society from the Fourteenth to Eighteenth Centuries" (Ph.D. dissertation, University of Illinois, 1992).

61. Jennifer Holmgren, "Observations on Marriage and Inheritance Practices in Early Mongol and Yuan Society, with Particular Reference to the Levirate," *Journal of Asian History* 20(2) (1986):182. See also the discussion in Birge, "Women and Property," pp. 262–270. The connection between the change in rules on dowry and state recognition for widows who remained chaste would be worth exploring in some detail. On the recognition of widows who remained chaste see Ann Waltner, "Widows and Remarriage in Ming and Early Qing China," in Guisso and Johannesen, *Women in China,* pp. 129–146; Mark Elvin, "Female Virtue and the State in China," *Past and Present* 104 (1984):111–152; and T'ien Ju-k'ang, *Male Anxiety.*

62. Mann, "Grooming a Daughter for Marriage," p. 204.

63. See Craig Clunas, *Superfluous Things: Material Culture and Social Status in Early Modern China* (Urbana: University of Illinois Press, 1991), pp. 1–39, for examples of how books that taught taste became commodities for the first time in the late Ming; see Cynthia Brokaw, *The Ledgers of Merit and Demerit,* for examples of how conceptions of morality and fate were in flux due to social changes; and see Richard von Glahn, "The Enchantment of Wealth: The God Wu-tung in the Social History of Jiangnan," *Harvard Journal of Asiatic Studies* 51(2) (1991):651–714, for a specific linking of anxieties about money and marriage.

64. See von Glahn, "The Enchantment of Wealth," especially pp. 682–704.

65. See, for example, the discussion in Clunas, *Superfluous Things,* pp. 141–165.

66. See the discussion by Patricia Ebrey in "Introduction" to Watson and Ebrey, *Marriage and Inequality in Chinese Society,* p. 5.

67. Liu Zongzhou, *Renbu leiji,* p. 107.

68. Wang Shijin, "Guimen dang su," p.104.

69. S. J. Tambiah, "Dowry and Bridewealth and the Property Rights of Women in South Asia," in Jack Goody and S. J. Tambiah, *Bridewealth and Dowry* (Cambridge: Cambridge University Press, 1974), p. 64.

70. Dardess, "Ming Historical Demography," p. 69.

71. Ko, *Teachers of the Inner Chambers.*

72. Tambiah, *"Dowry and Bridewealth,"* pp. 66–67.

73. On the variety of ways in which a young girl was prepared from birth to become a bride see Mann, "Grooming a Daughter for Marriage"; see also Susan Mann, "The Education of Daughters in the Mid-Qing Period," in Benjamin A. Elman and Alexander Woodside, eds., *Education and Society in Late Imperial China* (Berkeley and Los Angeles: University of California Press, 1994), especially pp. 20–21.

GLOSSARY

ding	丁	adult male
jinshi	進士	"presented scholar"; highest degree in the examination system
juren	舉人	"recommended man"; graduate of the provincial examination
li	例	administration regulations
li	里	a Chinese mile
liang	良	free
ling	靈	spirit; spiritual efficacy
lü	律	codes
renming	人命	human life
shang sheng huai su	傷生壞俗	harming life and damaging customs
yang ji yuan	養濟院	asylums
yin	陰	the feminine manifestation of the two primordial forces
yinger	嬰兒	infancy

8

Children of the Dream:
The Adolescent World in Cao Xueqin's
Honglou meng

LUCIEN MILLER

In relation to world literature, generically and comparatively speaking, Cao Xueqin's eighteenth-century novel *Honglou meng (Dream of the Red Chamber)* is not a work of children's literature. Absent are the magical yet foreboding fairy-tale world of the Grimm brothers' *Ash Girl* (Cinderella), the beauty-and-the-beast pattern of *Snow White and Rose Red*, the enfant terrible of Nepalese animal stories, the journey into fantasy of *Alice in Wonderland,* and the wondrous crossing of barriers seen in folktales by Yunnan minorities.[1] We cannot compare it to Western twentieth-century young adult fiction or "coming of age" ethnic autobiographies of adolescence such as Joy Kogawa's *Obasan* or Maxine Hong Kingston's *Woman Warrior.* But the *Dream of the Red Chamber* may be considered a children's book in a very precise and definite sense: it focuses primarily on the premarital life of young persons between puberty and marriage (roughly parallel to the fictional lifespan of the protagonist Jia Baoyu) as told by an autonomous narrator who sees through the eyes of children.

According to the periodization of ages in the Qing encyclopedia, the *Tushu jicheng,* the novel spans the stages of juvenile *(shaonian)* and young adulthood *(qingnian).*[2] However, the Western concept of growing up is "alien to the Confucian view of life," where aging is viewed as a lifelong process.[3] Certainly we do not find in the *Dream of the Red Chamber* definite stages of cognitive and moral growth considered archetypal in Western children's development.[4] In the Qing dynasty there is no culturally recognized period of adolescence or ritual marking of transitions from infancy to adulthood, though one should note that birthdays of young and old are a constant source of

family celebrations in the *Dream of the Red Chamber*.[5] But if there is
no socially acknowledged teenage period and if the self in traditional
Chinese culture is typically transient, conditional, and evolving over
an entire lifetime according to role and circumstance,[6] there is no
question that Cao Xueqin singles out for attention the time of flux
and "becoming" of *shaonian* and *qingnian*—youth and adolescence.[7]
Indeed, I would argue that, by focusing on the psychological and
sexual conflicts of a group of youths who are no longer considered
children but are not yet fully adults, Cao Xueqin has discovered adolescence in premodern Chinese society.

In the novel, and possibly in the Qing dynasty itself, the period of
young adulthood (the teenage transition before marriage) is an elite
phenomenon.[8] The poor may witness that privileged world close up
as servants, or marvel at it from a distance beyond the walls of the
wealthy Jia family compound, but they lack the leisure and financial
resources, and the exquisitely refined sensitivity that ensues, necessary to experience youth as a time apart. To the extent that the *Dream
of the Red Chamber* is autobiographical, its world of incredible opu-
lence is a reflection of Cao family wealth and a reminder of the days
of Cao Xueqin's grandfather, Cao Yin, who, as bondservant to the
Kangxi emperor, enjoyed an enormous income through his appointment as imperial textile commissioner, rice distributor, and copper
purchasing agent.[9] The adolescents of the novel are elite too in the
sense often spelled out in the "Zhiyanzhai" commentary, where commentators stress the originality and unconventionality of the novel
and assert that Baoyu, for instance, is "too complex and too unusual
a character to be judged by any ordinary standard."[10] The story of
Baoyu, his female cousins Daiyu and Baochai, and their servants
and friends is by no means the only story of the *Dream of the Red
Chamber*.[11] But it is a story compelling the attention of the author,
through whom the reader vicariously experiences the ecstatic but
passing and troublesome world Tolstoy terms "youth, beautiful
youth."[12] Interestingly this ironic vision has been said to be the
source for the *Dream of the Red Chamber's* being considered by elite
elders a forbidden book. Children ought not to read the *Dream of
the Red Chamber*, not because it is sexually explicit or morally evil,
but because its tragic revelation of youth might cause young people
to lose their life's ambition.[13] The *Dream of the Red Chamber* is an
adult children's book.

The *Dream of the Red Chamber* provides us with a unique opportunity to explore the world of the adolescent in premodern China.

Young adults live apart from the adult world in an ideal garden setting, and under the guise of fiction we readers are free to observe
them as though we were guest parents in some laboratory school of
gifted children in mid-Qing China. Initially it seems to us that the
children of the *Dream* live in a utopia and are ideally suited to appreciate its carefree environment without adult tyrannies and responsibilities. Though they are elite members of the upper class, it appears
they can ignore class, gender, and hierarchical distinctions. But as we
explore the text our initial vision of blissful childhood undergoes a
radical change. Cao Xueqin reveals the adolescent world to be overwhelmingly serious and fraught with ambiguities and contradictions
that frustrate growing up.

THE ADOLESCENT WORLD

Youth in the elite traditional society of the *Dream of the Red
Chamber* are border walkers between adult and children's worlds,
and Cao Xueqin seems obsessed by their unresolved conflicts. Here I
want to investigate certain features of the young adult environment
in the novel that seem central to the pain of adolescence—the garden
world as a children's reserve and playland, the liminal existence of
young adults and their resultant identity confusion, the mixed messages from adults regarding education, sexuality, and family relations, and the presence of children's disease and mental illness in a
seemingly utopian setting. In my comments I shall limit attention to
the "premarital" chapters of the *Dream of the Red Chamber,* primarily the first eighty chapters of the hundred-and-twenty-chapter
novel, as it is there that Cao Xueqin's vision of youth is largely set
forth. Marriages occur sporadically throughout the novel, but it is
around chapter seventy-seven that the marriages of the Daguanyuan
(Grand View Garden) maidens and cousins begin to unfold in ear-
nest, marking the absolute transition from the world of youth and
innocence to adulthood and experience.

Kiddieland

In the unique and privileged adolescent world of the garden, where
the children of the *Dream* dwell, various forms of infantile behavior
are sanctioned. Baoyu acts and is treated like a baby. Yet the adult
world—his grandmother, parents, aunts and uncles, teachers, father's

scholar-friends, and older servants—expect him to grow up and
assume family responsibilities. The placing of Baoyu and his female
cousins in the garden is the first sign of contradictory messages from
elders—in the garden Baoyu is left carefree and protected, yet adult
encouragement of regression prevents him from accomplishing the
developmental tasks of adolescence.

One's initial impression of the garden world of the children of the
Dream of the Red Chamber is that it is frivolous. Playtime activities
for Baoyu and his female cousins include riddle guessing, Chinese
chess, puzzles, kite flying, bird watching, fireworks, boat punting,
fishing, calligraphy and painting practice, poetry contests, and flower
collecting.[14] Grandmother Jia (Jia Mu) and the children are ever fond
of celebrating birthdays and festivals with plays and operatic performances. Baoyu is continuously babied with tender treatment by
maids, female relatives, or lower-class acquaintances. When he visits
Aroma (Xiren) who is home one day with her family, her elder
brother takes care to lift Baoyu gently from his horse, while Aroma
carefully blows away the skins of pine nuts before handing them to
Baoyu to eat.[15] If she is away, he must have his maids Musk (Sheyue)
and Skybright (Qingwen) serve on night duty, for he is afraid of the
dark—he also deploys his fear as a strategy to get pretty maids to
sleep with him.[16] His maids dry his tears when he cries,[17] and even
come to his assistance when he urinates,[18] or has a bowel movement,
cleaning up after him and washing his hands.[19] Note that in the latter
episode, Baoyu is fifteen or sixteen years old.[20] He has a tendency to
regress to infantile behavior to keep maternal figures close, or to
become the baby needing comforting. Baoyu talks baby talk when
Aroma threatens to leave him.[21] Between the ages of twelve and fourteen, we find him fond of nestling in his grandmother and mother's
laps.[22] And of course, as everybody knows, he is a "naughty boy."
He is fond of collecting mirrors, for example, even though his grandmother says children should not look in them, for they give young-
sters bad dreams.[23] He indulges in girlish hobbies such as making
cosmetics, or likes to reverse hierarchical roles and play the female
servant, for instance, ironing dresses for maids.[24]

This tendency to infantilize—to hold onto the fantasy ideal of
being an irresponsible babe in toyland—is indulged and supported by
the adult feminine world as well. No one loves to "play" and
"party" more than Grandmother Jia. There is a list of "not-
supposed-to-do" things that she enjoys herself, or looks the other
way when others, such as children, are doing them. A prevalent

example is drinking. Baoyu is not supposed to drink, says his nurse, but he often drinks at home and is fond of getting drunk with his male companions.[25] Grandmother Jia and the adult married women love to drink, too,[26] while Baoyu and his young female cousins consider themselves seasoned drinkers who like to combine drinking parties and poetry contests.[27] Drinking is a celebrated social habit that flows from the adult world of Grandmother Jia to the children and back again, drawing Baoyu, cousins, and maternal dames into a community of conviviality. In the world of children, drinking to the point of inebriation is never considered a serious social problem. It only appears to become one in the world of adults outside the garden. Nonetheless, the ease and constancy of drinking mark the children's world as a world of difference unto itself, a place where adult guidelines can be forgotten or suspended in the company of adult co-conspirators, an oasis of pleasure that stands apart from the desert of "sober" realities beyond the garden wall.

Border Walking: Development and Identity

Despite the many diversions of the children's world and fun-filled moments of escapism and regression, there is a steady undercurrent of boredom flowing beneath the garden's stream of delight. The endless round of perfunctory morning calls that dutiful children must make to their elders[28] belong to a world in which, Baoyu complains, there are nothing but birthdays.[29] At times he is so bored with his children's world that Aroma must force him from his bed to go out and take a walk.[30]

This periodic boredom and the moments of infantile regression are clues, I believe, to the larger, ambiguous world of pubescent, premarital adolescence that so fascinates Cao Xueqin. To approach its dynamics, I should like to "colonize," so to speak, the garden world of the *Dream of the Red Chamber* with a couple of theories, one psychological and Western, having to do with adolescence, the other from traditional Chinese medicine, concerned with somatic illness or neurasthenia. I do not have in mind a reductive Freudian reading—Baoyu's view that boys are "dirty" while girls are "clean" reflects masturbation guilt (as does his boredom); his buffoonery and clowning reveal hidden phallic exhibitionism; his noisy outbursts indicate a fear of castration; his and his cousins' hypochondria implies they fear their mothers do not care for them; the children's following of doctor's orders and prescriptions signifies regressive forms of gratification; the youngster's fondness for painting and calligraphy suggests anal and urethral preoccupation. Such a reading would presumably open up the text in various directions, but the sheer bravado of such colonizing is in itself imperialistic. No, what I want to do is neither to be reductive nor to lay bare what is hidden. Instead, I want to look at what is plain and visible in the surface texture of the everyday life of elite, precocious, and precious adolescents in *Dream of the Red Chamber*.

What is on the surface and plainly visible for any reader to see is that the premarital life of the children of the garden belongs to a liminal world with hazy borders. In the context of rigid hierarchical relations between master, mistress, and servant, as well as strict rules of etiquette and protocol, the garden cousins seem to be suspended in an ideal paradise of freedom from time and adult responsibility. Yet they live "on the edge," so to speak, precariously perched on a threshold, across which various odd couples come walking hand in hand: innocence and sexual experience, conscious life and dreams, Confucius and Buddha, garden and urban values, married and unmarried states, heterosexual and homosexual love, private morality and public face, chastity and eroticism, earthly life and otherworldly existence.

I suspect it is his vision of the dicey nature of adolescent life that compels Cao Xueqin to embody premarital youth in exquisite detail and to fix upon his major border walker, Baoyu, a loving but honest gaze. The liminal world offers the writer major opportunities for fictional exploration and elaboration precisely because, for the adolescent, it is fraught with pitfalls and ambiguities regarding identity. In the case of Baoyu, to focus on the most dominant example of premarital youth in the novel, we have a child who may be viewed in relation to the Eriksonian model of adolescent development.[31] With the onset of puberty, childhood ends, youth begins, and the developmental task of the adolescent is to achieve self-identity. Failure means role confusion. Baoyu provides several instances of the drive to sort out identity, its concomitant challenges, and its fruit in a confused yet compelling fictional self. He lives largely within a female-dominated environment, surrounded within the garden by his female cousins and maids, while immediately adjacent are his grandmother, mother, and aunts. His father is distant and authoritarian, and Baoyu is unable to ally himself with older, hierarchical, masculine role models; instead his sense of self-continuity is gathered through endless conversations with females, especially Daiyu. His own confused sexual identity is continually marked by others who are struck by his femininity. Daiyu marvels at his feminine appearance when she first meets him.[32] You Sanjie, the voluptuous beauty who slits her throat over her unrequited love for the actor, Liu Xianglian, declares Baoyu is girlish and effeminate from spending all his time in the women's quarters.[33] The matriarch, Grandmother Jia, remarking on the strange fact that her grandson, Baoyu, spends all his time with young maidens, suggests that Baoyu may have been a girl in a past life and perhaps he should be one now.[34]

Baoyu's strong libido has to be worked out in terms of sexual identity, which he explores through bisexual relations. A confused sexual identity is indicated by his clannish overidentification with an elite clique of girls, excluding difference, a confusion that is further signified in delinquent behavior and radical shifts in mood. His endless falling in love is yet another sign of the self's attempt to achieve identity, whereby he repeatedly projects his diffused self-image onto the female other, whether it be Daiyu, Baochai, Aroma, or one of his maids. His adolescent mind is the mind of the moratorium, an ideological mind (seen in his tirades about Buddhism and Taoism), existing between childhood and adulthood. One suspects that for Baoyu, his developmental needs are not met and he must find satisfaction elsewhere—thus his infantile regression, his boredom, and his constant need for rapprochement with male and female friends to find security. His role confusion is exemplified too in his inability to face the future and look forward to the promise of a career or marriage. Baoyu's is a diffuse personality marked by role confusion, aimlessness, and an underlying anxiety.

While we are not considering the ending of the novel here, one remark in passing is relevant. From the standpoint of fictional closure, Baoyu's identity crisis is resolved when at the end of the *Dream* he finally affirms marriage and Buddhism, two complementary opposites that lift him from his garden world. But according to the Eriksonian model, Baoyu's ending may be problematic, as it appears he does not resolve the conflict between intimacy and isolation that follow the discovery of identity.[35] Since his marriage and fatherhood are meaningless and merely perfunctory to Baoyu, it seems he does not achieve true intimacy. Ironically, becoming a monk may be motivated by a fear of ego loss and self-abandonment, a reversion to isolation and self-absorption that marks adolescent regression. Yet Baoyu does not abandon the world meanly, so to speak, as one would expect were his final stage one of stagnant isolation. He is not intent on destroying filial, paternal, or marital values. His combative relation to father and Confucian system ends. Perhaps Baoyu's marriage and procreation suggest a concern for the future of the world left behind, an ethical sense that, Erikson notes, is a sign of the adult. In turning to ultimate reality, Baoyu simply transcends. The fact that the end of adolescence in the *Dream of the Red Chamber* may be read in two opposite ways—as an achievement of intimacy or final isolation—is consistent with the portrait of young adulthood throughout the novel: premarital life is conflictual, ambiguous, and charged with contradiction.

Now let us return to our study of the premarital chapters of the *Dream of the Red Chamber* and explore further theoretical implications of this Western conceptualization of adolescent development. Other contradictory aspects of the adolescent world that are emblematic of its drift between chaos and order are close and distant primary family relations, traditional and liberal notions of education, and the separation and integration of the sexes. A Chinese understanding of premarital youth will be explored in the second part of this essay in relation to somatic illness, neurasthenia, and sexuality in the novel.

Primary Family Relations

In the Jia family, while there are hierarchical, gender, age, and class distinctions, relationships are often ambiguous or contradictory, underscoring the vulnerable, precarious nature of premarital adolescence and the mixed messages children receive from adults. The extravagant, complex atmosphere in which the children of the elite exist in itself contributes to their insecurity.[36] One thinks of the division, jealousy, and infighting that take place in the huge wealthy household between family members and servants of higher and lesser ranks—seen, for example, in the episode where Mother Ma (Ma Daopo, Baoyu's godmother) works her black magic to destroy Baoyu and Wang Xifeng (Phoenix) on behalf of the concubine, Aunt Zhao (Zhao Yima), who wants them out of the way so that her son, Jia Huan, may become the family's favored son.[37] There is bribery, graft, and corruption in intimate circles—Wang Xifeng's husband, Jia Lian, gets her maid Faithful (Yuanyang) to steal things from Grandmother Jia to pawn in payment for debts.[38] In the huge household, vast amounts of money are spent on ancestor worship, funerals, and payments for ladies and servants. (Grandmother Jia, Lady Xing, and

Lady Wang each receive twenty taels of silver per month; Baoyu alone has sixteen servants.)

In a tradition where the mother or a maternal figure is in a vital affective role regarding the socialization of morals, Baoyu's mother, Lady Wang (Wang Furen), is both distant and close to her son.[39] She is wont to speak harshly of her eccentric child.[40] When Baoyu is nearly beaten to death by his father, Jia Zheng, and even as Lady Wang holds his disfigured body, she laments the death of her first-born son Jia Zhu, saying she would not have regretted the loss of a hundred sons had Jia Zhu survived.[41] Her distant relation to Baoyu means that other women play her maternal role, such as Baoyu's sister, the imperial concubine, Yuanchun,[42] or his maid Aroma.[43] Yet she is strangely close when it comes to protecting him against maids she considers "impure" and corrupting, such as her own Golden (Jin Chuan'er), though it is Baoyu, in fact, who tries to flirt with Golden.[44] Her role as purifier of adolescent morality drives Golden to suicide, and her lies about the cause of the suicide[45] lead Jia Zheng to believe Jia Huan's story that it is Baoyu's fault, resulting in a merciless beating.[46] In a parallel "defense of virtue" episode, we see Lady Wang as purifying mother in her attack on Baoyu's maid Sky-bright (Qingwen).[47] In fact, Lady Wang considers all of Baoyu's maids potentially corrupting.[48]

Lady Wang, then, is a contradictory figure as mother: distant in affection yet rigid and defensive regarding her son's sexual life. Her rigidity may be due to her distance from Baoyu, a paranoia born of her ignorance of his needs. One wonders to what degree she engineers the punishment Baoyu receives from his father. Cao Xueqin never explores such ramifications, but in creating the paradoxical image of a mother who is both near and distant, affectionate and spiteful, he highlights adolescent confusion and insecurity.

Baoyu's relation to his father, Jia Zheng, is similarly distant. Indeed, at one point in the novel, when both Baoyu and Wang Xifeng are deathly ill through the black magic machinations of Ma Daopo, Jia Zheng wants to let them die, believing that they are fated and nothing can be done.[49] But for the most part, the ambiguous signals Baoyu receives from his father are a paradoxical combination of contempt and pride. Jia Zheng is always criticizing Baoyu for his failure to study; he expresses contempt for the boy's love of poetry and humiliates him in front of friends.[50] But secretly he is proud of Baoyu's knowledge of aesthetics and feels tender toward him as his only heir.[51] On rare occasions, a father's solicitude for his son is revealed. Jia Zheng tells Baoyu he has his eye out for a likely bride for him, but he must first prove himself in his studies.[52] Once, his affection for Baoyu is revealed in a father-son outing, a shopping spree for presents.[53] Again, as in Baoyu's relation to his mother, the combination of opposite attitudes in Baoyu's father fosters identity confusion and psychological disquiet in the son.

In her relation to grandchildren and servants, Grandmother Jia alternately appears trustworthy and unreliable: the fun-loving elder who loves without reserve and the authoritarian head-of-the-house who maneuvers family ties. Daiyu is initially her pet, her specially favored one,[54] treated with the same favoritism as Baoyu,[55] then Baochai becomes the most loved girl in the family.[56] At one point she says that her maid Faithful (Yuanyang) is superior to all other women in the household. She dotes on Baoyu, loving him more than her own son, Jia Zheng, and loathes her other grandson, Jia Huan. She favors Jia Zheng and Lady Wang over Jia She and Lady Xing and exhibits great affection for Wang Xifeng. Her partisan perspective blinds her to what is really happening in her family,[57] and she "spoils" Baoyu, suspending him in a narcissistic adolescent world.

The contradictory closeness and distance in Baoyu's relation to grandmother, father, and mother are important sources of the fragmentary, troublesome character of adolescence.

Notions of Education

Amidst an atmosphere of role confusion and countersignals of favoritism and distance, education has an ambiguous significance, contributing to the general tension between chaos and order in the garden. To Jia Zheng, Baoyu's education is deadly serious, for it ensures the future well-being of the Jia family clan. For his family, as for many wealthy Qing clans subject to partible inheritance, downward mobility is likely, while passing the imperial examinations means access to power and security. In this social context, Jia Zheng's savage beating of Baoyu is comprehensible—in fact, it is part of an old Jia family tradition of beating boys to discipline them. (Jia Zheng was beaten by his father, for example, and Jia Zheng's brother, Jia She, beats his son, Jia Lian.)[58] Despite the threat of being disciplined, Baoyu's reluctance to master the required canon and move out of the garden is understandable—other pampered male Qing readers probably sympathized with an elite youth's lack of self-discipline and his unwillingness to take the civil service examinations.[59] In contrast to Jia Zheng's pragmatic view, Baoyu's preferred reading of literature is personal, narcissistic, and emotive. He and Daiyu see the romantic protagonists of the *West Chamber (Xixiang ji)* as extensions of themselves,[60] while their reading of the text leads them to imitate its story.[61] Baoyu hints of his love for Daiyu through such romances, which he smuggles into the garden, sparking her romantic interest in him.[62]

Jia Zheng's complaint that his son is ignorant or uneducated, however, is simply not true. For one thing, while Baoyu's early training is not described specifically, his general level of literacy assumes he acquired the typical preschool education for a Qing elite boy, which included the "San-Bai-Qian" *(Trimetrical Classic, Hundred Names Classic, Thousand Character Classic)*—some two thousand characters by age seven, followed by the study of the Four Books *(Analects, Great Learning, Mencius, Doctrine of the Mean)* and the Five Classics *(Book of Changes, Book of History, Book of Songs, Book of Rites, Spring and Autumn Annals).*[63] Except for some general allusions to plays, children's theater, novels, and one or two morality books, there is little discussion in the *Dream* of popular literature. Surely a boy of Baoyu's class and temperament would be familiar with the popular novels and dramas, street entertainment, ballads and songs, detective and ghost stories, popular encyclopedias, cartoon illustrated stories, and morality books that were such a significant part of the times.[64] Deng Yunxiang notes that Baoyu is learned in poetry and aesthetic theory, while his general knowledge and level of culture are good but not unusual according to Qing standards.[65] I would add that his broad knowledge of plants and flowers, revealed in the tour of the garden with his father, is quite remarkable.[66]

Baoyu's doting elder sister, Yuanchun, gives him oral instruction and teaches him several books—he may have learned two or three thousand characters prior to home study with a private tutor.[67] With a tutor, possibly for six or seven years until he is twelve or thirteen and enters the family school, Baoyu reads the Four Books (4,466 characters), three books of the *Shi jing*,[68] many Tang and Song poems, and several *guwen* essays and prose poems *(fu).*[69] While his length of attendance at the Jia family school appears brief—clearly Baoyu does not follow the family tradition of spending ten years of formal training in school—he obviously reads much on his own, often citing his literary favorites *(Lisao, Wenxuan, Zhuangzi, Xixiang ji).*[70]

How, then, are we to understand Jia Zheng's constant criticism that Baoyu is not fond of reading? Jia Zheng means that Baoyu lacks training in the "eight-legged essay" *(baguwen)*, an examination necessity. But mainly the father is pointing to the fact that while his son *kanshu* (reads by looking), he fails to *dushu* (recite aloud and memorize).[71] And Baoyu's own limited list of texts he has memorized supports his father's reservations.[72] Baoyu loathes canonical learning that he feels is corrupted by association with ambition to become a scholar-official. He resists Baochai's encouragement to study, not wanting to be a career worm,[73] and rejects Shi Xiangyun's advice that he should meet official visitors to build future connections.[74]

The popularity of the *Dream of the Red Chamber* during the Qing attests to the idea that a positive view of education for women was attractive to numbers of intellectuals.[75] In the novel, adolescent women are literate and learned, revealing their talents as poets, painters, and calligraphers, and usually possessing greater sensitivity and ability than their male counterpart, Baoyu.[76] But there is a tension among the girls regarding learning. Baochai's theory of reading for young people is that bad books have an evil influence and that it is unhealthy for girls to have a literary reputation.[77] Of course her criticism is disingenuous, as she herself is highly educated and exhibits her profound grasp of the poetic tradition in poetry contests. Daiyu is said to have been raised as a boy, that is, educated in texts such as the Four Books,[78] and is wont to quote dynastic histories.[79] She is a poetry master, an effective tutor,[80] and proud of her skills.[81] Both she and Baochai have a better knowledge of Buddhism than Baoyu, as he only too fully realizes. The girls' intellectual superiority may reflect the author's theme regarding the general superiority of women, but it is also a forum for the expression of their rivalry.

Underneath the garden fun of poetry contests and riddle guessing, there is an unsettling disquiet between an aesthetic "art for art's sake" model of erudition and a classical, analytical "art for official-dom's sake" that pressures and splits adolescents. The conflict between Daiyu and Baochai over Baoyu is mirrored in differing concepts of proper reading for girls. Baoyu and Daiyu use poetry and plays to flirt. Jia Zheng judges poetic knowledge unorthodox and useless. The division over education in the *Dream of the Red Chamber*, its means and ends, earmarks the tensions of the adolescent world.

Sexual Intimacy and Separation

The idea that the garden is an idyllic, timeless paradise inhabited by innocent children is a stereotype that continues to prevail.[82] In fact, the incestuous relation between Baoyu's aunt, Qin Keqing, and her father-in-law Jia Zhen (Cao Xueqin deleted her consequent suicide at the insistence of commentators) casts a pall over relations among children in the garden that cannot be undone. Baoyu's nap in Qin Keqing's bedroom and his subsequent dream-world initiation into sex is hardly "innocent," since his nap is arranged by the seductive Qin Keqing who leads him in his dream.[83] That Baoyu is allowed to live intimately in the garden with his female cousins, while major adult figures such as his grandmother, father, mother, and Wang Xifeng are remote, means the Jia family's normal rules of relationship and the mid-Qing standard of the strict segregation of the sexes are in abeyance, hinting at a "disregard for ultimate consequences" that the Zhiyanzhai commentators imply will result in ruin.[84]

Cao Xueqing's emphasis on the absence of separation and individuation is a corollary to his marking the close proximity of opposite sexes in the garden. A common practice in both the Jia and the Zhen families is to give girls boys' names.[85] One of Baoyu's eccentricities as a child is his inability to recognize distinctions between persons, whether they be relatives or servants.[86] His dream ideal of the perfect female is a combination of Daiyu and Baochai.[87] Unable to appreciate the difference between an image and a live person, he goes to comfort a beautiful woman in a painting whom he thinks must be lonely.[88] That the lines between the sexes are unclear is most commonly seen in the easy access that Baoyu and his female cousins have to one another's sleeping quarters. He and Daiyu are noteworthy for having slept in the same bed as children.[89] The pair share intimate bedroom conversations and morning toilettes together.[90] As Baoyu grows older, however, both Daiyu and maids such as Nightingale (Yingge) reprove him for touching them.[91] Here again the blurred lines between traditional accepted mores and their absence—the purity and separation of the sexes as opposed to sexual intimacy— are evidence of the ambiguous, fragile nature of adolescence.

Baoyu idolizes the pure and unsullied state of his girl cousins; indeed, his deepest fear is that they will one day marry and become "polluted." He asserts that when girls marry, they become infected by men. Unmarried girls are good; married ones are bad.[92] Within the novel as a whole, the premarital state of garden women is one of purity and virtue, while married women, such as Wang Xifeng, Lady Wang, and Lady Xing, acquire vicious traits that belong to the world of men. Of the numerous suicides in the *Dream of the Red Chamber*, all but one are by women, and almost all are the result of their chastity being maligned.[93] Baoyu venerates Grandmother Jia's maid, Faithful (Yuanyang), for committing suicide rather than compromise her purity.[94] The positive view of women's suicide in the *Dream of the Red Chamber* is reflected in general attitudes among elite women in Chinese society: it is an honor to die a chaste widow. Through suicide one avoids conflicts with the natal or marital family that might ensue should one remarry; it is an effective act of rebellion or criticism; and one's ghost may seek revenge against the family.[95]

The problem with Baoyu's idealization of the unmarried state is that it fixes him in an impossible, impermanent state of adolescence, one that radically conflicts with his own libido drives and his extensive sexual experience with both men and women. He constructs an imaginary boundary between married and unmarried women and then divides young girls into inaccessible virgins (his cousins) and the sexually exploitable (maids and actresses). The latter may not be "polluted" in the same way as married women, who become empowered and corrupted through marriage, but they are sexually experienced and less innocent. The easy sexual accessibility of the maids and actresses contrasts to the invisible hymen between Baoyu and his virginal cousins. Baoyu lives in a tense space where there are practically no borders between himself and his cousins. What separates him from them, sexually, is obvious: they are relatives with whom one should not have premarital sexual relations. Qin Keqing, however, in her incestuous relation with her father-in-law, did the unthinkable, and while it seems to be beyond Baoyu's conscious intention to seduce Daiyu, Baochai, or Shi Xiangyun, he is constantly manipulating them into situations of boudoir intimacy, ever broaching the borderline of forbidden pleasure. In the garden mix of virgin cousin and sexually experienced maid, "pure" suicide and "impure" marriage, we have a deepening vision of adolescence as a precarious and threatened state and, moreover, a clear demonstration of Baoyu's conflict between the emergence of adult sexuality and his childish recoiling from it.

THE *DREAM* AS ADOLESCENT ILLNESS NARRATIVE

Cao Xueqin's fascination with the ephemeral quality of adolescence is epitomized in his portrait of illness in the *Dream of the Red Chamber*. Baoyu's identity crisis and role confusion, the mixed messages of parents and elders, the exquisitely empty nature of garden life—all mirror a general malaise that is replicated in the pervasive health concerns of adolescents, the pressures they face and the conventions they must uphold regarding education, and their ambivalence over sexuality. Poor health and health worries frequently mask moral problems, or else they may be a somatic manifestation of psychological disquiet. The peculiar nature of the passing life of children is unfolded through an illness narrative, a kind of allegory of sickness that belies the golden world of childhood.

Arthur Kleinman, who has written extensively on health in Chinese society, defines illness as a cultural and patterned way in which a sick person perceives and interprets symptoms and disability. An illness narrative "is a story the patient tells, and significant others retell, to give coherence to the distinctive events and long-term course of suffering."[96] To the extent that Cao Xueqin's *Dream of the Red Chamber* is autobiographical, as Hu Shi and others have claimed, it may be considered the author and commentators' own illness narrative, an attempt to come to terms with the decline and fall of the Cao clan. But I think that from the fictional perspective of the text, there is a more persuasive argument: the *Dream of the Red Chamber* is the illness narrative of adolescents about adolescence.

Children and Disease

Among the garden children, and the Jia family adults and servants as well, health issues are a pervasive, daily concern, reflecting, perhaps, Qing social realities even among those with the best access to medical resources. Twenty-two of the Kangxi emperor's fifty-five children died before age four, and 50 to 60 percent of the sons of each of the three eighteenth-century Qing emperors died before they were fifteen.[97] In the *Dream of the Red Chamber*, consumption, tuberculosis, and smallpox—common Qing diseases, the latter especially feared among children—are frequently alluded to.[98] Wang Xifeng's baby daughter, for instance, becomes infected with smallpox,[99] and Aroma suffers tuberculosis.[100] There is a steady and broad-ranging stream of curers (most of whom are useless cheats, says Baoyu's maid, Skybright),[101] making sick calls on the Jia family—doctors, exorcists, black magic practitioners, Taoist longevity experts, fertility specialists—offering a host of diagnoses and remedies based on medical texts, popular lore, and a vast pharmacopoeia.[102] Baoyu brags to his mother about his knowledge of pills.[103] The family is keen on acquiring special medicines and health foods available only to the elite,[104] including foreign drugs like snuff.[105]

But in the *Dream of the Red Chamber*, health worries among adolescents often border on hypochondria. The maids of the household get used to the fact that Daiyu is always sickly and moody.[106] In fact, she practically lives on medicine.[107] Baochai suffers from a recurrent illness for which she needs steady bed rest and rare prescriptions.[108] There is a whole panoply of female disorders that the novelist hints are related to the onset of puberty—hormonal changes, menstruation, pregnancy—and one thinks of Qin Keqing's mysterious "illness" from which she dies, quite possibly an abortion.[109] For young women who must contemplate wedlock, marriage is a health threat to themselves and family, linking gender and disease. Wang Xifeng, a young woman in her upper teens, suffers a miscarriage and years of chronic hemorrhage through marriage, not to mention an uncaring profligate husband, Jia Lian.[110] The connection between her female illnesses and her mean and vindictive spirit is formulaic in the novel. "Pure" and good adolescent virgins become "impure" and evil adult women by marrying and achieving domestic power.[111]

While unmarried girls are emblems of virtue, they are at least potentially a source of pollution and familial disruption through menstruation and pregnancy. On the other hand, men are seen as the polluters of adolescent women. Baoyu becomes self-conscious about his own impurity following a youthful dream where he has his first sexual experience.[112] Throughout the novel he is certain that all men are equally unclean, like himself.[113] Terrified by the possibility of becoming Jia She's concubine, Faithful, Grandmother Jia's maid, cuts off her hair, threatens suicide, and swears that she will become a nun in order to stay unpolluted.[114]

Somatic Suffering and Neurasthenia

The significance of adolescent illness in the *Dream of the Red Chamber* is not simply that it is something which happens to an innocent, unmarried person. Stylistically it is important because it becomes a narrative discourse in the novel through which individuals relate to one another and make sense of their lives. Medically speaking, the somatic manifestation of illness seen in Cao Xueqin's work reveals an understanding of adolescent illness that may be particular to traditional Chinese culture.

Somatization is the expression of distress through bodily complaints and seeking medical help. Often taking the form of prolonged preoccupation with illness and becoming part of everyday behavior, it is normative and adaptive—an idiom of disability that is learned and is part of the ecology of the local system of family and culture.[115] In China, depression commonly has social and cultural origins, rather than private and individual ones, which manifest themselves in nervous exhaustion, chronic fatigue, and weakness—a collective syndrome termed neurasthenia.[116] In the *Dream of the Red Chamber*, adolescent distress and depression are always manifested somatically and are never understood by family members as mental health issues. If Baoyu acts in an aberrant manner, as he is wont to do, leaping about or smiling vacantly or mumbling incoherently, the diagnosis is physical, never psychological. He needs a change in diet, or medicine, or environment, not an analysis of his relation to his parents or his sex life.

Examples of neurasthenia and somatic illness are manifold. Baoyu, his female cousins, and the garden maids, like many adults in the novel, commonly complain about nervous exhaustion, fatigue, and weakness. When Baoyu hears the news of Qin Keqing's death, he spits blood.[117] He becomes physically sick at the thought of a marriage proposed by a Buddhist abbot.[118] A lover's quarrel with Baoyu or a reflection on mutability will drive Daiyu into a profound melancholia that reveals itself physically.[119] Her depression manifests itself somatically, making her speechless and prohibiting her from expressing her true feelings to Baoyu.[120] When the lovers are falsely told they will soon be separated, Baoyu turns numb, while Daiyu coughs so hard she loses her breath. The cause of illness and its remedy are both physical, reflecting the somatic understanding of stress. Aroma blames Baoyu's condition on the weather. Daiyu's maid, Nightingale, tries to cure her mistress with a massage.[121]

In the *Dream of the Red Chamber*, most of the adolescents, but especially Baoyu and Daiyu, prove themselves to be skillful at manipulating their illness narratives in order to influence others, gain support, express emotions, or conceal them—strategies typical of somatic cultures.[122] Daiyu, for example, the outsider and orphan, is a person of unequal power in the family, even among the garden cousins, so she tries to negotiate the meanings of her illness to attract Baoyu and gain security. And, of course, Daiyu and Baoyu are continually using their illness narratives to manipulate one another. The difficulty for both is that their neurasthenia is not simply private and acute, but public and chronic, and they become "problem patients" within the family.[123] As their ill relationship is felt to be messy and threatening to others, it ends up being disregarded or repressed by elder adults, cousins, and servants. Baoyu and Daiyu cannot be left free to manipulate one another through their illnesses because such manipulations only exacerbate their painful interdependency, leaving their relation at center stage. When Baoyu's grandmother and mother secretly decide it would be best for Baoyu to marry Baochai, they need to lessen his focus on his relation with Daiyu, forget about their own admiration for her, and overlook her illness. Besides, as the fortunes of the family decline, treating the pair of sick adolescent lovers becomes inordinately expensive.

In the last analysis, the illness narrative that adolescents weave in the *Dream of the Red Chamber* appears culturally specific. When read superficially, the children's narrative reveals no pathogenic disease for which adults are responsible. But as we listen to the latter's mixed message of opposing ideals—filial piety and duty to elders versus the indulgence and infantilizing of young adults, sexual innocence versus intimacy, distant versus close familial relations, art for art's sake versus art for officialdom, private versus public morality— we discern that, for the adolescents inextricably wedged between contradiction, the message and the social body that voices it may be considered psychopathological. The adults seem not to be aware that they are playing games with their children; nor do they understand why they are doing so or realize what the consequences might be. In promoting the creation of an impossible garden, the adults are perhaps projecting their fantasies and walling out personal and social realities from memory. As noted earlier, these realities—uncertain identity, traumatic relations with parents, sexual tensions—are not to be denied, although the garden world cannot equip children to deal with them. The adults are the hidden children of the *Dream*, helping to build a kiddieland while shouting that the children must grow up and behave. They provide no ladders over the wall and construct few bridges between adolescent and adult worlds. Perhaps this is why the children's story is largely an illness narrative. Suddenly one day the elders precipitate the end of youth by arranging marriages—in effect, closing the garden.

Within the world of the novel, the treatment of Baoyu is largely somatic. He has no psychological problems. But one might argue that his and Daiyu's illness is the mark of a children's disease in mid-Qing elite society that is culturally induced, rather than a matter of fate, as suggested by the Goddess of Creation (Nügua) and the Goddess of Disillusionment in the novel's initial chapters. It is this sickness in the social body that Cao Xueqin lays bare through his illness narrative. In short, the problem of adolescent illness lies within an elite culture that is unable to perceive its own disease, typified in the contradictory demands and messages of its adults, a disease that Cao Xueqin reveals to be pathogenic and destructive, stranding children in a borderland between inner and outer worlds.

Sexuality

On the surface it appears that adolescent sexuality is clearly bifurcated in the *Dream of the Red Chamber:* elite girls are expected to be moral models of purity and innocence, while boys are free to explore sexual desires so long as they are not disruptive to family or society. In the novel such male explorations do become *luan,* chaotic and disruptive, and receive considerable attention from Cao Xueqin, for they are central to his vision of premarital adolescence as a tertiary world that is both desirable and abhorrent, timeless yet vulnerable, and emblematic of life as a whole.

Baoyu is sexually experienced at an early age: his first sexual experience is with his maid, Aroma, when he is twelve (thirteen *sui*).[124] By the time he is fifteen, he proves himself to be a connoisseur of erotic paintings, showing off to his friends by identifying pictures by the Ming-dynasty artist Tang Yin.[125] He is subject to "pure," nonsexual love for his cousins Daiyu, Baochai, and Shi Xiangyun and to "impure" sexual relations with maids Aroma, Patience (Ping'er), Parfumée (Fangguan), Musk (Sheyue), and Skybright (Qingwen), among others. As remarked earlier, Baoyu is also a "pretty boy" *(mei nanzi)* noted for his feminine appearance and preference for girls. He is sexually aroused when he meets girlish-looking boys, such as Qin Zhong,[126] and female impersonators, like Jiang Yuhan.[127] He carries on a homosexual love affair while attending the Jia family school,[128] and he blackmails Qin Zhong into having sex with him while they are attending the funeral for Qin Keqing.[129] Baoyu dresses up Parfumée as a boy, finding her more attractively exotic. In a lengthy commentary underscoring the theme of adolescent bisexuality, the Stone narrator remarks at this point in the *Dream of the Red Chamber* that there are many transvestites in the Jia household and much interest among the girls and their maids in dressing up as boys.[130] As the Goddess of Disillusionment comments—she confesses that this is the reason why she herself finds Baoyu so attractive—Baoyu (in the guise of the stone) is the most lustful person in the world![131]

A Western psychologist might trace Baoyu's bisexuality to various

familial factors such as his lack of a male model with which to identify or his emotional distance from both father and mother. Contemporary Chinese commentators find its source in Baoyu's luxurious,
pampered life, where he is surrounded night and day by a bevy of
beautiful young female cousins and maids and separated from
elders.[132] But we might note that Baoyu's sexual orientation accords
with the Qianlong cultural context (1736–1795), an era in which
male and female prostitution flourished and homosexual relationships with female impersonators became stylish, official puritanical
prohibitions notwithstanding. The aging emperor's own fondness for
a handsome young Manchu, Heshen, "gave an unspoken encouragement to such relationships."[133] In this regard the text reflects the cultural texture. For example, Jia Zhen and Xue Pan, Baochai's brother,
carry on affairs with male prostitutes during a period of mourning
for Jia Jing, deceased head of the Ningguo branch of the family.[134]
One reason why Jia Zheng nearly beats his son to death is because
Baoyu lies about his involvement with a female impersonator, Jiang
Yuhan, whose stage name is Bijou (Qiguan), a favorite of the Prince
of Zhongshan.[135] What is wrong with Baoyu's relationship is not
homosexual sex but a breach of etiquette: Bijou belongs to a member
of the imperial household. This same female impersonator, Jiang
Yuhan, is given a special sash to wear by another royal admirer, the
Prince of Beijing.[136] Such episodes suggest imperial sanction of homosexual relations or at least officialdom looking the other way. It is
also possible that, in the mid-Qing era, adolescent homosexual love
is viewed as a permissible stage a young boy may go through, as it
was in the late Ming.

Whatever the source of Baoyu's bisexual orientation, his bisexual
activities inside and outside the garden appear to be accepted, as are
those of other young males such as Jia Lian, Xue Pan, Qin Zhong,
and Jiang Yuhan, so long as they are not disruptive to the family. But
in fact they are disruptive—recall Baoyu's heterosexual involvement
with Golden which ends in her suicide, his homosexual relationship
with Bijou which brings court officials to the Jia household to find
him, and the homosexual love affairs at the Jia family school which
erupt in the disintegration of studies. Often the culprit in an adolescent sexual relation in the *Dream of the Red Chamber* is mercilessly
punished or develops a somatic illness. There is a taste of homophobia or moral criticism of homosexuals in the novel: Liu Xianglian
tricks Xue Pan into thinking he will be his lover, then horsewhips
him;[137] Aroma admits to Baoyu that she is disgusted with his involvement with homosexuals, whom she finds contemptible.[138]

What is strange, in the face of so much sexual activity, is the defense of male adolescents' innocence by well-meaning elders, especially women. We previously noted Lady Wang's protection of her "innocent" son. When young Baoyu, naive about incest, asks Wang Xifeng about sexual innuendos he has overheard regarding Qin Keqing and her father-in-law, Jia Zhen, Wang Xifeng quickly hushes him, saying that such filthy talk is bad for children.[139] There is a great uproar in the family when a purse with a pornographic picture of sexual coupling is discovered in the garden—the horror of sex is invading the world of adolescent innocence. Adults are upset because, while it is acceptable for an adult couple like Jia Lian and Wang Xifeng to have such a purse (married persons are a source of impurity), the children of the garden are supposed to be innocent.[140] To ensure that innocence and purity perdure, Aroma urges Lady Wang to move Baoyu out of the garden, as he and his cousins are growing up, and their continued dwelling together makes the family look strange to outsiders.[141] Oddly, late in adolescence, Baoyu does not understand the sexual jokes of a Taoist priest who comes to cure him of a somatic illness, revealing a simplicity and naïveté despite a world of sexual experience.[142]

I think this emphasis on innocence and naïveté suggests that surface appearances of broadmindedness belie the reality that adolescent sex is highly problematical in the Dream of the Red Chamber. Marital sex in Chinese culture might be suggested as a contrast to adolescent heterosexual sex in the Dream of the Red Chamber, the former being comparatively egalitarian and healthy.[143] In the Dream, illicit heterosexual relations and somatic illnesses are inextricably bound together. Jia Rui, the frustrated lover of Wang Xifeng, dies in a pool of semen after repeated illusory acts of intercourse with an image of Wang Xifeng he sees in a magic mirror, which are actually acts of masturbation.[144] Baoyu's close friend, Qin Zhong, younger brother of Qin Keqing, creates evil karma through a love affair with Sapientia (Zhineng), a Buddhist novice, and perishes in a profound depression, surrounded by spirits who sweep him off to the underworld.[145] The love affairs between two male profligates, Jia Zhen and Jia Lian, and two unchaste sisters, You Erjie and You Sanjie, end with the women committing suicide and You Erjie acknowledging that her misery is retribution for her sexual sinfulness.[146] When Baoyu is deathly ill, all women are prohibited from visiting his bedroom, except for his grandmother and mother, and this period of enforced celibacy required by a Taoist monk restores him to health.[147] Yingchun's maid, Chess (Siqi), feels deeply guilty over a love affair with another servant, and when he runs away, she takes to her bed, eventually dying with symptoms of neurasthenia.[148]

Heterosexual sex is not only morally polluting. With the exception of a rare miscarriage or induced abortion,[149] it is not procreative, whether licit or illicit. There are few little children in the *Dream of the Red Chamber* and practically no babies, despite the sexual proclivities of the Jia males. A reader may assume a widespread Qing practice of birth control or abortion. But what is apparent in the novel is a sexual impoverishment, a kind of spiritual lack, which is not fulfilled through exploration.

One wonders if Baoyu's sexual freedom really is "innocent" or whether its expression is at the root of his constant acting out, his somatic illnesses, and his eventual turn to Buddhism. Baoyu seems haunted by a sexual anxiety that becomes palpable in his first sexual experience as a twelve-year-old, an ambivalent adolescent experience of masturbation and intercourse. In that episode, Qin Keqing puts him in her bed for an afternoon nap and he dreams of a nightmarish sexual encounter with her, ending with his awaking from a wet dream and having sexual intercourse with his maid, Aroma. Baoyu's repugnance for boys and reverence for girls, presented in the *Dream* as an unexplained innate aspect of his character, does not stem from moral guilt—his relation with Aroma is sanctioned by the family. But that innate repugnance which predates sexual experience comes to the fore and intensifies in the boyish shame felt from self-pollution through the ejaculation of seminal fluids—a cold, sticky presence that embarrasses both himself and Aroma.[150] His self-discovery is quickly suppressed through intercourse with Aroma, where sex becomes acceptable, but I suspect this polluting experience clouds his psyche. In the Chinese cultural context, the loss of semen *(jing)* through nocturnal emissions, masturbation, or too frequent sexual intercourse spells a worrisome loss of vital energy *(qi)* and is potentially life-threatening.[151] One is tempted to conclude that Baoyu's psychosomatic illnesses, his manic-depressive states, his obsessing over the purity of girls and the impurity of boys, his addiction to bisexual relations, and his fear of the loss of Daiyu and other female cousins through marriage are all related both to this first masturbation-intercourse experience of sex—described by Cao Xueqin both more explicitly and with greater innuendo than any other sexual episode in the novel—and to the sexual experiences that follow. The episode, a brilliant elaboration on sexual shame and pleasure, lies at the base of Baoyu's subsequent and paradoxical attitudes and relations, an endless play of attraction to and repulsion from that which is pure and impure in adolescent sexuality.

How else are we to understand why the adults paradoxically defend and demand the sexual innocence of children when in fact they know the children are not at all innocent? Why is there an emphasis in the *Dream of the Red Chamber* on Baoyu's adolescent sexual innocence when everyone is aware he is experienced? Aroma is a family gift. Flirting with maids is a daily garden adventure. Partying with bisexual male friends and female impersonators is fun, too. I think that innocence is defended because, beneath the surface appearance of sexual permissiveness, innocence is essential to a deeper, spiritual grasp of ultimate reality, and adults unconsciously know it. For Baoyu, his heterosexual, homosexual, and bisexual experience is something to be gone through and transcended, a stage that must be mounted and surmounted, on the road to Buddhist enlightenment. While my focus on premarital adolescence prohibits detailed discussion of Baoyu's Buddhist transcendence, which occurs in the last chapters of the *Dream*, there is no question that Buddhism (and certain Taoist corollaries via *Zhuangzi*) eventually guides Baoyu in a spiral movement from innocence to experience to final innocence. The death of Daiyu, a disappointing marriage to Baochai, the loss of garden childhood friends, the emptiness of ambition— all are privations that turn Baoyu away from the world, propelling him on his quest, but none of them individually or collectively provides a path to transcendence. That path is innocence, achieved through the full exploration of the "Red Dust," the Buddhist term for the ephemeral world that is both beautiful and disintegrating, like youth, beautiful youth. Sexuality, so problematical to adolescents in the garden of the *Dream*, and never reducible to mere genital experience, is emblematic of that world. For most of the children, desire will bind them to the Red Dust, as it does nearly all the adults, perhaps because their desires are circumscribed. In Baoyu, the most lustful person in the world, the exhaustion of the Red Dust enables his return to innocence and transcendence. Only he is purified by experience.

CONCLUSION

It is difficult to read the *Dream of the Red Chamber* as a portrait of Chinese children in elite Qing society, since so often Cao Xueqin parodies and weeps over its conventions. Adolescent youth are freighted with a burden of rules, etiquette, hierarchy, convention, educational standards, and fixed notions of morality. For the author, the saving grace of the garden world seems to be that he can posit another world, one that contrasts radically to whatever is normative in the culture. Cao Xueqin's focus is on children as border walkers in an adolescent world that is precariously balanced on the edge of time and adulthood, a land where rules may be suspended by well-meaning adults and where youth are both transient and vulnerable and inordinately bright and attractive. Living a liminal existence in a risky world, where elders seem contradictory, parents distant, grandmothers inconsistent, young girls pure and unpure, and young men bisexual, there is indeed identity confusion and disquiet. But even as adolescence unravels as a somatic response in youthful bodies to social disease, it is transformed into a golden allegory of health and ultimate well-being, and the illness narrative of Cao Xueqin and his cast of characters rises, like the proverbial phoenix, from the ashes of youth to the pleroma of Buddhist emptiness and transcendence.

NOTES

1. See Karuna Kar Vaidya, ed., *Folktales of Nepal* (Kathmandu: Ratna Pustak Bhandar, 1971); Lucien Miller, ed., *South of the Clouds: Yunnan Tales*, trans. Guo Xu, Lucien Miller, and Xu Kun (Seattle: University of Washington Press, 1994).

2. Richard J. Smith, *China's Cultural Heritage: The Ch'ing Dynasty, 1644–1912* (Boulder: Westview Press, 1983), p. 216.

3. Tu Wei-ming, "The Confucian Perception of Adulthood," *Daedalus* 105(2) (Spring 1976):110–112.

4. Lawrence Kohlberg, *The Philosophy of Moral Development: Moral Stages and the Idea of Justice: Essays on Moral Development* (San Francisco: Harper & Row, 1981); Lawrence Kohlberg, *The Psychology of Moral Development: The Nature and Validity of Moral States* (San Francisco: Harper & Row, 1984); Jean Piaget, *The Child's Conception of the World*, trans. Jean and Andrew Tomlinson (Totowa, N.J.: Littlefield, Adams, 1976); Dorothy B. Singer and Tracey A. Revenson, *A Piaget Primer: How a Child Thinks* (New York: International Universities Press, 1978).

5. Susan Naquin and Evelyn S. Rawski, eds., *Chinese Society in the Eighteenth Century* (New Haven: Yale University Press, 1987), p. 80.

6. Robert E. Hegel, ed., *Expressions of Self in Chinese Literature* (New York: Columbia University Press, 1985), pp. 15–20.

7. One vital form of "becoming" in the adolescent is Baoyu's Buddhist

salvation quest. It is not investigated here as it flowers mainly in the final "postmarital" third of the novel, which covers later adolescence. Baoyu's Buddhism is inextricably bound up with questions of marriage and evolves when most of the maidens have been married off and his own forthcoming marriage is inevitable.

8. Smith, *China's Cultural Heritage*, p. 219.

9. Jonathan D. Spence, *Ts'ao Yin and the K'ang-hsi Emperor: Bondservant and Master* (New Haven: Yale University Press, 1966), pp. 85–89, 116.

10. John C. Y. Wang, "The Chih-yen-chai Commentary and the *Dream of the Red Chamber*: A Literary Study," in Adele Austin Rickett, ed., *Chinese Approaches to Literature from Confucius to Liang Ch'i-ch'ao* (Princeton: Princeton University Press, 1978), pp. 196, 205–206. "Zhiyanzhai" is here used in the collective sense, meaning the composite work of the several commentators found in various eighty-chapter manuscripts of the novel. For a collected edition of commentaries see Yu Pingbo, ed., *Zhiyanzhai Honglou meng jiping* (Shanghai: Zhonghua shuju, 1963).

11. Wang, "The Chih-yen-chai Commentary and the *Dream of the Red Chamber*," p. 202.

12. Leo Tolstoy, *Childhood, Boyhood and Youth*, trans. Louise Maude and Aylmer Maude (London: Oxford University Press, 1957).

13. Sa Mengwu, *Honglou meng yu Zhongguo jiu jiating* (*Dream of the Red Chamber* and the traditional Chinese family) (Taipei: Dongda tushu gongsi, 1977), p. 176.

14. See, for example, *HLM* 23:180; *SS* 23:460. Chapter and page citations of the *Dream of the Red Chamber* are from: *Honglou meng (HLM)*, ed. Rao Bin (Taipei: Sanmin shuju, 1973); *Honglou meng bashihui jiaoben (HLMBSHJB)*, ed. Yu Pingbo (Beijing: Renmin wenxue chuban she, 1958); and the English translation of David Hawkes and John Minford, *The Story of the Stone (SS)*, vols. 1–3 (Harmondsworth: Penguin, 1978–1980).

15. *HLM* 19:144–145; *SS* 19:379, 381.

16. *HLM* 51:429; *SS* 51:520.

17. *HLM* 57:489; *SS* 57:100.

18. *HLM* 78:693; *SS* 78:561.

19. *HLM* 54:454–455; *SS* 54:25, 27.

20. Daiyu is fifteen *sui*, or fourteen, in *HLM* 45:376; *SS* 45:397; Baoyu is one year her senior.

21. *HLM* 19:149; *SS* 19:391.

22. *HLM* 25:194; 43:354; *SS* 25:490; 43:346.

23. *HLM* 56:483; 57:490; *SS* 56:87; 57:101.

24. *HLM* 44:368; *SS* 44:377.

25. *HLM* 26:209; *SS* 26:523.

26. *HLM* 40:334; *SS* 40:298.

27. *HLM* 62:535; 63:547–548; *SS* 62:203; 63:230–231.

28. *HLM* 37:298; *SS* 37:213.

29. *HLM* 52:436; *SS* 52:537.

30. *HLM* 26:206; *SS* 26:515.

31. Erik H. Erikson, *Childhood and Society* (New York and London: Norton, 1985), pp. 261–263.

32. *HLM* 3:113–114; *SS* 3:100–101.

33. *HLM* 66:576; *SS* 66:294.

34. *HLMBSHJB* 78:886; *SS* 78:556.

35. Erickson, *Childhood and Society,* pp. 263–266.

36. Sa Mengwu, *Honglou meng yu Zhongguo jiu jiating,* pp. 11–16, 21–25.

37. *HLM* 25:197–198; *SS* 25:496–497.

38. *HLM* 72:632; *SS* 72:423.

39. Richard W. Wilson, "Conformity and Deviance Regarding Moral Rules in Chinese Society: A Socialization Perspective," in Arthur Kleinman and Tsung-yi Lin, eds., *Normal and Abnormal Behavior in Chinese Culture* (Dordrecht, Boston, and London: D. Reidel, 1981), p. 122.

40. *HLM* 3:22; *SS* 3:97.

41. *HLM* 33:268; *SS* 33:150.

42. *HLMBSHJB* 17–18:177; *SS* 18:358.

43. *HLM* 19:149; *SS* 19:390.

44. *HLM* 30:245; *SS* 30:101.

45. *HLM* 32:263; *SS* 32:138.

46. *HLM* 32:263; *SS* 32:138.

47. *HLM* 74:650; 77:682; *SS* 74:463; 77:535.

48. *HLM* 77:463; *SS* 77:535.

49. *HLM* 25:200; *SS* 25:502.

50. *HLM* 9:71; 17:126–128; *SS* 9:203; 17:340–343.

51. *HLM* 23:179; *SS* 23:457.

52. *HLM* 72:638; *SS* 72:434.

53. *HLM* 78:693; *SS* 78:559.

54. *HLM* 3:18–19; *SS* 3:88–89.

55. *HLM* 5:34; *SS* 5:124.

56. *HLM* 35:283; *SS* 35:180.

57. Sa Mengwu, *Honglou meng yu Zhongguo jiu jiating,* pp. 43–55.

58. *HLM* 45:375; 48:402; *SS* 45:391; 48:455–456.

59. Naquin and Rawski, *Chinese Society in the Eighteenth Century,* pp. 35, 52, 57.

60. Haun Saussy, "Reading and Folly in *Dream of the Red Chamber,*" *Chinese Literature: Essays, Articles, Reviews* 9(1–2) (July 1987):35.

61. *HLM* 23:182; *SS* 23:463.

62. *HLM* 32:260; *SS* 32:131.

63. Evelyn Sakakida Rawski, *Education and Popular Literacy in Ch'ing China* (Ann Arbor: University of Michigan Press, 1979), pp. 48–49.

64. Ibid., pp. 111–115.

65. Deng Yunxiang, *Honglou fengsu tan* (On social and cultural life in *Dream of the Red Chamber*) (Beijing: Zhonghua shuju, 1987), pp. 262–273.

66. *HLM* 17:129; *SS* 17:339.

67. *HLM* 18; *SS* 18.

68. *HLM* 9:72; *SS* 9:204.

69. Deng Yunxiang, *Honglou fengsu tan*, pp. 266–270.

70. *HLMBSHJB* 66:736; *SS* 66:293.

71. Deng Yunxiang, *Honglou fengsu tan*, p. 271.

72. *HLM* 73:638–639; *SS* 73:436.

73. *HLM* 36:290; *SS* 36:195.

74. *HLM* 32:259; *SS* 32:130.

75. Mary Backus Rankin, "The Emergence of Women at the End of the Ch'ing: The Case of Ch'iu Chin," in Margery Wolf and Roxanne Witke, eds., *Women in Chinese Society* (Stanford: Stanford University Press, 1975), p. 41.

76. *HLM* 50:418; *SS* 50:495.

77. *HLM* 42:349; 64:558; *SS* 42:333–334; 64:256.

78. *HLM* 3:23; *SS* 3:100.

79. *HLM* 76:674; *SS* 76:517.

80. *HLM* 48:405; *SS* 48:463.

81. *HLM* 18:139; *SS* 18:367.

82. Ping-leung Chan, "Myth and Psyche in *Hung-lou meng*," in Winston L. Y. Yang and Curtis P. Adkins, eds., *Critical Essays on Chinese Fiction* (Hong Kong: Chinese University Press, 1980), pp. 167–168.

83. *HLM* 5; *SS* 5.

84. Mary Scott, "The Image of the Garden in *Jin Ping Mei* and *Honglou meng*," *Chinese Literature: Essays, Articles, Reviews* 8(1–2) (July 1986): 91–92, 94.

85. *HLM* 2:16; *SS* 2:82.

86. *HLM* 5:34; *SS* 5:124.

87. *HLM* 5:43; *SS* 5:145.

88. *HLM* 19:143; *SS* 19:377.

89. *HLM* 20:158; *SS* 20:411.

90. *HLM* 21:161; *SS* 21:415.

91. *HLM* 32:260; 57:484; *SS* 32:133; 57:89.

92. *HLM* 77:681; *SS* 77:534.

93. Louise Edwards, "Women in *Honglou meng*: Prescriptions of Purity in the Femininity of Qing Dynasty China," *Modern China* 16(4) (October 1990):12–14.

94. *HLM* 111.

95. Margery Wolf, "Women and Suicide in China," in *Women in Chinese Society*, pp. 112–113.

96. Arthur Kleinman, *The Illness Narratives: Suffering, Healing, and the Human Condition* (New York: Basic Books, 1988), pp. 3, 49.

97. Naquin and Rawski, *Chinese Society in the Eighteenth Century*, pp. 107–108.

98. Ibid., p. 108.

99. *HLM* 21:165: *SS* 21:424.

100. *HLM* 77:688; *SS* 77:548.

101. *HLM* 52:440; *SS* 52:547.

102. Jonathan D. Spence, "Commentary on Historical Perspectives and Ch'ing Medical Systems," in Arthur Kleinman et al., eds., *Medicine in Chinese Cultures: Comparative Studies of Health Care in Chinese and Other Societies* (Washington, D.C.: U.S. Department of Health, Education, and Welfare, 1975), p. 81.

103. *HLM* 28:221; *SS* 28:45.

104. *HLM* 60:518–519; *SS* 60:165–166.

105. *HLM* 52:436; *SS* 52:536–537.

106. *HLM* 27:22; *SS* 27:23.

107. *HLM* 52:437; *SS* 52:538.

108. *HLM* 7:53–54; *SS* 7:167.

109. *HLM* 10:79; *SS* 10:219–220.

110. *HLM* 55:463–464; 72:630–631; *SS* 55:45; 72:420.

111. Edwards, "Women in *Honglou meng*," p. 14.

112. *HLM* 5:39; *SS* 5:136.

113. *HLM* 20:157; *SS* 20:407–408.

114. *HLM* 46:384; *SS* 46:416.

115. Arthur Kleinman, *Social Origins of Disease: Depression, Neurasthenia, and Pain in Modern China* (New Haven: Yale University Press, 1986), p. 3; Arthur Kleinman and Joan Kleinman, "Somatization: The Interconnection in Chinese Society Among Culture, Depressive Experiences, and the Meaning of Pain," in Arthur Kleinman and Byron Good, eds., *Culture and Depression: Studies in the Anthropology and Cross-Cultural Psychiatry of Affect and Disorder* (Berkeley: University of California Press, 1985), pp. 473–474.

116. Kleinman, *Social Origins of Disease*, pp. 34, 66; Kleinman, *The Illness Narratives*, p. 100; Kleinman and Kleinman, "Somatization," p. 467.

117. *HLM* 13:97; *SS* 13:258.

118. *HLM* 29:237; *SS* 29:83.

119. *HLM* 30:241; 23:183; *SS* 30:93; 23:467.

120. *HLM* 32:260; *SS* 32:134.

121. *HLM* 57:486–487; *SS* 57:93–95.

122. Kleinman, *The Illness Narratives*, pp. 11, 15.

123. Kleinman describes the "problem patient" syndrome in *The Illness Narratives*, p. 17.

124. *HLM* 6:44–45; *SS* 6:149.

125. *HLM* 26:208; *SS* 26:520.

126. *HLM* 7:58; *SS* 7:177.

127. *HLM* 28:227; *SS* 28:61.

128. Chapter 9.

129. *HLM* 15:113; *SS* 15:300.

130. *HLMBSHJB* 63:706; *SS* 63:237.

131. *HLM* 5:43; *SS* 5:145. Of course, as the goddess goes on to explain, she is not simply referring to physical sexual activity but to "lust of the mind," meaning desire in general, which in Baoyu's case is usually linked to emotion, sensitivity, and intelligence, thus distinguishing him from sexual addicts such as Baochai's brother, Xue Pan.

132. Sa Mengwu, *Honglou meng yu Zhongguo jiu jiating*, p. 59.

133. Naquin and Rawski, *Chinese Society in the Eighteenth Century*, pp. 62–63.

134. *HLM* 75:664; *SS* 75:493.

135. *HLM* 33:265; *SS* 33:143.

136. *HLM* 28:228; *SS* 28:61.

137. *HLM* 47:397; *SS* 47:443.

138. *HLM* 28:228; *SS* 28:63.

139. *HLM* 7:61; *SS* 7:183.

140. *HLM* 74:648; *SS* 74:459.

141. *HLM* 34:275; *SS* 34:164.

142. *HLM* 80:714; *SS* 80:609.

143. Smith, *China's Cultural Heritage*, p. 225.

144. *HLM* 12:94–95; *SS* 12:252.

145. *HLM* 16:122–123; *SS* 16:321.

146. *HLM* 69:608; *SS* 69:365.

147. *HLM* 25:201; *SS* 25:505.

148. *HLM* 72:630; *SS* 72:418.

149. See You Erjie episode, *HLM* 69:608–609; *SS* 69:366.

150. *HLM* 6:44–45; *SS* 6:148–149.

151. Kleinman, *The Illness Narratives*, p. 23.

GLOSSARY

baguwen	八股文	eight-legged essays
dushu	讀書	to recite out loud and memorize
fu	賦	prose poems
guwen	古文	classical literature
jing	精	semen
kanshu	看書	to read by looking
luan	亂	chaotic
mei nanzi	美男子	pretty boy
qi	氣	energy
qingnian	青年	young adulthood/adolescence
shaonian	少年	juvenile/youth

PART THREE

Early Modern and Modern China

Overleaf: Portrait of a woman and girl. Courtesy Peabody Essex Museum, Salem, Massachusetts.

9

Relief Institutions for Children in Nineteenth-Century China

ANGELA KI CHE LEUNG

This chapter explores how new ideas on the destitute child emerged and developed in the nineteenth century through the organization of relief institutions. These views are significantly different from those that informed early and mid-Qing foundling hospitals (established in the mid-seventeenth and eighteenth centuries) and have already been the subject of several studies.[1] Recently, the Japanese scholar Fuma Susumu has published several ground-breaking studies on nineteenth-century institutions for children in the Jiangnan region.[2] Consequently, that these institutions were, with few exceptions, essentially initiated, managed, and financed by the local people under elite leadership is now a generally accepted fact. Yet there are still many aspects of these hospices that invite further study. The change in the idea of the child as a social being is one of them.

My study is based essentially on institutions that had the richest resources and fullest experience in welfare provision for destitute children—those in the Jiangnan region, or roughly the Lower Yangzi area. In other parts of China, similar provisions could also be observed in better-off commercial centers. Hongjiang, a town *(zhen)* close to the Guizhou border in Hunan, is one example I will cite to show that Jiangnan cities were not entirely unique in their concern for child welfare.[3] But it is probably true that as a region Jiangnan had the highest concentration of institutions for destitute minors. We can therefore surmise that the new ideas behind these institutions were initiated in this region and later spread to other parts of the country.[4]

MODIFICATIONS OF THE RELIEF SYSTEM

The need to improve care for unwanted infants was felt as early as the end of the Qianlong period (1736–1795). Complaints about foundling hospitals in urban centers suggest that the hospices were badly organized. Corruption, negligence, and high rates of mortality and morbidity among the assisted children were among the charges leveled against them. The hospices in Yangzhou and Suzhou, for instance, two of the oldest and most important institutions in the Lower Yangzi area, were plagued with scandal at the end of the eighteenth century and were repeatedly "cleaned up" by local officials until their collapse at the arrival of the Taiping rebels.[5] The mismanagement of the hospices, of course, was at the foundlings' expense. Indeed, the reputation of the Yangzhou hospice had become so notorious around midcentury that local people called it the *shaying tang*: "hospice for killing infants."[6]

The Yangzhou example was certainly not an exception. In fact, mortality inside many of the institutions remained high throughout the nineteenth century. Fuma Susumu has calculated that as many as 48 to 50 percent of the babies died in certain Songjiang hospices in the late 1860s; 41 to 53 percent died in a northern Shanghai orphanage in the late 1880s; 31 to 39 percent died in the orphanage of Haining in the early 1890s. These figures conform to the claim made in an 1876 official document of Jiangsu province that only five or six out of ten babies could survive inside the average urban foundling home.[7] Mortality might have been even higher in less developed areas. One example is the hospice in Hongjiang, the Hunan town, which had accepted 133 infants (13 male and 120 female) between 1880 and 1887—of whom 89 died in the institution (7 male and 82 female)[8], representing a mortality of almost 67 percent within these seven years.[9] Though this exorbitant mortality might be traced to many causes, people tended to blame the bad management of the hospices.

Many were also aware of the limited access of these urban institutions, which were geographically beyond the reach of the rural families most likely to drown or abandon their newborn out of poverty or other considerations. For this reason, as early as the early eighteenth century, philanthropists of some of the more prosperous and urban areas started to organize in the more remote districts relay stations called *jieying tang* or *liuying tang*. Here babies were collected and eventually transferred to central institutions in major metropolitan centers. In some of the more populous towns, these stations actually functioned in much the same way as the standard foundling homes in big urban centers.[10] From the late eighteenth century on, the network of philanthropic institutions was rapidly branching out, at least in the Jiangnan area, until the momentum was interrupted by the Taiping Rebellion.[11]

Some, especially members of the gentry, began to question the effectiveness of the relief methods of the existing system, which concentrated all efforts on the inmates of the institution. They asked if a more flexible system, one with "outdoor relief" to the families of unwanted infants,[12] would not be more practical.[13] Wang Xisun, an Anhui merchant living in Yangzhou around 1845, noted that a better solution to the problem of infanticide and high infant mortality was to give monthly stipends to the mothers of unwanted babies. The mothers, who were bound to be more caring than the generally indifferent wet nurses, would therefore have more incentive to nourish their own children.[14] A contemporary from Hunan, Ouyang Zhaoxiong (*juren* 1837), made a similar suggestion:

> The wet nurses [of the foundling home of our city] all had their own children whom they nursed with their own milk. They therefore secretly fed the children under their charge with rice soup.... Soon these children died. Thus the method should be changed: all those who send in their baby girls should be given an identity card with which one could receive a monthly stipend of 600 cash as well as clothing. The baby would be nursed by her own mother. After having nourished the baby for some time, the mother would acquire a deeper sentiment toward her offspring and the child would no longer risk being drowned. After a year or two, the identity card could be withdrawn.[15]

The existence of another project, this time stated in a pamphlet proposing the organization of "Societies for the Preservation of Babies" *(baoying hui)* written in 1843, suggests that the idea of providing monthly stipends to the mothers of unwanted infants had probably become widespread by this time. The principle, devised by Yu Zhi (1809–1874), a member of the Wuxi gentry, was to give rice (one peck) and money (200 cash) every month to the needy parents of a newborn for a period of five months.[16] After five months, if the parents proved too poor to bring up the child, the baby could be sent to the city foundling home. Special allowances were also given to children whose fathers died before their birth. The argument was that parents would thereby be discouraged from drowning babies at birth. It was also argued that this plan would result in fewer children being sent to the hospices since parental love for the child would normally develop within the five months. It was proposed that the society should be financed by members who would each donate shares of 360 cash. To render the work more manageable, only children within ten *li* (about five kilometers) of the locality could receive assistance from the society. Yu Zhi not only set up the society in his hometown in 1843, he actually spent the next decade preaching his ideas through the community lecture system *(xiangyue)* of nearby regions until the eve of the Taiping Rebellion, which inevitably destroyed his entire project.[17] Nevertheless, his tracts and his ideas survived the upheaval and the example he set up in Wuxi was to inspire a whole new vogue of social assistance to the child in the post-Taiping period.[18]

POST-TAIPING PERIOD

Changed social circumstances in the wake of the Taiping Rebellion (1851–1864) helped to establish the new direction of welfare policies concerning children.[19] Led by Hong Xiaochuan, an unsuccessful scholar and convert to Christianity, the rebellion began in Guangxi province and eventually affected all southern provinces with enormous devastation and loss of life. Though it was finally put down by the Qing state with the help of provincial strongmen, the decade-long unrest had ravaged the social fabric.

The immense loss of life caused by the upheaval fostered the conviction that more lives were now urgently needed to recover social equilibrium. Equating a populous society with prosperity, many social reconstruction activists of this period explicitly cited the preservation of life as the main goal of the welfare system. In the preface to a set of rules for the city's *baoying hui* published in 1865, a gentry member of Tongxiang by the name of Yan Chen wrote:

> At this moment right after the pacification of the upheaval . . . the number of households in each county was reduced by 70 to 80 percent, or in the best of cases, by 30 to 40 percent. The destitution of the people is even worse than before. Not only do they drown their baby girls as before, but at times they also drown their baby boys. . . . The function of the foundling homes during the time of peace was merely to prevent the foundlings from dying, whereas the function of the societies for the preservation of babies after a great upheaval is to let life spring forth. Their importance is greater still.[20]

Statements concerning the urgent need for more lives appear in many other documents on the *baoying hui* of various places.[21] In other words, for the post-Taiping philanthropists concerned with children's welfare, more practical social needs outweighed the lofty ideals of earlier social activists.[22]

Another development that influenced policy was the appearance of an increasing number of seasonal refugee or mendicant children above the age of four or five in many urban centers. This phenomenon was of course not novel in the 1860s; it had already come to the attention of local leaders in the earlier half of the century. The causes of this disquieting phenomenon were closely linked to the general loosening of the socioeconomic fabric from the end of the Qianlong reign onward. Such a development was common in many regions of China. In Wujin, for example, a *xugu ju* (bureau to give relief to orphans) was established in 1836 to accommodate children ages five to fourteen from the tenth month to the second month of the following year.[23] This initiative had apparently triggered a series of similar attempts in lower Jiangsu province.[24] In Shanghai, the Englishman W. C. Milne visited one of these asylums in 1850:

> The asylum was but temporary—only for a few months, to meet the peculiar exigencies of the juncture. . . . The number of children, when I visited it, amounted to two thousand, one-third of them girls. Each child was well clad, and seemed well fed. A ticket was put on each, and a minute registry kept of the place from which the child was brought; so that, on the breaking up of the asylum, it might be restored to its proper guardians. . . . The average ages were between three and ten.[25]

Homeless children were getting attention in the 1830s even in a peripheral province like Guizhou. Between 1836 and 1845 the governor of the province, He Changling (1785–1848), set up a *jiyou tang* (home for the young) that gave relief to more than one hundred children ages five to seventeen and provided them with basic education and training in various crafts. These children, too old for the foundling home and too young for the general hospital, "not only lacked jobs to keep themselves alive but also had no one to discipline them."[26] He's main concern was that this youthful lot should be properly guided lest they turn to banditry.

Wandering bands of juveniles were clearly the cause of much anxious concern, for the influx of such children into the cities seems to have increased dramatically since the Taiping Rebellion. Now they were not just seasonal refugees but tended to stay in the big metropolitan centers where they could beg for a living. Such a sight was said to be common in Shanghai around 1866:

Hundreds of refugee children, most from other regions, beg inside and outside the city wall. When asked what has become of their parents, they answer that they have been killed or kidnapped or have died of illness, of cold or of hunger. . . . These children's clothes and shoes are torn, their hair and faces dirty. They almost do not look human.[27]

The situation prompted the establishment of the "Bureau of Relief and Education" *(fujiao ju)* in 1866, which provided shelter, food, clothes, and medical care, as well as basic education and training in various skills, to some 250 children under sixteen years of age.[28] In Changshu three centers were set up to accommodate refugee children *(nantong)* shortly after the rebellion was pacified.[29] Clearly the more complex social character of the needy child—that is, the child considered within the context of the family and society and not merely as an inmate of an institution—affected the thinking of post-Taiping philanthropists when they designed relief projects for children in their hometowns.

Another new phenomenon that affected relief policy was the existence of foreign missionary foundling homes, which were often targets of popular suspicion.[30] Many, especially the authorities, believed that a wider network of native foundling homes and orphanages would offset the effect of this foreign presence:

Most of the incidents involving Christian missions were caused by hooligans slandering the missionary foundling homes with such calumnies as the charge that they brutally killed the babies. Thus the establishment of [native] orphanages is absolutely necessary to improve the situation.[31]

The authorities believed that the insufficient number and the poor organization of Chinese institutions provided the best excuse for the missionaries to set up their own orphanages. Indeed the establishment of more native foundling homes was no longer simply a manifestation of compassion but now was seen by the authorities as an essential political measure to counter imperialism:

For the sake of the missionaries, unless their orphanages are closed, the suspicion of the people cannot be laid to rest; for the sake of the country, unless orphanages are widely established, the missionaries will take advantage of this deficiency to continue operating.[32]

Missionary foundling homes not only aroused popular suspicion, they also hurt the pride of the Chinese authorities, who considered the presence of foreign charitable institutions to be a mocking comment on their own incompetence.[33] The tactful diplomat Xue Fucheng (1838–1894) knew better than anyone that foreign orphanages could not possibly be closed down. He therefore recommended stricter supervision of the institutions by local bureaucrats and gentry in order to weaken their humiliating autonomy.[34] Anxiety over the missionary foundling homes, more than any other factor, accounts for the renewed bureaucratic interest in native institutions after the Taiping Rebellion. It may also help to explain the widened gentry interest in child welfare, especially in places where foreign presence was conspicuous.

BLOOMING OF THE *BAOYING* SYSTEM

Though the model of the idealistic early Qing foundling hospital survived the Taiping Rebellion, it proved inadequate to cope with the overwhelming social problems left by the destruction. Besides the rapid and spontaneous growth of relay stations and smaller hospices in the *zhen* and even *xiang* (a settlement smaller than the *zhen*), Yu Zhi's idea of giving outdoor relief to all babies of poor families, not only those abandoned by their parents, found its most receptive audience in this period of reconstruction. Sometimes the *baoying* society was the only system available in a locality; more often it was combined with existing foundling hospices or relay stations. Numerous societies of the same nature but bearing different names also emerged after the Taiping. Some of the better-known ones, called "six cash societies" *(liuwen hui)*, were financed by members donating shares of 6 cash each.[35]

One easily finds detailed records of the regulations governing *baoying hui* in gazetteers of major cities from the 1860s on, some of which explicitly trace the origin of the system to the 1843 society in Wuxi. The following summary is based on three detailed sets of regulations: one published by Jiangsu province in 1876, another published by Nanxun *zhen* (a town under the jurisdiction of Wucheng of Zhejiang province, at the southeastern edge of Lake Tai) in 1868, and the last one published in 1888 in the *zhen* of Hongjiang.[36] The similarities of the regulations published in places of different geographical and administrative importance suggest the remarkable consensus on standard practices. But of equal interest are some of the minor variations in the rules. Regulations from several other places will also be cited here to supplement this account.

The main principle of the post-Taiping *baoying* system, as initiated by Yu Zhi some thirty years before, was to provide outdoor relief (money, rice, and clothing) to the newborns' families in order to reduce the chances of poverty-induced infanticide. At this time, however, the regulations became more detailed and allowed for different kinds of assistance depending on a family's individual needs. Families with male infants, for instance, would have more difficulties getting relief in Hongjiang, since it was less likely that boys would be drowned at birth.[37] Boys had to have lost a parent in order to qualify. The same principle applied to firstborn babies, whose families had to prove that they were more destitute than others in order to receive aid. Furthermore, more aid would be given to infants who lost one or both parents at birth. It is obvious that the post-Taiping organizers were more conscious of the complex motives behind infanticide and were becoming more realistic in their approach to the problem.

Table 1 should give us an idea of the principles behind the various levels of assistance available to needy infants.[38] In these institutions, although the monthly amount of aid for the "normal" child was

TABLE 1: CASH RECEIVED AND DURATION OF AID TO INFANTS

Location and Year	"Normal" Infant	Infant without Mother	Infant without Father	Infant without Parents but Maintained in Family
Jiangsu, 1876	600/9 mos.	600/2 yrs.	600/3 yrs.	?
Nanxun, 1868	600/5 mos.	1,200/2 yrs.	boys: 500/4 yrs. girls: 400/4 yrs.	800/4 yrs. 600/4 yrs.
Hongjiang, 1888	600/1 yr.	800/2 yrs.	800/2 yrs.	1,200/3 yrs.
Luodian, 1878	600/1 yr.	1,200/1 yr.[b]	600/2 yrs.	600/3 yrs.
Wujin, 1875	400/6 mos.[a]	800/1 yr.	400/18 mos.[a]	800/18 mos.

Note: Besides money, clothing, and bedding, sometimes food was also provided.
a. 800 cash for the first month.
b. Could be extended 8 more months.

about the same (600 cash per month), particularly needy infants received special treatment.[39] The differences can be summarized as follows: an infant without a mother was given a considerably higher sum for about two years, while an infant without a father or without both parents was given a moderately higher sum for a considerably longer period of time (maximum four years). The reason behind this scheme was obvious: if the mother was dead but the male head of the family was still alive, he would need aid to pay for a wet nurse for one or two years; but if the breadwinner was dead, the widow (who could nurse the infant) or the family of the infant would need aid for a longer period of time. Fuma Susumu, who has consulted sources concerning the Shanghai *baoying* societies, has provided several concrete examples of families thus assisted.[40] That a great number of post-Taiping foundling institutions made provisions which were not at all common among the early Qing foundling homes suggests a significant change had been made in children's welfare policies: attention and effort were now focused on the *families* of abandoned children instead of expensive institutions housing large numbers of abandoned children and wet nurses.

This new policy kept pace with and complemented the growing vogue of institutions for "Preserving Women's Chastity" *(baojie)*. In the late eighteenth century, such institutions for women appeared slightly earlier than *baoying* societies and became widespread after the Taiping Rebellion.[41] So that widows would not have to sacrifice their virtue (i.e., fidelity to a deceased husband) in a second marriage, *baojie* institutions provided them with basic life necessities. More often than not, institutions for women and infants were closely linked. One especially interesting example was to be found in Nanjing, where the foundling home was administratively combined with a chaste widow institution after the Taiping Rebellion. Children of the inmate widows could stay in the foundling home until they were aged fourteen (boys) or sixteen (girls). By 1886, the institution's authorities claimed that children kept inside the foundling home were mostly children of the widows; the number of children whose parents had both died had by this time decreased.[42] An institution in Wujin founded in 1875 also combined the functions of preserving both the lives of infants and the chastity of widows by giving relief money to infants according to the general principles cited above as well as offering assistance to local widows (500 cash per month, 800 cash if she had a widowed mother-in-law in her charge, 700 cash if she had a child).[43] That providing relief for infants was often linked to similar provisions for widows becomes all the more obvious if we look at one supplementary condition stipulated in most of the *bao-ying* societies' regulations: if the mother of the assisted child ever remarried, aid would automatically cease.[44] In fact, a portion of the stipend for infants without fathers was usually called "money for the preservation of chastity" *(baojie qian)*.

Other innovative measures were also devised to accommodate the newly decentralized system of outdoor relief. First of all, the managers were required to collect more accurate information about the families who asked for aid. This was one reason why the amount of property owned by the families had to be declared. In Tongzhou, for instance, those who were proprietors of more than fifteen *mu* of land, or who had the right to cultivate more than twenty *mu*, or who "had other ways to earn a living," were not qualified for aid. The same requirement was made by the foundling society in Taixing, which, moreover, excluded mendicants and alien households *(kemin)* from the program.[45] To ensure that the claims made by applicants were accurate, foundling society directors asked neighbors or local elders to guarantee reimbursement of all relief money in the event that the assisted family later proved to have lied about their poverty.

A new method of donation, which called for the financial "adoption" *(renyu)* of a number of needy infants by local benefactors, also helped to diversify the institutions' resources and simplify their fiscal organization. Local people were encouraged to donate a monthly pension for several babies to receive assistance from the *baoying* society. In Jiading, a red label inscribed with the number of infants thus assisted would be posted on the donor's door as a token of recognition. The method was said to have some success in various localities. The foundling hospital in the vicinity of Rugao claimed that after implementing this method, the number of infants assisted (inmates as well as recipients of outdoor relief) increased from less than seventy in 1868 to more than two hundred in 1873.[46]

Since these new methods required more precise information about potential beneficiaries, the area in which the society functioned also needed more specific definition. Most of the societies, in fact, limited their help to families within four or five *li* (about two and a half kilometers) of the headquarters or, in certain places, a maximum distance of ten *li* (about five kilometers).[47] Some societies did not specify exact distances but required proof of local residence. The Nanxun society only gave help to the inhabitants of the twelve hamlets *(zhuang)* of the *zhen,* whereas that of Hongjiang had application forms indicating that only residents of the *zhen* were entitled to relief.[48] Besides the obvious considerations of limited finances and the need to verify information about applicants, there was another reason for the geographical limitation of services. To ensure regular distribution of relief and efficient inspection of the children, the headquarters of the society had to be within a one-day walk of assisted families. The *baoying* societies of the late nineteenth century were clearly a much smaller and closer-knit enterprise than the earlier metropolitan foundling institutions.

From the incomplete sources available to us, one gains the impression that in the late nineteenth century the number of infants assisted was greatly increased in places where the *baoying* system was implanted. Besides the example of the Rugao foundling home cited earlier, Fuma Susumu has observed that between 1874 and 1875, in a little over a year, the *baoying* societies of the Shanghai district had assisted some 370 families compared with the 120 or so infants (24 inmates and some 100 outdoor recipients) aided by the pre-Taiping Shanghai foundling home—a threefold increase.[49]

Another interesting example is the case of the twenty-one *baoying* societies in Tongxiang that, since 1872, gave relief to some three to four hundred infants each year, making a total of more than four thousand by 1887. Thus each of Tongxiang's *baoying* societies helped an average of twenty infants per year. Moreover, "less than one-tenth died." Accurate or not, this impressionistic figure suggests that the new system had a much better record than the *xian's* (county) foundling hospital in which 3,128 foundlings died within the six years after its reestablishment in 1866. Similarly, Shanghai's *baoying* societies' mortality of 20 percent was considerably lower than the 48 percent in the municipal foundling home.[50]

A Suzhou *baoying* society that only accepted infants within five *li* had a quota of fifty infants per year at the beginning of its organization in 1866.[51] Some of the bigger societies might assist up to seventy infants a year, as shown by the case of the Hongjiang institution:[52]

1880:	12	1884:	56
1881:	12	1885:	57
1882:	21	1886:	77
1883:	37	1887:	51

We should consider these figures in the context of a limited *zhen* area, which was on the average ten to fifteen *li* (five to eight kilometers) in diameter. By comparing the Rugao figures of the early Qing and those of the late nineteenth century we can better appreciate the growth of its relief system: between 1668 and 1775, the annual average number of inmate infants in the county's hospice was 156, whereas by 1873 an institution in the county's neighborhood assisted more than 200 a year.[53] Clearly the new system touched a far greater number of families and infants.

THE CHILD AS SOCIAL BEING

Early Qing foundling homes made every effort to save the lives of the foundlings, but they did not seem to pay much attention to the reintegration of the child into society when it grew up.[54] By contrast, late Qing philanthropists not only assisted children in greater numbers but thought of them in very different terms. If the newborn embodied the abstract symbol of life for the earlier foundling homes, the initiators of late-nineteenth-century institutions tended to see children in a concrete social context—namely, as potentially useful or dangerous social elements in flesh and blood.[55]

One indicator of this change in perception was that the organizers of the *baoying* societies now took a more aggressive approach to recruiting needy infants for assistance. For example, the society in Luodian (a town some twenty-five kilometers northwest of Shanghai) compensated the guarantors of families who requested aid (from 100 to 160 cash) or local constables *(dibao)* who came to report new births in needy families of their neighborhood; those who came from more distant quarters (but still within the society's sphere of action) would receive slightly higher sums for their extra trouble.[56] The Jiangsu authorities suggested that the province's *baoying* societies should compensate midwives who discouraged families from drowning their newborn infants and who reported such families to the society (200 cash for each case); a much more handsome sum (1,000 cash) would be awarded to any midwife who reported unyielding families still prone to infanticide. But a midwife who was accomplice in any such act would be punished.[57] At the same time, foundling hospices, which were often combined with programs offering outdoor relief, also went a step further to locate abandoned infants more actively. People who collected exposed infants and brought them to the hospice would be awarded money. The Nanxun society suggested that these people should be generously compensated: "After the heart is stimulated with profit, it will also incline toward goodness."[58] The new urge to preserve life after the Taiping upheaval had certainly pushed the philanthropists to confront the problems of infanticide and child abandonment more realistically, inspiring in them more aggressive strategies than waiting idly for infants to be brought to them as most of their early Qing predecessors had done.

Moreover, the problem of high mortality inside the hospices was addressed in more pragmatic ways. Special health care for the child was another conspicuously new element of the nineteenth-century institutions. Advice offered to caretakers on hygiene and medical care for assisted infants was becoming more detailed and specialized as the nineteenth century progressed. As organizers acquired better knowledge of common children's diseases, the basic medical care they provided tended to be more professional. The Hongjiang institution, for instance, recorded that more than half of the mortality was due to smallpox, while 20 to 30 percent died of other illnesses such as convulsion (jingfeng), tetanus neonatorum (qifeng), and various scabies (chuangjie).[59] Many prescribed a certain "sanhuang" soup for all newborns, a medicated plaster to extract the fetus toxicosis (taidu), as well as hot baths as soon as the infants were sent in.[60] Pamphlets published by late-nineteenth-century "six cash societies" included not only tracts and songs condemning female infanticide but also prescriptions for common childhood diseases.[61] Some of the richer institutions now stored expensive medicines for children's diseases and even employed wet nurses and doctors in permanent residence to take care of the infants.[62] But no innovation showed the organizers' determination to curb infant mortality better than their efforts in promoting vaccination.

As smallpox and measles (which were often confused) were found to be the most common cause of death among children, Jennerian vaccination was provided by an increasing number of foundling hospices and societies. We know that traditional variolation using human pox was offered free to local children by at least one early-nineteenth-century charitable institution before the general application of vaccination in China.[63] By the 1840s, vaccination was provided sporadically in several foundling hospices and baoying societies in the country. By the 1860s, free vaccination, sometimes alternated with variolation, became a widespread public service offered by foundling institutions, which often set up subsidiary "vaccination bureaus" *(niudou ju)* to carry out the job.[64] For some, vaccination was one of the main projects of the new relief system. The Hongjiang institution, for instance, generously paid a specialist of the new technique (8,000 cash per month, a salary just below that of the general manager of the institution, who received 10,000 cash a month) to prepare the pox and vaccinate children of the whole district.[65] In one sense, the task of the "vaccination bureau" was not only to serve the foundling institutions but was itself an independent charitable act.[66] The provision of medical aid to children had actually become one of the most widespread features of welfare in China from the early nineteenth century on. The extensive assistance offered by the bureau and the provision of more sophisticated general medical care for the child (as well as for the mother or wet nurse) were further indicators that infant mortality was now perceived as a problem to be solved by coordinated social efforts. Merely collecting sick or moribund infants for institutional treatment was no longer enough. Like the *baoying* societies, the vaccination bureaus began reaching out more energetically to the populace.

The growing importance of the child in society could also be seen in the treatment of deceased children. In the mid-nineteenth century we begin to see the development of charitable children's cemeteries. One of the first such cemeteries was established in the town of Hongjiang in 1846, and there appeared to be rapid growth of this institution after the Taiping Rebellion in the Jiangnan region.[67] Nanjing built one of the first post-Taiping children's cemeteries in 1876. In the county of Changshu, local philanthropists constructed a children's cemetery in 1895 to bury infants who died of various illnesses inside and outside the city wall. Within seven years, it had buried more than one thousand children.[68] The memorial of some gentry members of Suzhou, calling for the creation of a local children's cemetery in 1892, tells us more about the importance of such institutions:

> In the past, dead children never had any special burial ground. Especially in the Suzhou area, rich families do not bury their children in their ancestral ground for geomantic reasons. As for the poorer families, they only wrap the corpses with cloth or weed and place them on empty ground; within days, the remaining bones and decaying flesh are exposed. It is a miserable sight. We gentry have discovered that in 1876 the *Tongshan tang* of Nanjing initiated the institution for burying dead children. By now, they have already buried more than 15,800 children. It was indeed an unprecedented charitable act.[69]

As in the undertaking of other charitable tasks, these gentry members organized themselves, donated money, found empty ground, and employed gravediggers and other workers. In the same year they began to offer free burial for local children who died of various illnesses. It is important to note that the cemetery also accepted dead children of well-off families. In fact, the cemetery's name, *"daizang yinghai binyuan"* (children's cemetery), was such that it would not be confused with the poor man's charitable graveyard, the *"yizhong,"* thus saving the face of the rich who nonetheless had to bury their children in this public ground "for geomantic reasons."[70] It was therefore not for the poor that this new institution was started; it was clearly for the children, and for them alone.

If in death the child was now given a new special place, we can very well imagine the new considerations given to living children. Consider, for example, the ways in which the foundling institutions prepared children for the challenges of life after they left the institution. Early Qing institutions invested all hope for the children's future security in the possibility that they would be adopted by local people. But there were no controls over the adoption process, nor were there any follow-up procedures.[71] To some extent, the late-nineteenth-century institutions also relied on adoption, but now the procedure was more closely supervised. By continuing to subsidize adoptive families for a period of time, for example, many institutions encouraged poor families to adopt girls as wives for their sons *(yangxi)*. Guarantors were required to ensure that the children were not sold into prostitution or slavery. Except in cases where the child was severely handicapped, guarantors also had to ensure that children were not adopted by Buddhist or Taoist temples, as monks and nuns were despised by mainstream Confucian society.[72] Moreover, all adoptions had to be reported to the local bureaucrats, who kept official records on each case. More important still was the requirement of some institutions that the adoptive family take the girl or boy to the institution for a yearly inspection until the child was sixteen.[73] Increased control over adoptive procedures may be attributed in part to competition between native institutions and missionary orphanages, as such procedures would minimize the number of children taken away from native foundling homes to missionary orphanages while enhancing the credibility of native institutions. With the advent of tighter controls native authorities could now use the unreported, thus illegal, acquisition of children as an argument against the presence of missionary orphanages.[74] Whatever the key to this change, the result was that assisted children no longer ceased to matter once they were adopted, as was the case for most of the early Qing institutions.

The increasing numbers of refugee and mendicant children also heightened concern over the future of institutionalized children. Already in the 1830s, He Changling had advocated education and vocational training for destitute youth. Many post-Taiping foundling institutions also adopted vocational training as a key item in their relief programs. Indeed, institutions were beginning to realize that keeping children alive was not enough; children needed to be prepared for life outside the walls of the institution as well. The establishment of charity schools *(yixue)* in the foundling institutions was part of a bigger movement of popularizing elementary education that began in the early Qing period and had gained enormous momentum by the nineteenth century.[75] Now many foundling institutions obliged boys over seven or eight to attend the charity school either attached to or outside the hospice. In the Nanjing institution, boys were sent to the attached charity school when they were seven *sui.* There they would study until age thirteen, at which time they would be allocated jobs. The institution in Funing, a county in northern Jiangsu, offered a similar educational opportunity to boys over seven *sui* who "showed that they were intelligent enough to study." In the more peripheral region of Hongjiang, boys were sent to the outside charity school for three years beginning at eight *sui.*[76] While these examples are fairly common in nineteenth-century sources, schooling was rarely mentioned in the programs of earlier Qing foundling institutions.

More important still was the vocational training provided by the institutions. The Shanghai hospice for refugee children, which since 1866 accepted juveniles under the age of sixteen, provides a most interesting case. All of its inmates would undergo two months of schooling—just enough to foster basic reading skills—and afterwards would be trained for one or two years in a craft, either character engraving, printing, tailoring, shoemaking, bamboo weaving, fan making, forging, two kinds of weed weaving, or shaving. Money and basic tools would be given to them when they had acquired the basic skills to make a living.[77] At this time many foundling hospices also provided training for the children. The same Funing hospice would send boys over twelve and of average intelligence to shops and artisans' workshops as apprentices for three years. During the apprenticeship, they would still receive a yearly subsidy of 1,200 cash. More significant still were the special consideration and training given to girls and handicapped children. Girls in both the Funing and Nanjing institutions were generally taught needlework or cotton weaving from about age seven *sui* until they were thirteen, when they would be married out or adopted. For their labor, they were sometimes paid wages that they could use to prepare their dowries, as in the case of the Hongjiang institution. Blind boys would usually be taught fortune-telling. Those who were too handicapped to learn anything or to get married would be transferred to hospices for adults, or to religious institutions, when they came of age.[78]

Though it is difficult to evaluate the quality of schooling and vocational training provided for such children, we can at least deduce from these new policies that late-nineteenth-century philanthropists now believed that to integrate these children into society at large was as important as safeguarding their fragile lives.

LIMITED BUREAUCRATIC INVOLVEMENT

I have argued elsewhere that bureaucratic intervention in charitable institutions generally declined toward the end of the eighteenth century.[79] But official interest in these organizations, particularly their financing, seems to have recovered in the reconstruction period (the 1860s and 1870s). It was obvious to all concerned that membership fees were not sufficient for the high expenses of the societies, and it became a common practice to rely on revenues from silk, salt, tobacco, and other local commodity taxes. Some institutions obtained subsidies from the *lijin* tax, grain transport tax, real estate transaction tax, and commercial taxes from local shops.[80] Such subsidies, granted by individual officials and local authorities, were usually given to the institutions in addition to the endowment of land, houses, and salaries.[81] Clearly, as Fuma Susumu has suggested, in the reconstruction period, official interest in the charitable institutions increased in absolute terms.[82]

Yet it is also true that the initiators and organizers of the institutions, the people who actually ran the system and controlled it, remained essentially extragovernmental gentry members, merchants, and other wealthy citizens—what Mary Rankin calls the "managerial elite."[83] William Rowe fairly sums up the respective roles of the state and the elites during the post-Taiping reconstruction in his study of Hankow: "Though lagging considerably behind urban commercial elites, the state, too, was adapting to the realities of social change. What had passed from state to societal hands was not, then, *participation* in social-welfare activities . . . but, rather, *initiative* and *control* over such undertakings."[84] Rowe somewhat simplifies how the initiative and control of charitable undertakings passed "from state to society," however, as society had always had a hand in these enterprises.

In contrast to its relative withdrawal in the early nineteenth century, the state in the post-1860 period approached foundling institutions with a renewed interest, albeit one partly prompted by xenophobia. Despite this enthusiasm, however, it seems clear that it was now too late for the state to take the lead in fulfilling a responsibility it had long relinquished to local society. Although the state assumed some of the financial burden of maintaining post-Taiping charitable institutions, its share of moral leadership in public charity had in fact further declined, at least in the Jiangnan region under study here. One obvious indication was that the network of foundling institutions in the average city, with their subordinate relay stations *(jieying tang)* in various suburbs or *zhen,* rarely respected the official administrative hierarchy. Indeed, the network increasingly adopted a geographical and social logic of its own.[85] Another sign was the gradual disappearance of the systematic eulogies of the state in the descriptions of charitable institutions in local gazetteers. Organizers of late Qing welfare institutions seemed not to share their earlier Qing counterparts' feeling that lip service had to be paid to the state, which, at least on paper, had to take most of the credit for providing relief to the needy.[86] This final breakdown of verbal formalism tells us much indeed about changes in ideas concerning relief institutions for children.

FROM PATHETIC CHILD TO COMPLEX SOCIAL BEING

We have seen two parallel developments in the assistance of children during the nineteenth century. The first was the emergence of the destitute child as a social being belonging to the community. The pitiable abandoned infant extracted from the family was no longer the dominant image of the assisted child, though he, or more probably she, certainly continued to exist in huge numbers in the late nineteenth century. The strategy employed to reduce infanticide and infant mortality had been shifted from providing institutional care to assisting needy families, especially widows with children. Moreover, it was not only the child's life that was safeguarded by the late Qing institutions but also its future role in the community. We may attribute the diversification of relief strategy to the emergence of a more sophisticated view of the child on the part of post-Taiping philanthropists, who increasingly understood the child within the context of family and community and from the vantage point of superior medical knowledge.

The second development was the further decline of the state in its role as the sacred protector of life. In this respect China's experience was completely different from that of the West. In France from the late eighteenth century onward, the state institution became "synonyme de sécurité, de protection de l'enfance malheureuse."[87] In China, it was the reduction of the state's moral lead in providing social assistance to children that allowed the final takeover of the child by the community. Late Qing society after the Taiping Rebellion was in desperate need of reconstruction; the charitable institutions had as their goal not just the spiritual gratification of philanthropy but the satisfaction of working for objective social needs.

The pragmatic characteristics of the post-Taiping institutions, however, were not only a result of the particular circumstances of the time. We have seen that changes were already taking place in the early nineteenth century—namely, the branching of the network of institutions and the diversification of assistance including various forms of medical aid and outdoor relief. The unique conditions of the post-Taiping society—specifically, increased poverty and competition from missionaries—only helped to accelerate the changes. Even though the state at this critical time provided concrete financial contributions, it had irreversibly lost its moral leadership, which it had maintained, at least formally, until the mid-Qianlong period. From then on, the destitute child began to shed its image as merely miserable and pathetic and gradually emerged as a more complex but real social being.

NOTES

1. Fuma Susumu, "Shindai zenki no ikuei jigyō" (Foundling projects of the early Qing), Toyama daigaku jimbun gakubu kiyō 11 (March 1986): 5–41; A. K. Leung, "L'accueil des enfants abandonnés dans la Chine du Bas-Yangzi aux XVIIe et XVIIIe siècles," Etudes chinoises 4(1) (1985):15–54,

which is a largely revised version of the Chinese article "Shiqi, shiba shiji Changjiang xiayou zhi yuying tang" (Foundling hospitals in the lower Yangzi region during the seventeenth and eighteenth centuries), in *Zhongguo haiyang fazhan shi* (Taipei: Academia Sinica, 1984), pp. 97–130.

2. Fuma Susumu, "Shindai Shōkō ikueitō no keiei jittai to chihō shakai" (Management of foundling homes and local society in Songjiang in the Qing), *Tōyō shi kenkyū* 45(3) (December 1986):479–518; "Shinmatsu no hoeikai" (Societies for the preservation of infants at the end of the Qing dynasty), *Shirīzu sekaishi e no dōi,* vol. 5 (Tokyo: Iwanami Shoten, 1990), pp. 163–190.

3. A *zhen* is a nonadministrative town, usually a market town of modest size near a main administrative city. Populations of *zhen* vary from place to place. The biggest towns in late Qing China had populations of more than 100,000: the *zhen* of Hankow, for example, had an estimated 180,980 people in 1888. See William T. Rowe, *Hankow: Commerce and Society in a Chinese City, 1796–1889* (Stanford: Stanford University Press, 1984), p. 39. The *zhen* of Hongjiang here is more than fifty kilometers from the administrative center of Huitong and was known as a busy market town in the late Qing period. Population figures are uncertain, but at the end of the nineteenth century they may have ranged between 10,000 and 20,000.

4. One concrete example of such direct influence was the case of the Maxiangting Institute in Quanzhou of Fujian province. As the 1873 orphanage was the brainchild of a magistrate who was a Jiangnan native, its principles of operation were thus identical to those discussed in this study. See "Tang nei guitiao" in *Maxiangting zhi,* 1893, app. *xia,* pp. 47a–49b.

5. Liang Qizi [A. K. Leung], "Qingdai cishan jigou yu guanliao ceng di guanxi" (Charitable institutions and bureaucracy under the Qing), *Bulletin of the Institute of Ethnology, Academia Sinica* 66 (1988):89. For a recent analysis of this important event see Philip Kuhn, "The Taiping Rebellion," *The Cambridge History of China,* vol. 10, pt. 1 (Cambridge: Cambridge University Press, 1979), pp. 264–317.

6. Wang Xisun, "Yuying yi" (Suggestions on the care of foundlings), *Cong zheng lu* (1845), reprinted in *Jiangdu Wang shi congshu* (Shanghai: Zhongguo shudian, 1925).

7. Fuma Susumu, "Shindai Shōkō ikueitō," pp. 74–75; "Shinmatsu no hoeikai," pp. 171–172; "Shi jin ninü bing quan she baoying hui" (Notice to forbid female infanticide and to encourage the organization of societies to preserve babies), in *Jiangsu shengli,* vol. 1, 1876, pp. 2a–3b.

8. *Hongjiang yuying xiao shi* (Brief account of the foundling institution in Hongjiang), 1888, *juan* 2, p. 9a ("Shi jingfei").

9. Anyone familiar with the same problems in contemporary Europe would not be surprised by these figures. In the foundling institutions of Rouen in the late eighteenth century, for instance, 90 percent of the abandoned children being taken care of died before they were one year old; in Paris, only 7 percent of the children in the Hôtel-Dieu lived till their fifth

year. See Jacques Gélis, *L'arbre et le fruit: La naissance dans l'Occident moderne XVIe–XIXe siècle* (Paris: Fayard, 1984), p. 428.

10. According to sources available to me, the earliest such institutions were established in the Jiangsu-Zhejiang border area in the Yangzi delta where the *zhen* and even *hsiang* (communities smaller than *zhen*) were already quite urbanized. The institutions listed in Table 2 were all established before the Taiping Rebellion.

TABLE 2: THE EARLIEST FOUNDLING INSTITUTIONS

Institution	Jurisdiction	Year	Functions
Nanxiang	Jiading	1702	transfer babies to Suzhou
Pinghu	Jiaxing	1706	transfer babies to Suzhou
Deqing	Huzhou	1734	transfer babies to Suzhou
Huzhou	Huzhou	1707	transfer babies to Suzhou
Nanxun	Wucheng	1737	transfer babies to Wucheng and Suzhou
Lili	Wujiang	1738	nourish babies of the area
Puyuan	Jiaxing	Qianlong–Jiaqing	transfer babies to Jiaxing and Tongxiang
Xiashi	Haining	early Jiaqing	transfer babies to Haining and Tongxiang
Luodian	Baoshan	1813	transfer babies to Jiading
Jiangwan	Baoshan	1813	transfer babies to Nanling *zhen* (under Taicang *zhou*)
Yangxing	Baoshan	1813	transfer babies to Nanling *zhen* (under Taicang *zhou*)
Shenghu	Wujiang	1816	transfer babies to Wujiang
Zhouquan	Shimen	1820	nourish babies of the area
Yuxi	Shimen	1820	nourish babies of the area
Qingzhen	Tongxiang	1839	transfer babies to Hangzhou
Zhangyan	Louxian	1847	nourish babies of the area

Sources: Fuma Susumu, "Shindai zenki no ikuei jigyō," pp. 28–30; *Nanxun zhi*, 1920; *Lili zhi*, 1805; *Puyuan zhi*, 1927; *Haining zhou zhigao*, 1922; *Baoshan xianzhi*, 1882; *Luodian zhenzhi*, 1881; *Jiangwan lizhi*, 1921; *Shenghu zhi*, 1925 (1874); *Jiaxing fuzhi*, 1877; *Wuqing zhenshi*, 1936; *Chongji Zhangyan zhi*, 1919.

11. It is interesting to note that because of the overflow of abandoned infants in the capital as well as in the major cities, France began to decentralize its foundling system in the same period. See Gélis, *L'arbre et le fruit*, p. 431.

12. "Outdoor relief" consists of distributing money and other material aid to the needy outside charitable institutions in contrast to aid given to inmates of institutions. The term is generally linked to the workhouse system in nineteenth-century Britain. The workhouse not only provided aid and training to its inmates, but also gave aid to the poor, mainly paupers, outside the institution. For details of the system see M. A. Crowther, *The Workhouse System, 1834–1929* (London: Methuen, 1983).

13. It should be pointed out that some of the earlier foundling homes had already compromised somewhat by allowing wet nurses to stay home to nurse the babies. Chen Hongmou (1696–1771) mentions this common practice in Suzhou in his recommendations to a foundling home in Yunnan in the early 1730s. See Chen Hongmou, *Peiyuantang oucun gao*, 1896, *juan* 1, p. 35b ("Wenxi").

14. Wang Xisun, "Yuying yi," *Cong zheng lu.*

15. Ouyang Zhaoxiong, *Shuichuang chun yi* (Springtime dream talk behind the moistened window) (based on the 1877, 1902, and 1911 eds.; Beijing: Zhonghua shuju, 1984), pp. 20–21.

16. In the period 1801–1850, ten pecks (one *shi*) of rice cost about 3,267 cash. Thus one peck (about ten liters) cost about 300 cash. See Peng Xinwei, *Zhongguo huobi shi* (History of Chinese money), 1958 reprint ed. (Shanghai: Renmin chubanshe, 1988), p. 844.

17. Yu Zhi, *Deyi lu* (A record of charitable acts) (Suzhou: Dejianzhai, 1869), *juan* 2/1, pp. 1a–14b.

18. Fuma Susumu's recent publication on the *baoying* societies has shown that under Yu Zhi's influence, seven such societies established in the Shanghai *xian* in the year 1874–1875; see Fuma, "Shinmatsu no hoeikai," pp. 176–178. The 1885 gazetteer of the *xian* of Danyang near Nanjing also reported that its 1874 *baoying* bureau was initiated by Yu Zhi, who died later that very year; see *Danyang xianzhi*, 1885, *juan* 25, p. 12b.

19. For a general background of welfare linked to the bigger reconstruction project after the Taiping Rebellion see Mary Rankin, *Elite Activism and Political Transformation in China: Zhejiang Province, 1865–1911* (Stanford: Stanford University Press, 1986); and William T. Rowe, *Hankow: Conflict and Community in a Chinese City, 1796–1895* (Stanford: Stanford University Press, 1989).

20. *De yi lu, juan* 2/1, p. 37b. For further details on Yan Chen see Rankin, *Elite Activism*, p. 66.

21. For example: "Shi jin ninü bing quan she baoying hui," *Jiangsu shengli*, vol. 1, 1876, pp. 2a–3b; *Nanxun zhi, juan* 34, p. 11a; *Tongxiang xianzhi*, 1887, *juan* 4, p. 3b.

22. For a discussion of the ideas behind early and mid-Qing charitable

institutions see Fuma Susumu, "Zenkai, zentō no shuppatsu" (The origins
of charitable societies and institutions), in Ono Kazuko, ed., *Min-Shin jidai
no seiji to shakai* (Kyoto: Daigaku jimbun kagaku kenkyujo, 1983), pp.
189–232; A. K. Leung, "Mingmo Qingchu minjian cishan huodong di
xingqi" (The rise of the popular philanthropic movement in the late Ming
and early Qing), *Shih-huo Monthly* 15(7/8) (January 1986):69–70; Joanna
Handlin Smith, "Benevolent Societies: The Reshaping of Charity During the
Late Ming and Early Ch'ing," *Journal of Asian Studies* 46(2) (May 1987):
309–337.

23. *Wujin Yanghu hezhi*, 1886, *juan* 5, p. 28b.

24. *De yi lu, juan* 4/1, pp. 1a–5a, "Dongyue shouyang yihai tiaocheng"
(Regulations for accommodating children in winter), Wuxi-Jingui area.

25. William C. Milne, *Life in China* (London: Routledge, 1859), pp.
47–48.

26. He Changling, *Naian zhouyi cun gao*, 1882, *juan* 4, pp. 32a–33a.

27. *De yi lu, juan* 13/4, p. 4a, "Quan tuiguang fujiao ju gong qi" (Public
announcement to encourage the propagation of the bureau of relief and
education).

28. *De yi lu, juan* 13/4, pp. 1b–4b.

29. Lu Yun, *Haijiao xubian* (Sequel to the Book of the Corner of the
Ocean), original ed. 1868, in Ke Wuchi, *Louwang yongyu ji*, based on the
Guangsu ed. (Beijing: Zhonghua shuju, 1985), p. 140.

30. See Paul A. Cohen, *China and Christianity: The Missionary Movement and the Growth of Chinese Antiforeignism, 1860–1870* (Cambridge,
Mass.: Harvard University Press, 1963), pp. 91–92, 230–231.

31. *Shanghai xian xuzhi*, 1918, *juan* 2, pp. 37b–38b; see also *Wujiang
xian xuzhi*, 1879, *juan* 2, pp. 5b–6a; *Jiangsu shengli*, vol. 2, 1891, "Zheng-
dun tuiguang yuying zhangcheng," pp. 1a–2b.

32. "Yushi En-pu zou yi guang she yuying tang yi qing luan liu shu"
(Memorial by En-pu to urge for wider establishment of foundling homes to
stop the chaos), 1891, in Wang Minglun, ed., *Fan yangjiao shuwen jietie
xuan* (Jinan: Qilu shushe, 1984), p. 315.

33. Note also the following letter to foreign embassies from the Zongli
Yamen in January 1871: "In each of China's provinces, such charitable
activities [foundling homes] are numerous and there is no reason why west-
erners should meddle in these affairs"; *Fan yangjiao*, p. 382. Or this 1863
memorial of the Hunan governor: "Well, the babies belong to our land
(neidi), so why should they need the nourishment of people from overseas
(waiyang)? After all, the nourishment of foreigners' babies is not a concern
of our people. Moreover, there are already foundling homes in every place in
Yuezhou—all the more reason why one must not exploit the foreigners'
good intentions"; *Fan yangjiao*, p. 289.

34. Xue Fucheng, "Nishang yuying tang tiao yi" (Proposal for [foreign]
foundling homes), 1892, in *Fan yangjiao*, pp. 396–397.

35. More details of the *liuwen hui* can be found in Hoshi Ayao, *Min-Shin*

jidai shakai keizaishi no kenkyū (Studies in the socioeconomic history of the Ming and Qing periods) (Tokyo: Kokusho kankokai, 1989), pp. 377–380. The value of the cash was reduced after the Taiping Rebellion. Between 1861 and 1870, one *shi* of rice cost 4,480 cash. Thus one had to pay 448 cash for a peck of rice, instead of 300 before the uprising. See note 16 above.

36. "Baoying zhang cheng," *Jiangsu shengli,* 1876, vol. 1, pp. 4a–12a; regulations of the Nanxun society in *Nanxun zhi,* 1920, *juan* 34, pp. 12b–21b; *Hongjiang yuying xiaoshi,* 1888.

37. The majority of the babies (62 percent) assisted by the Shanghai *baoying* societies were female; see Fuma, "Shinmatsu no hoeikai," p. 183.

38. *Luodian zhenzhi,* 1881, *Wujin Yanghu hezhi,* 1906, *juan* 3, p. 7b.

39. This sum, though modest, represented almost two pecks of rice in post-Taiping Zhejiang province. The daily salary for a worker of the first category (e.g., stonecutter, boatbuilder) in the immediate post-Taiping period in Zhejiang was 100 cash; 60 cash for the second category (e.g., carpenter, harvest worker); and 40 cash for the third category (e.g., tailor, bamboo worker, ordinary farmworker). Thus 600 cash should represent the ten-day salary of a second-class worker. See Xu Yingpu (1892–1981), *Liang Zhe shishi conggao* (Manuscript on the historical events of Zhejiang province) (Hangzhou: Zhejiang guji chubanshe, 1988), pp. 395–397.

40. Fuma, "Shinmatsu no hoeikai," pp. 178–185.

41. For recent studies on institutions for widows see Raymond D. Lum, "Aid for Indigent Widows in Nineteenth-Century Canton," paper prepared for the panel "Philanthropy and Public Welfare During the Ming and Qing Dynasties" of the 1984 Annual Meeting of the Association for Asian Studies; Fuma Susumu, "Shindai no jutsurikai to seisetsudō" (Societies and institutions for chaste widows in the Qing), *Kyoto Daigaku bungakubu kenkyū kiyō* 30 (1991):41–131; Angela K. C. Leung, "To Chasten Society: The Development of Widow Homes in the Qing, 1773–1911," *Late Imperial China* 14(2) (December 1993):1–32.

42. *Jiangning fu chongjian puyu si tang zhi,* 1886, *juan* 1, pp. 1b–2a, 20b–21a.

43. *Wujin Yanghu xian zhi,* 1903, *juan* 3, p. 7b.

44. *Nanxun zhi, juan* 34, p. 16b; *Hongjiang yuying xiao shi, juan* 2, p. 6b ("Shi guitiao").

45. *Tongzhou zhili zhouzhi,* 1875, *juan* 3, pp. 65–66; *Taixing xianzhi,* 1885, *juan* 8, pp. 6b–7a.

46. *Jiangsu shengli,* 1876, 11a, "Jiading baoying zonghui banfa ge xian xiang cun jianbian zhangcheng" (Brief regulations distributed to the Xian, Xiang, and Cun by the Jiading general *baoying* society); *Rugao xian xuzhi,* 1873, *juan* 1, pp. 13b–14a; another example is the society at Taixing: *Taixing xianzhi,* 1885, *juan* 8, pp. 6b–7a.

47. The *baoying* society of the Xiashi *zhen* of Haining gave help to families within four or five *li* of the town; see *Haining zhou zhigao,* 1922, *juan* 6,

p. 6b. That of Qingpu accepted infants within eight or nine *li;* see *Jiangsu shengli,* 1891, vol. 2, p. 8a. The set of regulations proclaimed for *baoying* societies of the whole province of Jiangsu in 1876 limited the maximum distance to ten *li;* see *Jiangsu shengli,* 1876, vol. 1, p. 7b.

48. *Nanxun zhi, juan* 34, p. 22a; *Hongjiang yuying xiao shi, juan* 2, pp. 8b–9a ("Shi guitiao").

49. Fuma, "Shinmatsu no hoeikai," p. 185; Milne, *Life in China,* p. 43.

50. *Tongxiang xian zhi,* 1887, *juan* 4, pp. 2b–4b, 8b; on the mortality in Shanghai institutions see Fuma, "Shinmatsu no hoeikai," pp. 184–185. In effect, the society of Luodian *zhen* (about fifteen kilometers west of the administrative county seat, Baoshan) also claimed to have given aid to some twenty infants a year since 1869 (*Luodian zhenzhi, juan* 3, p. 10b); the one in Zhouzhuang *zhen* (thirty kilometers southeast of Suzhou) had given relief to some ten to twenty infants since 1867 (*Zhouzhuang zhen zhi,* 1880, *juan* 2, p. 22a).

51. "Sucheng zhun ban baoying hui qi" (Preface for the Baoying society organized in Suzhou), in *De yi lu, juan* 2/1, p. 43a.

52. *Hongjiang yuying xiao shi, juan* 2, pp. 9b–11a ("Shi jingfei").

53. See Leung, "L'accueil des enfants," p. 37.

54. For details of the idealistic principles of earlier Qing foundling homes see Leung, "L'accueil des enfants."

55. I have argued elsewhere that the late Ming and early Qing philanthropic institutions (of which foundling associations and institutions were the first) owed more to the ideological changes of that time than to strong social pressures; see Leung, "L'accueil des enfants," pp. 40–44. Fuma Susumu has traced the close relation between late Ming institutions and the Buddhist idea of *"shengsheng"* (let life proliferate) much in vogue since the late Ming; see his "Zenkai, zentō no shuppatsu."

56. *Luodian zhenzhi, juan* 3, p. 11b.

57. *Jiangsu shengli,* 1876, vol. 1, p. 6b.

58. *Nanxun zhi, juan* 34, p. 20b; for other examples see *Zhouzhuang zhenzhi, juan* 2, p. 22a. The Shanghai hospice would award more money to those who collected babies in cold seasons or in dark hours. See *De yi lu, juan* 3/1, p. 11b ("Xu ying zouyan"). This provision was in fact very common for foundling institutions all over China in the latter half of the nineteenth century.

59. *Hongjiang yuying xiao shi, juan* 2, pp. 1b–7b ("Shi guitiao"); pp. 4a–b ("Shi niudou fangyao").

60. Ruan Benyan, *Qiu mu zouyan,* 1887, reprinted (facsim.) in *Jindai Zhongguo shiliao congkan,* vol. 27 (Taipei: Wenhai chubanshe, 1968), *juan* 8, p. 7a (On the foundling hospital of Funing in Huaian); *Jiangsu shengli,* 1891, vol. 2, "Jieying zhangcheng ba tiao" (Eight rules of the *jieying tang* of Qingpu), p. 6a. A detailed set of regulations of a hospice of the late nineteenth century in Jiangsu province was also particularly concerned with

medical and hygienic problems; it even contained an appendix on "The Best
Way to Nurse a Baby" *(Yuying liangfa)*; see *De yi lu, juan* 3/1, pp. 9a–13a.

61. *Baoying bian* (Brochure for the protection of infants), Zaoxuetang
ed., 1890, includes eleven such prescriptions.

62. For instance: the Nanhui hospice, which was established in 1873,
as well as the prefectural hospice of Songjiang; *Songjiang fu xu zhi*, 1883,
juan 9, pp. 13b, 7b.

63. I have conjectured that an institution in Yangzhou established in
1807 practiced free variolation for local children before vaccination arrived
in the Yangzi region. See my "Ming Qing yufang tianhua cuoshi zhi yan-
bian" (Preventive measures against smallpox in the Ming–Qing period),
Guoshi shilun (Taipei: Shihuo chubanshe, 1987), p. 246.

64. I have found that at least in Nanjing, Jurong, and today's Xi'an in
Shaanxi there were foundling hospices with vaccination services in the 1840s.
For examples of foundling institutions offering vaccination in the 1860s and
after, see *Guoshi shilun*, pp. 250–251, n. 74.

65. *Hongjiang yuying xiao shi, juan* 2, pp. 4b–5a ("Shi niudou fangyao"). It is noteworthy that vaccination was first practiced in the Hongjiang
institution in 1883 but was stopped due to shortage of resources. When
severe local smallpox epidemics forced the organizers to rethink their strategy, they came up with the bold initiative of offering a handsome salary to a
prestigious vaccination expert of Wuling (present-day Changde) to induce
him to come to this provincial town as resident doctor of the foundling
home.

66. The bureau of the locality usually vaccinated children, poor and rich
alike, free of charge. There were seasons for the vaccination: most bureaus
did this in the midwinter months; some also offered the service in the late
autumn.

67. *Hongjiang Yuying xiaoshi, juan* 2, p. 7b ("Shi guitiao"); *juan* 3, p. 1b
("Shi ceyin").

68. *Changzhao he zhi gao*, 1904, *juan* 17, p. 7b.

69. *Jiangsu shengli*, 1892, vol. 3, pp. 1a–1b.

70. Ibid., pp. 2b–6a.

71. See Leung, "L'accueil des enfants," pp. 35–36.

72. The institutions in Haining and Hongjiang, for example, explicitly
forbade adoption by monks and nuns; see *Haining zhou chongshe liuyingtang zhengxinlu*, 1891, sec. "Liuyingtang zhangcheng yibu," p. 1b. It is
interesting to note that children rescued from brothels were now authorized
by the law to take refuge in foundling hospices: in 1881 and 1884 the
Hongjiang institution accepted two young girls who had been sold to
brothels; see *Hongjiang yuying xiaoshi, juan* 1, pp. 14b–15b ("Shi
yuanqi").

73. For adoption and guarantors see, for example, *Hongjiang yuying
xiao shi, juan* 2, pp. 5a–6a ("Shi guitiao"); *Jiangning fu chongjian puyutang
zhi, juan* 5, pp. 20b–21a; *De yi lu, juan* 3/1, p. 6b ("Yuyingtang zhang-

cheng"); *Jiangsu shengli,* 1891, vol. 2, p. 7a (regulations of the Qingpu institution). On the yearly control over the adopted child until age sixteen, see *Qiu mu zouyan, juan* 8, p. 9a (on the Funing institution in Huaian).

74. In fact, this was one point in the open letter to foreign embassies in January 1871 on which the Zongli Yamen elaborated to counter missionary influences. The Zongli Yamen accused foreign institutions of failing to report to local authorities about the children they kept and never allowing adoptions by outsiders—practices that caused popular suspicion. These are two reasons cited by the Zongli Yamen in their request for the total abolition of foreign orphanages. See *Fan yangjiao,* pp. 381–382.

75. On the earlier Qing charity school movement see my paper, "Elementary Education in the Lower Yangtze Region in the Seventeenth and Eighteenth Centuries," in Benjamin Elman and Alexander Woodside, eds., *Education and Society in Late Imperial China, 1600–1900* (Berkeley: University of California Press, 1994), pp. 382–391.

76. *Jiangning puyu tang zhi, juan* 5, pp. 21a–b; *Qiu mu zouyan, juan* 8, p. 9b; *Hongjiang yuying xiao shi, juan* 2, p. 7b ("Shi guitiao").

77. *De yi lu, juan* 13/4, pp. 2b–3b ("Fujiao ju zhangcheng"). In Zhejiang most of these jobs were in the "third category," which allowed the worker to earn about 40 cash a day in the immediate post-Taiping period. See note 39.

78. *Jiangning fu chongjian puyu tang zhi, juan* 5, p. 21b; *Qiu mu zouyan, juan* 8, p. 10a; *Hongjiang yuying xiao shi, juan* 2, p. 7b ("Shi guitiao"); *De yi lu, juan* 3/1, pp. 5a–b ("Yuying tang zhangcheng").

79. Liang, "Qingdai cishan jigou yu guanliaoceng di guanxi," pp. 92–94.

80. *Lijin* was a commercial tax created in 1853 initially for financing the military suppression of the Taiping Rebellion. After the rebellion, it became a local commercial and toll tax managed by local officials. Most commodities were taxed from 1 to 10 percent.

81. Mary Rankin has written a detailed description on the financial aspects of the institutions in Zhejiang; see *Elite Activism,* pp. 98–107.

82. Fuma Susumu, in his detailed study on the Songjiang foundling institutions of the late nineteenth century, observed such official involvement in the institutions; see "Shindai Shōkō ikueitō," pp. 483–501.

83. Rankin, *Elite Activism,* pp. 111–119.

84. Rowe, *Hankow,* pp. 131–132.

85. The excellent example of Songjiang is provided by Fuma Susumu, "Shindai Shōkō ikueitō," pp. 501–512. For another example, see note 8 of this chapter. Rankin provides illustrations of networks of elite activism independent of bureaucratic hierarchy; see *Elite Activism,* pp. 137–142.

86. Examples of such early Qing eulogies can be found in Leung, "L'accueil des enfants," pp. 24–26.

87. Gélis, *L'arbre et le fruit,* p. 432. Geremek characterizes the official social relief reforms since the sixteenth century as "un élément de l'idéologie de l'Etat moderne"; see Bronislaw Geremek, *La potence ou la pitié* (Paris: Gallimard, 1987), p. 261.

GLOSSARY

baojie	保節	to preserve chastity
baojie qian	保節錢	money for the preservation of chastity
baoying hui	保嬰會	society for the preservation of infants
chuangjie	瘡疥	scabies
daizang yinghai binyuan	代葬嬰孩殯園	children's cemetery
dibao	地保	local constable
fujiao ju	撫教局	bureau for giving relief and education
jieying tang	接嬰堂	hospice for receiving infants
jingfeng	驚風	convulsion
jiyou tang	及幼堂	hospice for the young
kemin	客民	alien residents
li	里	Chinese mile
liuwen hui	六文會	six cash society
liuying tang	留嬰堂	hospice for keeping infants
nantong	難童	refugee children
niudou ju	牛痘局	vaccination bureau
qifeng	臍風	tetanus neonatorum
renyu	認育	adoption
sanhuang	三黃	a kind of soup given to newborns
shaying tang	殺嬰堂	hospice of killing infants
sui	歲	year
taidu	胎毒	fetus toxicosis
xian	縣	county
xiangyue	鄉約	village lecture
xugu ju	恤孤局	bureau for orphan relief
yangxi	養媳	girls adopted as daughters-in-law
yixue	義學	charity school
yizhong	義塚	charitable graveyard
yuying she	育嬰社	society for the nurture of foundlings
zhen	鎮	town
zhou	州	prefecture
zhuang	莊	hamlet

Remembering the Taste of Melons: Modern Chinese Stories of Childhood

CATHERINE E. PEASE

There was a period of time when I would frequently recall the vegetables and fruits I ate as a child in my old hometown: water chestnuts, broadbeans, wild rice shoots, muskmelons—all these were most delicious, and they all bewitched me into missing my native place. Later, when I'd been away for a long time, tasting them still had the same effect; the flavors from the old days lingered on in my memory alone. Maybe they will fool me all my life, making me look back now and again.[1]

—Lu Xun

CHILDREN OF A NEW ERA

Born in the last decades of the Qing dynasty (1644–1911), early modern Chinese writers grew up in an era of radical social change.[2] With the abolition of the Confucian bureaucratic system, intellectuals began to reassess their very function in society and developed a strong sense of mission, perceiving themselves as shapers of new modes of thought and behavior. Their most important tool was a revolutionized literature that they hoped would broaden their base of influence and give voice to those seldom heard from directly in the past, in particular, women, peasants, and children. Through the new literature of the 1920s and 1930s, writers tried to increase their own and others' understanding of society at all levels and, by so doing, reevaluate their own social and individual identities.[3]

Many found it especially instructive to look back to their early years for insights into themselves and the development of the new society as a whole. Historically their transition from childhood to adulthood—the process of *cheng ren* (literally, "becoming a person") —took place within the context of China's entry into the modern world: their paths toward individual personhood paralleled China's progress toward modern nationhood. They viewed their childhood worlds, therefore, with a mixture of nostalgia for the "flavors from the old days" and a sharp, often painful, awareness that those flavors had to change.

In some measure, their protests resonated with the voices of reformers in previous transitional eras. But instead of seeking solutions in ancient wisdom, as their earlier counterparts had done, early modern writers turned toward the future, reached beyond China's borders, and embraced the new in an attempt to assert China's place and ensure its survival in the modernizing world. Their interest in children and childhood was a natural outgrowth of the promotion of "newness" as a positive, indispensable value. Children had always played a role in Chinese culture as symbols of renewal, but modern stories place particular emphasis on the freshness of the child's perceptions and the relative ease with which the child moves across traditional social barriers. The nostalgia pervading many childhood narratives is not, therefore, so much a longing for the way things actually were in the old days as for the child's unjaded palate and unclouded vision.

Ironically the very effort Chinese writers expended on looking back into childhood reveals doubts about their own effectiveness as social reformers. As Wendy Larson has observed: "The dilemma of the intellectual in modern China is encapsulated in the fate of these twentieth-century writers, who attempt, literally and figuratively, to go out into society, but are held back by their association with their work."[4] The advantage of focusing on one's own childhood was, first of all, that a writer could work from within a familiar world to open windows on society at large. Moreover, writers could thereby avoid the trap Lu Xun warned against—namely, acting as mere mouthpieces for the "ordinary people [who] have not yet opened their mouths."[5] Writing of their own relatively privileged childhoods was an intermediate step toward dealing with more socially distant groups, since, in contrast to their social relations as adults, as children they had interacted more frequently with servants, laborers, and peasants. This relative social flexibility forms a major motif in early modern childhood narratives. The message of many such stories is that the world of adults is excessively stratified and humanity would be better off if the child's less prejudiced view were to prevail.

Three of the stories I discuss in this chapter, Lu Xun's "Guxiang" (My Old Home, 1921), Bing Xin's "Fen" (Parting, 1931) and Wu

Zuxiang's "Chai" (Firewood, 1934), illustrate the advantage children have over adults in social flexibility, as does Cao Xueqin's pathbreaking eighteenth-century novel *Honglou meng* (Dream of the Red Chamber). Predictably, these personal narratives of childhood are far more convincing than stories narrated from the perspective of a character who is socially distant from the implied author. As Yi-tsi Feuerwerker points out, stories of the latter type often reveal "little understanding or conviction" compared to those told from the angle of people from the author's own social milieu.[6]

Whatever the narrative angle, twentieth-century Chinese stories of childhood portray children of all social levels as an oppressed group. The suffocating atmosphere of childhood in elite households as well as the hardships of lower-class children both form important motifs in early modern fiction.[7] As offspring of the educated elite, early twentieth-century writers had felt hemmed in both by child-training practices that emphasized filial piety and by a classical curriculum that bore little apparent relevance to the modernizing world.[8] At the opposite end of the social spectrum, children from poor families (mostly girls) were frequently sold into servitude, concubinage, or prostitution; many became victims of infanticide.[9] Bringing the child's vision to the foreground not only created a broader view of society but also drew attention to children's needs.

Nonetheless, it is highly significant that even in the most childcentered of these stories, the adult consciousness behind the child never disappears entirely. Moreover, these works derive much of their didactic power and emotional force not from the child's vision alone but from the interplay between the child's untrammeled perspective and the adult's often disillusioned view of social reality. The influence of traditional social hierarchies is clearly evident in the adult's controlling hand. Even so by ascribing validity to childhood perceptions and treating childhood as a primary locus of crucial personal experience, these stories represent a major literary innovation in Chinese fiction.

Concepts of childhood in China and elsewhere have changed considerably in the last century or two, and the importance of childhood in literature has increased along with its rising importance in other spheres. Given the symbiotic ties that have always existed in China between writing and social process, a brief overview of Chinese attitudes toward the treatment and upbringing of children will clarify the social context in which narratives of childhood gained prominence in the twentieth century. Both indigenous processes and developments in other societies influenced these changes, and in certain respects Chinese views of childhood have evolved in parallel with those elsewhere.

Modern Attitudes

Progressive intellectuals blamed traditional moral codes and education for many of the problems afflicting children and the family system. They called for new approaches to learning that would directly address current social, economic, and political needs, and at the same time they sought to discard what they saw as the moribund Confucian canon. In his book *Legacies of Childhood,* Jon Saari traces the evolution of early twentieth-century attitudes toward the nature and role of childhood: "By the end of the New Culture period (1915–1921), a veritable tide of feeling and arguments against filial upbringing and authoritarian education had swept through coastal and literate China. By then a historic restructuring of the process of growing up had occurred."[10] Part of this "tide of feeling" arose, Saari suggests, from the personal oppression younger intellectuals experienced through old-style schooling or arranged marriage. At the same time, awareness of more far-reaching social crises was growing among the elite, intensifying the search begun by late Qing reformists for remedies outside the pale of Chinese tradition.

Many intellectuals supported reforming children's education as the first step toward resolving the social and political problems of the late nineteenth and early twentieth centuries. Rising interest in pragmatic subjects—namely the social and natural sciences—signaled a determination to save China from Japanese and Euro-American expansionist designs by building up China's technological and military capabilities. Educational reformers were eager to incorporate into a new system, beginning at the primary-school level, whatever outside ideas might help bolster China from within. As Saari asserts, foreign ideas played an influential, though not a generative, role in the processes of reform and revolution.[11]

In 1919–1920, John Dewey, a mentor for many early modern Chinese intellectuals, expounded his child-centered educational philosophy in a series of lectures delivered in China and later published in Chinese.[12] He advocated ending the traditional "preoccupation with subject matter" and urged devoting attention to the child instead, giving children credit for a natural motivation to learn and also stressing their need to move around and participate in the learning process.[13] His views resonate with those of many Western missionaries and other educators in the late Qing and early Republican eras who criticized traditional Chinese schools for overemphasizing rote learning of ancient texts and not incorporating physical activities into the curriculum.

But the ideas of Dewey and other modern reformers actually echo earlier Chinese efforts of the Ming and Qing dynasties to approach education in a more spontaneous, experiential way rather than concentrating on inculcating sets of time-honored principles without assessing their current relevance.[14] Although those earlier attempts at reform had succumbed to the "chilling winds of official proscription" blowing from the orthodox Neo-Confucian authorities, by the late Qing intellectuals were becoming increasingly receptive to new educational theories.[15] The abolition of the Confucian-based examination system signaled official recognition of the fact that traditional education was no longer able to meet the needs of the modernizing state. Many early modern intellectuals had suffered as children through years of classical schooling only to find that once the exams were gone such learning no longer prepared them for government careers. Chinese educators further realized that if literacy were to spread, as would be necessary for the promulgation of new ideas, educational methods and content needed to change along with goals. As Saari points out, the difficulties of mastering the classical language and content of traditional education exerted a "deadening impact on children" that could hardly foster wider access to learning.[16]

The leading writer and educator Ye Shaojun (1894–1987), whose satire of the examination system, "Horsebell Melons," we shall discuss shortly, wrote an essay on elementary education appearing in 1919 in which he compares young students to young flowers or grass. If planted in impoverished soil, using inappropriate methods, plants will surely wither. In the same way, he says, elementary students cannot flourish under the care of teachers who "lack the art of cultivation." He cautions that the goals and values of primary education are still a matter of dispute, but his priorities are clear: "Elementary education is for the elementary students, and elementary teachers are there to cultivate elementary students," an idea inverting the traditional focus on the child's future adulthood. He continues by noting the importance of childhood *(younian)* as a critical stage in the formation of a sense of direction—an "outlook on life" *(ren-shengguan)*—and places responsibility for proper guidance on the shoulders of teachers.[17] Ye took up these themes in many of his stories, from the point of view of both children and teachers, as in "Ah Ju" (1920), "Fan" (Rice, 1921), "Yi ke" (A Lesson, 1921), "Malinggua" (Horsebell Melons, 1923), and the novel *Ni Huanzhi* (1929). His views call to mind Mencius' exhortation to retain a "childlike heart" and to cultivate the sprouts of morality innate in every person.[18] But Ye goes beyond traditional notions of child training by stressing the need to nurture children as individual beings rather than to prune them into predetermined shapes.

Ye Shaojun and his contemporaries welcomed educational approaches that focused on the people they felt had the most potential to improve China's capacity to deal with threats on all fronts: their own generation and the children who would follow them. Lu Xun (1881–1936), himself a father figure to modern writers and highly conscious of his personal roots in the old system, wrote an essay in 1919 entitled "Fatherhood Today," which called for a reversal in the traditional parent/child relationship. The views expounded in the essay parallel the realignment of teacher and student priorities Ye Shaojun advocated. Lu Xun goes on to cite progressive developments in other parts of the world while criticizing stagnation in his own culture:

> Standards should be set by the young, but are set by the old instead. We should give weight to the future, but instead we emphasize the past. . . . I mean that from now on, those who have already awakened must wash away the false ideas of the Eastern tradition, increase our sense of duty toward our sons and daughters, and do our utmost to quench concern with our own rights, in order to pave the way for a moral order in which the young set the standards. Moreover, the young, having gained their rights, will not hold them forever; in the future they, too, will have to fulfill their duty to their own young. In short, everyone will play the role of transmitter, those who come first to those who follow.[19]

His reference to older generations as "transmitters" echoes Confucius' view of himself as a transmitter rather than a creator, though the knowledge and attitudes Lu Xun advocates transmitting ironically reverse the Confucian emphasis on the lessons of antiquity.[20] He also turns Confucian hierarchical relationships upside down. Though Confucian thought had always emphasized the reciprocity involved in the "five relationships" of society (ruler/minister, father/son, husband/wife, elder brother/younger brother, friend/friend), in practice the sense of obligation extended more upward than downward, an inequity Lu Xun deplored. Lu Xun goes on to cite modern European, American, and Japanese family systems as examples of positive change and urges a more child-centered perspective:[21] "Only recently, owing to the research of many scholars, have we come to see that the child's world differs entirely from the adult's. Those who don't make the effort to understand this, but just blunder ahead blindly, will greatly hinder children's capacity to flourish."[22]

Wu Zuxiang (1908–1994) expresses similar thoughts in an essay written in 1925, several years before he had children of his own. In this essay he outlines the ideal childhood environment:

> A home ought to be near natural scenery; the best place would be in a conveniently accessible rural village, giving children frequent opportunities to draw close to Nature in its true beauty, thereby not only influencing their temperament for the better, but also allowing them to study Nature's textbook, enabling them to obtain knowledge both practical and interesting. In the house, aside from beautiful furnishings, there should also be provided all kinds of equipment suitable for children's recreation, games and exercise, to make their lives more active and amusing, stimulating their intellect at the same time.[23]

Wu condemns traditional Chinese attitudes toward children—chiefly paternal severity toward sons and practices like training girls early in the "three submissions and four virtues" *(sancong side),* which required women to submit first to fathers, then to husbands, and finally to sons and to go about their women's work quietly and diligently.[24] His essay, like Lu Xun's, reveals a sense that China had a long way to go toward the emancipation of children. But he makes few practical suggestions about alternative modes of behavior for children to follow, and the ideal children's environment he sketches was completely beyond the reach of most Chinese families at the time. Still, the essay shows that new ideas about children's status had made definite inroads, at least among progressive intellectuals.

Bing Xin (b. 1900), who devoted much of her career to writing for children, also perceived the child's world as one quite distinct from that of adults. In her preface to *Bing Xin quan ji* (The Complete Works of Bing Xin, 1932), she affirms her commitment to keeping that awareness alive and to maintaining her close connections with children. Criticizing her own writing, she says she knows her understanding of "children's unaffected innocence" is overburdened with "the complex psychology of adults." She concludes the preface with a hope: "I wish only to have children following me around all my life, to live surrounded by them!"[25] Many of Bing Xin's early stories, poems, and essays about children and childhood display views as idealized as that expressed in Wu Zuxiang's essay, but she shows an unusual level of interest in children's thoughts and feelings along with a genuine desire to communicate with them.

The Rising Prominence of Children in Literature

Paralleling the role of the parent or teacher outlined by educational and social reformers is the persistent presence of the adult as a guiding force in modern Chinese narratives of childhood. The adult in the background enables the child to speak, presents the child as someone worth listening to, and anchors the child's voice in the wider context of social issues.

Elsewhere in the world during the nineteenth and twentieth centuries, we find a similar rise in the use of children as literary subjects and centers of consciousness. In European and American literature, child-centered narrative fiction reached an unprecedented height during the nineteenth century—Mark Twain, and Charles Dickens were prominent proponents.[26] Fiona Björling underscores the idea of children in the nineteenth century as objects of social concern: "The romantic and realist writers approached the child from without, as an object, the redeemer or the victim of a corrupt social order. . . . From the end of the eighteenth through the nineteenth centuries, children represented a measuring rod by which to establish patterns of right and wrong, good and bad; from the metaphysical as well as from the social point of view."[27] By the early twentieth century many Chinese intellectuals had come to view their own society as corrupt and likewise turned to children as both social "measuring rods" and inspirational models. Saari contends that "children and youth are significant for innovation inside a society because as a group they are relatively indifferent to the prevailing customs and ideals."[28]

David Grylls, noting the "enormous popularity" of childhood as a "literary symbol and theme" in nineteenth-century British literature, finds embedded in such narratives a direct challenge to adult authority. Dickens, he says, gives little credit to adults for moral capacity and clearly implies that children are the proper models for virtuous conduct. As Grylls puts it, Dickens' "pantheon is crammed with a soft-boiled array of credulous infantile adults" and his child characters found very few of their elders worthy of respect.[29] John Sommerville likewise sees a tendency in the Victorian era to portray adults as villains and children as moral arbiters.[30] Certainly modern Chinese fiction often treats adults with similar disdain, especially in satirical pieces like Lu Xun's "Remembering the Past" and "Kong Yiji" (1919) or Xiao Hong's "Jiazu yiwai de ren" (Family Outsider, 1937). Discrediting adult authority naturally entails depicting a convincing selection of unsavory examples, next to whom even quite unprecocious children seem better qualified than adults to inherit the earth.

Not only modern Chinese writers, but Japanese, Korean, and writers from other parts of Asia, also began to delve into the experience of growing up in a world of change.[31] The development of child-centered literature within modern Asia as well as between modern Asian and Western cultures deserves a detailed comparative study. The common thread seems to be that the profound familial and larger social disruptions occurring in each of these societies in the transitional era spanning the nineteenth and early twentieth centuries prompted a significant increase in the consciousness of childhood. From this new perspective, childhood was viewed as a distinct and critical phase, one that held the potential for a renewed vision of human capability at a time when the validity of traditional models appeared to have crumbled.

In genre as well as in theme, modern Chinese narratives of childhood have antecedents in premodern literature. Children frequently appear in traditional fiction and occasionally in other genres such as autobiography and poetry.[32] But until the twentieth century children seldom appear either as narrators or as the primary focus of narration. When they appear in premodern works, the emphasis frequently lies less on their attributes and perceptions as children than on their role as future adults or on their relationship to adult protagonists. As Anne Behnke Kinney's and Wu Hung's essays (Chapter 1 and 3 in this volume) demonstrate, stories of precocity typically describe children who act like miniature adults or juveniles whose profound reverence for parents distinguish them as exemplars of filial piety. This tendency reflects the traditional attitude that childhood itself is not a significant stage of human development. As John Dardess puts it: "It did not matter so much that one was a child. What mattered was that one was a son or daughter, older or younger than the next child, and a regular family member or a child of the servant class. Each child had its proper *place*."[33]

When children do play major roles in traditional Chinese works, as in Cao Xueqin's *Dream of the Red Chamber,* they often figure in contexts that challenge predominant behavioral norms such as filial piety, submissiveness to authority, and the observance of other conventions based on the hierarchies of gender, age, and class. Such child characters take on a subversive function, asserting the power and value of the child's natural insight and substantiating Dardess' observation that, efforts to maintain hierarchical distinctions notwithstanding, "human desires and passions often ran in one direction, whereas the body of Confucian principle cut in quite another."[34] Modern narratives, by bringing children to center stage, develop this subversive function much more fully, to the point where it is no longer subversive but overtly revolutionary.

In modern narratives, an increasing tendency to focus on the details and emotions of personal experience also facilitated the emergence of child-centered stories. Modern autobiography and fiction are closely intertwined, as is readily apparent in the reminiscent narratives of childhood we shall examine. A few premodern autobiographical accounts hint at the approach taken by modern writers toward evoking their childhood worlds. By showing glimpses of life from the child's perspective, these accounts contrast with the typical traditional autobiography in which childhood flies by in a few lines.[35] Children and childhood figure more frequently in traditional fiction, most prominently in the *Dream of the Red Chamber,* the first major work of Chinese fiction to concentrate on the world of children and youth. Although this novel concerns adolescence more than early childhood, it contains several explicit references to childhood as a distinct stage of development and is unique among traditional works in the extent to which it explores the psychological and emotional dimensions of growing up. It has inspired many modern writers dealing with youth and childhood, among them Ba Jin, whose novel *Jia* (Family, 1933) contains many "new youth" echoes of *Story of the Stone.* Although modern narratives seldom incorporate the allegorical and mythological dimensions so central to *Story of the Stone* and other traditional fiction, they share with it the clear implication that the child's seemingly naive and unformed view of the world often contains more truth than the adult's more sophisticated perspective. Furthermore, the Qing novel's psychological penetration and its exposition of a wide range of social concerns foreshadow modern efforts to depict society from underneath, from inside, and from the perspective of people whose youth, gender, or class traditionally deprived them of public identity or authority.

ANGLES OF VISION IN MODERN NARRATIVES:
WHO AM I, WHO ARE WE?

It is plain that the emergence of children in modern literature has traditional roots. It is only in the modern era, however, that childhood
becomes a common and favored narrative theme. The rise of child-
centered narrative goes hand in hand with the rise of personalistic
autobiography and first-person fiction. These narratives demonstrate
the preoccupation of modern intellectuals with figuring out who they
are both as individuals and as social beings. Looking into their own
childhoods led modern Chinese writers to explore the influences that
shaped their individual worldviews within the context of the emerging new society. As Milena Doleželová-Velingerová notes: "In many
modern Chinese short stories, the first-person narrator's experience is
combined with the search for his own identity in a world wider than
his private universe. The basic question 'Who am I?,' obsessive in
Western fiction, is in China overshadowed by the query, 'Who am I
in my society?' "[36] Turning back to childhood is a natural way to
begin the search for the roots of personal identity. By exploring the
social relationships of children, modern Chinese writers have simultaneously addressed the wider question of how social identity forms.

The Dual Lens: The Adult Behind the Child Narrator

The modern development of the first-person point of view, influenced
by both Western and Japanese trends, is a key feature of the stories
discussed here. Significantly, in these childhood narratives the angle
of vision is not unitary but dual-layered: the adult behind the child is
always there. The balance between the two layers varies, but the
respective roles of child and adult remain the same. The child's view
functions as a touchstone for a fundamental reality, while the adult
self acts as a mediator, anchoring the child's perspective in a wider
social context. As Wayne Booth says, the presence of an "I" telling
the story makes us instantly "conscious of an experiencing mind
whose views of the experience will come between us and the event."
At the same time, getting the story straight from this "experiencing
mind" enhances the narrative's credibility.[37] When two levels of an
"experiencing mind" are present, some of the biases (which contribute to what Booth terms the narrator's "unreliability") tend to cancel
each other out: the child is naive but clear-eyed, while the adult
"knows better" but has creeping myopia. The adult and child narrators represent two phases of the same person, but they take on sepa-

rate, complementary identities, akin to the "composite characters" frequently found in traditional Chinese fiction.[38] The socialized, educated adult, aware of status distinctions, complements the unbiased, undiscriminating child. As in *Dream of the Red Chamber*, the adult sees social reality while the child sees social possibility. The overall vision projected by a narrative reflects the relationship between these two aspects of the first-person voice.

True child's narrative, of course, would come straight from the child. Such narrative is rare, however, owing largely to the fact that little of what children have to tell ever gets recorded without adult mediation or interference. As Rosemary Lloyd says, "the fact that the narrative voice is almost invariably adult reflects less a philosophical choice than a stylistic difficulty."[39] The two-layered narrative is a compromise: the child's account is recorded by an adult, often the child grown up, who participates in the narrative process by filtering the child's words and organizing the presentation. The adult consciousness mediates the child's voice and message, which in turn provides the sense of fresh, uncluttered vision. The adult mediator acts as either a hidden or an overt interpreter of the child's perceptions, drawing on accumulated experience and hindsight.

These dual narratives depend on complementarity for their effectiveness: the child gains credibility by being relatively free of judgmental constraints, whereas the adult, despite having duller vision, inspires confidence because people tend to listen to the "voice of experience," a fact of which even the antiauthoritarian young writers of modern China took advantage, consciously or not.

The Child's Privileged Point of View

Modern Chinese narratives of childhood communicate a distinct sense that the child has access to views of the world unavailable to the adult. Limitations on the adult's vision result from social restrictions imposed on people as they mature and become preoccupied with making a living or running a household. The adult's life therefore becomes part of a stratified social system. Again, as awareness of social reality increases, so too does blindness to social possibility.

Children also have a natural inclination to watch and imitate, picking up details an adult might take for granted. Writers often endow child narrators with what Joy Hooton terms "preternatural powers of observation and honesty."[40] A child telling a story differs from an adult narrator in two fundamental respects: both in the child's sharp-eyed vision and in its lack of ulterior motives that might color the selection and presentation of detail. Frequently the child is to some extent an outsider and views the world from a different vantage point, physically as well as intellectually: a child can wriggle through a crowd to get a front-row spot, crouch unseen in a corner, sit atop an adult's shoulders, or scramble up a tree to look out over the courtyard wall.

The usefulness of the child narrator also derives in part from the child's ability to see both the attractive and the seamy sides of life with little prejudice. Even the relatively well-to-do child growing up in twentieth-century China was aware of the devastating effects of warlord campaigns, foreign encroachments, and widespread economic disruption. Modern stories frequently deal with the hardships of servants, tenant farmers, and itinerant laborers, often drawing on the experiences of people working for the writers' own families. Children were not only in a better position than adults to observe and interact with such people; they often took more interest in them. Their observation of suffering is "innocent" in the sense that they had had little practice in assessing people and situations according to prevailing sociocultural norms. What children witnessed in those years, though, was often far from what adults might consider appropriate for a child to view. Modern Chinese writers have used this contrast between naive vision and dark subject matter to heighten a story's shock value: to the adult reader, a child's description of a landlord beating a starving indigent, as in Xiao Hong's "Family Outsider," is potentially far more disturbing than an adult's rendering of the same scene, because the child tends to present observations in a straightforward manner, making no attempt to soften the picture. By the same token, a child's portrayal of a beloved wet nurse, as in Ba Jin's "Nanny Yang," is more poignant for its natural bridging of the class boundaries that the adult reader has learned to recognize.

Of course, there are many aspects of lower-class lives that these elite children did not see, and the result is not infrequently a skewed or romanticized picture. Still, capturing the child's vision narrows the gap between the world of the elite adult and the world at large—and, again, stresses both the need and the potential for people in the new society to transcend traditional social categories.[41]

Looking Backward: Self-Conscious Reminiscence

In the most straightforward type of dual child-adult narration, the adult narrator looks back on his or her own early years from an adult perspective, consciously filtering the memories, so that the reader is fully aware of the adult's controlling hand. Drawing on the years of experience accumulated since childhood, the adult reevaluates the child self. The adult "knows" more, has seen more of the way the world works, and has come to accept certain constraints on social behavior, or at least to know what they are. On the other hand—and it is in this aspect that the ironic thrust of these stories lies—excursions into memories of the child's own mind create the sense that the child's moral instincts are purer than the adult's. The older self, in other words, evaluates the younger from the stance of informed hindsight, while the reader gains the impression that the world would be better off if the younger self's more spontaneous, less value-laden vision were to prevail and if the adult narrator could somehow avoid what Albert Stone, writing of *Tom Sawyer,* calls the "grown-up's compromising connection to society."[42] Society, especially the "old society," is often the biggest villain in modern Chinese literature, and many of these reminiscent stories associate socialization (moving out of childhood) with degeneration. As Yukio Mishima put it not long before his suicide: "The longer people live, the worse they become. Human life, in other words, is an upside-down process of decline and fall."[43] Nostalgia for the child's world and regret over adult ineffectiveness dominate the adult narrator's mood.

A poignant early example of the reminiscent narrative is Lu Xun's "My Old Home" ("Guxiang," 1921), about Lu Xun's sale of his family property in Shaoxing in 1919 prior to his move to Beijing.[44] The adult narrator's bleak present forms the temporal framework, but the moral thrust of the story is intimately bound up with the memories of his childhood that surface when he arrives in his old home village for the purpose of selling the remaining family property and moving his family to the city. The narrator's opening description of the wintry, overcast weather underlines the dreariness of his family's current circumstances. Then he poses a rhetorical question that sets the stage for the story's interplay between present adult consciousness and memories of childhood: "Ah! This couldn't be the old home I had so often recalled over the past twenty years."[45] His nostalgia-laden answer points explicitly to changed perceptions as the key difference between childhood and adulthood:

The old home I remembered wasn't like this at all. My old home was better by far. But if you wanted me to conjure up its beauty or detail its finer points, I had no particular image in mind, nor words to describe it. It seemed there was no more to it than this. So I came up with an explanation: my old home had always been like this—and although it hadn't gotten any better, it wasn't necessarily as forlorn as I felt it to be. It was simply my own state of mind that had changed, because this time I was coming home in an entirely cheerless mood.[46]

The nebulous good memories he associates with his old home may not accurately reflect the whole spectrum of village life in the old days, but he admits that his own current perceptions might be interfering with his ability to see things as they are. In this passage lies the first indication that his adult vision has grown cloudy.

As the story progresses, however, several important facts come to light. The villagers of the story were indeed materially, physically, and perhaps spiritually better off before: the narrator's own family was wealthy, the beancurd shop proprietress Auntie Yang was still known as the "Beancurd Beauty" (Doufu Xishi, perhaps more aptly rendered as "Helen of Soy"), and his childhood companion, Runtu, had a plump, ruddy face and wore a silver necklace. Now the narrator has come back to sell everything off and move his family to the city, committing the ultimate transgression of abandoning the family estate. Auntie Yang has grown sticklike, the very image of a drafting compass. Runtu's face is now sallow and lined; he and his family, like everyone around them, have fallen on hard times. Runtu's own small son, Shuisheng, is a pale shadow of himself as a child, and the silver necklace is gone.

Clearly more than the passage of time has intervened. The village and its people are now in decline, a common enough state of affairs in the early decades of the twentieth century, so that in fact the narrator's warm memories of childhood are not all that far off the mark— his old home was indeed better. At the same time, there are clues that as a child he lived in a world of illusion, unaware of the realities of the life Runtu and other poor villagers led, and unable to foresee the hardships that lay ahead for them. At his mother's first mention of Runtu a storybook image flashes into his head:

In the deep blue sky hangs a full golden moon, beneath it the sandy shore, planted to the horizon with jade-green watermelons. Amid the melons a boy of ten or eleven, a circle of silver around his neck, clasps a steel pitchfork and stabs as hard as he can at a badger. But the badger twists around and scurries away between his legs.[47]

The narrator calls this image *shenyide:* "magical."[48] There is nothing about the scene that could not have been real, but the feeling he recalls resembles in its ethereal quality the rest of his memory of the young Runtu: a boy who knew all manner of strange creatures and who lived in a world beyond the narrator's imagination:

> Ah! Runtu's head was filled with an endless store of curiosities, things my usual friends knew nothing about. There was a lot they didn't know, because all the time Runtu was out by the seashore, they, like me, saw only a square of sky above high courtyard walls.[49]

These walls appear again, not only in this story but elsewhere in Lu Xun's writings and in many other modern works, as a symbol of class division. The high-walled compounds of the gentry did in fact separate them physically from their poorer neighbors. The "protection" those walls afforded also cut them off from the life Lu Xun's narrator paints so vividly, first in the luminous hues of his childhood memories and later in the gloomier shades he sees as an adult. He makes plain his feelings about these walls toward the end of the story after observing his own small nephew and Runtu's little boy getting acquainted with none of the constraints he and Runtu now feel as adults locked into a master/servant relationship: "I only sensed all around me an invisible high wall, closing me off in isolation, all but suffocating me."[50] The wall has intervened between Runtu and himself, and he feels no more capable of breaching it than Runtu does. But he hopes there will be no wall between the boys, that they will live neither a "wandering" life like his nor a "benumbed" one like Runtu's.[51]

Despite the positive value he ascribes to the children's attitude toward life, Lu Xun's presentation of the story implies that it is the adult narrator who sees things realistically, as he suggests later by saying that the "flavors from the old days" would "fool" him into recalling his childhood.[52] Things may have been better when he was a child, and his childhood memories are more appealing than what he sees of present reality, but he also recognizes that those memories represent a romanticized vision. The fact that the narration never really varies from the reminiscent mode reinforces this impression; the dominating presence of the narrator's adult voice implies that the child's vision requires reinterpretation. We do not travel back in time to stand inside the child's shoes except through a few fleeting and fading images. We also share the jolt of disillusionment the adult narrator feels when Runtu, never shy around him as a child, arrives and addresses him as "Master," refusing to call him "Brother Xun" as he had before. Runtu explains that "I was a child then, and didn't know any better."[53] What Runtu says ironically reverses the story's moral message, which is that adults who "know better" actually have succumbed to society's artificial constraints. Yet the narrator explicitly endorses the *moral* sense of the child by expressing the hope that things will be different for the new generation. The narrator's memory of Runtu as a child may be romanticized, but the story implies that the child's perception should be the model for the future.

Like Mishima, Lu Xun vilified the process of growing up. As William Lyell notes: "For Lu Hsün, 'growing up' was necessarily bad. It meant assimilation into a social structure which he saw as evil: maturing was equivalent to being corrupted."[54] In "My Old Home" Lu Xun stresses the ironic distance between both his selves— the adult and the child—to make clear that the way he saw things as a child was a better way though less realistic. Discouraged with the kind of life he and his generation have achieved as adults, he knows that any future disappointments his nephew and Runtu's son may face will derive not from their "unrealistic" perceptions but from the social walls crisscrossing adult reality.

For all the doubts Lu Xun expressed about his own effectiveness in the cause of social change, and despite the gulf he sensed between himself and the children of the new era, he continued to maintain hope that the next generation would be able to live "a new life, one we have never lived through."[55] Here he was following his own exhortation to adults expressed in "Fatherhood" to pass on their "rights" to the young—to let the young determine the shape of the new moral order.[56] Memories of childhood in Lu Xun's stories form a collage of elusive images and half-forgotten flavors. Yet the child's angle of vision is a powerful element in a number of his works. Significantly, "Diary of a Madman" ("Kuangren riji," 1918), the short story that launched his literary career, ends with the plea, "Save the children . . ."[57]

Shifting Consciousness

In contrast to "My Old Home," where the adult's interpretation dominates the child's vision, the narration in Wu Zuxiang's "Firewood" ("Chai," 1934) operates on two distinct levels: an essay about cutting and selling firewood and a story about an itinerant woodcutter dubbed "Big Brother Egret" ("Lusige") by the boy narrator. The essay belongs more to the adult narrator, whose minutely detailed descriptions of woodcutting form a context for the boy's character sketch of Big Brother Egret. But the essay mediates the child's vision less overtly than the adult narrator in Lu Xun's story. A nostalgic tone still surfaces, but it intrudes only subtly between the child's view of his big friend and the reader's perception. As in "My Old Home," the child becomes a link between social classes; but in "Firewood" we see much more detail through the child's eyes. In place of the narrator's dreamlike memory of seaside melon fields of "My Old Home," in "Firewood" we find sharply defined images and stark evocations of the hardships of rural life. Undoubtedly the gap of a decade and a half between the two stories influenced the authors' foci and choice of images. By the 1930s, at the urging of literary leaders like Lu Xun himself, writers were directing their efforts more and more toward in-depth portrayals of peasants, workers, and other disadvantaged social groups.

Owing to Wu Zuxiang's extensive use of the boy's relatively unbiased viewpoint in "Firewood," the woodcutter emerges as a more completely individualized character. The boy's portion of the narrative also presents an opening for Big Brother Egret to tell the boy a little of his own story in his own words. The child thus gains insight into the woodcutter's mind that the adults do not possess or even seek. Just as Lu Xun's Runtu is shy of adults as a child and of socially "superior" adults when he grows up, the woodcutter, to the adults for whom he works, is one of the "silent masses"; but to the boy he talks freely.

The segments of the adult narrator's descriptive essay that frame the boy's story also shape the reader's interpretation of the boyhood recollections. The essay accomplishes this by supplying facts about the historical context and the woodcutter's social background. The essay begins with a general description of woodcutting in that region and then moves into a highly typicalized picture of the relationship between landowning households, like the narrator's, and the woodcutters who worked for them:

> Households buying wood liked to buy from the same old hands they'd always dealt with: their wood was always top quality. The ones selling wood also liked old customers, who gave better weight. So people usually stuck with the same old hands for eight or ten years unless some unavoidable problem came up. Sometimes people traded off, buying

from one this year and from another the next year or the year after, but even then they got to know each other pretty well.[58]

Gradually the narrator begins drawing a more specific picture of his mother's dealings with the woodcutters she has customarily hired, describing boyhood memories while still speaking in a reminiscent mode. Though he paints his landowning household in a benevolent guise, the narrator does not gloss over the socioeconomic gap between his family and the woodcutters. Indeed, he details the hardships the woodcutters endured:

> Then my mother would weigh the wood. The loads brought in by the younger men and those in their prime she'd weigh one at a time, the kids' loads and the old men's in twos, and as she weighed it out she'd call out the amount to me and I'd mark it down. All the while she'd be urging the fathers to give the children less to carry, because when she asked how old they were, it would turn out they were all eight or nine, though they looked more like five or six, and she'd say it was because they worked too hard, so their health had suffered. At the same time of course she'd be telling the sons and grandsons to let their grandpa off easy, not to let him overdo it next year. Everyone listening felt grateful for her words, though they answered like this:
>   "You're right, you're right, Grandmother. But the kids're always showing off, won't listen to their elders!"
>   "Lots of mouths to feed, Grandmother. They've all got to pull their own weight."[59]

The narrator here refrains from evaluative comment, more so than the narrator in "My Old Home." His boyhood self is a participant in the scene, but the organization and presentation are still generalized rather than recalling any specific episode from childhood. The passage suits the adult narrator's overall purpose, which, as the closing essay makes clear, is to show that through these years the woodcutters' lives went from bad to worse due to the widespread economic crises of the 1930s.

As the narrative moves on to introduce Big Brother Egret, we see more from the child's angle, even gaining the impression of looking up at the rangy woodcutter from a child's height. Although the diction in this section of "Firewood" is still close to that of an adult, the kinds of observations the narrator makes and the sense that he is an observer and listener, rather than a full player, suggest a child's way of looking at things. Big Brother Egret's ungainly eccentricity isolates him from other adults but fascinates the boy, who supplies a vivid, elaborately detailed image of him. In the following segment, the imagery comes straight from what Peter Coveney calls the "phantasmagoric world of childhood."[60]

> His face was wizened and gaunt, looking a little like the axehead he chopped with. He was almost frighteningly tall; his legs were especially straight and slender, as if he were on stilts. At first, I was a little afraid of him, imagining he looked like the death-spirit, but gradually as I got used to him I discovered that he liked me, and really wasn't scary at all, so my fears went away. I gave him the name Big Brother Egret, and he answered to it with no objection. At the time he was close to fifty; I was just a child.[61]

The final sentence is superfluous, as their relative ages are obvious enough from the description. Adding it, though, subtly emphasizes the irony of the child's use of "Big Brother" (ge), rather than a term more appropriate for someone so much older. The boy may have decided upon that term instead of the more respectful "uncle" or "grandpa" because of his awareness of the woodcutter's lower status. But the choice also suggests that the two of them can form a bond across the status barrier, even as it underlines the narrator's perception of Big Brother Egret as more overgrown child than awkward adult.

Many modern Chinese stories portray working-class or peasant characters as having an affinity with children. The tacit implication is that children can cross class barriers far more easily than adults because they can still see through those barriers. "Firewood" also expresses the sense that the child and the peasant or laborer are comrades-in-arms, as neither has achieved full personhood in the traditional elite view. As in "My Old Home," what is important here is that by ascribing fundamental truth to the child's view—and, by extension, to that of the child's lower-class companion—the story challenges the validity of traditional social hierarchies.

The following passage, describing Big Brother Egret's eating habits, further clarifies his subservient relationship to the adults in the narrator's household and simultaneously reveals more of the boy narrator's interest in him. The big woodcutter takes small bits of the tastier dishes only if urged and eats the way he works, looking rather comical but doing a thorough job:

He ate very fast, a full bowl of rice raised till it bumped the end of his nose, half a bowl gone in one mouthful, down to the bottom in two or three. But the manner in which he ate seemed very deliberate and polite, not at all greedy, perhaps because his mouth was so wide. He didn't chew much; I never actually saw him chew, though he did in fact have very good teeth. After he'd finished, he would go over the cracks between his teeth with his tongue, blow his nose, bend his big frame to pick up the axe and go off back to work. He never dared steal a moment of leisure.[62]

Again, this description has the organization and diction of an adult's writing, but the selection of images conveys a vivid picture of the young boy sitting across the table watching Big Brother Egret's every move, taking in the smallest details of his mouth and teeth, staring at him intently in a way most adults have learned not to do. As a result, we come to know Big Brother Egret far better and take much more interest in him than if we had only an adult's description.

When Big Brother Egret tells his own story, Wu supplies short passages in the woodcutter's own words with the narrator summarizing his childhood memory of the rest. Here the child becomes a mediator for the woodcutter. The tale is a tragic one, as the woodcutter laments his inability to control fate, especially in such hard times. There are holes in the story, arousing the reader's curiosity about motives and circumstances, but it is more detailed than Runtu's brief and generalized complaint in "My Old Home." Moreover, Big Brother Egret talks to the child with less hesitation than Runtu in speaking to his now grown-up "master." Again, the adult narrator refrains from judgmental comment, instead relaying Big Brother Egret's own explanations for such unfortunate events as the loss of his son, which the woodcutter blames on bad luck and the shrewish woman he married. His story reveals a possible reason for his interest in the boy: he misses the son he never got to raise. He also asks the boy not to tell anyone else, thereby drawing a circle around the two of them: the boy and the social misfit, neither one fully assimilated into the adult world. In terms of experience, Big Brother Egret is far beyond childhood, but he trusts the boy more than he trusts adults, and the boy in turn feels pleased to have such a big friend:

Up until then I had never met an adult who would confide in me so seriously, and without being aware of it I began to listen quietly and attentively like a grown-up, feeling a little ill at ease but also rather elated.[63]

"Firewood" differs from "My Old Home" in two key respects. First, the central object of the narrator's reminiscence unlike the child Runtu is not a romanticized figure although Big Brother Egret, like Runtu, proves to hold a store of knowledge about things such as different kinds of wood, hunting, and strategies for keeping vicious dogs at bay. The details shown of Big Brother Egret through the child's eyes create a stark, largely unretouched portrait with little of the magical quality Lu Xun's narrator remembers from his childhood encounter with Runtu. In "My Old Home," Runtu's appearance as an adult gives the narrator a way to measure the child he remembers, and by comparison the younger Runtu looks better. In "Firewood" Big Brother Egret does not reappear in the narrator's adult life. The narrator merely comments on his lingering memories of the sound of Big Brother's axe and his face, now as nebulous as Lu Xun's childhood flavors:

> Even today, I still seem to hear dimly the heavy, slow thud of the axe and to see the watery eyes in his gaunt, ugly face, his wide mouth aslant as he munched away. But as for the man himself, he must be long gone from this world.[64]

While in "My Old Home" the narrator's memories of the young Runtu are more fully integrated into the narrative, here there is a separation between the adult's generalized recollections and the child's detailed descriptions, which are as vivid as if narrated by the child in his own time. The narrator in "Firewood" does not simply look back but actually moves back into his childhood world, giving us a fuller, more tangible picture of what he saw. These distinct shifts between the adult's and the child's angle of vision lend more independence to the child's perception than in the more overtly mediated reminiscent mode of "My Old Home."

There is no implication, as in "My Old Home," that the boy's view was less realistic—only that what he saw was but a detail from the whole canvas. What the narrator sees as an adult supports the truth of the boy's impressions. The adult narrator of "My Old Home," by contrast, constantly reevaluates the "real" meaning of his boyhood memories in light of his present circumstances and adult knowledge. Nonetheless, the two stories share a similar social message: the adult narrators may know more but do not necessarily "know better." In each case the children are able to transcend artificial class barriers with ease, while the adults, having grown up with the barriers, are less flexible.

The Lurking Adult

Ye Shaojun's "Horsebell Melons" (1923) tips the narrative even more toward the child's perspective. The narrator, a young victim of the dying imperial examination system, tells the story with little overt interference from his adult self, recounting his inside look at the Confucian literati world he had been trained for, a world rapidly losing its viability in the face of political and educational reforms. The examination, his "rite of passage," is the *yuankao*, or first-level state exam, which Ye Shaojun himself took and failed at age eleven in 1905, the last year they were administered.[65]

"Horsebell Melons" shows up the exams as a farce and of little relevance for a scholar's future—a broad-ranging, foreign-influenced curriculum and new educational methodologies were already replacing the orthodox Neo-Confucian learning on which they were based.[66] The boy's experience taking the exam graphically demonstrates that he is at the threshold of a new era and that his own generation will be responsible for creating new values and new ways of choosing political leaders. Here the child is not exactly a "moral arbiter," in Sommerville's phrase, because he as yet lacks a cohesive moral code, but he still has what Coveney calls a "corrective influence" over his own adult future.[67]

The adult narrator in "Horsebell Melons" intervenes only minimally, though the humorous tone and much of the diction belong to him rather than to the child. The title, referring to the melons the narrator's father gives him for fortification during the exams, immediately alerts us to the young examinee's priorities (food for thought is more important than thought itself), as does the opening description of preparing for the big event:

I was carrying a handy bamboo basket, packed with two horsebell melons, seven or eight steamed buns, a packet of ham, and other things to munch on like watermelon seeds, peanuts, and cured olives. My mind dwelt on the two melons: each big enough to fill a rice bowl, their jade-green rinds charmingly mottled, just the thought of them making my mouth water. The day before, I'd told my father, "If you want me to go, I have to have two horsebell melons to take along."

My father smiled, and magnanimously agreed. "And why not? Two it will be." That afternoon he did indeed come home with two horsebell melons, saying as he gave them to me, "Put these in your lunch basket." Utterly delighted, I set them gingerly in the basket and covered them with paper before I put in the rest. That evening when it was time to set out, I hastened to take the basket, leaving all the other stuff for my uncle to carry.[68]

The "other stuff," of course, includes the tools of the scholar's trade: writing brushes, paper and ink, and a selection of classics and reference works. He sums up his thoughts on these texts succinctly: "When I looked at their small, fine print and close spacing, I guessed that these were works of great depth. It didn't even occur to me to think how I would look things up in them."[69] The language and thoughts here, in keeping with the child's point of view, are simple. The exam itself is much farther from the boy's mind than the treats in his basket, but the adult self's critical eye is aimed at the exam system, not at the boy. By refraining from comment, the adult self implies that in fact the boy is right about the books. They may look fascinating, but they have little application to real life and are more abstruse than profound.

This passage sets the tone for the ensuing description of walking in the dark to the examination hall: the whole procedure is obscure, mysterious, and ultimately meaningless to the child. The boy's confusion stems not just from his age but from his dim awareness that the exam system is on its last legs and there is no clear moral or intellectual authority to replace it. By taking the exams, the boy is theoretically practicing for adulthood, but this training is a dead end. We can predict from the beginning that he will fail the exams. His adult self, however, with the benefit of historical hindsight, presents the boy's failure as comical rather than shameful. Success would have little bearing on his future life; indeed it would be a kind of sellout to the old system.

The images of mystery that pervade the story reinforce our sense of looking through the boy's eyes and recall both the "magical" quality of the narrator's childhood memories in "My Old Home" and the awed fascination with which the boy in "Firewood" watches his woodcutter friend. As they approach the examination courtyard near dawn, he gazes at the bustle of peddlers and passersby in the streets: "I sensed an aura of ghostly gloom about all these shapes and sounds and clutched instinctively at Uncle's long gown." He follows his uncle "as if hypnotized" to join the others waiting at the gate. When it is time to enter the courtyard, he tags along "like a sleepwalker."[70] A big shadowy figure scoops him over the high threshold. Inside more enigmas await: "As I turned around, another mysterious scene spread out before me. A great hall stood far in the distance, dim and indistinct. Near it were a few dots of lantern light and some blurry human shapes."[71] Looking around for his examination cell, he at first misreads the character denoting his assigned place, making him feel "frustrated, like a weary traveler deep in the wilderness at night, unable to find lodging."[72] Throughout the time leading up to the exam itself, the images the narrator uses to refer to himself and his perceptions convey an impression of smallness, weariness, and timidity. As in the boy's descriptions of Big Brother Egret in "Firewood," the physical angle of vision is definitely that of a child.

The narrator's adult self stays covert until a disruption occurs when a new-style middle-school graduate kicks up a row over another examinee who has registered under a false birthplace. By this time, the boy has eaten most of his food, horsebell melons first, but has nothing on paper except for the exam questions. Naturally, he welcomes this new distraction. Here the narrator steps into his adult shoes briefly to explain the background of this incident: new-style middle schools were springing up to replace the old Confucian academies, but their students were forbidden to take the traditional exams. Uncertain of the career possibilities of the new system, however, students sometimes tried to sit for the exams illegally in order to keep two irons in the fire. The complainant raising the ruckus, nicknamed "Heavenly King Du" (Du Tianwang), has signed in under a false name himself, so the fuss he raises over the other impostor is hypocritical and absurd. Nobody dares cross him, though, as he is the son of a powerful local family. The incident underscores the corrupt state of the whole examination procedure.

After this brief aside, the narrator quickly reassumes his boyhood guise to describe at some length the captivating tale of how Heavenly King Du once led a gang of middle-school students in smashing up the statues in a Buddhist temple, raising a revolutionary battle cry: "Only if we tear them down can we destroy ignorant people's superstitions!"[73] The boy is anxious to get a look at this fellow, not because of anything to do with the exams, but because of his heroic exploits at the temple and his imposing looks. When the "hero" has bullied the unfortunate "impostor" out of the courtyard, everything gradually settles down, and the boy's wise reaction is to fortify himself with a ham-stuffed steamed bun. What the adult narrator has added as background information about the conflict between the new and old systems is artistically superfluous, a brief distraction from the child's point of view, though it does reveal that early versions of educational reform had so far proved inadequate. Ironically, Heavenly King Du, who is fond of spouting revolutionary slogans, puts the supposedly progressive side of the debate over education in a bad light by behaving like a typical young gentry bully. Superficial reforms obviously will not solve China's educational crisis.

The boy's observations supply another perspective on the incident. It is from his point of view that we watch the crowd beating up the accused, blows still resounding when the boy can no longer see him. The boy appears more sympathetic than the crowd of adults. As a child, he has little sense of why the man's dishonesty—in this absurd context—should cause such a violent reaction. The boy's last image of the man as the clerks lead him out of the compound is a glimpse of his queue, symbol of Chinese subjugation under the nearly defunct Manchu dynasty and a vestigial remnant of the old order. Again the narrator presents the image without comment. What we infer is that both the old system and the new reforms are riddled with hypocrisy, to which the boy reacts with an appropriate mixture of puzzlement and apprehension. The context of the incident is clear from the information the adult narrator has supplied, but the emotional response to it derives from the child.

In the end the boy does buckle down to work, and here the narrator interjects a comment that reaffirms the basic congruity of attitude between his adult and child selves. At one point the boy stops to count up the number of characters he has written, finding only two hundred out of a minimum three hundred. "How could I stop at two hundred?" he asks. "I didn't consider at all how good the composition was, but I certainly wanted them to read it. This really made no sense."[74] The child's voice is indistinguishable from the adult's in this comment. The boy has begun to realize the pointlessness of the whole exam, and the adult confirms its absurdity. The old system is all washed up, and it matters not a whit that the boy has spent his day eating melons and peanuts.

The boy's perspective prevails all the way to the end: on the way home, he thinks neither about the exam itself nor about the consequences of failing it. He concentrates instead on his plan to ask his father for two more horsebell melons when he gets home, a request he feels is "fully justified." The adult narrator again refrains from comment, implying agreement with the boy's thought that "this kind of scorching hot day was just the time to be eating horsebell melons."[75] Throughout the story the adult narrator, by not intervening, lends mostly unspoken support to the boy's views, thereby allowing the boy's consciousness to dominate the picture. As a result, we gain the impression that although the road ahead is uncharted, it will lead to a better place so long as those leading the way are youthful enough to remember the taste of melons.

The narrator of "Horsebell Melons" is, like his American counterpart, Huck Finn, the protagonist of the story he tells. Also, more than in "My Old Home" and "Firewood," the social commentary in "Horsebell Melons" emerges from the boy's consciousness, just as Huck's unpracticed eye and his voice "are made delicate instruments for registering social truth."[76] The adult consciousness in the background functions primarily to confirm rather than interpret the boy's impressions. Ye Shaojun made no attempt to reproduce a child's diction and storytelling style as closely as Twain, but the angle of vision is still distinctly more the child's than the adult's.

Reading this work alone among Ye Shaojun's stories and essays would give an incomplete picture of his complex attitudes toward the world of children. But the impression it leaves strongly reinforces what he expresses elsewhere from an adult's perspective—that we have something to learn from the child's observations of the adult world and his responses to it. The story also encapsulates a confluence of events that preoccupied early modern writers and aroused their interest in childhood: the parallel paths of the modern intellectual's growing-up process and China's incipient transition into the modern age.

Into the Mouths of Babes

Perhaps the ultimate child-centered Chinese story is Bing Xin's neonatal narrative, "Fen" (Parting, 1931), written six months after the birth of her son.[77] Though the piece is not autobiographical, contemporary critics contend that the story comes directly from her experience with her own newborn child.[78] It is easy to imagine Bing Xin watching her baby and wondering, as new parents often do, what on earth he is really saying when he cries. The entire story is told by a newborn from the moment of birth to the time he leaves the hospital ten days later.

In "Parting," the adult consciousness, never taking on a personal identity, serves merely to translate and transcribe experience. Though the infant understands adult speech and thinks complex thoughts, he cannot yet speak in a way intelligible to adults, nor can his tiny hands do much more than wave about. Adult assistance in writing it all down is therefore essential. Yet the adult "ghostwriter" does not participate overtly in the telling of the tale. The message of "Parting," however, is most definitely adult-generated and anything but subtle. The narration is highly contrived, as the diction and level of thought belong to an articulate adult, not to a preverbal baby. Still, for the most part, Bing Xin preserves the baby's angle of vision. Moreover, despite the control exerted by the adult consciousness, Bing Xin creates the overall impression that the baby is the one who really knows what's going on.

From the very beginning of "Parting" we look at the newborn's world from his physical perspective:

A gigantic paw broke through the fine-meshed net of dark pain and pulled me out, and I cried my first sad cry.

I opened my eyes. One of my legs was still upside down in the grasp of that giant paw, and I could see my red, delicate hands waving about in the air above my head.

With another gigantic paw carefully supporting my middle, he turned, smiling, and said to a woman lying on a white wheeled bed, "Congratulations, a fine big baby boy!" and laid me gently in a basket lined with a white cloth.[79]

The baby knows certain things we do not usually credit babies with being able to understand: he distinguishes a man from a woman, he knows some colors, he recognizes objects like "bed," "basket," and "cloth," and he sees that both the man's hand and his own are the same kind of thing despite their vastly different size. The baby also understands adult speech, along with some sensory and emotional concepts: "grasp," "gentle," "sad." At the same time, his perspective does differ from an adult's: what is "giant" to him is "normal size" to an adult, and his hands waving "above" his head are probably "below" it from an adult's point of view, though he does say that the doctor is dangling him "upside down." He also seems acutely aware of his helplessness in the hands of these giant adults. This mixture of conceptual sophistication and infantile perspective continues throughout the story, suggesting that just because infants cannot express themselves in words adults understand does not mean that they are really inarticulate or cannot comprehend things on a complex level. In fact, quite the opposite impression develops: it is the infant who is aware, truly aware, of himself and others, while the adults, hulking obtuse things, have lost touch with reality.

Soon after the baby is born, he is taken into a big, sun-filled room lined with cribs, each holding an infant. Some are sleeping comfortably; others are yelling, "I'm thirsty! I'm hungry! I'm hot! I'm wet!" But the nurse holding him just moves quickly and calmly down the row of cribs as if nothing is wrong.[80] Later, when he tries unsuccessfully to nurse at his mother's breast, the nurse reassures his mother that her milk will certainly come in soon, and "anyway, he doesn't mind yet," to which the baby protests, "I really *did* care, but nobody knew it."[81] The adults construct feelings and thoughts for the infants that have little basis in fact.

The notion of such a cognitively advanced baby looks especially preposterous in light of traditional Chinese concepts of infant development. Charlotte Furth has described these concepts, beginning with views of early infancy as an "immature, vegetative, and vulnerable" state, advancing to a stage at several months of age when the child begins to respond to adult influence, and then progressing to the level of "developed consciousness and faculties" at about a year and a half.[82] Bing Xin's narrator debunks the idea of the baby blob. If adults only listened to babies harder and watched them more closely, the story implies, we would see that they know quite a lot and even have a few things to tell us. The narrator of "Parting" is puzzled and bemused by adults' obtuseness—like the twin babies in P. L. Travers' *Mary Poppins,* who share their own very articulate language with the sunlight, the wind, trees, stars, a starling, and Mary Poppins (an enlightened adult).[83] What adults term the "innocence of babes," Bing Xin implies, is really a greater wisdom. In a similar vein, Taoists in the Chinese tradition advocate becoming "as if stupid" *(ruo yu)*— that is, recapturing the infant's supposedly unencumbered state of mind. Bing Xin's story shows that growing up means becoming truly stupid—that is, forgetting the wisdom we were born with.

In "Parting," the sense that infants know better is crucial to the story's social message, which attacks the artificiality of class lines. During his first bath in the hospital, the narrator encounters another baby, a round, robust savvy little guy who regards the narrator with "condescension and pity" for being so delicate and pale.[84] It is immediately clear that the two are from opposite ends of the social spectrum. The first clue is the fragility of the narrator and his parents, contrasting sharply with the hardiness of his tiny companion and his "swarthy" mother. They compare birth experiences:

> I said, "I ached all over, four hours of struggling by the time it was over. It was really hard—how about you?"
> He smiled, and made a little fist. "Not me—only took a half hour to squeeze through. No pain for me, or my mother either."
> Silent, I sighed and looked all around. He said soothingly, "You're tired, go to sleep. I'm going to catch a few winks too."[85]

At this point the narrator experiences his first identity crisis. Suddenly he is whisked over to the glass door, where a crowd of kids has gathered to have a look at him "as if they were standing outside a window staring enviously at a display of Christmas gifts." They point at him, discussing which parts of him resemble which relatives, "seemingly ready to gobble me up piece by piece," an image calling to mind modern Chinese fears that foreign powers were carving China up like a melon *(guafen)* among themselves. The baby cries out, "I'm nobody but myself! I don't look like anyone else, let me go take a nap now!"[86] Xiao Feng, Bing Xin's biographer, notes that the family circumstances of the narrator and his new friend determine from the outset their future social status, even their occupations.[87] The narrator's early rebellion against such categorization echoes the protests of China's modern youth, who were restricted on a personal level by traditional social stratification and threatened on a national level by foreign encroachment.

As the babies get acquainted and other differences emerge, the question of identity takes on further dimensions. The narrator's mother is in a private room, the bedside table piled with books, flowers everywhere. His father, a thin, pale teacher, says he will come home every day after class to help with the baby—a modern dad. His little friend's mother, on the other hand, is in a big room with a dozen other new mothers and babies—"real lively," says the little friend, "and all the little guys've got plenty to eat," unlike the narrator, who is starving.[88] Their futures are already being mapped out for them: the narrator's parents wonder what kind of "specialist" he will become and decide that a scientist would be nice because "China needs science"—one of the twin hopes of the modern age, "Mr. Science and Mr. Democracy."[89] The other baby already knows he will be a lowly butcher like his father, and though he suppresses a tear at the thought of his family's poverty, he rallies himself enough to describe the trade with relish:

> A pig butcher! What fun, a clean blade goes in, a red one comes out! When I'm big, I'll do like my daddy, butcher pigs—not just pigs, also kill all those piggy people who just eat and don't work![90]

As Xiao Feng points out, Bing Xin endows this sturdy little friend with a brash self-confidence that outweighs the passing envy he feels for his richer friend's material comforts.[91] In doing so, Bing Xin reveals the kind of self-doubt Larson describes as plaguing modern Chinese intellectuals who see themselves as inferior to the working class.[92]

Even before leaving the hospital, the two babies, born at the same time in the same place, realize that they belong to different worlds and will never again be together the way they are now. For the time being they are friends, dressed in identical hospital clothes and treating each other with solicitude and friendly curiosity. Outside, the narrator will have every material advantage, while his friend will not even have the mother's milk he has been thriving on these first few days—his father has already sold his mother's services as a wet nurse. Ironically, the narrator will drink powdered milk at home because his own mother is too delicate to nurse him herself.

Despite the hardships facing him, the narrator's small friend neither pities himself nor asks the narrator for pity, again contrasting favorably with his proto-intellectual pal in physical capability and determination:

> "You will always be a little potted flower, delicately blooming in a greenhouse, where wind and rain can't get in and the temperature stays even. But me, I'll be a blade of grass by the road, have to put up with people's trampling feet, fierce wind and rain. You'll see me from far away, looking out your glass window, maybe feel sorry for me. But I'll have the endless sky over my head, butterflies and crickets chirping and fluttering freely around me. My brave, lowly companions cannot be burned or mown, but will dot the whole earth with green!"
>
> I felt so awkward I wanted to cry. "It's not me who wanted to be so delicate!"[93]

This small tough kid embodies not only the bravado of the *haohan* (roving heroes) of traditional fiction but the spirit of the modern revolutionary masses as well. The narrator, on the other hand, feels weak and marginalized, belying the rosy vision his parents have of his future and implying that their self-image is distorted.

For all their differences, both babies grow sad at the prospect of parting. When they finally get dressed up to leave, the narrator in his coordinated outfit of soft white and green wool and his friend in patched blue cotton hand-me-downs, a new kind of reality dawns on the narrator: "From now on we'd go our separate ways, parted forever in spirit and in flesh!"[94] The thought makes him shiver. Two identical little hospital gowns lie on the floor to remind him of their brief companionship. When they finally leave the hospital, he glimpses, secure in his mother's embrace inside the private car, a small sturdy shape shutting his eyes defiantly against the cold winter wind, being carried by his father out into the big anonymous city. "Look, precious, what a smooth white world it is!" says his delicate mother. His only response, closing the story, is to cry.[95]

What happens to these two infants results from forces already at work in the adult world outside. The title, indeed, could be translated "The Division," referring not to an imminent separation but to a preexisting one; it also suggests the homophone *fen**, meaning one's share or allotment. Even in the hospital they are treated unequally, the narrator carried by a nurse to see his mother in her quiet room, his friend wheeled on a cot with a bunch of other babies to the open ward. In fact it is only through the help of a benevolent association that the butcher's son is in the hospital at all—his siblings were all born at home. The narrator's parents are already planning his education, while the other will work on getting streetwise. Yet they do not let these class differences impair their friendship. The butcher's son will undoubtedly "grow up" faster, learning much earlier how to cope in a harsh world. The narrator is almost envious, thinking as he watches him go, "He had already started to enjoy his struggle."[96] He, the "child who has everything," as he hears his parents say, and his friend, who has to fight for whatever he gets, have experienced an ironic inversion during their first days of life that challenges the assumptions of the adults who run the world, or think they do.

Bing Xin does not attempt in "Parting" to convince the reader that the infant narrator's language is authentic.[97] The extreme youth of the narrator makes it impossible to conceive of the text as anything but an adult "ghostwriter's" construction, despite the fact that the angle of narration is consistently the child's. Bing Xin had already experienced the difficulties of assuming a child's voice, as she had first attempted to do in a series of letters addressed to young readers during the three years she spent in the United States between 1923 and 1926. "The more I wrote, the less my writing resembled [a child's] way of speaking," she said.[98] In "Parting," the very impossibility of the narrator's voice throws the focus back on the adult's message. To whose vision is the narrative true? This adult narrator is, on the textual level, more covert than those in any of the other three stories, yet the adult's didactic agenda is the most overt.

The age of the children in these narratives is one factor affecting the reader's sense of the relationship between child and adult consciousnesses. In the other three stories, the children are all old enough to make relatively complex observations of society around them and to perceive social conflict, even if they cannot articulate their observations as fully as their adult selves and even if they are less aware of the whole context. They are already in some measure social participants. And there is another factor affecting the degree of adult/child mediation: the infant narrator of "Parting" is the adult "ghostwriter's" son, not her own child self. In stories where the two levels of narration come from different phases in the life of the same person, the child's thoughts and the adult's are more closely associated, even if growing up has affected the narrator's outlook. In "Parting," the class alignment between adult consciousness and child narrator is still present, and the author still has a personal connection with the narrator, but the child's voice is much more an artificial construct than in the other three stories.

Bing Xin's neonatal narrative may be unique among modern Chinese stories of childhood. "Parting" would strain the credulity of most adult readers on a literal level, since neonates are supposed to be preverbal. Yet the seeming absurdity of the narration provokes the reader into wondering just how early children's perceptions of a divided world actually begin. The story also points to the negative impact of adult social structures on children's natural feelings and inclinations from the very beginning of life. Gloria Bien notes that the story, in contrast to Bing Xin's earlier works, "at last tackles head-on the problem of social inequality."[99] Fan Boqun and Xiao Feng also emphasize how much Bing Xin's attitude toward childhood in "Parting" has changed in comparison to her earlier stories.[100] No longer does she see childhood as a paradise watered by universal motherly love; from the time of birth, she now recognizes, social inequality can cause physical suffering at one end of the scale and spiritual deprivation at the other. The hand of the adult puppeteer behind the baby narrator in "Parting" is quite obvious, even intrusive. But in most of the story, Bing Xin manages to focus on a view of the world that adults ignore or have forgotten. To emphasize how fragile and fleeting that view is, after only ten days of life, out go the babies into a stratified, unjust society that will part them irrevocably.

By choosing an infant as narrator, Bing Xin dramatically highlights the position of children as victims of society: perceptive and intelligent but helpless. The end of the story contains no note of hope, only a sense that the adult world has sadly distorted true morality and impeded pure human feeling. Bing Xin expressed a similar view of childhood in a poem published in 1923: "Ah, childhood! / Truth in dream, / Dream in truth, / Tearful smile of memory."[101]

COMING FULL CIRCLE

China in the early twentieth century was struggling to "grow up," to assert its place among nations it viewed as more sophisticated and more progressive than itself; those nations, by and large, also saw China as backward. But its long, rich tradition made it anything but childlike as it entered the modern era. In fact, many early modern intellectuals felt that China by the end of the Qing had become senile—that it had entered the infantile phase of old age. Renewal, reform, and revolution were the watchwords of those who hoped to pull China out of the morass into which it seemed to be sinking. As had been true in earlier eras of transition, progressive intellectuals placed high value on the freshness of youthful vision. It is only natural that writers turned so often to the child's voice as a narrative mode, just as modern writers elsewhere have made use of the child as a "creative symbol," the seed of "hope for human salvation."[102]

The social criticism embedded in these dual child-adult narratives derives much power from the fact that the reader sees society not solely through the trained eyes of an adult but also from the standpoint of a relatively disingenuous observer. Nonetheless, the adult consciousness is always present, controlling the reader's reception of the child's observations. The agenda generally derives from adult concerns because, despite the new perception of childhood "as a time for the unfolding of a distinct personality in children, a time when children had needs of their own and a vitality *(xingling)* to develop," the adults writing these stories could not quite abandon their traditional role as guides and mentors for the young.[103]

Adult mediation takes various forms: interpretation, contextual-ization, confirmation, or transcription. More highly mediated texts, by tending to focus attention on the adult into whom the child has grown, cast the validity of the child's view in a relatively ambiguous light. The children in "My Old Home" (both the narrator's child-hood self and his own nephew) represent hope for a world in which the barriers of class will disappear. But the adult narrator's cynicism about the present combined with his romanticized images of child-hood lead us to question the pragmatic value of the child's perspec-tive. Children may embody true morality, but is that morality viable in the real world—especially in a world as troubled as that of early-twentieth-century China? In "Firewood," the adult mediation is apparent but not highly interpretive. The adult's perspective brackets the child's, providing a frame of reference while maintaining the integrity of the child's view. The adult's description of social reality confirms the child's "true vision" of Big Brother Egret. Although there is no substantial hope for the itinerant woodcutter's future, let alone any continuing friendship with the boy, the adult narrator's lack of commentary on his boyhood impressions implies that he con-tinues to believe in their validity, even if he now sees the plight of those like Big Brother Egret in a more "realistic" way.

More covertly mediated stories like "Horsebell Melons" and "Parting" imply greater congruence between the adult's vision and the child's. In "Horsebell Melons," it is sometimes impossible to dis-tinguish the boy's views from those of his adult self, but a child's way of looking at things predominates. The adult consciousness does not question the boy's responses but functions instead to back them up. The two levels of narration merge with few seams. The adult hand in "Parting" is hidden yet obvious; the congruence between the adult "ghostwriter's" consciousness and the infant's is virtually complete. Their shared attitude toward social injustice contrasts dramatically with the attitudes of the adult characters in the story, who appear either blind to social reality (the narrator's parents), deaf to what is really being said (the nurses), or inured to hardships over which they have no control (the parents of the narrator's small friend). It takes the newest of new people—with the cooperation of an adult tran-scriber—to see through the web of injustice, if only for a few brief days before social reality obscures the picture.

The impulse to recapture the freshness of youthful vision, to remember what melons actually tasted like in childhood, is doubtless as old as humanity. Examples of adults pursuing that goal appear frequently in early Chinese texts: in the *Dao de jing* passages associating an infantlike state with true virtue, in Mencius' maxim that great people do not lose their childlike hearts, and in tales of Lao Laizi who as an old man wore bright-colored clothes and cavorted like a child to please his even more venerable parents. In such texts, however, the child is an idealized abstraction. Only in the modern period did Chinese writers begin to give children a major role in telling their own stories. In so doing, modern writers were both exploring the roots of their own identities and speaking through children for a new kind of world.

In modern Chinese literature, traces of tradition are still evident in the tendency to make children's voices serve adult purposes. In many modern stories of childhood, Confucian patterns of social hierarchy underlie the reluctance of adult authors and narrators to relinquish the role of moral guide, and Taoist ideals still gleam through the romanticized nostalgia for childhood simplicity. Yet there is also a renewed sense of responsibility toward children in these stories, a feeling that children are worth attention not as the perpetuators of an ancient tradition but as a potent force for social change.

In his essay on modern fatherhood, Lu Xun summarizes the role of "awakened" adults in the modern world, a role paralleling that of the adult consciousness in modern child-adult narratives:

> [Those who have awakened] must liberate their own children. Bearing the heavy burden of tradition, they can put their shoulders to the gate of darkness, holding it open for the children to pass through to the land of open space and light, to spend their days from that moment on in happiness and rational harmony.[104]

Tsi-an Hsia traces this passage to a legend about the fall of Emperor Yang of the Sui. Those passing through the gate are rebels, one of them the future Tang Emperor Taizong. The gate finally crushes the "Herculean bandit" holding it open.[105] By urging adults to "hold open the gate of darkness," Lu Xun expresses the hope that adults will give children the opportunities and the freedom to develop a strong and healthy new society. In modern stories of childhood, the adult narrator plays just such a role, that of facilitator, with more or less of a controlling hand. Without the adult to open the gate, the children would remain imprisoned; but if the adult is willing to be crushed by the gate—to be sacrificed along with tradition—there is hope that the children will live on in a new and better world.

NOTES

1. Lu Xun, *Zhaohua xi shi* (Dawn blossoms gathered at dusk; 1927), vol. 16 of *Lu Xun sanshinian ji* (Three decades of Lu Xun's works; hereafter *LXSSNJ*) (Hong Kong: Xinyi, 1969), p. 6.

2. The writers concerned here generally fall into the category of "May Fourth era writers," referring to those who produced most of their work in the decade or two following the May Fourth demonstration in Beijing in 1919. Given the disputes over precise periodization of the May Fourth era and over the attributes of May Fourth literature, however, I prefer in this context to use the more general term "early modern writers."

3. See Wendy Larson, *Literary Authority and the Modern Chinese Writer* (Durham, N.C.: Duke University Press, 1991), pp. 47, 59–60; Jon L. Saari, *Legacies of Childhood: Growing Up Chinese in a Time of Crisis, 1890–1920* (Cambridge, Mass.: Council on East Asian Studies, Harvard University Press, 1990), p. 69; Vera Schwarcz, *The Chinese Enlightenment: Intellectuals and the Legacy of the May Fourth Movement of 1919* (Berkeley: University of California Press, 1986), pp. 9–10, 147–149.

4. Larson, *Literary Authority,* p. 60.

5. Lu Xun, "Geming shidai de wenxue" (Literature of a revolutionary era; 1927), in *Eryi ji* (No more to be said), vol. 17 of *LXSSNJ* (Hong Kong: Xinyi, 1967), p. 24.

6. Yi-tsi Feuerwerker, "Women as Writers in the 1920's and 1930's," in Margery Wolf and Roxane Witke, eds., *Women in Chinese Society* (Stanford: Stanford University Press, 1975), pp. 162–163.

7. See Lu Xun's "My Old Home" and Bing Xin's "Parting"; Wu Zuxiang's "Firewood" and Ba Jin's "Yang Sao" (Nanny Yang; 1931); and Shen Congwen's "Xiaoxiao" (1929).

8. Modern writers had as children experienced at least the milder forms of these restrictive practices themselves, as illustrated in Lu Xun's early reminiscence "Huaijiu" (Remembering the past; 1911) or Ye Shaojun's account of taking the imperial examinations in "Malinggua" (Horsebell melons; 1923).

9. Jonathan D. Spence, *The Search for Modern China* (New York: Norton, 1990), p. 309. See also Maria Jaschok, *Concubines and Bondservants: The Social History of a Chinese Custom* (London: Zed Books, 1988), for case studies and statistics regarding these practices in nineteenth-century and early twentieth-century Hong Kong; and Ida Pruitt on Shandong, *A Daughter of Han: The Autobiography of a Chinese Working Woman* (New Haven: Yale University Press, 1945; Stanford: Stanford University Press, 1967).

10. Saari, *Legacies,* p. 39.

11. Ibid., p. 53.

12. Chow Tse-tsung, *The May Fourth Movement: Intellectual Revolu-*

tion in Modern China (Stanford: Stanford University Press, 1960), p. 29, n. 216.

13. John Dewey, "Work and Play in Education," in Robert W. Clopton and Tsuin-chen Ou, trans. and eds., *Lectures in China* (Honolulu: University of Hawai'i Press, 1973), pp. 197–202.

14. Saari, *Legacies*, pp. 24–26.

15. Ibid., p. 26.

16. Ibid., p. 45.

17. Ye Shaojun, "Jin Zhongguo de xiaoxue jiaoyu" (Elementary education in China today), *Xin chao* (New tide) 1(4) (April 1919):62–63.

18. Wing-tsit Chan, trans. and comp., *A Sourcebook in Chinese Philosophy* (Princeton: Princeton University Press, 1963), pp. 65–66, 76.

19. Lu Xun, "Women xianzai zenyang zuo fuqin" (Fatherhood today; 1919), in *Fen* (The grave), vol. 2 of *LXSSNJ* (Hong Kong: Xinyi, 1967), p. 118.

20. Confucius, *The Analects,* trans. D. C. Lau (New York: Penguin, 1979), p. 86.

21. Lu Xun, "Fatherhood," pp. 119, 123.

22. Ibid., p. 123.

23. Wu Zuxiang, "Wo jiang zenyang zuo fumuqin" (How to be parents), *Funü zazhi* (Women's journal) 11(11) (1925):1723.

24. Ibid., pp. 1722–1723.

25. Bing Xin, "Wode wenxue shenghuo" (My literary life), in Ba Jin et al., *Chuangzuo huiyi lu* (Recollections of writing) (Hong Kong: Wanyuan, 1979), pp. 184–185.

26. See Louis D. Rubin, Jr., *The Teller in the Tale* (Seattle: University of Washington Press, 1967), pp. 56–80; Peter Coveney, *The Image of Childhood* (Baltimore: Penguin, 1967), pp. 112–127, 215–225, 314–318; Albert E. Stone, Jr., *The Innocent Eye: Childhood in Mark Twain's Imagination* (New Haven: Yale University Press, 1961).

27. Fiona Björling, "Child Narrator and Adult Author: The Narrative Dichotomy in Karel Polàcek's *Bylonàs pet,*" *Scando-Slavica* 29 (1983):5.

28. Saari, *Legacies*, p. 60.

29. David Grylls, *Guardians and Angels* (London: Faber & Faber, 1978), pp. 35, 142–144.

30. C. John Sommerville, *The Rise and Fall of Childhood* (Beverly Hills: Sage, 1982), p. 173.

31. Higuchi Ichiyo, Kawabata Yasunari, Tanizaki Junichiro, Inoue Yasushi, and Mishima Yukio are among modern Japanese writers noted for their evocations of childhood and youth. The works of the Korean writer Hwang Sun-won, as Edward Poitras shows, frequently portray children as central characters and deal with the interplay between generations as a major theme. See Donald Keene, *Dawn to the West: Japanese Literature in the Modern Era (Fiction)* (New York: Henry Holt, 1984), chaps. 8, 20, 21, 27; Robert Danly, *In the Shade of Spring Leaves: The Life and Writings of*

Higuchi Ichiyo, a Woman of Letters in Meiji Japan (New Haven: Yale University Press, 1981), pp. 11–20, 118–120, 125–128, 254–287; Makoto Ueda, *Modern Japanese Writers and the Nature of Literature* (Stanford: Stanford University Press, 1976), pp. 186–190; J. Thomas Rimer, *Modern Japanese Fiction and Its Traditions: An Introduction* (Princeton: Princeton University Press, 1978), p. 85.

32. In drama young children play few if any significant roles, and in poetry images of children are generally more important as motifs or symbols than as individual portrayals. I am grateful to Stephen West, Clara Yu, and Samuel Cheung for confirming my impression that young children do not figure significantly in traditional drama.

33. John Dardess, "Childhood in Premodern China," in Joseph M. Hawes and N. Ray Hiner, eds., *Children in Historical and Comparative Perspective: An International Handbook and Research Guide* (New York: Greenwood, 1991), p. 88.

34. Ibid.

35. The Ming Buddhist master Deqing's (1546–1623) autobiography is a rare example of a premodern autobiography in which the child's perceptions come to the foreground as critical to the formation of adult consciousness. See Pei-yi Wu, *The Confucian's Progress: Autobiographical Writings in Traditional China* (Princeton: Princeton University Press, 1990), pp. 142–147. Another autobiography in which certain sections evoke the child's world is Shen Fu's early nineteenth-century work *Fu sheng liu ji* (Six records of a floating life), which both Jaroslav Prusek and Pei-yi Wu cite as transitional between Qing and modern narrative. See Jaroslav Prusek, *The Lyrical and the Epic: Studies of Modern Chinese Literature,* ed. Leo Ou-fan Lee (Bloomington: Indiana University Press, 1980), pp. 11, 25–27; Wu, *Confucian's Progress,* pp. 235–236.

36. Milena Doleželová-Velingerová, "Narrative Modes in Late Qing Novels," in Milena Doleželová-Velingerová, ed., *The Chinese Novel at the Turn of the Century* (Toronto: University of Toronto Press, 1980), p. 72. Rosemary Lloyd notes a similar trend in nineteenth-century France: "For the aristocrats, the Revolution of 1789, together with the uprisings, wars, and revolutions of the nineteenth century, swept aside many of the values that had allowed for self-definition in terms of name, family, and state, and forced a re-evaluation of the self along far more individual lines." See her *Land of Lost Content: Children and Childhood in Nineteenth-Century French Literature* (New York: Oxford University Press, 1992), p. 14. Chinese society has remained more group-oriented than modern Western societies; in China, therefore, such "re-evaluation of the self along far more individual lines," as Doleželová-Velingerová asserts, is subordinate to a larger social reevaluation.

37. Wayne C. Booth, *The Rhetoric of Fiction,* 2nd ed. (Chicago: University of Chicago Press, 1983), p. 152.

38. Robert E. Hegel, "An Exploration of the Chinese Literary Self," in

Robert E. Hegel and Richard C. Hessney, eds., *Expressions of Self in Chinese Literature* (New York: Columbia University Press, 1985), pp. 28–30; Andrew H. Plaks, "Towards a Critical Theory of Chinese Narrative," in Andrew H. Plaks, ed., *Chinese Narrative: Critical and Theoretical Essays* (Princeton: Princeton University Press, 1977), pp. 343–344.

39. Lloyd, *Lost Content*, p. 25.

40. Joy Hooton, "Miles Franklin's *Childhood at Brindabella*," *Meanjin* 46(1) (1987):61.

41. The examples cited later all have male narrators; although gender differences in socialization have hardly been eradicated in modern times, many basic notions about childhood apply to both sexes. Childhood narratives from a female perspective deserve a detailed comparative analysis. For the time being, however, examples have been chosen more to illustrate various models of narrative structure and function than to analyze the precise types of messages carried.

42. Stone, *Innocent Eye*, p. 85.

43. Keene, *Dawn to the West*, p. 1205.

44. William A. Lyell, Jr., *Lu Hsün's Vision of Reality* (Berkeley: University of California Press, 1976), p. 133.

45. Lu Xun, "Guxiang" (My old home; 1921), *Nahan* (Outcry), vol. 8 of *LXSSNJ* (Hong Kong: Xinyi, 1970), p. 80.

46. Ibid., pp. 80–81.

47. Ibid., p. 82; the word *zha* (translated here as "badger") is, according to Lu Xun, the local dialect word for a badgerlike animal. He made up a character to go with the word; see Lu Xun, *Diary of a Madman and Other Stories*, trans. William A. Lyell (Honolulu: University of Hawai'i Press, 1990), p. 91, n. 2.

48. Lu Xun, "My Old Home," p. 82.

49. Ibid., p. 85.

50. Ibid., pp. 92–93.

51. Ibid., p. 93.

52. Lu Xun, *Dawn Blossoms*, p. 6.

53. Lu Xun, "My Old Home," p. 90.

54. Lyell, *Vision of Reality*, p. 305.

55. Lu Xun, "My Old Home," p. 93.

56. Lu Xun, "Fatherhood," p. 118.

57. Lu Xun, "Kuangren riji" (Diary of a madman; 1918), in *Nahan*, p. 27.

58. Wu Zuxiang, "Chai" (Firewood; 1934), in *Fanyu ji* (After-dinner pieces) (Shanghai: Wenhua shenghuo, 1935; Hong Kong: Yimei, 1956), p. 73.

59. Ibid., p. 74.

60. Coveney, *Image of Childhood*, p. 307.

61. Wu Zuxiang, "Firewood," p. 76.

62. Ibid., p. 77.

63. Ibid., p. 79.

64. Ibid., p. 82.

65. Ye Zhishan, ed., *Ye Shengtao* (Hong Kong: Sanlian, 1983), p. 263; Jin Mei, *Lun Ye Shengtao de wenxue chuangzuo* (Ye Shengtao's literary creation) (Shanghai: Shanghai wenyi, 1985), p. 60.

66. Saari, *Legacies,* pp. 63–64.

67. Sommerville, *Rise and Fall,* p. 173; Coveney, *Image of Childhood,* p. 204.

68. Ye Shaojun, "Malinggua" (Horsebell melons; 1923), *Xianxia* (Under the line) (Shanghai: Shangwu, 1925), pp. 97–98.

69. Ibid., p. 98.

70. Ibid., pp. 100–101.

71. Ibid., p. 105.

72. Ibid., p. 109.

73. Ibid., p. 114.

74. Ibid., p. 119.

75. Ibid., pp. 119–120.

76. Stone, *Innocent Eye,* p. 144.

77. Gloria Bien, "Images of Women in Ping Hsin's Fiction," in Angela Jung Palandri, ed., *Women Writers of Twentieth-Century China* (Eugene: University of Oregon Asian Studies Publications, 1982), p. 27.

78. Fan Boqun, *Bing Xin pingzhuan* (A critical biography of Bing Xin) (Beijing: Renmin wenxue, 1983), p. 146; Xiao Feng, *Bing Xin zhuan* (A biography of Bing Xin) (Beijing: Beijing shiyue wenyi, 1987), pp. 204–205.

79. Bing Xin, "Fen" (Parting; 1931), in *Gugu* (Aunt) (Shanghai: Beixin, 1932), p. 50.

80. Ibid., p. 52.

81. Ibid., pp. 58–59.

82. Charlotte Furth, "Concepts of Pregnancy, Childbirth and Infancy in Ch'ing Dynasty China," *Journal of Asian Studies* 46(1) (1987):24–25.

83. P. L. Travers, *Mary Poppins* (New York: Reynal & Hitchcock, 1934; New York: Harcourt, 1962), pp. 138–146.

84. Bing Xin, "Parting," p. 53.

85. Ibid., p. 54.

86. Ibid., p. 55.

87. Xiao Feng, *Biography,* p. 205.

88. Bing Xin, "Parting," p. 61.

89. Ibid., pp. 62–63.

90. Ibid., p. 60.

91. Xiao Feng, *Biography,* p. 206.

92. Larson, *Literary Authority,* pp. 59–60, 81–85.

93. Bing Xin, "Parting," pp. 65–66.

94. Ibid., p. 69.

95. Ibid., p. 72.

96. Ibid.

97. Linda Britt describes the Costa Rican writer Carmen Naranjo's creation of a child's narrative voice, referring to such narratives as "idioreliable, that is, totally true to their own view of things but unrelated to a 'reality' perceived by others." See Britt, "A Transparent Lens?: Narrative Technique in Carmen Naranjo's *Nunca Hubo Alguna Vez*," *Monographic Review* 4 (1988): 128.

98. Bing Xin, "Wode wenxue shenghuo," p. 182.

99. Bien, "Images of Women," pp. 28, 36, n. 24.

100. Fan Boqun, *Critical Biography*, p. 146; Xiao Feng, *Biography*, p. 204.

101. Bing Xin, *Fan xing* (Myriad stars; 1923) (Shanghai: Shangwu, 1933), pp. 1–2.

102. Coveney, *Image of Childhood*, p. 340.

103. Saari, *Legacies*, p. 259.

104. Lu Xun, "Fatherhood," p. 115.

105. Tsi-an Hsia, *The Gate of Darkness: Studies on the Leftist Literary Movement in China* (Seattle: University of Washington Press, 1968), pp. 146–147.

GLOSSARY

fen	分	to separate; to part; to divide
fen*	份	allotment; portion; share
ge	哥	elder brother
guafen	瓜分	to carve up; to partition (lit., carving up a melon)
haohan	好漢	brave man; hero
renshengguan	人生觀	outlook on life
ruo yu	若愚	as if stupid; seemingly foolish
sancong side	三從四德	three submissions and four virtues
shenyide	神異的	magical
xingling	性靈	vitality; spirit
younian	幼年	childhood; infancy
yuankao	院考	first-level civil service examination in imperial China
zha	猹	badgerlike animal

Revolutionary Little Red Devils: The Social Psychology of Rebel Youth, 1966–1967

MARK LUPHER

This essay examines and reinterprets the social psychology of rebel youth during the tumultuous opening phases of the Cultural Revolution. From late spring 1966 until Chairman Mao Zedong's September 5, 1967, national decree, urban youth in China played the leading part in a social and political convulsion that shook the Chinese Communist system to its foundations. Set in motion and legitimated by the leader of the Chinese Communist Party (CCP) himself, the Red Guard movement galvanized legions of university and middle school students, including millions of children in the true sense of the word. This youthful upheaval has become infamous; the enduring image of the Cultural Revolution remains one of mindless Red Guard destruction, violence, and frenzy. In China and the West, the eruption of youthful energy and rebellion in 1966–1967 is still predominantly viewed as an aberration and a nightmare.

These images of Chinese youth during the Cultural Revolution are not wholly inaccurate, but they are incomplete. As I will detail in these pages, rebel youth in 1966–1967 articulated deeply rooted tensions in Chinese society; in so doing, they confronted issues of fundamental and recurrent importance in Chinese culture and history. Specifically, rebel youth attempted to come to grips with issues of power and domination characteristic of both traditional and twentieth-century Chinese political culture. In addition to illuminating the essential features of the Chinese Communist social and political system of the 1950s and 1960s, therefore, the social psychology of young rebels in 1966–1967 also has much to tell us about authority relations and the position of youth in Chinese culture generally. Far from viewing the convulsions of the Cultural Revolution as aberrant, I argue that the youth rebellion was triggered by cultural, political, and social tensions of recurrent historical significance. These tensions remain largely unresolved and were underscored by the tragic events of June 4, 1989, in Tiananmen Square.

A full account of the many factors affecting the thought and action of Chinese youth in 1966–1967 is beyond the scope of this discussion. Sociostructural factors were, for example, a crucial motivational ingredient. As Hong Yung Lee first demonstrated, the formation of Red Guard factions in Peking in summer and fall 1966 was shaped by political and social cleavages. Young people from good, or "red" *(hong)*, class backgrounds—such as the children of party officials, People's Liberation Army (PLA) officers, and revolutionary martyrs—formed the first, elite Red Guard organizations. Young people from bad, or "black" *(hei)*, class backgrounds—such as the children of former Kuomintang (KMT) officials, ex-landlords, or "bourgeois" intellectuals—were persecuted by the elite Red Guards, subsequently formed their own Red Guard units, and, in due course, turned the tables on their persecutors.[1] Sociostructural cleavages thus underlay much of the conflict and violence of the Cultural Revolution.

The youth rebellion of 1966–1967 must also be understood in light of Chinese Communist political culture in the 1950s and early 1960s. Political campaigns, mass mobilization exercises, and incessant ideological exhortation were all part of the daily experience of urban Chinese youth in the years preceding the Cultural Revolution. Prior to summer 1966, these processes were always initiated and controlled by the party organization in the schools; in contrast, the power monopoly and institutional domination of the CCP was attacked and delegitimated during the primary phases of the Cultural Revolution. The chaotic and violent behavior of rebel youth in 1966–1967 was linked in significant measure to this volatile and contradictory combination of mass mobilization and suspended organizational controls.

By focusing on the social psychology of rebel youth, this essay seeks to reinterpret the role of cultural and attitudinal factors in the rebellion that erupted in the summer of 1966. Western analysts have developed two very different interpretations of the social psychology of rebel youth in this period. In *Mao's Revolution and the Chinese Political Culture*, Richard H. Solomon advanced his provocative and compelling thesis: there exists a fundamental ambivalence toward authority in Chinese culture, an ambivalence that is rooted in the socialization process and is manifested in the child's simultaneous awe and resentment of the remote and commanding father figure. Politically this ambivalence toward authority resulted in what Solomon has termed a national psychology revolving around the polarity of "unity versus conflict." In Solomon's words: "Both philosopher and peasant share common ideals of peace, harmony, political unification, and the 'Great Togetherness' *(datong)*, and fear of confusion *(hunluan)*, social disintegration, and violence."[2] Thus, he concludes, "as the Cultural Revolution progressed, the young students came to manifest the age-old Chinese ambivalence toward authority in their combined 'fervent love' for Chairman Mao and a growing mistrust for any concrete authority and organizational discipline."[3] In Solomon's view, therefore, the attitudes and behavior of rebel youth must be understood in light of the ambivalent social psychology of authority relations in Chinese culture. The more recent findings of Jon L. Saari tend to support this view. Rather than speak of an "ambivalence toward authority," however, Saari focuses attention on "the minority phenomenon of mischievous children," considers the limits of parental authority and conformist behavior, and emphasizes the wide range of individual responses to sociocultural indoctrination in early modern China.[4]

Solomon's interpretation was challenged in Anita Chan's *Children of Mao: Personality Development and Political Activism in the Red Guard Generation.* As her title indicates, Chan links the attitudes and behavior of rebel youth to distinctive CCP and Maoist political indoctrination and socialization processes. In Chan's view, the social psychology of the "first generation brought up under socialism" exhibited a pervasive "authoritarian personality."[5] This authoritarian personality stemmed from two closely interrelated processes: a pre–Cultural Revolution "educational system which gave precedence to iron discipline and competitive submission to collective and higher authority" and "the black and white Manichean worldview of Maoist teaching," which enjoined a militant and harshly uncompromising stance when students confronted the "people's enemies."[6] Rejecting Solomon's attempt to view rebel youth in the overall context of authority relations in Chinese culture, Chan concludes: "Our discussion has belonged to a period of modern China's history that undoubtedly cannot be resurrected. The particular climate that encouraged the development of the authoritarian 'social character' no longer prevails. The 1980s are not the 1960s; and the children of Deng are not the children of Mao."[7]

This essay will show that the interpretations of Solomon and Chan are not contradictory; indeed, the social psychology of rebel youth in 1966–1967 can only be understood in the joint context of Chinese culture broadly defined *and* post-1949 Chinese Communist and Maoist political culture. But I do not believe that both interpretations are equally persuasive. Whereas Solomon's attempt to view the social psychology of rebel youth in light of authority relations in Chinese culture generally may be fruitfully refined and updated, Chan's more narrowly formulated argument must be qualified and, in significant measure, rejected.

My discussion is based on a close textual analysis of a key Cultural Revolution document: *Selected Big Character Posters of the Great Proletarian Cultural Revolution (Wuchanjieji wenhua da geming dazibao xuan).* Officially published and distributed in massive quantities nationwide in fall 1966, this document contains a collection of big character posters and Maoist editorials arranged in generally chronological order.[8] With one exception, the big character posters were written by middle school students, children at the upper end of the age scale in the Chinese cultural context; the editorial commentaries were supplied by *People's Daily* and *Red Flag.* This document is not an unmediated primary source. Rather, like the *Analects,* it is didactic; politically correct rhetoric and themes are spelled out, appropriate targets and labels are defined, certain forms of political and social behavior are legitimated and encouraged, and other forms are condemned. The document thereby performs many of the interpreting, organizing, and confirming functions of "adult mediation" that Catherine Pease discusses in Chapter 10 of this volume. The text presents a detailed picture of the Maoist rhetoric and imagery in which Chinese youth were immersed in summer 1966, along with a vivid impression of the youthful response to the Maoist message.

The interaction of Maoist ideology and youthful rebellion is the most interesting and significant aspect of the document. As noted, the big character posters are arranged chronologically, beginning with junior philosophy instructor and future radical leader Nie Yuanzi's famous Peking University manifesto of May 25, 1966, and ending with an August 23 big character poster from Peking No. 1 Girl's Middle School.[9] The editorial commentary at the end of the document then underlines, amplifies, and endorses the response from below, pointing up the interplay of Maoist ideology and youthful upheaval in this period of building political momentum. The document also describes and denounces from a Maoist perspective the political behavior of the party organization in the schools, thereby providing an impression of the language, tactics, and outlook of the CCP power structure that was subjected to attack during the primary phases of the Cultural Revolution. A close look at the language and imagery of the document reveals that rebel youth were not simply reacting to Maoist exhortation from on high; the students were simultaneously rebelling against an authority structure and educational system they had experienced as oppressive, confining, unfair, and boring. In sum, the document provides a detailed picture of Maoist ideology, authority relations in the pre–Cultural Revolution school system, and the social psychology of youthful rebellion in the summer and fall of 1966.

YOUTHFUL REBELLION AND THE IDEA OF REVOLUTIONARY RENEWAL

The origins of the Cultural Revolution are complex. Power contests and policy disputes between Mao and other CCP leaders were a key element; these political conflicts dated back at least to the Hundred Flowers episode in 1957, the Great Leap Forward in 1958–1960, and the Socialist Education campaign in the early 1960s.[10] By the mid-1960s, the political and ideological estrangement between Mao and other leaders of the CCP civilian apparatus had escalated into a complete break, spurred by Mao's conviction that the CCP was rapidly turning into a "new class" of corrupt and privileged communist officials. These events are not unique. Central rulers throughout history have regularly engaged in struggles with political and economic elites who have sought to undercut their power and appropriate their authority.[11] As I have written elsewhere, central rulers have attempted to contest elite challenges in two ways: "from the top-down, with assertive personal rulership and the deployment of centrally controlled power structures; and from the bottom-up, with appeals to the masses and alliances with nonprivileged social strata."[12] In China, the Ming founder, Zhu Yuanzhang, waged precisely such a war against bureaucratic and landed elites. As emperor he "repeatedly issued orders that men of merit be recommended by central and provincial officials for government service with almost no consideration to be given to the social status of the recommended" and "made a point of letting his distrust of officialdom be known to the people."[13] In the communist systems of the twentieth century, Leninist leaders regularly attempted to mobilize nonprivileged social strata against elite groups under the rubric of "class struggle," while reformers like Khrushchev and Gorbachev also tried to revitalize the Soviet system by bringing political pressure from above and social pressure from below to bear on entrenched communist officialdom.[14] Mao's appeals to and mobilization of Chinese youth during the Cultural Revolution fit these patterns.[15]

In the summer and fall of 1966, however, Maoist rhetoric explicitly linked processes of youthful rebellion with the idea of systemic revitalization and revolutionary renewal. This linkage originated in the historical experience of the May Fourth period. As Pease suggests in Chapter 10, the idea that young people were uniquely dynamic, vital, and insightful was central to the thought of the May Fourth period. But the dynamic and historically progressive activism of youth was not conceived as harmonious or peaceful. On the contrary, the rhetoric of the May Fourth period was iconoclastic and confrontational; young people were called upon to destroy the false idols of Chinese tradition and attack all manifestations of Confucian hierarchy, ritual, and propriety.[16] Thinkers of the May Fourth period viewed the overthrow and destruction of the prevailing social and institutional order as a necessary step in preparing the way for the construction of a healthy new society. In the 1920s and 1930s, these ideas became fused with the Western, Marxian principles of violent class struggle and radical socioeconomic transformation that would shape the ideology of emerging Chinese Communism; yet the notion that young people should mount uncompromising attacks on tradition predates the rise of the communist revolution.

As we shall see, this militant vision of youth resurfaced in more tumultuous and violent form during the Cultural Revolution, spurred by the remarkable personal sponsorship of Chairman Mao Zedong. Mao's "real" motives in launching the Cultural Revolution were murky and will never be established with certainty. Yet it is apparent that Mao was not simply using Chinese youth against his political opponents in a cynically Machiavellian fashion during the Cultural Revolution. In the Maoist rhetoric and imagery of the summer of 1966, we repeatedly encounter conscious attempts to recapture the vision of youthful dynamism and revolution that first surfaced during the May Fourth period and then figured so importantly in the victorious rise of Chinese Communism.

REPRESSION AND CONTROL IN THE SCHOOL SYSTEM

Virtually all accounts of the Cultural Revolution, primary and secondary, Chinese and Western, concur on one basic point: the system of education in Communist China in the 1950s and early 1960s imposed harsh pressures on students. Chan correctly stressses the "iron discipline" and "competitive" conformity of the Chinese Communist school environment; but this authoritarian educational environment was hardly the novel creation of Chinese Communism. Rather, Chinese students in the 1950s and early 1960s had to survive in an educational system that fused traditional Chinese pedagogical approaches with CCP discipline, ideological exhortation, and mass mobilization. This amalgam of tradition and modernity forcefully upheld all the orthodox values historically inculcated in Chinese youth: veneration of classic works, social hierarchy, submission to adult authority, and, of course, endless preparation for crucial examinations. In this "neotraditional" system, the pressures on students in elite schools were particularly intense.[17]

To be sure, there were new elements; in the place of filial piety, the *Analects,* and Confucian rectitude, students were called upon to be politically and socially active, to revere the CCP and the Marxist-Leninist classics, and to participate in physical labor. But the priorities and reward structure of the pre–Cultural Revolution educational system were entirely familiar. In his memoir, former Red Guard Gao Yuan describes the public display of the names and test scores of students admitted to Peking and Qinghua universities in 1964:

> Red paper, gold characters. The imperial examiners of the Qing Dynasty had announced the results of the court examinations in the same way. Now things were different, of course. High marks were not supposed to mean power and prestige. . . . Still we looked with awe upon the names of alumni who were now students at these famous universities. . . . I looked at the Beida names so many times I knew them by heart.[18]

We will find that the tensions engendered in this high-pressure academic environment figured pivotally in the youth rebellion of summer 1966.

If much of the bombast and accusatory rhetoric of the Cultural Revolution did not arise out of the daily experience of young Chinese, the Maoist charge that authority relations in the school system amounted to "various forms of revisionist domination" *(zhongzhong xiuzhengzhuyi kongzhi)* struck a responsive chord among many students.[19] Numerous university and middle school students, and in the elite schools most of all, readily related to denunciations of educational authorities in the pre–Cultural Revolution school system and their sponsorship of "that heavy and stifling atmosphere at Peking University where 'ten thousand horses are muted as one' " *(Beida nazhong wanmaqiyin de chenmen kongqi)*.[20] Indeed, the most consistent themes in the big character posters discussed in this essay call for and celebrate the freedom, release, and empowerment of youth. Even the Mao personality cult, which for most of the Cultural Revolution decade (1966–1976) functioned as a rigid and unrelenting control mechanism, was linked with exuberant images of youthful freedom, release, and empowerment in the summer and fall of 1966.

THE LANGUAGE AND IMAGERY OF ORTHODOX AUTHORITY

If Chinese students were subjected to an especially burdensome amalgam of Confucian and CCP authoritarianism in the 1950s and early 1960s, by the late summer and fall of 1966 the tables had been turned completely. Big character poster denunciations of adult authorities, the suspension of normal CCP political and social controls in the schools, the formation of Red Guard organizations, the convening of mass rallies—all had been sanctioned by official decree and Mao's personal endorsement. During the preceding months of May, June, and July, however, the school system in Peking had been the scene of intense struggle, as CCP authorities opposed to the emerging Maoist line attempted to rein in the incipient youth rebellion with a variety of devices. In June and July, the CCP civilian leadership dispatched "work teams" to the Peking school system; in conventional CCP fashion, these work teams asserted the party's power monopoly, attempted to control and limit the writing of big character posters, suppressed dissenting views, and upheld orthodox CCP doctrine.[21] Consequently, the big character posters and Maoist editorials examined here contain detailed descriptions and rebuttals of the language and methods CCP authorities used in this attempt to control rebel youth. The orthodox authorities' view of youth is both familiar and revealing.

As the big character poster of Nie Yuanzi et al. described, party officials and school administrators at Peking University sought to contain the impending upheaval with conventional CCP paternalist authoritarianism. Their conceptual vocabulary stressed orthodox CCP control and mobilizational methods, such as "strengthening leadership" *(jiaqiang lingdao)*, "active guidance" *(jiji yindao)*, "normal development" *(zhengchang fazhan)*, and the "correct path" *(zhengque daolu)*. As always, it was the role of orthodox CCP authorities to "guide the movement to develop in the correct direction" *(yindao yundong xiang zhengque de fangxiang fazhan)*.[22] In accordance with standard CCP organizational procedure, such "guidance" was very much a hands-on process with little tolerance for unstructured input.

In an important account of the Cultural Revolution in Shanghai, Lynn T. White III focuses attention on "the importance of labeled status groups"—that is, the division of people into "proletarian" versus "bourgeois," "red" versus "black," and "revolutionary" versus "counterrevolutionary" social categories.[23] As White notes, the practice of labeling was well established in traditional Chinese culture and also functioned as an essential CCP control device prior to the Cultural Revolution. In May, June, and July 1966, the labeling process was initiated by CCP authorities attempting to check the incipient youth rebellion; it was insubordinate students who were first labeled by party officials, school administrators, and the work teams. The labels affixed at this time provide a familiar picture of prevailing adult attitudes toward youth in Chinese culture.

Youthful insubordination was denounced as a violation of the CCP power monopoly; labels like "counterrevolutionary" *(fan geming)* and "disciplinary infraction" *(weifan jilü)* were affixed accordingly. As noted earlier, however, the pre–Cultural Revolution education system was a synthesis of traditional Chinese social norms and communist institutions and control methods. In the eyes of the orthodox "power holders" *(dangquan pai)* and "authorities" *(quanwei)* in the school system, therefore, CCP hegemony and paternalist authority were one and the same; their indignant admonishment to unruly students was "Your elder is the party itself!" *(laozi jiushi dang)*. In fact, it was the challenge to orthodox models of youthful decorum that appear to have most outraged school administrators and CCP work teams. Rebel youth was "too one-sided" *(tai pianmian)*, "too crude and boorish" *(tai cubao)*, "too excessive" *(tai guofen)*; insubordinate students were accused of "creating a disturbance" *(nimen dao luan)*, they were "spoiled" *(zao toule)*, they were "ill-behaved and childish" *(nimen kuangwang, youzhi)*. As far as the elders in the school system were concerned, rebel youth "smelled of mother's milk and were not yet ready to attend to affairs" *(ruxiu weigan)*, an assessment with which any Confucian schoolmaster or traditional clan elder would have surely concurred.[24]

YOUTHFUL REBELLION AND THE MAOIST RHETORIC OF EMPOWERMENT

The affixing of labels by school administrators and CCP work teams was countered in midsummer 1966 with a ferocious Maoist labeling campaign that ridiculed and sought to undercut the paternalist authoritarianism of the opposition. In the Maoist view, the "old gentlemen power holders taking the capitalist road" *(zou zibenzhuyi daolu dangquanpai de laoyemen)* and the "reactionary academic 'authorities' " *(fandong xueshu "quanwei")* were "old antiques" *(lao gudong)*; it was under their aegis that "layer after layer of old thinking, old culture, old customs, and old habits had piled up for thousands of years" *(ji qiannian lai cengceng duiji qilai de jiu sixiang, jiu wenhua, jiu fengsu, jiu xiguan)*.[25] While attempting to discredit and delegitimate established authority figures, Maoist proclamations simultaneously advanced a rhetoric of empowerment that challenged the traditional polarity in Chinese culture of youth and ignorance versus age and wisdom.

The Maoist rhetoric of empowerment was phrased in language that was both classically Marxist and traditionally Chinese. Youthful rebellion was linked with the essential Marxian premise that conflict and struggle play a historically progressive role; as one *People's Daily* editorial put it, "from ancient times, those who dared to make revolution, those who dared to start new things, were primarily 'childish' young people."[26] In Mao's view, at least, this premise had been validated by the rise and triumph of Chinese Communism and now needed to be reaffirmed. More paradoxical, yet nonetheless culturally resonant, was the way the Maoist rhetoric of empowerment sought to link the youthful upheaval with such traditional Confucian values as "virtue" *(de)*, "talent" *(cai)*, "wisdom" *(zhi)*, and "right principle" *(li)*. In rebel youth, Maoist editorials proclaimed, "virtue and talent are prepared as one" *(de cai jian bei)* and "wisdom and heroism are both complete" *(zhi yong shuang quan)*. In attempting to fuse traditional Confucian values with Marxian principles of mass dynamism, the rhetoric of empowerment produced such contorted phrasings as "revolutionary youth has perfect wisdom and animal vigor" *(geming qingnian you zhihui, you boli)*, as well as the definitive Cultural Revolution slogan: "Rebellion is justified" *(zaofan you li)*.[27]

The widely shared sense of youthful enpowerment that resulted is nowhere more vividly conveyed than in a big character poster entitled "Sally Forth with the Attitude of Master of the House" *(Nachu zhuren weng de taidu lai)*. According to this especially brazen manifesto, Chairman Mao had called upon youth to "liberate themselves, teach themselves, administer themselves, and make revolution themselves." To do so was a matter of "daring to think, daring to speak, and daring to do" *(gan xiang, gan shuo, gan zuo)*; above all, it was a matter of "becoming master of the house" *(dangjia zuozhu)*.[28] This confident, strident, and arrogant tone is typical of youthful pronouncements of the period; all the big character posters proclaim the shared assumption that youth had been released from the constraints of customary adult authority. Unapologetically they proclaimed in the colorful language and vibrant imagery of the day: "Smashing down the palace of the King of Hell, the revolutionary little red devils are liberated" *(dadao yanwang dian, geming de hong xiao gui jiefang le)*.[29]

THE ASSAULT ON AUTHORITY

The Maoist rhetoric of empowerment sought to redefine the position of youth in society by delegitimating the bases of orthodox paternalist authority and mocking conventional models of appropriate youthful deportment. Marxist-Leninist ideological and organizational principles were challenged and undercut. On June 2, 1966, the *People's Daily* editorial "Hail the Peking University Big Character Poster" *(Huanhu Beida de yizhang dazibao)* publicly denounced the university party committee, put quotation marks around such previously sacrosanct terms as "party" *(dang)*, "organization" *(zuzhi)*, and "party secretary" *(dang shuji)*, and heretically proclaimed "your 'party' is not a real communist party but a fake communist party."[30] Such an unprecedented assault on orthodox CCP principles and institutions was, in and of itself, bound to have profoundly destabilizing consequences. But these were only the opening salvoes; the editorial went on to question principles of social order, social propriety, and social hierarchy in general.

It did not matter how "high" an authority's "position" *(duo gao de diwei)* or how "old" an authority's "credentials" *(duo lao de zige)*, the editorial stated; the "black organization" *(hei zuzhi)* and "black discipline" *(hei jilü)* of such people would be smashed regardless.[31] By the same token, revolutionary youth was now solely accountable to the even higher standard of "Chairman Mao's highest instructions regarding rebellion" *(Maozhuxi guanyu zaofan de zuigao zhishi)*.[32] In their confrontation with "high officials doing what the common people dare not attempt" *(zhouguan fanghuo)*, rebel youth was now armed with "invincible Mao Zedong Thought" *(zhanwubusheng de Mao Zedong sixiang)*. With "old literary styles, old forms of proper behavior, old forms of social order" *(jiu zhangfa, jiu guiju, jiu zhixu)* out the window, youth was truly liberated, released from oppressive social conventions and constraints, free to mock and defy their delegitimated elders. As one poster put it, "why is it necessary to respond bashfully" to authority *(hebi xiuxiu dada de ne)?*[33]

Yet the hold of traditional models of appropriate youthful deportment remained strong, and some students were clearly uncomfortable in their new role as rebels. In addition to attacking principles of seniority and hierarchy, many of the big character posters contain appeals to still deferential and quiescent fellow students. Aren't you ashamed, the Red Guards of Qinghua University Middle School asked their more reticent classmates, to "adhere to precedent and tread properly" *(xungui daoju)* and "respectfully answer in assent" *(weiwei nuonuo)*; "how can you live with yourselves?" *(nimen zeme huo de xiaqu ne)* the rebels demanded.[34] To continue to relate to authority in traditionally deferential ways, the Red Guard manifesto proclaimed, was nothing less than a betrayal of Chairman Mao's wishes and "highest instructions."

IMAGES OF FREEDOM AND DESTRUCTION

Many young Chinese experienced a genuine sense of freedom, release, and "liberation" *(jiefang)* in 1966–1967.[35] Youthful freedom took many forms. Fall 1966 was the period of "linking up" *(chuan lian)*, when state-financed transportation and living expenses were extended to tens of millions of young Chinese, and middle school and university students were granted the unprecedented opportunity of traveling the length and breadth of the country. According to

Chan, many of her interviewees recalled the "free exchange of ideas to which they became accustomed" in the primary phases of the Cultural Revolution.[36] Certainly the "excitement" *(renao)* of this period provided an exhilarating contrast to the pressures and constraints of the pre–Cultural Revolution school system. Tragically, though not surprisingly, youthful freedom was manifested in many unhappy ways as well; indeed, images of freedom and liberation were explicitly linked with images of destruction and violence in these big character posters.

Some depictions of youthful freedom were benign—an especially prominent image was that of the free bird. Thus revolutionary youth were exhorted to "soar" *(aoxiang)* like "brave sea swallows" *(yonggan de haiyan)* and "heroic falcons" *(xiongying).*[37] As the predatory image of the falcon suggests, however, the role of revolutionary youth was militant, uncompromising, destructive, and violent. The words "beat" *(da),* "beat down" *(dadao),* "break" *(po),* and "smash" *(za)* are recurrent in the big character posters and Maoist editorials. Liberating youth from the constraints of "old thinking, old culture, old customs, and old habits" was defined as a matter of "breaking the four olds" *(po sijiu).*

In the summer and fall of 1966, "breaking the four olds" took the form of a violent Red Guard assault on all symbols and vestiges of the past, human and inanimate. Youthful violence during the Cultural Revolution is well known and amply documented. One of Chan's informants described this scene in early fall 1966: "It was the beginning of the Cultural Revolution. . . . We were trying to take the train from the Peking railway station, and we saw those secondary school students beating people, completely out of hand. Whap! Whap! They were whipping some former landlords and whatnot. Blood all over."[38] In fact, behavior of this type was implicitly, and often explicitly, sanctioned in Red Guard manifestos and Maoist proclamations in the summer of 1966. One big character poster mocked the hallowed Confucian principle of "human sentiment" *(ren qing)* and called for a "great fight and great slaughter" *(da bodou, da sisha);* such incendiary rhetoric was then amplified and endorsed by Maoist editorials with lines like "the dialectic of revolution is without sentiment" *(geming de bianzheng shi wu qing de).*[39] In this setting, youthful enactment of "freedom" *(ziyou)* assumed all the unruly, chaotic, and self-indulgent forms that this concept connotes in Chinese culture and the Chinese language.[40] Of course, the violence of the Cultural Revolution cannot be explained solely in terms of inflammatory big character poster rhetoric and editorial imagery. It was the fusion of everyday grievances and tensions with the ideology of revolutionary renewal that fueled the youth rebellion. As sociostructural cleavages, pent-up tensions, and score settling were fused with and exacerbated by militant Maoist rhetoric, there ensued a chaotic, irresponsible, and destructive outburst of youthful energy and violence.

AN INDULGENT AUTHORITY FIGURE

I have argued that the youthful upheaval of 1966–1967 was not simply imposed from on high. When the opportunity presented itself, many young Chinese were ready to attack an authority structure they had personally experienced as oppressive, unfair, confining, and boring. At the same time, the students were responding to the rhetoric of empowerment and rebellion emanating from the top: from Mao. While the Maoist message struck a responsive chord by addressing old grievances, these latent tensions would never have become manifest had the process of youthful rebellion not been initiated by Mao. The central element in this interaction between exhortations from on high and youthful ferment from below was the Mao personality cult. Contrary to conventional notions of mindless Red Guard fanaticism, youthful perceptions of Mao in summer 1966 were as complex and ambiguous as the Maoist message itself.

As put forward in *People's Daily* editorials and reflected in the big character posters, the Mao personality cult was paradoxical and multilayered. Mao was depicted as the ultimate patriarchal authority figure; the posters incessantly invoked Mao's "instructions" *(zhishi)*, "repeated teachings" *(zhunzhun jiaodao)*, "limitless expectations" *(wuxian xiwang)*, and "abundant hopes" *(yinqie xiwang)* for youth. For their part, young people had the special virtue of being "especially attentive to Chairman Mao's teachings" *(zui ting Maozhuxi de hua)*.[41] In the traditionally Chinese manner, Mao was intensely interested in the process of "cultivating successors" *(peiyang jiebanren)*. Rather than carrying on the family line in the usual fashion, however, these "successors" were charged with the Marxian task of "continuing the revolution" *(jixu geming)*. Thus the Maoist rhetoric of empowerment, while couched in familiar patriarchal language, upheld a confrontational, energized, and unruly image of youth entirely at odds with the prevailing view in Chinese tradition.

In the summer and fall of 1966, Mao's authoritative injunctions were very benevolently and permissively phrased. In the words of the editorial "A Salute to Revolutionary Youth," the "heroic little marshals" *(yonggan de xiao jiangmen)* were "so very lovable!" *(duome keai a)*. These "lovable little marshals" were assured, moreover, of the long-term protection of big daddy himself, since Chairman Mao "looked after revolutionary youth like a loving father" *(xiangci fuban de guanhuai geming de qingshaonian)* and "the future belongs to revolutionary youth" *(weilai shanyu geming de qingshaonian)*. With such explicit encouragement and legitimation, it is not surprising that many young people came to believe sincerely that "Chairman Mao has turned over great power to us" *(Maozhuxi ba daquan jiaogei women)* and took seriously the notion of "seizing power" *(duo quan)*.[42]

The unleashing of youthful attacks on authority via the endorsement and protection of an indulgent paternalistic authority figure constitutes the fundamental social-psychological dynamic of the period in question. Young Chinese were willing, indeed eager, to rebel against the established structure of authority, but they were able to do so only when given permission by the ultimate authority figure: Mao himself. When the youth rebellion got out of hand and became mired in violent factional conflict in 1967 and 1968, Mao personally ordered an end to Red Guard political action and feuding and remarked: "Young people won't listen to criticism; their temperament somewhat resembles my own when I was young. The subjectivism of children is strong, exceedingly powerful, and it seems they're only capable of criticizing other people."[43] By the end of 1967 and 1968, Maoist permissiveness and benevolence were things of the past, and endless study sessions, rote memorization of Mao Zedong Thought, the coercive disbanding of Red Guard organizations, and forced rustication had become the lot of millions of rebel youth.[44] In the summer and fall of 1966, however, the exuberant and unruly playing out of previously unmentionable acts of youthful rebellion and freedom was interpreted as faithful obedience to "Chairman Mao's highest instructions."

THE LEGACY OF THE CULTURAL REVOLUTION

In February 1967, massive military intervention in the Cultural Revolution signaled the beginning of the end for the youth rebellion; it was at this time that editorials in the central media began to criticize the "shortcomings" *(quedian)* of rebel youth. According to a *Red Flag* editorial in early 1967:

> Of course, the young revolutionary fighters have shortcomings and mistakes. They lack experience, are not yet mature politically, and at crucial turning points in the course of the revolution, they frequently cannot see the direction clearly. . . . Young revolutionary fighters, too, must seriously remold their world outlook.[45]

By fall 1967 and into 1968, the "remolding" of rebel youth involved an increasingly rigid and often draconian combination of military control and ideological indoctrination, as Red Guard organizations were forcibly disbanded and millions of young people were first exhorted and then compelled to move to the countryside, where they were supposed to settle for life. I do not propose to detail here the painful fate of rebel youth in the later phases of the Cultural Revolution.

What was the legacy of the Cultural Revolution for Chinese youth? Western analysts conventionally speak of the youthful apathy and disillusionment that resulted. In some respects, this interpretation is persuasive. When Stanley Rosen speaks of a "skeptical youth" who in 1978 had "seen through" *(kantou le)* everything, and so believed in nothing, he accurately describes the contempt with which Maoist dogma had come to be viewed by Chinese youth.[46] Other commentators reach more sweeping conclusions. In William A. Joseph's view, the Cultural Revolution bequeathed China a legacy of "pervasive political apathy and ideological cynicism."[47] Anne F. Thurston argues that young Chinese today "remain cynical and more preoccupied with their own advancement and material comfort than with contributing to their country. The major legacy of the Cultural Revolution among the young is a profound sense of anomie."[48]

But these bleak views of Chinese youth in the 1980s were contradicted, albeit briefly, by the events of April, May, and June 1989. As in the summer and fall of 1966, Tiananmen Square was filled with exuberant, defiant, and idealistic young demonstrators who waved banners, wrote big character posters, demanded political, social, and cultural change, and condemned the prevailing structure of authority and power in China. Of course, fundamental differences separate the youthful upheavals of summer 1966 and spring 1989. In contrast to the militant Red Guard rhetoric of class struggle and proletarian dictatorship in 1966, rebel youth in 1989 called for democracy and the rule of law and espoused a philosophy of nonviolence. Furthermore, the youth movement in 1989 was not sanctioned from on high; there was no indulgent authority figure to summon rebel youth forward and benevolently protect them.

Yet suggestive parallels do link the upheavals of 1966 and 1989. As in the summer and fall of 1966, the target of the youthful "pro-democracy" demonstrations in spring 1989 was the established Chinese political and social order itself. In April, May, and June 1989, familiar grievances were aired with tactics wholly reminiscent of the opening phases of the Cultural Revolution. A collection of writings and speeches from this period show a "large allegorical drawing at Peking University, in which a massive rock of feudalism is crushing the Chinese people while officials plunder the land's riches."[49] The collection contains a big character poster entitled "Unless the Net Is Torn, the Fish Will Die," which condemns "huge networks of personal connections" and declares:

> In the forty years since the founding of the People's Republic, the struggle against feudalism has never been interrupted, yet feudalism's ancient roots disappear only to reappear, tugging on people's souls. The older a person, the greater the accumulated power of the specter of feudalism in his heart.[50]

As the editors of this collection therefore observe: "The Democracy Movement was as much a protest against 'bureaucratism'—in Chinese eyes, the arbitrary exercise of power or the abuse of power by Party officials—as it was a demand for democracy."[51]

As in the repressive later phases of the Cultural Revolution, moreover, it was young people who bore the brunt of official repression in 1989. In both cases, the coercive might of the Chinese state was used to curb and then crush the youthful upheaval. Yet the symmetry is less complete in this respect. Whereas the PLA deployed a combination of ideological appeals, veiled threats, and brute force in suppressing the youth movement in late 1967 and 1968, Chinese rulers used overwhelming military power to crush youthful protest in June 1989. Perhaps the enduring legacy of June 4 for educated Chinese youth was one of apathy or cynicism. In June 1993, *The Washington Post* reported that Wang Dan, a young leader in the Tiananmen demonstrations, "has traded in his glasses for contact lenses, his headband for a tie, and his loudspeaker for a beeper." The newspaper

noted: "The one-time firebrand, 24, appeared almost bored by questions about democracy. What he would like now is the chance to go
into business and get rich."[52]

THE PATTERN REMAINS

Expanding on Richard Solomon, this essay has interpreted the social
psychology of rebel youth in 1966–1967 in the broad context of
authority relations in Chinese culture. Historically, China's authoritarian social and political culture has placed youth in a subordinate
and oppressed position; we have seen that this pattern continued
under Chinese Communism and remains in place today. Usually
there is little to be done. As the big character poster suggests, people
tend to accept the traditional culture and ideology, get older, acquire
seniority, and gradually work their way into positions of relative
dominance. This was the reality that thinkers of the May Fourth
period feared and sought to overturn when they equated maturity
and age with decay and corruption. Yet the pressures for youthful
freedom and release remain ever present. During the primary phases
of the Cultural Revolution and in April, May, and June 1989, this
latent demand was reinforced and made manifest by ideologies of
change, reform, revolution, and empowerment. Of course, the imagery and much of the rhetoric of these two periods were very different,
not least a deified Mao and "proletarian dictatorship" versus the
Goddess of Democracy and the rule of law. But I have suggested that
important parallels do link the substance of youthful upheaval in
1966 and 1989. Above all, processes of authoritarian control and
CCP dictatorship were subjected to a fiery youthful critique and
assault in both cases.

Chan's thesis that the attitudes and behavior of rebel youth in
1966–1967 were dictated by now defunct CCP and Maoist socialization processes is too narrowly formulated and must be revised fundamentally. Orthodox communist socialization processes were attacked
and delegitimated in 1966–1967; for much of this time, Mao held
forth and sanctioned a rebellious vision of youth that sharply contradicted the ideals and reality of the pre–Cultural Revolution school
system. While the youthful demonstrators in spring 1989 did not
employ the dated and discredited Maoist vocabulary of class warfare
and Mao Zedong Thought, many of the grievances and demands
that were aired can be traced back to the youth rebellion of 1966–

1967. Where, after all, did the idea of publicly criticizing corrupt CCP officials and the prevailing political order with big character posters and mass rallies in Tiananmen Square originate?

Because the hold of China's traditional social and political culture has proved so tenacious, it appears that the concerns and aspirations of the children of Deng are not so fundamentally dissimilar from those of the children of Mao. Cynicism, apathy, and consumerism did not precipitate the youthful demonstrations and attacks on CCP authority in spring 1989. Just as young Chinese sought to redefine and reshape authority relations in Chinese culture during the primary phases of the Cultural Revolution, so too were the youthful demonstrators of April, May, and June 1989 motivated by similar concerns.

NOTES

1. Hong Yung Lee, *The Politics of the Chinese Cultural Revolution* (Berkeley, Los Angeles, London: University of California Press, 1978), p. 5. The centrality of social cleavages in Red Guard factionalism was subsequently documented in Canton by Stanley Rosen, *Red Guard Factionalism in Guangzhou (Canton)* (Boulder: Westview, 1982), and in Shanghai by Lynn T. White III, *Policies of Chaos* (Princeton: Princeton University Press, 1989).

2. Richard H. Solomon, *Mao's Revolution and the Chinese Political Culture* (Berkeley, Los Angeles, London: University of California Press, 1971), p. 99. This thesis was most explicitly challenged by Thomas A. Metzger, who rejected Solomon's "either/or" view of authority relations in Chinese culture and spoke instead of an "ongoing psychological drama of competing moral claims" in Confucian society, in which submission to authority in one arena did not "necessarily mean the suppression of psychological processes of self-assertion." See Metzger, *Escape from Predicament: Neo-Confucianism and China's Evolving Political Culture* (New York: Columbia University Press, 1977), p. 46.

3. Solomon, *Mao's Revolution*, p. 501.

4. Thus "Chinese parents and educators intervened early and forcefully into the lives of children to attempt to ensure . . . that the child's self-understanding and social roles would be shaped by its elders. But this outcome could never be guaranteed." Saari goes on to pose the question: "But were the father's intermittent instructions enough to check the spread of mischief?" He notes, moreover, that "unconventional activities, especially immoral behavior, could not be openly encouraged; but uncommon vigor and intelligence in children could win secret approval from parents." See Jon L. Saari, *Legacies of Childhood: Growing Up Chinese in a Time of Crisis, 1890–1920* (Cambridge, Mass.: Harvard University Press, 1990), pp. 60, 99, 245.

5. Anita Chan, *Children of Mao: Personality Development and Political Activism in the Red Guard Generation* (London: Macmillan, 1985), p. 1.

6. Ibid., pp. 17, 184.

7. Ibid., pp. 224–225.

8. Big character posters *(dazibao)* are powerful vehicles of political communication and political protest. Slogans, polemics, and detailed articles are handwritten on sheets of paper, displayed on public walls, and read by thousands of people. Historically deployed by the CCP as propaganda and communication devices, big character posters were turned against the party during the Cultural Revolution. This process was set in motion by Mao Zedong, who wrote a big character poster entitled "Bombard the Headquarters" in August 1966, thereby legitimating their use as vehicles of popular political protest and mass political action.

9. The origins of the Nie Yuanzi big character poster are complex. It went up on May 24 and then, according to Lowell Dittmer, "on June 1, Nie's poster came to Mao's attention, and he called Kang Sheng to request that it 'should be at once broadcast and published in the newspapers.' " See Lowell Dittmer, *Liu Shao-ch'i and the Chinese Cultural Revolution* (Berkeley, Los Angeles, London: University of California Press, 1974), p. 78. At the same time, Nie was part of Mao's inner circle and a Jiang Qing confidante.

10. See Roderick MacFarquhar, *The Origins of the Cultural Revolution*, vols. 1–2 (New York: Columbia University Press, 1974, 1983); Dittmer, *Liu Shao-ch'i and the Chinese Cultural Revolution*; Richard Baum, *Prelude to Revolution* (New York: Columbia University Press, 1975).

11. For a classic account of this process see Max Weber, *Economy and Society*, ed. Guenther Roth and Claus Wittich (Berkeley, Los Angeles, London: University of California Press, 1978), vol. 2, chap. 12, "Patriarchalism and Patrimonialism."

12. Mark Lupher, "Power Restructuring in China and the Soviet Union," *Theory and Society* 21(5) (October 1992):665–701.

13. Ho Ping-ti, *The Ladder of Success in Imperial China* (New York: Columbia University Press, 1962), p. 216; John R. Watt, *The District Magistrate in Late Imperial China* (New York: Columbia University Press, 1972), p. 117.

14. Sidney I. Ploss, "A New Soviet Era?," *Foreign Policy* 62 (Spring 1986):46–60.

15. Of course, students in the Peking school system were often very privileged in relation to other young Chinese. In the context of the authority structure of the pre–Cultural Revolution educational system, however, these students were very much "nonprivileged social strata."

16. Chow Tse-tsung, *The May Fourth Movement* (Cambridge, Mass.: Harvard University Press, 1960), pp. 182–186, 300–312.

17. Andrew G. Walder describes as "neotraditional" the fusion of "communist institutions designed to exercise political control" with personalistic

networks of patron/client ties; see Walder, *Communist Neo-Traditionalism* (Berkeley, Los Angeles, London: University of California Press, 1986), pp. 6–7. In Walder's view, "communist neotraditionalism" is a distinctly "modern" sociopolitical configuration. In fact, it was the emerging synthesis of traditional Chinese social relations with communist ideology and organization that Mao feared and sought to combat during the Cultural Revolution.

18. Gao Yuan, *Born Red* (Stanford: Stanford University Press, 1987), p. 32.

19. Nie Yuanzi et al., "Whatever Are Song Shuo, Lu Ping, and Peng Peiyun Doing in the Cultural Revolution?" (Song Shuo, Lu Ping, Peng Peiyun zai wenhua da geming zhong jiujing gan xie sheme?), in *Selected Big Character Posters of the Great Proletarian Cultural Revolution* (Beijing: People's Press, 1966), pp. 1–4.

20. "A Letter to Nie Yuanzi and the Seven Comrades" (Gei Nie Yuanzi deng qiwei tongzhi de yifeng xin), *Selected Big Character Posters*, pp. 5–9.

21. Lee, *Politics of the Chinese Cultural Revolution*, pp. 27–41.

22. *Selected Big Character Posters*, pp. 1–4.

23. White, *Policies of Chaos*, pp. 10–15.

24. "Long Live the Proletarian Revolutionary Rebellion Spirit" (Wuchanjieji de geming zaofan jingshen wansui), *Selected Big Character Posters*, pp. 10–12.

25. "A Salute to Revolutionary Youth" (Xiang geming de qingshaonian zhijing), *Selected Big Character Posters*, pp. 23–28.

26. Ibid.

27. "Long Live the Proletarian Revolutionary Rebellion Spirit One More Time!" (Zailun wuchanjieji de geming zaofan jingshen wansui!), *Selected Big Character Posters*, pp. 13–14.

28. "Sally Forth with the Attitude of Master of the House" (Nachu zhuren weng de taidu lai), *Selected Big Character Posters*, pp. 17–18.

29. "A Salute to Revolutionary Youth," *Selected Big Character Posters*, pp. 23–28.

30. "Hail the Peking University Big Character Poster" (Huanhu Beida de yizhang dazibao), *Selected Big Character Posters*, pp. 19–22.

31. *Selected Big Character Posters*, pp. 1–4.

32. "Long Live the Proletarian Revolutionary Rebellion Spirit for a Third Time!" (Sanlun wuchanjieji de geming zaofan jingshen wansui!), *Selected Big Character Posters*, pp. 15–16.

33. "Long Live the Proletarian Revolutionary Rebellion Spirit," *Selected Big Character Posters*, pp. 10–12.

34. *Selected Big Character Posters*, pp. 10–12.

35. In Lowell Dittmer's words: "From a psycho-cultural perspective, then, the Cultural Revolution implied an opportunity to smash taboo barriers and emancipate culturally and psychically repressed vital impulses of all kinds—an opportunity that many Chinese young people found exciting."

See Dittmer, *China's Continuous Revolution* (Berkeley, Los Angeles, London: University of California Press, 1987), p. 89.

36. Chan, *Children of Mao*, p. 187.

37. "Long Live the Proletarian Revolutionary Rebellion Spirit for the Third Time!" *Selected Big Character Posters*, pp. 15–16.

38. Chan, *Children of Mao*, p. 169.

39. "A Salute to Revolutionary Youth," *Selected Big Character Posters*, pp. 23–28.

40. The term "freedom" *(ziyou)* has many pejorative connotations in the Chinese language: e.g., "liberalism" *(ziyou zhuyi)*, "going one's own way without discipline" *(ziyou sanman)*, and "unrestrained self-indulgence" *(ziyou fangren)*.

41. "A Salute to Revolutionary Youth," *Selected Big Character Posters*, pp. 23–28.

42. "Sally Forth with the Attitude of Master of the House," *Selected Big Character Posters*, pp. 17–18.

43. "Conversations at the Summons of Responsible Persons of the Capital Red Guards Congress" (Zhaojian shoudu hongdaihui fuzeren de tanhua), July 28, 1968, *Joint Publications Research Service* no. 61269-2, February 20, 1974.

44. Thomas P. Bernstein, *Up to the Mountains and Down to the Villages* (New Haven and London: Yale University Press, 1977), p. 263.

45. "Cadres Must Be Treated Correctly" (Bixu zhengque duidai ganbu), *Red Flag* 4, 1967.

46. Stanley Rosen, "Prosperity, Privatization, and China's Youth," *Problems of Communism* (March–April 1985):3.

47. William A. Joseph, "Foreword," in Gao Yuan, *Born Red*, pp. xxvii–xxviii.

48. Anne F. Thurston, "Urban Violence During the Cultural Revolution: Who Is to Blame?" in Jonathan M. Lipman and Stevan Harrell, eds., *Violence in China* (Albany: State University of New York Press, 1990), p. 168.

49. Han Minzhu, ed., *Cries for Democracy* (Princeton: Princeton University Press, 1990), p. 156.

50. Ibid., pp. 36–38.

51. Ibid., p. 27.

52. Lena H. Sun, "Chinese Militant Swaps Protest for Business," *Washington Post*, June 2, 1993, p. 1.

GLOSSARY

chuanlian	串連	linking up
dangquan pai	當權派	authorities
duo quan	奪權	seizing power

geming qingnian	革命青年	revolutionary youth
hongxiaogui	紅小鬼	little red devils
jiaqiang lingdao	加強領導	strengthening leadership
po sijiu	破四舊	breaking the four olds
renao	熱鬧	excitement
weifan jilü	違反紀律	violating discipline
yonggan de xiao jiangmen	勇敢的小將們	courageous little marshals
zhengchang fazhan	正常發展	normal development
zhengque daolu	正確道路	correct path
zuigao zhishi	最高指示	highest instructions

Contributors

Kenneth J. DeWoskin received his Ph.D. in Chinese literature from Columbia University. He is now professor of Chinese at the University of Michigan. His recent publications include *A Song for One or Two: Music and the Concept of Art in Early China; Doctors, Diviners, and Magicians of Ancient China: Biographies of Fang-shih;* and in collaboration with James I. Crump, Jr., a complete translation of the *Soushenji.*

Charlotte Furth holds a Ph.D. in history from Stanford University and is currently a professor of history at the University of Southern California. Among her writings on modern Chinese intellectual history are *Ting Wen-chiang: Science and China's New Culture* and *Limits of Change: Essays on Conservative Alternatives in Republican China* (editor and contributor). In recent years she has published a number of articles on the history of Chinese medicine with special attention to gender issues.

Anne Behnke Kinney is associate professor of Chinese at the University of Virginia. She received her Ph.D. in Chinese language and literature from the University of Michigan. Among her recent publications are *The Art of the Han Essay: Wang Fu's Ch'ien-fu lun* and "Infant Abandonment in Early China." She is currently at work on a book-length study of children in early China.

Angela Ki Che Leung received a Ph.D. in history from the Ecole des Hautes Etudes en Sciences Sociale, Paris. She is research fellow at the Sun Yat-sen Institute for Social Sciences and Philosophy, Academia Sinica, Taipei. In addition to her shorter publications in English, French, and Chinese on Ming–Qing sociocultural history, she is currently completing a book on Ming–Qing philanthropy.

Mark Lupher received his Ph.D. from the University of California at Berkeley and is currently assistant professor of sociology at the University of Virginia. His publications include "Power Restructuring in China and the Soviet Union" and the forthcoming *Power Restructuring in China and Russia.* Professor Lupher spent four years of his youth in China between the years 1964 and 1968.

Richard B. Mather is professor emeritus of Chinese literature at the University of Minnesota, specializing in the literature and intellectual history of the early medieval period (ca. A.D. 200–600). He received his doctorate in oriental languages at the University of California, Berkeley. Among his major publications are *Shih-shuo Hsin-yü: A New Account of Tales of the World* and *The Poet Shen Yueh: The Reticent Marquis.*

Lucien Miller received a Ph.D. in comparative literature at the University of California, Berkeley. Specializing in East-West literary relations, he teaches Orientalism and Occidentalism, Contemplative Literature, Hyphenated Texts and Cultures, and Children's Literature and Folktales. Among his publications are *The Masks of Fiction in Dream of the Red Chamber; Exiles at Home: Stories by Ch'en Ying-chen;* and *South of the Clouds: Yunnan Tales.*

Catherine E. Pease holds a Ph.D. in modern Chinese literature from Stanford University. Her publications include an article on Wu Zuxiang's wartime novel, and she is currently at work on a study of Chinese childhood in the late Qing and early modern eras. She teaches East Asian Studies at Western Washington University.

C. John Sommerville, professor of English history at the University of Florida, received his Ph.D. from the University of Iowa. He has published a number of articles on the cultural history of childhood as well as two books, *The Discovery of Childhood in Puritan England* and *The Rise and Fall of Childhood.*

Ann Waltner, associate professor of history at the University of Minnesota, holds a Ph.D. in Chinese history from the University of California at Berkeley. She is the author of *Getting an Heir: Adoption and the Construction of Kinship in Late Imperial China,* "The Moral Status of the Child in Late Imperial China," "On Not Becoming a Heroine: Lin Daiyu and Cui Yingying," and a number of other articles dealing with gender, religion, and kinship in China of the Ming and Qing dynasties.

Wu Hung, Centennial Distinguished Service Professor in Chinese Art History at the University of Chicago, holds a Ph.D. in art history and anthropology from Harvard University. His book, *The Wu Liang Shrines: The Ideology of Early Chinese Pictorial Art,* won the Association for Asian Studies' Joseph Levenson Prize for the best book on traditional China of 1990.

Pei-yi Wu, Ph.D. (Columbia University), teaches Chinese at Queens College, City University of New York, and Columbia University. He is the author of *The Confucian's Progress: Autobiographical Writings in Traditional China.* His article "Education of Children in the Sung" is included in the anthology *Neo-Confucian Education: The Formative Stage.* His most recent publication is "Memories of K'ai-feng," which appears in *New Literary History.*

Index

References to illustrations are in **bold face**.

abortion, 170–171, 195–196, 234, 240
adolescence: as developmental stage, 6, 8,
180, 181; as elite phenomenon, 220;
224; as liminal, 224; in literature, 8,
219–242; and sexual identity, 224–
226, 231–232; for women, 230–232.
See also puberty
adoption, 260, 265–266
Analects (Lun yü), 73, 112, 324
ancestors, and inherited character traits,
64–67, 165
aunts, 87–89, **87**, **89**, 105
authority: ambivalence toward, 322–323,
338–339; in education, 327–328; and
Mao cult, 334–335; rebellion against,
328–334; and top-down, bottom-up,
325

*Baihu tong (Proceedings from the White
Tiger Hall)*, 91
Ba Jin, 288, 291
Ban Gu, 39, 51n. 59, 68
Ban Jieyu, 50n. 43
Bencao gangmu, 160
big character posters *(dazibao)*, 324–325,
328–334, 338, 340n. 8
Bing Xin, 280–281, 285–286, 305–312
Biographies of Filial Sons (Xiaozi zhuan),
83
biography: and autobiography, 37, 130–
133, 220, 288, 289; and charactology,
61–62, 76, 288; contrasted with the
West, 72; as didactic discourse, 57–59,
130; genres of, 59–60, 129–133; and
narratology, 59, 61, 75–76, 288;
women's, 26, 60
birth: age at, 167; breech, 25; supernatural,
66–69
bisexuality, 237–238, 242
bodies: and conservation of sexual substances, 178–182, 240; as microcosm,

17–18, 45n. 4, 158–164; as parents'
property, 113, 177; and ritual, 158, sexual development of, 35, 158, 178–182;
sexual differentiation of, 163–165
Bohu tong. See *Comprehensive Discussions
at the White Tiger Hall*
Book of Changes (Yi jing), 28, 39, 157,
159–160, 229
Book of Documents (Shu jing), 130, 131
Book of Odes (Shi jing, Book of Poetry),
27, 30, 39, 130, 229
Book of Rites (Li ji), 27, 113, 157, 181
boys: parents' strategizing for the future of,
123, 208–210; and sexual exploration,
237; stereotyped depiction of, 5, 144
Bo Yu, 99–100, **100**
breastfeeding, 95, 137, 172, 177–178, 309.
See also wet nurses
Buddhism, 162, 171, 185n. 25, 241, 265
burial, 113, 138, **139**–140, 141, 143, 149,
151, 264–265. *See also* mourning

calendrics, 24, 31, 163–164
Cao Cao, 122
Cao Rui (Emperor Ming of the Wei), 140–
141
Cao Xueqin. See *Dream of the Red Cham-
ber*
Cao Yin, 220
capping ceremony (and hairpinning), 34,
97, 157, 181
cemeteries, 106n. 6, 264–265
Chan, Anita, 323–324, 338
Chao Cuo, 46n. 12
Chao Yuanfang, 159
chastity. See virginity; widows
Chen Hongmou, 199
Chen Ji, 114, **118**
Chen Jiru, 131
Chen Longzheng, 136–137, 153n. 17, 195
Cheng Hao, 130, 131
Chenghua emperor (of Ming), 205, 209
Cheng Yi, 130, 136

347

Production Notes

Composition and paging were done in
FrameMaker software on an AGFA AccuSet
Postscript Imagesetter by the design
and production staff of University of
Hawai'i Press.

The text and display typeface is Sabon.

Offset presswork and binding were done by
The Maple-Vail Book Manufacturing Group.
Text paper is Glatfelter Smooth Antique, basis 50.